MILKBOTTLE H

MILKBOTTLE H

Gil Orlovitz

DELL PUBLISHING COMPANY
NEW YORK

813.5
O72m

108547

Let this book stand as a tribute
to my beloved wife Lynne,
without whose patience and enduring
dedication none of my work would
have been possible

MILKBOTTLE H

dont you think if a thief wants to come in, a locked door wont make any difference;
he takes a walk,
he goes flying,
he crouches and he creeps
a small moth, making a mild twang against the summerscreen, becomes a slate folded wingclip against the metal mesh; Lee Emanuel nods at the white mottles on the body, the canted wings, three quarters of an inch arrowhead, tiny black twinks of eye each pocked by a pop of glisten
leaning by a yield Lee
;scrubby antennae, halfstarved, halferect, tucked shrug. Category of the eaters of light
reaches for his cigarette lighter, fizzes wheel against flint
black balloons gray
susurrating into blue, scutiform, yellowtipped the Philadelphia
ADELPHIA HOTEL
HORN AND HARDARTS
LINTONS
THOMPSONS CAFETERIA
JOKES; YOU'LL KILL ME YET SAMMY TAKE WHAT IN THE MIDDLE OF THE OI THAT WAS A HARD
FRANKFORD EL
MARKET STREET EL
TRAFFIC EASTBOUND ONLY
TRAFFIC WESTBOUND ONLY
FIFTH STREET A RUMBLE OF GRANITE BISON BLOCKS THE CARWHEELS RIDING HERD LEVI EMANUELS SOLE SURVIVING ACCIDENT IS THAT A FACT IS THAT A FACTS
Lee Emanuel has a midwife in attendance at his birth let me remind you that Rabbi Jonah Silver of the Brith Mikveh Synagogue
the route of the Number 5 trolley begins at Frankford Avenue and Orthodox Street connecting with the A Bus that traverses the Roosevelt Boulevard, Hunting Park Avenue, 33rd Street, Benjamin Franklin Parkway to turn south on Broad Street and terminate at Federal Street, whereas the Number 5 trolley passes the

5

grocery-delicatessen, proprietor Solomon Goldstein, at 3892
Frankford Avenue
  gas streetlamps all yellow
  GAKWOOSH more phosphoresce than the cigarette lighter
  and Rena Goldstein. Then eat it. The belly detaches commences a parachute end-over-end descent toward the moth
  and Esther Goldstein in all her crinkled vivacity whose lyre-
black hair when untrammelled lyres beneath the waist for silver
troikabells to tinkle light from in the night and ice outside Odessa
to bobbin glint from in the day. A head shorter than Rena; up
and down and around, half the size of Rena; her laughter
a maidens, v for vagabonded virginity, lyreletch, My daughter's
a little horse, isnt that right, Nate
  ,carrying a flickering blue and yellow nutriment.
  Hidden redgold lavastitches underamong Esther's hairblack,
volcanic virginity flow.
  The mothsize flame licks at the moth's undercarriage. The insect moves not. The Leebelly pendant from the screenmesh, being
a basic bag, stuffs itself with canted arrowheads, shoot-the-chutes,
drowsy glory, Lord High Flex the Elocutioner Muscles, let them
eat cake and :
  Subtitle : The Ruthlessness of Trivia. Like the Sadist who
would—
  PINPOINT EXPERIENCE
  Jeanne d'Moth
  indeed, the bellys a curious vicinity, where a brain eddies, ethers
a whorl, Dr Kitzmiller gruffs Hell the boy's tonsils have got to
come out, Ill arrange for a private room at the University Hospital, Kitzmiller rosy toque upon toque, irongray mustachios flowing from the eyecorners, mothsize as humans go; does Dr Kitzmiller grow toward the earth? Yes, conservatively
  theres a species of emotion that may be the belly with its mouth
slack, the whale flopping on the sand, tailflukes slapping against
the flexible airscreen while an acidulous snake sneers, sniggers,
singes, squirts a velvet sugar
  the moth moves not
  one

6

three
five seven
eight ten
twelve
thir

teen four flame flick, a blueyellow caroling against the lyre-meshnight

teen fif greedy tenacious goddamned trivial moth strike the belly because Lee takes over, the cigarette lighter an application of iodine on the inside of his thigh, sunlight on the wet iodine on the soapscrubbed ringworm wounds, the Atlantic City boardwalk and then the ocean slate and blue

teen sixteen

the Pacific ocean mudded pineroot brown from the rock and earth dumps behind the stubby lighthouse to shelf out a new beach

drownEEEEEEEEEEEEEEEEEEEEEEEEEEEEEEEEEEEEEEEEEEEng the moth sticks a stac of cato touchofa, shriek, into Lee's eye and plummets backblackward, but the creature hasnt been trained to die, like some involuntary volunteer. Lee's nose hurts, burns

Got too much salt water up it, he tells pregnantwadded Norma, secondwife.

Not the kid with the hoop, she says.

The snapshot shows Rena, age eleven, in Fairmount Park, standing beside her bicycle. My girlfriends

Carla Coffman has a headache again, shes in bed

used to tell me they couldnt understand why I was never raped, her smile faintfoulfatuous, her white teeth perfectly even but showing the gaps of her eyes, riding around the park, you can see I was very developed, her udders twin monoliths, why when I was twelve the Young Communist League said I could help them a lot so they stood me outside their summer camp about a mile down the road beside a sign in a tight sweater so I could direct anybody who wanted to get to the Camp right there, we never had any trouble because the cars stopped right at me

I know. The couple watching with the child.

Not the man and the woman.

7

I know. The boy.

Yes.

Lee's body itches. Friday night. Time for a bath at 236 Roosevelt Boulevard, before the synagogue evening services.

The boy. The fife of the dancing ant axes off the surf.

MOVIES FRANKENSTEIN STANLEY THEATRE 17TH AND MARKET
FOX EARLE FAMILY KEITHS
THEATRES FORREST ERLANGER LOCUST ST

The rubystained bedroom door is secured to the goldpainted radiator beneath the window by one of Lee's discarded neckties, strung out taut and knotted at either end, so that the strong breeze flowing along the second storey hallway from the open window at the rear of the boy's room to the front room at the opposite end of the corridor (the nonexistent polarity misleads the antipodes; geographical situations at best are geographical; it is in their unawareness of each other that opposites tend to develop their most potent tensions most validly related; in awareness, and believing in opposition, the parties containing the tensions slip by each other, and are astonished that a satisfying explosion does not occur, although there may be the illusion of such, but the hate or love tends to continue for the most part unaltered, the really unopposed tensions slipping by each other a raw wrenching lie of loss, for it is duty only that dictates loss in that moment—and to feel that someone is lost when he actually is not promotes a spurious grief engendering a real grief, that regret that the loss has not come about, from which anger ensues, and that anger in turn must be inhibited; grief over inhibition is one of its most appalling expressions, and the subject may be seen wearing a very nearly ludicrous mask : facial contortion made urbane) where his mother and father sleep will not slam the boy's bedroom door shut. The boy's mouth is open too, and will not shut, tightly ajar in the pleasure at the prospect of acquiring intimate knowledge of Rachel and Levi Emanuel. That sweats him. The hot summer night sweats him. The brown shade paralleling the length of his head puffs like a rolltop desk in the breezes from the window opposite the next-door neighbors. His pajamas are luke ice wet over his plumpness. Propping his arms behind him, Lee squirms his body

8

inch by inch off the bed. The voices of his mother and father linger as hums. Even his mother's nag remains a remote but highly enviable possibility. He feels that perhaps the voices, not Rachel and Levi phonating them, will slice each other to bits; that the sounds themselves will stab and wreck each other. He gives his pajama-lowers an uptug; in the effort to be as noiseless as possible, he has all but slipped out of them, and the breeze lightly itches his anus. He halfcrouches at the chiffonier chased with the same fecalbrown whorls that adorn walls and ceiling. Out of the canted eye through the summerscreen mesh of the rear window he tips the arclight hanging from the L-shaped piece beyond and above the Emanuel garage; but its brilliance tonight is jaggedly sectioned by one more calcined within rubbing the anus lightly, a batted baseball having cracked and dispersed part of the glass bowl encasing it, to reveal the illuminated underbelly of the glowing insect within, a torch held to the undercarriage but the arclight moves not

Brilliance can suffer from concussion, Flikker remarks

Theres Lee Primus with the blood of light oozing out.

Take away your cigarette lighter from your younger brother. Its really quite impossible that he should return in the form of a moth and adhere to a summer screen.

Thats what Im getting to.

As a little boy?

Yes. My brother's interned at the end of the corridor and thats precisely where I intend to burn him

Shes burning

Who

Mrs Sherman

Mr Sherman bought her a chinchilla.

A what?

A chinchilla the linger leaks down the corridor and aggregates into the plumpfaced boy's plumpear in a burr, a scoot from the sectioned arclight featherlighting one riskroll of one large brown eye

go to sleep Rachel. The bedsprings roll over, sharp ends sticking out

9

What do we need with a car the Shermans dont have a car
YOU need a car just to ride down to the business so why cant you
take a trolley like Mr Sherman does so Mrs Sherman can have a
chin
    linger.
    what do I
    Ra
    dont you dare go to sleep when Im ta
Closer. The long suck from the opposite end of the hallway.
The rolltop shade flaps. The frontal part of the skull a tent the
sides sloping, the breeze billowing the skullflaps in and out; taut,
though yielding, bone to cartilage to viscid fluid, but the fluid
strapped in an ever tightening band around the nose and bulging
in the back of the throat, the boy wants to curve back into bed,
relinquish the arclight. Hell its somebody else's batted ball, not
mine
    In the cherryred breakfast room at 236 East Roosevelt Boule-
vard the highboy with its Japanese Buddha on either cabinet door
remains; the long cherryred lowboy on the opposite side of the
room remains; the tapestry above the lowboy, however, with its
loosetitted Spanish dancing girl and her sportive tambourine
hatching a hip before two lewdeyed male admirers—this is gone.
The oblong glasstopped table is gone. The chandelier and its pendant prism is gone. Gene Hertzog manages to obtain a hospital
bed that occupies most of the space. Lying on the bed, encysted
in the July heat of Philadelphia, covered from the waist down by
a thin white sheet, is Levi Emanuel, seventyseven years of age. A
rubber tube issues from under the sheet and curves down into a
bottle standing beneath the bed. From the tube into the bottle
piss drips, quietly. Levi Emanuel lies on his side, his head raised
by two pillows propped under. At his back is yet another pillow,
to ease the agony of two huge bedsores located just above his buttocks. Levi Emanuel's body is bevelled and canted; his son, Lee,
coming upon his father from the diningroom with its crystalware
and huge round table, will vouch for the simile that has his
father's body very much like that of a moth's; but it is not that of
a moth particularly at rest, not altogether, that is: for one mem-

10

ber, in Levi's case an arm, the right arm, as a matter of fact, is
restive; not that the arm swings, nor thrusts, nor swipes, nor declares itself in any form whatsoever, for it attaches itself by gripping fingers to the bars running the length of the bed—loosely
gripping;
    tentatively gripping;
    alternately gripping and half-uncurving:
    Aaron Emanuel comes
    and Aaron Emanuel goes;
    Aaron Emanuel's feet are encased in shoes two and a half times
the necessary size. Of all things, Levi is searching for these outsize
shoes. Of all things, Levi's fingers are paying a longdelayed tribute to the wisdom of his brother's swimming feet. Of all things,
Levi is succouring and salving his dead brother's feet, for they
are sore, chilblained from the winter cold in the Levi Coal Company Yard, weary from many directions decided on simultaneously, let us put balm on Aaron Emanuel's feet, only second in
command in leading the Hebrews out of Egypt, the chariots are
loaded with black anthracite and the second in command must
twice and yet thrice rest in the desert while the scholar of the tribe
climbs to receive the order from on high, but let us have Aaron
superintendent while Levi is gone to face the angry cloud of
Jehovah upon the mountaintop
    shall I bathe the feet of my Lord while I am upon the earth?
    My Lord is my younger brother
    What ghost, then, at the other end of the hallway? What fatted
golden calf slain by the Mother and Father of men. What do they
worship, these Gods at the other end? his fingers
    loose at the bars,
    touching himself?
    Levi's right arm pulses. Shivers. A touch of a tremble. Stops.
A roulade of a tremble. Stops. The ridge of a vibration. And stops.
The gutter of a quiver, as a quiver mounted atop a tickle, and
stops. But the head of Levi Emanuel,
    The skull of Levi Emanuel,
    The brain and the occiput and the cheekbones and the
meninges and the eyes and the chin and the thin lips and the hair

11

of Levi Emanuel are those of a man, fullskulled, fullheaded, full-brained, fullnerved, yea unto the seventh generation shall the skulls of his forefathers be visited upon Levi Emanuel

The man is his head.

But the body of Levi Emanuel has come to this moth teetering backblackward into

Lee halfrolled into crouching boy at the door to his diningroom-bedroom, the sweatlight a magic beadwork along his collarbones, itching:

must take a bath

but little Nina cant sleep. On 21st Street between 7th Avenue and Broadway, a third floor loft in the garment district converted into a studio, the walls hot and cold with canvasses, a raucous electric bulb near the plateglass tundra of the frozen front window, a squat bulbous easel bearing the most recent of her work, a painting, Picassolike, of a boy whose outstretched arm fingertips a bird perched thereon. In the tiny bedroom off the stairway of the twofamily house at Fourth Street and Girard Avenue in Philadelphia

BURKS FRANKFURTERS

FRANK & SEDER

FROZEN MEATS

she all but trips over the toy monkey, her long heavy flannel nightgown hooping Nina Brody Nina Tarassoff, clear thick swart flesh hooping about the juicy brown mounds of her eyes half billowing out of her face over the weighted protuberances of the sloppily sinuous lips licking at the brawlsounds keeping her awake, a motherandfather sound and a maleandfemale stranger sound booming and ricocheting, snarlscooped and baying, laughter-whanging and slugging slap, the sucksound of a torrent down the kitchendrain, she mumbles in her heavy white flannelgown toward the door, remembers to pick up the toy monkey she stammers to Lee, the juicy brown mounds of eye anxious at the rickety cardtable, nasal stammer, the rich thick brown voice pushed up into her nose, I boiled some coffee want some I know you sure you do its ready, hustlesloppying over to the twoburner gas stove, A friend of mine tapped the gasline, ConEd dont know

12

the goddamn difference, the raucous electric light shattering into glass laughter fragments in her throat, I have to walk down a half a flight of steps, the monkey clutching at her throat, doing trapeze-work inside her nose, its not a toy monkey at all, it chatters and it screeches and its awfully cold, it wants to get inside my nightgown those dirty sons of fucking bitches. A beerbottle full of pulpy brown cockroaches smashes against the wall, foaming with their insides. The monkeys cold even though Lee knows its summer-time, but the monkeys going to talk

LETS CHANGE PARTNERS

at once, changes

gaSHWOOL an electriclight in a scalloped bowl on the wall be-side the little courtyard where the stairway rightangles narrow and dark to descend, the little girl Nina at once believes shes a rightangled stairway bearing a scalloped electriclight gashwool-ing like the gaslamp on the corner of Fourth and Girard

LETS CHANGE P, her thick clear swart flesh very stern. The stair-way says lets descend. But the monkey stammers no. Because the monkey is quite cold. It wants to go through the doorway of the little landingway courtyard. Nina tells the monkey to be quiet, but it clambers up and down the girl, clasps her neck, tugs her nightgown, it is supposed to be a trained bird, a newborn falcon, an eaglet, and Nina is supposed to be a boy a hunting we will go a hunting we will go. It is impossible to subject a newborn animal to such intense cold. Tenderness overcomes the sternness on the girl's face. All the monkey needs is a little warmth, a mere breath of it, a touch, and all will be well. Thats not true, Lee says. He warns her not to open the door. He warns her to keep going, go down the stairs. I'd rather go back to bed, Nina says. Its far too warm in your bed, the monkey'll smother there. Theres got to be a middle way. My husband Sys a middle way. Hes a way to leave Philadelphia. As soon as we live in New York itll be a matter of time and then Ill get out. It isnt that I dont respect Sy. But Sy cant leave. Philadelphia isnt the place for you, Lee writes him from the Garden City Army Airfield in Kansas. Letter after letter. Youre responsible, Nina gives the laurel to Lee, he finally under-stands he cant paint in his mother's house. But you keep importun-

13

ing him, Lee tells her. Certainly I cant stand that mother of his in that bed upstairs. Tachycardia. Her name Riva Tarassoff, short, yellow, thin, her face hangs down in thin saffron strips. Get out, Sy, Lee writes from Garden City, the airforce Ground Safety sergeant, abominating Riva Tarassoff, her thin voice treacling from the thin mouth Why cant you paint regular portraits like the Chestnut Street portrait painters do, you could make an awful lot of money, youre so wonderful at likenesses, Sy, and you can paint them so quickly day in and day out from the upstairs bedroom. No, its Maurie Tarassoff, the younger brother, whos responsible, the whole family has ears like the enormous machine reapers of grain on the Kansas wheatfields, only the Tarassoff ears are red, red as the Kansas setting sun an Indian heirloom on the dead-white plains, because Maurie cant paint at all while his brother Sy is around, he cant put a simple charcoal line to paper seeing his brother's nimble nerve scurry lionrabbited and rabbitlioned across the white plains, to hell with having heirlooms of red sun around but wholl heirloom our mother, snagwhine-voiced Riva Tarassoff blipped by tachycardia and mongolyellow in the upstairs bedroom, Sy you can bring up my supper now you fucking Rachelbitch I refuse to let any living mother alone Lee swears to Rena in the Garden City farmhouse Nina says Mrs Tarassoff thinks Im responsible, she doesnt approve of my painting too, its enough theres one nut in the family Riva descants as Lee writes Danny Naroyan in my opinion Nina is a peasant, shell always remain a peasant, I thought Id never forgive you for that Nina assures Lee in the studio at 21st Street, loving him, loving Lee, jesus I had a case on you when I first met you Lee so youve no idea how you hurt me and I felt so sorry for you because Rena told me she didnt love you. I mean I really shouldnt tell you that, Lee, should I? Im talking out of turn. But now I guess it really doesnt matter, does it? Tremulous Nina, anatomize Lee while mothering him, its all right, its all right, Renall pass, shell pass, believe me, dont cry, you want to sleep here overnight you can if you want, duckwaddling across to the coffeepot, the fine medium tits nearly circular under the flannel nightgown, the monkey chattering her weighted lips. What if mom dies, Maurie Tarassoff

14

says. She wont die because Im going to New York, and she wont get any better if I stay. Maurie is bleakly young. There is a whole race of the bleakly young, age teetering back and forth on his perfectly triangular skull with their great red wheatgatherers pluming out. Maurie says the least you can do is stay till she dies. Its impossible to say how long thats going to take, Lee writes from Kansas, isnt that true? It can happen tomorrow, five years from now. Kill all the mothers, especially during the wartime, nobodyll notice that we get rid of them. Nobodyll notice how I get rid of my friends while Im in the army and they are not. Nobodyll notice how I tweak their desires in wartime because Im in the army and theyre not. Im justified in whatever kind of letter I write. I have no responsibility, its all theirs, and Ill give advice because I hate the three of them, Sy and Nina and Riva Tarassoff. I hate them from a distance in their little warren on Wellens Avenue in Philadelphia where absolutely nobody belongs, all the two-storey houses along the street and all the streets should be gutted, set fire to

What about the Shermans house?

I have nothing to do with that.

You like fire?

Certainly I like fire. During rocketfiring practice on the range a rocket misfires and sizzles straight up the ass of the captain in command of the battery and for one whole moment his insides are incandescent, the entire internal grid lit up clear as day through the transparent flesh like a marvellous colored chart. It takes him six agonized hours in the field hospital to die. I tell you its like a colored chart

to which the chattering monkey has access for the heat of the day in the night GASHWOOL flares the narrow chart through the strip of door Nina opens LETS CHANGE PARTNERS a squashed beer-bottle full of liquefied foaming cockroaches runs down the parlor wall her monkey father with his nightgown pulled up around his ears and teetering back and forth on the carpet patterned with fake purple chinese monograms. I have a little father, Nina says, and he looks like a monkey, but very wiry. He has a thin wire hanging from the patch of hair on his groin and the two boarders,

15

Mr and Mrs Rakmil, are rocking him back and forth on the carpet while Mrs Brody Nina's mother is trying to forcefeed him with another beer bottle. Mrs Brody is vastly naked, a vast woman not with an eaglet head nor yet that of a young falcon. Bite him says the falcon. The head of a fullgrown falcon, a female eagle twentyfive years of age with greasegreen eyes, diamond greasegreen, absolutely diamondshaped ramming her gaze along a bulwark nose which has chunks of coruscant white teeth in either nostril and sluicing behind her spillways of anklelength bronze hair, the greasegreen eyes with their green lyreing through black and violet and bronze, Mrs Brody never stops eating except to take a breath. When she dreams, she eats. When shes on the toilet, she chomps a sandwich. When shes taking a bath she slices a salami. Mrs Brody doesnt laugh as she tries to forcefeed the chattering monkey of her husband imitating a rockingchair on the chinese monograms. Mrs Brody never laughs. She hulks and hunches on the top of her mountain of nakedness and looks for game from the greasegreen violetblack bronze eyes, the bronze hair peristalting behind her. The game is this monkey on the floor now, her own bronze groinhair spattered with beer as Mr and Mrs Rakmil try to hold the monkeywire down LETS CHANGE PARTNERS ILL GET THIS GODDAMN BEER INTO HIS MOUTH WHILE YOU SIT ON HIS THIN CHATTERING LITTLE MONKEY MAKING LIKE A TRAPEZE Mrs Brody bellows, Ive got a toy monkey I could contribute little Nina whispers but nobody hears her, nor sees her. TAKE OFF YOUR PANTS RITA RAKMIL Mrs Brody bellows you cant do a goddamn thing to him that way, and little fliptitted Mrs Rakmil puckers out of her pants YOU GET BEHIND ME IKE RAKMIL Mrs Brody commands that thin tall melancholy man, his mustaches weeping with beer and half loony with sleep, and the last thing Nina sees is her mothers hulking haunches reek with gnarling muscle and spreading her whales of thighs for the skinny lurching Ike Rakmil who doesnt know if hes coming or going or quietly shutting the door Nina

has no further suggestions. The very silent nightgown with the dead serious monkey in it

the dead serious monkey in the long flannel nightgown clutching its toy nina takes slow steps down the dark narrow stairs. Lee clutches a toy lee.

Theres no point in one pole going down to visit another, especially when one knows one will discover that the characteristics of one are very much like the other's; worse, for as one becomes laden with such confirmations, one has to struggle back to one's original point and reestablish that the opposites are strangers to each other, insist on the alienation, in the realization, constantly, that such has not occurred. Lee would like to go back to bed and fall asleep, but he is girt now with the weapon of realizing intimate hatred, a great weapon for a boy, and he is loath to relinquish it. He must bring the weapon of himself down the hallway, like a cumbrous miniature fieldpiece, his mouth like the aperture of a small cannon. A changing traffic-light hangs at the corridorend, whether amber or green or red he does not know, and the monkey begins his crouching creep.

Monkey nee Nina in its heavy white flannel nightgown and holding out before it a little tin toy cup. She hears an organgrinder tune behind her in the dark, up the street, up wide Girard Avenue and its double line of cartracks passing through her bedroom a little man in a black corduroy coat turns a handle on the side of the organ he steadies on its single middle leg

sanTAAAAAAAAAH lucheeAAAAAAAAAAAAAAAH.

Monkeynina will find pennies for him so that he can change partners. He will be the monkey and she will be the organgrinder. Maybe there will be somebody with pennies outside. To go outside she must first descend the narrow dark stairway. Since shes a monkey she wont have to talk. Her mother and father do all the talking anyhow, especially her mother. She leans her elbows on the rickety cardtable. Behind Lee is a cardboard closet containing her wardrobe.

Somethings wrong with Nina, Sy says, puffing worriedly on his pipe. The table bearing his painttubes is meticulously neat in the spacious fifthfloor walkup apartment at 3rd Avenue at 36th Street, the southeast corner. Sy goes about his painting with exemplary exactitude, never a wasted motion; he stretches and sizes his own canvasses; completed, he frames them. In the midst of a

17

painting, Sy never breathes rapidly; he stands back a few feet, makes a rapid survey, narrowly appoints an estimation and proceeds once again to the brushstroke. He mixes his paints carefully, slowly but with perfect surety. On shelves he has built himself he has arranged an array of the requisite chemicals. Multifariously adept, he utilises gouaches, watercolors, oils, lithographing and etching to equal effect. During his WPA days in Philadelphia he invents a carborundum process for prints but must defer in ownership to the federal government. Two of his pastels are so prized that they hang in the extraordinary collection of the Barnes Foundation in Lower Merion, outside Philadelphia; a lithograph is owned by the Metropolitan Museum. In New York he makes a modest living teaching arts and crafts in a settlement house on the lower East Side three afternoons a week. Unperturbed, whenever he has a free moment, he paints, he pastels, he oils, he watercolors, he charcoals with perfectly undramatic deftness, pausing every now and then to relight his pipe or tamp down fresh tobacco. Dont know how you can smoke cigarettes, Lee, they make me nervous, Sy swivels forth a grin. I dont understand him, really, Lee tells Rena as she brushes her hair in the Garden City farmhouse, fifty strokes a night before going to bed. Sure, Ive seen him worried, Ive seen him pretty deeply grieving over his father's death, but Ive never really seen him angry. I want to stir him up a bit. He needs stirring. Rena looks up at him from the edge of the bed, the hair the color of rotten oranges sashaying over her sloping naked shoulders. Hes just got to get out of Philadelphia, its no place for him, and Ive written him that. You know I think youve lost some weight, he surveys her. You are happy Im here, arent you? Rena puts up her face to him with a sweet dubiety. You make the army a helluva lot more bearable.

Seriously?

Yes.

You know when I got here I weighed exactly two hundred and twenty pounds? Did you know that?

Yes. But you were very beautiful, nevertheless. Youve got the height.

You mean that, dont you? You didnt mind how heavy I was.

No. It was all proportionate.
But you dont mind my losing weight.
No, its all right, if you dont lose too much.
Rena giggles grandiosely. Oh, Lee, you cant mean that.
I do, I do. Honest.
Well Im down to a hundred and eighty now.
Dont you dare go under a hundred and fifty, Rena.
But thats still too much.
No it isnt, youre almost five eight.
You dont want me skinny, do you?
No.
All right. A hundred and fifty.
Promise?
Yes I promise. Im losing weight because Im a lot happier, you
know that, dont you?
Yes.
Im a lot happier, Lee I can't work the way Sy does.
I know.
I think Im plenty jealous of him if you want to know. Nina is
sloppy in her painting. Her tubes of color helterskelter. Her black
hair splattered all over her face, paint smears on her forehead,
her cheeks, slashes of green and red and yellow up her arms. She
goes about her work with a clatter and a fumble. It takes Sy
fifteen minutes to ready himself for an oil. Half an hour for
Nina. Sy is noiseless, Nina trips, bangs, spills the paint thinner,
her whole frame stammers, blurts. As often as she cant find the
word to express a thought, and wildly waves her head and jumbles
her arms and contorts her neck and pushes her body this way and
that to painfully find the phrase to say what she means, many times
going absolutely dumb in the process so that she blushes, breaks
out into a twisted dazzle of laughter, goggles of guffaw, brays, hee-
haws as if shes hacking up her throat—just as often she cant
snatch up the right thickness of paintbrush, or furiously whirls the
carbuncles of color around on the palette to scramble around for
the right one. Sy is pleasantly tired after a painting session; Nina
is exhausted, throwing herself into an easychair, jeesus she rants
at the ceiling, who the fuck ever told me I could be a painter, if

19

I ever find the guy so help me Im gonna murder him, Ill rip him like a piece of canvas. And then, squeals delightedly at her own exhaustion. Im some helluva sight, aint I? she screams. Christ I want a houseful of kids, but how the hell could I paint, heh? Theyd be at my tits all day. Ah, to hell with them, I guess Im a schizophrenic at heart, but Im nice, aint I? But Ill never make it, she glowers the next moment, Im a naturalborn suicide, shit! Come on, Lee, have another cup of coffee, I made all the stuff for you, you drink tons of the stuff goddam it, DRINK she

looks all right to me, Lee shrugs.

No, Sy says. Shes breaking me. I dont make that much money as it is, and you know what shes spending it on? New dresses, thats what. Each week she comes home with a new dress. What the hell. Somethings gotta give

the monkey some pennies, because the monkey knows how fetching she is in her long white flannel nightgown. The dark has a mirror, and she can look into it. I used to think I could see myself in the dark, put up a black mirror and there I was, all lit up, she giggles at Lee. The monkeys very quiet. There arent any trees in her bedroom, she cant swing back and forth, and if she cant do that then shes got to go down on a stairway. The little monkey with its faintly protuberant brown eyes and round swart face and long warm black hair under the nightgown softly sinks down the stairway holding its toy tin cup out before her and then it opens the door to the street. And it goes out. And then it stops. And then it just stands there in front of its house on the street at four oclock in the morning, in the slate still cold. The shining cartracks go south on Fourth Street, and then north on Fourth Street, shining either way in their slate gleaming. The monkey extends her toy cup. But nobody passes. Theres not a soul in the black mirror, and Nina cant see herself, either. She cant see anything, or hear, or taste, or smell. She can only feel her monkey becoming stiller and stiller because the organgrinder tune has stopped : the organgrinder, she knows, has been welcomed by her mother and father

LETS CHANGE ORGANGRINDERS. Ah. Ah. Thats it.

20

Well, now, you cant do that and keep a little monkey alive and chattering

LETS CHANGE ORGANGRIND

Straight out, stiff, rigid, extends Ninas arm, the toy tin cup at the end, and stares up at the slate dark sky from which a penny is supposed to fall

BUT NOT IF THE ORGAN IS ANGRY WITH ME

the flannel nightgown stiffening in the dark stillness in front of the house. She wants to say the words but she cant, Mister gimme a penny, mister gimme a penny

the meanings standing for the people, you see,

are chopped up, hacked up into littler and littler pieces, till they arent recognizable, and they jumble

LETS CHANGE OR.

Or what? Theres no alternative for the little girl. You cant say a goddamn thing if theres no alternative

OR LETS CHANGE ANGRYORG. Partn. Change parts. Greasegreen eyes wont mix with water, float on top, embed themselves in the trafficlight at 4th and Girard, at 71st Street and Central Park West Lees got to get there, whether hes animal or no santAHHHHHHHHHHHHH lucheeAHHHHHHHH. She doesnt want to go anywhere, Nina doesnt. Solved. She's a trafficlight, shes the greasegreen eyes, shes green, shes amber, shes red, shes amber, shes green, she can change colors all in one role, one part, one stance, standing still, not saying a word, and everywhere else the traffic can go, and pass, and return, and flow, but all she has to do is stay in the same place, changing red amber

green

RED

green

AMBER

shes

the

organ

all right. but cold, not a feeling. not a sense. simply: three colors

ni

21

na
ni
na
ni
whats. She looks at the man. The traffic stops in a white coat. Your name. Nanin. No thats not it. Nanin, doesnt bother with it. Nanin, nanin

Dont you know you can catch an awful cold standing out here like this
nanin.

A little girl like you shouldnt be standing out here this time of night or this weather whats your name

na. nin. no. A monkey that has no tree is a trafficlight. Lee must climb, too, up 71st St where do you live

Na, no. He has a white truck like a buildingblock spelled, block for block : na, nin, no, ni. And—there are six bottles of white, three on each side, in his right hand, puts them down, bends to her, Harbisons Milkman

Where do you live?

Nani.

I said where do you live.

Nani. Penni. Monki. Parti. Mommi. Daddi. Moni. Nini. Ah. Ah. Ah

I cant hear you.

Na. Ah.

Did you have a bad dream? Did you walk in your sleep? Do you want some milk? Why cant you talk?

The cartracks shine slate gray. There are stone snakes between each twostorey house across the street so that you will not fall when you go down the two concaved marble steps from the door. You hold the snakes with your left hand or your right. The sky is monkeyhair black. I see a white block lying on its side because its chimney in front, also white, is also on its side. The block and the chimney have one wheel each. Gray smoke idles from the white block's chimney. The block says HARBISONS MILK. The pavement is dark gray walk in your. It is cold in your bad sleep, and you cannot move.

If your body cannot move, your lips cannot move, and your head cant hear you live or catch an awful cold or walk your name when you are a little leegirl, but the milkman at the end of the hallway should understand that you have one red eye, one green eye and amber teeth. They have names upstairs. They have names in bed. Everybody has a name except as a child. It is not true children have names. Oh no. Charlotte Nathanson Lees cousin does not have a name watching her mother and grandfather through the keyhole. Even Lee six feet two and one-half inches walking toward Central Park West has no name; nor when he bends his head to enter the Constellation at the Los Angeles International Airport he has no name. She would like to ask the milkman his name, but that would spoil it. He is nameless. So he is joking, of course. But she does not smile. The joke makes her look even more stern. You have a responsibility to be more and more grim as the joke becomes more and more funny. As everything becomes louder and louder you must be quieter and quieter. Suddenly, though, the milkman stops talking, and Nina knows that she must at last open her mouth and say something about lets change partners, clearly. And in that instant she shuts her eyes, so that she will not see the milkman's silence and can keep on standing there and can keep on being dumb

dumb; he rings the doorbell

dumb; he waits patiently

dumb; Mrs Brody is a stuporous unsteady ton of bronze hair in the doorway in the purpleflowered housecoat the greasegreen eyes crackling with cartracks and wrenching in her daughter's hand;

dumb; maam I guess shes I found her out and she wont

dumb; yeh yeh gimme the milk I got her

dumb FORCEFEED HER the bottles of squashed white cockroaches against the throatwall. There are three people in my family. If I were older I would be silent for three years. But I am a little girl, so I will be silent a month for my

mother a month for my

father and a month for

Nina. Me? Me? Oh : I dont count. I wish I couldnt count Lee

23

thinks glumly on the snowslugging corner of Frankford Avenue and Somerset Street at four-thirty Sunday morning, three blocks from the Goldstein Delicatessen. I wish I didnt have to count the seven days before Rena will let me put my prick into her big cunt next Sunday afternoon. He chews slowly on a rapidly cooling hotdog in the shelter of the Greek's hotdog stand that has a brief tin cowl over the counter running its sevenfoot length. The Greek proprietor stands completely protected behind the small slidingglass window sections. Sometimes Lee goes in to clench with two or three other men beside the Greek behind the counter, but tonight he prefers to weather the cold and the snow as he waits for the trolley, his overcoat collar high and snug around his ears, but they are beginning to burn. The snow particles snap at him, nicking his wayward nose and pelleting through the chinflesh to icily heckle the bone. Dim white mammoths stable against the granite church and parochial school directly across, and his sullen eye, winkbrittle in windsting and snowshot, curtly dismisses the dark tailorshop on the other corner and the black threestorey residence on the third. Cold and hot in the overcoat, warm and cool in the pajamas, drowsy and hot on the Pacific beach he wishes he doesnt have to count the number of times a four-year-old girl with a bare minimal hipshrug whips a plastic hoop around her waist. Twelve. Sixteen. A master. Everyone on the beach eyes her enviously. The glintshot from the bisonwaves nick his eye. The palisades behind twist his neck around. FLAGS RESTAURANT, concrete slabs behind it buttressing the soft palisade. The palisades slide. They slide a quarter mile down the Coast Highway, they slide a quarter mile up. At Flags, no slide. But the warm air slides. The shadows slip. The water slips and slides. The afternoon slides under the noon, under the bathers darkly in the water, under the beach umbrellas, under the baretorso men and the bikini girls. Thirtyfour, thirtysix, forty, the circling hoops of the gulldusk slide under the day, lifting it over and beyond the palisades. The slipping sun slides over a swimmers saraband arm, the bisonwaves shot, foamstaggering at the shoulder as the little hunterbirds with bowandarrow beaks race mustanglegged parallel to the herd

The end of the Western Scout, Lee offers Norma, takes place

24

before your very eyes on the California shore. What am I to do with Rena as the Germans march through Poland, fortyone, fortytwo

Oh the hell with the hoop, Norma says. Naturally, many pennants, varicolored, fly from toy poles affixed to FLAGS RESTAURANT, the poles like one side of an aisle whose sabres are upraised, quite military, and on whose points are transfixed multipasteled paper triangles, tattling in the breeze, here comes the bride,

here comes the bride Rabbi Dr Jonah Silver officiating waiting beneath the canopy. David and Betty. Lee and Rena. But no music. Weeping from the immediate family, but no

fortyeight, fifty

Over the textile mills of Philadelphia's Kensington, above the Frankford El, can be seen day and night, illuminated diurnally by the natural resplendence of the sun, and nocturnally by banks of spotlights at its base, a gigantic reproduction of a MILKBOTTLE erected on the roof of the dairy it symbolizes and advertises. The MILKBOTTLE is dumbfoundingly and magniloquently white, and in cursive Tudor Black is the gigantic letter H on two sides of the MILKBOTTLE, arrogantly denoting the initial letter of the company whose cows and bottles serve the populace: Harbisons. True, there are the other milk companies, Breyers and Supplees and Abbotts, whose wagons on puffy rubber tires first are pulled by horses and at last by engines. But if one raises one's eyes skyward, the Philadelphia horizon is instantly purified to a supernal degree by Harbisons MILKBOTTLE, WHITE AND SQUAT, hereinunder known by the lets change parties of all parts as MILKBOTTLE H

fiftytwo

sixty the hoop around the little girl goes blind. The faster the spiculed spindle, the dimmer the hoop. But the man and the woman with the little boy between them continue to stare at the spinner. The man and woman each hold a hand of the boy between them

The boy, Norma says, dammit the boy!

The little girl herself who spins the hoop, Lee says, and the boy. Norma hunches her eyebrows at Lee. Yes, he says. Possibly, she says. Mrs Sherman has hunched eyebrows, quizzical, the crows-feet at them as her spiked high heels, spindled. Her thin auburn hair, dyed and waved, wrinkles out of the latest copied Paris chapeau. In winter, chinchillad; in autumn, minkstoled; in summer, boldly haltered and in shorts; in spring, pasteled; in all seasons, spindle-heeled, clattering from her house next to the splinter faction synagogue at B and the Roosevelt Boulevard to the Number 50 carstop at Rising Sun Avenue, her fingers bediamonded, besapphired, berubied, gems pendant from the corners of her mouth, the spikeheels gabling one shoulder higher than the other, she moves at a tripping teeter, the smile glittering as Rachel Emanuel the furry squirrel crooks her index finger at Lee, See see see Mrs Sherman her husband doesnt have a cent to his name, not an automobile, and yet look how proud she holds herself, she looks so high and mighty with her rings and her high heels and her dyed red hair

You sure Rena dont dye her hair, Rachel insinuates at Lee.

Im sure.

How can you tell, hah? You noticed the streaks in her dark parts. Only somebody dyes their hair and lets it go has streaks

I can prove, mother, that

Dont prove me dont prove, Rachel turns away disdainfully. A mother knows. Ask your mother she can give you the benefit of her experience look look look at Mrs Sherman. Dont she look a little crazy?

Not particu

What are you talking. Thats all she has. Her furs and jewels. She has to take the trolleycar. You know what her son turned out to be? He tried to go to medical school, ah, a nothing. Too dumb. He tried to be an accountant, but for that you need real sense. So what do you think he is?

I cant possibly guess

Try. Try.

Mother I

All right all right. A chiropodist, yet. Curiously, then, sly, to her son : Aint that what Renas brother is?

Thats right.

26

But he aint so dumb. Hes successful. Mrs Shermans son isnt so successful. Poor thing, like me, shes got no satisfaction from her children. One son was enough. Me, I got two dumb ones. Well, one. Dave. Youre smart already, and still youre dumb. When you think of it, Daves not so dumb either, its just hes got no sense. What did I do to deserve such look look look Mrs Sherman with her fancy clothes has to take a streetcar shes so smart. But you got to give the devil his due, a good president of the Brith Mikveh Sisterhood she was, raised lots of money, always on the go, and what speeches, one of the best presidents we had, you got to give her credit she keeps herself so young, always faputzed, like shes got no troubles, but one thing shes lucky, her son loves her, he cant do enough for Mother why dont you stay overnight, weve got room, why go back to an empty house, dad wont be back from his territory for another week yet

No no no, Mrs Sherman says

and a long thing for her cigarette yet, Rachel points out

Its called a cigarette holder

So why didnt you tell me. Other sons tell their mothers when theyre making mistakes. You want me to sound like a fool?

Ill feel better in my own house, Mrs Sherman spikeheels up the mouthcorners at her son. Ill sleep better.

Mrs Shermans son a hulk of a man, slips and slides inside him that break up his face, dark, into pallid planes under heavy eyebrows. You still having trouble with insomnia?

Grinning, Mrs Sherman admits it. So I read myself to sleep.

I'll feel better if you sleep here overnight.

Mrs Sherman jiggles her head. I'll be all right, dont worry, what could happen to me in my own house? Your father would feel better knowing Im home. He might phone. Hed feel better if I talk to him from the house. Goodnight, son. Kissing him and her daughterinlaw, she clatters, the past president of Brith Mikveh Sisterhood, hardly balancing herself on the spindles, spicule pains slitting up her feet through her calves, having her hoist a shoulder, down fourteen steps to the street, the trolley, Roosevelt Boulevard, the maples in stuporous procession, lustreless green at summerend, up sixteen steps to the wooden half pillars saggingly

27

imitating the classic Greek painted a wan white on either side of the front door its many tiny panes of glass stretching and separating the features of Mrs Sherman. There is a moment before she removes the key from her brocaded handbag, startled the first time by the splay of her face in the tiny glass panes, the perpetual onesided smile stuttering all over the door, the auburn ringlets now here, now there, now everywhere stuccoed upon the front door, the eye pouches brocaded by the eyelashes into the handbag of the face, the orange lipstick having come loose and sunk into spicules of orange into the tiny lines under the lips, the powder knotting and flaking and offsplotching from the frizzled flesh, the head unbalanced on the neck, the one shoulder onesidedly smiling, the jewels as spotlights shining through the translucent jowls, rending the thin neckflesh limb from limb, the vertical cords of her neck prominently displayed, but her blue eyes still fizzingly blue, fresh as far and as beautiful as only fear can be exclusively in the eye, Itll be only right if he phones me Ill be in my own bed she tells herself reassuringly, only for a moment having the faintly horrifying vision of her vertical neckcords become horizontal

Vertical. Yes. The boy between the man and woman watching the girl spinning the hoop. Hes blind.

I know hes blind, Norma says impatiently, but why is he jumping up and down up and down

like a flamefitter

holding on tightly to the hands of the man and the woman. Because he cant possibly jump back and forth on the beach, this way and that, Lee responds savagely, if hes new to the beach, so hes got to move inside a blind hoop, the girl spinning the hoop quite silent too, not a word, precisely as the boy, why should the spectators be watching the little girl alone, the two of them should be stared at in the afternoon sun, the blind boy springing up and down

sixteen eighteen

thirtytwo fortythree

how long will the two of them keep it up, the jumping loinclothed boyflame, shuddering, as from a launching platform, up, only to descend, the guyropes of the man and woman committing him to limiting error between their static hoop, Norma and Lee choicing the boy, the others the girl, when all of us should encircle both, because the blind boy would like to use the man and woman holding his hands as a hoop he in the middle and roll down the sand, roll down to an object he could fling himself against or immerse himself in, instead he must partly shinny up the air like a Ninamonkey as the little girl seeing the blind one from the stared perfection of her hoop thinks to herself he should have a hoop then he wouldnt have to jump up and down, nobody suggests it to him, I would myself if everybody wasnt staring at me so I have to make a record number of hoopturns, I got to establish a challenge so I cant help him

its the fault of everybody on the beach that I dont give the boy my hoop look at his mother and father stupidly looking at me while they remember to keep fast hold of their boy, backblackward, no sun for the boy except the sense of the heat which he must plunge up and down in, if not for the little girl everybodyd be watching him, commiserating, this way the pity is confined to Norma and Lee, and Lee can but glance from time to time at the goddamned little missile on its sandy launching platform restrained from flight by the handropes. He wouldnt fly anyway, thats sentimental, he gruffly dismisses it. Hes blind as a hoop. The little girl mentally withdraws her prospective offer, because the hoop if he uses it must only torture him, but maybe even that would be good, hed have an agony inside him rather than outside

Lee.

Whats the matter.

Time to get up. Its six oclock Rachel calls standing outside the bathroom, heavyhipped and heavylowbreasted in the heavywhite flannel nightgown with its thin pale lavender stripes, her dyed black hair in pincurlers, her bunioned feet in felt slippers splitting at the seams, her calves in white and blue stripes of flesh and vein and fretworked in volutes of purple where the veins make their small explosions under the skin, all the little fireworks of delicate degeneration.

29

I got fifteen more minutes, Lee mumbles.

Youll be late. You dont want to be late for the Army

jesusCHRIST

Dadll drive you down to the bank, Rachel calls. Hes waiting downstairs now. He cant wait forever. Hes got to get down to the Yard. The trucks are waiting for him

All right, all right, Im getting up Lee tosses aside his eyelids with the bedcovers and springs to an upright sitting position on the bed, anger chesting him to absolute wakefulness and the winter cold freezing his mouth into grimace. For a moment the world in its perfect clarity is perfectly blind. Through the rear window the arclight is extinguished for the day, and its frosty glass protective cover a wrinkled sheen in the morning sun over the garage and the corner of Ruscomb and Rockland Streets. Tell them youre blind, Lee jabs a joke at himself, and unfit for military service. Because its impossible to move. Anger and cold immobilise him, his jaw jutting, his arms clenching at the bed-sheets. Stairs descend just off the middle of the hallway. It is impossible to crawl completely to the other end. The trafficlight meaning STOP is white or gold or blue, never red. The whitegold-blue trafficlight of the early morning never changes. Lee can stay here, crouching on the bed, his broken ankle in a cast on the open-porch mornings of five and a half years of age ruminating on the Boulevard traffic flowing by. Fractured blind bones, the world-hoop spinning around the blindboy. Everybody look : see how many times the earth can revolve around me, whats the army and military service compared to such a feat? And I can jump up and down SIMULTANEOUSLY as the hoopworld revolves about me. Sheer magic. Im exempt from the draft. Definitely, Rena, you need not come down to the station to see me off. I dont want you seeing me off, Im angry, the little boy jumping up and down between the man and woman like flame practice is furious, in a vertical rage. Rage isnt horizontal at all, because its blind, and it doesnt know where it is, so its got to spring up and down. Naturally I cant be expected either to go forward or blackbackward. I must sit here on the bed. I will. I wont move. Nobodyll make me. Ice and rage but

30

WHATS HE DOING UP HERE RACHEL TELL HIM TO HURRY UP
to water

all right its toothpaste on the teeth and a squat on the toilet
and a comb through the black hair and the heart snarling around
its pumps, sonofabitch the blood comes up easy, sonofabitch how
goddamn modern can the body get, turn on the throatspigot and
the red blood pumps up like a geyser, hot or cold or luke anyway
you feel and its all there in the bellysink with its navelstopper so
youll have a whole basinful which Lee doesnt ordinarily do, he
usually uses the two spigots of hot and cold water, washing first
in the one and then switching to the other, now he balances both
in the small reservoir

Lee your eggs are ready

all right Im coming Im coming

sluicing down the jellyeggs, his father on the porch, pacing.
Levi paces late at night, from porch to kitchen, arms finger-
clasped behind him, frowns cluttering his forehead, pacing out the
night, so many steps to morning, so many steps up the narrow
way to the second floor of the Levi Coal Company where he sometimes pauses for fifteen minutes or so during the workingday for a
rest, or to eat his lunch away from the noise and the clamor, Max
Pollacks been blind twentyfive years, Lee

Rachel hovers over her son as he hunchmunches away at the
kitchen table. At the stove two feet away. Sure you dont want
some cereal, Lee, youll have something in your stomach for
the trip, till they feed you.

No, mom.

I could make it easy, it just takes a minute.

I dont want any cereal.

Cereal sticks to the stomach, its good for you.

The eggs are plenty.

Its no trouble, Lee, she smiles worriedly.

I know it isnt but the eggs are

All right all right, I was only suggesting, dont get huffy.

Im not hu

I only meant well

31

I realize

Some fruit?

No.

I can make a little something for you to take along with you,
youll get hungry before they feed you

No I dont like carrying any bags

Whats the matter you feel ashamed to carry a

I dont feel ashamed. Its just another load, and I dont like
things in my hands

Itll be light, whats so heavy

No.

Coffee?

Yes.

I didnt have time to make it regular. All I got is instant.

I like the instant better. I cant stand that no caffeine stuff.

Whats the matter no caffeine. The other keeps you awake.

Not me.

Not you? Thats funny. Me it does. Thats why I changed. You
know how hard it is for me to fall asleep anyway, I lay awake all
night thinking, I hardly got any sleep last night in the bargain,
worrying.

Theres nothing to worry about.

Thats what you think. What do sons know. Wait till you have
children of your own. Who knows when youll be back. She begins
to sniffle.

Ill be

I hope you will, Rachel heavily giggles, suddenly, I hope you
will. Then, absolutely certain. Of course youll be back. But you
get colds. You should keep your overcoat buttoned around your
neck, you know you get colds.

Ill make sure.

You always forget. You got a habit of forgetting. Can you remember that?

Ill remember

Sure you dont want a cheese sandwich, it wont take me nothing to make.

Thank you, mother. No.

On the train youll get hungry.

Im sure they feed you.

Not like your mother.

Lee chuckles at last. No, not like Mrs Emanuel.

Whats so funny.

Oh, mother, sometimes youre very funny.

Was I funny? She laughs outright, hovering at his side, elbow over stove. You watch out for the girls, Lee. They like to rope you in.

I got Rena, remember,

Rachel makes a very mysterious shrug. Who knows. Things can change before you know it.

We wont change, mother.

Always youre so sure. Life plays funny tricks.

What funny tricks?

Who knows? Do I know? Im just saying.

So stop saying.

I was only talking. The white flawlessly clean crinkled cotton halfcurtain over the window blurs the sun, but the forms of the backyard can be made out. The bare vines, stripped of honey-suckle, frowning, backtracking, wavering, scraggling and climbing over the rear of the garage. The stubby black fences on either side. The red brick wall of the garage and its monklike single window. The untaut clotheslines whipping in the morning winds, ready for the wash. The grass behind the dark hedge brown and patched. The rose bramble and no roses. The snowball bush with no snowball floral bursts. The scar on the little finger of his right hand throbs from the slicecut made by the glass washboard splinter

Another cup of coffee, Lee?

No thanks, mother.

Lee I cant wait forever, his father appears in the breakfastroom doorway.

Im ready.

Theres time for another cup of coffee, Levi, Rachel reprimands her husband.

So give him another cup.

Lee stands. Ive had enough. Lets go.

His mother wipes her hands on her apron. You going out the back way, Rachel inquires.

Wouldnt it be foolish if I brought the car around front, Levi says, it only takes more time.

So dont get excited, Rachel says, Im just asking.

Im not excited. So lets go already, he tells Lee.

Put on your overcoat. Wait, Ill get it for you, Rachel scurries out of the kitchen.

Mom, mom, I can get it myself

Here, I already got it, no trouble, you take so long Lee, she raises her forearm and waves her hand at him in affectionate derogation.

Levi tacks the two, cysting his mouth. So say goodby already, Lee.

Yes, yes. Goodby, mom. Any moment his eyelids will float away on the original Noahflood. Take two of every kind, the Lord says, two of the bird, two of the reptile, two of the beasts of the field, and let them go into the ark. Take two handkerchiefs, Rachel says, you blow your nose so much he bends down, the tall Lee, to kiss his mother on her lips which are warm and dry, cool and moist, wrinkled and smooth, Levi has his back toward them, in the pantry, his hand on the doorknob, opening the door, out on the step, his heavy muscular figure stooping forth into the ark, two of every kind, one father and one mother, one son and one daughter, but there are no sisters in the Emanuel children, both boys, two hearts if you have them because you blow your heart so much, and two arks because one is already capsizing on the motherwaters, Rachels underlip gouging into her upper, her fists at her mouth fighting her mouth

Be a good boy.

Yes.

Theres nothing to be afraid of.

Yes. Blind. He cant see in the blind water that floods over his skull, two by two, take two thoughts, but only one scald enters, burns, burns, fire in the modern American freezer, FIRE, FIRE

IN THE FREEZER ARK behind the eyelids noah noah noah ahno ahno ahno

ahno

go already, Lee, wiping her hands in her apron. A stiff board rams down his neck, youre a stiffnecked Jew

Ill see you as soon as I can, mother

Take care

Yes.

Write Dad and me the minute you can, hear? The mailman always stops to say hello.

Yes.

It doesnt have to be a long letter. A couple sentences. Put up your overcoat collar, and button it, she commands severely. Didnt I teach you anything?

Ill be in the car.

Never mind never mind, youll forget when you get out. You want to go to the Army sick?

All right. That better?

Yes.

Goodby, Mom.

Dont say goodby, its unlucky

half out the door, Lee turns, grinning, Mom youre so superstitious sometime

Never mind never mind

LEE

Go already, your fathers so impatient, so thick with hydrants is Rachel that she appears chinless. Raises her apron to her face watching her son's tall lean back bend through the garage door, watching from the pantry window over the gas refrigerator, through the small pane of glass, fitting her chinless face into the small pane, like a small animal in the glass underbrush peering out on enemy and lover. But she must call the butcher and the grocer, and wheres the colored girl, if only she didnt have to Gertrude Forsten on the upper level backyard pavement crunching her skinny redspeckled arms on the black iron fence Lissen Mrs Emanuel I have the same trouble

Im telling you Gertrude you always have to pick up after them

35

Aint that the truth Gertrude shrills Mrs Emanuel, her redhair wash in tiny wirered balls jiggling in the mondaymorning slaps of the white wash flipping corners and snapped unleashes in the slatecolored waspwind

No matter how you keep after them theres always something they dont do, theyre lazy goodfornothings but howm I going to get along without them

You cant. You just cant

You got to follow them around like they were babies, just like your children

I was telling my husband just the same thing the other day

How is he

Oh you know Mrs Emanuel, Gertrudes face shrinking, shagging, shelling, puttying, pressing, peeving, pewling, He works so hard

Yeh

So hard

Yeh

He comes home he dont want to do nothin

Yeh

But he does, Gertrude perks, packs a smile in swiftly, yes he does, he mends a screen, he waxes the floors, he

Hes a good man, Gertrude. Let me tell you hes a good

Dont I know it Gertrude scales highlow down at Rachel Emanuel, dont I know it

He certainly loves you, Gertrude.

Yeh.

Thats a man you dont have to worry about.

Well Mrs Emanuel hes not the only one. Now take your Levi

Yes hes a wonderful man, then giggles, only I dont tell him that too often

Well now, Mrs Emanuel, gee, Gertrude winds up her eyebrows, spreads her hands palms out, You just cant do that

You cant pamper them

Thats right

Once in a while I tell him, Rachel grins secretly.

You got to be careful

36

With everybody a persons got to be careful, Rachel says very seriously. The colored girls especially. You turn your back and they take advantage of you, Im telling you Gertrude you have to have eyes in the back of your head and you know, she frowns, I cant run up and down the stairs like I used to

I know I know Mrs Emanuel, Gertrude Forsten is very grave. You got to take care of yourself

But how much can you take care? Theres a limit Oh my goodness, Rachel huffpuffs back to the pantry steps, My roast, my roast, I can smell it a mile away oh it mustve burned to a nothing. Not that Levi would know the difference by the time he gets home sometime the meat is shrunk away to practically nothing rolling over the as yet unpaved section of Ruscomb Street past the patchy farmhouse structure of the Chalks where on the steps their son Ernie is already out with his right hand plucking away at an invisible guitar and his left hand down at his side vibrating

But Levi isnt trying to hurt anyone, theres the difference. Perhaps Levis right hand is indeed plucking away at the parallel bars running the length of his sickbed, but he isnt bullying anybody Lee: Lee: Lee: he says in a strenuous tone, as if his entire chest is lodging in his nose, Lee you got to tell me

What do you want me to tell you, pop.

Tell me what you want. Tell me what you want, the once gray-green eyes opening darkly on his son, hard and dark, with no sheen and yet not dull, not sunk, not buried, but bold, his hands cupping his eyes in their sockets

the Ernie Chalk plucking at the invisible guitar, the Gus Nathanson strumming at a quite visible butterfly, the two of them fitted one into the other and lying on their side in the sickbed, the white butterfly circling the bed, the guitarbody of Levi Emanuel groanplucked and wanting to discover a small boy he can torture and diminish and utterly reduce. There is no stature in the dying, there must be somebody smaller than I, there must be somebody who can crouch in fear beside me, whom I can lean over, LEAN over

)Levi tries to raise himself, DO SOMETHING he renoseancestrains at Lee. Do something,

37

do
something,
What?
The pain. In my back
im
a
small
b
o
y
(BULLY BASTARD ROOM ITSELF TOWERING OVER LEVI CHALK
THE VAST NIGHTSKY OF THE CONTINENTAL UNITED STATES OF
AMERICA TOWERING OVER LEE IN HIS SEAT FORWARD OF THE
WING IN THE CONSTELLATION THE CHALKDOTS OF LOS ANGELES
RECEDING)

Uncle Ben on the phone in his muted boulevardier voice Lee.
Yes.

Norma sits on the bed, her body chinning itself without motion,
focussed on Lee

I think you can guess why Im calling you

Theres an itching in Lees throat. It needs to be scrubbed with
soap and water. The ringworm has got to his throat, the fungus
is slowly mapping out his swallowsystem. Soap and hotwater,
then iodine painted inside his throat, to be then liberally coated
with cigarette smoke, one after the other, he scratches at his neck,
lamentation as iodine deep red, staining the inside slowly, biting
slowly, lamentation is not black, it is a deep ruddy winecolor, that
itches, burns, stings

You promised me you werent going to fly. Not ever, Norma
wrenches her lips to form the words

I said only in an

emergency the vertical boy springs up and down in the continental hoop of the United States of America, the engines move
slowly into a slideup revving leviathanic roar

Everything slides. The hand from the other hand. Mrs Sherman reads a book in her bed, smokes a cigarette. She drowses, her
fingers unshrug, her housecoat humps at her breast, her arm

38

slides from the book, the book to the floor, the cigarette to the sheet, the burning tip the color of her dyed orange hair itll be nice if he calls me Ill be at home her son with the sliding dark planes of faces one over the other like palisades sliding onto the darkening highway as Rachel Emanuel playing an old Indian woman peeps over the top of the palisade to keep a sharp lookout for the unwary pioneer urging the weary covered wagon down the Roosevelt Boulevard Mrs Sherman still one of the snappiest drivers

well wed better go now if Im to see him alive at all, Lee tells Norma. Ill call the Union Pacific for rates.

Well mother told me she and dad would pay the fare for Stefanie and me

The foetus rides free, Lee says from one side of his teeth. Did the doctor say itd be all right? he touches Norma's bucking blond curls,

if we go now, she says. Another month and itll be too late.

I hate to go at all, he says.

Yes, I know.

I do and I dont

I know

But Ive got to

I know. Norma spells out his whole body with gravity, grace, hunger. I love you, Lee

And I you, very

I told Uncle Ben I just had absolutely no more money to come in for to the corner of B Street and Ruscomb where Brith Mikveh synagogue begins, now once again an empty lot I guess somebodyll be building on it soon, he remarks to Levi.

Yes. Somebody. Tear down and build up, build up and tear down, Levi says heavily, as if the very banality of the process, as an overladen overweighted species, must suddenly crumble; himself an overweighted banal crawl behind the wheel of the Buick. I guess down B to Wyoming will be quickest, he intones to Lee. Where is the draft office?

Its the basement of the Wyoming Bank and Trust Company, Lee nibbles at his own short smile

and the paintbrush nibbling at his eyes :

39

the paintbrushes are faucets, hot and cold : Lee in heavy black
curls with Sy Tarrassoff's receding chin rides in the front seat of
the Buick. A son, who washes his hands under the hot and cold
running water faucets, graygreen waters. A father doesnt quite
understand why his sons chin should be receding, seventyfive
thousand dollars worth of David Emanuel

$$\$75,000$$

riding on the horses. Got one thing paid for, nevertheless. Got
away over the state line, nevertheless. Dave makes certain. Coaled

$$\$75,000$$

closer,

COLD

is a bankruptcy, Shun and Gadstreet, whats my credit fleeting?
Credit is a receding chin sitting beside him, heavy black curls, the
younger son a ffffffirile stroking moilmale washing his hands under
hot and cold, the hot water in the Emanuel bathroom steamingly
hot, dazzleicing down a vertical scald, the quick wash with the
soap and rinse under the hot, such a scald that he shifts to the
cold stream to reestablish toleration, then back to the hot for the
balance of the clean, Lees face can be seen longoblong, black-
curled, heavy tho Syrecedingchinned through the great Egyptian
pillars of hot and cold running water,

the very sparrow of a

sphinx,

small sphinx at the florists shop. Hothouse greens. The double
line of Wyoming Avenue cartracks compose the Lee torso down
which Levis Buick runs, fitted for flame, morning category, graygreen. He washes his hands of Dave, Lee's brother. Only theres
an old older brother in Levis manifold with Levis tough heavy-
chin, greenbearded, he will shave the greengray stubble later. The
hot is very hot. LETS CHANGE PARTYFAUCETS, Ninas hot and cold
monkey and greasegreeneyed mother, but Lees mothers plump,
rosyrose where do they take you down to broad street station

at the bottom it is
dusty brown the sunlight
is dusty brown falling
from tawny skylights ten

40

      thousand

                            $75000

feet above the pale lavender
flame scallops from the
Constellation
cold now. Make Levis run. Lee caught threequarter canted, moth-
wingfold in the Buick against the winterscreen, fire fire, how can
Levi turn on both at the same time for at the top of the blind boy
is 5th Street, where the morning sun is so blinding that the whole
top of the canvas hurts the eye one son in the Texas League,
nothing holding Lee back, my loins itch, he wants to take his foot
off the accelerator. Size of Levis shoe: $7\frac{1}{2}$. Quite small for a man
five feet ten inches in height. The size of Lees shoe is $11\frac{1}{4}$, D width.
$7\frac{1}{2}$. Accelerator. $11\frac{1}{4}$. We miss the brake. I omit it from the
canvas. I do not have seventyfivethousand dollars in the Wyom-
ing Bank and Trust Company Levi knows, thats how sons are.
I trusted him. I trust Lee. Insist on the canvas that both sons enter
underneath the vaults, I have a hoop of a wheel between my
hands, I give it advice on turning, in Hebrew letters. Dave runs
in a new car, paid for, thats all thats paid for. Theres a sleek
sprint offcanvas. Turn on the cold, the cold. Quartzhot crystals
babble through Levis blood, spray Lees skin; son hunches, the
cartracks converge abruptly into pointed pyramids, the hose at
Lees groin squirting cold water over the tops of the pyramids.
Diamonds of pinheaded men in ticktacktoe cravats are disposed
in crannies of goggles, staring through blackly curled goggles at
a rising sun, a scald of orange, cold water on the eye, sir, cold
water on, ice the heat on the retina Levi never calls Lee son, nor
David does he call son, each has a specific name he must drive
down to Run and Hadstreet, rankbrupt, to labor into his seven-
ties to pay every goddamned cent he owes on his son David,
Clancy Mann, ho, Clancy yet the sardonic snoirl, Lee separates his
feelings on his thighs, one hand on each, steel cartracks plunging into his legs: one line backtracks, pushes against an absolute
perpendicular, then we: absolutely make no relation between
one line and another, paralleling, a horizontal that may connote

41

an automobile bumper rams its elbow into the diamonds of pin-
heads before granitegreen bulge of a structure

ASSETS $1,548,492

LIABILITIES $1,548,492

MEMBER FEDERAL RESERVE I assure you, insured
up to, interest compounded at the rate of five minutes early :

GruffJove : I can wait five minutes.

Sure.

They got a lot this time. JoveGruff.

Pretty much, pop.

They all look so healthy. In Lithuania flakeccent.

1A. He dares a look at his father's hands, on the hoopwheel.
Greengray hairs on ruddy handbacks. Intolerable, than he can but
spring up and down within the carwheel. Intolerable, that, Lee,
has his hands fixed under both hot and cold running water. One
side of his body flaming; one side in a freeze; and a block of continental territory to his left, dark under the Constellation, his
father is named Los Angeles, then Omaha, then Chicago, then
Pittsburgh, then Harrisburg, then. And all the land between his
father is: heavy, bulging, continental, mountainous, ravined,
valleyed, laked, rivered; is alkalid and sagebrushed, is forested
and forestfired; his father is a globe, a capitol, a hemisphere ruddy
and graygreen, heavychinned in the nightsky, revolving, and revolving, and revolving beside him in the Buick while he sits in the
middle of the hoop watching for the chance to spring out without the sides of his father's body touching him, avoid the revolving and the revolving and the revolving for he your father may
spin you into spumeflake and spiculespray, hurtle you beyond

ASSETS

and

LIABILITIES

:

IS

he worth more than seventyfivethousand dollars Levi grunts. The
dollars have pain. The dollars have chunks. The dollars have
charcoal bags. The dollars have great loads of crap he has to get
rid of nightly in the Emanuel toilet on the Roosevelt Boulevard

my son. Dollars are my Lee, whom he does not look at in the front
seat, fearful he may hurl his entire dollarbody upon him, belly-
smothering the young dollars, hold him down for gods sake the
   oi oi oi the slim young egyptian
   oi oi oi the secondborn for he the jew he jew Levi must flee
Egypt and here his egyptian bastardson will stay behind, my god
my god why hast thou created us father and son has father and
son created He them. Tear Czar. So do the Russian borders retaliate. Out of one army into son's another, the Egyptian drowns
in Rocky River, at the bottom of the river as the drowning man
locks Lee Lee pictures his father in a Buick before
                    ASSETS
                    LIABILITIES
my loin has no more dollars. Rachel? She: no compound inter-
locking. No fuck. Less Lee. Fuckless. Slip and slide
   o healthy five m
   nts
   fi
   Here take it. Lee looks at the five Levi folds into his hand, ah,
laughing, (
   laughing,
laughing,
ahahahahahha: ho: in the five bucks, the loaded crap dollar-
pain father and son hands touch
   What i
   You might. Maybe youll need it. Take it
   Well all r
   miscellaneo
   us. Yeah. Little things, razorblades, vaseline hair ton, cigarette
   s
   Ill send you more.
   Thanks, pop looks like theyre getting ready. Well. The faucets
have stopped running. Neither hot nor cold. Across from the
bank a newsstand. Morning papers. Bulletin, Daily News, In-
quirer, Ledger
   Behind the newsstand a florists shop. Wait for Number 50
trolley. Down to work, they stare at the draftees. Work. Germany.

You know. Itll just be a year, pop
Yeah.
Hitler wont
Guess not
Glad mom has low blood pressure instead of
Yeah, shes lucky.
Its time for me to report
I know, Lee. Speedometer. Oil gauge. Gasoline indicator. Battery, charge, discharge. Lights. Horn. Clock. Glove compartment. Dashboard. Back seat. Armrest. Rearview mirror. Fender mirror. Windshield. Windshield wiper. Clock, oil gauge, gaso, speedome, choke.
Choke.
Choke.
Choke.
Choke.
Choke.
Choke.
Choke.
Choke. Choke. Choke. Choke. Choke. Choke. Choke. Choke. Choke. Choke
CHOKECHOKECHOKECHOKECHOKECHOKE NOT NOT NOT NOT NOT NOT NOT NOT NOT NOT NOT NOT NOT NOT
lee.
No, Sy Tarassoff will not substitute. Not this morning. No, nor will Rachel Emanuel substitute this morning, Rachel nibbling at the morning wash, here I am in a sheet, mother, for fathers keep, so youd better register for the draft. Theyll train you to be me. Levi rages at Washington DC, whats my wife doing in the army, its illegal. Mother, youre illegal. Go instead of him, Levi bellows. Ah, no, Rachel says. Not this time, Ive got my wash to do, its Monday morning, how can I leave the colored girl all by herself, you got to keep watching them, you wont have anything clean to sleep on she tells Levi, would you like that?
I guess not.
Youre betraying me for the Monday morning wash, Lee guffaws, do you realize that?

I have to sleep on a clean sheet, Levi says, defensively.

Can that be defended as against sending your wife to war?

Do you have to smoke so much, Levi asks.

A new experience, Lee says. The army.

Ah, Levi deprecates. Youll see itll be nothin, a boy of your intelligence.

Sure. Youll be late at the Yard.

So once Ill be a little late. Itll run without me.

You never said that before.

I dont like to think that. I like to think the business cant do without me. Of course thats nonsense. Itll go on after Im gone. We like to think nothing can do without us.

I wont want to do without you, pop.

Nonsense, nonsense.

No, no non

Yes yes, Levi shakes his head. Youll get over it, mark my

A Number 50 trolley can be seen down the long dip of Fifth Street going north, ascending toward them. Clangclang distantly metal. The trolley labors up, gray green distantly, clangcl. Stops at a corner to take on workers

Clangcl

Should be replaced by busses, Lee says. Phillys so slow.

Yeah. Politics. Thats something you should think of going into, Lee. Look at all the great men. Lincoln, Teddy Roosevelt, did I tell you I once heard Teddy Roosevelt speak. Five hours he spoke, Lee, and would you believe it not a piece of paper did he hold in his hand. Not a note did he need. A great man, believe me. Bryan I also heard. Silvertongue orator. Five hours he spoke too, without notes. Extemporaneous. You heard of Clarence Darrow I guess.

Uhhuh.

Six hours he spoke I heard him. Extemporaneous. Lee you could speak like that

Oh pop

Yes you could. Youre good on your feet. I could still send you to law school you want to go?

Pop

I mean it
I better get out and report.

HORN AND HARDARTS RHONA LRYIAN
DIANE VALIN
CELIA RENN
MARK FAHN
SILAS KLEIN
ACHILLE VOLPE
ROSA CABY
BARRY HANDLER
FIONA AND CORNELIUS NURI

JAY across the square table in the Statlers diningroom downtown Los Angeles, series of vertical triangles from head to toe, the thin bloodless lipline If you remember, Lee, I used to write those ballet stories but I stopped doing that a long time ago. Had to. No, sir, couldnt go on doing that, the voice the thin bloodless lines running through. Couldnt exist on that, no, sir. Not with three children and a wife. Ever hear from Rena?

No.

Not with a wife and three children nosir, Lee. Got a pretty fair job now you might say, the triangle series and its bloodless thin lipline teeter precariously, the top trianglehead thrust back, the middle battened down in black charcoal business suit, black tie, white shirt, white cuffs, cufflinks protrude from the triangle hands; you might say; with a watersoftening outfit in Racine. Sales manager. In LA to expand the sales territory you might say. All expenses paid, order a steak, Lee, the company pays for it, you have to sell yourself, I found that out, yessir. Sell yourself. Nobody elsell do it for you, the triangles protrude from his chest, from his eyes, a snakeline on his lips, a faint blue snake, horribly undernourished, the slightest of blue curls to his underlip. Yknow tho one of the best ballet stories I ever wrote was the Minotaur and the Labyrinth

You want to hear my story Jay directs at the girl in the scarlet dress, then shrugs his lipline, the red girl in maybesmiles at the young man to her right, the cafeteria thronged with the musiclovers after the Saturday evening concert of the Philadelphia Or-

46

chestra. The girl simply cant hear Jay, who then turns to her friend in the purple dress. The red girl simply sits in her maybesmiles as the young man to her right talks around her, she inserting response to each circle, tangent and entering, shaking her rotten orange fruits of hair in sorties down her broad tawny forehead, shoulders sloping from the powerneck into the bisonbosoms lowering and kicking under her scarlet shortskirted frock, her ankles arent thick Lee jubilantly pronounces, theyre big not not thick, in suitable proportion to the long, generous calf and the spread of thigh under the scarlet, the wide hazel then brown then black then tawny eyes spattered with saltant riant flickerings, immune from cosmetic the whole face he growls over, kneels over, except for the mouth scarletthicked as her dress I will be with her all the days of my life his groin fizzes the hot faucet, I want to lay my mouth on hers

did you say your name was

Rena Goldstein, she labyrinths her fingers of both hands, strong long thick fingers you say yours

Lee Emanuel

They strike each other with catoninetail grins, Rena and Lee, got to have my ringworm treated and cured once and for all he reminds himself. Grins. Her teeth brilliant bones, the fingers labyrinthing about them

Are you here often?

Snack of a laugh, we will refer to, cavalier specialist Lee, depreciating, an impossibility not to be in The Heel

That what they call this H&H?

Yes. Practically every night.

Really?

Im an addict.

Oh. What do you do?

Plays. Write pl

Do you do you Im glad you

Are you?

Yes. Thats wonderful

Not really, its n

47

Yes it is, the effervescing glory in tawny precipitations upon her strong humped nose
And you?
Oh I. Me? Go to school, naturally.
Where?
The University of Pennsylvania, Rena says most ingenuously. In my sophomore year, her heart hoops at the sight of him, the Lee, the boy, the young man, hoops at his days growth of beard, the fizzes of black curls on the big black bony head and the slashingly white skin, the eyes closeset,
   in angina vectoris
   at the doublebreasted fecalbrown suit the boy, the young man, this Lee wears. Clips of pain in her, her heart the canted bevelled wingfolded smallmoth against the Leescreen, her heart with the tiny black twinks of popglisten eyes tacked on his screen, breath laborious, breath not at all, immune from breathing clipped against the black and white tall lean Leescreen, hes so skinny, doesnt his mother feed him properly, he probably drinks only coffee and coffee and coffee and he smokes incessantly, I wont have to breathe with Lee, my eyes will do all the airing, her nipples the small scarletbrown moths folding out toward him oh Lee youre so skinny Ive got a whole delicatessen store, youll have salami and bologna and pickles and my mother makes wonderful potato salad hes not handsome. No. But hes black and white, and very tall, and longthinfingered, and blackbrowneyed, my eyes yours, his profile is a boys, so young, hes so very young and tall and he must have a long turkeygobblet my brothers run around upstairs all the time dressing and undressing I see their pilgrims progress all the time Lees must be my nose isnt as perfect as Lees Ill sing for him he doesnt know I
   live? 3892 Frankford Avenue, yes write it down, and
   236 East Roosevelt Boulevard
   Hey you two want to get some beer at The Bloody Bucket Jay laughs in thin lines at the two of them, their tongues practically
   Bloody Bucket, Rena momentarily spicules at Jay, whats
   The Clock, actually, Lee instantly interposes, on Arch Street, would you like some beer Rena

48

Oh, wigglewhirling at her friend, say yes, say yes, say yes
The purplefrocked friend, gogglegiggling, All
Yes, Lee, Id love

Lets go. I mean I havent that much, you know, I hope you
dont mind, a couple anyway, you sure you dont mind if there
arent four or five beers because I forgot to

snappaining for the young man, Rena douses him with plumes
of pride, No no no, I only want one, lets

Rising, the two, Lee, Rena, preceding the others, Jay and the.
Pre. Ce. Ding. By her side, Orangered boomtitted girl, by MY
side, past spectators, past all men, all women, talking about them,
SEEING the two, turning, Rena and Lee, the girl the girl my girl,
this is she, yes, yes through the revolving door onto Broad Street,
downflitting his skull to her upgaze I want to tow her mouth to
mine, please, crooking his arm, an elbow, here you are, Rena

Yes?

Mumble. He mumbles. Hard to say it. But must. Sort of a,
well, suggestion? You can if you want you dont have to if you
dont want but, you know

Do take my arm

Yes.

Oh, he smiles. She grips his arm. No mistake about that. North
on Broad, they PRECEDE the others, fast, faster, a half block ahead
they leave the others behind

Do you like music?

Oh yes, yes Lee. I play, too

What?

Oh, piano City Hall the mausoleum ahead, black ponderous
granite squat. Not very well, youll hear

Will I?

I dont see why not

I mean I want to see you again.

Do you?

Yes.

I want to see you again, Lee.

I want to see you again very much.

I want to see you again very much, Lee.

Very.
Very.
They swell to a halt for a moment in the sweet cold on Broad Street. A bank. A Guaranty Title and Trust Company. A subway entrance, Chestnut Street, NORTH ON BROAD. Cars susurrate. Lees mouth has ears on it, Lees ears have mouths, the wind swears Renas rottenorange hair back. They are slings of gravity in the stiff black icy night. The two are ironbound in the gravity, effacing and facing each other, changing position without a move, mist hushing from her lips Lee darling she tries to herself, Thy belly is as a heap of mist, Lee tries to himself, the cold is a buzzardhoop circling them, they have each others hands, hands that can explore, extend, move in, turn, hit, smooth, but the hands do nothing but hold each other, all exploration done, all smoothing finished, all hitting lapsed, all extensions immobilized. These are our hands, her tweed coat open from top to bottom, the scarlet frock telling her whole body, his trenchcoat slapping his calves

I will see you again, Rena. Quickly.
Yes.
The buzzardhoopwind upmarauds their chins.
Quickly.
I want you to. Waits. Still as the buildings, City Hall, squat granite. Guaranty Title and Trust, squat granite, cars gunning, pulling out from the curb, turning down Chestnut single cartrack line, but the young man, the young woman, face each other effacing, hands in each other, covering and interlining, tall gaunt Lee, hes so gaunt, hes so, sumptuous rubescence of a Rena, shes so voluptuously volute

I want to see you tomorrow night.
Where?
At The Heel.
All right, Lee. I'll be there.
About ten.
Yes, about
By yourself.
Yes, by

50

Alone.

Alone, Lee

They swear exultant chuckles at each other. Turn toward the others nearly at them on the quartzgrained pavement. Now they can walk four abreast, and sit two across from two at the Bloody Bucket, and Lee is no longer afraid, and Rena is not afraid.

Hoppy Zitin, jewellers apprentice, not Morrie who introduces Lee to Rena, whose single appearance in The Heel for the introduction is his own foreclosure, Imagine that Danny Naroyan squeals to Pinky the Pomeranian on his Lindley Avenue verandah, he doesnt like us intellectuals, Ah its not that Morrie slickhair disclaims, that crowd just aint for me, but Ill tell you something, Danny, yes you tell us something tell us Danny violently shakes Pinkys head the goddamn rugs can wait he bawls at his fourfoot eleven mother standing balefully in the doorway, if it wasnt for guys like me that there friend of yours. Lee? Yeh. Chances are heda never met that girl, heda just sat there and looked. So what kind of a girl is she Morrie, tell Pinky and me, Pinky wants to know DONT you Pinky Danny flips the Pomeranian on its back and ferociously tickles the dogs belly, Pinky yelping, yapping all of its four legs in a furry desperate jabber of frustrated locomotion Christ I dont know, she looks like a juicy enough cunt CUNT you hear that Pinky thats what Morrie thinks of girls, thats all theyre for, theyre brainless, hysterical, capricious creatures ARENT you Pinky, all they want to do is just lay down before any male that comes along pinky Pinky PINKY you stupid hysterical female creature you Danny yaps at the dog if they dont have somebody to take care of them theyre witless Whats the matter Danny dont you like women Of course I like women fuchrissake Danny growls at the nagsmiling Morrie, but theyre pathetically stupid take this coloratura I sometimes accompany at a recital, why the poor girl is madly in love with me, cant let me alone, calls me once a day. Beautiful voice, great voice, seriously interpolates, no getting away from that. But no sense, HAS she Pinky, squealing again at the Pomeranian and barking, Pinky yipping right back as he jumps one step toward Danny and as Danny bends to her she jumps three steps back yip yip yip the pink fur fierce. Half German half Jewish. Maybe that accounts for her Pinky? No, you idiot, Danny growls, the coloratura aria from where asks Lee. I cant place it, Hoppy, and switches again toward the revolving door. Shell be here, Silas Klein heavily reassures him. The other three at the cafeteria table contribute confirmation, Jay, Achille Volpe, Mark Fahn. Well maybe not, Lee lightly counterposes. Pretty heavy snowfall. Not many around altogether.

The six at the table are a heavy concentration in the otherwise deserted cafeteria. The female brownhaired buddha who bears a brooding resemblance to Herbert Hoover sitting on her stool at the end of the row of steaming urns, hotplates, casseroles, trays, has no checks to punch with her steel tweezers, and gossips with the coffee-server, Caucasian. To the left of the cafeteria revolving doors, as one enters, an aged male sits on a high chair, the cashier, an employee loyal for twenty years in the dispensing of food, promoted at last to business suit and a charming small adding machine, both enclosed in a booth half marble and half glass, featuring a circular aperture in the glass for exchanges between customer and cashier at approximately liplevel, and a slit at the bottom of the glass for payments of the check and the making, if any, of change

prague; neville ch

;to the right a check dispensing machine, at roughly hiplevel, manned by a foodhandler, if he can be spared, who extends the courtesy of the establishment by pulling up a check from the slot of the machine as it automatically protrudes another and smilingly proffers it to the prospective customer; if business is tense, the customer himself pulls out the check, a little startled at the quite musical clang that accompanies the separation of pasteboard from slot, temperately reminding one of the more brutal clang that a trolleycar motorman summons forth with his foot to warn errant motorists or feebleminded pedestrians surprised on the cartracks

a Number 50 trolley slowly ascends Fifth Street toward Wyoming. Will it be Number 50 or Number 75? If the trolley that appears is the wrong one for the person who waits, the habi-

52

tué of public transportation will have to linger another fifteen minutes. In cold weather, and always at night, he can be seen agonizingly stepping off the pavement to the street to peer anxiously in the distance, desperately gaping to make out the number

I guess youll take the 75 to the Frankford El, Levi says, and thatll take the whole bunch down to Broad Street Station. Well I guess you wont be the only one, Levi is ponderously jocular. I see everybody else is going

Yes. Everybodys

at home tonight. Except the repossessed, Lee sourly sickles the group. Heavy snowfall.

Never heard you talk about the weather before, Silas Klein hoo hoo hoos in his basso.

Come on, Silas, get those goddamn books off the table, crowded as it is, Jay tremblethins at him without a glance.

All right hold your horses, hold your Silas reddens from pedestal neck to pediment skull, two thick red blocks, the squashed nose and forehead pimpled by sweat, the ancient snapbrim hat nobody ever sees him remove but his mother a sweatstained chocolate. Lee offers him a cigarette, to which a shy halfgrin, You never remember, Lee, I dont smoke, SAVE A LOTTA MONEY THAT WAY Silas suddenly juts at him, would you believe paid my way through lawschool no cigarettes and selling papers. Pumping his skull up and down, then halfyelling, Youre a good boy though, Lee, yessir

Jesus you dont have to smart my ear off, Mark Fahn tugs at it aggrievedly. Modulate, Silas, modulate

Yeh nearly forgot I had a composer next

Well it isnt that Silas I was raised in a family of six sisters.

Six! Achille Volpe cavils. Evil, evil, he sardonically shakes his globules—eyes, cheeks, chin, each of which seem to bubble forth from a globular crater of face. But one eye he must pull round to its perfectly normal brother; it is the left one, whose cornea lags to the left, a backward brother and filmed over with a thickening milky substance; backward, yet curiously canny, for sometime it seems to hold back from proper focus as if, in its straggle, it would

53

essay a better view, become a kind of observer before deciding to join the other eye : Achille finds it invaluable for his sculpturing though that eye steadily loses its power : one could see it being stricken in the knowledge that Achille and the sculpture will one day have to ignore that eye altogether. So the eye already is a sad stray, and imparts a mood of somewhat helpless struggle to the Volpe face otherwise vulgar and savage in its constantly convexing globuling

alsace

while Marks precisely ovoid skull at nineteen years of age is sweetly bald, the relic of a light blond fuzz softening the highlight glare on it; a gentle face, in loose oviforms of youth, except for the mouth long on one side and short on the other, ripped on the longer by a rending sneer of lustreless lechery wiped by a rasping hate, the lips pale pink and the surrounding flesh a verdant pearl, the nose a mere smudge of cartilage

sudetenland; a globule Churchill fattening a bench in the House of Commons

Dave

Yeh pop

So let Lee come down a couple weeks, its going to hurt the Club?

Its not that itll hurt the Club, pop, but we just aint got the room Id like the kid in Wildwood as much as you would

Dont tell me you cant make room

Well Ill see. Maybe he can sleep in my room, the whole house is nothing more than an old shack. You think hed like it? Ballplayers are a pretty rough bunch. Dave Emanuel, or Clancy Mann, is heavier than his father, but the deep chest is somehow disappointing in the excessive slope of the shoulder and the bold width of the hip; redeemed by bulgemuscled thigh and thick calf. His hair is as black as Lees, but rapidly thinning in the deep corners and on the pate; his head resembles Levis in its foursquare quality, but is more rounded at the edges, in this wise tinged by Rachels structure; the nose is a big piece of meat and cartilage, like a shoulder of lamb, humped and broken and bulbous; the forehead lines are cut more deeply than anyone else's

54

in the family, are more numerous, more jagged and more striking to the observer; but when he takes off his shirt in the room
back of his office in his coalyard at 22nd and Lehigh, it is the bicep
on the man that first impresses the eye, as Levis impresses Lee :
it has the width and the curve of a butcher's cleaver, and a shark-
like slash when the arm is in motion. The weakness and intensity
of Dave's harrowing worry are relieved only when the man tells a
story of one of his cronies or escapades, and is altogether erased
when he talks baseball

My Dear Brother Lee : As God is my judge, I intend to repay
every line of his calligraphy, each letter, is floridly formed, very
nearly rococo in its frill and arabesque; it is a handwriting at once
rigorously copybook and forbiddingly ornate, agonizingly neat
and decoratively indecipherable, while Lees, equally illegible except when he takes considerable caution, is from letter to letter
crabbed, sprawling, now ascending and now descending, now
oblique and now upright, a most obnoxious hodgepodge in the
heaviest possible strokes, at worst childlike and at best confused,
two characteristics Rachel displays in her own blurting scrawl.
Levi rarely writes a letter; sometimes, a note; pressed, a signature;
feeling that he has never mastered the script adequately and
would make far too many errors; he is diffident in the extreme
about the matter, and foregoes it with every possible pretext.

Hoppy did you ever consider trying to be a music critic? Lee
says to the redheaded Zitin.

Nah, Hoppys nose dodges and deflects, whos got the money?
He blinks rapidly, as if to blink his nose away, which occupies
most of his phiz; a nose something like the sideview of a peeling
axe splotched by pale orange freckles; the rest of his face seems
to shrink away, hide, run back quickly away from the nose; even
the puffy eyes have tried to be unobtrusive by way of their watery
pale gray, by their dimming and squint, not wanting to discern
the nose; they constantly tear, and he just as constantly blows his
nose Yeh my eyes are getting bad, its all that close work on the
jewelry, my doctor told me to quit but who can quit, its a living,
I sure as hell envy the bunch of you

Youre talking to the wrong man if you include me, Silas hoo

hoo hoos at him. As a hardworking lawyer I must take exception
All right, so youre excused. Did you see Rosa tonight?
I saw Rosa tonight. Part accusing, part envying, to Lee, She still
loves you
Id be sort of sceptical
Sceptical my ass. Im telling you the girl
In a dry capervoice, Hoppy wags his nose at Silas, Girl. Shit.
She's forty if shes
Now how the hell do you know. It happens I got the facts. I
make sure of the facts, its important to get the facts, Hoppy
Facts are dated, Silas, Hoppy rags his tones through the pejora-
tive nasal—all the time.
Its impossible to argue rationally with you, Hoppy, Silas grips
his mouth together, reddening violently, averting his face. Its
clever as hell to call facts dated but that doesnt tell the truth about
them
Lee withdrawing in the cheerlessness of momentarily remembering Rosa. You know she got so goddamn jealous of my coming to The Heel he interrupts Silas
Well yeh, you know how a woman
Tell us, Silas, what about a woman, Hoppy jeers
Aw let the man alone, Jay steers in disgustedly, his fingers
spidering around a coffeecup.
Let him talk, Jay, let him talk, Silas beefs his face on the block,
this dissembler of facts. Neville Chamberlain returns from Hitler
and assures the English that the man assured him thered be no
war, but this is too dated a fact for our friend Hoppy Zitin
You wouldnt know the time, Mark Fahn slyly interjects to Lee.
Oh. Yes. Its a quarter after. You bastard, he laughs, his brother
in fifty below Believe me, dear brother, I dont relish being in
Alaska, but I did want to write you because mom hasnt answered
any of my letters and its no use writing pop I just dont think either
of them understand The clock its numbers in Roman numerals is
situated just above the water faucets on the wall
I still say shes forty if shes a
Middle thirties, Silas pronounces authoritatively, in the tone of
having thoroughly tracked down all available facts. Married once,

56

and shouldnt marry again, all the statistics are against marriage, did you know that, Lee?

No I

Dont marry, my boy, dont marry. Take my advice. They all end in divorce. Ive had cases, shaking his head in curt abhorrence, naturally I cant discuss them. Referees in divorce cases are forbidden. Sexual incompatibility at the bottom of most. Very lurid, believe me, Silas uses his head as a stomper. All of them are sordid, he pronounces sweepingly, without exception. Then, benignly, sweetly, confidentially, Which is why I never got married. Not me. Marriage is completely corrupt. Money can be used to far better advantage. Another five years, Ill be taking my second trip to Europe. About ten and its twenty af. Fizzi Galleries, my boy. I shouldve had a sister, Donna Zion crawling over near Garden Pier Atlantic City on her belly then propping up torso on elbows Lee theres a lot you dont know just dont know What is it Donna her lowslung breasts dragging on the sand Lee lying flat on his back as Donna overheads him the breasts squirming on his ribs Russ is lucky to have her for a sister we could roll over each other, and over, over and lying on his back in his bedroom an eagerness to be a girl, to spread his legs with a great brutal muscular man over him about to Donna lisps slightly if I could only tell you Lee, well then, tell, but youre really too young to understand about two months in Paris Silas is hyphenated in a dashing codes of creases each at right angles to each other rubicund each crease with a bright bulb lit underneath, a tinkle of festooned tiny flashing bulbs on a blockparty holiday face I should be able to finish all my notes of course I know the Left Bank Hank Monahan is still over there he knows Joyce quite well matter of fact look up some of the old transition back numbers some of Hanks articles are there talks just like he writes in a bad automobile accident they got him back in Germantown. Yeh. Nothin but a wino now Silas hoohoohoos, but still talks as he I cravebound your pardon Silas, peoplost me stymie ago did you agknow your numb is Lassi somewit keenverted? Matter of fact Joyce was to some degree influenced by Hank Monahan, Silas gleehoohees

Now what the hells so funny about that, Hoppy Zitin clicks off a sneer, as he prods some jello, his adamsapple largesse humming up and down his throat a hunk of quiver with a helicopter all its own. I will ignore that, Zitin. You were born to it, Hoppy admits sadly. Hank Monahan is a pathetic case, I know that, Silas puts aggrievedly. Are the notes for the book, Lee queries politely, gently. Yeh. Long as Ive known Silas, Achille hulks in his black suit and trailing eye, fifteen years, right? Ri Hes been working on that Well Ive got most of the notes now, the unifying factor of all the arts, the element common to each, rhythm. Rhythm. Requires enormous documentation. The Law is simply a method of making twenty five minutes after ten a good living for my mother and myself I take no trolleys I have no car his face pounds up and down on a red block the small chunky man calls for order

ORDER IN THE KLEINROOM

did you know I walk everywhere? Yeh. He belligerently knocks the face of each of the five at the table. I walk to the library, I walk to the law office he shares with five other lawyers, I walk down to Second Street from Broad, and then down to Federal, a distance of a good five miles wouldnt you say Achille? The trailing eye pufflip broads assent. It doesnt matter what the weather is, nosir in Alaska its fifty below with Sue, Martin and Gregg, Sue working for the biggest lawyer in Alaska, she shoulda gone through lawschool Clancy miserably shakes his head drunken old sonobitch my boss is Sue blearnasals through her eight scotches and soda they call him for a case and I gotta go from bar to bar lookin for him, seventy if hes a day thats how you save money you young squirts wouldnt know a thing about that would they Achille rain or snow or hail I never mind. His ontogeny brought to book, Hoppy whispers to Jay. The equation is Labyrinth minus M, Jay clears his throat. I caught that, Silas chews at Hoppy. In mock horror, Thats the last thing Id want to do, Hoppy relents, is anger Silas. Nobody can make me angry, Silas blunts

Barry Handler, the black moss of hair combed back as far as it will go from the approximately two square inches of his forehead, his body a beaver and otter, small hands the slippery flippers of seals slapping them in the zoo pool as they beg for food from the circling onlookers, regrets to Lee that its certainly true

that Silas Klein is a veritable Brittanica. A pause, timed. Then :
the 1915 Edition

Im like that client of mine, naturally I cant disclose his name,
Silas confidentially leans to Lee its nearly ten thirty who finds it
expedient never to become angry you wont recognize her. Thats
good. The mind is a revolving snowflake out of the backblackward. For purposes of memorable study the crystallization does
not endure, running off in trickles from the dark eye looking down.
She wont come through the revolving snowflake. If one had an
invisible magnification, theres the solution. If I could pass around
and through her with the enlarging, she would adopt the same
principle, and we'd cancel each other out, become the magnification itself, his Roman numerals circle the cafeteria table,
pointing at each of the males, accusing Youve got time, I havent,
I wont recognize her, wherever she is I wont know her, I will have
got back here without a single smart

promises are idle wounds

she doesnt have to be at the army exhibition of the captured
German collection of paintings includes a long narrow Botticelli
panel the background absolutely dense black while through the
center with hair the color of rotten oranges

this is all I remember

like eves friend furling over the groin Aphrodite stands in amber
fleshtones, wait, Lee stands before the painting for half an hour,
were it not for the nose

this is all I remember

this is Rena do you think the Germansll march into the de-
militarized zone Ive got to move away from the painting

I may remember more

theres the whole rest of the collection to cover, Ive got to get
to the other end of gallery away from the Botticelli Youve looked
at the painting long enough Lee, Rena says. No, I the coffeecup
jiggles in the saucer the Roman legions lock boots across a de-
militarized zone dont you see Im, truce after Diane and Rosa
and Celia and Valerie and Jennifer Hazlitt the littlefingerscar
jiggles the saucer in his throat promises are idle wounds without a
single smart Lee rubs his hand up and down his beard. Whole

areas become sensitized for cutting by desensitization. You can mark the places, and the five males become the missing of the having of the sister well this client suspected his wife of infidelity how can a girl possibly be unfaithful to one if there is no prior relationship. Comforted, be comforted, Lee. Lap at

MILKBOTTLE H that protrudes through the revolving door and spills its contents Lee urges himself forward with the gigantic saucer

He likes milk. So does his father. Cold. Ridiculous, Renas contenting cream so he pulled the usual gambit of pretending to be out of town and that night he softly lets himself into their apartment and there his wife is on the bed with another man. You know what my client did? Jocund Silas vast in the moment before the climactic brilliance, stained snapbrim pushed back a quarter of an inch, no more, not a soul knows what the top of his head looks like the top of my head is a saucer of milk from which I cant remember is lapping he merely looks down the two of them, in handkerchief delictu you might say, doesnt say a word. Puts his hand in his pocket, pulls out a roll of bills, peels off a five and flips it over to the man, Here, he says, go get yourself a good lay. And he walks out. MURRAYS R

south on 2nd Street on an icechapped Sunday Morning Lee rides with his father in the Buick over the shockenspieled cobblestones. The trolleycar overhead cablewires black bisects corner after corner past the grayred rows of threestorey houses against the retina whitehissed swatchblue of sky. Churchgirls, ribbonhatted; churchboys all chin above the gripping sundaysuits. The Fifth Cobblestoned Baptist Church of the Redeemer clappers against a bell carved from iron cobblestone, then, a storefront boyhood and return, whose plateglass windows are blinded by long posters side by side reading MURRAYS ROACH DOOM MURRAYS RAT DOOM MURRAYS FLY DOOM MURRAYS ANT DOOM in thick black letters against an ochre background MURRAYS WORM DOOM Lee blows his nose, stuffs back his handkerchief. Takes out his handkerchief, blows his nose, stuffs it back certainly the goddamn bastards are going to go to war Silas thrusts himself back from the table contempting at Hoppy Zitin. He has hardly any legs, Lee notes with sudden surprise, theres no point in Lee starting out at any kind of work if theres going to be They wont let Adolph remilitarize the Rhineland, everybody knows he hasnt got the troops to take an armed outhouse the female Herbert Hoover has chins growing on her hairs, look at her flintsquinty eyes cavilling back and forth admiringly Silas grins at Lee, then to the others ticking off his jaw at the boy Handsome bastard aint he theres no point doing any job at all Ill teach you how to drive the car Levi offers. No, Im not really interested. Im telling you theres nothing to it Rachel poopoohs, havent I got a license? So why arent you driving Levi heavily inquires. Whos got the time Rachel objects, who needs it, when I could use it youve got it down the Yard so I should go somewhere at night. Then could you tell me why you keep renewing the drivers license year after year, Levi rattles down the paper in some irritation. I keep it up, why shouldnt I, what are you talking about Rachel sopranos aggrievedly, its a nice thing to have, if I ever need some kind of identification the license is always up to date and who knows when Ill have to sit behind the wheel. But you havent driven ever since you passed the test. Im telling you whos got the time. Dont you think I could pick it up again in a minute if I had to? All right Im sorry I mentioned it, I cant reason with you really want a job Lee Wally Singer the field CIO organizer butts at Lee in The Heel one night, Lee nodding seriously, by christ hes got to find a job, be independent of his family, exsocialist Wally, exhighschool crony, a mahoganystained baritone where the hell have you been. Down south, organizing, Wallys bitterly amused. Hows it going? Slow, but its going. Rough? Wallys beak stirs the onionsoup, the bald brown eyes hovering somewhat over their sockets, circling, moist, forever wondering if they should settle back, the lean body, shoulderless, crabbed in the chair, crabbed in its walk, crabbed in its sleep, Wally the exdebater of Olney Highschool, exdebater Lee of the infamous cracked Liberty Bell uterus speech yeh, rough, kicked out of the mill towns, youve seen the stories. Its true. But we are organizing. They cant stop us. Not when the cadres of negro and white form. But I can get you a job, Lee, if thats what you really want. You sure? Yes. Wally scribbles a

61

name and a company on a scrap of paper, this guys the superintendent, see him Monday morning, Ill speak to him tomorrow, youre set the trolleys grinds along Allegheny Avenue and Lee steps off at G Street, a black unlaundered sheet in the Monday morning winterwind, hundreds of men carrying their nicked black metal lunchboxes, overalled, cap brims down in the scissile blue-cold sky scraping its icy feet along pavement and cobblestone MILKBOTTLE H rearing over Kensington, the Philadelphia mill and factory section, the trolleys flapping open their green door to clatter down the two gray wooden steps down which the passengers brogan and highheel, leather and woollengloved, a last cigarette before growling into the mill SCHLICTERS JUTE CORDAGE CUNEO PRINTING HILLS PAPER COMPANY Lee frozen into a butcher counter of cold meats. Ridiculous, he should turn back now, whats he. But an apartment maybe. His own unreported comings and go might as well go ahead with it MILKBOTTLE H

Cross the street, lights red, cars wait. Cars wait, lights red, cross the street. Lights red you see, actually, the American people want war, shivers, Im not dressed for the job, I cant go ahead with RED, whatll the superintendent whats his. Fumbles for the slip of Wally paper Mister MacLennihan, G and Allegheny HILLS PAPER COMPANY, its in the basement I ought to have overalls RED, the plaque on the building entrance lists HILLS who? Look at the paper again. Amber. Green, have to wait for the next trafficlight nineteen years of age Levi says the least you can do is get some kind of job Lee if you dont want to work at the Yard, yes, Ill I really want to Wally, takes out the paper scrap once again its Mister MacL. Heat circulates under his clothes amber RED MILKBOTTLE H lunging across Allegheny the black unlaundered sheet flapping in his mondaymorning heatwind HILLS PAP down the metal stairs to a door with a frosted glass pane HI a steelspectacled suspendered grayhaired sixfooter purple blotches on his face standing at his desk near an open door through which on the lower level ten billion women white and negro girls jabber through the slang of pulleys and the throatcutting cutting machines, the sixfooter splotch glancing up from his timesheets Im Lee Emanuel

Whats that. You gotta talk louder over those, he shrugs at the lower level

Lee Emanuel. Wally Singer phoned

Oh yeh. Yeh. Youre the new man. Benevolently, his eye hefts the boy. Gimme your Social Security. Aint much of a job, Emanuel, but you wanna work, that it?

Thats r

Buck ten an hour, that okay?

Yes its

Simple enough job, Emanuel. Wont take you a minute to get on to it, come on down

Lee sees nothing. Girls faces swivel, laugh, giggle, chatter, their hands independent of their faces, their chatter and swivel. Their fingers deploy, turn, scurry, fold, shove, pick above tables at which they stand, bend over sections of cardboard sliding along the conveyorbelt, the factorywindows high on the wall in their blue laps of light, augmented overhead by banks of fluorescent cylinders, a blueblur glow over the long cellar and its swivelling faces laughing, chattering, giggling at the lanky Lee

HE gonna work here

miomi

aint he somethin now

All right, girls, Mister MacLennihan holds up a musclestuffed paw the cutting machines slanging through the retchhigh cardboard Lee stiffly sees nothing MacLennihan leading him to a long table opposite the line of eyerolling breastskipping girls piled high with flattened out cardboard boxes trafficlight RED, red. Mistake. Error. Altogether. Hes not dressed properly, thats the whole trouble Better get off your coat Emanuel MacLennihan Joell show you where to HEY JOE to the far end of the basement, the lithely sprung one head shorter and sprightlyfaced young negro slips and slides down the row of tables, checking the machines, spotting the work, Joell show you what you do, ever tie knots Emanuel

No I cant say I

Dont give it another thought, youll pick it up in no Joe heres your new man, Lee what was that?

63

Emanuel

Yah. This heres Joe Ritter, the foreman, you can pick up your card in the office, Joell take care of ya, and MacLennihans back up the stairs Lee cant see. Cant hear. Gently Joe tells him to remove his overcoat.

Yah I was going to

Ever tie knots, Lee?

No I cant say I

Nothing to it. You a friend of Wally Singers?

Yeh we went to highschool togeth

Nice guy

Yeh he the pulleys snarl among themselves. The cutting machines screech, jabber, giggle, female cutting machines, the pulleys blabber you mean he gonna work HERE

big strong man now aint he Youll get used to the noise, Lee

Oh, sure

First time in a factory is it?

Yes it

Sure, sure, Joe nods sagely. Dont take much sense to do this job though. Five minutes youll be picking it up. You see this pile of cardboard? Uhhuh. All right. Now you take this here twine, Lee, and you pass it under the pile. Like you was wrapping a package. Youve wrapped packages. Uhhuh, Lees mouth is trying to find his reticulated tongue, hes got to quickly find it because its flaking off, layer by layer and then bunching up in small prickly balls in his throat, hes just not dressed for the job, this is the whole trouble, his mother shouldve warned him to take a pair of overalls dollar ten an hour the cutting machines rip and screech through the cardboard, the hands of all the girls at the conveyorbelt line are cut off, they operate all by themselves, the fingers scurry, snatch, snap, pick, pull, weave, jabber, gossip, brown hands and white projecting from the factoryblue worksmocks while the girls themselves gossip jabber snatch at each other shrugging off their fingers entirely because they yield to the cutting machine, theres no reason for attachment because their mouths move happily over each other about what are you eating for lunch and mikes almost got the last payment for the car and

64

theres a new guy by the name of gary at the church social and my goddamn sister you know i put her through college shes got a bs degree and she goes and gets married and gets three kids and dont dress up i told my other sister the beautician i just aint gonna have anything more to do with her and she aint gonna set her hair no more why you know she can play the piano shes real smart and look what she done the fingers play brown and white over the conveyorbelt

Then you tie a knot. Not a regular knot, Lee, we got one specially for this and it isnt hard to catch on to. Should take you about three seconds

three sec : under once with the short end of the twine, then over once with the long end, then a twist and one half, Lee, to the right, and then two twists counterclockwise, once over then with the short end, double S with the long and a figure 8 with the long, then you put your finger down, give a hard tug, take the scissors here and cut. Then you take the pile youve tied and stack it with the others. Three seconds and youve got it, now thats pretty simple, isnt it? Ill do it once again, slowlike, and then you can try no no, Lee, its a figure 8 with the long, a double S with the short. No, one twist counterclockwise wont do it, the bundle wont be secure, you can understand that, cant you? Sure you can. We cant take the trouble the piles getting loose in the shipment, I think youll do better when Im not hangin around, makes some people nervous, I understand, Lee, you just take it easy for a couple minutes, and Ill be back in a little while to see how youre

The tall boy screws himself to the task. What is it now. Over once with the long end of the twine, then under once with two twists to the right, then a twist and a half counterclockwise. Shit.

Here lemme showya a loopsmiling negro girl deftly ties the knot

Get back to your table Marie Joe calls, sauntering back to Lee, the screechmachines chewing at the pulleys, the fluorescent lighting in a sweating blur, Lees fingers slopping amidst the twine, his left foot a clod of spiculed flameflickers How you doin Lee

Not so

Well I think youre just a little tense. Relax, theres nothin to it,

65

the left foot now incapable of movement, the shorts beneath his pants a bed of squirming knots, his penis shrunk and a flattened-out piece of tissue, the testicles in figure 8s and double S's, lets try it again, Lee. See what I mean? Give it a hard tug No Im not interested in driving, pop Youve been at this for about half an hour havent you Lee

Thats r

I think MacLennihan wants to see you in his office

Im sorry Mister MacL I dont know what it is I just cant seem to

Dont give it another thought Emanuel, lets just say it didnt work out, the purple splotches curiously jag over the boy. Got a dime?

Yes I think

Well heres a buck, pay you for the hour, Emanuel, I took out the deductions. Ninety cents.

Thanks Mister MacLennihan.

Sure. Good l

The iron steps lift him to the street. The winterwind lays a flat slab of ice on the heatpooled body, the left foot a maze of hot spindles, bent and twisted, counterclockwise. Stupidly, the boy takes a streetcar. Everybodys at work. Mister MacLennihan, Joe Ritter, his father

MURRAYS ROACH DOOM

everybodys at. Not Lee. He shouldve thought of the overalls himself, he cant go to The Heel he might see Wally Singer and Wallyll. He doesnt know what to say, Ernie Chalk the Ruscomb Street idiot presses him against the Diebele garage wall, bending his forearm back, Lee the gears work this way, youve got to use the clutch when you shift do you think you could do it yourself. Id like to try sometime, pop.

Why not now?

Oh Id just rather not, now. Id like to watch you a little bit more.

Try it now, Lee, you can get into the drivers seat.

No. No, pop, Let me watch you a little

So howd you make out on the job, Rachel greets him, youre back early.

66

Well I didnt feel so good, Lee mumbles.

Didnt feel so good, whats the matter already, you caught cold?

I started to feel chills, he says.

Ahf mein sonim she screeches disgustedly. Why didnt you keep the muffler around your throat like I told you.

I did

Screaming: I can see its loose, what are you telling me

I dont feel so good

GET UPSTAIRS INTO BED YOU WANT YET YOU SHOULD CATCH PNEUMONIA Ill have to run up and down the stairs again thats what you get when your sons dont turn out ah fa chop, the ch the yiddish throat guttural, get upstairs right away and undressed and in bed get the thermometer and take your temperature Ill be up in a little while if its not down tonight Ill call Dr Newman

All right, mom. Quiet. But you dont have to yell

ILL YELL IF I FEEL LIKE IT WHAT OTHER KINDS OF PLEASURES DO I HAVE FROM MY SONS

In a very low whisper, Please dont yell mom, please dont, please. One week is required before the fever and coughing subside. Another week to convalesce. His father takes a look at him; grunts. Youll find another job. Sure, pop. Dont talk about jobs already his mother scolds Levi, what are you worrying him for? Whos worrying him? I just mentioned

So stop mentioning. The main thing is he should get better. Helplessly, Levi smiles down on his son, sees the pile of books on the dresser. At least you got an opportunity to do a lot of reading.

Abashed. Yes.

Dont encourage him, Rachel scolds, its not good for his eyes, hell strain them and hell be in bed even longer

MURRAYS FLY DOOM

please. His shoulders hunched over the cafeteria table, dont you see, the American people want war, more than any other people. If they dont Rena get directly involved in the one coming up Rena theyll see to it theyll become directly involved in the world war thatll follow Rena Goldstein, Rena theyll.

In anger plied by smiles Silas tackles Youre out of your mind,

67

Lee, whats got into you, that sounds like the Communist line.

The hell it is, Im as privysluiced as you, Silas, to the trials where Radek and Zinovieff were railroaded. At fifteen years of age the verbatim transcripts of the trials were sufficient to corroborate for me the Kulak slaughter and the uprooting of populations and the emergence of Stalin as a High Hangman Priest the like of which in quantity of enemies enemad into confessing the ecstasies of imminent mortality has never been equalled. Nor does Toynbee persuade me that despite the gross inequities and cruelty on a broad bureaucratic scale Russia may nevertheless be the valid matrix of socialist revolution—and you will recall that Toynbee has been attacked by Marxists for not having encased his Study in dialectical materialism though his Yang and Yin in terms of their polarity amount to very much the same thing. The Marxist and the Toynbean make the same enormous error in the formulation of opposites to produce synthesis, to which Freud and y Gasset contribute their buttressing fallacies of ego, superego and id, they, you and I; the sorry concept being that there is an Outside and an Inside. None of you can sit here and tell me he can sense whatever it is that an enclosure encloses. You have a sense of the volume of your body and the volume of other bodies, and if there is any truth at all it is that which understands that all phenomena are outside, outside Rena Goldstein outside. You may tell me that the thoughts you think are incontrovertibly within, but this is incapable of any demonstration; you will the more accurately describe the process by stating once again that as a sensing volume you sense another volume possessing the attribute of mentation. You can understand the ludicrousness of the paradox of inside and outside if for a moment you imagine the construction of phenomena as a theory of spheres, one inside the other, or, one outside the other in ascending or descending dimensions of Rena Goldsteins colored scarlet if shcs out in the snow they will have become etiolated, round tits of snowflake theyre so good they melt in the mouth so that you are inevitably led to the falsity of infinity in one direction or the other like trying to tie a knot around cardboard boxes that are constantly being flattened out which is what the matter really is which is really whats the

68

matter. Consequently in the one direction all phenomena are Inside; in the opposite direction they are all Outside one another. I say if theres any truth at all it is that which holds the doctrine of the Outside, or, if you will, altogether the Inside. But it cannot be both, Lee and Rena are incapable of performing Opposites, and if they do it will be illusory and they are in trouble as all humans are who attempt similarly I shouldve taken a bath Mark and Achille and Silas and Jay and Hoppy are itching on my flesh. A memory of Rena itches like a filigree on my skin, ten million seahorses of Rena drying and caking on my skin at ten oclock in the evening the point being theres neither Inside nor Outside first you take a washrag and dunk it in hot water and saturate it with soap and then you bend over the bathtub in which your father always takes a bath before you do at a quarter of eleven on the cafeteria clocks it is impossible that I shall ever be able to have black roman numerals absolutely clean because the time of Levilee is dirty and nothing Rena can do can clean and you painstakingly you wash away the black ring of dirt your father leaves, dirt and scales of skin because your father itches too and his flesh comes off little by little as your flesh comes off little by little at the itching memory of Renabody lying upon various areas of your skin that you must scratch and scratch till the dirty orange blood of her hair is washed off the memory of her is not in the mind, no, never, she is like a series of orange strips of insect leeching upon the flesh and all the mind is is a revolving cafeteria door

Around and

around

and

a

till the enamel of the bathtub is pristine white snowflake painted and frozen thereon do they have to have it so goddamn hot in the cafeteria when its freezing outside

You see its impossible to elude the semantic, Lee, Silas hawfully interrupts

Oh fuck, Lee dismisses the case, all one can ever sense is a series of planes without any describable dimension sliding one upon and through the other. We will have microscopes eventually capable of photographing minuscule acts of energy, and if we continue with the foolishness of ideating Inside we will be slapped on the eye by Limit : we will have to say something resides within the minutest act of energy. We will have to build space ships which will make forays into Inner Space. I can see the entire race of mankind attempting to crawl into itself Evil evil evil Achille Volpe overreaches his chortle, as evil as six sisters. Silas' body duckwaddles with laughter, Jay shakes his head in tiny no no no, his mouth forbidding its own smiles, Hoppy sniggers and Mark Fahn displays a whole cultivated acreage of rotten teeth over vermiform inflamed gums of tickle at Lees picture

War.

War.

War

Youve got to admit youve gone pretty far afield and well get to the questions of epistemology another time, Lee, but Ill withdraw the Communist line accu

Please come back, Rena. Her knitted wool sweater in black and white horizontal stripes, a heavy gray flannel skirt, the long strong tawny legs, the feet in gray pumps 1829 Clearfield Avenue MILKBOTTLE H the Kensington El grinds and grunches and crunchsteels by a quarter of a block away, Nate her oldest brother with Hannah his wife in the kitchen background regard Lee seriously Hiya Lee howya doin he stammers and Hannah draws him back into the kitchen Come on you idiot they want to be. There is this strangeness to Rena : all over her body she appears to have black eyes, as though somebody has been punching her and then pasting her eyes over the blackandblue marks I think we can talk better in my brothers office, she says, the black eyes making her smile pulpy and unbelievable, a kind of cruel tenderness in metal staples through all of her softness Is Rick waiting to hear from you Lee cannot resist scratching at her. This is mine. Theres no Rick. He is unbelievable, he does not exist Ive seen him Nina says, I didnt believe it, I didnt believe it Norma says, hes thin and stringy and he looks like hes got dirty unwashed black hair ITCH, get it off, take a bath but the footdoctors instruments in the office are polished to a high lustre, this is the white

70

enamel pan that he puts the cornparings of his patients feet in, they sit in a barberdentist amalgam of a chair his patients swear by him they adore his stammer his boyishness the rough josh of his approach they wait in lines outside his office, two bucks a visit to have their feet treated, the factory workers that stand at the assembly lines all day, the salesladies on their feet all day, the old Irish biddies with their misshapen bogs and quicksands of feet to have them kneaded and washed and alcoholed and pared ah that feels a whole lot better Doctor Goldstein it does now, the chorusgirls that cab up from the Philadelphia downtown district to have their feet touched and trembled and tucked and tickled and smoothed by the capable boyish fingers of Doctor Goldstein Hows that arch feel now Billie but Im afraid you will eventually have to wear orthopedic shoes, we call them corrective he stutters prettily Hurry it up Rena Im due at the links so if Im going to drive you to Oh shut up you idiot Hannah hushes him What is it that you want to say Lee Rena inquires gently

MILKBOTTLE H thats what he wants to MILKBOTTLE Youre crazy to want to go back with her Nina worriedly pronounces I have a little monkey INSIDE of me he says that wants to clamber all over Rena offering his little tin cup

of a mouth toward the revolving door WAR WAR WAR he docsnt have to marry anybody he doesnt have to work for anybody he doesnt have to make any money, he can be death personified, yes, the actor who carries a small coffin on his index finger in a silver setting, onyx, I seal all my communications thus, death absolves from him all living problems WAR WAR WAR. Not that she has to come. Nobody has to come to anybody. Nobody has to make an approach, all approaches are reconsiderable, there is simply the statement of schedule on Broad Street the evening before. Trains. Momentary schedule of meeting, the trust of what is now. He values the appearance of Rena at seventyfive thousand dollars, precisely the amount his father stakes his brother to for two coalyards successively, he peels off a bill from the heavy wad he carries here Rena Goldstein go get yourself a good lay. In the final impotence, the impossibility to destroy, running through all the impossibilities, what shall I take the torch to the sulfur tips

71

of his fingers knock against each other, theres smoke under his fingernails, smoke under his doublebreasted suit, a whole smudgepot of curling blacks because theres a frost tonight, keep the fruitballs from being ruined, theyre delicately balanced, a whole crop waiting to be transported you cannot destroy. The wildness in any man

in any man

due to the fact that he wants to destroy but that in all the destruction that ensues he destroys nothing so that he stands back or he sits back in the cafeteria chair with the concept of destroying Rena but twentyfour hours in the knowing of her and yet knowing that whether he puts torch or knife or garrote to her whether he sets fire to his mothers and fathers house whether or no he sends all the men and women he hates to the gaschamber that the weight of the stuff he believes he has destroyed remains exactly and precisely and horribly the same. Lee feels light, light, light with the sense of incapability of destruction, as if all weight has run away from him. Light wildness. Delicate wildness. Feminine wildness. A very fag fashiondesigner light wildness at the impossibility of the perfect creation. God. God. God. It is a matter of creating her. He all but lifts himself out of the chair as he keeps sitting there. The wildness to make a figure, make a Rena, which he has destroyed in the notdestroying. The wildness of the sameness of his self before after and during, which also is quite impossible. You breathe, but thats impossible. You see, but thats impos. You hear, but. You. So. You turn an inch in your chair, another, still another, the seat wet with sweat, reconseater. But the mere commonplaces can hold her up, delay her, which is what Lee must repudiate in all situations. Nobody but Lee must be susceptible of succumbing to the commonplace. For everybody else but Lee the reason, the deter, the prod, the motivation, the barrier must be extraordinary. He refuses to live in a world that may be defined by the commonplace; only Lee is permitted the dull and the tedious and the boring within himself. Everyone else must caper, clown, roar, whisper, tumble, play; he and he alone can remain seated, doing nothing and wondering on the fabulous circumstance in which all other men and women behave

WELL JESUS CHRIST IF IT ISNT TIMMY LASCAR the table greets the blueeyed blondhaired deckweaving sailorman Yeh docked at Baltimore and took the train in he grins Christ nothings changed youre still at the same goddamn table talking

intimately Timmy Lascar can confide to Lee You think you got problems. You think anybodys got problems. Minor stuff. Trivia. Let me tell you what a problem is but I expect you to say nothing. Nothing to anybody, understand. I dont want any pity. If you want to know the truth, Lee, Im dying

Lee nearly giggles, but restrains. Im sorry to

No youre not, dont wig me

Well, what is it that youre

Softening, Timmy Lascar confides, his round shoulders reflected in his foreheads crouches, pastyfaced, You can see I got no color. Im on the deck and I get no color, plenty of sun, heh? Sure, but no burn. I cant burn, thats the truth of it. Because Im softening. My bones, Lee, my bones. Ever hear of decalcification? Well, nodding his chin up and down, the grim soft childing light of his blue eyes leaping and frolicking over Timmy Lascar, Im losing the calcium. Oh its slow. Itll take another twentyfive years sure, but in time Ill be just a heap of jelly, nothing more, Keep it under your hat

Lee here says the American people want war, want direct involvement

Not only that, Lee cuts in, but they want to be defeated, decimated, holocausted, ruined, devastated

Hes right, Timmy Lascar swipes a chair from another table, turns it backward and straddles it, he knows what hes talking about Silas

The whole goddamn American people wants its bone structure decalcified, they want to be a heap of jelly

Hes right, Silas, Timmy Lascar does a soft grin around the table

Jesus what a bunch of boobs Hoppy Zitin says disgustedly. For once I got to side with Silas. What youre talking about is an action of mass suicide, and I dont believe in looking at people as a mass, theyre made up of one two

73

three

four five

six seven eight nine

the little girl whips the hoop about her how many times can she do it. One becomes many, one wants to be many. No one. A single digit is impossible, you see, Hoppy

What the fuck are you talki

Nothing single, noth. One is one billion. Two is four hundred and sixtyeight trillion. One is seventyfive thousand he hackhaws to himself.

Do you consider yourself

and plus Rena, thats how I reconsider, Im already two. And before, yes, theres Levi and my brother dont I have his worry his frownlines, dont I if he whores and plays the races not think fantasy of whoring and. Multiples, clusters

I cant quite subscribe to that, Mark Fahn

What are you saying, youve got six sisters youve got to sub

now wait

no you listen to the Ark two by two God could think of one and one only

well there was noah

and his wife

and his sons

the ark of man is multiple in the raging flood. God did not visit his wrath on one man because He couldnt see one man, he never created a singular, he was distraught at the beginning, he caught his error didnt he

evil evil evil

remembered he had a rib he could deal with

never one elephant, even the beasts plural of the field I cannot go on single Rena Rena Rena

for GODS sake you understand I call on

MASS, Hoppy Zitin, you cant get away from your multiples, your attachments, your planes flowing and sliding one and through the other

Was there more than one Minotaur at the end of the Labyrinth Jay attempts

74

there were a whole bunch of priests at the end of the labyrinth and Jason slew them all, eh, Theseus?

well why did he report one minotaur

fabulous wasnt it? how much more persuasive the gigantic myth rather than a group of priests the mammoth beast he a man slew to hell with slaying other men what the hells that thatd been done over and over

well I for one have no desire to be decimated; urge himself at himself Lee considers, reconsiders, multiconsiders, urge Hoppy at his manynesses, have him slay the hydraHoppy happyhoppy arent you with your apprentice jewelership arent you eh

I didnt say I

your eyes smart and sting and you tell us youre going slowly blind doing it but you call it a living and what else is there to so its obvious you hate it you hate you, imagine the enormous area of hatred in you Hoppy Zitin

well that doesnt mean that everybody else

let me take you on an American tour while you sing your excerpts from the great compositions of music Hoppy Zitin, sure, you sing for the American people, Hoppy, you do an extract from the Art of the Fugue to the Pittsburgh steelworker and ask him where its from, you whistle a melody from the Trout Quintet to the Nebraska farmer and ask him what its taken from, isnt that what you want to do

Who the hell wants to sing to the Pittsburgh steelworker or the Nebraska farmer you got rocks in your

You dont give a fuck whether they live or die do you

No I dont

You think they give a fuck whether you live or die

No they dont but whats that got to

I like that indifference to another mans existence, hey Hoppy. That perfect marmoreal crystallized indifference

You fucking sonofabitch Lee you motherscrewing Hoppy hiccups his laughter·

Who are you waiting for? Mark says to Lee flatly, and the table takes up the chorus WHO ARE YOU WAITING FOR

What a bunch of cruddy pricks Timmy Lascar

75

That doesnt disprove Lee bellows

All right all right Silas gavels the table, youve both had your innings

Hoppy turns on Silas, Who appointed you the referee, his adamsapple jiggling like a marble in a stoppedup rainspout, The American people want to die let em die Lees got a point theyre like their own gobblers stuffed and overstuffed with peace

Lee feels exhaustedly triumphant, the hell with Rena, the hell with girls, subject then to a commonplace fantasy he has on numerous occasions, that of all the males in the whole world murdered except Lee Emanuel, who then proceeds to slide his prick into the vagina of each and every living female, the female dirges of lamentations broken by the regular grunts, gulps, whimpers and fartsighs of each woman being satisfied

man is a fartsighted animal, Lee drawls

jesus youre evil Achille shakes his head.

The cafeteria courtroom is gravely silent. The figures at the Moscow Trials are: Kaminev, Zinoviev, Radek and Emanuel, Judge Silas Klein presiding, Achille Volpe the State Prosecutor, the dirtyskinned white bad eye a dog at his feet Your full name is, please

Rena I beg you beg you beg you beg you

Lee Primus Emanuel

You admit that you had established communication of a surreptitious nature with the American People.

I do so admit, sirrep.

Will you kindly inform the Court as to the methods you employed to seduce the American People to commit acts of a hostile nature against the citizens of the Soviet Union.

Yes, sirrep. The bad whitish eye leaps to its feet, goes about nuzzling and lapping at the crowd in the courtroom, whispering Evil, Evil, its all because he has six sisters, you see, one of whom is named Rena Emanuel, the worst kind of agent provocateur who committed acts of an unspeakable nature in her early childhood, unspeakable. Oh, yes, Whiteye holds up his finger, and as the official blind organ and hoopster of the Soviet People it is my duty to have you privy to these acts. I make my living teaching the art of sculpture to deserving students of the Workers, but in my spare time I am a believer in the plastic as the essence of life. I make small figures, you see. And this small Rena Emanuel is one of my masterpieces. At three years of age, in the city of Baltimore, her birthplace—the United States of America, after all, a surreptitious and subversive choice—leading us to comprehend that sabotage and treachery begin, you see, at the very moment of conception, in which the foetus selects its forebears and thereby the nation of the forebears—we have begun to detect, you see, that the Lysenko theories of environment after birth do not always quite apply—we must investigate environment prior to parturition—well, then, as I was remarking, this Rena Emanuel, at three years of age, observing that the aunts who comprised her family were far too numerous, conspired with her brother Lee, when her mother and one sister had gone to shop in downtown Baltimore, to set fire to the family house in which were slumbering five sisters and brothers of her mother. These sleeping brothers and sisters perished in the flames, except for one brother, who was badly burnt but who managed to live. Live, as a matter of fact, to the age of fifty. But he died, at last, too. Not from scars, you understand, no, nothing so clearly obvious. Died from his skin.

Oh, yes, the white eye breathes heavily, the brother of Rena's mother died from his skin. The fire, you see, had affected his flesh in such a manner that at age forty-five he developed a cancer of the skin. He began to scratch at his skin, the itching of the cancer intolerable. He was shunted from one hospital to another, given one drug after another. Nothing was of any value. In his fiftieth year, Citizens, driven mad by the itching in his head, in his feet, in his scrotum, under his nipples, behind his ears, under his navel, in the small of his back, the itching behind his eyeballs, on his scalp, far enough up his anus so that he could not intrude a finger to relieve himself—driven mad, I say, by the itching of his flesh, he excused himself from his hospital bedroom, walked to the toilet, opened the window and hurled himself out to his death six storeys below. He died, continuing to itch, for the attendants, coming

77

upon his body, in which all the bones were broken, observed his right index finger flexed and twitching at—it is unspeakable, Citizens, utterly unspeakable, but it is my duty to—twitching at his soul. We in the Soviet Union do not acknowledge the existence any longer of the Soul, but in this man's case, since he was an American, the Soul in all its treachery and subversion had not yet been eradicated. Treacherous, disloyal Soul to this poor man, I say, typical of all that is corrupt and decadent in the Western World. For his Soul had got itself Infected with the Cancer which had itched the flesh of the man. So that the Soul, after the body's death, mind you, continued to itch. In America it is still itching, poor forsaken thing. Rena Emanuel, therefore, is responsible for an Itching American Soul, an itch that was communicated as well to her brother, Lee Emanuel. A complex saboteur, Rena Emanuel. I give you her background so that you can watch her the more acutely. She is a pyromaniac and a carcinomaniac

Yes, sirrep. A very simple method, Lee Primus says very softly, not wishing to disturb his brother Secundus at the other end of the hallway. It is not that the American people were overstuffed with peace that they desired war. No. I simply persuaded them that as a people they did not as yet have the opportunity of enjoying the knowledge that in destruction they could not finally destroy. European and Asiatic peoples had already demonstrated that, but the American never believed the foreigner. It was very simple to plant the idea that they needed the demonstration for themselves. But they are good people, you see, and good people must commit suicide. I should be decorated, Comrades, not held for Trial. I have done you a service, I do not have to tie any knots, I am free

america is the last of the free peoples I will not die in war

I can hardly see now, Hoppy Zitin says, so Im not eligible for the draft.

I support my aged mother, Silas Klein says, so Im not eligible for the draft.

I have a feeble eye, Achille Volpe says, so Im not eligible for

I have six sisters, Mark says, so Im not

I will have a wife and two children, Jay says, so Im

Im practically boneless, Timmy Lascar says, so

78

Yes. I guess theres too much snow, Lee says, rising, Id better get back to the Boulevard myself. Goodnight, gentlemen. Eleven oclock the Roman numerals, and they walk Arabic toward the revolving door but Lees reflection in the glass pulls back his torso, a bare thrust of oneeyed hair falls to the shoulder of his trenchcoat

You werent going, she starts and stops in her own breath, the dismay tap of her smile fulltugged at her mouth, her body all but a series of full bundles emerging from the glass vanes, bundle by bundle, spewed by the revolvingdoor machine, melting snow a needled porcelain web stammering over her falling hair over one eye the color of rotten oranges with dark brown pits of gaze. A nylon bublitchki tipsy at her hair. A crinkly transparent plastic raincoat cottoncandied about her body. Shoes, but no galoshes. Semiprecious jewelwet. A great black bulky knitted wool sweater done by her mother rolltopped over her bosom and hips under the plastic wrinkles. Wet. The shoes soaked. Her body titters, her remotely mochacolored flawless skin. Five feet eight inches, a draw of brawn canted and bevelled, brownblonde, cornercurved, the power and the muscle of the girl, this Rena, spiculed and siphoned off in the mocha clarity of the skin, the shadowed hazel of the eye, the capsizing corners of the gravely weighted mouth withal volant, vacant, visceral, vortical and veiled in turn oh I have no chin she merrilys to Lee, theres enough of one he insists, not even as much as Sy has, who has a kind of minuscule trimmed goatee of a chin one might say but compensated by a determined thrust, not so Rena's, which shyly backs in a bit, like me, she merrilys. Im very undetermined

a days growth of beard, blue on white, she tells herself about Lee, the shoulders rumpled in the trenchcoat, somewhat bent from the waist, as if he must remember not to be roundshouldered because of his height, but inevitably bowing while the torso is kept straight. Taller than I am, much taller, too much vaseline in the black wavy hair that he arranges in a tousle over a forehead corner, carefully, spending at least fifteen minutes before the mirror combing and recombing so that the tousle will fall precisely right, heavily dousing the hair with water, again and again, so that

79

streams pour down his neck, wet his shirt, pool on the tile bathroom floor while he defecates at times mapping out an imaginary area in whose bounds he endeavors to count the tiny hexagonal tiles, white once, now faintly yellowed, tilted, canted, a few missing from the floor now cracked in several places from the gradual settling of the house, the cracks chorusing up the walls and down the ceiling, reflecting in Lee's features, faint jags on the forehead and down the cheekbones where Renas are high, her face from the front a delicately inverted delta, the two faces somehow somewhat crooked, offcenter, his on a turtleneck and hers on a neck a shawldrop and perfectly valenced on either side to their broadly sloping shoulders, white on blue the Leeman, and his slenderlong fingers fixing the water saturating in his hair then with fat wads of vaseline, petroleum jelly the jar label says, the thick long heavy eyebrows of him, his eyelashes any girl would give a fortune to have Mrs Goldstein giggles, but not the hairs growing from the tip of his nose, which he plucks from time to time, hair all over him, hair even on your ears, Rena says wonderingly, mockingly, a thick white fuzz on them, the ears themselves arranged in two concentric semicircles and heavy lobes, the boy and the girl touch not a moment away from each other untouching, a crosshatched penumbral fuzz between, an arc of table, a hyphen of a rail, a spigothandle at the waterfountain, the polished marble floor, and the quiet of the all but deserted cafeteria, a group of men welling up at them from the rear, a roman-numerald clock jowling down and oblique upon them, the entrance plateglass window frosted over but evoking a half of a heft of her here, the raffish segment of his trenchcoat collar there, the bottom margins of the revolving doors footed in heavy rubber to slow the whirl down, slowing, now ending, the shush of the rubber against the wet marble halting, tatters of water at the girls feet, her cheeks smudged red from the cold, you dont have to wear any makeup at all he tells her, never, never. Oh, maybe a touch of lipstick. Thats all? Thats. Take that goddamn eyeshadow off. All right, Lee. No rouge. Yessir! she merrilys at him. No mascara. Yessir! she shoots at him, Aye aye captain. No jewelry. Just a little costume jewelry? No, nothing, you dont need it. Yessir! Oh, Lee. Rena, Rena, Re. Trembles trip all over her. You must be freezing. You werent going were you. I thought the snowstorm pretty heavy. But I said Id come, didnt I? Yes. I told you Id come sweeps aside everything and anything from her eyes but the Lee proscenium. Clear all, not another stick, bare stage, simply the overhead light, nothing in the rear, no group of men, no clock, no rail, no female Herbert Hoover, the hair looped back from the broad shore of the forehead, her forehead for his entire hand. But the snow, youre wet, youre cold. Oh a little snow cant melt anybody. Do you go out like this all the time, in all kinds of weather. Yes even in the rain. I like the rain, I never catch a cold, I dont care, what harm can a little rain do. It just took me a little time to get out of the house. My mother thought I was crazy, so did my father and brothers, and then I had to wait for the trolley, and the trolley took an awfully long time, I was so afraid you wouldnt wait, Lee, but I did get here as fast as I could. Were you afraid, really afraid I wouldnt. Seriously, slowsweetedly, she nods. Yes. But I wouldntve let anything in the world stop me. Oh you cant mean. Yes, yes I do. I was afraid youd. Were you? Honestly? Yes, she has a faint smudge of down on her upperlip, sometimes I think its quite a mustache. Oh, no, it just looks a little darker, but not like a. Youre sure? I always think people think. But they dont. No? Its not really that dark? No. Oh youre just telling me that it. No, Im not, Rena, Im not one for just telling for the sake of telling, I never do that, I cant spare feelings, you should know that, Im not given to idle compliments, when I do compliment then you will know I mean it absolutely, without equivocation, youre beautiful. Ah, Lee. No no, you are, I told I dont. All right. You believe me. Yes I bel. I simply thought that the storm, you know, and such, wouldve. Im here. Touching in the penumbra crosshatching between, Rena not looking away from him, not glancing at another living or inanimate thing, not at a rail, nor the floor, nor the clock, nor at herself, but simply and believingly at Lee, tall, blue on white, slim, the trenchcoat rammed up behind his head like a mediaeval ruffle, stiff and daring, Im ruthless in what I say Rena, maybe I sound a little harsh, but theres no point in not being truthful. Yes, Lee. The swart gold of her.

The depth of the mocha coloring, like the layers of the Venetian glazes, the fathoms of unglistening lustre, you dont have to wear earrings either tho they become you, yessir yessir yessir! He jackles with laughter in spite of himself. She joys and she dazzles at him, she brings him in at her, around the dinner table, she heaps his plate with her, take more of this and of that and of everything, take it all, do you want some of, do you want of this and of that, do you, Ill get up and go to the kitchen for, Ill run upstairs for, no its nothing, will it please you, will it make you smile, will it fatten and elate you, can I get you coke from the store no it wont break my father he can afford it, and my brother Herb drinks a case of cokes a day, would you like some creamcheese, a sour pickle, Ill run across the street for some lox, how do you like your chicken, Lee, have you had enough, no you havent, youre not telling the truth, mother hes so polite, isnt it wonderful my father has a delicatessen, now you just sit still

   darling

   darling

   darling

touching, in a moment. Another day, another night, not for a windbit, a whilethin, a waver and a thimble of Im so glad I didnt miss you, Lee. I am too.

Are you.

Yes.

Im awfully glad, Lee.

I am too.

Where we going?

You still want to go out?

I dont care. Whatever.

But youre still wet, and youre trembling.

Oh Ill dry, Ill be warm. Dont worry, Lee.

Its not that Im worrying but

Ill be all right.

Will y

Oh, y

s. Then? Where shall we go?

Where would you like to, Rena?

It doesnt matter. Wherever you want to

Ive no particular preference. Havent you some

No. You tell me. Anywhere, Lee, you want to go or be. I dont care.

You sure?

Yes. Any

Well I thought wed go over to Roberts, its a very good delicatessen just a block away. I like rolled beef, do you

Anything.

And coffee.

Uhhuh.

Lets go, he grins up and down at her, straightening out all the crosshatches, circumnavigating his skull with his grin, lopsiding his face with the grin, the big girl of her and the littleness, as though there are a hundred little girls in the girl all jostling inside of her, and tumbling

and hooping and crazily balancing like a pagoda of acrobats housed in the tallness of her, under the breasts of her all grown up and out and like enormous hoops of cannonnippled tit but the girls inside of her, the little ones, on bicycles, on hoops, on jackintheboxes, on the peeps at the lookouts of the eyes, balanced on the whoop of the lip outside they plough into the snowdrifts, her plastic raincoat gnarling and knocking and whipping and crunching in and out of the high wind walloping the snow around them, down their collars, blurting at their flesh, she lowers her head, twisting it then up at him, tearsmiling from the brassy, driving, dancing, chapping, chunking cold, My hands, oh my hands

You take my arm, he firms at her, ordering. Yessir. Oh my hands. Can you stick one of them in my pocket will it be all right you wont think Im

She shakes her head one hundred billion times

All right. Here.

She shoves one hand into his coatpocket and he grips it. The other hand she crawls up her own sleeve and contrives it into the sweater. But the one in his pocket he grips, tight as a stone jungle creeper, laced and interlaced, a double S a thousand times under, a figure 8 counterclockwise around and through, then tieing without cutting, and the powerful Renafingers countergrip, counterknuckle, clock him round the wristtrack as the cold tumbles away in patches, and the grim warmth works its way laboriously through palm and knuckle, the boy and the girl fistfighting through whiteblack spinnakers of snowfurl and windfjord, a snowplough tediously inching down Broad Street clearing a Blackred Sea transitory asphalt and cobblestone way

Schenleys whiskybottle puffed in snow atop the Philadelphia Rapid Transit Building, the night graywhiteblack around and above the statue of Billy Penn atop the City Hall, holding his iron quaker hat, gusts of chindimpling ice ramming down the chins of the boy and the girl, bitterly breathless

godDAMN the snow he bellows at her

godDAMN the snow she batters her voice against the wind

and momentarily they straighten, on top of themselves as they turn the corner of Broad and Walnut

SCHULTES CIGARS want to wait in the doorway a sec

NO lets go on she mockheroics my other hand is coming off

then lets change pockets

all right they scream, the snowgnats snapping against the hot backs of their open mouths, against the hot inside throat, Lee and Rena coughing like a couple of mangy animals, manged with the snowstreaks and winddigs, faces scrawled with the double 8s and supertwisted horizontal S's of hot and cold, not another goddamned soul on the streets we must look crazy to anybody looking out of the window

I dont care she says

I dont care either he says I got your other hand

I didnt know she yells at him happily

I cant feel my ears he bellows

Why dont you wear a hat

I DONT LIKE HATS I NEVER WEAR HATS I HATE HATS I THINK THEYRE STUPID IM AGAINST HATS I DONT LOOK WELL IN HATS AND I GUESS THATS THE REAL REASON I ABSOLUTELY REFUSE TO WEAR HATS

ALL RIGHT she gulplaughs

BUT MY EARS ARE COMING OFF

WHY DONT YOU WEAR EARMUFFS the tears are tumbling down her cheeks

I WOULD LOOK VERY FUNNY IN EARMUFFS

WHAT DIFFERENCE WOULD THAT MAKE

WOULDNT YOU MIND RENA

NO I WOULDNT CARE

WELL I STILL WONT WEAR THEM I WOULD LOOK STUPID WHY DONT YOU WEAR THEM

WILL YOU MIND LEE

NO I WONT

THEN THE NEXT TIME I

Promise?

Yes they clump clump clump up the steps at last of Roberts Delicatessen, thrust open the doors and stand, breath racing, wordless, absolutely stupefied with each other, faces burning, shaking off the snow, Rena holding her ears, Lee beating frantically at his own ears a nest of clashing needles, his nosetip very white you dont think its frostbitten Rena do you?

Oh no. Is my nose very white?

Yes. You dont think its

Oh no. He touches it with a finger, presses. Can you feel?

She waves her head, touches his nose. Can you

He gravely shakes his head, and they both clatter with laughter. He seizes her arm, she thrusts it to him in the seize, and they stride

Wait a minute she says, my legs arent as long as

Sure they

Well maybe almost but yours are

Ill slow down. As they clip past the delicatessen freezer

I like to sit almost in the rear. All right?

She bobbles her head.

I dont feel comfortable in the front or in the middle, he tells her. I like to be in back where I can observe. Of course theres not much to observe on a night like

Its pretty empty.

Except for that little crowd in the last booth.

Its a funny crowd, isnt it?

Yes, I dont think Ive seen them in here at all before. With Rena, Lee begins to drop the tight tendency toward a suspiciously British accent. Not that theres a pretense involved. The accent emerges about the time hes fourteen, picked up from the stage English and British English he hears in the movies, and partly the outcome of a wish to hug in his speech, to curtail response to it by virtue of near unintelligibility. He does not want to open up his throat to most listeners, in the fear that what he has to say will either be sneered at or laughed at. So he talks far down in his throat, keeping his lips as static as possible. He manages with the habit, mainly because he has very little to say, his paucity of small talk constantly causing him embarrassment. It is principally to the female, and then only to the female he sexually responds to with great strength, that he finds sudden release and incessant fluency; and to his three close friends in early adolescence, Al Gordon, Sy Tarassoff and Danny Naroyan; in middle adolescence, in The Heel, he discovers too that topics of intellectual nature on which he can be combative, contemptuous and negative, enable unimpeded speech—and that because he can retaliate at length and venomously in argument. But the clipped English has its first real softening with Rena; and the ease at smalltalk is never at such a spate as it is with Rena. He has never before felt so perfectly unself exacting with a girl, never felt it so unnecessary to activate a goal, as with Rena. She is neither old nor new; she is neither stranger nor innerly domestic intimacy; she is the girl, not that he feels a belonging to him, but to whom he easily belongs

walking down the delicatessen aisle, striding;

and sitting, casually, in the booth at the back. Why dont you take off your raincoat.

Later, maybe, her eyes glaring with dark, shaking off the bublitchki chunks of argument tossed from behind, in the booth back of them with five girls and one man Youll hafta go out again Jodie You lost your, on a night like, Whats the matter with the Broad St Sta, I been to the Family an its loaded with fags

Dr Kitzmiller makes a motion to the anesthesiologist and a rubber Halloween mask, a tube attached is fitted over Lees nose

86

and mouth Now you start counting Lee and breathe deeply count and breathe deeply of Rena, there is a kind of hissing of ether proceeding in concentric circles from the dark glare of her eyes and Lee breathes deeply, counting her, the humped nose and the wide red mouth, the unbuttoning of her black knitted wool sweater over the soft rayon blouse and the rise and the fall, the fall and the rise of her own breathing lying on the operating table taking in the young man, there is an organ being taken out of both their throats, going from one throat to another through the masks that are the faces themselves, through the tubing of breathing between them, how many times must the hoop be whirled about the two of them before their supremacies are established one over the other in simultaneity, in a halloween cafeteria in which everyone else is unmasked, the waitress who walks toward them an order book in hand, the delicatessen man behind the counter, the elderly lady cashier behind the register, the customers selecting their salamis, the ether hoop, breathe deeply in order that the operation be a mutual success, a suck and a cess through the dark glare of Rena and the grave venomous merriness of Lee, both masked in that ultimate nakedness be portrayed, for in the unmasking is no hooping together, in the bald everydayness of this is what I am there is no anesthesia, count his long skinny neck like a turtles, his shoulders wide and upturned in pointed bone lapels, the small red mouth Ill be godDAMNED if Im gonna go out in this kinda Youll go out and like it so gimme the bills take ten what the fucks the matter withya take ten I got rent to I got I need fifteen if I need a Shut up

Ready for your order

What would you like Rena

You order Lee

Isnt there something special youd

You order. Rena momentarily worried, a slip of a frown on the undereyelids

Two rolled beef Coffee Rena. Yes, thats theres something I ought to

Wait a minute. You know, theres. Youre cold arent you

No Im not its just that Ive got a sort of little chill

Youre a goddamn stoic, Rena

Oh no, no, Lee, its just that the little things dont disturb me very much, like the weather. He gouges an ear with his little finger, looking at her doubtfully. Does it itch?

Once in a while.

And, at once, an acrobat grovels on her lips Ive got a drinkin aunt Lee who has that kind of trouble oh I guess its a lot worse than yours though, Aunt Lilly youll like Aunt Lilly shes got a sort of southern drawl because shes lived in New Orleans for I guess oh about fifteen years and she visits us a couple times every year shes married to a great big fat man by the name of Walter Bergstrom, anyhow youll meet her and get to know lots more about her but shes got a terrible thing with her ear I think its a kind of ringworm infection oh nothing really serious

Lee slants down

Something the matter

Oh no, I

you know as long as you keep it under control nothing awful can ever happen but you cant cure that kind of thing either its far too deep down in the ear and Aunt Lilly keeps scratching at it and scratching and then she says Well I guess now Ill have to have little nip I just cant stand this itchin anymoh a woman has just got to have some peace so she opens up her handbag and takes out a pint and takes a swallow straight from the bottle Now I want youall to understan Im still a lady but a lady can take a drink from a bottle just like a man besides Im here with family and you dont mind now do you my earll just be feelin fine in a couple minutes an Ill be happy an gay again you sure wouldnt want me sad on my visit up noth now would you my Aunt Lilly says Rena mimicking the accent perfectly

What were you going to tell me.

Oh. That. You promise me you wont mind.

I wont mind. Is it so bad?

No its not that bad I guess. It was just a little lie. I was scared for a little while because you said you know you dont keep back what you

he leans back, relishing her discomfiture

88

think

I keep some things back, Rena, and Im not altogether immune from lying

Oh thats a relief. It wasnt much of one and I so much wanted to impress you last night you wont mind will you

No. I couldnt possibly mind.

Sure?

He nods. Very seriously

Well when I told you I was going to the University of Pennsylvania.

Youre not.

She shakes her head no, ruefully.

Well, where are you going Lee is indulgent, paternal. She chuckles on her mouth, on her hands, the fingertips hidden as much as she

Im in my last year at the Kensington High School for Girls, is it all right, the long waving hair of her touching the side of her chin, donkeys of innocence stubborn all around her

I dont care where youre going, Rena, or studying.

It doesnt make any difference to you?

Not one bit.

I mean it doesnt make any difference I lied?

No.

Because I did it to impress you.

I know. All Wisdom Lee, Omniscient, Omnipresent.

I mean I wont ever do it again

You dont have to promise me anything, Rena whats the matter with your hands?

Oh. Startled, she jams them down at her side on the seat. You mustnt look, Lee, theyre awful

They cant be that

Yes they are yes they are she assures him with quiet wildness, and you musnt look at them

But Ill have to see them sometime, he says with surpassing gentleness, reaching out for her arms. Come on.

Promise me you wont laugh or make fun or

I promise.

Really.

Yes.

She jabs her hands up and forward and spreads them on the table. Lee laughs uproariously

You promised you wouldnt l

But Im not, not at you, Rena

Then at

But you just bite your fingernails, nothing more, I dont see what you were so

But theyre not just bitten, theyre dirty.

He holds them. She trembles seriously at him. He straightens out the fingers, touches them over with a thumb. She gives a faint start, as if to pull them away, but he tightens over them. She shakes her head, once, violently. Im so ashamed of

You musnt be. I dont want you to be ashamed. At any time. Of anything.

You mean every word, dont you?

Every word. A moment, a breathing, count their slow whirls about each other, losing count but continuing, the whiteblue Lee and the mochaorange Rena, and then their hands glide away from each other

You better eat something, Rena

Oh I will I wont waste it

You dont have to eat it if you dont want to

But Im going to. Im just very slow about eating, Lee.

Are you? I eat very fast. I take after my father.

My father used to eat very fast too Lee but he stopped when he got his ulcers, and now he eats very

You can take all the time

I guess I get my nervous stomach from my father. My mother too perhaps. Youll meet her.

I want to. Very much.

I told you where I live, my father has a delicatessen

Yes

We live behind and over the store. It isnt very special. You wont mind, will you? Because you live on the Boulevard. Lots of

my familys friends have moved to the Boulevard, but pop never
made that much money

I wont mind. I dont care where you live, Rena, youve got to
understand that. And theres nothing so special about the Boulevard

Its green, there are trees. But you know we have a very funny
little tree in the backyard, it grew out of the cement. And we always have a lot of food from the store, anything you want But I
used to study classical music with Constantine Zinov at the Philadelphia Conservatory do you know him

No I guess the only important musician I know is Danny Naroyan youll like him hes a dynamo and awfully funny he studies
composition at Curtis one of my closest friends is it getting late for
you Rena?

I dont want to go All right girls dump the bags Ill count the
bills the five girls in the rear booth disgustedly scoop out all the
cash from their pocketbooks the coin tinkles on the table christ
Jenny youll have to do a lot better than what hell dya think Im
settin those guys for

but I guess I better.

Ill take you

Oh no you dont have to Lee its perfectly all right all I have to
do is grab a trolley on Walnut and it takes me to 3rd and then I
get the Number 5 going north and it lets me off practically at my
door

Not on a night like this

But youll get home awfully awfully late Lee

Its all right. I want to take you home.

Thank you, Lee.

Dont be so formal.

Okay. Her voice smudges off, a contralto, wisps of baritone
and soprano curling through.

ICE NEVER FAILS

MILKBOTTLE H Ive got some very bad habits Lee shouts through
the swizzing eyecracking slingshots of the snow lifting his arm to
help the girl down the gray wooden steps of the Number 5 trolley
for the moment halted opposite the ISIS THEATER on Frankford

Avenue, her smile plasticrinkling through the snowchattering raincoat, the bublitchki flaring back from the brighteyed hair Youll have to jump the snowdrifts the pale salmoncolored cirquelight from the front of the trolley humped and floundering among the drifts of the black and white up and down and askew on the street All right here I come landing solid and warmcold girl against him, the face of the girl quickly and incontrovertibly serious This is where I live what are your bad habits Lee. The trolley tugs itself into motion CAPILUNGOS BUTTER & EGGS SCHILLERS BAKERY ISIS THEATER, its black rod scaring ground sparks from the overhead wire against the swizzing black&white gray overhead night and the girl and the boy take jerky WHITMANS SAMPLER high goosesteps over the snowdrifts and the transitory clearing between the cartracks GOLDSTEINS DELICATESSEN Thats our store Yes I her right arm building up the drifts of her whole body into it, the drifts of the girl wedged into the side of the boy till the little alcove This is the door to the store and this is the door to our bedrooms upstairs I hope I can find my key she wipes the streaming cold from her face. Lee flaps his trenchcoat, swiping the white snowpellets with red knuckles from the coat Rena lunging her fingers into her pocketbook Yes here it, I thought for a minute Id have to ring the bell and wake up. Facing him. Rena is a whole open space facing Lee, a white clearing peering up at him. Her keys tingle in the tight cold alcove air Well one of my bad habits is that I eat so quickly and so much Rena that about right around the middle of the meal I suddenly have to stop short and belch and sometimes it takes me very nearly five minutes to bring up the wad of air stuck in my stomach and I have to do that before I can go on eating because I feel so very full I got to get rid I dont know why Im talking about eating and belching, Rena. His shoulders lower. She puts the tingling keys in the lock and turns to him again. I have to say goodnight Lee its very late.

Yes, I know. He grinds his teeth, takes her hands, I knew there was something I wanted to ask you

You can ask me

her fingers in his hands, holding, he puts them in his hands again

92

and again and again. Rena is worriedly patient

because I really dont want to be talking about eating, you understand. Im not hungry.

Im not either. Thank you for taking me to

Oh, please, it was

No, no, I enj

Rena.

Yes?

Well what I want to ask you is, the teeth snagging the voice. I mean are you in love with. I mean with, oh. You know. Somebody, are you in

Quite gravely she regards him

I mean is there somebody youre attached. I. I believe its referred to as something steady

No, Im not going steady, Lee. Im not in love with anybody. Her fingers are lavishly cold

I cant seem to warm your

Dont worry about them

the two in the alcove, the girl bulky, the boy thin, the air tight with cold, the wind snowfizzing down the avenue he glances away Thats Schillers Bakery she says across the street. Theyre German. Next doors Capilungos Butter & Eggs but theyre a front for a bookie joint and I know a good story about their son hes going to be a cripple for life because he beat up the guy that made his sister pregnant so the guy ran over his legs with his car and next door to them is the Isis Theater and Marcus Kronthal owns it hes very dashing even though hes fiftyfive with a ruddy face and curly black hair and smiles all the time and comes into the store to see my mother and my father doesnt like it at all youre not in love Lee are you? Marcus Kronthals wife is a very sick and bedridden all the time so she doesnt

No Im not Rena. His hands are very cold, as cold as Renas, his nose spreads and his mouth spreads and his eyes narrow and his forehead clenches and unclenches and clenches and his ears are racked up and back

and youre not going with anybody

no im not this is sort of sudden Rena but I want to ask you I.

93

Theres something would you. Id like to see you, you see, all of the time, I mean I rather you wouldnt go out with, except, I know its an awful lot to ask, request, because I dont have the right, you see, it was just last night that we her nose humps hes got blackheads he looks a little like Lincoln a little bit like some movie star yes almost a double for hes awfully skinny but her hair, her hair, like the color of, and her skin, the flesh, her one profile is awfully bad I know I must be awfully young yet because hes something Ive

you can see me as many times as you like Lee

to kiss you taking then, letgo the hands, he puts up his hands to her head, holding her head as her hands, with tight looseness lays his mouth upon her icewarm lips

You are

unkissing, they heap themselves upon each other, skulls ramming side by side, bonedrifts, her neck back for axes, their teeth grind together, he sucks apart from her

darling, she has. Her head lowers, hands on his arms

Youd better go in, Lee says, transcendental imperious, limits locked momentarily, they must, to resume, in the great vacuum of the commitment of the two, like a globe each adhering to, between them, hard icerocked vacuum they are curved to

Yes Ive got school tomo

Ill call you before supper

Yes Ill be

Rena Rena Rena come here, come here, come

They cant keep, her hand falls from the keys, swerving round to the boy she. Lee, swe

your mouth. your. He wrenches her hair

oh not so

you. You. Lee, my

Get in, now. All right, I, shes on the two wheels of a three-quarter face at him. Humble

Ill phone

yes

goodnight

I wont sleep

I wont either. But youve got to, theres school
oh who cares about
Youve got to care
Well if you
Ill phone.
Yes. She races up the stairs, sinkgloomed in the. Goodn
Goodnight, night, night, night
War will not be declared.

Theres one thing, Rena. She twists round on the bench at the upright piano in the Goldstein livingroom, the new wallpaper of vertical magenta stripe against a cream background, a narrow horizontal mirror crested by ornamental silver, Lee standing a little hunched in the late night in front of the overstuffed unbalanced easychair.

Theres nothing wrong with the way I do the song, is there?

It has nothing to do with that

What? Tell me. She twirls round on the bench, crossing arms over bosom.

You dont have to hide your breasts, Rena.

The girl momentarily drops her head, shrugs, her face stumbling, color lowering her, she takes her arms to stiffen them against the bench, shakes her head, Is that

No, its just that I think I have another name for you. Rena doesnt suit you altogether.

She tickles her face up at him. Oh. She stands, swings, her skirt swinging toward him, her hair swinging over her eye, Lee lightly clasping his arms around her waist as she leans lightly back from him, in the peeling of pressure, as their bodies lightly begin to come off from each other and there is an effervescence within the tip of and down through the center of his penis, the volatile powders of her beginning to fizz in the boy's blood, as if she has dusted his genitals lightly, her loins lisping against his softly, lending them a lisp she pats him with her hip, then with the other hip, then the light joust of loin against loin his penis stumbling through the left side of his trousers at the folds of her skirt

What do you think suits me, she looks up at him with delicate

95

gluttony. They stand quite still against each other. There is simply the stern hardness of his genitals against her

Red, he says. But thats not enough. I think if I called you Saint Red that that would properly

I like that, I like that

Saint, Saint Red. That suits you, that he grabs her head, his mouth stamping out the color from her face, forcing the crimson back from her lips, dunning her breath, raking her lungs with his tongue till the girl is out of bellow, is a full volume of flesh hanging from him, airless, his skull enclosed by her airlessness he desperately pushes her back till she loses her balance against the sofa under the mirror, the vertical magenta stripes running into the girl, the creamy mocha of her neck, heaving her shoulders back and lifting her legs till she is a supine length, her skirt pleating above her knees Lee falls upon her, his leg ratcheting her thighs and a shovel of his hand upon her right breast and she rattles her skull and clenches his hand No I dont want you to hold it there, Lee, no I dont want you to, please, Ill let you know when you can, but not yet, please, Lee, my brothers used to catch at them when I ran around upstairs everybody has made fun of them because theyre so large even when I went to Hebrew school the teacher used to squeeze them and I couldnt do anything about it when I told my father he slapped my face he refused to believe me and neither did my mother, please, Lee, you can touch me anywhere else you like but please dont now on them, just give me some time and youll be able to

All right

Anywhere el

All right Saint, and she lifts her skirt up further

Anywhere el

Yes

But not with your hand down there, not yet, Ive got to get used to, you can use your leg. Yes. Like that, like. I dont mind how hard

Is that

Yes, oh. Lee, Lee. All of you. Get on top of me, because your leg hurts, its rough, thats

96

Like that

Yes. Thats better, that much. Only slower, slow

Like

Thats perfect, thats, only youre so heavy, could you rest on your

All right?

Yes. There, right. Now, wait. She pulls her skirt up to her chest and upflexes her legs, the spade of her groinhair flattened under her cream panties, now you can. Thats, yes. She crosses her ankles above his waist, Thats much. Gripping him, she chunks her loins against him, hurls her loins against him as he blunts himself against her, again, and again Im getting awfully wet Lee do you think Ill stain your

Its all right

No dont take it out, please, not yet, Ill let you know, no it wont be long Lee, I promise you, Ive got to get used to, please keep him in, please, just give me more time

Its been weeks and weeks and

Just be a little more patient just oh Lee Im

Saint, Saint. Grinding, the tip of the blunt against steelwool, his teeth curdling against hers, the pain of the unbared teeth of her thrusting through the pantied meat against the bunchedup penis

Darling Im, her loins cluster to him, a whole series of bunched-up groins of her to him, Lee, Lee her hips tumble down distances, her legs slide down from him, her thighs slab against the cushion Darling did you

No in just a, just keep your legs up a little while

All right is that Im sorry I

Its all right dont wo. He slumps, biting on his crowded tumescence, biting, the musclejaws of buttocks, hips, belly clamping down on his genitals

Lee, darling, I l

What?

Nothing, darling, I

What were you going to

Its just that I adore you I adore you I

But what were you going to, you had something

97

No, no
Rena, my darling, my
Yes, say it.
I cant, I
Dont worry, Lee. You musnt frown so. Oh, wait. Id better get
my skirt down, you never know about my mother, shes liable to
have heard and she creeps down the stairs and tries to did you
hear anything
I dont think I
will make up for every penny as God is my judge, Lee. I dont
know how just yet. But the breaks have got to come. It cant always be like this Mrs Shermans cigarette is falling asleep the book
falls to the floor the cigarette tip is a merry orange spurt against
the white sheet the bedlamp bolds brightly through the bedroom
shadows, a tiny black iron ring with jagged edges makes way before the merry orange of the cigarette tip its got to change, my
luck will certainly change and then Ill be in a position to help you
as well Lee I guess mom and pop are pretty angry with me
I havent heard a word. Well let me tell you its been pretty tough
all the way around, dear brother. Its sure no fun being way up
here in Alaska, this running an automobile agency just isnt a
cinch but Im managing to save a few pennies here and there but
I guess army life isnt such a cinch either is it brother? You can tell
mom and pop when you write them that Ill make it up to them
someday so pop can retire and take it easy like he should, he works
like a dog and he shouldnt and of course I realize Im somewhat
responsible. But Lee youve got to understand I certainly didnt do
anything deliberately, it was just an unfortunate series of circumstances and I swear Ill make up for it so maybe mom and pop can
find it in their hearts to forgive me. Theres got to be something
in the works for me. I just cant help feeling that someday Ill certainly strike it rich and then we can all be on easy street. Ive been
working awfully hard for that day to come, let me tell you as God
is my judge, nobody knows this better than I do, Sue has given
me two wonderful children you should see them, theyre very
bright. I guess mom cant find it in her heart to forgive me, even
more now because I married a shiksa, but let me tell you Sue is

as good as any Jewish girl and these children after all are mom's grandchildren whether she likes it or not, so she could send them something if she really wanted to. Of course there are doctors bills that make it hard to save anything. Martin the oldest son hes got something a little wrong with his eyes and needs glasses badly and Gregg the youngest, well, I hate to tell you this and dont let mom know, but he was born with a clubfoot. I dont know, maybe its God punishing me, and I guess Hes right if He wants to. But two more wonderful kids a man couldnt have, theyre very intelligent and they get a lot of that from their mother, shes got some Indian blood in her, way back, of course, it goes to the Cherokee. Her great great grandfather was a Chief of a tribe so she's got some royal blood in her veins. Shes got quite a temper sometimes but it just isnt easy up here as you can well imagine. It sometimes gets to be fifty below and you have to go around bundled up all the time. But life cant continue being this hard. I think what Ill do eventually is get back down to California, Ive had some offers from the Pacific Coast League to umpire, you know the same thing I was doing with the Texas League. Do you ever see Betty and the kids? Ill bet Fay and Richard are nearly grown up. Gee but Id love to get to see them, especially Fay she must be almost a woman now. But I dont know when Ill ever get back to Philadelphia if I ever do, thats the farthest from my mind even though I do want to see mom and pop its close to seven years since I saw them. Seven long years. I wish I could tell you everything thats happened but it would take too long. Suffice it to say its been very rough, dear brother. I sure wish I could make it up to everybody but at the moment I dont know how. But surely as God is my judge theres got to be a silver lining to the dark clouds and a rainbow after the storm. They say theres a pot of gold at the end of the rainbow and I know thats just nonsense but you know what I mean, Lee. Im bound to get mine, and when I do well then everybody will benefit. You know Im not stingy. Ill take care of mom and pop and you and Fay and Richard. Id like to see Richard too. If you saw them when you were on your furlough will you sit down and write me the way they look? From what you tell me about Richard he looks a lot like Betty so he must be a pretty handsome boy. Betty was awfully pretty, theres no denying that, and its just too bad we couldnt hit it off finally. But thats the way things are. Its better we got divorced all the way around, Betty wanted it as much as I did. Theres no denying she was a very good wife, Lee, but we just couldnt seem to hit it off. How is your wife, dear brother? I certainly do remember her from that time you brought her to see the game at the Broadwood, those were the days all right. I was a pretty good basketball referee if I do say so myself. But whats done is done, whats past is past, isnt that right? I sure wish mom and pop could see it that way, but I guess they wont and theres no use crying over spilt milk is there? If you do go east again I wish you would tell mom and pop that I think about them all the time and Im awful sorry about what happened and wish they could find it in their hearts to forgive me. In the meantime, brother of mine, you take care of yourself you hear? and remember me to Rena, shes a pretty handsome girl if I recall correctly, and give my love to mom and pop, Your loving brother, Clancy

Dave swerves the Olds on two wheels off Lindley Avenue
EXIDE BATTERY
the Philadelphia to New York milktrain rumbles over the Broad Street overpass. The factory workers on the way to the graveyard shift lean patiently against the granite curve of the overpass foundation, waiting for the Broad Street bus. The all-night red and green neoned diner lounging against the overpass has a sliding door through which two drunks slide out and down the steps. The overage newsboy, sweating in his t-shirt from the hot whiffless Philadelphia night, spits into the gutter and waves his papers at the passing Broad Street traffic on the tardrenched street, the rolling tires picking up the slick GIT YER MORNING INQUIR GIT YER MORNING INQ the rolledup shirtsleeves of the cabby across the street reading the sheet by the yellowgreen gash-wool gaslight his torso half out the taxi window chewing on his time, he flicks his paper to the seat, jacks himself over to the door and blabs it open for the lone passenger discharged from the milktrain who slumps down the stone overpass stairs CAB MISTER

making a left on Warnock and drunkenly slamming on his

100

brakes against the curb opposite the Dave Emanuel apartment Christ almighty shes still got a light on what the hell I told her not to bother to he tools his heavy body across Warnock, the frownlines scratching at the thinning hairline, flakes of dried vomit cracking on his lightweight pongee summersuit I dont suppose Ill be able to make it up to her tonight he halfchuckles, rakishly, uncertainly, stabblingly, stuporously, nettledly feeling his key into the frontdoor lock Betty lets Forever Amber fall into her housecoated lap. Now where the hell have you been, Dave, and whats the idea coming home this time of night, dont you have any concern for the children at all? Theyre your children too, you know. You are their father.

Oh jesuschrist Betty not now.

Nows as good a time as any, Dave, even though youre still half drunk.

Whos drunk, christ I can put away more

Oh yes you can, youre great at that, Ive never seen the time yet you could hold your liquor and keep your voice down if you dont care about the children why then I certainly do.

Tipsiness sticking little tacks all over him, Dave scrutinizes his wife through the tacky scrutinies, the tacks winking up at him, brassy, sassy, little puddles of light leaking from the mahoganycolored spinet he steadies his hip against Who the hell is gonna play this spinet anyhow its made of Red Ash

What are you talking about Dave

The goddamn anthracite thats what Im talking ab

Never mind that.

Yeh, never mind, nev, he keeps sticking tacks all over the surface of Bettys body. What about the spinet

Its a lovely piece of furniture and its going to stay there, upright the Betty sits on the sofa at 236 East Roosevelt Boulevard in the quarter light.

This is Betty, Lee, this is the girl Im going to marry.

Oh, Im very pleased to meet you, Betty. The girl is rivetingly thin, scathingly, reprimandingly thin, a very seethe of thinness as she sits right upright angle up rightup stiff on the sofa, Rachel Emanuel sniffing merrily at the sight of the girl and her firstborn,

Bettys vast cutglass blue eyes something the sun drops blue fizzing powders in Lee narrows his eyes at her, the narrowing of his eyes something like the squeezing of his groin to sight the girl, his nostrils pinched sitting in the great chair in the semidark corner of the livingroom the dusklight leaning on one side of the girl in the pain of the exactitude. Exact, except for the sunfizzing powders in the blue eyes, exact in the grim straightedge of the nose, exact in the measured curve of the lips. The neck. Lee knows the neck, very special, rivetingly and scathingly thin neck as the hollow where the neck joins collarbone we have left a hole here, Lee cannot detach his stare from the beat of the hole of the hollow of Bettys neck where the well of her blurts up, blurts, someone pumping steadily from her inside, theres going to be a strike, the girl has a secret gusher her modest frock over the small but exactly clumped teats to slim hip and exactly long and shall we have a curve of calf, this is permitted with the teat as the sole gust in an otherwise scathe and punishment of thinness, an excoriation of loveliness, loveliness flayed alive and yet kept to the skin of the girl where each bone very nearly is articulated to the open scoops and screws and batters of light and shadow, a grief of flesh over the presence of skeleton, the poniard that the bulky Dave perhaps keeps at his side, the dagger of the girl strapped to his thick waist, he seems the Renaissance middleclass prince with the stolen gem, the priceless up and down and slimness of her not arrayed against the sofa, not displayed, not sumptuously bared to the gaze, but scrupulously presented through a niche Lee cannot keep his throat from holding the throat hollow of hers where perhaps is her only clenched fist, the sole ram she can muster driving up and down at the base of her throat, the exact cool of the glade in the dusk, the precision of springtime against the jagged burs and forestration of David Emanuel in whom gentle mammoths graze, sweet behemoths for all his curse and crack of the bat and bounce of the basketball and the sweat of the locker and the growl over pussy here, Betty, is that which he must oil and clean and put in the firearms case till the cleanliness of the girlyouth somehow insult him, Lee must edge away as he peers at her, tastes her, go into background where he may glimpse, for the pounding hollow at her throatbase dismays him, halts his breath, he must cavort in a cry at her, the boy hold this amaze at her for century upon century seeing the blue conflagrations in her eye, the bursts of blazes wake up Mrs Sherman wake up charred twostorey house wake up unbelievingly the boy walks slowly past the gutted blackened Sherman residence wake up Mrs Sherman the cigarette tip burns a steadily widening hole in the white sheet the blue tip burns a steadily widening hole in Bettys face impossible that this alter, impossible that the cheekbone arches crumble or be overgrown, dust perhaps, ruin might be, but not the glaciality and pump, yes, as if the throat hollow finally strikes and the glue, the mucilage, the glutinous squeezed back year after slowly circles to the surface, layer after layer, slab after slab as in the beginning with the appearance of the first child the grip of her thinbones slumps, with the second child gives way altogether

yes, of course, it is her pelvis

yes, of course, it is the pelvis which, thrust aside, jostled, pushed, elbowed for the two successive births, loses its notch and the whole pelvis settles back, becomes an overstuffed easychair for the rest of the body that wells out of it, enabling the pelvis to swell with pride, vanity, venom and move up upon the girls body so that the hollowbase of throat no longer throb but rest, rest, the girl in her insane thinness needs rest,

needs fat,

upon fat, upon

fat, from ninety pounds of scathing thinness to

threehundred pounds of

PELVIS

from which all other children flow. There will be no other children. Known by all and sundry as, The Pelvis's Revenge, you sonofabitch Dave. Squat, Mighty Pelvis, upon Bettys neck

three hundred pounds of Forever Amber in the housecoat Lee stands paralysed

MILKBOTTLE H floodlighted. The Milkbottle H of Betty, floodlighted. Putrefying cream, her blue eyes lap at

You almost didnt recognize me did you she chortles at Lee

Well I wouldnt say

Oh go on, I know Im fat, Im not sensitive about it

Well you do look as though youve put on a

Im just plain gloriously fat she squeals at Lee. Thats why your brother doesnt like me

Shes gotten fat mom, she didnt have to let herself go like that, Dave complains dolorously

Sure she didnt have to let herself go, so whose fault is it Dave

Well it aint mine

Youd better think again Dave

Well, he growls, shes gotta help herself. Shes been to the doctor, the doctor told her what to do and she dont do a thing about it, she just keeps on eating, shes got to exercize some willpower

Im fat she triumphantly announces to Lee, you can look, I dont mind, Im not sensitive, Im as fat as they come and whats more I dont care

If you treated her right, Rachel tells her oldest, she might be able to help herself

where do you put the thin parts of her, Lee asks himself. What do you do with them? Where can I keep them so that everybody will know? How can I handle them so that Betty will know what do I do with them. I have them, he urges to himself. I can give them to you at any time

Do you want them Betty

Shes quiet, she sits straightup on the sofa, the hollows bursting in her throat in sleepless black rings to the boy. I have them, any time you want them he tells the girl on the sofa, his brother's wife, he loves her in his boyhood, he loves her in the smallness of himself far down, and far away and on the edges of his manhood he adores the girl his brother will have for wife, you musnt be gross, you musnt give way he holds his small tin cup toward her Nina come out of the cold we love you. I do, anyhow. But Betty scathes

Theres nothing you can give me, Lee.

No, he is not God, small as he is. In the divinity of childhood, he is still not God. He can take, infinitely, but cannot give back, not in childhood, and yet he wants to. He wants to give Betty back her shadowiness, but he does not hate his brother for being un-

104

able to do so either. His brother cannot commit error. This is the gross incompatability involved in loving Betty and loving his brother: neither can commit error, and yet the two, wife and husband, are connected. If he were God, he could comprehend the link. He can hate Dave, he does hate him as much as love him, but in hating him he also cannot blame him for what occurs to Betty, for it is a hate limited to Lee's feeling for Dave, Lee hates him for Lee's sake, nobody else's, so that whatever Dave does to anyone else other than Lee, well, that is Dave's right of movement, not Lee's, so that Dave is a purity to Lee as far as Betty is concerned, and Betty a purity to Lee as far as Dave is concerned. How perfectly hateful such purity, for it tells him nothing of the link between Betty and Dave

she revels, bodily, in the fat

Christ youre fat, Dave sits on the spinet bench, working his hands through the thinning hair, how the hell can you stand bein so fat, heh?

Lee I have a question to ask you, other boys answer their mothers questions you should too I shouldnt look so dumb with the other mothers first get some water for the plants they look droopy the morning sun drops incendiaries into the Emanuel porch scrambles of sparkle, shinnies of glint, burrs of whitegold jackal geranium and newmown panes of glass, slaps and woodpeckers of sheen on the enamelled stone wall under the windows, shackles and trickles of incandescence on the bright yellow chintz wicker coverings, fizzes of popping bluewhite through the uprolled brown shades and their tiny spark holes Lee can but stand with breath akimbo at the Saturday morning autumn scooting whirling pinpoints of blinding scathe through the porch torn off from the blue sleetstickers of the sky among the nakeding maples along the Boulevard, morning Lee, morning Rachel her legs widespread and plopped extending from brownpainted steel porch chair its rocking springs facing the front door the dyed black hair of his mother showing iodine tones at the temples and on the forehead the iodine roots sinking into the white scalp and the broad peasant base of her nose spread in a canny smile, morning of mornings for Lee, very nearly too much for the human eye to bear, very nearly no right for a soul to see such a conferring of light upon the world

patiently : Put some water in a bottle and water the plants. Is this all right the boy returns with Milkbottle H thats right now water them all around and make sure the water gets to the roots he pushes aside the leafage and diligently pours careful Lee careful you shouldnt get the water on the floor Georgiana just cleaned yesterday I want to know why shes so thin there must be something wrong with Betty you read a lot so tell me what does it say?

Theres nothing wrong, shes just built thin

How can a person be built so thin? All you see is her bones. I admit a beautiful face shes got. But a face isnt enough. Dave will need doctors for her youll see

Marriage can make a lot of changes, mother

Rachel shakes her head, brooding merrily. So thin. How does a person come to be so thin? Like a stick, a rail, a piece of wire, a string. Its unhealthy. Her eyes stick out all over her face, Lee. Its a sin to be so thin how can a person get so. She eats. Not like a bird. Like a horse. And? Nothing. Where does it go? Its wrong. I tell Dave and he laughs. Wait. We'll see how he laughs at Nina sitting with the monkey and the tin cup on the Emanuel sofa the fold of Bettys brown dress looped over her chest to give the illusion of increased depth and substance

I didnt know you could have a breast in the middle Nina says

Its because I dont have one on either side Betty says. Primly. Somethings wrong because Im so thin you see people dont believe I can be so thin. Well in a way thats like me Nina says because I dont have a mother on one side and a father on the other so I have this monkey in the middle

water the plants you dont have to worry about pushing aside my leaves Lee Bettynina says because Im straight up and down what everybody doesnt know is that Im a

so thats why Im so

Its all very clear. Certainly : my father has cancer of the throat. A surgeon removes it. All my father can do now is whisper, Ninabet explains. Then my father has a heart attack. Well, hes still alive, but hes got to lie on his back for six months. Now, you see, my mother dies years ago. I have two sisters, both fullbodied and bigchested. All right, she says matteroffactly. Whisper, and stay in one spot, thats all I can do. People not only inherit lower animal characteristics. They inherit plant attributes too. I dont want to move from this sofa. My monkeytit can move, its attached to a Dave. You see : I let people water me. Im very fragile, at least I think I am. I let people take me out of my pot, and put me in a car, and drive me, and put me to bed. Plants are very vain. Youve seen the Walt Disney cartoons. Very well, then. But theres something left out. I feel I move around incompleted when Im an animal. Completed, when a plant. You see, I vary from one to the other. Which makes for something of a conflict, and people cant make up their minds. Thats the great pathos : the worst thing that can happen to a person is when other persons cant make up their minds about him, her. This is awful, Rena has something of this trouble too, nobody quite comes to conclusions about her. Theres something even worse : before you know a person, and after you stop knowing her—thats a sort of homicide. Because in all the years of not knowing her before, you bring to her just that : cipher, and the cipher cant ever be filled, just dabs and daubs in which the person trying to fill in about herself does injustice to herself, and everybody else does too whom she may get to testify; then, later, in the notknowing after the knowing is another bunch of hoops, so, take a person, and you see her going around with ciphers all round her. What can one do? You get tangled up in the ciphers. No wonder that blind boy jumps up and down in his hoop. Will somebody please water him? Norma says but all we have here is salt water, and thatll make him more thirsty. Give him a series of stairs, Lee says. No no, Levi replies, I want nobody up here in my private office even if he is Max Pollack you remember Lee dont you Max. Bessie Pollack his wife nudges him in the Levi Coal Company office. Listen if I know Lee, Uncle Aaron shuffles in with his oversize shoelaceless shoes flapping, you do too he grins floppily. Bessie Pollack has a wide slit of a smile something like a Chinese dress only horizontal : slit at the ear to open on the horseteeth which she displays like a pair of handsome legs, Bessie nudges and pokes

107

at Max who is squat and grinning and has his eyes wide open displaying
  his blindness
  showing off his blindness, sires, like a magnificent pair of biceps or a great brain
  he stands squat and still, turning his head this way and that. Lee how are you, his greasecavalierism tones. Give me your cane Bessie pokes at him. Christine Novak looks up from her ledgers in pained mockery, grinds round in her seat to open her drawer WOULDYA LIKE A DRINK MAX

Oh no, no, Max holds up pudgy hand. Bessie says He dont drink Christine, maybe at a Barmitzvah thats all. Christine twists off her smile like a piece of chewing tobacco and slams the desk-drawer shut. Hey Levi Im waitin to be weighed Gene Hertzog bawls through the tiny window at the scales I gotta get out on the street Lee takes Max's hand, soft and pudgy Gee I remember you when you were so high Max grins

He does too he does he does yeh yeh Max remembers, Bessie pokes Lee, giggling. So what are you doing now Max says, very serious. Im helping pop in the office

Thats good, thats very good, yes, you must persevere.

Turn your head this way, Bessie shrieks at her husband, Lee is over here. Oh yes, yes, so he is, so he

How does he continue in business, pop, Lee follows his father up the narrow twist of chew tobacco stairs to the private office, pausing to glance through the sootseamed windowsquare over-looking the Yard the massive coalbucket slowly ascending pulled by a cable from the concrete bin into which the coalcars from the railroad dump their cargo the bucket in turn transferring the White Ash into the silos Cal Lacefield leaning from the window of the tin shack housing the controls squinting the bucket ascend. Here its a little quieter up here Levi lowers himself into a gutted leather armchair here I meant to talk to you about your mother you know after all she doesnt understand everything you under-stand, Lee. So you shouldnt yell at her, sometimes she doesnt know what shes saying, he tells the boy gently. Do you think you should yell at your mother? No, I guess not, Lee softly allows. Youll try to remember. Yes, I will, pop. Its quieter up here, Lee, its where I like to come and relax a little. Its a shame Max Pollacks blindness, I didnt want to say anything down there, his wife does all the work, the accounting, thats how he stays in business. She lets him think hes doing the most important figuring. Shes a very smart woman Bessie Pollack, takes care of the business, takes care of him, drives him all around. Any children, pop? No, no children. So tell me, Lee, what should I do with you? because you after all know best of all, I want to do right by you, and a person should be happy in what hes doing, theres no sense in doing anything else because hell fail. And Dave, well. So. There are the silos. Its a going business, you can make a good living out of it but you have to pay attention, you cant be thinking of something else. I built it up, by myself, you can step right into it, how many boys do you think have such an opportunity. Very few, pop. Thats right. Well, but its no sense talking, your heart isnt in its

your fault, Dave, thats how I can stand being so fat.

Waddya mean my fault. Jesus. Red Ash. Jesuschrist. You burn it in the furnace and what happens. It makes iron, thats what. It looks like iron. Big enormous clinkers. Dont drop through the grate thats what

s that got to do with the children Dave? With Fay and Richard.

He nods, one buttock off the spinet bench, Nice kids. I like em. One daughter, one son. Very evensteven family. Half a chortle to suit the one buttock off the stool. Aint that nice?

Youre drunk, I cant talk to you, go to bed

No no no well talk you stayed up goddamn it so well talk christ youre fat.

Is that so?

Yeh, thats so.

Whose fault is it?

Your fault, Betty, you let yourself go

Do you think you can remember why I let myself go as you put it? Its because I havent been watered, she wants to cry but how can she if she hasnt been watered

109

I never knew a woman who had a tit in the middle of her chest jesuschrist that can make any man

You put it there. You couldnt find one on the left side, or one on the right so you pushed from either side and bunched all the flesh together and stuck a cherry on top and lo and behold I had a breast in the middle of my

What would any man do I ask you. A clinker. Youre a Red Ash woman. You burn and what happens, you got a clinker on your chest. Well goddamn it you think any customers gonna reorder after that? The hell he is, hes gonna go to some other company. Shit. An iron tit. Who shipped you, Betty? The man at the mines said you were a terrific shipment. Levi looked at the stuff too. Shiny black anthracite. Good stuff, the best. And what happens, you fuckin Red Ash woman he brings his elbow down on the spinet keys

Youll wake up the kids

Oh I dont wanna do that. Dave begins to cry. He reaches into his backpocket for a handkerchief, blows his nose in a great trumpeting bellow. Sssssh, he holds his finger to his lips, dont wake up the kids.

Dave, she softens to the highschool fourletter man, the catch of Germantown High, she sees the frowning man kick the soccer goal, dribble the basketball down the white lines, an endaround run and kicking the tiescore, and a triple play to Emanuel tossing his glove contemptuously into the air CLANCY CLANCY CLANCY whats the matter, tell me whats

He shakes his head. Nothing, Betty. Im all right. Im sobering up. But his other buttock slips off the spinet stool and he lands with a clump on the floor. Ooops, he laughs up at his wife. Grins stupidly and hauls himself up and sits by her side Why are you so fat? he drops his hand into her lap

Oh stop, she flings it off, Ill make some coffee for you, and he lumbers after her into the kitchen.

You know theres another Lee Emanuel one coffeecoccus confides to his twin, their flat surfaces nose to nose, the one thats three years younger than Dave, not particularly interested in ballplaying, nothing that he concentrates on, anyway, and you must admit

110

its a challenge. Were not supposed to be on this toiletseat anyhow, well never be transmitted, I cant understand your suddenly believing in a myth, we cannot infect a plant. Yes but shes a cross between a plant and an animal Dave get the red rubber ASH pump, the toilets stuffed Betty says Ive nothing to do with your brother lumbering worriedly behind, he doesnt lumber, well Im not paying much attention to the new Lee either and hes thirteen years younger. Is everyone younger than you, Dave? He takes the red rubber pump and lowers it into the stuffed toilet, veils of turd irregularly scudding the waters, and leans on the long wooden handle, whose is that down there Lees or Bettys or Fays or Richards. Are you too drunk to clear the toilet Betty says, half her fat in slabs hanging down one side of the bathtub toward the drain, and half her slabfat hanging down toward the tile floor. Hurry up she says Ive got to go. Theres nothing the matter. Look its true Randy Miller took me for everything I had in the first coalyard I was never around I was out whoring around but the second coalyard pop gave me I was determined to make a go of it I worked day and night I was there all the time brother I slept in that goddamn little cubicle off the office I dont know how many times and there wasnt a redhead around

theres always a redhead around Betty says

does she know you Rena says in the afterhours spot on Delancey Street

You sure your names not Clancy now the redhead says

No thats my brother

Well ah knew your brother so well the redhead heaves out a great bosomy smile at Lee you look just like him

You dont look just like him Rena dryly observes

Its the dim light Lee tells the redhead

The coffeecoccus says look as an exponent of pathos as against tragedy I demand a terminus. Dave wants us. He doesnt want any more children from her younger than he is. He wants another woman, the point being that hes experimenting;

certainly : he wants to find a woman who will bear him children OLDER THAN DAVE EMANUEL. Its the dim light. Maybe you dont know that the first Lee is a coffeecoccus, thats whats caus-

111

ing all the trouble between us, Betty, he doesnt want you to have any more children, hes sterilizing you, hes a plant

get out of my vagina

GET OUT OF MY VAGINA DAVE youre a clinker, a red ash cl

goddamn it Im trying my best to get the turds down Betty, its just that its been a lousy shipment as god is my judge.

God is your inflammation, Clancy.

God is the firstborn, Clancy says, and He swings the bat without knowing Who Hes hitting. I want a divorce

Oh no, Betty says, Ive got to go, I wish youd finish

Christ Im pumping as hard as I can, Clancy sweats over the longhandled suction, ploop ploop ploop Leeturd the First, the ponderous sloping shoulders crouched over the enamel bowl ploop ploop and its a

HIGH BALL STRAIGHT OVER CENTERFIELD IN THE MERRY MERRY MONTH OF PARK ONE DAY

reach for it, the coffeecoccus yells to his twin

thats not the way I break balls the twin shrugs back

REACH FOR IT ITS A HIGH BALL STRAIGHT OVER YAY CLANCY MANN YAY CLANCY MANN

Its not my policy simply to infect the air, twin coffeecoccus says, its true gonorrhea is sufficient coffeegrounds for divorce Betty admits but you cant go back that far.

Him. Orangesunorrhage of the futerus before I know who he is hes taken away. Thats what you cant do to me, Dave, I wont let you take yourself away before I know how much damage you can do to me, concussion of the clitoris, my skull is bleeding at the sex. Thats impossible, Lee the Second says

My plant, you see, Betty explains, has to be watered, if only by a gonorrheal discharge, then such I must accept, if the test is his being the animal of me, then I must close myself up, but he, the animal, has got to draw the line of how he is me. You see you really dont hate me for that, Dave triumphantly announces.

Thats true. Its not your fault that I inherit you, Dave, Betty says, and yet youre the one who comes out in me, you invade me, youre my fat, youre the animal by which I shall feel nothing at all, so therefore why should I let you go when you continue to

112

insure my callousness, FOURLETTER BETTY, Im the obese athlete

ram the suction up, ram the suction up the coffeecoccus urges his twin

inflame the urethra

the struck baseball as the sterilizing factor, Lee, this is one boy who wont get at Betty or at any girl with sperm

You know hes crossing the park at noon today. He always crosses the park at this time. You give us enormous credit for synchronization. Two brothers should have

Youre the cause, Betty

What?

I said youre the cause for my killing my younger brother.

Lees alive, what are you

Im talking about the first Lee goddamn it the first the first and the last

You had the idea

I did and I did not. Ideas are BETWEEN people

Dave I had absolutely no idea that you were in the park, you couldve been on any ballfield as far as I was concerned

ITS THE GREAT AMERICAN SPORT, Dave weeps copiously, dont you understand, it proliferates, its in every possible open space. Do you often strike at a gonorrheal ball

Mother doesnt know. Its not simply a baseball. Its got two coffeecocci on it. At first, when I see the ball coming to me from the pitcher its a small one, a thin one, a flat one, a lovely white circle, lovely as Betty, we pitch BALLS, man MANN, we pitch the feminine ball, the single, young and slim and white, Betty BETTY, leaving the pitchers hand it grows larger, it gains weight, the baseball becomes LARDFAT WHITE HUNKED LARDFAT I GOTTA SQUASH Someones crossing. A boy. Any boy. It doesnt matter the bat SLICES AND UPROCKS the ball its supposed to be a canopy over us Rabbi Silver my bride stands thin and leaflike under mother doesnt know. I

I

I dont know, really. Only that my eyes must be watered, Bettys leaf grows over them. Ploop ploop ploop I SHOULDVE KILLED HIM IF I DIDNT

113

no, Lee says, thats my you pay the secretary that Polack more than you give me money for the house Rachel complains. Oh for gods sake Levi grunts in the dark

Sues not so lucky as I am Betty crows three thousand miles away

Keep your mouth shut

Oh Im not going to say anything to her dont you worry Dave, not me. You can tell her yourself.

Dave, Sue says.

Yes.

I dont want to move back to Redondo Beach. She remains thin. She battens on thinness. She fetishes thinness, she starves her bones, she only fattens her green eyes with lustre, she drinks her eyes at the green Pacific, her cheekbones glisten with spray.

Youve got to go back, youve got to face it.

But Dave thats where Phil died

as god is my inflammation

I know.

I cant go back. I keep seeing the tyke in the big chair where I held him, her cheekbones glisten with fume, the green Pacific scuds in her eye. I wish I had a suction pump, Dave thinks, a red rubber pump, I could clear her eyes, theyre stuffed up with Phil-turds, I keep killing, automatically, without feeling, casually

where I held him.

how can a great big sentimental slob like Clancy Mann be a killer? Its because hes soft, he doesnt know what hes handling

I know, yeh, Sue, yeh

Why did he have to die?

I dont know.

Yes, you do.

Dont be foolish. How could I know.

You do, you do know, youre keeping it from me, the boy was only a year and a half, thats no time to get leukemia, its too early, what was wrong

I dont know. But we have to move back. Its economical

Its a matter of money.

Yeh.

114

I thought you said its something I have to face.

Its that too.

Cant you make up your mind.

Its both, dammit, its

Gimme another beer.

Youve had a dozen.

Gimme another, dont I deserve it?

All right.

Lissen you kike sonofabitch Ill drink as much as I want.

All right.

Im Cherokee, Im royal blood, and here I am going to bed with a Jew. Married to a Jew.

Youve had too much to drink.

The hell you say. Phils dead, I dont have enough. Martin has weak eyes, Gregg has a clubfoot, whats wrong with you Clancy, whats wrong with

Nothing. I dont understand.

You understand all right, youre just not talking

As God is my judge

Yeh yeh yeh. Nobodys older than Dave Emanuel. Theyre all younger, more ablebodied, theyre getting ahead, four years in a row hes skipped over for umping in the major leagues, its because hes old, hes a Jew, hes honest, hes impartial, he doesnt suck ass, flaw his children then, hobble them, cripple them, kill them because theyre not older than he, the toiletbowl wont clear, the coffeecocci keep coming up, maybe the father of the little blind boy has gonorrhea Lee says. Betty says shes a hoop

she wont give me a divorce can you imagine that he plaintively confides to his brother in the cubicle behind the office at seven in the winter evening, 21st and Lehigh Avenue.

Oh Im an athlete and I have five letters oh, B-e-t-t-y, she sits at the spinet, not playing, the sounds lidded down for the night, this stadium of female flesh, the greatest athlete that the plant-world has ever known, for no air can stir her in the apartment on Warnock Street, existent without watering, but her roots hurt from standing up all day as a saleslady in a womens lingerie shop, her fatface faintly green and waxen, insentient to the insects of

115

light and voice and rustle that crawl over her

Why dont you get married again, Betty?

Oh Im perfectly happy as I am she trills, what do I want with another man? the beating hollow in her throat endlessly overcome at permanent high tide, a seabird flying high over it, there is something that the bird is missing is the tale told on her waxen face, Ninabet, the night flows at hightide in roombirds over the fat woman at the spinet, the birds in the circling memory of the plunge, Levi Emanuel is her secondman

Even pop was taken in, Dave nods worriedly at his brother.

N'Muxt is snowed in go shovel a path to the road Levis father delivers the edict the Wyoming Bank & Trust Company must have a clear way to its vaults

I HAVE RED ASH CLINKERS IN MY CHEST he doesnt ask for Dave. Lee. Yes, pop. Lee. Yes

Youre

his hand along the grates of ice, when will the ash fall through I cant move whats burned up through the grates I cant get rid of it. Why doesnt the boy go already, he can get nothing out of that Bank. Im a scholar, why should I have to shovel a path

There is an undulant grate on Daves forehead. My father should fall through my head, I carry him up there

You dont have to carry your father anywhere, Levi roars to his eldest three thousand miles away

I havent gone anywhere, Lee. You know that. Im not going anywhere, its simply I have to shovel a path through the ice and snow

Pop was that Mr Diebele by our house waving goodby

Mr Diebele is very prim two houses away, I will use him for a path, the Diebeles have no children. Its a curious bed that has grates death is White Ash that sifts through easily, burnt from the high quality black anthracite dont kill me Dave dont kill me

I swear to you pop you saw the stuff yourself

I see a thousand things, must I have your coalyard and mine and your mother and Christine Novak to be responsible for shes dying of pneumonia

You saw it yourself

116

Youve got to rely on your own judgment Dave

I rely partly on your experience

Youve got to judge my experience Im a scholar who had to become a practical man. You must take that into account

But youre seventyseven and youre running too.

Youre not an old man, Dave, Lee says very quietly in the cubicle off the main office.

Thanks, brother; the proferred kindness of the boy settling for a moment on Daves frowns as he changes his socks, leaning forward from the fat upholstery of the easychair. You dont have to stay, Lee, its late. Did you get your money for the day? Lee nods. Dave says I wish it could be more but right now I cant afford

Thats all right.

You got a date you oughta

go with them already at 5th and Olney the snow is level with the rooftops Levi stands back in the seat of the automobile, leaning against the concussion of the morning theyre all dead :

A man dying thinks that everybody standing around him is dead, and he is grimly amused

Ive got no date Mrs Sherman is asleep. A small flame nibbles at Levi, and the white sheets of the winter sky over 5th and Wyoming catch fire

Youll come back, Lee

Yeh Ill be here in the morning Dave says how come no date Lee you got no girl how come

Lee shrugs

Ah dont be in a hurry youll have one theyre pushovers Dave sneers feeling his feet theyre still in pretty good shape, pressing his thumb in the flesh between the bones

So hows the business coming along?

The business? Dave jacks out a snort. I guess all right, Lee. Just there hasnt been any reordering it was a lousy shipment a real lousy shipment he prods his heel with the shoehorn and jams the foot into the shoe sometimes I feel like I got big clinkers up in my head my brains wont reorder. Know what I mean?

my son is an athlete. My son likes to hit baseballs. My son is

117

an umpire watching balls fly and hit. My son is a man who enjoys the sport that kills my second child

WELL WHAT THE HELL DYA EXPECT ME TO DO POP GO DOWN THE DRAIN IN SOMETHING I LOVE BECAUSE LEE IS KILLED BY A BATTED BALL AM I SUPPOSED TO FEEL I DO IT

I never say you should feel

No. You never say jesus you dont have to say, Lee.

Its all right.

Im going downtown. You want me to drive you?

Im going home first and have supper.

Oh, sure.

Businessll pick up, Dave.

Ah Im not worryin. Its not your concern, brother, so dont you go thinkin about it. You gone home first you said? Lee nods. Well say hello to mom, heh? Lee nods. Dave croaks out a grudging laugh. How she feelin?

The usual aches and pains.

Yeh. Theres not a goddamn thing wrong with her, shell outlive us all but dont tell her I said so. Lee nods. Think youll see pop? Yes. Tell him Im gonna drop down Monday. All right. Dont ever do what you dont want to do, Lee, hear me? Lee nods. I had four goddamn athletic scholarships offered to me at Germantown High, from four different colleges, I turned em all down. The fire advances in a slow circle around the bed of Mrs Sherman Im expecting a phonecall from my husband on the road she smiles, the gems on her fingers fizzing with the augmented light that Mr Diebele is a good neighbor keeps everything spick and span he waved his clean prim spectacles cleanly collecting odds and ends of light smiling at Lee departing for the Army if I couldve cleaned you, son, put clothes upon you, washed you, daubed off the fecal matter from the infants buttocks why then you would know I am just as much a mother as Mother

I said goodby to mom.

Not to me.

Youre not her.

Look on me as such, Lee, look on me as

Youre not her

118

yes. so. you wipe the spectacles clean. That fathers cannot be mothers are the tears in the mans eyes, in this Levi. That fathers cannot give suck, nor carry sons or daughters in the womb, makes stern rippings in the man of Levi. That for the space of nine months this man Levi cannot divest himself of his maleness and carry a fetus beclouds the cars windshield Lee steps into the trolley and the elder cannot start the car. He wants to follow. For a moment he knows he must follow the trolley to its destination. For a moment he knows he must board the train with his son, go to the war with his son, die in front of his son stop his son from dying there has been one dead already from a comic white ball, but the sweat dissolves his clench on the wheel, dissolves his foot from the accelerator. Levi is still, his motherness has left him. Peculiar matter, as his eyes dry: that he has just felt as if the son who left is his own mother Lee Lee. Yes. The pillow. What? Fix

the PILLOW

FIX the

mother is in the trolleycar, so she cant be by the bed. His arm rests on the rolleddown window of the Buick I must clean the Yard, Diebeles yard at eleven antemeridian in the morning of the night the sun melts all the snow in an instant the mother is clean and blue overhead, his hands are cold STRIKE THREE somewhere in a Texas ballfield he must catch his heart a flyball in the cold blue above the Wyoming Bank & Trust Company

Tell pop not to worry, the ordersll start comin in Dave hunks himself into the pinstriped doublebreasted suit. No use worryin is there brother he grins at Lee. The boy nods a potted fat woman Fay and Richard popll take care of em well Im going straight downtown you take care of yourself. Over the weekend, Lee, hear? Sure, nodding. All right, Dave grunts, all right they walk past the coalbins might be a helluva lot different with a decent shipment of White Ash Dave mumbles, yeh, yeh, a lot different, well theres no use worryin is there brother? Lee nods. Youll be down again next Saturday, heh? Lee nods, the skinny one round-shouldering himself by the side of his brothers bulk in the night against the lowquality anthracite, very black, very shiny, and sometimes if you look closely you can see the imprint of ferns, of

119

plants thousands and thousands of years ago and Lee crawling up the trunk of an ancient fern and then out on one of the black leaves to catch bloodcurdling sight of his prehistoric brother lumbering toward him, nibbling at him, then lumbering away and Lee left as an imprint on hard black anthracite a half a mile underground, sensing the footsteps of his lumbering brother receding. Youve got to dig some coal out he tells Dave, as though he, Lee, would like to feel the pick and shovel of his brother discovering the finely burning coal that would slip through Dave and partake of some of the heft of Daves shoulders, the heft of his scrotum, the redhead in the dim light, Id like the girls to mistake me for my brother. Drunkard. Infected with gonorrhea. Fourletter man but he feels the imprint on Red Ash, the lousy shipment thousands of years ago

Well so long kid his brother leans out of the carwindow, Im goin straight downtown dont forget say hello to mom and pop, shifting his slow easy laughter through all gears, mockingly, lovingly, decks of sliding laughter, one over the other, his broad bulbous nose leaning out of his face at Lee, tell em not to worry

Lee takes the washrag, saturates it with water, rubs it furiously against the bar of soap concaved a frontdoor marble step and then scours off the black dirtrings left by his father on the sides of the bathtub. YOU READY SOON WE GOT TO BE THERE NINE OCLOCK FOR THE SERVICES LEVIS faint yell through the mahogany-stained bathroom door ILL BE READY IN TIME. Then he turns on the hotwater faucet and with the washrag sloshes the soapy dirt from the bathtub sides, flicking the washrag at the reverse swirls of dirty water which the clean water pushes toward the back of the tub because he doesnt want to get his hands dirtied from his fathers muck, terrified at the possibility, sloshing the dirty soapy water gradually toward the drain at the front of the tub where it mingles with the clean water and little by little is sucked down, the tub now being comparatively clean he observes, relieved, obtaining the stopper and shoving it into the drain and then turning on the hot and cold water faucets full force but there isnt the force he has always expected and never got. The mingled hot and cold water a slow trickle. It will take fifteen minutes to

120

fill the tub. So there is time to take a shit. He removes all his clothing except his undershirt, to guard against a chill, and then he
lifts the toiletseat and squats, lightly toying with his penis, lightly
tense at the picture of his father and mother downstairs in the
livingroom, his father impatiently scanning the Yiddish newspaper
while Lee presses thumb and middle finger against his penis which
begins to harden, the noise of the trickling water from the faucet
sufficient to form a buffer between his tension and the picture of
his parents in the livingroom, urging his sphincter on to defecate
between the squeezings of his fingers, the hot water steam skulking a dim milky cloud over the long tilted mirror, the boy
again wishing that it is possible in bed to make himself into a hoop
so that he can insert his penis into his own mouth and suck it and
on numerous occasions attempting exactly that, bending his torso
over as far as it will go and rubbing his penis into erection
and straining forward at the same time that with his hands he
lifts his buttocks so that the organ will come closer to his mouth
but failing, always failing by a few inches because the older he
grows the taller he becomes and the further his skull from his feet
and his loins even though his penis becomes longer there is always
the space of a few inches though he strains and he heaves, his
spine burns, his coccyx nearly cracks as he curves himself double,
but still he misses the penistip push though he does, knead the
member though he does so that it will elongate, he all but splits
his neck in the exertion and the gap remains the steam from the
faucet completely covering the mirror now as his penis flushes
and the boy leans back, his fingertips barely touching the organ,
teasingly, his face in a grimace, the water in the tub growing more
deceptive in its turbulence as its depth increases, the water nearly
at the faucet edge as the image of a naked woman in the boys
mind shoves her vagina at his face like a fist the sperm spits and
with a sudden lunge Lee stuffs his penis into the toiletbowl pointing it directly at the bowlwater so that the sperm catapults at the
white enamel spillway jesuschrist the water, the water in the tub
it might overflow Lee closes his whole fist around his penis and
grips and rubs and grips so the last goddamn ounce is propelled
and twists his torso round and grabs the toiletlever, the flushing

121

of the bowl simultaneous with the sperms last spurt so that there will be nothing telltale and the turds wash down the sex and he can race to wipe his ass in sufficient time to bound up and turn off the spigots and no tub overflow result, breathing stertorously, grinning, glancing at the door, victorious, victorious in that nobody has managed to break in and catch him in the act. In spent elation he puts one foot into the tub. Too hot. He turns on cold water for a moment. Again the foot. Acceptable. He wont be scalded. Gingerly, nonetheless, he lowers his buttocks, they are the first to go into the water but he makes sure that he holds his testicles aloft so that the scrotum will not be singed and he can gradually immerse them, and at last his testicles and buttocks are fully submerged and he can commence the bath proper, though with considerable effort because he remains somewhat enervated from the orgasm, though it is possible, he thinks, what with the presence of the soap and the always delicious prospect of massaging his penis with the smooth silky soap, that he might choose to have still another erection and another orgasm which of course the soapy water would diffuse, nevertheless somewhat shy at the possibility that the sperm odor might linger in the air and the next user of the bathroom become suspicious and besides because of the Friday Evening services at the Synagogue there may not be enough time for yammeke and tallis and Bruch ataw adonai no its not right we should use the Buick Levi says maybe on a very cold night it would be all right but its not that cold and we can walk down the Boulevard youre too idealistic Lee youll have to get rid of some of it. I dont see why I should, pop. I just cant see any justification in the City spending fifteen million dollars building an Art Museum when everybody knows it can be built for five, somebody, the contractor, is making an awful lot of graft and thats money which could be used in slum clearance and the like. But you dont understand, Lee, graft is necessary the cold red and amber and green light in the distance at C and the Roosevelt Boulevard slitting its colors through the naked treebranches nothing can be done without graft. Thats how things are built. Nothing would be built at all if somebody didnt get graft, would that be better? No I guess it wouldnt. So what are you going to do?

Isnt it better to have an art museum? I really dont know if it is, pop. Youll learn that nothing is accomplished if somebody doesnt make more than he should, if there isnt some stealing Levi smiles down at the plump youngster rapidly walking at his side down the Boulevard, the chill yellow radiance of the gas lampposts bumping the boles of the trees and glazing the dark tar of the street the first thing he does is take the scrubbing brush and rub it so hard against the cake of soap that furrows are gouged and then he begins to lay the brush with furious fleshtingling strokes against the skin of his arms, digging out the dirt from the bend of elbow and the elbow tip and then along the flat of the forearm, the sweat sluicing from his forehead. After he has thoroughly scrubbed his arms he does not dip them in the water. No. He wishes to preserve the virginal purity of the water for a while, theres a purpose he religiously observes. He takes a long wooden handle from the side of the tub and fits it into the scrubbingbrush and then applies it to his back. That finished, he disengages the long wooden handle, carefully replaces it at the side of the tub and with desperate vigor, for the whole process is beginning to bore him mightily, he wants to get it over with as quickly as possible, the few smudges and flakes of dirt that he cannot prevent falling into the bathwater have begun to nauseate him, he tries to edge his body away from them and supplements that by gently pushing clean water against the dirtscums without contact from his fingers so that the motion of the water will push them away from his body toward the front of the tub he wishes they could be at the traffic light at C and the Roosevelt Boulevard, it is always such a huge expenditure of energy to reach a given point, it doesnt matter where, his mind already present at the destination, but the goddamned body inevitably lags behind, he becomes dizzy with the breath of frustrating anticipation, there is a kind of jerking madness in the boy when he isnt where he intends to be, more than impatience, it is a flogging, a twitching weariness that besets him, as if he cannot locate himself in the motion itself, that he does not belong to where he is as long as he is not where he wants to be, so that he itches, he squirms, he curses, he hates wherever he is in the process of going somewhere, there is no fairness to it, he is being discriminated against, he is being punished by having to enact the process of going, he forces himself not to look ahead, he forces himself not to think that there is still his chest to scrub, his belly, his crotch, his buttocks, there is still the appalling area of the lower limbs to deal with, it is impossible that he should ever finish, he will be taking a bath and walking to the light at 71st Street and Central Park Boulevard with his father forever and ever, he cannot reach it, his lower limbs mock him, their vast area taunts him, he would like to blot them from his sight theres something I have to tell you Lee what is it Rena whats the matter over the phone must he go through supper must he take a bus must he get on a subway must he walk down steps and up steps and then south on Broad Street before he can see Rena St Red so many things must be got through before a point of enjoyment is possible, in which there is a fine madness indeed, a very hurlyburly of damnable painful sport of nonmeaning, we cannot enjoy a moment of pleasure without its predecessors of punitive action, someone else punishing you, and you yourself, as though one must be whipped toward the area of gratification, you cannot go straight to, cannot at the desire immerse yourself in it because this possibly would mean a greater punishment of notbeing at all goddamn Lloyd Engle and Noah Hudsen the two fags in the apartment beneath his on 75th Street listen Lee theres something youve got to know I just cant stand around and watch you WHY cant they just stand around and watch me why must they appoint themselves guardians of my past and future Shes not the one for you Terry Shannon reappears in negligee at her bedroom door in the New York apartment the following week I meant to tell you when you brought her here last week but somehow I didnt find the moment either its graft his father says or. Or what? Or men must do it for nothing, theres got to be either a plus or a subtraction. Not only must men build for nothing if theyre not going to do it for graft but they must lose practically after they have, often their lives. Thats the way things are built. By making much more than the actual cost, or a lot less. You never pay the socalled real cost, because that isnt the real cost, in the terms of the dollars and the cents. The cost is all in taking advantage, either of other men or yourself. That is the lesson you have to learn, Lee. I dont want to learn it. Then youll be hurt, and I dont want my son to be hurt, Im lots older than you, I can tell you how not be hurt, what am I here for if not that I cant go along with that Terry I Yes I know you think you But I do. There are a lot of other girls in the world and you should marry one who has a lot of money for you because youre going to need money because youre not going to make any yourself and Rena might for a while but shes so constituted that she wont continue. I cant agree. I knew you wouldnt I have scotch I have bourbon I have rye which would you like Lee? Oh, scotch. With soda or over the rocks, its very good over the. All right. Going to the portable bar she gestures at the large wide flat book in the center of the coffee table Did you look that over. Lee, tight, resentful, because Terry Shannon of all people shouldve been able to Rena with the brassy orange darkcolored hair vertical 8-ing over her broad forehead No. Well, do, theres an interesting photograph in there, youve heard of him? Scarne Xender, yes, one of the truly great photographers. The only one, she sharply corrects him, I wouldnt work with anybody else, look for the one American Winged Victory, its a nude. Yes. Its a magnificent body, Terry, but its impossible to tell who posed, he tentatively grins up at her, taking the drink and nibbling at it, not really liking the taste of scotch its too damn much like iodine but it feels very expensive You like the scotch. Oh, yes. You ever buy scotch make sure its. Oh, yes, I will. Nothing like it. Very few people know of it, Americans dont understand a damn thing about whiskies anyhow well what do you think of the photograph. Lee humbles himself in his insides, he crouches over himself, he does obeisance before himself as he fantasies rising before himself. I like it, I like it very much, theres not the usual soft focus. Yes its clear isnt it. Very sharp and cl she stands over the young man a moment as he leans back in the chair, then she grins one-sidedly and haunches herself down to a hassock close by, turning the tall glass one quarter filled with scotch over the rocks in her strong red and white hands, the knuckles heaping up white over the coarse red grains, the pugnosed hoyden ugly of a face compassionately sneering up at Lee, the violently slap of the red tumbled almost crimson hair in wild heaps and huddles and swirls and unevens and tangles and thistled curls around her skull and blurting and brambling over her shoulders curving in and deepening the raw gap of her high wide breasts, the gap closing at the waist and clothing itself in broad hips letting out the long slim legs straddling the hassock, her whole body arrayed before the young man even unto the nippletips tucked forward, forward-tucked and spikeheeled through the negligee, their roots tapping nervously against her ribs, the high heels of her tits stamping, stamping impatiently against her bones, what good is the prod of flesh unless it can tap itself against the bone, it has no meaning lest it in its unfinishedness try itself and test against ultimate hardness, to sense its plastic, to revel in its yield without losing structure well they Whos they My father and mother they think its not quite right you know I should go by myself into town Lee they think a young man if hes interested should Oh Im sorry no, no. You dont have to be sor But I am I should have thought of that myself and certainly Ill come down and pick I think I guess partly maybe they want to meet you You have to get on the damn A Bus and take it to Frankford and Orthodox and then transfer to a Number 5 trolley I know Lee its an awfully roundabout way Its all right Red Ill I think thats wonderful of you Lee I shouldve Oh no, no, its their fault Ive got to stop now darling I think I hear a clicking my mothers upstairs and she often goes up just to About eight is fine At a special synagogue meeting with Dr Jonah Silver present the board responsible for reporting on the status of the Rabbi brings up the charge against the will of Wohl and Zusserman and Levi Emanuel that perhaps Dr Silver is perhaps becoming a little overage and might require the services of another rabbi in attendance so that Dr Silver might be readied for retirement is the opinion of Melinkoff and Degen Dr Silver rises touching his goatee Now gentlemen you must understand that it is somewhat embarassing for me to be present when my status is under discussion. Levi leaps up No its all right Rabbi you stay right here theres not going to be such action with slower and slower strokes Lee gouges the rubbingbrush over his belly, extruding his navel

126

as much as he can and taking an instant to insert his forefinger
and dig out the strange yellowgray lint and waxy substances
that smell so good when he brings them to his nostrils and takes a
long breath, something very special about one's body secretions,
he shivers with pleasure his penis small and aimless now between
his thighs he can see immediately Terry Shannon carrying a penis
around to review the troops, Colonel Terry Shannon of Her
Majestys Light Turd, yessir, yessir, yessir in her whipcord breeches
and the insignia of bone on her shoulders of course and naturally
the baton she carries and snaps and whips and lifts an errant pri-
vates drooping chin the baton, ladies and gentlemen, I am a bit
of a sideshow she tells Lee, that baton is a prick GOT

GOT

the archaeologist quietly tells his audience in the darkened auditorium the University of Pennsylvania Museum the colored slides
gently leaping off and committing smudges of suicide in the darkness

GOT

in the Borneo headhunting tribes they periodically scour the
bush for their enemies, and, upon flushing them out, kill them
immediately, castrate the males and remove the penis which they
thereupon preserve by special oils and unguents and hypodermics
that spurt in calcium so that they have a hardened erect penis,
why, yes, the lecturer drawls on, when you enter one of their huts
on East 68th Street in New York City you will see the dried penises
hanging from the ceiling

NOT SHRUNKEN MIND YOU LIKE THE HEADS OH NO THIS WOULD
BE A VAST SHAME

lees little penis sweetly rattling in his pants as he walks by his
fathers side

BUT ERECT YESSIR TERRY SHANNON whips that prickbaton
around like she OWNS it

STRAIGHT LEE

GET YOUR SHOULDERS ERECT

his mother tells him, look people straight in the eye Terry shoves
her baton straight at him so who do you think posed for Scarne
Xender. It was Terry Shannon, of course, he wanted my torso and

127

legs and since naturally there could be no identification by leaving out the head I was certainly flattered and amenable.

Magnificent body, eh? she rises before Lee. In the photograph, of course. Oh, not that the body hasnt declined a bit, but its still pretty much what it used to be, she slaps her thighs, what the hell, Lee, Im forty years of age, did you realize that? No, I wouldntve believed. Nonsense, boy, nonsense. I look every pinching year of it. But not the body as a whole, that hasnt decayed Melinkoff is a great tall man with bones of bulging iron, iron bulging from his head in the eyesockets, iron clanking through his neck, an iron girder comprising his jaw and chin, awkward iron burdening the man, the heavy iron bones of him making him stoop from the crushing weight, the legs massive and stiff in their irons, linked by irons he takes small steps for such a huge ironness of a man, the iron dolorous, steeped in gray massive melancholy, drenched in metal the emotions, the bowels, the turds that grind out of him and clang chillingly against the enamel toiletbowel, Melinkoff wants Dr Jonah Silver to resign, Melinkoff himself is eighty years of age, the iron of the Old Testament in its revenge and frozen gore hanging in brutal gray metal around his ears, like muffs to the mortal world, the Old Testament shuts it out, clangs huge brazen iron doors over the American years, there are no American years, they are all subject to the clangors and the proscriptions and damnations and the revenges and all other people shall die who contest the supremacy of the Lord and his Chosen People Dr Silver is getting too old, he does not spring about, he has no spring for the old Melinkoff who demands this weakness be expunged from the Congregation Brith Mikveh. The torso is done, there need be no more frantic scrubbing there, but now comes a most delicate procedure: the contaminated soapfoam swirled and caking his entire torso must now be laved and got rid of, but Lee must make absolutely certain that, after rising from the horizontal position in the water by which he will rinse himself of his own scum, he must lift himself out of the water in such a manner that the water that has become dirty because of his torso must not be in the vicinity of his torso at the point it once again becomes perpendicular, which means that his torso will emerge perfectly clean.

128

In a series of plump grunts he lowers his torso flat against the bottom of the tub, and with his hands he disturbs the dirty soapings and liberates the torso from them. The filth, then, remains relatively on the surface of the water. The problem now is to emerge without attracting the filthy water to his scrubbed and cleansed flesh. To this end, craning and straining his neck so that he can see what he is doing, Lee arranges his hand into a scraper whose blade is perpendicular to the water's surface and commences to urge the dirty surface water toward the foot of the tub, but, realizing that if his motion becomes in any way turbulent he then risks initiating a force that will not only send the dirty surface water toward the foot of the tub but back again toward the rear so that his whole purpose will have been negated—his scraping, sweeping motion is delicate and gentle, and the wavelets serenely carry the scum away from the upper body of his body. The last area to be cleared of the dirty water is that encircling his neck, which he accomplishes, cautiously, with his fingertips—first from about his neck, then urging the wavelets to the sides of the tub near his arms, finally past his waist and thence to the foot. Now comes the climax of the problem. Though he has with gentleness and caution accumulated dirty water at the foot of the tub, so that the upper part of the tub shows clean water only, the boy knows that the motion of the water has not ceased : his very breathing is sufficient to make the water rise, fall and circulate around the tub. Therefore, he must seize the moment at which the last particles of surface dirt reach the foot of the tub, and those particles that have got there first are about to return in the direction of his torso, in which to hold his breath and, as he narrowly watches for this point to occur, he tenses his muscles and rams his torso out of the water, swiftly looking about him to see if any dirt from the foot of the tub has escaped his eye and clung to his torso. He grins. The mission is accomplished. But as swiftly as he grins, lugubriousness returns. His legs must be dealt with, and this is an even more ticklish proposition. Besides, his torso has begun to itch a little. He is distinctly uncomfortable. He is far from completion. Through his entire adolescence he is far from it. Dr Jonah Silver is far from finished, this is the most valuable part of his life Levi thickly as-

129

serts, and Wohl and Zusserman nod emphatically in agreement, Wohl's nods referring to his own body that is short, stumpy, and Zusserman's nods like his body, tall as Melinkoff's, the bones as heavy as Melinkoff's but the tallness and heaviness as slabs of hardened fat, as yellow as fat, so that his nods are meltingly ponderous in the Brith Mikveh auditorium where the male congregation meets to consider Dr Silver's case, You want a virgin to come into the congregation Levi sarcasms toward Melinkoff and Degen, the latter too a tall man but in a distinctly pinched and parsimonious way, his skin repulsively white and his lustreless brown hair lank and falling over one side of his forehead, and owning a body that for all its tallness cannot quite straighten up, it is moreover irregularly bowed, one shoulder higher than the other and both slumped, the mouth twisted so that it falls obliquely across the lower part of the face, he glances away from Levi, detesting the man and his concern for the Brith Mikveh school in which the Jewish boys learn their Hebrew and their ancient culture, the schoolrooms running down one side of the auditorium, Miss Degen his daughter sitting at a desk in the rear taking notes, a replica poor girl of her father, the same lank lustreless brown hair, the same sour expression but pathetically tinged with the fairness and sweetness and opposition of youth to the paternal exposure, the same bowed hunched tall body with the most apologetic breasts, the whole girl clothed in a ghastly purple, of the same color of the burgeoning flames at the foot of Mrs Shermans bed, the sapphires and diamonds on Mrs Shermans fingers seizing and hurling the glow into themselves as if to run from the puffs of smoke blabbering toward the bedroom ceiling. Mrs Sherman stirs. A task of pain teases her sleeping features, then passes. She smiles, but her breathing is deeper, and a little more labored. She appears to be drugged. Then a frown, but a faint one. If the frown would be deeper, there might be communication to the legs, but they lie inert, not like Wohl's congested features furious at the enormous insolence of Melinkoff and Degen in bringing up the question of Rabbi Silver at all, furious that it should occur at this time of all times when he is forced out of his paint business, compelled to sell it and, indignity of indignities, to work as a salesman for the same

company, otherwise he would have no job at all, this stumpy stub
of a fellow bankrupt at fortyfive for all his furious agressiveness,
for all his domineering selfassurance that leads him to be president of the Brith Mikveh Congregation three times at various
periods, Wohl riding roughshod over contrary opinions in the
running of the Congregation, the thick spectacles softening the
hard busy blue eyes, everything rolled into balls within him, hard
knocking balls through the circulatory system, hard balls in his
stomach, the congested man, but loving Dr Jonah Silver, though
admittedly theres more pity than love in him for the rabbi, but
what right has he to pity the balls are flung at him by his own fists,
a worse insolence on the part of Degen and Melinkoff, that they
arouse that pity for Dr Silver when all his pity should be for himself, exclusive, the dirty kikes Degen and Melinkoff, the latter a
monster of orthodoxy and the former a furniture store owner,
thats where his hair got so brown Wohl savagely tells himself, from
the goddamn brown furniture, cheap stuff that moves fast not
like his paint company where the paints are of the highest quality,
which has been the whole trouble, you cant have high quality and
sell it Terry Shannon says, or its highly unlikely, but the itching
to be somewhere that you want to be, this is like my uncle, the one
dying from cancer of the skin Rena brightly remarks to Lee as he
surveys his lower limbs, Lee wants to tear at himself, wrench out
the necessity of transition, the whole experience of the passage
from one point to another a deadly proliferation, wildly multiplying, a body ceases to have unity, it spreads like wildfire over the
whole landscape, like a spray of napalm, consuming the sense of
what you are, because the transition is a multiplication of self,
in the arrival at the destination as in the transition itself one had
acquired at the very least the visual characteristics of the point
reached, the danger being that the proliferation of selves, of acquired exteriors introjected, will not have ceased, because in the
irritation of transition is as well an ecstasy, the overriding pleasure at not being unified, so that one wants constantly to be in
transition, to be a kind of fiery spray over the landscape of oneself
so that one is perforce driven to hunt all ones separated particles
in several directions at once, and nobody can find you, much less

yourself, who, indeed, coming on Lee in the bathtub can find the boy, for he is intent upon the anger, exhaustion, hate, frustration, farce, the hiccuping breath as the boy regards the fantastically stupid spectacle of his lower limbs waiting,

waiting,

that he should have to pass through this spectacle, render it null and void by the elementary acts of scrubbing brush and soap, is too much for the senses to bear, he wants to quit but cannot endure the idea of getting out of the tub half clean and half dirty, he can positively see the dividing line, his lower limbs will drive him mad in their filth and his torso wish to draw away, he will cut himself through the middle, half clean half dirty, and everyone will certainly see that Ive been looking all my life for beauty, just beauty Terry tells the seventeenyearold as she stops the car for a moment along the East River Drive in Fairmount Park and offers the young man a smoke, her orange red haggle of hair disarrayed over her pugged and rutted face, the green eyes scouring the dark, the traffic swiftly shrugging by the halted car in the drugged summertime because everything is so dirty all Im looking for is a little beauty her hoyden voice drops to a rusty whisper grated through the muted red hair, a light spray of pathos daubing her here and there as she quietly sights the boy along her cigarette, the smoke cupping her eyes, do you know I feel so dirty personally, she says, that I average at least three showers a day, all seasons, and even great literature is unnecessarily dirty Terry avers, dont you think, even that magnificently beautiful Ulysses, for example, why there was no need for Joyce to inject all of those dirty passages and spoil an otherwise beautiful book, I just cant forgive him for that, what do you think Lee, but he finds it impossible to reply, the words crawl up his throat and then lie abject on his tongue, you know you do make it difficult for me, Lee, I have to keep talking all the time Terry complains. Well Terry its just that Ive never met anyone like you, he says, abashed, I mean with all your experience and knowledge, its hard for me to say anything which would add to Oh dont be a silly boy, thats not true, of course Ive done a lot and Ive picked up a few things here and there but do you know something Lee I broke an engagement

I had tonight, no I wont tell you who he is, hes fairly high in municipal administration. He wants me. I know he wants me, and I really dont care one way or the other. But I preferred to be with you, Lee, youre extremely talented. Thank you. Oh dont thank me for gods sake, Ive had people being grateful to me all my life and Im sick and tired of it. The only two people who were never grateful to me were my mother and father, and Im grateful to them for that. What sort of man is your father, Terry? Oh, hes dead. He was a Senator from South Carolina. Lee is doubly overwhelmed, her father a United States Senator, a United and I know something about art, Lee, I made my debut as Sieglinde in Vienna when I was seventeen. Lee, dismayed, Why havent you continued singing? She flicks the cigarette through the window on the road and starts up the engine. My mother wasnt grateful, as I told you, Lee, and she had absolutely no knowledge of my limitations, and certainly I didnt the trees and shrubbery seethe past in clumps of blur, the rear red lights of the cars ahead in the distance round the curving East River Drive, the moonlight in caduceus silver across the Schuylkill and GASHWOOL of the posts of the gaslamps along the riverbank in soundless vacillograph of reflected yellowings across the flowing river waters ICE NEVER FAILS high and scarlet above the trees, the PSFS of the Philadelphia Saving Fund Society just above the rest of the skyline consequently I made my debut in Wagner before my voice was really ready

My voice broke, Terry states flatly, and I had a nervous breakdown the following day.

I never sang again, she asserts, flatly, her hands steadying the wheel.

Oh, I still have something of a voice, she flatly states. But not for grand opera.

Im sorry, Lee feels he must say.

Oh Ive gotten over it. Its just that I keep looking for a little beauty, thats all I want out of my life, and its so hard to find, so very very hard, Ive been searching all this time, Im never in one city for too long. Im so tired, Lee, so very tired. But the wheel is steady, her eyes brim with traffic judgments, curve judgments,

speed judgments, her body refuses to let up, is perfect in its compromise in the drivers seat, relaxed but ready, cavalier but cautious, swift but easy she may be tired from wanting to be tired, but this is located, this weariness, only about the eyes where the skin is a little bunched up, wary, jumping uncontrollably in its weariness, a crafty skin dumping itself into deep hollows, at the bottom of a very circumscribed pit of skin under the eyes may exist weariness, as though this is where she may feel it and store it, in these pouches, warily weary, and Lee has the feeling there are moments when she closes her eyes without the lids coming down, as Harry Ring, and is blind, so that she may not be recognized, it is unnecessary that Scarne Xender lop off her head in photographing her, but that probably matches her desire, she does not wish to be recognized as unrecognizable, at least not permanently recorded as such, so that the decapitation is more natural, more
   beautiful
   the trouble is that Joyce was an Irishman and Im Irish of course and I understand perfectly why he had to inject all that filth, because all he was looking for was beauty too and he couldnt find it and he dirtied himself in a kind of revenge oh I could kill Joyce for that, I can never never forgive him, she protrudes her lip fiercely. He will not be able to tell Rena hes a virgin standing on the corner of Frankford and Orthodox because it is all due to the ringworm he tries every possible cure desperately Dr Newman sits him under ultraviolet meanwhile discoursing on Lees habits How many packs of cigarettes do you smoke a day. Two and half. How many hours of sleep do you get a night. Between five and six. Well at least Dr Newman observes you are breathing oxygen in its purer state for six hours. How many hours do you work at your desk. About five. Is the window open. Yes. And youre smoking all the time. Yes. Do you feel stimulated or drugged by the presence of all the smoke and carbon dioxide. Mostly stimulated. I see; well I suppose its true that carbon dioxide can be stimulating, and I understand your desire to work in concentrated periods I myself when I was studying for my medical exams went out on the Atlantic City beach, thinking the bright sun would help me concentrate. Of course I fell asleep and got a severe case of sun

poisoning Dr Newman constructed in small yellow oriental puff-balls, something like a miniature Buddha bouncing in utter still-ness as he leans over his desk this ultraviolet might help the ring-worm. But it doesnt. The ringworm returns. Lee has tried every-thing but plain rubbing alcohol, and it is purely by chance that in a moment of thinking of antiseptics his eye falls on a bottle of rub-bing alcohol his mother keeps around for her aching bones, and decides to apply it to the afflicted area and nearly rips a hole through the bathroom ceiling when after a bath he douses the redsplotched skin on the inner part of his left thigh near the groin with the alcohol and dances an extremely avant-garde dance as the alcohol tangles the nerve endings in stickers immediately rip-ped off and replaced by firecrackers whose main constituent is sulfuric acid, the boy's mouth gaping with hoops and swallowed howls, the pain unable to be halted, his eyes bounce up and down in the sockets, he crouches, he straightens, he crouches again, he squats, gently drawing the scrotum away from the alcohol, the scrotum also spattered and shrinking in utter horror, he fans him-self madly, first with his hands, then with a towel, then jumps up and down to implore the air to dry the alcohol rapidly, he shakes, shivers, an agonized marionette WHAT ARE YOU JUMPING UP AND DOWN IN THE BATHROOM FOR his mother yells up IM NOT JUMPING UP AND DOWN he yells back savagely and squats again, his legs as far apart as he can spread them, squats and rises, rises and squats, breathing like a maniac in the inspiration that relief can come by air swallowed, ventilating the thigh inside and out till at last the pain begins to subside, the boy sweating and giving thanks to whatever powers powers can be. The astonishing con-sequence is that the ringworm does respond. The point is will it respond quickly enough so that when he disrobes in front of Rena euthanagia the Kensington El train smoothly stumbles on the tracks overhead, the wheelsparks making momentary lavender scabs on the secondstorey windows as the train passes the store-front red and green and yellow and prickly tinsel displaying the Christmas toys euthanagia look its not a question of bringing in a virgin Degen sourly chews on a cigar Levi, its a question reliev-ing the Rabbi. As his spokesman suppose I say he dont want to be

135

relieved you think everybody when they get older wants to ridiculous and unfair Wohl sputters. Fair fair whos talking fair Melinkoff, we all want to be fair to Rabbi Silver, nobody wants bread from his mouth, its just he cant get around like he used to, hes got too many funerals too many children getting born too many young people theyre getting married euthanagia, the iron swinging from his jowls, it aint right he should be alone, especially a rabbi. I got a few words, Levi interposes angrily, to say to Melinkoff, of course what Im going to say is theory, only Levi omits the h so it comes out teory. A hypothetical case, he says, feeling more sure of himself. I know the hypothetical cases Lee remarks, like the woman with the three children who wouldnt give her husband a divorce so he could marry the woman hes in love with Im not talking about love Christine Novak who could certainly satisfy Melinkoff, shed soften his iron My wife is dead Melinkoff heavily reflects you cant dig up my wife what would Rabbi Silver do in such a case would he rename her? Thats whats Im talking about Melinkoff permits the smallest gleam of advantage to burnish his iron, say somebody rises from the dead Rabbi Silver needs an assistant that something hed need two assistants to do something for because it would be a crime and he would have to get her to lay back in the ground where she belongs BELONGS Melinkoff is close to a bellow euthanagia euthanagia five sons this man has is the hypothetical case Levi raises his voice to interrupt the pounding of the iron and his wife is dead and the five sons dont give a damn for the father who is eightytwo years of age they let him alone but he cant admit how he wants them to come to him to succour him in his old age I myself dont give a damn what my sons would do. I expect nothing from them. Thats the best way then you wont be hurt the all-male congregation is totally silent in the auditorium, Dr Silver blushes rose and silver is the rabbi behind the black goatee, rose and black and silver what can I say in my sermons he smiles faintly, apologetically to Lee in the Emanuel livingroom I cant say anything disturbing they just wouldnt follow me, you understand, Lee, eh? Nu, what can you do, you compromise yes yes what would Rabbi Silver do if my wife came back from the dead hah? Melinkoff flushes a deeper

136

gray, the flush of the iron, never mind the theory of the five sons, I could even say I have five sons who go away, but, BUT he lifts his iron all gouged and pitted from the surface mining, five sons I made, MADE for the giving away, got rid
of them, rid
of them, rid
of all five in myself, who WANTED FIVE SONS IN HIMSELF euthanagaia EUTHANAGIA. That, understand it, a man should have this many males inside him is a curse, all young, all infants the iron clangors away, theyre a burden, so you give them to a woman's womb and she brings them forth for you and sends them out, and away, who wants to see them, I got five sons
to give me back myself. So much for your
TEORY he catapults at Levi, and sits. The old ones, Wohl thinks, they are all crazy, crazy with age, sputtering within Wohl does, they hate having been spared, they hate the iron clamping over their eyes, their flesh, they hate the reverence given them, a mark of their senility, so they fume, they rage to seek the conflict that is no longer in their hands, and make for a disordered disorder in the world
A compromise, Levi rubs his grin lightly. When Melinkoff's wife rises from the grave, put in the minutes Miss Degen Dr Silver should get an assistant, then and then only I call for a vote you ought to forgive Joyce Lee suggests. Terry gives a short giggle. Whats the matter with you Celia Renn whispers to him her face a peeled potato with the eyes, warts and excrescences left in ICE NEVER FAILS the scarlet sign clear from the Girard Avenue Bridge spanning the Schuylkill dont you know what she it isnt that Rena isnt a splendid figure of a female I admit, but really, Lee, shes quite vulgar, you know, and she lies terribly well I dont know what lying is and Ive never heard her lie he lies true and false is a false configuration anyhow why do you lie to me Lee his father sweetly inquires. I wouldnt mind anything so long as you wouldnt lie and I cant understand that do I hit you
No
Do I deprive you of anything
No

137

Do I threaten to punish you in any way

No

So why do you lie can you tell me yes but I cannot tell you since you are the truth of my father I cannot believe in the incontrovertible there is something monstrous in that which cannot be denied. Undeniable, therefore deceivable. Inexorable, therefore evadable. Turning. Theres a solid confronting me. Suppose I dont want to escape the solid but only to have it less substantial. I will go around it, faster and faster till it becomes a blur the boy jumping up and down in the hoop is a father, and the hoop circling him is the son. I can make you circle round my hips if I go around you, you understand? The point is, that I want to give birth to you, to a father, what is more important, that is already here, so that I can circumvent having one who will be younger than I. I want one younger than I but he must already be here older which is why I apply alcohol to my ringworm and dance up and down in the hoop, blind with pain. If one is blind with pain, then one must lie that one is seeing. Do you follow? No, I cant. Well, then. I want you to follow me all the days of my life, so that I lie to lead you on. If I told the truth, you would not follow, everything would be simple and clear. I must obfuscate, deceive, dissemble, dissimulate so that you keep on being born to me, for if I told the truth I run the risk of losing you you must not think of me as your father Rena St Red, but if that is the only way you can keep me, then lie, fabricate, embroider, for you know of course that as soon as you stop I wont. I wont stop, but it places an extreme burden on me, from which too I must escape. You see, father, you want to escape me, and I cant have that. But Rena is not related to you, and I am, shes a handsome filly. You keep away from her, pop, she doesnt like your breath, it stinks. Do you actually say that to me. No, never, I simply turn my face away, but she doesnt, and Dave doesnt, she accepts stinking breath, I can see the look in your eye, pop, when you look at her, resting on her tits, her legs, why must you embrace her so tightly and then out of her presence impugn her, call her a liar, you think because she and I are together that we must both be liars and that such is catastrophic, that at least one must tell the truth. But do you tell me the truth, can you even imagine what truth is, will you put yourself up on a cross for truth? Thats what Jesus Christ thought he was doing and HE was a liar, perhaps the most grandiose of all, knowing that Pilate had finally pierced HIS lie by asking what is truth, so Jesus martyred Himself knowing he was a liar, knowing He was not the Son of God but that he had to carry the lie through OR HE WOULD LIVE, and living with such a lie was out of the question. Well Im not the Son of God, Im only the son of a father, and I but half lie, and you need not crucify me for that and bring me then back from the dead, like the supposed resurrection of Melinkoff's wife. Never mind YOUR resurrections, Ill do them for YOU. Thats my job, and each time I resurrect you with a lie, I did attend classes, I did study, I did spend the money on food, I did talk to the professor, I will make you proud of me, I will not lie again, I will not spend your money foolishly, I realize you want to do nothing to Rena when she is here LIAR LIAR LIAR YOU WANT TO FUCK HER and of course she regards you as a male, a fuckable one that is a truth I will lie about to myself. Shouldnt I? Dad, she says. Dad. Dad I have no clothes she wobblelips up at you. You know that as a professional singer I need a wardrobe. Dad, pulling your belly to hers he sleeps he snores on the Atlantic City sand in the shade, his face in the shadow under the boardwalk suddenly I see he has a belly. Standing, its not too noticeable. Lying, its obvious he had me under the boardwalk the one time I thought I might. What, Rena? I wanted to, Ill be honest with you Lee I wanted to, but when he nearly was about to put it in I twisted away because I thought of my mother. Oh, wonderful mothers day. I thought of my mother. Liar, liar. He had no contraceptive on, thats why, fuck your mother. He was barepricked. My father has the contraceptive of fatherhood on. Lee laughs and laughs and laughs, Im a genius, you see. My father as he was conceiving me with Rachel intoned the special prayers that a pious Jew using the Apocrypha should intone during coitus to insure that the child will not only be male but be a signal honor to his people as well, so the prescription is, as you are sliding your penis in and out of your wife, to recite the list of the Hebrew Prophets and, at the moment of orgasm, to grunt Tetragrammaton,

Tetragrammaton, the Almighty, the Lord King of Hosts and lo, and behold, the child thus conceived will be mighty in brain and in brawn. The brawn isnt so necessary. My brother has brawn, good old Dave YAY CLANCY MANN CLANCY MANN Celia Im sorry I cant oh forget it Lee its just that its so hot anyhow Terry says the ride is cooling us off does it always get so hot in the summertime in Philadelphia hows that little Armenian magpie friend of yours. Danny Naroyan? Yes, hes a busy little thing isnt he. But limited, you understand, Terry is quite grim. Lee is confused. Limited? None of his intimate friends are permitted to be limited. They must all be extraordinary, they must all be huge successes, transcendental. He could cry if they are not Well I dont want to confuse you, Lee. I think hes a great composer, Terry. Do you? All right she strides back to the bedroom door and strikes a pose euthanasia. The mercy killing of the young, in that they are precisely that if they do not serve their prime purpose, the servicing of the aging and the aged all I want to do she writes Lee in her precise script from Seattle on the letterhead of the Consulting Engineers interior decorator National Youth Administration executive architect Sieglinde at seventeen oh yes. And by the way heres a novel I wrote, Lee, its not bad, its not unique, it was published which is about all I can say for it is to find a little beauty before I die no you may not read the novel, Lee, its a waste of time will you excuse me for a moment Ive got to take a shower. Dr Newman is the result of that long Atlantic City exposure to the sun, poisoned with gold now turned to yellow, oriental puffballs no I cant go into an extended description of Levi's symptoms he snaps over the phone what are you bothering me for Ive got a whole officeful of pregnant women his case is hopeless, hopeless, now stop phoning me Ive got a whole officeful yes of course Terry sweeping out again from the bedroom in an offwhite negligee ah that feels much much better this New York heat is would you like another drink? Lee whispers yes. This is the most difficult part of the bath. In order that his thighs not be contaminated by the increasingly squalid water he must furiously push it toward the foot of the tub again and again and again and meanwhile raise his thigh, scrub it with frenetic speed and, that effected, keeping the

140

thigh aloft, dash the dirty water toward the front of the tub quickly enough so that he can lower his thigh, but the exertion is fantastic because, as he scrubs his thigh he must lean his torso back on one elbow, then, the scrubbing completed, the water pushed, rise from his elbow, lower the thigh, dunk it and keep pushing pushing pushing the dirty water away, and repeat the process with the other thigh, the knee, the calf and, straining his arm to the utmost, daub more than scrub the ankle, which is insufficient, he knows, he is trying to escape the inevitable, for the ankle will not be cleansed by such a method, so he must raise his leg as high as it will go in the air, push the water and bring the ankle close to his face so he can properly reach it, grimacing all the while, gnashing his teeth, sweat pouring down his forehead and stinging his eyes how often do you take a bath Lee? Once a week he admits abashedly to Terry. With a sense of dread he imagines the form of Mrs Wohl, the wife of the paint salesman. Mrs Wohl is a pretty woman, a woman of girlish bones whose lyric laughter beginning low on the scale rises to a high note, girlish but with firm breasts and slim legs. The trouble with Mrs Wohl the wife of the paint salesman, the girl who constantly softens the pugnacity, the bite, the clashing balls of Mr Wohl by the laughter rising from the low to the high, a coloratura, she begins as a girl and ends as a girl; as her hair grays, the coloratura laughter still is present; after the death of a son, the girlish rise from a low of her tripping laughter emerges after a week or two; the lines that deepen on her faintly equine face do not extend into her throat where the day forever remains the morning; she is helpless to forbid her girlishness at fifty years of age, at sixty her laughter helplessly rises; there is a Fairmount Park spring of cold and sweet watering laughter in her throat. What will Mrs Wohl do on her dying day Lee thinks as he covertly scans Terry Shannon. The trouble with Mrs Wohl is that even after her death the girlish laughter will yet be welling up from her throat as an extra organ that never belonged to her body at all. Its possible that each of us have extra organs that refuse to die, which have absolutely no chronology. Ive got to find mine, Lee concludes seriously, and then Im going to mark it, and after I die Im going

141

to look for it. Not that Mr Wohl is going to be haunted by his wife's laughter; no, because it really is never related to him; it parallels him and vocally is a lenitive, but the laughter never issues because of him or for him or against him; the laughter issues anywhere, accompanying a selfmodestying his wife does constantly, as though she really isnt present anywhere at all, only her laughter is here, the rest of her doesnt matter. Dr Jonah Silver expresses his gratitude to Levi on the pavement outside the rabbi's home. You dont owe me anything, Levi shakes his square face. Owing is no good, I dont believe in it. Still and notwithstanding, the rabbi protests. Never mind never mind Levi stops it, your salary is too low as it is. Well whats true is true the rabbi says, Im telling you Levi if it werent for the gas furnace I installed I dont know what Id do, I hated to do it you understand because I always bought coal from you and I felt badly, but you have no idea how efficient it is. Yes its more expensive I realize, but the efficiency makes it less expensive than coal. I know I know Levi admits, theyre putting gas into all the new developments, and when you think of it its only right even though it affects my business, you dont know how bad its cut into it. Im not going to have gas in my house Rachel swears, it will smell up the whole house she tells Levi. You cant smell the gas, it dont leak, he says. Never mind never mind, suppose theres a leak the whole house will explode and what will it look like for a coalman to put gas in his house, hah? The least you could do, Rachel, is consider installing oil because after all Im handling oil as a sideline. I dont care how youre handling it you should hear sometimes what its like when they put the oil on next door Im telling you Levi I cant stand it. It pounds so. I get a headache from it, and I can hear the smell. Mamma you cant hear a smell Lee tells her patiently. What? I said you cant hear a. So what should it be? You smell an odor. Im glad you corrected me, Lee, other boys correct their mothers so they shouldnt sound foolish in front of others. What did you say you dont hear a smell? Thats right, you smell it. Oi Im telling you my mind isnt what it used to be. Oh for chrissake how can you admit that Lee? A bath once a week when she takes three showers a day, boyman Flikker grins darkly at him from his white

142

face, his wide shoulders a little hunched besides youre late he includes Norma. Im already drunk how do you like the barony? He flourishes a limp hand at the upper East Side basement apartment. How the hell did you promote it? I met one of the girls at the ad agency I was just fired from, thats why were having the party. Can you imagine that, Lee, I was fired because I made half a dozen calls to Texas to a client, I was only trying to locate him to inform him his layouts would be somewhat delayed. Of course, I was responsible for the delay, and I guess an airmail special delivery letter or a telegram wouldve been sufficient, but—he airily waves an arm—I felt like calling Texas. Youre way behind, have a drink while I take care of your sensual wife who looks like a prim golden Sundayschool teacher. Im not innocent am I, Norma skids over her shoulder as Flikker leads her away. Hi, Xena Ritchie says behind his back and, as he turns, continues, Oh no, no, I didnt come with Flikker, at least I dont intend to leave with him, the girl built in elongated triangles and carefully grading them at every possible moment to make herself more acceptable for modeling, so far, however, managing only stocking and slip ads. Shes really not a bad girl, Flikker confides to Norma. Uhhuh, Norma says dubiously. I mean its certainly true that she changed her name from Rakowsky, and that shes still married to a painter shes been separated from for two years, and that she keeps a little red book full of names. Why should she do that, Norma feels she might as well please him with the conspiratorial question since Flikker is bent as usual on revealing every possible scrap of information he knows about anyone. People strongly doubt the truth of the revelation and, indeed, diminish their respect for the betrayer, which is precisely what Flikker wants; he hopes people think him a liar as he tells the truth, a process he considers a kind of cream of the jest; and if I please him with this conspiratorialness he will be, somehow, less nasty to me, perhaps say nothing of me at all to anyone, I dont want him, specially, talking about me, I dont want anybody talking about me particularly, not that I want particularly to perpetuate a picture of me as a Sundayschool teacher, she is a little petulant I need a drink she tells Flikker and he leads her into the kitchen and starts to mix. How many drinks have you had, she asks curiously. Half a dozen, he says quietly. They dont show, she says. They never show, he snarls suddenly, but I dont want you interrupting while Im talking about Xena Ritchie's little red book. Are you jealous of your husband? he darts at her. No, she replies quite evenly. Well in that little red book Xena has the name of every man who has ever laid her. She writes them down after each lay and makes a count of how many shes had at the end of a week. She has slept with eightytwo men to date, he looks at Norma raffishly. Norma says It sounds like she has a project. Flikker chuckles. She has; she wants to sleep with any man she can lay her hands on. You know what she does after she undresses and a man is about to make love to her? Ill tell you : she makes an entrance from the bathroom and strikes a modeling pose and says Isnt my body a perfect dummy? SNYDER-GRAY MURDER CASE, GRAY SENTENCED TO ELECTRIC CHAIR, SNYDER GETS LIFE. They are both found guilty of conspiring to murder Mrs Snyders husband for the insurance, but the State spares the woman Lee eagerly chews at his rolledbeef sandwich at the kitchen table during his lunchperiod from Clara Barton grammarschool. The famous baldheaded explorer and archaeologist stands to one side on the platform at the University of Pennsylvania Museum auditorium as with his long pointer he taps on the colored slides jerked into the darkness TITLE : HUNTING FOR THE DINOSAUR EGG IN THE GOBI DESERT. THE GIANT FOOTPRINT OF THE DINOSAUR here you can see Dr and Mrs bending over to examine the footprint. The shadows resemble splotches of ink awkwardly split. There is a frozen tumble of rocks. The scientists are in khaki, their shirts shortsleeved and open at the neck; they wear woollen stockings ending just below the knee. They have flaps on their breastpockets. One scientist is bald; another, his wife, has long hair, and accompanies her husband everywhere. Into the dinosaur's egg? Its size should be suitable for an apartment. I never knew dinosaurs laid eggs sponsored by the University of Pennsylvania. Im going to give you a bath now Mr Emanuel, the female negro nurse says with grave sweetness; I do it with alcohol she explains to Lee. Lee, his father looks at him. Yes, dad. Lee help me. What kind of help do you want. I want

144

you to decide what I should do, its hard for me to decide, but
you have to know what its all about. Anything you say, Ill do anything you say, Lee says in low tones. Then call Hertzog right away,
tell him I want him over right away. I have Mr Hertzogs phone
number the nurse volunteers, I'll call him. But Victor Nathanson
is only indicted for the murder of his motherinlaw, he is never tried
while Snyder is tried and convicted. Mother never ventures an
opinion as to her brother's innocence or guilt, she doesnt want to
come to any judgment at all. It is sufficient evil to the day thereof
that Victor is locked up in Moyamensing Prison. There is neither
guilt nor innocence is the way Rachel Emanuel has it; there is
simply an error, but she will not even ascribe causation to the
error. It is ERROR, capitalized and mysterious, and possessing a
life of its own, in which her brother is caught. It is the same kind
of error that catches Aaron Emanuel when shortly after his im-
migration to the United States he is drafted into the army and
driven mad by the sound of the BOOMBOOMBOOM of the great guns
on the riflerange. The Emanuel family assigns no culpability. I
am an intermediary, Flikker whispers both to himself and to Xena,
this is my major life role. What do you want me to do?
Xena poses as in a lingerie ad, her long triangles lopped off by
curves. I want you to get me Henry James, her long mothgray
eyes steadily fluttering at her fingertips that tread at Flikker, bring
him into the bedroom. Didnt Henry James and you have an argument over Lee Emanuel? Flikker sways at his shoulders, tilting
his nose up at the girl a good head taller than he and then looking
down at the boy in the bathtub. Itd be very difficult for me to
bring Henry James into you, Xena, hes taking a bath and, frankly,
Id like to keep him there, hes having trouble, bloodless and limp
though Mr James avers him to be. Oh I can cure anybody's style,
Xena crows. As you cured you husband's, Xena; I dont think I
can forgive you for making him paint all his canvasses on their
frames. Xena laughs whitely, You must admit its quite a depar-
ture for an artist. Theres certainly no doubt in my mind, Flikker
concedes, that I hate Henry James, but hes having trouble taking a
bath, and my sympathy goes out to him : he's very dirty, the wiz-
ened sourness says, and he tries so very hard to lift up all the layers;

for this I have a grudging love finders peepers FINDERS PEEPERS he cackles at her. You cant see the bigness of his body, she jabs at him, its like a big building that you walk by and you hear a voice. Its Henry James' voice. You rarely look up at the building, Flikker, but you can love a voice, cant you? Passably, Flikker admits; I love in passing. That is the quality of old men, Xena condescends. I need another drink, Im becoming irritated, Flikker flings at her, and dont be so critical of old men and their loving in passing, the old within the young, the advantage is the very feeling of retrospect as one engages in youthful actions, one's sense of fantastic frailty, brittleness, that one may break off from an engagement at any time with an adversary and leave him your youth, leave her your youth, he grins abruptly at her, as you scoot away in your old age, Flikker cowers from the girl, as though at any minute he may run through her spread legs, Flikker the nonagenarian child. Go get Henry James, Xena persists in a low tone. If I love him, why should I bring him to you? In passing, she cries, purely; leave him your youth, he should do well with it : wouldnt you like to have yourself clothed in him as he bends over me in the bedroom; you could reach my lips without my having to bend down evil evil evil Achille Volpe whispers from his crouching eye finders peepers you could watch from the doorway, watch from anywhere, watch through the wall, watch from a thousand miles away, youre rather talented at that, perspective being the attribute of the noncommitted. He has a wife, he says softly. Well, then, watch with his wife, Xena cries fiercely, watch through her, this is the best sort of observation for an intermediary, is it not? when that which you observe is distorted through the medium you observe; watching by yourself would not be a finality, would not be real; you find the truth of things by having them reflected on another object. Thats all you can tolerate, Flikker, is reflection. Direct examination is much too painful, much too—she pauses, sweetly—uncivilized. Civilize us for gods sake, the tall grayeyed model reels back against the wall, civilize us, she chatters, excitement trickling from her mouth in chips of teeth, go get Henry James, go get him go get him go get him on the subway with Lee and Norma Flikker's face sways, pales, Ive got to get off at the

146

next stop he tells them fondly, the wrinkles low on his forehead, his nose creeping slowly but surely toward the space between his eyes, his smile fixed, his eyes a stainedglass agate. Are you sure youre all right, Norma puts in with concern. Oh Im all right, I guess Ive had just a little too much to drink. Lee shakes his head. Not that much, Flikker reassures him. You look green, Norma says. Thats all right, Flikker says; is it a pale green? Yes. Then as I say Im all right—with pale green. It will not deepen. The A train stops, Flikker bites his lip. Goodnight, folks the domeliner passing through Wyoming

(Bank &)

the rock formations are like Flikker's face, magnified, Lee turns to Norma; as though lava erupts on Flikker's face, and the flow ceases when it reaches his chin; but in pale green, lavender, gray, and touches of crimson he stares through Flikker, the long window giving out on the landscape eruptions, Flikker's face are these in miniature, snarled stubble, gnarled, anciently youthful, as though a face erupts from the earth and abruptly stops at the rim. You can talk about him directly, Norma says. I dont think hell die before we get there. If he sees me, he might want to go on living. The fact that I come may give him the will to live, Lee turns to her. Thats possible, Norma tells him gently. I mean I think my father wants to die, and if I can tell him that thats foolish, that thats . . . he trails off, the thought of his father suddenly stopping at the rim of a heaving in him what are you worried about Norma? The wheels, were right on the wheels. Oh god dont deliver now. Maybe wed better stay in the domeliner for awhile, its more cushioned up here than in the compartment (Bank & Trust Company) Lee. Yes. Lee. Yes. Terry strides like a striding male up and down her apartment, pacing. Is she looking for a dinosaur egg? One has the sensation that she searches for the prehistoric. Will they find a little dinosaur in the egg do you think? Norma do you carry a baby dinosaur? Does he resemble my father? Is it possible that what the scientists are looking for on the Gobi desert is a father whos a dinosaur, so that they can lumber him across the stage of the University of Pennsylvania Museum auditorium now theres an idea, giving birth on the Gobi

147

Desert, the purple and gray and green lava formations erupting from the womb, I found Him

I found HIM at last in a dinosaur's egg

I can keep him now

I can exhibit him

I can charge admission price

He is petrified

He exists for all the ages dont deliver now Norma for gods sake not now the compartment buckling over each separation in the rails buckle

Buckle Him down

put Him between the spaces of the tracks

Listen

Is He coming

for christs sake for Lees sake DONT SQUASH THE DINOSAUR EGG NORMA NORMA NORMA I DONT WANT HIM TO DIE

I know

WHAT THE HELL LEE, Terry Shannon speaks imperiously, whats wrong with me, you can tell me, what makes men act the way they do with me

Xena

Norma I wonder if I can borrow him for a moment I want to talk to him. Certainly.

I tried to get Flikker to bring you into me and he said he would but somehow he seems to have got lost, hes drifted away.

Flikker has a way of drifting. Xena takes Lee James by the arm and guides him to the bedroom, moving murals on the walls embodied and envoiced and with drinks in their hands the murals may be spoiled Lee idly drifts with Xena to the foot of the bed and she languids her arms about his waist and leans back from him, her weight pulling at him, Im losing my balance she cries at him with drunken cheer, fall down with me

FALL DOWN WITH ME she taunts, cries, whispers, invites, wheedles, at arms length from him, oblique over the foot of the bed, fall down with me she murmurs and lets screw the hell out of Lee Emanuel hes spineless gutless bloodless NOT like Henry James she giggles, her head toppling back, the murals on the wall turning

148

toward them, pretty bad murals Lee thinks, coming off from the wall already, pretty cheap paint as he stiffens himself, the fingers about his neck now tugging. Well the point is that Ive got myself scrubbed now from head to toe and my fathers waiting for me. Mr Emanuel make him fall down on top of me. But hes just a little boy, Xena, you certainly dont want to put him in your little red book. But Terry Emanuel says she doesnt care whether hes a boy or not, its a matter of modeling before a male, old or young, weve got to keep in practice. Terry Ritchie says now theres the girl for you, that Norma, I have opposing Ritchies as you can see, theyre stuck there by Flikker, he enjoys juxtapositions green as he is, I cant get the picture frame to lie down all my life Ive been looking for beauty on the frame Xena Shannon avers Henry James and James Joyce, isnt Henry the one on the frame, thats why we tore Joyce out of the frame, hes filthy toppling from the wall. The services, the services, Levi calls, Ive got a tallis around his neck Xena offers, Im a good Jewish girl, I was circumcized Norma Ritchie volunteers. My flesh tingles from all the scrubbing, Im itching, I always itch after a bath thats because you dont take more than one a week Rachel authoritatively maintains. No, its because Dad has his fingers under my skin, he left them there, he forgot where he was, he SHOULDNT FORGET HIMSELF IN HIS SONS the lava formations rests its head against the doorway to the bedroom doodling its Flikkertongue at the scene, the room clickclickclicking over the rails, theres a train riding over me Lee thinks and I mustnt drop into any of the spaces between the rails youre a man Norma rails at him you tell me whats wrong with me. Levi seizes Xena around the waist, let me go she yells up at him, let me go I cant I cant he feels himself falling

whos pushing stop pushing whos pushing Flikker are you pushing he wriggles a long monkeyarm at them no Im asking for pennies Nina watches the struggle from Flikker's childhood youre such a little milkman she says softly to him, you do carry white bottles of milk dont you youre the little man who deposits MILK-BOTTLE H on the doorstep sweetly and silently in the morning for all the children in the world to drink

SHUT UP Flikker bellows at Nina Emanuel you have no right

to intrude your little boy with the bird on the canvas, because Xena has torn them all out, Sy paints only on the frames now, wise man, hell make a fortune. Hes not her husband. Well then Sy ought to take a tip from her, be a gigantic miniaturist on the frames, hes good at frames, he can make them fifty feet wide and thrity feet long and the art will be mammoth, stretch from Los Angeles to Philadelphia

You see, Lee, Norma confides, the rails are paintings, thin, narrow, three thousand miles long, no canvas between, you will be famous for the death of your father

cruel

thats very cruel

sons

sons

down the line one after another famous for the deaths of their fathers. Fame erupting all over death, death erupting all over fame, theres death in Flikker's face, of course, thats why he gets off the subway stop, because in another minute he will be death, he doesnt want to frighten us and its been such a wonderful party

Im sick and tired of men looking at me as though I were on a pedestal Terry Shannon flings at Lee hoarsely, whether theyre taking a bath or no Ill have them

come clean

(he laughs)

come clean

she stands at the bedroom door. Norma sighs with relief : its Terry.

All your life youll be sighing with relief, Terry hurls at her, so stop it, stop it

Im trying. Very hard, Norma backs away, Im

Terry brings up her hands and scours her skull through her blinding crimson hair I dont want them peering up at me as though Im on a pedestal

she says, now, quietly. Reflective.

Calm.

Low tone.

Nearly—drab.

Yes. Drab. Quite still. No tremble. No fuss. A lonely smile. Controlled. The words adept. One can hardly hear her. Lee cups his pants, makes a megaphone out of his groin WHAT

Dont be loud. Ssshhh. She says. Very simple. She flutes her lip Ive

simply

wanted them to, you might say, take me by the hair and

(curiously, a slight upzip of mouthcorner at Lee, testing? Ruminative, ah)

drag me, you might put it, yes, you might put it perhaps in such a fashion. Modeling the idea for Lee, the lingerie of the face and

Lee wrenches himself from Xena, she falls backward, laughing drunkenly, laughing

Flikker from the doorway, shrugging, You didnt quite ma

returning to the body of the party, Norma, oh N

Someones behind you, Norma says.

Terry you didnt quite fini

There are so many people in the apartment, Terry swallows. A moist eye, so many, I didnt expect, I just havent got enough liquor

from the pedestal into, ah

Terry falls backward into the long low chair

the bedrooms are upstairs you have to go to them as I went to them the other night through this outside door or you can use this door from the store, you see

and, well Lee takes the last of his drink, cooling off the hot mouths in his throat that are coming up from his stomach like jellied moths flying and sticking in his esophagus, the flying things of Lee in so multiple a number that they weigh him down, an enormous presumption in rising from the earth :

the lava eruption of Lee stays at the rim; and

rape me;

because, for its age and youth visavis Terry Shannon, the lava eruption must be petrified, for exhibition. Further, Lee feels quite dirty. I havent taken a bath this week, he mutely adores Terry Shannon through the bathtub scum

I just havent taken a

Well I guess you might just as well come in through the store, Rena says with bright fatalism, and meet my father first.

Yes, you do that, Terry dryly counsels, meet her father, if you can; meet them all, all the fathers, and the mothers, too, if there be such, and give them all some reverence, and pity, in that they are recordable, and no more. She smirks, lightly, never one to gouge the role; the voice is subtly hoarse, a feather of rust; she commits the error of surplus only on the side of freckles, with which the entire area of her skin is cluttered. You will forgive the ramblings of an old woman, she writes to Lee in her sprawling hand. I wish I could have introduced you to a lot of important people, but, you see, I really dont know many too well, though I guess Ive met them all, and it would have been important, for your sake, that I had been on intimate terms with them—but most of them were much too vulgar for my taste, the men and women of the theatre, specially, who could have done you some good, they who define the greatness of a play in terms of the number of sides for a given role, and its susceptibility to a complicated series of topographical patterns on the stage. Besides, you were a boy. Somewhat mysteriously, I suppose, I tried. You understand, of course, I can make light of fathers and mothers because I myself have no children, and certainly intend not to have any. Mysteriously. You saw my flights at sculpture. Some of them have been bought, you know, and repose on tables here and there across the country. Francesca thought well of them. But I shall do no more. A novel, Sieglinde, interior decorating, architecture, executive administration, a toy monkey, a design for a contemporary, a really contemporary milkbottle. What I have not composed is an Ode To A Boy, or, if you will, The Hymn of Old Women To A Boy, by the headless Winged Victory. So, you see, I discarded most of the Important People. As I grow older I discard more and more, and feel less and less alone. When I was a child, like your Rena, in an experience precisely duplicating hers, I became lost on the streets of Richmond, and wandered about till an old man took me by the hand and led me to his apartment, up many flights of rickety stairs past Mr and Mrs Brody and Mr and Mrs Rakmil who were all swimming about in a tank of foaming beer, except

152

that all their skulls had been replaced by bottletops continually popping, so that those poor people found that the sole use of their arms consisted in trying to bang the bottletops back on their necks —a most unusual preoccupation, but understandable. I remember that, once in the old man's rooms, I began to cry. An odd thing about him : he had no beard, but his chin was as long as a beard might have been, and as soon as I had noted his steamshovel chin I stopped crying. I suppose he was grateful for that; at any rate, he took a top out of one of his drawers, and a string, rolled back the rug from the floor and, without a word, began to spin the top. There he was, that ancient, on his haunches, his chin three feet long and resting on the floor—and spinning the top for the little girl. I no longer felt lost. I could not keep my eyes away from the spinning top. And I smiled for him. Well, there, you see, Lee? That is part of my vision of the world, an Old Man Spinning A Top For A Little Girl. Rather sentimental, I should say—except for his chin. I have the strange feeling that as we grow older there is a settling of the whole body into the chin, which drops, so that our mouths are forced open, and kept that way. No matter. Quite rightly, because I mentioned it so often to you, you ask me to tell you what I think beauty is. May I refer once again to my abortive attempts at sculpture? Francesca had a penchant for them, too, when I lived in Portugal as a girl, and helped her translate some of Camoens into English. A very brave woman, Francesca, and you might have taken a bath, after all, fauns in the forest do, though as a mother I dont really mind, Im writing this at Pacific Palisades where Im staying for awhile, Lee, to recoup my health, I had a gallstone operation, of all things. A painful ordeal, Im very tired. A hysterectomy has been performed, too. Hysteresis. My intentions not to have children, you see, are quite honorable. In a way, Im glad the Depression occurred, because it enabled me to meet you, Lee, although I dont think Mrs Roosevelt would have approved the National Youth Administration for such a purpose —it was her idea, you know, not her husband's, who has the distinct impression that he is God, oh theres no doubt in his mind about that. You ought to try to do a play on him some day, his special brand of arrogance, his special perversion originating in

153

his infantile paralysis affliction, which gave him his overwhelming charm, the paralysis that everyone in contact with him had
to reckon with in the backs of their minds, meeting his reckoning
with it in the back of his mind, so that, you see, he really never
met anyone face to face—it was actually back to back, as though,
upon meeting him, you were compelled to walk away a certain
distance, as at a most formal kind of duel, yes, take a number of
paces, then turn, Lee, and when you thought you were going,
finally, to come into conflict with him, you couldnt, because he
was already crippled for life, and you couldnt bring yourself to
do a mercy killing. We couldnt. Stalin was the only one who could,
he had no compunctions, did he? You see, what you do
is, put a character like Stalin into the American scene, construct
him as Roosevelt's antagonist, a man who will destroy a cripple
as he would a man in full health. But the strange thing is, of
course, that the American People as a Body did kill Roosevelt, by
forcing their whole weight upon him three times successively, saying, in effect, we will give him his perverted due, we will divest
ourselves of all of our major decision making and impose it upon
the President, upon a Defect, upon a halfman who produced a
number of sons in his own right, Potency out of a Wheelchair,
Virility out of Steel Braces, this vast presumptuousness, all right :
we will give it to him. At any point, Roosevelt could have cried,
Enough, enough. But he did not. A disgusting masochist, the spectacle of a man seeing how much he could endure. Any such spectacle is disgusting, Lee, but we enjoyed it too, did we not? The
more lives medicine manages to save, the more we fiendishly test
the salvaging. A cripple desires international responsibility? Give
it to him, let him have it, because : why should a man in full health
ask for responsibilities which keep multiplying, which have no end?
Give it to someone who is sick, and we will indulge in the
spurious grief of standing in multitudes to watch the dead body
roll by to its last resting place. Disgusting, Lee, utterly disgusting.
He turned my stomach. But, then, most men do. Beauty is Henry
James, the mind distilled. This is precisely why I keep my little
red book, to record all the men I sleep with who are utterly unlike Henry James. I have him on my night table next to Keats.

154

The Ode To A Nightingale is one of my favorites; I have often
persuaded myself to sleep with a feeling of joy by reading his Ode
aloud, softly, before turning my head on the pillow Levi and
Rachel cannot hear. Well, I am not your mother. The trouble
was that you could not look upon me either as a mother, or a sister,
or a wife, or a mistress, or, indeed, as a woman of any sort. Obviously, however, I was not nor am not now a man, nor ever re-
sembled one, so that I couldnt have frightened you by maleness.
What of me did frighten you? I confess the cause is mysterious.
That, perhaps, I was difficult to characterize; but, then, anybody is to a young man of seventeen—he finds it hard to differ-
entiate one human being from another, they are all shooting off,
like veils twisted into whips, in his mind. I think that, perhaps, I
was a kind of false piece of art to you, whose sex had been abrog-
ated. Mediocre art, yes. On whom sex had later been tacked. That
I was so full and you were so empty, that you would have been a
kind of film over me, with no more dimension than the thinnest
transparency, and that you had no right to be so moulded, that
I was a kind of snake, if you will, that shed skins, three showers a
day worth. You were repelled by the series of transparencies you
saw falling off from me. What was it? What? I wanted you so
very much. You knew goddamned well how obvious it was. You
saw it. Was a woman of forty so repugnant to a lad of seventeen?
Was it this face of mine that we all agreed would be better off
from the Winged Victory, showing my body only? Was it the
advertisement of the Photograph that stopped you? the admission of guilt? the face featured of erupted lava stopping at the
brim? That you would perhaps do me offense? Your body pre-
suming upon a cartoon? What? Oh, Lee, I think it was the fear
that you would leave off something. It was the fear that your face
would be a kind of deposit upon my own, and that the juxta-
position would be a horror unto Nature, a gross insult to yourself.
You were afraid of humiliating yourself, mortifying yourself to
be in contact with me. It was as if you had told yourself that to
have committed a sexual act with me would have been to admit
your own inadequacy with women of your own age. Pride, goddamn it, sheer pride. You flung your pride at me. Oh, not really

155

flung. You sat in it, you were stubborn in it, unyielding. The fact that I communicated to you with everything short of words that I wanted you you interpreted as danger, or as a mockery of you, as an Error. I was making an error. It was not Lee that Terry wanted, you told yourself, but a particular kind of experience in which the special ingredient called Lee was not involved. You thought I looked past you, around you, not on you yourself. Now, then: pride and ego in you rejected me. Indeed, why should I have wanted you to drag me from the pedestal by my red hair, why should you have been so characterized as selected to do that, eh? What right had I to say that I wanted that of you when I complained I wanted it of men? Again, I insulted you. Insulted you by singling you out as a possibility for such an action, and what right had I thus to compliment you? The compliment was loaded with a responsibility I wished to impose on you, and where did Terry Shannon find her presumption? So, I narrowed you down. I put you up for a role. I all but said you are the one to rape me, at least to show invincible male aggressiveness toward Terry Shannon. I wanted to force you, I did my best by my suggestiveness. You felt the force, and you proved unyielding. I dont know where I got the right to ask it of you, Lee. There was no right, I suppose, that was involved. It was the sentimental determination of a fortyyearold female to ask you to touch me, to take me to bed, to let me teach you. You know of course, you knew, what was worse, that I wouldve had to teach you, and that was appalling. Why couldnt I have understood that? But I didnt want to think that I would have had to initiate you—the whole idea was contrary to your taking me. So, consequently, what I must have wanted to discover was the flaw in your maleness, so that I should have had to take over, and rectify it, and this would have been intolerable to you—you thought! But would it have been intolerable? Would you not at last have enjoyed it? enjoyed me? You could not penetrate to the final aspect, which would have been joy, for that would have been to be natural to yourself, to your body. Thats what I was asking, really, at bottom, that you be natural to your body, and you were incapable of it, but I shouldve known that and gone about the matter differently.

156

Why didnt I? Because, my unnaturalness matched yours. At forty, no different in the final effect from yours; and, extrapolating, I knew that you would be incapable in unnaturalness, and therefore I undertook no different method because I really didnt want it to turn out any other way, which you incontrovertibly sensed. Did you not? Oh, dont tell me, please dont tell me, I dont think the old lady could bear it, to remember the walks down narrow little Cherry Street to the cool saloon, sitting on the great grass lawns in front of the Bord of Education Building, the model of the Wright Brothers biplane in front of the Benjamin Franklin Museum, and the flagrant vulgar summer of the night on the East River Drive, the fortyyearold woman sedately indulging her noncontact orgy with Lee Emanuel. Hysteresis. Well, the sculpture should have told you. Francesca knew. Beauty, what is beauty? I certainly have been diligently looking for it, and here I am in Southern California, and will be elsewhere, persisting in the search, really an old lady, not that Ill stay in California, because the winters remind me too much as I am now, quite warm to the touch, you see, when the sun is up, during the day, but, withal, the most extraordinary kind of feathery chill in the very heat of the day, as if the heat is pale, a frail and brittle warmth. Yes, it is too evocative of myself, and it strikes me that what we both wanted was a kind of orgy of noncontact : people do go through such phases, I wish I could stop listening to you reply, well, what is beauty, Terry? Surely you must know what you are looking for, if only to recognize it when you see it. Perhaps the orgy of noncontact was something we both recognized simultaneously, and chose to pass by, finally, by our not being together at all, because we were both terrified; a recognition that this was all that anybody could have, anybody anywhere, orgies of noncontact, and that we decided, well, let us look upon it as it is and see if a relationship can be thus conducted. I am beginning to wonder if my sculpture was not its expression. But Francesca would have told me, directly. But perhaps she knew that though she would tell me directly that that in itself would have been a deception, and she desisted. She was careful, possibly, not to tell me the truth of things because she felt I would have taken truth to be truth, so

157

she forebore. I think perhaps the happiest time of my life was with her, in her forebearance, in her delicate strategy to live directly in the indirect. After that first marriage of mine, to a boy with whom I had grown up, it was probably what I needed most— after that, and the voice breakdown following Sieglinde. It wasnt that my husband had not known how to make love, but that I simply didnt care for it, then. I owe Francesca that, too; she made me care for the physical aspects of love, by the very fact that she was a woman, you see, by the very fact, Lee, of her indirection— being a woman she could be only a surrogate; at first she made it seem not bad at all, then, at last, little by little, absolutely marvellous: she acted within the indirection of female to female, which I could accept without knowing what it was she was proving, so that, afterwards, years later, with men, I could still revel in the indirect ecstasy, and throughly participate in the experience as it is actually to our minds—secondhand. How could I accept Francesca? That was comparatively simple: because I knew she was not a male. And on her, on that woman, all successive males were reconstructed. Did you feel that you might have been thought of by me as a reconstruction? Well, then, now we can see, I suppose, that all the men I slept with were experiences of an orgy of non-contact, and that you were intuitively aware of that, and that I was, so that another kind of noncontact—contact itself—did not occur. Because, in any case, Lee, direct experience between us was impossible, is impossible, is impossible between and among human beings. The only direct experience a human is able to have is his own, or her own, thinking. Dont you see? Do you already know that? Is that why you were so astonishingly silent most of the time with me? Knowing that when another area of our bodies is involved in an experience that it transmits the message of the experience to the mind, but the message is already of the order of the past, so that the mind cannot know what the experience directly is that the other part of the body is having. All the mind in presentness and directness experiences is the nature of the message to it, and the mind's thinking about the message, just as the other part of the body cannot directly experience the actual thinking of the mind and acts upon the message concerning the

158

thinking when it is received. I am speaking of the conscious mind, of course, which is all, in all of earth and time, we can be sure we are conscious of. The sole direct experience a man or woman can have is the thinking of his own mind; all other experience is vicarious—to the conscious mind; the direct experience is, exclusively, the presentness of the recording the mind makes. It is a rigorous and awful limitation, though of course capable of enormous richness in itself; but it is rigorous and awful, Lee, because it is as much cut off in its limitations of directness as are all other phenomena. We are friendly strangers to the rest of our bodies—always a bit afraid of what the other parts of our bodies will do, though we often quite successfully tell them what to do and they tell us they have done it, but they may not report the whole truth, really, and theres no absolute way of checking up on them—we do it only circumstantially—and they might act quite dangerously before we can stop them, as other humans do to us, and suddenly, inexplicably, we are lost before we realize it. Yes, what is beauty, indeed? I guess what I have been searching for all these years, and now I realize that I will never, never find it, is the surcease from the loneliness of my only availability, accessibility—that of direct experience limited to my thinking. The beauty I look for is the beauty of nonloneliness, to have a direct experience not limited to my own thinking. Oh, Lee, is that what the two of us did?—recognized such an impossibility, that the two of us, a woman of forty and a boy of seventeen, each at that moment in their lives were looking for that with an intensity neither had before known, and that then we met and were related in the sympathy of the impossibility? I suppose that is it. I suppose that all human beings are lonely because at bottom they know they experience only their own thinking. I guess I should have been able to see that a long time ago, looking at my sculpture

her essential terror, Lee notes, lies in her unwillingness to take her belief one step further. She is fully aware of it, but he is afraid to look on its face. She must draw a line when she knows damned well theres no line that can be drawn. She must know, in short, that no direct experience is available at all. She must know that the socalled direct experience of thinking is in fact no more than the idea of thinking: one thinks that one thinks, a series continuously prolonged backward or circularly (whatever the nature of the arc) into time. What seems to occur is a curious circuit of indirection; that, because the given object contacted possesses no definable boundary, one is forever one step or god knows how many steps removed from direct contact. One can, therefore, never break off contact just as one cannot break into contact. She is terrified at the prospect of imagining a nonindividuated world; indeed, horrified at what to her is the monstrousness of the Spinoza formulation that we and all of nature are attributes of what he called God; that we are parts of the circuits of this Beast is too formidable for Terry to look on. She is afraid, in brief, of becoming antiSemitic

Francesca would touch me, looking at my sculpture—which I think, now, I should like—oh, not to crush, not to break up— but, simply, to discard altogether, to shove aside, to wave a wand over and have them painlessly disappear—all those papiermache little cubes cunningly put together in the shape of women's hats, sometimes, in the shape of a deck of cards suddenly flung outward and boxed in, in the shape of reconstructed sails on an invisible deck, from which the wind had abruptly departed so that I could rearrange them in cubes, hollow cubes always, and each with two sides omitted, so that from whatever direction the light was coming the light would always manage to go through—in the shape of an ocean reef on which the land would be caught, things fighting to be abstractions, abstractions struggling to be things, a pinwheel that had got senile, a crank that had got surprisingly straightened out, breasts that had become caves for boys of light to play and hide in and discover themselves in, sculpture, Lee, that never made one cry or bellow with laughter or empty oneself out, the cubes were charms, amulets, if you will, to hang around the neck of a moment to frighten mock demons away—shaman Terry Shannon, medicine woman Terry Shannon, bracelets and necklaces in sculpture, African masks degenerated into a white woman's cubes, I—I am almost ashamed, I think. I wanted, here, to make a Hymn of Old Women to Boys, but the hysteretic hysterectomy seems to be preventing me. I think of Francesca dying in

160

her great house outside Lisbon, of cancer, and touching me as she dies. I didnt need the money, but she left me a little income, so that I should never have to worry. Not for a moment did she mention death—she welcomed her visitors with great abandon, and continued to touch me to the last, even while the visitors were there. She thought Camoens a great poet, and he isnt, and her thinking of him that way saddened me—I knew there was no one from whom I could expect perfection of judgment, infallibility. The hot sun falls here with its little feathers of chills. I think I will be going to Oregon next, to Portland, a firm of consulting engineers would like me on their staff, I will live on the Roosevelt Boulevard with Nick, my new husband, and my three children, your darling Rena, sleep sweetly, in Philadelphia. I tell you what I, Terry Shannon, will do, though, in the California winter, because I cant gather together all my sculpture in a heap, Id have to travel too far and too wide to do so, but what I can do, what I promise you the old lady will do is to gather together all my freckles. You remember my freckles, Lee? Im practically covered by them. Well, Im going to rake them all off my body, and put them into a little heap and then burn them, like autumn leaves, in a rusty little fire, Mrs Sherman has freckles too, and thats her trouble, because in her sleep shes gathering them all together and putting a flame to them, I know what she feels like. And then my skin will be pure white, unmarred, and then perhaps you will have me, hymn and all, veined as the cliff crouching over the young boy sleeping on the sand beneath. I think I love you rather fiercely, beyond, if you will forgive the play, beyond rapprochement my own mother Sadie Schwartz did as much as she could for me I must admit. Difficult, too, with my straight black hair dense with dandruff. It was simply that I could never stop giggling, old as I got, giggling and trying to stop by sharply sucking in my breath. I giggled all the way through the University of Pennsylvania on a scholarship, just as my younger sister Ethel did, the one who got cancer of the breast so that she had to get it cut off, which her husband the architect Myer Kaplan never said he minded, but then hed never admit anything intimate, nobody seems to, ever, to me. And I never got over being so tall, which is

161

why I walked with bowed shoulders, giggling, sharply sucking in
my breath, I knew I had to try to stop somehow, even with the
thirtyfive thousand dollar dowry my mother had for me. I giggled,
Lee, and I bowed, and I had a big white face and a big white
high forehead and low big breasts and I always looked like an old
maid and I began teaching school because of that, giggling at my
little blackhaired bowed mother walking fiercely along the Boulevard with her prayerbook to the synagogue. The man who
sold realestate in Trenton, Louis Garber his name was, he wanted
me, but that wasnt good enough for my mother, who demanded
what she called a professional man, oh, I giggled a lot that night,
in my bed, over that, I sucked in my breath so sharply so many
times that my throat felt cut up by little terribly sharp barnacles
of giggle, but at that Im not as badly off as my sister, who owns
only one breast now, and when Dr Adolph Anderman came
along yes, young boys, The Student Prince at Garden Pier I
leaned over Lee too, as I do now over the palisades, and I finally
told him about Alex Bradlow, who was only at that time a young
law student on scholarship, though my brother Russell never got
one, but he's equally brilliant, yet Alex had no money at all, he
was working as he went to school, and he was tall, as you, Lee, and
darkly sweet, and Im going down the beach in ten minutes or so to
meet him, you can meet him too if you like, if you go right away,
Lee, and my brother likes him, likes him a great deal, and Alex
doesnt mind the impediment in my speech, I had a cleft palate
when I was born and it had to be operated on, have you ever
noticed the impediment, Lee? If it only werent for my mother. It
doesnt matter to my father. Hed go along, hes so much softer than
my mother, I really dont want to go to Beaver College, I just
want to be with Alex, youre really too young to understand all of
this, Lee, much much too young even though Im an old lady, but
you dont have to understand anything at all, we old women
dont want understanding, really, just the vision of a boy who wont
mind old women without their breasts. We dont ever really want
to see you again in the flesh, Lee, just the picture of you rising
from the little heap of burning freckles. Because if we saw you,
we would want to keep you forever, never let you go. Because,

162

too, we will have other children in the flesh. Ethel Schwartz and Myer Kaplan have two children, and after they grow up they can take a trip to the Grand Canyon and Myer rises very early so as not to miss it and he urges Ethel to rise, to put on her dressing-gown because it wouldnt be nice to look at the Grand Canyon with one breast obviously missing. Donna Zion and Roy Lindauer, twenty years older than she is as Dr Anderman is twenty years older than Clara Schwartz, have three children in the flesh. We can let all of them go. But we couldnt you, Lee. We would dismember you first, even as Penthiselea murdered her own son when she discovered him, disguised, not recognizing him, watching her and the other women in their secret sexual mysteries —tore him down from the tree, she and the other women, killed and dismembered him, only to find that she had done this to her own son. Because, you see, the boy the old women are in love with watches them at their mysteries, at their secret ceremonies of their barren and unproductive selves. So, as at my little heap of burning freckles, the old women bend over their memories of the sunburnt boy, mumbling, holding aloft the severed breast, the boy the cancer itself growing in that breast, he did it, he started it, he whipped the cells into their spectacular growth so that we had to cut him from us, and be the ancient myth that all old women are, Onebreasted, hopping about from palisade to palisade in the California warm winter. Stealthily we watch you, lying warm and brown on the beach, a bumblebee buzzing about you, we raise our hands, he shall not sting you, we will swat the beastie as we go about the world swatting all the flying stinging beasties who would threaten young goldenbrown boys preenprone on the sands, may your member forever lie flaccid under its curling black hair, may the tawny sands forever stumble gently against the sides of your lean long body, may no high heel of the wind and the storm gouge you, may the sun forever mock a myeast of honey over your brow, may the Lourdes watch over you and protect you, sleep, boy, sleep, for the old women are forever awake, forever full of revenge for having given birth at all, like that old Hollywood biddy I know, whom I sucked off the other night, shes one of those who will take it wherever she can find it, I happened

163

to go into a restaurant on the Sunset Strip and there she was with a man at her table. I sat down, of course, at the same table, but she hardly said a word to me, concentrated on the man,

the poor woman didnt want to damage her amateur standing have mercy on my memory, Lee,

it is about all anyone can have any mercy on, and we hardly take advantage of it

Daniel Naroyan introduced us . . .

DANIEL HAGUE (THE SAME) MUSICAL SATIRIST TOWN HALL FEBRUARY TWENTY-SEVENTH AT EIGHT THIRTY THERE HE IS IN HIS EIGHTEENTH CENTURY WIG AND THE GRIN OF A CLOWN ON THE PROGRAM PHOTOGRAPH UNDER MANAGEMENT BY UNDER PERSONAL REPRESENTATION OF THE PROGRAM WILL CONSIST OF CHARLIE CHAPLIN VISITS THE GALLERY SHOWING THE PAINTINGS OF SHEP THE CHIMPANZEE A LITTLE BOY ACCOMPANIES HIS MOTHER TO A SHOWING OF WOMENS HATS GOTTERDAEMMERUNG OR GO HOME YANK

a fag introduces us. Fags ought to have hysterectomies. Fags ought to have babies, goddamn it, theyd sure as shit quit aping women then. Let them go thru childbirth, thatd cure em. See if they could pout with their labia majora, simper with the clitoris. Let the fags get menstrual periods and see how long theyd swish their hips, Ive had enough of them too, Lee, believe me. Yes, I know, Francesca. But you do see the difference between fags and female inverts. Thered be no pain in being men. You know that female inverts detest fags, dont you, Lee? Its not common knowledge, because we tolerate their presence, as a kind of common rebellious front against the heterosexual prigs. But at bottom, they nauseate us, we think theyre all liars and frauds—all us women do, and all women are inverts, and all women are aware of their innate homosexuality, do you think we enjoy the pain of childbirth? Theres a big myth, if you want one, and you get it ripe and choice from male doctors with their blarney about natural childbirth. The male is full of shit, generally, and that includes the male invert—yes, I know, I never used fourletter words before, but Im an old woman, Lee, and I feel perverse, and out of sorts, with my freckles burning in a little heap, because my pure

164

white skin wont make you come either. I know one great tall fag, he must be sixtyfive if hes a day, still erect though he suffers from arthritis, which he deserves, who used to be an aerialist with the great European circuses, I met him through Francesca, and hes here in Hollywood now, saw him last week as matter of fact. Very courtly. Bows from the tip of his nose, as you might say. Scouts for Ringling Brothers and trains young men, is a consultant to the movie studios. Punctually, once every three years, he falls in love with the young man he trains. Raises them from anonymity and squalor, as he announces to all and sundry, to fame and fortune, to be Somebody. And falls in love with each one. Expects each one, and each one does, to desert him in time. A pale big man, with muscles of plastic metal and faintly freckled. Says he loves falling in love with a young boy. To mould them, he says. To make something distinctive out of what was once dirt, filth, the other side of the tracks. Speaks impeccably, you cant for a moment imagine him sucking cock. Terribly clean. Takes FOUR showers a day, more than I do, Lee, Im still at my old three a day. Very courtly. Lights your cigarette, whether youre man or woman. Seats you at the table. Likes to talk, of course, about Diaghilev, the fantastic Russian balletomane fag, who slept with each of his leading men, and who visited his leading man of the moment at any hour of the day or night to exact his toll. He performed as an aerialist in drag, a tall, palefreckled woman with false breasts. He amused me. Im not too amused now, with my little heap of freckles burning like autumn leaves. I want to wake you up, Lee, from where you are on the sand on the beach, and have you dash at the palisade in an effort to climb to the top and take me, and if you cant do that then dash your body against the palisade till its bloody and torn and dead. For old women must wish young boys all dead, so that

the tides of the old women will come from the sea, with their rusty red and dirtywhite tresses, trailing the flotsam and jetsam of their hysterectomies, and claim all the young dead boys on the beach, and take you back to where you belong, in my clean pale bloodless gums and jaws, so that I can tear at you and chew your dark brown eyes way out at sea, where nobody is looking, not a seal

165

can sue, play with your dead body as a dog with a dead rat,
shake you
bite you
tear your head from your shoulders, gnaw at a limb, crunch
your genitals between my teeth till theyre mashed bubblegum
because :
you,
you,
you were on a pedestal.
You, Lee, were on a pedestal with your long black hair crying
to all women that you wished they wouldnt be so circumspect, so
respectful, so afraid, but that
theyd come and drag you by the hair into the bedroom.
Thats what you wanted me to do to you, didnt you?
So, give me back my freckles, I burn my hands sticking them
into the fire on the top of the palisade, and getting them out and
pasting them back on to my flesh, only
its so hard
so hard
because my flesh is aging, aging, and its hard to stick anything
on it, either rouge
or lipstick
or freckles
they wont stay;
they keep falling off;
and its your fault, Lee, your fault :
that :
I :
cant :
be :
Old again;
Im anciently young and for that, Lee,
                    I hate you,
                    I hate you,
                    I hate you,
                    Terry Shannon.
    PS : Is it possible that youre a fag?

166

Listen, Rena, Im telling you that he, Nate Goldstein begins, his stuttering worse than ever. Oh shut, Rena says fiercely, just shut up, shut up

This is my father, she says, and the middleaged man leans his light brown eyes against Lee from behind the spring scales.

Its time about, Solomon Goldstein gently chides his daughter.

Daddy, she corrects, taking Lee by the hand and leading him through the space between the end of the counter and a meticulous display of pretzels and potato chips to the chapel door opening on to the livingroom, Daddy youre supposed to say Its about time.

Whats the difference, Solomon lifts his chin at Rena, if the heart is in the wrong place. Anyhow, he shakes Lees hand vigorously, Im glad to know youre not my daughter's imagination. I guess youre too tall a boy to make up. How tall are you?

Six feet two and a half.

Of course the hair makes you look taller. Lee Emanuel?

Thats right.

Any relation Emanuel the plumbers?

No, they spell theirs with two m's. Were always confused. I sat behind their daughter in high school for four years.

Nice girl? Solomon inquires perfunctorily as he cleans the meatslicer.

Well, she walks sullenly, a hybrid turkeyduck

Daddy its not necessary to

I was only sending the time of the day. But Ill tell you, Lee, I could use some of your hair.

Look at all the kisses on the top of your head youd miss, Daddy.

Ah, they give me sunstroke in the winter, Rena. She tells me your fathers in the coal business.

Yes, thats

Wholesale or retail? He owns a mine?

Id like him to but he doesnt. Retail, Mr Goldstein.

Well its still a good business. Now you take the delicatessen business like this lousy store and little by little were forced out of competition. On Kensington Avenue, Rena, you knew theyre opening a supermarket

167

Wheres mom?

In the kitchen with the fishcakes, as soon as shes through Im going upstairs.

My fathers supposed to take a nap every afternoon, she explains to Lee.

On account of once I had a bagful of ulcers. All right, Rena, take him in back, I see a customer shining his face in the window. Ill talk to you later, Lee, its good to know youre in existence the bald hunchnosed Solomon Goldstein assures himself and Lee; and proceeds to arrange his features in the best possible smile of annoyance with which both to welcome and intimidate the prospective customer to whom he shifts the light brown eyes, the wobbling belly, the fine array of faintly gray false teeth and the abruptly sloping shoulders emptying into the bowl of the wider hips; in Rena the shoulder slope is more judiciously gradual, and her hips are superbly contained by the thighs. The goblinesque clutch of Solomon Goldstein's features is released in elfin quantity on Rena's face; the fixed location of self in the father's expression is undone in Rena's: the tales told about her may not be so, but I may surprise you, Irish for Jewish she implies, and you may swear you have seen me, but I may not believe you at all, she retreats, a tilting raft of retreat in her look as Lee's fingers clutch, goblinesque, swearing in the drowning North Carolina river that he can save her

Jesus loves me yes I do

Jesus loves me yes I do she bassomimicks the Salvation Army choristers, strutting around the livingroom thumping the big bass drum of her face, her hair then a trilling tambourine the color of rotten oranges save me from what?

Lamely, there seems to be a law that you should be saved

men make up laws, she dances

heavy makeup, Lee says

And you know I wear hardly any. Do you want me to wear more makeup?

No he says rather savagely.

Except on the lips.

Except on the

Did you kiss the man in Rocky River? she asks curiously and in the letter to Lee at Fort Benning she inquires as to whether or no he has any objections to her posing in the nude for Sy Tarassoff

His telegram immediately dispatched I absolutely forbid it and a letter follows I realize Sys a great artist and of course I trust him completely but posing in the nude for him is absolutely out of the question its not a question of morality at all or my false modesty

Lee sweats on the bunk

its simply that Im the only one who has the right to see you naked I just dont want anybody looking at you in that condition youve got to promise me immediately airmail special delivery that youre not going to permit this I love you I love you I love you

at the stone balustrade on the verandah outside the senior high school dance held at the countryclub Rena in a white gown youre going to tell me

please please please youve got to assure me instantly or else I swear Im going AWOL and taking the next train north to Philly you just cant pose in the nude not for Sy not for anybody I just cant stand the idea of anyone staring at your it drives me wild I feel in a panic Ive never felt so close to hysteria when I think of somebody with his eyes I Im begging you really Im on my metaphorical knees youve got to promise me instantly

Lee I just hadnt realized please I beg you calm down I cant stand the pitch of your emotions dont get into any trouble will you wire me that youre

A stupor of relief reading her reply

Did you kiss the man?

Well its true he has a gnomelike face coming up to me while Im sitting on the grass at Robin Hood Dell listening to the strains of Brahms by the orchestra outside the gates and reading The Magic Mountain at the same time What are you reading

The

How delightful gnomeface and knucklebody leans over the book Ive got an enviable collection of Manniana. Are you implying that the removal of your clothes for the purposes of posing releases a goblin homosexuality in you Rena

169

Well it was so hot and were all girls here she merrilys in the crabbed apartment on South 16th Street after all we havent removed our panties and bras have you ever seen Wilma's collection of blue ribbons

I know its an awful place to keep a dog, Wilma admits, but I just cant let him go, I just cant let him be put to sleep, hes got a certain type of mange, you know, thats quite incurable and its going to get worse and I know hes in pain darling darling arent you but youre being so good Wilma revels her fingers over the shepherd's face so awfully good I just cant bear letting you go oh Im treating him with a special salve the vet made up for me but its just no good the sweaty tears greasing down her lovely infant face, unlined, uncalloused, patrician infant Wilma as she opens the closet door to search for the thinnest possible blouse thus revealing on the obverse innumerable ribbons, blue, red, white for this dogshow and that the others are in the kennels of course I rent them but I just cant put him out darling darling she kneels by the sloped shepherddog whose throat quotes mincing brief motifs of pain and its the heat the damned heat I dont want to have him sheared come darling she persuades him to the pullman kitchen let me apply some more salve

I practically grew up with a girl next door who had a tremendous German police dog, Rena tells the story in brutal elfinesque. Of course she was much older than me so I really didnt get to be friends with her but I could see down into her yard from the upstairs window when she walked out. The dog would be waiting for her and spring toward her the whole length of his long thick steel chain. But before she would feed him shed tantalize him

Danny Naroyan drives the Army surplus ambulance he has bought for his family's rugcleaning business. He is silent in the presence of another sound. On the two bracehung padded steel seats running the length of the ambulance Rena Goldstein and Lee Emanuel, both heavily clad in winter attire against the slitslanging bonescraping derisive rain in the autumn night, hump forward opposite a hunched tall girl in a dyed muskrat fur coat. Her name is Gail Greene, an old musician friend of Danny's. She has been singing in an undistinguished yet quite pleasant mezzo the

170

bawdy verses of an old cavalier tune in which is recounted the story of a rogue who step by step advances upon the virginity of an aristocratic lass prettily remonstrating in calculated astonishment at each of her successive surrenders to the rogue's tactic; just as Gail reaches the stanza at which the honor of the lass is about to become a nostalgic memory, the singer is abruptly harrassed by a fit of coughing; between the spasms Gail hectically apologises that she has contracted a stubbornly severe deep bronchitis, a most unusually virulent case that has her commute twice weekly to New York for treatment by a specialist. After the usual polite assurances by Danny, Rena and Lee that no apologies are necessary, they all fall silent in the face of Gail's uncontrollable hoarse expulsions of staccato breaths; these are dry stabbing coughs to which the girl holds a wad of kleenex; intermittently, lapses of light circling in through the two small round windows in the rear doors of the ambulance from an occasional streetlamp momentarily brush away the dark from the cougher's face, at first startling by the length of its equine construction, but the short loops of her black hair falling shoulderlength dispel the onlookers' anxiety at the girl's resemblance to a horse; and the terrible grin drawing back over the great white teeth down which her heavy-lidded and monumental black eyes stare to demand the utmost from the observer in retaliation against conventional symmetry hushes the onlookers' unconscious cry; we see a clavichord quality to the flesh under which high cheekbones poke; no tuberculotic spots redden the checks, but there seems to be a kind of hidden blush, the low sound of a secret fever, and slimness spiculed throughout the entire height of the girl, some six feet and one and a half inches; for one so tall, the tiny balledup hands rushing the kleenex into the mouth seem but sportive sprouts; still the cough straddles the girl's throat; still she must lurch back her head as the cough rams up Do you think I ought to turn back and take you home Danny worriedly offers No. No. No she whispers. Your friends are waiting for me, theyve been looking forward for weeks to hearing the South American songs. Rena turns her fingers into Lees arm, a faint smile ungovernably minnowing about her features. The autumn rain fizzes, magnified a hundredfold by the

171

metal body of the ambulance against which the downpour strikes. A smoky iciness suffuses the ambulance interior, a suffocating cold, Rena and Lee feeling the very bulkiness of their woolen garments has bulwarked a frozen damp against their skins to press it against them. Danny drives slowly, carefully, but Gail, at the very extremity of her coughing, as if an anchor gone amok bounces frantically along her bottommost chambers, an anchor that she must somehow lift, drag up from the stoniest, dryest plumbs, throws down her whole torso, crashes it down on her hips, both balled hands stuffing the kleenex into her yawning jaws, Lee then stiffly leaning across the intervening space to steady her, to right her, yet the girl shakes her head sternly as a turn of Danny's around a corner rocks the girl to the side so that she thrusts out an arm and, her fists removed from her mouth, the whole whiplashing length of the anchorchain cough unimpededly spews forth, a snaking gash through her lungs in the final hot and stinking and dry eruption. Shaking, Gail slumps back, a frail anchor of spit hanging from her lower lip that at last she manages to daub at and remove, quietly remarking that the whole coughing spell must have been stimulated by the stanza of the sound she had been about to sing, in which the virginity of the lass would have been no more. It mustve been too much for me, she frailly smiles. My head feels a little heavy but otherwise Im all right now

You get his shoulders and head the Nurse advises Lee. Put your arms under his and lift when I tell you. She neatly and quickly disconnects the tube from the bottle under the bed and then she extends an arm around Levis loin and another under his knees Are you ready Lee?

Yes.

You might think that for one so ruthlessly thin

This is how you can get thin Levilee at last informs Betty, Dave's first wife

You neednt tell me, she trills, oh you neednt tell me. You see, I began dead. Im dead to the point I have my first child, Fay. You see, Levi, its very simple. Now you have no children, so you start your thinness. True, you may have taken your children back

172

into yourself, I dont deny that she runs her fingers over the spinet or over the clavichord that she never plays, nor does her daughter, nor does her son, nobody plays

Didnt you know, Betty cries, sniffles, didnt anybody understand that I didnt have the spinnachord around for anyone to play. I have it around because the instrument is so thin. I buy it when I begin to put on weight. I know whats coming. Theres got to be the slim instrument in the livingroom that I can dust

polish

see my image in

Take all your children back she fiercely advises Leelevi

Im in the process he snorts

Here, here, here, Betty reaches close to him, can you see your face in me,

oh

(she draws back)

oh

she says, absently. Its home. Ive forgotten it

what are you going to do about us

your son has run away

Ive got to get across the state line

Ive got to get across the state line

Ive got to get across

Lee, you understand, Clancy voices it from Texas, a man has to run if in the lifting of his fathers body which actually is felt to have a goodly amount of weight that the weight even in your lifting has shifted to the mans head, the tonnage, the Red Ash tonnage, the lousy Red Ash clinker tonnage is in Levis head,

yes, theres the clinker, dropping through my gratehands

But Im not running, Lee thinks :

I want to have my fathers head but in the lifting of Gail Greene in the afternoon in the Jewish Hospital. They are taking her down to the xray room. The medical staff deems it advisable to commit as many studies as is feasible before her death so that perhaps by an acquisition of a further piece of knowledge we may perhaps save another's life. No,

she wont feel anything.

173

Under heavy sedation.

It is a law: no feelings permissible at this point. Dont break the law Lee whispers down at the sleeping girl. But not even her head hath weight. Certainly not:

Is she thinking?

Certainly not: therefore, no weight.

Is Levi thinking. Yes. That explains the lightness of his body where no thought dwells, all thoughts funneled into the head. When his body under the head, beyond the head, no longer thinks
he all but belches it out
then his life is at a critical point.

A magic hoop encircles Gail Greene's body, and she is effortlessly lifted

Kanovsky, who insists upon being referred to by that name alone, speaks in cumbrous highly exaggerated Russian accents to Lee and Paul Moyle the multilinguist and veteran of the Lincoln Brigade in the Spanish Civil War. You know something darlings, I buried my wife today. Look at him, Kanovsky suddenly blubbers his weight in the chair at Whelans Drugstore, corner Locust Street and Broad, look at the manager, have you ever seen such stupid arrogance, ah? he gestures broadly at the tall immaculate doublebreasted floorwalker type, gardenia lapeled, dryly issuing his order to the waitresses behind the counter. Who does he order around I ask you, Kanovsky demands of Paul and Lee. Not the cook, not the dishwasher. But the girls. For two cents Id smash his floorwalker face in. Im telling you, for two cents, I feel very ugly tonight, very ugly indeed, Kanovsky curls his pendulous lip, purplecolored and as fat and ripe and unblemished as his heavyfleshed, heavyboned square loopchinned face is pocked and pimpled and purplescratched, Lee I want you should meet my wife, Anne in the transparent oiliness of the Philadelphia summer afternoon in the kitchen of the house in clogged Strawberry Mansion You want some beer, Lee? Anne get him some beer, good for you in this hot weather, this lousy Philadelphia summer Ah you should see the Mediterranean. Anne peers at her husband's undershirted torso in the stuttering adoration of her blinking eye You are a great playwright and I am a great director he dispenses

174

the dictum expansively, what more natural you and I should get together, hah? he claps Lee on the shoulder and blubbers his purple mouth around the white foam of the beer. Her parents' house, he nods sagely at Lee. They left it to her, his fatty brown eyes squint and dim I just had an operation in the shoulder they removed a tumor he lets on to Lee in the Italian restaurant on 45th Street between Broadway and 6th. I dont feel so good yet. I drove to Philadelphia were you to Philadelphia recently he demands of Lee. Well Im telling you it makes me sick to go there, sick. Ill never go there again. Sick

Im a little scared, Lee, Rena admits to Lee on the hard wooden rolltop seats on the upper level of the doubledecker A bus as it crosses Girard Avenue in the summer afternoon, to her left through the window the slim river called Schuylkill whisks the single scullers from under the bridge into the flashing black sunlight

I stayed in the cemetery after everybody else left Kanovsky dully tells them. It was raining.

It had to be raining, Paul Moyle says expressionlessly.

What do you mean by that you sonofabitch.

Nothing, nothing why should I mean anything

Allright you sonofabitch, I tell you I feel ugly, dont cross

Lee, crossing the parquet floor of the apartment at 119 West 75th Street, the apartment occupied by the two homosexuals Lloyd Engle the chorusboy and Noah Hudsen the actor, can still hear the modulatedly virile tones of Lloyd as he crouchprances on top of the sofa, Get rid of him, Noah, get rid of him right away

How do you know its a him the horsehair dark handsomeness of Noah Hudsen calls from the broomcloset.

I dont know, it can be a her for all I care. It probably is a her, Noah, but kill it, kill it

Lloyd a mouse cant possibly do you any harm

I dont care, I dont care, I dont care, Im not taking any chances. Have you got the broom yet?

Cant you see me?

Im looking at the mouse.

Well look at me.

I cant. Im staring at the mouse.

175

Do you think itll go away if you look at me?
No, it might jump up and run up my leg. I couldnt stand that.
If I keep looking at it
Her, Lloyd.
Her, it, then it wont jump up. Im looking her in the eye.
CHRIST NEVER FAILS
MILKBOTTLE H
BUT CHRIST NEVER FAILS
in slowly revolving scarlet neon atop the belltower of the church at Fifth Street and Lindley Avenue. Levi, opening drawers in the front upstairs bedroom of the Roosevelt Boulevard house so he can find a clean change of clothes, snorts a glance at the slowly revolving scarlet neon
CHRIST NEVER FAILS
You got to see her tonight? Look how its snowing, Rachel complains
BUT CHRIST NEVER F
(signs and milkbottles, signs drinking from milkbottles, signs being children; what milk did little Jesus drink but that from the spring Moses struck, yea, from the rock in the desert as the children of Israel fled from Egypt; even so doth David Emanuel smite the Levi rock as David fleeth in the night, milk from Jesusfay and Jesusrichard. Question: what doth DavidClancy lead through the desert? Why, sirrah, his sperm who traileth behind him. Can sperm be spat? Verily. In contempt. Yea, in truth. Is Levi the rock? Aye, smitten and resmitten. Doth he protest? Well, sirrah, shall a rock protest the smiter when the function of the rock is to be smitten? Poor stone he that protesteth. Pale pebble he. Rocks are to be smitten and to be gushed. But this Fay and this Richard, how are they prophets of a new faith? Oh, sir, they are children, and all children are prophets, all children are to be crucified, all children will die to rise again. That they are undistinguished is the desirable irony
I got to thrash it out with Betty once and for all.
Let her go out and work, Rachel says harshly. Its our responsibility Dave left her and the children? Maybe youll get up four oclock in the morning now to go to the Yard? Maybe youll come

176

home ten oclock at night to a burnt dinner so you can have the
burden of your grandchildren. Whats the matter with Betty's
father?
He cant do it, Rachel. You know that.
No, only Levi can do it. So whats to thrash out? Tell her on the
telephone you get through raising three of your own children with
one killed by a baseball so now youre ready to make money and
raise two more children. Tell her. Tell her your wife is very content with the same fur coat now for ten years, tell her, shell be
happy, she has a big mouth to laugh small with
Its late I got to go
In the snow
In the snow
Wear a tie.
Why do I have to wear a tie?
Look presentable.
Its my own daughterinlaw. Levi laughs bulkily;
driving the Buick slowly west on the Roosevelt Boulevard
there have been the garage doors flapped open in the dark; there
has been the shovel to clear the snowdrifts so that Levi can back
out; there has been Ruscomb Street to the rear and the Shatsky
house on the corner, the porch of which is empty in the winter
night, the snow piling on the porch and on the rockingchair and
the memory of the paralytic Shatsky rocking in the chair, the snowdrifts on the top of his skull; there has been the grim conceit in
the mind of Levi of snowdrifts atop his own skull and the thought
of the Lord God Almighty taking a shovel to clear a path)
so that, stopping for the red light at 5th Street, where he will
make a right to proceed to Lindley Avenue and thence a left, the
tires themselves sounding as highpitched engines when the treads
gape at the snow and slush, shifting into second for more efficient
traction toward the daughterinlaw's apartment at Warnock
Street and Lindley Avenue, the treetrunks tapped for white rubber
streams and white maple syrup, the treetrunks lashed by shaggy
white ropy animals their torsos crawling up the black trunks, the
wind blistering the drifts, the windsucks hollowing them, sucking
up CHRIST NEVER FAILS

177

There is this reflection in Levi : For Lee and for David me and
Rachel are dead people; for them the mother and the father no
longer got any meanings; that is why they are embarrassed when
they see us, talk to us; that is why they are horrified; they wonder at an awful thing, why we are still alive in the body when in
their minds we are dead to them; when they see us, we are ghosts;
they have no feelings for us now; all their feelings are for us when
we meant something to them, years ago, when they were small
children; so, they wait for us to die in the body, they feel that
everything will be all right only when we die in the body so
that will fit our death in their minds; yes, they know us; yes, they
speak to us; but their food comes up in their throats when they
see us because they see us already dead

Then Flikker courteously opens the door of the Buick after Levi
parks in front of the Dave Emanuel apartment.

Its not often, Levi says in astonished admiration, that one so
young as you should be wearing galoshes.

Fortunately, I wear no vanity on my feet, Flikker explains. I
wear it, as most of us do, on my head. Notice Im bareheaded. Your
son Lee cannot abide wearing a headpiece either : it would destroy his carefully set waves.

Where is my son?

At the moment he walks down the heavily carpeted stairs of
an apartment house on West 75th Street in New York. He has
been told a piece of information by two homosexuals that
he would rather not have heard.

You will excuse me. I must go to my daughterinlaw.

But your son will be walking, cumbrously, toward a red light.

I cant concern myself with that. He thinks of me as dead.

And the children of your daughterinlaw, Betty, inside the apartment you will shortly enter, will think of you as alive?

Yes.

But they too will finally think of you as dead.

If Im murdered enough, it will be all right for me to be dead,
the squarebodied, grayheaded, foreheadmuscled, grayeyed man
peers up at the ceiling of the schoolrooms of the Congregation
Brith Mikveh. You can never tell about those contractors, the

178

cheap materials they maybe used. There could be leaks. Already there are cracks. The children after all are entitled to the best, there should be any leaks, the children should be studying. Why arent they here the old man gazes up at the breakfastroom ceiling

Nurse

Yes Mr Emanuel

Nurse

Yes, Im here, Mr Emanuel, theres nothing to be excited about

Nurse why dont you attach the rubber tubing to the cracks in the ceiling. Theyre leaking. The children will get wet, theyll stink from my piss while theyre studying their Hebrew lessons Where are the children make the connection

MAKE

the connection

Lee you got to tell me what you want Im not dead

Im

not

dont be

embarrassed

should I give Donald Schwartz powerofattorney How long you going to be here

Not

I know you got to get back to Los Angeles

But pop theres a limit how long I can stay

Limit, limit, limit. All right. I understand. Tell me the truth. Im here, pop. I want you to live.

Hertzog hates Donald Schwartz. If you have powerofattorney

But I can only stay two weeks

Russell Zion says Are you so wedded to Los Angeles that you cannot consider returning to Philadelphia

Im not wedded, Russ, its simply that television

All right

You have to have a number of children murder you in order to feel justified to die, Flikker sallowly puts to Levi Emanuel. The two figures stand in the jagged hollows of the snow, the snow-scallops building up at the behest of the wind around them, two figurines in white niches. Christ almighty what a smiting you must

179

absorb, Levi, how many lives must be smashed against you before you can find the courage to disintegrate yourself. Quietly, though.

All is quiet in you, Flikker goes on in curious tones. The quiet endurance. The soft power. A sly ego that nobody suspects, the sweet enormity of you

thats your son, too. Thats Lee, godamn it

Festive, the Constellation touches down at the Philadelphia airport, the big Levibody

My father is a plane touching down at the airport,

festively

Lee's cousin, tall blond Jared with the long blond face oddly gray in his grayblond hair younger than Lee by five years. Jared, with his little son

I want you and Norma to come over to our house,

whose little colonial lamps outside shedding their little colonial radiance

But I know all there is to know about surgery, Jared says quite without conceit. Surgery itself knows all there is to know about surgery. Yes, there will be mechanical improvements, of course. I am already a great surgeon. All I want is a very great quantity of money. I dont really want to practice surgery any more.

Binnie, his wife, curving near the concealed television set in the Tudor interior

let me take you on a brief tour, Binnie graciously insists, the childrens game room

Humpty.

Yes, you see, the toys are all stacked away in concealed

Dumpty.

Very polished floor. Vast

Scarlet bathroom, scarlet toilets, scarlet spigots. The Goldsteins' crimson kitchen. The manicurist comes in to do the spigots

My fathers

manicured

Oh, money.

Yes, Jared says, drinking the Irish whisky cautiously, I want to travel, I want to do nothing. Travel, yes. Surgery

at night the surgery on his face does a lovely plastic gray job, all the instruments are curved sweetly. My uncle, you know, Binnie frankly informs Norma and Lee, left me a baby oil well, so each month I get a check for

Jared and Binnie and Lee and Rena cautiously teeter into a canoe at Neshaminy Creek.

Go into your children, Levi, and murder them so that you can die as Lee emerges

numb and terrified at the death of the father in Rena. What will he do? His jaw hanging, his mind lusting after total disorientation while at the same time he knows he cannot afford that, the tall boy stretches forth his hand as if he must touch a bannister, one slanting down the steps at 236 East Roosevelt Boulevard, mahogany, but none here on 75th Street in the springtime, no bannister, simply the stone balustrades fronting the basement apartments of the houses along the street, rough to the touch, hes got to go somewhere. There are people walking, looping their lips, he does not wish to be seen by them. At all costs he must avoid their eyes; he must avoid everyone's eyes. But on the other hand, he must be with people. Anybody, but at all costs not by people along the street, hes afraid of them, but he cannot walk quickly. Theres indescribable mass to his limbs, as though he walks against enormous drifts of something, infinitely light, that he passes through effortlessly and yet which impede him. He must phone someone. The first person who comes to mind is Sy Tarassoff. Sy has married again. A girl named Ada. She sings. She wins a Marian Anderson award in Philadelphia. Ada. But its Sy he must get to. Sy is a person. Lee steals away his own face, looking neither to right nor left, and enters the drugstore, a phonebooth, a dime, a slot, a ring, a dial, a number. What is Sy's number. Lee has a small black book. Flicking his lips, his breath scurrying, fear dialing through him, the dial wheeling back, he cannot go on, he cannot open the black book with the numbers in it, too much of an effort, the wrong page opens up, the wrong page, theres got to be a right one Rena, Rena theres. Hes got to get to. Rena. Rena. No. Sy? Sy this is Lee, I got to come over is it all right. Sure, Lee. Right now? Right now, its all right. Is there something wrong? No I just have to be with you. You mustnt mind me. I may not talk much. Just let me sit there, all right? Yes, are you sure youre all right? Yes. Are you sure youll make it here all right? Yes I got to, dont mind me if I dont say anything while Im there. No I wont mind. Will Ada mind? No, Lee she wont. All right, Ill be there in a little while he cradles the receiver. Now.

Now:

He must go out of the drugstore. He must walk south on Amsterdam Avenue. No. Yes. Amsterdam is all right. It wont be so crowded with people. But his limbs are very heavy. Do you see there, in the distance, 72nd Street? Yes. Well, I must cross that street and go to 71st which is quiet and dark and has few people walking on it. When I get there I must turn left, east, and walk up to Central Park West where I will wait for a bus which will take me to 3rd Avenue and there I will board a bus which will. No. To 34th Street. Then I get a bus there and go down to 3rd Avenue and then walk to 36th Street. Im walking slowly, god almighty, but my breath is not in me. I want to sit down on the curb and cry and then an ambulance will come and they will take me to a hospital for the insane. No.

I must not sit down anywhere.

I must keep walking.

Its such a long walk.

But Sy.

To walk up 71st Street is to walk up a child's long

Theres nothing to it, Lee, Clancy Mann writes him. When you get off the railway station in Wildwood, the boardinghouse the teams living in is one block away.

You dont have to be afraid, Lee tells Rena on top of the A bus as it jounces north on 33rd.

I was afraid you wouldn't be at the Heel that night, Rena confesses again.

It is a matter, Jared Emanuel, surgeon, Lees cousin, says, staring out over the television terraces at the suburban Philadelphia colonial night, of cutting along the dotted line. A tall young man, Jared, the dusk conferring gray sideburns on his cheeks. Did you know that, Binnie, he switches his rasp to his wife, a dark maid whose long legs stilt up her tuppence breasts, who implies that a

182

veil should film down from her eyes and that her belly should be bare, and that she should pass around her navel, even so, as a plate heated on the brazier of the East, a Jewess of the burning sands. Im watching the show, Jared, she replies evenly. Dont be stupid, Jared paces the sunken den recessed in the sunken livingroom recessed in the sunken television terrace recessed in the sunken foyer recessed in the sunken door, by god were recessed in the bowels of the sunken earth Jared exclaims joyously, the very earth is constructed in split levels, we Americans have ingeniously taken advantage of the implication of strata, but as I was saying, Binnie, were born anatomically in dotted lines. Why, he pounces on it, we even think in such a fashion. But, you see, when you start dissecting a corpse you get into trouble; a corpse leads one into fallacies because there the dotted line has solidified. The secret of a great surgeon, he muses, is to cut and pause, cut and pause, since in the space of the pause there is absolutely nothing to cut; the scalpel skips, Jared's voice cocks up a note and he grins, across the space between the two dotted lines. You dont follow me, Binnie, because your mind has dispensed with the dotted lines altogether. I wonder, though, he tilts up his head to ponder, I wonder if God is made in a dotted line. Suppose one were called upon to do an operation on the Almighty in the Great Amphitheatre as the student angels looked down in their white gowns upon the human surgeon, the fabulous Jared Emanuel, about to perform without his gauze mask, for God after all cannot possibly be septically susceptible, for the microbes whom He Himself had created would stand off at a distance, respectfully, in their proper category, Virus Cherubim and Seraphim. Therefore, what strange disease could the Lord God Almighty have contracted so that Jared Emanuel would be summoned in emergency? Of course, of course, God would have got to suffer from Jesus Christ, and Jared would be called upon to cut out Jesus Christ from the body of Our Lord, the climax of Jared's career. For this, then, Binnie, he gleefully tosses it at her, as in stubborn anger she sits at her vanity table and smears on the white television screen cream, her features suffering in the agonies of a hundred projected dramas, spastic in the jerking cockadoodledoos of the com-

183

mercials, I shall harden my tubes against Jared, I shall admit only electronic impulses to my womb, they shall be as a salve against the lesions of three children of Jared's, and I shall shall paint the black mustaches of my baby oil well on my genitals so that Jared's penis will crumple in laughter—for this, then, Binnie, Jared unshackles his boyish laughter, are the Jews pogromed, for the Hebrew Jared Emanuel cuts out Jesus from the body of God, Jared's greatest feat, the Jews' greatest feat, but for which they are accused of murder. Why, says Jared, I only did the Lord a good turn, for He was being infected in the only possible way He could be! Very difficult sectioning, Jared nods, for there were neither dotted lines nor spaces in the Lord Adonai. He speaks professionally now, quickly, in a staccato dotted line. Jesus by that point had metastatized in God; the son was all over the Father, in every organ, breeding copiously. Never saw anything like it, Lee, he confides to his cousin. Youdve never thought that thin sonofabitch had any balls at all; well, Im here to tell you he had them in his Father. And Mary, Lee? Shit, Mary couldnt care less. Of course, she brought soup into Him, she arranged His pillow, God used to say only Mary could properly arrange His pillow. But you know, Lee, all wives want their Gods dead. Isnt that so, Binnie? No use, you cant budge her away from the television set, shes the kind of woman whose channels you can change by remote control. Anyhow, the worst of it, Lee, was that damn splinter I had to remove from God—Jesus had taken the damn thing in with him, imagine his presumption—wood into flesh, what the hell did he care—he said he had to go back into God from out of the cold, the poor sonofabitch said hed been rejected, so he drags that splinter cross in with him that was encrusted with all kinds of filth, bits of humanity barnacled on there, loaves of bread, dead fish, dried up salt water, money from the temple—where did he think he was going to use that currency do you imagine? Well, Lee, let me tell you the operation was a success

but the Patient

(as we say)

d

So we Jews were accused of double murder.

184

Sure, Marys alive,

Rachels got arthritis but shes a

Listen, Lee, its this way. Im in a canoe, and Im paddling down the Neshaminy, and the girl with me has an oil well. Did you know Bens going to marry again?

Your father going

Your Uncle Ben, yeh

Well, Mary had a little lamb, Jared snaps in dotted lines across the television screen, whose bones turn into fleece. Mildred

I always call my parents by their first names, Jared says. Ben I say to my father. Mildred I say to my mother, your bones are turning to fleece

Sssshhh, talk in whispers, somebodys dying softly, have mercy on your cousin who has mercy on nobody. Merciless Jared, sure. You need a refill on your bourbon, Lee, and I have to shave off my gray sideburns, nights here

Gail Greene, alighting from the plane in Santiago, Chile, the delicately lewd blue mountain traceries at the top of her eyes, the last country she visits on her mission for the Library of Congress to collect South American folk songs, hurries too quickly down the ramp and in so doing the man ahead of her gouges the heel of his shoe into her instep. It is a bad bruise but she dismisses it, the pain causing her little discomfort. A month passes and the bruise does not heal; it appears, now, to worsen, and the pain becomes more acute. Still, the matter seems to her a trivial one; but, after the second month, the bruise as bad as ever, the pain spiculing up through her leg, she feels it might be wise to consult a physician. Histories, as for most physicians, have a certain appeal for the Santiago doctor whom Gail calls on. It seems that Gail's left foot was afflicted once before when she was seventeen years of age; a wart on the sole for years had been giving Gail a certain amount of trouble, and at seventeen she had had it removed. Unsuccessfully, however, as it had turned out: the wart reappeared, somewhat larger than it had been before. Curious, the Santiago doctor admits to himself, and he recommends xrays. When they are developed, he instantly insists that she return to the United States at once there to undergo amputation of the left leg. In a

185

matter of days surgery is performed, Gail's left leg amputated just below the hip to prevent the further spread of the sarcoma. It is the earnest hope of the consulting physicians that the amputation has been effected in time.

It was in time, Gail smiles beautifully as she dispenses with her crutch while she eases herself into the sofa and picks up the guitar. If this damn bronchitis werent bothering me, Id be entirely hale and hearty she apologizes, angling her artificial limb under her. She coughs a little, the girl six feet tall does, her glossy black hair shaken off the tall horse forehead, lowering her head over the gut-strings as if in a stall and flicking her tongue over sugar, her mezzo sweet as a dark sigh, Danny Naroyan sitting humbly at her artificial foot

Waddya mean you cant shit? Danny demands, one leg under him, swinging on the Naroyan swing on the verandah of the spring night, the Pennsylvania Railroad New York Express shaking over the Lindley Avenue Bridge overheading North Broad Street. Goddamn trains, Danny mutters balefully.

Thats right, Lee, admits, I

You? You of all people cant shit? Danny hoohoohoos in a special masculinefeminine laughter. Pinky Pinky Pinky did you hear that? he tussles the pomeranian who scoots back and forth across the verandah in a merry rage, stopping short, yipping in soprano tattoo. Lee cant shit. No, Lee, I cant believe you. Impossible. Your bodily functions have always been exaltedly salubrious, enviously so. A passing phenomenon, Lee, nothing more, Danny airily dismisses it.

Morosely giggling, Lee reveals that the condition is at least a month old. I try, he tells Danny. Counterpointing the swing, Lee creaks back and forth in a rocker on the ancient boards. I try very hard, each morning, every night. What do I produce? I assure you, nothing more than a speck. Whichd be fine for a fucking fly, but not for Lee Emanuel, he adds dryly. What do you think I should do, Danny?

In the darkened moviehouse, the Stanley Theatre, at 17th and Market Streets, Lee sits watching the feature attraction, Frankenstein. At the point in the film at which Frankenstein's Monster

186

chances upon a little girl in a flowery dress playing serenely at the edge of a lake tossing plucked flowers into the waters, at which the Monster sympathetically smiles so that the little girl beckons to him to give him a flower, innocently unafraid of the creature who seems to her merely one more pathetic human, somewhat oddly got up, to be true, but nevertheless related to her own race, albeit awkwardly—miming to the Monster that he should do likewise with the flower she is about to hand him, the Monster then approaching the little girl ever more closely with that much blitheness a creature such as he might be capable of, Lee realizing that the Monster has absolutely no intention of using a flower at all to toss into the lake when the creature can make better do with a living little girl—for one can observe the conclusion in the Monster's eyes that a little girl is ever so much more graceful in an imagined arc into the water than a dissociated flower could possibly be—Lee finds it imperative to quickly shut his belly's eye

Little boys running along the path beside the reservoir, the eastern line of which parallels 33rd Street, cast stones with pomeranian yips into the water. The A bus yanks abruptly to a halt to pick up a passenger and Lee catches Rena before she rams her head into the seat ahead.

The infections Mr Emanuel, Rena grins at him and quickly covers her mouth. I dont like my teeth, she shakes her head.

At the Goldstein supper table, watching her mother and her oldest brother Nate openly flirting with one another, Rena is conscious of her own amusement rapidly increasing in malevolence. Why doesnt her father, at the head of the table, see it? But Solomon Goldstein rarely talks during the evening meal; he rarely opens his mouth during any meal except to ingest food; he rarely looks at anyone else around the table whenever he eats; and it is most exceptional, during a meal, when he condescends to listen to anyone talking. Solomon has vowed, since his bagful of ulcers has been cleared away, that he will during any given meal concentrate on nothing but food.

Is that the dog leaping the length of his chain next door, Lee inquires of Rena.

Esther Goldstein, Rena's mother, susurrates her hips from the kitchen into the diningroom; she bears a tray on which are folded at least three dozen yokes of tongue and a capacious bowl of potato salad Youve only had one sandwich, Lee, Esther vigorously accuses the young man, Now when youre in my house thats something I wont let you get away with. She bows the food to the immaculate tablecloth, a ripple of sweat across the strong black down of her upper lip, dotted lines of merriment plucking up her eyecorners; fine black hairs thread down her arms, and the length of her black tresses, dottedlined by sorrel, piles in a thick bun above her neck. Oh, my girdle, my girdle, she suddenly laughs with Rena. As a young man you shouldnt be hearing this kind of talk she shrilltrills

Oh they shot the dog, Rena rapidly advises Lee, dismissing it, each of her chewed fingers gnawing at each other.

What dog, Esther idly asks, You dont mind children if I sit with you a minute, Ive been on the go since six.

Mom you didnt open the store again this morning Rena rashes out in an irritated flurry. I thought Herb was supposed to open it.

Well you know how it is since Herb and Frances lost their store, he isnt feeling too good.

You ought to see her when she doesnt have any clothes on, Rena laughs across to her mother.

Rena, what kind of talk, Esther assumes a florid fluster, blushes blurting into her flesh, but anger huskying her tones.

Shes still a very beautiful woman, isnt she, Rena proposes to Lee.

Stop it, Rena, her mother highvoices at the girl, her grins nevertheless shuttling back and forth across her features.

Oh, mother, really, you know very well it wasnt that long ago a young man committed suicide over you. Was it five years ago?

Thats something I dont want to remember, Esther Goldstein finds little pieces of one thing or another to pick up from the tablecloth, Look we just cleaned

drove his car into the Delaware River

Rena

188

I dont see why something like that has to be hidden, mother, I really dont see

Dont you care a young man died?

Oh of course I care

But you make it something like a joke

Lee am I talking about it as if it were a joke. Youve got to tell me. Do I sound that way? Small tensing troubles raise and lower the girl's eyelids, tiny swinging doors whip back and forth under her cheeks

Well it would seem to me, Mrs Goldstein, Lee temporises, that your daughter isnt quite

Naturally I would expect you to take her side, Im glad for her, thats the way it should be, Esther triumphantly announces to Rena, heres a man for you, did you tell him about the party

Oh the birthday party, well. Rena breaks off.

Its a very special party, Esther nods happily to Lee.

Special? Lee is somewhat puzzled.

Oh he doesnt know how sp

No no no, mother, I havent

The mother and daughter scurry up a tower of laughter. Mother you werent supposed to

How long my daughter can you keep such a s. Lee, Esther twitches her face into a semblance of seriousness, the girl youre so serious about

Do you have to talk to him in that way? Weve only been going together for six months, I wish you wouldnt bother him. Please dont bother

Whos bothering him? Im just going into the facts

Well were not ready to go into the facts

Lee are you serious about my daughter now you dont have to answer you dont mind my talking to you this way after all a mother has certain concerns about her daughter

Im very serious, Mrs Goldstein

Well do you know shes going to have her sweet sixteen party? She didnt tell you how old she is, did she?

Lee cannot quite reign in his reaction. Very slowly, as if digesting the enormity to himself since hes five years older than the girl

189

and must take the whole five years at this point to ponder the matter, What youre saying is that Ive been going with Rena since she was fifteen.

Fifteen and a half Rena loudly interpolates.

Shes a baby Esther Goldstein half cries half laughs to the ceiling.

You didnt think I was a baby did you Lee she swings to him in her tailored jacket next to the bus's open window. His testicles yawn and crack their knuckles at the awning of her breasts rising in the blouse beneath the jacket. Theyre going to parachute over my body, and Ill knock a batted ball of a tooth at a nipple. He pains an open palm down her cheekbone. Her sorreltufted brown eyes are blown around and around the Leeboy. The Fairmount Park Reservoir awnings into a baseball diamond. The Victorian wooden houses of Strawberry Mansion along 33rd Street lower their pendulous rooves for shadow against the browsing hot afternoon sun. On one corner of 33rd and Lehigh knifehaired boys with rolledup muscles shuffle and shock and shinny around an icecream store with sidewalk tables in barbershop colors, and girls in candy skirts and lustresmeared legs jabber chips of tit and snuggles of spitspangled mouth into the scars of bluegold air left from the moving bites of the males, the icecream cones in melting white huts, and rasberry and orange and lemon sherbet slurring red lip and sunburned wrist and squashed rainbows on the gray pavements, bitter and challenging little boys scootering and slitting through the teenagers after hiccuping hogcalling little girls. On the opposite corner the PRT carbarn arranges the rumpfaced green trolleys in snubassed rows. Pausing motormen in black uniforms and visored toques lean loosely into the shadows to fumble at the halfcool while resting conductors carry their shiny change cylinders in their hands as they bend their way out of the lunchroom with coke bottle remains. Waiting prospective passengers mop their bellies and munch the hair off their forearms to ease away the heat, the men fluttering their testicles in the hope of a breeze, one woman blowing a furtive breath at the cleft in her breasts, and another vaguely fanning herself with her skirt

Its so hot Im not wearing any pants, Rena sniggers, but you didnt think I was a

I thought you were at least nineteen. Honestly.

The bus crawls on all fours behind itself, rears up and gives itself a mighty push; by a series of such maneuvers the engine at last comprehends the urge and bronchitically coughs ahead the entire vehicle, the passengers within silently bellowing of sore rump and crumpled coccyx; but the plasticity of the doubledecker bus is never so graphically demonstrated as it is on the top level where the steel rods that brace the wooden seats to the stippled metal flooring wrench curdlingly at their screws; the seats actually shift fractions while the bus is in motion, and the wooden slats on which one sits tend to corrugate the buttocks so that the anus must attempt to cope with itself in a jagged state. But the buttocks of Rena and Lee are never during this ride static in themselves, for Lee is forever turning to or catercornering away from Rena, and Rena is forever lunging forward, or slumping down, or bolting upright; sometimes Lee is half off his seat to deny or confirm what Rena is saying, and often Rena twists so much as to have her knees perpendicular to Lee's thighs. So at variance are both Rena and Lee to the chiasmic strains of the bus' upper level in their own bodily usages that for all practical purposes their buttocks are simply not in contact with the seats, but squirm, squat and spring on a superior plane.

But you know now I lied to you, Rena insists. About my age I mean.

But it was a perfectly ordinary thing to do, Lee shakes his head. I mean I dont think of it either as a lie or a truth.

I didnt want you to be frightened off, darling

I know, I know. I wouldntve been anyhow.

Look at the big girl of her, Lee stuffs her under his eyelids top and bottom. The trembling big. The bounding bowers of her brassy hair puffing enormous brass circles about her skull, the jugularly throbbing jawbones, the oldfashioned skirthoops of brassy hair arcing around the pitchedin roastbeefbrown eyecolor on the snowy corneas, the thrustup in the center her nose, the ugly hook she derides, that from certain angles tells that she is a cen-

191

tury and a half of age, the hook as a kind of boil in the center of her beauty, as if she is born anew each morning only to show the accretions of an endless time behind her and in her from the center of her nose at which the ancient boils up and is held by a stiff ridge, a tough bone transplant from the spine, while the chin recedes in the sport of the infantile, and the gross startle at what she is puffs out from the larkkeening eyes I know you but I will not know you Lee knows look at the big girl of her atremble against the scutiform sky, the skull, only, brought home from the wars on the childshield, for there is not room enough there for the body, the bodys down below, left on the earth for the scavenging Lee-genitals to find, pick up and consign to a certain anonymity within himself, her body an unknown or anyknown female thing within Lee while he does honors to her skull, an honor of error, perhaps, but think it a time honor, so far so in the bracket thereof and therefor no error while she tabulates the error again and again and again in the time wrestle, a corruption as far as shes concerned done upon her by him from which he must reel in stench, I smell I smell I smell she flares her nostrils towards him as he ruefully pinches his own nose, not very developed my sense of smell he avers, always deficient there he shrugs

Youre very sweet, he picks her off, he tucks her terrors back in her as an adult the covers over a sleeping child

TOUCH ME NOT

MILKBOTTLE H

A NIPPLE A DAY KEEPS THE DOCTOR AWAY

TUCK ME NOT

ARE YOU MY NIPPLES KEEPER

I BITE MY NAILS DONT YOU SEE THEYRE JAGGED I REALLY PLAY A LOUSY PIANO I FAKE I. I BITE MY NOSE THATS WHY ITS SO HUMPED I DONT WANT YOU TO SEE IT LOOK AT ME FULLFACE NEVER IN PROFILE I CANT STAND MYSELF IN PROFILE THATS HOW YOU CAN SEE SIDES OF ME

TOUCH TUCK TALK TALK TALK

Youll always talk to me wont you Lee wont you

Yes Rena yes

Because a couple years ago when my mother had a heart attack

192

and my father used to go upstairs to visit her every night and shed
be looking forward to it there in master bedroom overlooking the
backyard and that little tree growing up through the pavement
and the alleyway behind it and the brick wall behind that and on
the right the smell of piss from next door because they had a toilet
in the yard

Darling I gotta piss

Look Lee you dont have to go upstairs that way my motherll
know Im home just go outside in the yard and piss against the tree
nobodyll know any different and besides the trees got to be
watered its perfectly all right they do it next door all the time the
guys from the saloon but I never have any trouble with them even
though mom is always worried and there are fights going on Saturday night without fail so Lee stands with curved body and pisses
against the tree meanwhile lifting his eyes to the coldly braced
night and its crystal cockscomb stars that the nextdoor saloon
warriors piss into Saturday nights till the urine spreads into dawn
Rena waiting on grins and petals and preens and fettles

and my mother would be waiting for the talk of the day the
gossip a joke of the customers a phone call from Baltimore and
what does my father do but carry up under his arm the Jewish
paper and after perfunctorily telling her Esther youre looking believe me plenty improved he settles down in a wicker armchair
and rattles open the paper and he reads not aloud oh no the strain
would be too much on his new clean bellybag with no dozen ulcers

how much are ulcers a dozen

pop reads quietly while mom lays back on the pillows
little tattles of pain in her grins, reads silently for an hour till
its time to go back down into the store my father does

well always have something to talk about wont we Lee you
know how important that is to me.

Yes.

Theyre always saying Im lying, do you know that, Lee?

Who?

Oh, my mother and father and my brothers and thats why I
really dont have really close friends all except Carla Coffman youll
meet her she has such awful headaches, she gets one at least once

a month its not that she hasnt told her parents she has but they really dont believe her how bad the headaches are they think its because shes adolescent and becoming a woman but its funny. Funny. They humor her all right, they let her stay in bed when she gets a bad headache, shes lovely, shes small and dark not like me, more like my mother except Carla has no tits and my mothers are large and they still stand up I hope you wont be disappointed in mine theyre so big you know the tissues are broken and they, she shakes her head savagely, her brassy hair turbiding lashes and loops of black you believe me though dont you Lee

But why do they say youre lying?

They dont understand how people can be the way I describe them or do the things they do it sounds like Im lying but my own family here in Philly and in Baltimore nobody would believe what they are and what they do it all sounds fantastic but you know how fantastic people are dont you Lee

Of course, Rena, and I

Youll always have to believe me wont you

Yes

And trust me, trust me, tr

Y

I know youre the only person in the world Lee that trusts me all the time

And youre beautiful.

No, no Im not, Im too big.

I like you big.

My mothers petite.

I like you big.

Im five seven and a half.

Im six feet two and a half so youre not too big.

My mother wanted me small.

I dont care about her.

You wont ever doubt what I say will you.

No.

Ive never had anybody believe me so completely she furrows her eyes the late sun pecking little prickles into the back her neck

Who you carrying whats in your little finger Lee wheels on

194

Barry Handler shorter by a head behind him in front of Altmans at five in the afternoon on the summer day the metal benches in front of the department store tucking womens crossed legs in rendezvous the hunchpour of customers on 5th Avenue the five-hundred ton trucks scuffling over the cabs on 34th Street people of the male and people of the female and people of the thousand ages nicked by vacuity and plectrumed by gnaw shovelling, troweling, rocking around the tall one and the short one the Barry Handler related to the otter whose silken black hair smears low on the setting forehead the small scurrying shoulders spreading out into a run at either hip racing in the opposite direction hunter and trapper Barry Handler whose ripe whiteheaded pimples are stuck with pins from his eyes

Whats the matter with you Lee werent you expecting me

Yes of course

Im sorry I came up from behind

Christ even when you come up from front you come up from behind Barry

Steady, I apologise for

Im sor

I understand, but I didnt know

Im panicky

Youre shaking.

I guess I

Lets go somewhere to eat and then were visiting a friend of mine youll like him

I wont be any good Barry

Thats all right

I may fall asleep

That all right

I havent slept I

I didnt know it was that bad

Yah. Its bad youve got something in your finger when you touched me

I didnt mean to startle y

Touch, touch

Come on

195

Just a minute, just a Altmans. Men bowing too on the curved metal benches. Making the distance into bits, each approaching human has a numeral on his wristwatch. Somebody has a limousine to pick them up at Altmans, the chauffeur gravely opens the door, the fourteen year old child enters followed by Frankstein's Monster

Do you feel as if somebodys going to pick you up

Yes

Harm

Yes I havent slept. She. I cant get her out of youve something in your forefinger, Renas on

What? Barry laughs boldly.

Renas on the tip of your finger, it stinks Rena, youve

Get hold of your

Ive got hold of myself, Barry, altogether. What a grip, a sliding door grip, one thing tries to escape I slide the door there, another and I slide the door over there, Im turning round, always, on guard for the escapee, the little mouse. Lee laughs feebly. Two homosexuals and a little mouse come to think of it a little mouse under my fathers bed sniffing at the pissbottle my fathers not an old man. He really isnt. I never see him that way. I always see him young, young. Of course, older than I, but never aged. Immune to age

fathers are immune

untouched

thats why I cant be touched;

its all clear

because, you see, if you touch me then Ill be contaminated and Ill die. I wont live forever. Now, you see, I inherit this from my father Rena so you cant touch me

Thats why, Barry, to hell with you, fuck you, I hate you, you took me by surprise with Renas message shes killing my father

Youll feel better with food inside you.

Food is like sleep Rena lets eat Rena eat

I must tell you, Lee abruptly farts a laugh.

What is it the bus turns east on Allegheny Avenue otherwise

they would smash into the concrete abutment of the cemetery darling?

That immortal crack of Sys when a bunch of us were riding down here in a car toward the park as Sy glanced up at the cemetery

Oh what

Sy said it with the proper degree of brightness, dryness and utter matteroffactness and with something of the tinge of the spieler on a sightseeing bus turning round to us on the back seat said Sy with too a touch of the faintest surprise:

This is where the dead people live.

You see Barry the touch of death in your finger that touched me Renas message shes dead and she stinks and you had your fucking finger in her you think Im paranoiac?

I think you need help Barry snaps.

How long have you been going to your psychiatrist Barry?

Five years Barry replies matteroffactly. I hate my old man and I hate my mother and I hate my wife. Five years isnt too long.

Shit.

I take it you want to eat Barry says quietly after a pause.

You prick, the laughter in Lee licks at the terror.

And drink, Barry adds, the otter skinning the animal.

Lee grasps Barrys hand. Im glad you came. I. I didnt know where to go.

I know. Come on, Ill find a restaurant.

Why did two fags have to tell me why did two fags why Lee babbles

The solution is a simple one Jaredflikkerlee tells Lee in the privacy of his bedroom at 236 East Roosevelt Boulevard as he stands naked before the long mirror running the length of the closetdoor. A knife, a meat-cleaver and a saw, each brilliantly polished to a mirror finish (

it is instrumental that one see oneself in the process

), repose on the bed and reflect the curious milky sheen that is done from certain positions of the noonday sun coursing on a spring day through the window on burnished metal.

197

MILKBOTTLE H, IN SHORT, POURS AS WELL ON SURGERY as on the black underpinning girders of the

KENSINGTON EL

ACKMAN'S FURRIERS (parents of Hannah, Nate Goldstein's wife, Dr Nate Goldstein, podiatrist)

DR ARTHUR SHUMWAY, NECKBREAKER AND MEMBER OF THE AMERICAN MEDICAL ASSOCIATION

THE KENSINGTON EL CONNECTS WITH THE MARKET STREET EL FAR WEST ON MARKET

COFFMAN'S FURNITURE (Carla's parents)

The Kensington El does not proceed at a rapid rate but owns the virtue of making fewer stops along the way compared to the gross injustice of the PRT surface trolleycars that faithfully halt at the end of each block to pick up a passenger. There is always a passenger standing on the streetcorner. Except, of course, in the late evening or very early morning hours when the motorman, released, juices in the current from the overhead wire to charge the trolley along at its wildly maximum fifteen miles per hour. But the Kensington El at all times of the day and night majestically grinds ahead directly parallel to the second storeys of the houses to right and left in which one can observe humans in postures that, from the viewpoint of a twenty mile an hour rate, inevitably impress one with their naivete. But the Ackmans, Dr Shumway, and the Coffmans, who reside on Kensington Avenue, do not regard themselves as naive in any position. Inevitably, however, as Jaredflikkerlee takes the few steps to the instruments on the bed that swollen spring day, he must on the contrary hold himself wholly naive.

He halts, shakes his head.

Something isnt clear.

He detours to the chest of drawers on whose top rests a benzedrine inhaler. His nose is stuffed. Chronic sinusitis. Methodically he unscrews the inhaler cap and thrusts the torpedoshaped head into a nostril. Then he inhales, the sound because of the raucous ravaging intake of breath resembling the ripping of rags soaked in jelly as the acridities shear through the packed mucus till, when a passage is cleared, the sound alters to a shredded feline whistling.

198

He nods, satisfied. The way is clear. He can proceed.

Taking a glance through the window he immediately observes that MILKBOTTLE H is leaning precariously, a tower of white nostril. He sneezes, once, twice, three times, a fourth and fifth and a sixth sneeze. A dozen sneezes in all, his hayfever has always commenced in the spring

Dr Newman

Yes, Lee, the oriental jew quizzically regards the boy. The doctor is constructed in three yellow balloons, each smiling, face, torso and legs that, while he sits, tiptoe at the floor. Through life I shall carry three yellow balloons. Very symbolic, he nods at Lee. Though Im a general practitioner, my office is invariably filled with pregnant women. Im blown up, so to speak, into an obstetrician. My days are spent listening to foetal gossip. I dont see you often enough, Lee. I wish youd drop by whenever you like, without an appointment, Ill usher you into my office as quickly as Im through with whatever patient is in there when you enter. Let them wait. Im behind as it is. Im always behind; the perspective leads one to delay without guilt. Im a confirmed Russian, 19th Century of course. But let me get to your symptoms. Hayfever you believe? I suggest tests. Since in all probability youre allergic to but one type of pollen I dont think theres any harm in giving you right now a series of punctures, very simple, Lee, believe me, the length of your forearm. I will shoot several varieties of pollen into your system. The one you react to we can then prescribe for. Is it agreed? Good. Lets get on with it.

Lee sneezes. You see, doctor, the moment I emerge into sunlight or I find myself in a dense wooded area Joshua Nathanson my maternal grandfather inserts his entire body into my nostrils and I immediately discover that my snot is racing down my upper lip with the moos of a cow in plunging pursuit. Then a dancing ant inserts his fife into my nostril and I sneeze again. Then the ant axes off some surf with his fife and the spray makes me sneeze still once more. Then my father emerges from the Pennsylvania Station at 34th Street and 7th Avenue. As I go to meet him I see that he is walking, hobbling, with the aid of a cane. Four months before he has had his first heart attack. I can tell you why

199

Why, why

His blood has had to sneeze. His blood is allergic. Is that possible, doctor?

I tell you again, Lee, I miss our discussions. Please drop by whenever youre in the mood

Can blood be allergic?

To what?

To the veins and arteries, of course, doctor. To the manner in which the walls of these concourses have developed. They may be collecting dust. At any rate, the blood cells begin to sneeze. Are you denying that parts of me may not be primitive?

In what way?

Well, sir, when Joshua Nathanson entered my nostrils he did so because he had already died. All of us primitive natives know that when a man dies his soul seeks the apertures of his enemies. Once an opening is found, as Joshua found mine, it is entered by the soul who wishes his enemy dead. But Im young, you see, Im not quite grown up enough to accept my primitivism without a struggle. So, accordingly, I start sneezing. Im going to expel my maternal grandfather if its the last thing I do.

Then theres one matter you havent thought about, Lee, so I must warn you. If I succeed in curing you of your hayfever, you will cease your sneezing. How then will you expel Joshua Nathanson?

That possibility frightens me, doctor, but you must nevertheless go ahead. Ive faith in you. I feel the problem will be solved.

As you like, Lee.

Dr Newman secures a hypodermic and, successively from half a dozen ampules containing as many liquids, he punctures Lee's arm that many times from a point just above his wrist to a point just below his elbow.

Very curious, Lee, Dr Newman remarks as his yellow balloons study the effect of the injections as they signify on the flesh of the young man's forearm. Each puncture has begun to redden and swell. When you see your father hobble out of the Pennsylvania Station, is he alive or dead?

Oh, dead.

And your mother?

When I see her standing in the doorway at 236 East Roosevelt Boulevard calling after me to inquire if I remembered to take an extra handkerchief, she has already died, too.

Now, tell me, Lee

I will tell you that my heart action seems to have increased those are stirrups are they not for your genitourinary examinations of women

Yes

And thats a sterilizing cabinet and an ultraviolet lamp

Yes

Apparently youre a doctor I see you have a prescription pad and a diploma from the University of Pennsylvania Medical College. A lacecurtained window. A bookcase filled with volumes on obstetrics gynaecology diseases of the eye ear nose and throat the pathology of the endocrine system apparently

I want to ask you whether

But its not true. Actually you want us all out of the way. You want all the sick to file through your office so that finally the office will be empty and you will take your place with the healthy. But you dont believe the healthy really live out there until you rid yourself of all the sick. I wonder, even, if thats the case. I wonder perhaps if you do not put yourself here as the one healthy individual by whom the sick file by, so that you derive pleasure from being the isolated healthy one. You hardly leave your office, Dr Newman, isnt that so? You want to be surrounded by disease. You laugh at the sick. You prove to yourself again and again that you can remain healthy even though the sick forever parade by. True, you undergo peril at all times, which only gives the proof more zest. You expose yourself to danger and death innumerably more times than any big game hunter or mountain climber, but theres no courage involved; what is involved is the superior wit of your whole body against the dullard bodies of the sick

You forget my practice is composed mainly of pregnant women

No, I dont forget. Youve been rerouted against your will, doctor. Your wit has been spoiled by an even more witty antagonist : money. Your superiority has been levelled : by money

I have simply wanted you to tell me, Lee, whether or no you envision all the men and women you know in scenes after they have died

My hearts pounding, doctor, at rather a furious rate. I feel very hot.

A smile balloons at the corner of Dr Newman's mouth and yellowly ascends to a corner of a yellowly ballooning eye. Apparently, he says

A fantastic adverb

Whenever youre on Wyoming Avenue, Lee, I want you to drop in from the line of double cartracks, I want you to come down from your steeplejack position atop Milkbottle H, I want you to tear yourself away from Rena and come in and talk with me, take a walk down A Street and enter my door. Ignore the drugstore across the street. Ignore the knitting mill adjacent. Ignore the maple trees and the Wyoming library. Cancel everything and come in to talk with me, Ive hardly anyone with whom I can have a decent discussion the doctor gently wafts his yellow balloons back forth across Lees face buy a balloon for your daughter your son buy a balloon for every organ of your body and tie the balloon to your organ and watch it float gently aloft the kidney undulating into the blue, the heart translucently crimson against the sun, the stomach blue against the moon, the genitals disappearing behind a cloud, Ive balloons for every organ

Im finding it difficult to breathe

Well now here you take this balloon and let it lead you to my waiting room apparently youre allergic to just about every pollen encountered on the eastern seaboard

youve made an error

but youve been using apparently all along the yellow balloons guide Lee into the sitting room the balloons lifting Dr Newman to a height precisely that of Lees, six feet two and a half inches. Now you simply sit down and lean your head back. Yes

My head is blowing up, doctor, blowing, and I can hear my heart how many times is that child going to whirl that hoop around her

202

Youve a child around your heart, Lee, Dr Newman comments
sweetly
My father doesnt want to leave me, doctor
My mother doesnt want to leave me, doctor
My wife doesnt want to leave me, doctor
My grandfather doesnt want to leave me, doctor
Apparently, apparently, apparently, apparently
Nobody wants to leave me, doctor
Apparently
My grandmother
Yes, she too apparently
Sam Abrams the painter doesnt want to leave me either I cant
breathe doctor my heart is diamondshaped, one piece of anthra-
cite squeezed into the other
have a balloon
RINGLING BROTHERS BARNUM AND BAILEY the bearded woman
yells at Lee your heart has a beard your body is a succession of circus colored posters the elephant of possession sways dangerously
from side to side
Pop I didnt know your hand is an elephants long nose
I stick my nose down into my body and I smell sawdust and shit
and
my spine is the skinny man
the skinny mans hurty feet tall and my eyes peer out from atomic
reactors
my father roars he is a lion
my mother chatters she is a monkey
and the seesaw at Atlantic City is the aerialist over the immense
net of nerves pop
CORNpop
CORNpop
CORN
munchmunch, I hate cereal for breakfast the trumpeting elephant of the wind tramples over the top of the big tent confess:
the sideshow wants Lee dead STOP
the pounding on the big bass drum of the heart I need air, air,
air outside my body smelling of sawdust and shit I will not go to

the end of the hallway the little boy vows to himself but the circus is in town all the years of his life the animals in their cages at the opposite end of the hallway snarl and spit their claws flash in the black stillness of the summer night I want to stop now now I want to stop I dont want to hear them

why should they want me dead the little boy crouches on the hallway carpet the lisping breeze liltingly stammering against his ribs

I dont do anything to them I never do any harm

NINA NINA NINA

sssshhh, Lee, sssshhh, take your bath

But now the most difficult part of the maneuver presents itself

Dr Newman Im burning up

Lee must twist his torso over on its side in order to apply the harsh scrubbing brush to his thighs and calves while at the same time he fans the scumthickening water towards the foot of the bathtub so that neither his chest nor loins nor back will be polluted. Fortunately, he congratulates himself, scum sticks to the surface of water

Oh Lee thats great thats positively great Nina practically does a backflip in her studio, howling about scum insisting on clinging to surfaces, best thing to do she screamingly laughs at Lee, best thing you should clean yourself underwater put on a fucking diving suit and go down to the bottom of the sea and give yourself a bath oh Lee Lee Lee she reels back against one of her paintings holding her teats to prevent herself from total collapse now look what youve gone and made me do she whoops my fucking paintings going to come off on the back of my dress like a goddamn decalcomania the great art of the future Lee dont you see Rembrandt manufactures decalcomanias Modigliani doesnt jump

ahahaahaahaa she cries

Modigliani doesnt commit suicide by jumping into the street but by painting himself into a decalcomania

PYROMANIA MRS SHERMAN THE YELLOW BALLOONS ARE ON FIRE AND THE YELLOW SMOKE SPREADS THROUGHOUT HER BEDROOM IM WAITING FOR MY HUSBANDS PHONE CALL NYMPHOMANIA HEY RENA IS THAT WHAT

204

DECALCOMANIA THE NEW PSYCHOSIS

poor Lee
thats what hes got
he sees himself coming off from all mankind on somebody elses
flesh

THE DECALCOMANIAC

what are the psychiatrists going to do with this new psychosis
the museums are filled with decalcomaniacs
the walls are hung with them
the mirrors have all gone absolutely lunatic my fathers heart
is coming off in decalcomanic patches
quick quick quick :
get an impression
mothers waving handkerchiefs
fathers with canes hobbling across streets
a little child peeling off from himself

NINA YOU LOUSY FART

NO IM A YELLOW BALLOON IN THE CIRCUS

MY HEART IS A THOUSAND ANTHRACITES FILLED WITH EARTH
FROM WHICH MY MOTHERS GERANIUMS GROW ON THE PORCH
WATER MY HEART DOCTOR NEWMAN PISS BRIGHT SUNLIGHT ON
MY HEARTS RUBBERPLANTS

wear your rubbers, lee
dont get cold feet
put two pairs of socks on, lee
here Ill put on a mustardplaster
wear a hat you shouldnt get a cold in the head
Im giving you a shot of adrenalin, Lee.
All right, doctor.
Better?
Yes, but Im very weak.
Ill drive you home myself.
Yes.
I want you to stay in bed for a couple weeks.
Yes. My right nostril, doctor, each time air strikes I go into a
sneezing paroxysm.

Im going to stuff it with cotton, Lee. Youll have a fever for about a week.

Theres an uncontrollable tickle in my right nostril

parts of the body have the faculty of laughing isolatedly when other parts may be quite grim his hand grimly takes the gleaming cleaver from the bedspread, he faces the mirror, protrudes his tongue, places a heavy block of wood directly under it and brings the cleaver down upon it in a ponderous slashing motion to slice off half his nose and half his tongue. The apertures to his nostrils now are considerably enlarged, though somewhat more vertical in their appearance, and the blood thinly streaming down to make scarlet oriental mustaches from his chin has its course gummily impeded by snot. His tongue now more closely resembles a square-headed shovel, the crossectioned nerve borings and muscle striation, aquiver momentarily from the severance, instantly obscured by red tendrils dripping on his yellowed teeth and then overflowing his lower lip. The severed portions of tongue and nose, prettily bouncing as they strike an uncarpeted flooring near the mirror door seem now, quite unbloodied as they are, throughly anonymous,

if, for example, you observe Dr Clifford Gratz, a Philadelphia dentist married to Nadine nee Schonfeld (the sister of Guy Schonfeld, professor of sociology at Pennsylvania State University, the first husband of Jennifer Hazlitt who permits Lee to make abortive love to her during the early hours of the evening so that she can proceed during the later hours to be made love to by the more advanced years of Guy Schonfeld, the comparative youth and lesser status of Lee a necessary initiatory prelude to her acceptance of the total cynicism of Guy whose lovemaking progresses beyond the abortive, Jennifer observing a multiple amatory protocol in a graduatedly heightening glee, I have just sloughed off my callowness she informs herself as she slips into the practiced arms of Guy, the male of the species to Jennifer a sort of escalator clause, I want this at eight oclock at night she refers to Lee, and I want this at midnight she refers to Guy in the grand department store of her choices, all her men chromatically illuminated at her own bazaar, Jennifer a prototype of the afternoon television programs in which a brash type of talking woman magically concocts an already prepared dish while she explains ingredients and their very best commercial sources, Lee the best source for early evening and Guy the finest for later all the while as she whips them up together in the high polished bowl of the camera self, a vast unseen audience looking on, the greatest possible audience that of the unseen, Jennifer opines to herself, congratulating herself on her cookery already conceived by another, all her actions justified by her conclusion that she herself has been prepared by others and that she is doing her duty by a vast unseen audience of preconceivers by talking from the condition of one preconception to another, a talking escalator so to speak, her white buck teeth the escalator steps as her lips move up and up and up), in whom, we speak of Dr Gratz, may be injected Jennifer Hazlitt, since she is a tall girl who may occupy the considerable length of spine characteristic of Clifford Gratz, underscoring that male escalatorism, itself impossible of course without the infusion of the female without which it cannot ascend, and which Clifford must conveniently borrow since Jennifer is transitorily related to him by virtue of her husband, Guy, the brother to Clifford's wife, Nadine, though Jennifer is not present at Sy's and Nina's party at Sy's mother's house on Wellens Avenue, though Lee and Red (Rena) are. In Lee himself is the extrapolation of Flikker, that petite boyman, that grinning figurine who, though distinctly unotterlike, possesses the low forehead and nihilistic sans communistic commentary of Barry Handler, the nihilism more sweetly done and therefore more tolerable to the possession of Lee, so that, when Lee encounters Clifford Gratz, it is matter of unconscious solicitude with which he offers, so that it is most equably accepted, that boyman nihilism, that bowed sly upwardmerry destructive teethgnash of Flikker which, as it enters Clifford, partakes then both of the fanatic skepticism of Clifford Gratz himself lashed about by the dark skeptical fanaticism of Barry Handler while Lee's innate shyness, finding itself congruent with the physical height of Clifford Gratz, is reduplicated with considerably more incisiveness in Clifford Gratz who sits longlegged and darkly smirking by his wife Nadine whose beak, inordinately convex, tends to disfigure an otherwise

207

nocturnally handsome visage and tends, too, not to disfigure but
to be drawn into the very spine of Clifford, her husband, so that,
while often enough he stands straight, his attitude is one of vexed
and scimitarlike convexity that, as it cuts into his body, must accordingly continue on its way and slice into other humans as well.
The unique banality and the banal uniqueness of the matter is
that Lee and Clifford so closely resemble each other; and it is that
profound sympathy of Clifford's to his resemblance to another
that he must find, as indeed he has, a tomboy girl shorter than
Jennifer, and as brunette as Jennifer is blonde, but as brunette as
the man Lee, or any other male so colored, with that gnashing
teethlikeness of Jennifer which has been incorporated into Nadine
nee Schonfeld's nasal structure, a structure duplicating her
brother's. Obviously, she must have a brother. A brother is not
dispensed with. Consequently it is to her advantage that she feed
her nasal structure into Clifford as a characteristic, a connection
malodorously gratifying, to say the least, and one can observe
the essentially thin, pinched nostrils of Clifford attempting to
flare and never quite succeeding, but the intent is there, and that
suffices, so that they talk with each other as two in a cage and
from time to time they dart their sugars through the bars to lick
up the characteristics of those on whom they must feed to sustain
their own incestuousness, black and bitter sugars, the two, Clifford
and Nadine, the better to spit at each other with, the spitting evi-
dent even as they put their very mouths together and hurtle their
sugars into each other with the most twisted of smacking of belly-
tongues, Clifford's tongue of course owning one advantage: it
can sort out the cavities and decays in Nadine's teeth since Clifford
is the more professional dentist of the two. So, Clifford
Gratz is constructed of Lee, of Flikker, of Barry Handler, of Jennifer Hazlitt, of Guy Schonfeld and of Nadine. But, at the same
party, he encounters Harry Ring for the first time, and at the contact with such a freebooter as Harry is, such a commodious
cavalier, Clifford senses the flapping of his own concealed free-
booterism; but it can only flap; there is no room in Clifford for
the real thing, so that the sensing of expansiveness must torture
him, he cannot really span its width, but what Clifford Gratz can

do is mimic Harry Ring and construct the illusion to others that he, Clifford, is cavalier, is an actor of such proportions, for he is after all so much of womanmangirlboy that he believes he can make these characteristics assume the aspect of Harry Ring's lordly shrug. To Sy the ensemble is inevitably a painting. Lee quite thoroughly understands that when he telegraphs his objection to Rena (Red) against her posing in the nude for Sy. Lee knows that this entire ensemble is present in Philadelphia while he is an element in the Second Armored Division at Fort Benning in Georgia. The problem is compounded by Lee's realization that Sy is familiar with his hatred of Jennifer; it is further compounded by Lee sensing that very probably the offer to pose in the nude comes from Red herself; still further compounded by the realization that Lee has frequently touted the greatness of Sy as an artist to Red; yet further compounded by the fact that Lee has tacitly implied that he himself would wish himself female to pose for Sy in the nude, and that if it were possible to extract from himself his femaleness he would gladly establish it in a naked pose for Sy; more compounded by virtue of the fact that, in Lee's absence, Red is a surrogate and, further, takes over by her femaleness Lee's femaleness so that it becomes wellnigh a commandment that, while Red perhaps never voices the offer to pose in the nude, Sy hears it nevertheless and insists on painting Lee in the guise of Rena; compounded, too, by the element of Sy himself as the nude, just as, in his watercolor of Lee, Sy calculatedly infuses it with his own selfappositeness; it were vulgar, sure, for Sy to paint himself naked; this he has never done; but to paint Red thus, were acceptable, his own guilts thereby assuaged—so that the compounding as well involves Sys ridding of his own guilt, divesting himself via RenaLee, the more magnificently convenient and the more acutely esthetic by virtue of Lee absent some fifteen hundred miles away, which provides Sy a splendid perspective, the very naked body of Lee removed from the scene so that Sy in the hours of Rena may conjure it up with all the thrill of teat and mount of venus that could be ascribed to Lee, an inordinate magnificence, a richness of triune duality perfectly safe, the very sumptuousness of LeeRena pedestaled yet beckoning, a paradox holding the pot-

209

ential of assault for all of Sy's objectivity, for when is objectivity objectivity when in a moment of Sy's supreme hauteur he may very well enclose the poser, herselfhimself, within Sy himself. The lure of self is certainly the most seductive lure of all, and when it is projected on another it is wellnigh irresistible. To throw one's self on one's self is a sumptuous selfimmersion. True, the casting involves the application of paint on canvas; but when the paint on canvas is done, the self is not done; the curve of the action continues its arc; the esthetic completed, the body follows, just as the body completed, the esthetic follows. Besides, the canvas is the painter. You do not deny the artist once you have not denied his brush. Rena could well welcome the enormous distance of the Lee thrust in the presentness of Sy— the force of the distance itself a goad, a fantastically deceptive phallus, and what more glee could possibly ensue in Red than that engendered by the fantasy of the projection within the brevity of Sy's presence, a phallus that Rena could shake, could chastise for the agony Lee costs her, for the anger he has so often visited upon her, for the Nadine-CliffordLee sugars he has so often injected into her, and yet, yet— with the pleasure of the chastisement is the ecstasy of the brief reality itself, Sy's prick—drill, drill, drill, you painterdentist in Philadelphia. Come now, come now, Lee, Clifford Gratz issues the kind of vocal order that implies that the resistance to his specific reasonableness might well constitute catastrophic fatuity, the kind of tone that lusts after a world directed by Clifford Gratz himself in which must exist a whole genuflecting brotherhood of nastily sweet reasonableness, dont you think we can tackle the problem of Rena's posing or not posing in the nude from the angle, for example, of her mother, Esther Goldstein. I mean this way, he smiles indulgently and annihilatively at Harry Ring who while Rena strikes the basic chords on the Tarassoff piano thumps his own chest in time to the rhythm of a ribald Yiddish song whose stanzas Clifford has long ago assimilated, dehydrated and referred to the vault of his own crinkled quaintnesses that figuratively cuckold him with generations long past, generations that he cannot approach, so that in his Americanism he is rattled from time to

210

time by the ancient ring of Harry Rings dancing derisively around him

(BE THAT AS IT MAY, BE THAT AS IT MAY is the recurrent slogan that must grimly content the dentist, a contemporary magic disposeall, a professorial indictment of the impossible as impossible which, being the case, we at all times pounce feverishly on the possible, the possible being the sole catharsis of modern society, the impossible having belonged to the Greeks; as much as we may admire their art, we can no longer be Greek. Forget the Greeks, forget them, Clifford irascibly advises; do without them; they wont help you; youre on your own, he staccatos at his helpless listening possibles; were no longer capable of tragedy

Who isnt, Harry Ring blissblasts him. You mean Dr Clifford Gratz isnt capable of tragedy.

Well. Well, Clifford blastblisses, his smile fawning in innocence, Im—Im representative. Am I not? Am I not? Youll concede that, yes? BE THAT AS IT MAY)

If, Clifford begs leave to continue, if you think of Red posing in the nude as analgous to her mother Esther in the Odessa suburb in Russia staring out of the window during the winter at the moon, you cannot possibly, Lee

again, note, the simplicity, the viability of the possible, but, BE THAT AS IT MAY

you cannot possibly, Clifford begins to munch on the long curved fantastically sweet banana of a smile, you cannot possibly take offence. Look, after all, note, Clifford prods. The want of Sy to paint Rena in her naked state is after all much like a boy gazing at a full moon. Besides, after all, Sy sees Rena as her mother, he sees her, if you want to know, as simply a mother. And then, really, Sy is the full moon gazing down on the little naked girl. It is a kind of paternal romance on Sy's part that he certainly must recognize. Hes going to paint Rena's mother on a winter night enraptured by the full white moon in Russia. Both Sy and Rena are children. They are both enraptured by the full white lunar mother as a girl. So: Rena, Esther and Sy are three children posing in the full white lunar nakedness—the artist when he paints must certainly remove his clothes, no? What more innocent romp

211

could you possibly conceive of, Lee? Theres Rena in her nakedness romantically bemoaning her mother's lost youth, for Rena
has become the white full moon at which her mother gazes. My
child, my child, Esther sings in her heart to the moon, knowing
full well that the moon in reality is a blank white man posing
nakedly in the black sky. Will not Sy protect himself? Of course :
he assiduously invests the canvas. Rena has nothing to fear. You,
Lee, have nothing to fear. The whole composition is vacuous in
the extreme—no reflection on you, Sy, you understand. The
moon couldnt reflect on you anyhow : it shines on Lee. And that
is precisely the reason why Esther tells about that particular aspect
of her childhood to Lee : the moon, since her daughter is enamored
of Lee, is indeed Lee himself. Now what, Lee, could you
possibly object to? Esther praises you, the evoker. Her daughter
takes her mother's praises of you to Sy. Paint my mother's praises
of Lee, she tells Sy. Well, all right, I admit another element in-
trudes. There is in Rena's statement an implied criticism of her
mother. So : she has an artist, Sy, who will in turn as an artist
criticize the criticism and thereby possibly (POSSIBLY, BE THAT
AS IT MAY) invalidate it. So she wants to pose in the nude for Sy
so that he can exorcize her mother, and he would like to take her
up on it for the additional pleasure hed derive in exorcizing his
own mother who breathes her last upstairs. His brothers, after all,
are opposed to his leaving Philadelphia, as his wife is incessantly
coaxing him to, because the mother is dying and they believe it
only right that Sy should at least stay on at her side till she dies.
But that can happen tomorrow or five years from now. Nobody
can really make an accurate prognosis. Consequently, and further, as amelioration, Sy would like to paint his mother as a girl.
She would become, then, momentarily palatable. She would become esthetically violable as a matter of fact. Lee, Lee, how can
you possibly say no to such an intent? You yourself, later, from
Kansas, constantly urge Sy to quit his mother and Philadelphia.
True, by that time Rena is with you. But why not anticipate yourself? This would be gallant, graceful, youd be a man of the world,
because a man of the world you really arent. Dont misunderstand
me, now : I can hardly contend that any contemporary male can

212

be a man of the world. But certainly we can make stabs at being so from time to time. A stab, if you will, at Rena posing in the nude, a stab at accepting the quixotic white moon of her mother's. Could there be a more beautiful wintry picture? I say—no. Lee, Lee, Lee, her mother is giving you all her winter springtime in describing her memory. The mother's storybook. She tells you of listening for the sound of a troika, of a count and countess glistening by in the night past Esther's humble home. She sees the troika sliding across the moon in a flurry of light. She tells you this as Red sits by your side at the diningroom table, the mother's face the blank white one of her girlhood. Her daughter wants to be as naked as her mother. Would you deprive Rena of that? If you do, youre arrogant, more arrogant than I thought, and perhaps Rena wishes to antagonize that arrogance by mentioning Sy's willingness to paint her naked. She wants to tell you that she knows you dont believe her mother's story, and in all probability do not believe, therefore, her, Rena, that you do not even believe there has been an offer made by Sy at all to paint her. To oppose someone's request, Lee, is often to indicate one's disbelief in the basis of the request. In the extremity of your opposition you actually denounce Rena as a liar. No wonder the shock of her request persists over so long a time: it is the shock of your believing Rena a liar. And the development of Rena begging you to forget about the whole matter only confirms your belief. Still, you refuse to accept your feeling that she is a liar. You go on and on writing painfully long letters to her about your imagining of Red as naked before somebody else's eyes. What nakedness? She isnt posing. Youre actually talking about what to you is her characterological nakedness, your presumption that she is a liar.

Howmidoing Cliffordjaredlee swings on Renanadine with purposely demotic vulgarity, the vicious vagaries of surgery hollowing out a testicle and with a stick rolling it down a long hill in Fairmount Park so that the boy rolls over and over and over lengthwise through the stupefying cloy of the summergreen grass, burs nettling his flesh through the rayon shirt and the sky walloping itself against the grass and the grass thudding against the sky all the way down over and over to the bottom of

213

as it is known

tree and grass and sky and stone swinging round and round round as the three rise in a giant lariat tightening though persisting in its awesome mammoth circles around their skull;

Ill be only too happy myself to pose in the nude for Sy Renanadine says.

Listen if youre getting rid of testicles the men say why give them to us but Sy does not paint them in that fashion:

He paints himself, Al Gordon whose speech impediment causes an enunciative thickness, Danny Naroyan and Lee sitting around the Naroyan kitchen table. But, more than merely sitting in normal vertical positions, they all lean clockwise as at the same time they bend vulpinely over heaping platefuls of food:

Witches.

Thats what they look like Nina tells the clambering monkey in herself to be still stopping on the bottom step of the stairway

No, friends, friends back there at the Naroyan kitchen Lee pleads with her watching her eyeballs swell with monkeyrumps;

Forget it, Lee, forget it, her wrinkles retch out her face at him. Witches, now

(jesuschrist, mr and mrs brody her mother and father clutch at her spine for cover, jesuschrist, nina cowers all the way down to her younger sister, what kind of world have i come into where the men are not beasts are not my superiors are not my competitors, no, nothing like that her round swart face laps at a trickle of cream in a far corner, the men

are witches on PENIS BROOMSTICKS oh my god oh my god she ties a bublitchki round her round swart face and holds her head between her hands

and they are enemies of each other; and Sy knows it when he paints them in the Naroyan kitchen and offers to paint Rena in the nude.

Sy puffs tranquilly and contentedly at Nina with his pipe, he is the serene queen of the witches Nina knows, and in that moment knows as well she will finally not live with him. And St Red, that Rena, what is she but the King of Witches, Sy her consort. For

King St Red, Nina twitches her finger at her throat convulsively
—King St Red makes a unified batter of lie and truth, the two
are to the King, poor Lee, poor Lee, poor

So, its very clear, Al Gordon confesses to Lee in the great Bronx
apartment house, confesses with a loud softness, his kinky wart-
colored hair bunched up in his thick lips, as if there is a speech impediment to his whole body, Im giving up painting and becoming
a salesman for a pharmaceutical house because its very obvious,
you know, having paralleled Sy through the years, and observing
his canvasses, that I have at best a small talent, nothing comparable to Sy's. Believe me, more than anything else in the world I
want to paint, but how could I be so ridiculous? I know, I know,
Al holds up his hand, his thick neck swerving down, all the years
I went down to the settlement school to study, along with Sy.
Funny guy, Sy. Remember how he knew nothing of the world till
we taught him? Hed never heard of socialism, knew nothing of
economics—nothing of anything except paint and girls and caddy-
ing in New Hampshire. Al gives a short thick laugh. And dancing.
Good dancer, Sy. Well. Its good to be back in New York, my
fathers a lot happier teaching Yiddish here, and my sisters studying soil bacteriology. His graybrown eyes contain a thick seriousness edged by gayety. I hope youll visit every week you come to
New York, Lee. Your playwrighting professor any good?

Hatcher Hughes

Do you remember how you passed that scrap of paper over to
me in the algebra class at Olney High?

But, lying in the same bed with Al later that night, Lee cannot
sleep. He can sense the whole body of Al protruding thickly in
its snoring pores. He can smell Als thickness; tastes it. The sense
of the bulk of Al is overwhelming. It is too close. It is a solid with
a liquid threat that will engulf Lee. Lee is panicstricken at the possibility that Al will accidentally touch him. He lies awake all night
in that fear. He edges as far away from Al on the bed as he possibly can. Lee cannot sleep with a man. He cannot be in the same
bedroom with a man. If he visits Al again, the problem will be
present, but he cannot tell Al that, he cannot hurt him, for the
thick guttural oblongsquat impedimented young man that Al is as

215

tender as touch of wound in new skin. Lee makes excuses as he peers down at the aircraft carrier anchored in the Hudson, that broad, gray river at which the lovers idly toss down their faces to feed the images flying low over the waters.

Al Gordon's father teaches Yiddish to a dwindling number of children, a short pudgy man who looks on his son as a dumb one. The short pudgy mother bustles around her daughter studying soil bacteriology at the University of Michigan:

all over the Jews are getting closer to the soil, Lee thinks. Dirt through a testtube

he passes through when he examines that closely. He passes through the slide, beyond it to a feigned yet innocent innocence.

Rubbing thumb against forefinger in his eyesockets, Dr Clifford Gratz proposes that Lee consider the posing of St Red in the nude from yet another view

Hes the original allweather man Harry Ring barkroars from the piano. Cliff is out in all kinds of people offering them umbrellas, snowshoes, nudist camps, sunvisors. Cliff youre a branch of meterorology did you know that, hah? His face peers out through the isobars. Im telling you, Lee, throw him peanuts and he will snow, he will come off in flakes. How do you fuck, Cliff? I suspect maybe you send up a weather balloon in Nadine's vagina, you know—with a thermometer, Harry is drawling lugubriously, to test the smear currents, what the pressure was at noonday, how many birds are flying through the tubes, the suck statistics from way back, you know, Cliff—how she reacted when an embryo to her papa's lips at mamma's clitoris blowing now hot and now cold, the old fashioned meteorological dianetician

Are you finished Harry

No no Im not Im still testing the weather CLIFFORD Harry protests innocently because maybe you would like to paint Rena in the nude. You get the picture, Lee? Harry wags his ear at Emanuel. The amateur sculptor Clifford Gratz turns amateur painter at somebody else's expense. How would you do that, Clifford, Harry smiles baronially at the young man. Maybe youd turn Greek, hah? and put paint on a statue of the naked Rena —paint to suffocate her pores, blind her eyes, stop up her navel.

216

Tell me, Cliff, why do you hate her?

Thats ridiculous, Cliff puffs. Why should I hate her?

Dont you love Lee?

Love Lee? I wouldnt state it that strenuously, Harry

Then stay off Rena, Cliff. If you cant really hate her, stay off of her, dig? Dont take it out on her because shes another married woman

Ive nothing against marriage

Nadine pouts her nose at Cliff, the oils pour from her, her neck empties all its glands, she sends up Fourth of July multicolored coils in smearing sneers at her husband, passionate sneers, adoring sneers, she runs around him in an oily river, she arches her intestines before him

No of course you havent, Harry presses delightedly. You simply rub up against it to test the friction possibilities

No. Not Lee listening to the trainwhistle at Taps through the Georgia pines. Lee disabuses himself of Clifford Gratz, but not quite of cousin Jared, and shrinking at the possibility of ingesting Sy, for if Sy paints Red in the nude then he, Lee, will have Sy in the picture of St Red, and Lee will be more highly pitched in relation to Rena since he will have absorbed Sy. This Lee cannot abide. The idea of puffing a pipe at Rena, gazing tranquilly at her. He does not want to gaze serenely at Red. He does not want to see her as a composition, he does not want to be endangered by the possibility of viewing her abstractly, for that would at one and the same time both reduce the area of their touching each other and also have him touch her more serenely, without the sense of possessing her. A fine picture of her in the nude would not be his. The greatness of her in art would not be his. Worse, the loss of her through such abstraction would bring her more intimately close to him, in this wise : she has been abstracted now, she has been dealt with by art, now she must be mine altogether and nobody else's; there could be no excuses for a separation then of Lee from Rena, for another would have by then taken her as a pure arrangement and Lee would be left with her inescapably as body, an incontrovertible connection to Lee, and this chance he cannot take. Being melted down to him, to Lee, is an utterly insupportable

217

denouement. Sy, painting her, would be giving her absolutely to Lee. I want none of such gifts he snarls. I want none of such purities. And to paint her is to make, further, a rift through her. Hes not prepared to have that rift come about through a painting. Thats too easy, too soon, and again too absolute. Because the very clearcutness of the matter, the very confrontation by Rena of Lee in a painting must force him either to accept or reject, and the clarity of such a decision Lee cannot tolerate. He cannot have either men or women so clearly put to him, for this is open warfare, and Lee fancies himself a humanist. The boy is antiwar, meaning antipeople, antiemotions, antilife itself, but he does not put those facts to himself. He remains at the threshold of humanism. He knows that the true humanist is a monstrosity. Lee monstrous? He cannot concede this, and in the very concession is a tempering of the monstrousness. He wishes, he knows, to maintain the tempering in himself, to be tested, so to speak, without testing, to be hurt without hurting, to love without loving, to hate without hating, to live, in short, wihout living and, at the end, and here is his crux, to die without dying:

he locks his head between his knees.
He clenches his eyes.
To die without dying.
He clenches his eyes.

It is impossible. But he will maintain the attitude BE THAT AS IT MAY Cliff Gratz I

cannot see whats gained by having Sy paint Rena in the nude: I do not want to envision myself coming off in patches from her body, like the hair on Wilmas dog does from the mange

the itching is infamous: the more I clean myself the more I itch

and the echoes. Echoes are odd manifestations to Lee, the echoes positively wallowing in the melody of Taps among the nocturnal Georgia pines. Sy with Rena naked evokes Sy with rotund Laura Ingersoll at Provincetown. Sy has Lee's girl Laura for two weeks while the painter visits Lee there. One can be jealous of an echo the trainwhistle calls through the pines. One must be jealous of an echo because one possesses it, the echo never ends. In her

218

posing for Sy she must cease to be unique to Lee, she must become a commonplace. Very nearly Lee comes to a realization that this may be what Rena actually wants, to be a commonplace to him. But that very wanting of her to become a commonplace is commonplace in itself, and that banality he cannot delegate to her, for it is a taunt, and St Red does not, cannot, must not taunt Lee. She is incapable of it according to Lee. She does not know how, must not, nor will she learn how. She will not mock him, shes incapable of it, has not the talent for it, cannot even imagine mocking him. He shrinks, hearing the mocking scraping its asymmetrical feet in the cellar beneath him.

That would make Rena equal to you, Lee, Clifford Gratz wafts at him, if she could really mock you. It would make her extraordinary, not commonplace. You hear equality scrape its asymmetrical feet. Again, Lee, she seeks to love you

love you

love you

love you

for in her very lust for mockery is her reflection of you, a fantastic love

of course she wants to pose in the nude for Sy. It shows you how much she loves you.

I deny that.

Have you ever considered how very natural denial is to you? How easy? How uncomplicated?

I deny that. I know Rena loves me. Theres no need for her to show it.

What did you say?

Who the fuck or what the fuck is pressing her to show me she loves me?

You are, Lee. You are.

I deny that

Darling what was the first thing that attracted you to me? You dont have to tell me, I already know the bus turns north once again on 29th Street the Frankford High Athletic Field to the west and the Central High Athletic Field to the east there are the boys in jerseys and shorts

219

punting a football
and running track there are the boys in jerseys and shorts
slamming a boot in soccer and lacrosse
there are the boys in jerseys and shorts
the muscles in thongs and the hips in a flout
the football twirls through a funnelling shout
the tennisball grimaces the plexus of a net and a wild whistle
racks up a cleat for the boys in jerseys and the boys in shorts
in kneepad and skullpopping to slam down a ball and a bone-
jacked body tackled against the wall the sunsweat sprinting up in
blindmans blue
there are the boys in jerseys and shorts
no girls
no girls
no girls
Lee
Yes, R no girls no g. Oddly, he can visualise Rena in a basketball outfit, he can understand her instantly as an athlete
Im attracted to you essentially he grins because youre an athlete.
Oh no. No, thats not
He capitulates immediately. All right, what
(It is, really, that on occasion she seems to be a whole damned
team of athletic girls, opposing teams, a whole damned league
as a matter of fact with a schedule, and games called off because of
rain, home games and games out of town, and a playoff, and a
world series, and standing in a long queue to purchase tickets for
her series, Rena Goldstein's International Playoffs, Rena as the
Umpire, and the Coach, and the Manager the Owner the President of the League
he skims low over her broad forehead, sunburned and unlined,
her forehead infancy even as Wilma's, a blue ribbon securing her
hair into a chignon
well you know, Lee, the reason my teeth are like they are, somewhat buck
no, why
that night. Nate, my oldest brother. My mother and he are

220

openly flirting with each other across the dinner table and I say, very clearly,

Oh, mother, really, for gods sake, why dont you take him to bed with you. My mother blushes all shades of a cosmetician's red. Nate stutters so badly he can say absolutely nothing and Im holding a piece of meat up to my mouth on a fork while my fathers bald head turns violet, absolutely violet; you see, my mother is kissing the top of his head quickly, she positively gets up on his head like an acrobat, stands on it and bends down to kiss it and Im about to clap my hands in furious applause at her fantastic agility its not every wife who can stand on top of her husbands head and kiss it simultaneously and what do you think Herb does, hes my brother next in line, Im the youngest, Herb who hates Nate and loves him when Nate was drowning once at the bottom of a pool Herb rescued him at the risk of his own life regretting it before he did it and regretting it afterwards but knowing he had to do it, regretting the very regret, but wanting Nate alive because thats how Herb wants to appear and if his brother dies then Herb wont have the picture before him to make the comparison, the envy of how he wants to be, that very envyd be dead, and he cant stand the idea of the death of his jealousy, not, Lee, not the death of his brother, oh no, but the murder of his envy, he wouldnt know how to live without it, he wouldnt dare, so he rescues him all the time even though Nate calls him all kinds of a fool and idiot and her youngest son with contempt, as if she wants to disown him, as mocks him and treats him with contempt, my own mother treats if it were impossible that Herb is something she gave birth to, its a mistake

an accident, Lee, you understand that

yes, I understand that

my brother Herb with his moonface and moonbody that could crush Nate in a second how dare I make such a slur against Nate because that, you see, affects Herbs jealousy of Nate, his envy, it tends to cancel out the reason for such envy, it gives him all the reality he needs of Nate, and its too much, Im murdering his older brother, Im getting him out of the way and that sends Herb into a panic and he brings his open palm suddenly and viciously under my hand holding the fork and the prongs plunge directly into my gums

and my teeth, you see, theyre still bleeding out Red laughs merrily, engagingly

and still my father can say nothing, but now theres a certain joy in him that the fork is stuck in my gums because thats where that sonofabitch wants to see those prongs because he cant slap my teats around like my brothers can he cant give them a good feel like theyre allowed to to their baby sister)

Thats what it was, wasnt it, Lee, at least partly? that you were attracted to the baby in me, and to my mother protesting in me to the baby without your knowing the mother even existed. It was sufficient that she was countering both you and I in me, opposing. You were taken by that clash going on, taken too by my mother gazing down on me, so that you could, too, so that you could mother me and remove some of the motherhood sting, to say now thats all right, Red, thats all right, Im your mother now; and further attracted by the eventuality of you contesting my mother in me, and my feeling you in there as a mother without admitting you as such, and your own wrestle with your own disapproval of me being attracted to you, thats a big motivation, isnt it? Because youre taking over my own mother's disapproval, which is deeply satisfactory, youre winning her disapproval into you, and at the same time youre gaining her within me in order for you to put her down, to put her under your foot while of a necessity you put yourself down under your own foot in me, and you enjoy the stomping, the squishing of all those soft female organs, mine, my mothers, and yours become female, I make your bowels dizzy, dont I, Lee? Didnt I when I came down the Horn and Hardarts aisle all in scarlet? the color of our insides, the mating with the inside colors, theres no other color before me, is there, Im red, red, red

and brass gold, Rena :

the color of your foot. My mothers going with a young man, with Lee. Lee is going with himself, hes going to sleep with himself, hes going to indulge in an unparalleled masturbation

222

but, but, but : Anything you say, Lee, anything. I approve, I like, I want. I want your masturbation close to me, do you understand. I want to glory in your selfglory, I approve, Ive no criticism, and you knew thered be no criticism in me toward you, which is why you wanted me so much, because it certified your own noncriticism in the grandest of eroticisms

with my mother screaming at you in hideous anger because you were masturbating her as well within me and she could do nothing about it, this, as I moved my thighs against each other as I walked, sideling,

sidleeing

down the aisle

youre taking away my daughter from me by the foulest of means, by the easiest, really, because you so much court yourself, and that is nothing we can fight against, either my daughter or myself, that double supremacy of the male, side by side with himself in total mastery, oh, Lee, Lee, Lee, I adore you for it as you, while I kiss you, know I kiss my mother, and you can feel the motherdaughter lips against each other knowing the enormity of the disapproval of the mouths, you know her suicide in me for all the young men who committed suicide over her, hosannah, hosannah, youre getting even for all those and she knows that and loves that and approves you while disapproving, yes, that too attracts you to me as you see her plunging to her death in me, what a

grand leap it is that the mother does as she leaps from the dizzying heights of her age to her death in my hard pavement of youth, smashing herself at my bottom

because there she is at my bottom, all the broken parts of her, still warm, still so hurt, oh, my beloved, my beloved Lee, her hurting parts I feel in me

isnt that why you see me as athlete

my shoulderpads and kneepads and catchers mask and breastpads theyre all to be champion so my mothers suicided parts wont hurt so much in me

so you were attracted to the athlete, the big Rena, while you, the winner, take all, knowing you can take all, that knowledge, too, attracting you to me

and the knowledge of your future joy in watching her approaching my edge, mine, so that she can commit suicide over
you, over
you
my walking down that aisle you see the leap, the crown of gold on my head warped with roan, my mother readying herself, your intake of breath as you see the two of us, watch out you
cry
to yourself watch
out
at St Red, at the big girl, your
breath, held, while I never knew it, giggling, I giggled at the sight of you because I felt myself jump
I thought youd never come.
I had to.
The melted snow clicking flashes in your hair.
I was so cold, but not so.
I was afraid youd be sick, I was afraid you already were.
I know. I couldve had a temperature, Idve still come.
Would you?
Yes. They all tried to stop me, my mother, my
And you came.
Idve jumped to
No
Oh, I wouldve
But you couldve got hurt
Id come to you hurt.
Any way at all.
Any way at all because I couldnt miss you, I was afraid the storm mightve stopped you, Lee.
No storms could stop a morning, St Red. Storms are theoretical, then.
The sight of you, standing. You were going.
No, I had to think of going to stop my fear, so I put on an act.
I know. As soon as I saw you I wanted to lean against you, lean all the night against your dark because you knew the dark,

and I could give it to you for keeping, so Id never have the night again.

The trouble with Lee is, Barry Handler says at his sign of the Seal & Otter, his flippers resting one upon the other at the table in The Heel, a ballooned red and white pimple balanced on the tip of his nose while his laughter is carefully immersed in regret, his eyes roving among coffeecup and jello dish, his forehead barely pushing up a clear space before the silken black hair grayly sheened lowly takes over to conceal the neat small round head, the crinkled crimson roughcut of Silas Klein's face punching the shoulders back, the plucked sharp pungent chin of Sy Tarassoff munching on the stem of his pipe, the milkfed eye of Achille Volpe pendant from and swinging across the pallor of his churchface, the blond Easter Island skull of Cornelius Nuri with heaving effort bulging aside the great stone lids from his resurrecting gray eyeballs, the blubbering blue eyes of his wife Fiona approximately one quarter Cornelius' height hurriedly bringing in the week's dirty wash from her face, the ovoid Mark Fahn slinging back his mouthcorners to rest his icilyfractured frenzies while one hand taps a cigarette end as if it must be a billiard cue, the thumbsup lowerlip of Jay Gray's sniffing at his nose, the adamsapple of Mike Burroughs capapie atremble from two coasttocoast hitchhike trips with his wife Myra whose sight in one eye has begun to blacken at the edges from the Depression of the Thirties slowly sinking in as at a quicksand grave of vision, Charlie Doyle raring back his lips to insert his pipe between the gaps of his blackening teeth while a hand amusedly brushes at the dried stain of morning cereal milk on his pearlbuttoned black vest at which his commonlaw wife Minnie, who has given up her comic modern dance talent to stare owlishly at her love for commercial artist Charlie and inch by inch pull apart her thighs with the rusty wrench of her voice to expect the warm pipepuffing breaths of an oncoming child, bids him not to bother to pluck up the remains of his morning courage, the lank brown hair of Paul Moyle falling over his pucky applecheeks continuing their bubble from the memory of a story he told a full ten minutes ago of an American volunteer in the Lincoln Brigade during the Spanish Civil War who was

225

so astonished to find himself the cynosure of a number of rifle bullets outside Madrid that he turned incredulously to Paul to curse But theyre real, the bullets are actually real, the calcimine face of Rosa Caby that cannot disregard its tawdry resemblance to Hedy Lamarr and grimly in the jawline refuses to recognize its own beauty, and Lee himself unable to parry as everyone but Rosa permits the silent cackle to rise slowly and inexorably in the group throat, Lee already dried out at the bottom of the cackle, dried out and burning as Barry drops the light lemonpeel of his private primitive sun alone in the otter and beaver heavens puncturing each red and white Barry pimple, each strand of silken black graysheened hair, but his gods permitting from time to time one paring of that sun's lemonpeel to sack one tiny community of another human, what beaverotter sun will not allow its child occasional vengeance on the twolegged ones who walk upright over the painstaking dams of the ugly scurriers to hunt down beaver and otter without so much as the distant recognition of wit but simply as one towering animal over a smaller scurrying one, Lee knowing and in his knowing compassioning Barry and yet unable to release his own hunt that can occasionally take the lesser animal wit for wit but when unable then suspends the love in unforgetting and unforgiving hatred that Barry desires far more than the loving so that he can venomously strike up at Lee as often as he wants to vent his otterbeaver spleen, vent his dream of Lee's tall flesh skinned and leathered at Barry's father's leathergoods firm, the human built into the luggage for otters and beavers to carry, into gloves and attache cases carrying the valuables of the fourlegged scurriers, the brilliant talent of Lee, for so beaver Barry publicly concedes it and privately loathes it, cowhided and alligatorgrained for beaver feet, all damned four of those beaver feet.

the trouble with Lee is, Barry Handler says with bright childlike casualness as he gives his little beaverdam one last loving pat, is that since Everyman has had his day the only thing Lee can fall back on to proclaim his universality is to call himself

Everyboy.

The table in the cafeteria buckles and spouts with bellycrushed laughter. Even Lee cannot resist an explosive snort that has him simultaneously fart. The exception is Rosa Caby who stares at Lee with carefully composed tears in her eyes so that her makeup will stay composed. She whispers to him in her carefully modulated Russian accent that she doesnt think what Barry has said is very funny and adds in the roaring commotion that wont Lee please, please think about coming to see her at her 16th Street apartment because shes never never had the chance to talk to him without intruders, yes, Lee?

When?

Tomorrow night?

He nods. And Silas Klein takes out his tiny penknife, inserting the point under his blackrimmed nails to slice forth small curling worms of pliant dirt. And in Rosa's invitation is expunged for Lee the ruthless disservice of Barry's wit. Barry, alerted, slaps the table and perkily informs Rosa that she is a bitch. She shrugs, quite grandly. Do you understand that, Lee, Barry shrills at him, I lose, goddamn it I lose, and the beaver proceeds to chuckle remorselessly at himself and then confides to Lee that his wife Selma is still in the hospital from an operation in which her fallopian tubes have been tied up to prevent the possibility of another anomalous pregnancy occuring there. Which means no children, Lee says quietly.

No children, Barry confirms. But we can always adopt a dog, cant we?

Or a beaver, Lee adds.

Do you always hit an animal when hes on all fours, Lee? Barry inquires graciously.

That always means one less inhuman, Lee suggests.

What are you so happy about, Red asks her brother Nate as he gleefully enters the livingroom behind the Goldstein delicatessen.

I just got back from the Roosevelt Cemetery, he happily announces to the group at the diningroom table, his brother Herb, gulping at a Coke, looking up at Nate with a short scornful grin as Esther Goldstein stands, hands on hip, in the kitchen entry, Frances, Herb's brunette rotund wife, behind her, a wet dish in hand, and Solomon Goldstein, whose chin lifts sardonically, follows Nate. Esther grins nervously. Frances giggles in open

227

amusement at her brotherinlaw. Lee gently cradles the telephone receiver, having finished speaking to his mother to explain he wont be back for supper who in turn has informed him that Levi might visit the Goldsteins before he returns home this evening since it is felt by the Emanuels that contact with the Goldsteins in parental form is long overdue.

And? St Red wriggles her volumes up from the chair as she sorts out an apologetic glance to Lee. Thats my very silly brother, her glance informs him of her feeling. My extremely silly brother, my fatuous brother.

What did you say? Nate inquires with momentary crossness at his sister.

I said, Rena shouts, I said you dont have any trouble hearing when you really want to.

Thats a lot of shit and you know it, his crewcut boyface pouts at her. You know my hearing comes and goes.

Fa mach dein pisk, her mother sopranos at Rena, who shrugs. So what were you doing at the cemetery, Esther mollifies her son.

Beaming, Nate resumes his joyous stammering. What was I doing? What was I doing? Very important, let me tell you, but Im so glad I could do it, Im telling you I was in luck, you cant imagine how lucky. You know right next to the plots you and pop have there I managed to buy two more, one for Hannah and one for me, can you imagine how lucky I was? Right on the same hill, mom, Im telling you, overlooking the highway and U.S. Route 1, were right next to you, isnt that great? I never felt so happy and lucky in my life. Listen, Herb, he turns quite seriously to his younger brother, assuming the eldest brother role of father advisor you should start thinking bout getting one for you and Frances, I mean, have you ever thought seriously about it? I think you should because those plots are going fast, but I noticed theres still room for two more, why dont you go out there tomorrow and get it settled, youll feel a lot better let me tell you. Then, beaming joyously once more at his mother and father, stammering excitedly as before, Thats some view let me tell you.

Yeh, some view, Solomon says heavily, turns and goes back

228

into the store. I hear a customer, he explains, dont think Im walking out on you, Nate.

Man there wont be any customers at the Roosevelt Cemetery, pop, Nate chortles at his own humor.

Yeh, his father agrees, curiously commiserative toward his son, and goes out.

How can you talk to your father that way, Esther demands, irritation with Nate sneering across her love for the firstborn.

Oh mom Im kidding Im kidding dont you know when Im kidding? But arent you happy mom that Hannah and mell be there with you and pop? I mean with that view and all? Phew, thats a load off my mind, he turns to Lee.

Im glad its a load off your mind, my son, Esther drily observes.

Some load, Rena shakes her head at Frances.

Ah what do you know, youre just a little shit of a kid sister, Nate tells Rena. You got to excuse us, Lee, he turns charmingly to him, you know how a family is. Shes a good kid at heart, Rena is, but shes still wet behind the kotex.

Ah why dont you quit that kind of talk, Herb bawls at him. Shes your sister.

You dont have to get angry, Herb, Nate shifts towards his mother.

Well I dont like to hear it, see?

Frances is a little frightened. I want to see you in the kitchen, Herb, thats the fifth Coke youve had today.

Why dont you shut up, Frances, Ill drink as many as I like. How many goddamn pleasures have I got?

Thats a nice thing to say, Frances blushes, her lower lids fattening with tears.

Jesuschrist cant you take it? Herb yells at her.

Stop yelling at your wife, Esther rebukes him severely. Youre lucky you got a wife like Frances, a dumb one like you.

Frances starts in agony toward Herb, Mother, mother, you dont have to

Ah my mother dont know what shes talkin, Herb growls, Im gone in to help pop.

A stunned kind of sigh hangs a hush over Lee Youre such a

229

smart one his cousin Donna Zion rumples her brother Russ' hair as he lies with his head in her lap on the Zion porch on Roosevelt Boulevard FAH MACH DEIN PISK Bella, her mother, snarls at her.

one thousand nineteen hundred and thirtyfour

one thousand nineteen hundred and thirtyfive

one thousand nineteen hundred and thirtysix times Norma counts steadily the number of full revolutions the hoop has made around the hips of the little girl on the Will Rogers beach in California.

Perhaps the female of the species has at last chanced on an unchanging fashion, Lee ventures from his fawning drowse at the bottom of the sun, but only because of the specific relationship of that blind little boy to her, the blind boy who, connecting with his hands his known father and his father's unknown mistress, springs forever up and down as a spindle through the female hoop. Now the little girl finds it quite impossible to take her eyes from the blind boy; she gives him, since she discovers a permanent fashion, her sight, for all she requires is the fashion; and since she has the eyes of everyone on the beach, why should she need her own at all? Did you know, Norma, that essentially youre a scientist? You quite patiently count the number of turns, a quite scientific trait. Its a wonder to me that more women dont fancy going into science. I predict that in the far future, once women are thoroughy emancipated from childbearing, they will make up the bulk of scientists, and become science's greatest figures. Then art will become the special province of the male. Very logical, very just, Lee nods sagely to himself, his chin furrowing the cool undersand. Creative and noncreative human expression sexually and therefore perfectly divided. It is quite right that the female, having divested herself of the procreative, should evolve into the noncreative, science; while the male, always bored at bottom with counting and measuring, should evolve wholly into the creative, art. Then, you see, as individuals, the male and female will cease to be at each other's throats; only their expressions will bloody each other and thereby interfecundate. Who knows but what art and science may not one day be one, the equations of physics, for example, put down in colors and in composition on canvas; or a

poem revolving before the eye in a nuclear pattern, such rhymes
as there might be constituted of positive and negative endings. But
I suppose, he sighs, that such will come about only when Aristo-
phanes' fantasy, courtesy of Plato, is resatisfied when male and
female are one and the same

one thousand nineteen hundred and fortysix one thousand nine
that sounds more like your own hundred and forty private fan
seven tasy Norma drily observes.

But that hoop the little girl revolves is our publicly private fantasy, and the blind boy jumping is our privately public fantasy,
do you know that, Lee lunges up to a crouch and shades his eye
at the ascending and descending traffic on the Coast Highway on
the Roosevelt Boulevard because he must rack his stare away
from the Kotex Girl, as he characterizes her, his cousin Donna
Zion who sits her legs astraddle the footstool on the Emanuel porch
its so damn hot she says, the white narrow wad curving
longitudinally at her crotch in plain view of the fourteenyearold
boy, her graygreen eyes drooping their iris lips all the way down
to her derisive mouth whose spittle ticks dim glimmers all the
way down to her mount hair thumbing its little cilia noses derisively at the boy, the graygreen flesh of her inner thighs putrescently
browned by Lee's irises and blackening as his pupils widen to ac-
custom himself to Donna's graygreen dark, its cheesy stink spiculing through the boy's heart, you cant have me anyway her cunt
grins at him because you cant talk because your mouth is taped
together by Kotex; besides, youre too too young, youd dirty up
my Kotex, and I want my period to remain pure she scratches
at her pubic with a flash of nail but permits Lee's fingers to linger
in his fantasy christ its hot she complains to her aunt Rachel
Emanuel whom she visits periodically for consultation with respect to her little triangular amatory problem.

East and west, west and east the cars burrow through the
chatter of the early afternoon sun on the black bareassed macadam
of the Boulevard's two outer lanes, the one on the north
side, furthest from the Emanuel house, carrying westbound
traffic, and the south side, closest the Emanuel's, carrying the eastbound; to Trenton and New York; and to Pittsburg and Chicago;

231

while the two center lanes, adjacent to each other but separated from the outer lanes by broad green paralleling lawns measuredly bearing broadbeamed maple and chestnut, directionally conform. On this windless day the leafage is ponderous and cannot in its chlorophyllic course throw back the sunlight in carbonated disarray; the greenery must perforce invisibly stagger under the burden of the bright as it cumbrously, creeping along through its own dark flue, drags in its sustenance, managing only to refuse, repulsing, the glimmering remains of light. Above, from the section of the city known as Logan, the black neon of CHRIST NEVER FAILS atop the churchspire slowly revolves in the yellowblue sky. Here in the high shot scintillance of the summer day time seems to be calmly and gerentologically fought—forever young time stuporously battled by hoary perception, perception some fantastically storied monster paleolithically scaled and scarred by innumerable blinders fastened to it by the dying living who can hardly draw a muted breath before the struggle, ended, renews while the wind waits at the far distance of the heat, its maned skull in a tiny unseen whirlpool at the edge of the earth.

Roy Lindauer, realestate agent, eminently dependable executive assistant to HUBERT SONNENFELD, of HUBERT SONNENFELD AND COMPANY, Philadelphia's real property tycoon, conveyancer of trussed titles and bethicketed deeds, of physical assets and wooden tracts, of brothelled office building and sluggard slum, Master at Mortgages of the first and the second and the third descending powers, Assiduous Assassin at Amortizations, President At Large of the American Board of Realtors, Consultant at International Parleys For Spatial Physics in that questions germane to the settling of titles to the void untold parsecs toward the furthest constellations must be thrashed out to the ethereal satisfaction of all nations concerned, the training of RealEstate Astronauts, Cosmic Surveyors (deference shall accordingly be paid George Washington, Father Astrosurveyor) and the Like—Roy Lindauer, it is clear, to whom is funnelled the trying details of Interconstellative Realty not to mention the lesser but nonetheless multitudinous trivia of the metropolitan buying and selling of the good or putrefying (Donna Zion?) earth, leasing and renting of valuable cor-

232

ner properties and mere middleoftheblock old homesteads, bears the weight of the worlds upon his somewhat slurring shoulders. The man is no risk for a marriageable girl. He is fortytwo years of age, is Roy Lindauer. The boy to whom Donna gives birth is, facially, an approximate reproduction of Roy; the dental structure is such that the thin underlip, curving out from the keen indentation in the already receding and pointed chin, reminds one of the mouth formation, exceptionally protrusive, of a certain African tribe, except that the Caucasian variation has evinced a grim paucity of flesh; a long pointed nose lofts the faintly bulging graygreen eye trophies to the wide forehead shield that discourses back to the kinky zigzags of sandy hair; but the tongue, in Roy Lindauer himself when in familial relationship a patient, yielding though somewhat querulous instrument, the tongue in the child is Donna's as she slumps, slinks, slogs, slushes (be it summer or winter, spring or autumn), slings, slivers, slangs, stoops, stutters, strangles down the brick pathway along the calfhigh hedge to the sidewalk dutifully followed by Roy in doublebreasted suit and, oddly enough, in a doublebreasted skull of which the eyes are four buttons and the top of which flies off in opposite directions by virtue of two kinky wings. The more he follows, the more his shoulders slip down to join the species of the broadhipped male. He bears the faint patina of astonishment and a box of candy, Whitman's Sampler

Is there any place youd specially like to go for a drive Donna?

Oh shut up, Roy, Donna twistslumps at the cardoor, the lisp as ever low in her speech, the control gripped in the nasal passages, her flowered dress bouqueted at the breasts, those of considerable substance though possessed of a natural yet piquant sag, a kind of feverish fertility at large loose ends.

Did you hear my question Donna, Roy pipes higher, a moiety of pique in the register.

What question was that, she pejoratives, she hauls away, she dumps into the gutter, the heel of her shoe gouging at the soft summerearth, her hand pulling down the waist of her dress, her thin stinging nasality of tone pinching her blond highcheekboned face, making the underlids shrug painfully. Her darkly undulant blond hair sidles away from the fine forehead sweep. Her florid hips trouble the buttocks as she shifts her weight incessantly. Out of her eyecorners she petulantly twitchnotes the gray mottlings on Roy's sideburns. She cannot directly meet his gaze; she cannot even take him in from head to foot, though she quite well is aware of the rodent quality of his fingers and toes, having witnessed him in his swimsuit on the Atlantic City beach, those members in cryptic contrast to the paunch on his belly, the paunch on his thighs and the paunch on the calves of his legs, not to mention his fatty teats evoking the image of her father's, fatty but in their pendulous droop thin at the bottom, even as his underlip. Her stomach is quite tranquil. Nothing of Donna's insides churn; she has managed to extrude her nausea; her surfaces roil, capsize, turn green in the lavender bluegreen twilight; she is vomitously sick in the swerve of her neck, extensive skin areas enormously enlarging their pores shallowly to stir the flickers of bile playing about her exteriors; she is sick at her fingers, at her nostrils, at her scalp. When she marries Roy Lindauer and goes to bed with the man she is sick on top of her throat; her ecstasy at the mouth of her vagina is a vomitous stench; as she writhes beneath him, the palms of her hands wipe at the sheets as their lines discharge greenish sweat; she grunts high in her nostrils as the man bursts in her his swollen scab, her gums foul with the insucked scum of her lips; her rumps fart copiously as her cunt nags at his penis, and a thin black stool trickles from her anus as she grinds the scant and petulant sperm out of Roy Lindauer you dirty bastard Ill fuck the realestate all out of you she nasals at him in the dark, Ill deed your prick to the Society For the Advancement of Victorian Needlework, Ill lease your testicles for ninetynine years as circling satellites to Mother Donna, Ill scavenge your scrotum till you walk in a wobble like a castrated ape the nun Donnanadine screeches at him, her bignose crawling like a boaconstrictor along her lips while she waits for Roy Lindauer to catch up with her at the cardoor; but though she stands for a moment perfectly still he perfectly illustrates the syllogism in the grimming summerdusk, the Boulevard traffic discoursing east and west, west and east, by never quite reaching Donna Zion though he constantly approaches her, for he himself regards

234

it an inexorable law that he must never establish realestate contact with her for all her dire predictions; suck her succulent earth
he must, and does, but comparable to a hovering, widehipped
insect over her fruitfulness, buzzing with a yielding, tolerant, temperate, faintly querulous buzz, for he sucks her by a curious extension on the end of his penis, and that is his long sharppointed
nose he blows into her vagina, in an admixture of snot and sperm,
and this it is that causes her curses, her frantic hipshoves at him,
the mean malediction of his nose that he passes triumphantly on
to his son, Donna wild in her ecstatic nausea, she can never have
enough of that extension while Roy victoriously waves his white
handkerchief that, now, she sees protruding from his back pocket
as he approaches her, the handkerchief she wants to snatch from
him and tear into jagged strips, this the only part of Roy Lindauer
she can stare at, so he walks around to the other side of the car,
plumps himself in and releases the opposite door for Donna who
buffets her body in to the seat, smiling meanly straight ahead of
her through the windshield as she hears his mild womanish voice

her father who stands somewhat bowed on the lawn in front of
the Zion house holding a limp garden hose in his limp hand, Mr
Sidney Zion, fatly retired now in a mild fat and mild spectacles,
watering the dark blue grass of the lawn with a limp stream
of water, Bella Zion appearing at the porch door at the side of the
house, whitefaced and whitefingered in the night

the clock strikes the truth she says

Bella Zions graying blond straight hair drawn back into a gigantic bun on the nape of her neck, the high white arced forehead
chalkily displayed, a tall woman taller than her husband by a full
head, with big white hands and big white feet, the white hands
and feet widely displayed all over her whiteface, her eyes brilliantly and opalescently bluegreen and watered down both in her
son and daughter by the limp stream from the limp garden hose of
her husband Sidney

she stands, little tight upsprings to her mouthcorners as she
whitely gazes through the black night under the startling cock-
combry of stars at her future soninlaw's car, a madly quiet stiff
weariness to the woman, thinking of the eminently dependable

235

astrophysical realestate agent Roy Lindauer, quietly knowing as she does how white her bones have been for years, how their whiteness has flaked through her flesh to thoroughly whiten her complexion, her only color now in her eyes, their opalescent bluegreen grimly and amusedly contesting the rest of her whiteness, but her eyecolor fast, indomitable as she sees her whiteness strewn through space for the Roy Lindauers, to whom she is giving her daughter, to plot and to deed, to lease and to rent and to mortgage, for her bones

her bones

her bones in the catacombs of the void are the realty for her soninlaw and daughter. Let her bones sting their eyes. Let the quanta of her pulverized white bones be counted as they strike the earth. And it is from her bones that she awards her daughter to Roy Lindauer;

not from her eyes that are quite unreal;

not from her eyes in which the sea greenly crashes not for a moment whitely foaming but greenly, ever greenly, she has the sea under control in her eyes, Bella Zion, wideshouldered, narrowhipped that she passes on in minuscule to her son Russell, narrowhipped and wideshouldered but petitely so, minified in proportion, his blond hair in natural marcel, his hands in natural marcel, his toes so, the crinkles at his eyecharm so, the sweet hunch to his shoulders so, but her whiteness he also horrifyingly has, while his sister Donna has not. In place of the blackbrown viaduct known as the Chinese Wall that bears the Pennsylvania Railroad tracks to Broad and Market Streets, the Wall constructed in a series of arches to permit the numbered streets, running north and south and thus rightangled to the east and west streets, to complete their fluencies at Market, broad and open parking lots are now established, and a new east and west street created, named Pennsylvania Boulevard which, at 17th Street, locates the Philadelphia Suburban Station from which one may entrain to outlying metropolitan areas such as Paoli distinguished both for nouveau and ancien riche and for that internationally celebrated repertory house, Hedgerow Theater, whose male doyenne directs plays in rehearsal from a wildly lobbing adamsapple acrobating over the

236

terrifying safety of a netted but scrawny throat attenuating into a
body whose lower attire is secured about the waist by a frayed
rope; theater and members are organized communally, so much
so that produce for the members' food intake is grown on the
grounds, cause and effect nowhere more brilliantly displayed than
by Hedda Myers singing in a piping contralto Cockles and Mussels
alive aliveo at the Goldstein dinnertable just after midnight
of a weekday evening, Lee Emanuel and Rena Goldstein present
and gravely if diffidently affected, while the following week news
is received by Rena, who is a good if somewhat disloyal friend to
Hedda since Kensington Highschool For Girls days, that the little
redhead Hedda, hooknosed, one front tooth broken, mussel-
breasted as Lee at last rubs a daysgrowth of beard into her pale
red pubic hair one rainy night in Nina Tarassoff's studio and twice
scours an orgasm out of her as Bernie Lefkowitz, her vacillatingly
maniacal husband, frustratedly boards a Philadelphia bus at the
Port Authority terminal, unable, temporarily, to learn her where-
abouts or that of her baby son's, is committed to the hospital for
the insane, Byberry as it is affectionately referred to, the diagnosis
being dementia precox, after the Paoli police have been notified
by interested parties that one of the elect of the Hedgerow Theater
group, namely, Hedda Myers, though still an apprentice in the
dedicated thespian cause and consequently relegated to such necessary but lacklustre roles as ticketseller in the tiny sentry boxoffice,
usher, sweeper of the theater floor and radish picker on the communal produce grounds, is observed crawling,
     naked,
     under a full, refulgently silver summer moon,
     along a rutted dirtroad about one mile from Hedgerow
Theater,
     her long radishred wavy hair clotted with pebbles, a few black
ants, wriggling, a flattened dandelion, a petal from a violet, some
wood shavings, some flecks of tar; her freckled dimwhite body
abrased and spasmodic in its bellied progress; her wide blue eyes
cluttered with the flakes of dead tears; her long thin mouth in its
rusty huskiness iterating and reiterating
     cockles

237

and mussels
alive a
live
o; her pelvis thudding up and down
up and down up and down up and
down the ridges of dirt as she crawls, as she is intent on knocking the sense out of the head of her clitoris, her clitoris that she
judges an idiot, a looseheaded, spittlebubbling idiot whose head
has been wobbled and waggled and pinched and puckered and
nicked and knuckled and pulled and picked and slicked and
sleeked and battered and bottled and tacked and teased and
frothed and filmed and yanked and yipped and dented and
dunned and hacked and hammered and chiggered and chapped
and hovelled and hooked and jacked and jabbered and clicked
and clobbered and frisked and flapped and looped and leaded by
the thumb and forefinger of one
Mark Fahn, composer,
whose mistress she is and the offices of Russel Zion, Esquire,
who, purchasing a portable radio for his daughter, accompanies
Lee to the Buick the latter has temporary use of, courtesy Gene
Hertzog who now owns same courtesy Levi Emanuel in return
for certain sickbed favors, namely, the purchasing of a hospital
bed placed in the Emanuel breakfast room, namely, airconditon-
ing equipment whose purpose is to ameliorate the breathing difficulties of the dying Levi in the insufferably humid Philadelphia
summer, temperature of the day ninetynine, age of the sufferer
seventyseven, a quite typically humid Philadelphia summer, the
Roosevelt Boulevard maple trees massively still in the squat heat
of the early afternoon, the traffic east and west incessantly east
and west both for the sixyearold Lee his fractured left ankle in a
cast and the seventyseven year old Levi his ticktacktoe heart in a
cast, one more Philadelphia summer for him to count while his
bedsores itch and squeeze through themselves long freighttrains
of agate pain, I count you, I count you, I count you, grasshoppers
of numbers trangling their clippers in his bedsores and his tattling
heart, the magic numbers that insure the sibilant sequence in
squares, in triangles, in circles, in the edema slowly drowning his

238

lungs why are you draining it doctor let the pot fill up, let me overflow for
    gods sake LET ME OVERFLOW
    LET ME OVERFLOW doctor
    pop youre going to live
    dont lie to me Lee
    I believe youre going to live pop
    believe believe
    I believe
    thats better thats the truth
    I believe youre going to
    whereas Dave
    he somehow cant make it
    with his ballteam
    yes umpiring
    he dont have enough money
    I guess thats
    yeh dont lie to me Lee
    but I believe
    all right believe he cant make the trip because of money is that
    yes
    no I wont be here tomorrow
    yes you will pop
    maybe tomorrow but the days are numbered
    no
    the truth Lee the truth
    if you want very much to live maybe theres a chance
    no Lee
    but I believe
    I wont be here
    yes yes
    I wont be here la comedia
    no
    tell mom she dont have to worry
    Ill tell
    I got to have your advice its hard for me to think
    yes

very hard
what do you want to know
think
yes
very hard
yes
you got to tell me what you want
about what
tonight I wont be here
thats not true
one more night maybe and thats
no pop please dont
Lee
yes
Lee
yes
hard
hes asleep Lee the nurse says
yes
better let him sleep
yes
Ill watch him
yes
your mothers on the porch
I guess Ill go join her
Ill be here
all right so that Lee will drive Russ to his Germantown home, patiod and swimmingpooled, childrened and wifed, Juliana nee Melamed, blonde, gratefully gracious Russ rushes, crinkleeyed, You understand, Lee, the reason I dont visit your father, I had a concentrated dose from my own mother and father, one dying within a year of the other, I dont think I could watch

Yes, but slow down for godssake

No, its all right.

Youre paler than ever, Russ.

Its all right, actually, the doctor informs me my pace wouldve killed me some time ago were it not for my low bloodpressure.

Fortunately that saves me. What the prosecution fails to understand is that the beautifully inhibitory function of the law is nowhere so well illustrated as in the case of my sister Donna, your cousin, Lee and members of the jury, twelve good men and true, Miss Kotex as I believe you so aptly characterize her. Get in, Lee, get in, Ill drive you to the Broad and Huntington station, you can take the subway there, no? Women are curiously keyed creatures Russ chuckles putting his coupe into gear puttering his eye over the rearview mirror and tranquilly gassing the car into a traffic hiatus west on the Boulevard crossing Rising Sun Avenue and the Boulevard Realty Company Dr Milton Kastrow pipe in mouthcorner studiedly consulting The Evening Bulletin emerging from the candystore his breath stinks thats the trouble with him Lee casually mentions otherwise he seems a competent enough dentist plays chess, Russ. That so? There goes his wife still limping hot soup to her mother across the Boulevard more careful about the soup than the traffic but I dont understand why he isnt making out in the neighborhood people dont seem to have confidence in him maybe he likes to read Goethe too much funny thing about Faust. Whats funny about it Lee. Well the poetry of it really isnt too good, in facts its rather mediocre. Sure hes got all the meters and the technical skill and such but the metaphor, the metaphor, Russ, is pretty hackneyed. Ive the feeling Goethe wasnt a poet at all but a genius who chose verse on occasion to vent his prose profundities

CHURCH OF THE REDEEMER AT ROOSEVELT BOULEVARD AND MASHER STREET. A clapboard structure adjacent to a modern basement. Thats how they build, Lee. They raise enough money to build the basement, finish that, raise more money and proceed with the ground floor and so on. I guess that basement has ·been standing now for about a year. Expensive stone, eh?

Waspwaisted the Boulevard rises over the Pennsylvania spur at Wyoming Avenue This girl Ive been going with Lee, Russ chuckles, secrets crinkling his delicately blond miniature features, the nose barely adequate, the lips carefully sensuous, the frownlines artfully not craftily cutting the forehead, the wavy blond hair piquantly tapped from the widowspeak, Ive a penchant for in-

241

jecting secrets where there may be none. You know, one should. Theres a secret for example in the flush construction of my beautifully voluted ear against my skull, as if it were cocking itself to listen inside rather than outside. What Im getting at, Lee, really, is that theres a secret to the secrets that Ive never quite fathomed, which is why Ive forever got my head tilted, Im listening for the secret of secrets if it should suddenly give voice, his pale blue eyes mark the cars ahead through the windshield. Theres a secret, as I say, to each secret, the reason for the jammed confessionals— the outside secrets have no compunction about telling, but not really about themselves except how theyve been kept, his right hand resting lightly on the stick gearshift but dabbing at it from time to time, not caressing it so much as redesigning it, my friend and I go to a studio once a week, my only relaxation really, and we sculpture, using a model from time to time, he gestures at the small statuary for the benefit of Norma and Lee. Good? Oh, I dont know. You like them? Fine, Im happy, Russ grins bashfully. Perhaps the secret really is that I badly need a secret, or that I wish to project the air of having one that shall remain forever unspoken. Thats graceful, no? One should carry something of the sort about one's person. In its baffling it charms. My baffling charm. Disarming. That I need to have people disarmed may be the answer. Well, why shouldnt they be? Im not going to harm them. They can resume their arms once theyre out of my presence. But, while theyre with me, kindly—disarm. Oh, yes, I—I myself continue to bear arms, but—theyre small arms. I drill a hole in someone with my derringer and its closed before that individual realizes hes been shot. Both humane and esthetic of me, eh? A small hole, a small sound, a wound very nearly unknown. Ah, perhaps we approach. I like to make unknown wounds, a pain so small that I alone will be aware of it, never the wounded; a hurt so neat that the subject will never feel jagged edges. But, do you know, Lee, youre one of the few who can make me really angry, as, for example, when you jibed at Hal Shirmer, calling his columns shallow. I know the man personally, Lee, hes spoken at the Y, he knows eight languages and his political comprehensions are phenomenal. How can you call him shallow? Well, I suppose

I was angry with you because of the cavalier mess you made when you lectured so arrogantly on English Literature—my cousin. Goddamn it I couldve drawn and quartered you. Russ blushes. White and red, both pale. I bear small arms against my fellow man, he grins at Lee. But this girl, yes. I took her out, you see, dinner, a show, and so forth. And we parked. I kissed her. Nothing, no reaction. I touch her thighs. No objection from her, you understand, I bear small arms, he chuckles. But, no reaction. Shes quite cold. I run a test about her ears, the nape of her neck. She remains cold. Sweet? Oh, yes. Cooperative? Yes. But her breath remains temperate, her eyes quite open. I tantalize the clitoris. Reaction? None. She all but shrugs, but does me the honor to desist short of that. I cup her breasts. Nothing. By this point, of course, I myself am somewhat more than stirred. And, as I run my hands up and down her body I, quite by accident, touch her nipples that, somehow, I had avoided or missed or skipped, what you will. And, do you know, the very moment my fingers came in contact with a nipple, she brays, she all but gags, she jumps, she nearly tackles me with her thighs, she bites me and in a fury she grabs my penis and very nearly pulls it out by the roots in her efforts to lock it into her vagina. But, I inquire, what was the secret behind the secret of sexual excitation lodged in her nipples? Granted the beauty of the economical concentration, we must grant bodies their economies or dispersions, as they will. There is in economy the function, among others, of the challenge. As if the girl played a child's game with her breasts hidden in her inclosed arms against the tree as she counted blind breasts' buff. Find out where I really am, she faced the others, all children and —all children still. Why not? The finding of a woman comparatively unimportant. The finding of her nipples allparamount. One can be a priestess in numerous ways. This, perhaps, was hers, the nippletouch the magic ceremony by which, if you will, she unlocked the unlocker. It wasnt she who opened, eh? but it was I. I was really the constrained one. She liberated me by her— underground movement! Admit its a possibility. All right. But the secret behind that? The nipple Lazarus raised from the dead? Somehow, no. Was she giving herself permission to share her

243

secret when I touched on her exterior one? To share it, Lee, without knowing it. Surrounded by secrecy without comprehending it. But we in the law must unravel and comprehend secrets. I suspect the girl's secret is that her nipples are islands surrounded by a bodily sea, and that one must make excursions to those islands; I suspect her nipples are the sole points of her body in contact with the outside world, the exclusive sensorium through which she operates perception; it is after all terribly presumptuous of us to regard the accepted senses as the sole purveyors of impression. Absurd that the nipples should have preempted the other senses? But, we give more and credit to absurdity, do we not? It is as if we leap out of bed in the morning with our eyes absurdly open —or the girl's nipples absurdly erect—to encounter consciousness all marvelously ready for us—the window an oblong, the grass a green, the sunlight through the mist a cloud of seltzer, the woman a kitchen, the toilet a bowl. It is precisely so with the law, Lee: who takes the picture of a fourteenyearold Lee in his rented bathing suit in Atlantic City, his back to the ocean? The space between your two front teeth is a repulsive gap, your ears project asininely, your torso and lower limbs are a series of awkward tufts of bone, you grin all the way round to the nape of your neck, your spindly arms are crooked with your hands on hip, your wet hair saltshaped on your skull in ragged lumps. And I? I stand next to you, already exceeded by you in height, my blond hair dripping into my eyes, my muscleless arms akimbo, my kneeless legs bowed simianly. Next to me your father, more bulky and more shapeless than either of us, his belly a bulging patio on which his flabbyfleshed arms are folded; he smiles grimly, but a certain stupidity behind his face spoils the effect. It is all wrong, we say. We are very happy in this scene; we are on a vacation; our fathers have joined the families for the weekend; but there isnt an iota of grace to the photograph. Later, your father and mother and my parents sit in a roofless pavillion built out from the boardwalk over the sand at the foot of Virginia Avenue; they watch the Negroes push the roller chairs in which puffily repose men in white linen suits and their wives in mink stoles and hardened scabs of diamond and pearl slicing into reddened arthritic arms, fingers and necks.

Im burning up, your father says, I got too much sun. Didnt I tell you Levi not to stay so long in the sun, your mother responds, but no you wouldnt take my word for it she caustically turns to my mother for substantiation, your father's sister. Nu thats the way men are, my mother says, with her hearty laugh, her shoulders wobbling with laughter. Is that right, my father sniffs sardonically. What are you talking, Sidney, your mother says, Levi wont sleep all night and wholl have to suffer? Ill have to suffer, she concludes triumphantly. They slap at offending mosquitoes. My mother has a fan. Theres never been such a hot night, she says. Not a breath of air, your mother agrees, what did we leave Philadelphia for. Its the truth, my father says. Its such a shame, my mother says, the men come from Philadelphia over the weekend and this is the weather they get. Youll see tomorrow as soon as theyre gone the nights will be cooler. Why do we have to look at the people your father says, lets sit on the benches facing the ocean so we can look at the ocean, its so peaceful. Whats to look at the ocean your mother says, all day during the week I look at the ocean, at night I like to look at people at least theyre alive, am I right Bella, she turns to my mother. Well you know how Levi is, he likes to look at the ocean. Its so peaceful Levi says. What can you see in the dark Rachel demands. The waves, the waves, Levi says forcefully, thats what you can see in the dark; look, look, he turns his head toward the sea, cant you see the white there, itll be here when were gone he says just as forcefully. Oh dont talk so silly, Rachel is sharply out of patience, who wants to think of such things

nobody wants to think of such things

and my mother is whitely fair on the pavilion seat, Lee, for your father and my mother are sister and brother, and it is the evening of the sixth day, for on the morning of the seventh everybodys work will be done in the body of the Lord and they shall be at rest

STEEL PIER

HAMID'S MILLION DOLLAR PIER

FRALINGER'S SALT WATER TAFFY WE MAIL TO ANY PART OF THE WORLD CUT TO FIT THE MOUTH THE ATTENDANT TWISTS THE MASS OF TAFFY OUT OF THE MACHINE

FROZEN CUSTARD

GARDEN PIER

THE STUDENT PRINCE STARRING ETHEL BARRYMORE COLT IN GIANT WHITE BULBS EXTENDING OUT TO SEA THE FISHERMEN SQUAT ON THE END OF THE PIER BAITING THEIR HOOKS OUT HERE THE WIND BLOWS WITH CRUSTY FEROCITY AND AS FRESH AND CLEAN AS THE WIND BLOWING ITSELF APART AND BLOWING CRUSTILY ON ALL ITS PARTS AND BLOWING THEM TOGETHER AGAIN AND THE LEVIATHANIC COMBERS ON GRADUALLY ASCENDING AND CONVEXLY CURVING ABDOMENS AGGREGATE ON THE HORIZON AND WITH BLACKENING GREEN RISE TO GIGANTICALLY VENTRAL PROPORTIONS TO BASH THEIR GREENWHITE FOAMING BELLIES IN ON THE PILINGS

And the law is? Lee inquires of his cousin.

The law, Russ says, as if his smile is a coldly converted tear, the law is not the picture. My sister Donna believes shes in love with Alex Bradlow, the poor but honest and brilliant scholar studying the law on a scholarship at the University of Pennsylvania. Alex is a very handsome young man, conventionally tall, conventionally dark, traditionally handsome, the prince on a somewhat spavined white horse, and the prince himself conventionally thin, his eyes thinly black. Three years must elapse before he is graduated. At least ten more years must elapse before he develops an income from law practice sufficient to support Donna and himself. On the other hand we have Roy Lindauer, eminently successful realtor, conventionally ugly, conventionally rich, conventionally twice the age of my sister. Roy believes he is in love with my sister. I plead my mother not guilty.

Who is the plaintiff, Lee inquires.

Bella Zion leans back in the chair, a white gentleness in a slow neverending fall from her body, her smile gently falling, her hands gently falling down her lap. I do whats right, she avers, a person can only do whats right. Its not that I care Alex Bradlow has no mother and father. For that I feel sorry for him. He hasnt got money, well, thats all right too. Sidney Zion and me have enough money. I give Donna a fine dowry. We could support Donna and Alex without too much strain till Alex would build up his prac-

246

tice. And its not important to me, believe me, as the clock strikes
the truth, that Roy Lindauer has money and can take care of
Donna in fine style. To me it doesnt matter Alex is handsome and
Roy is ugly, no. But it does matter to me how crazily Donna pleads
for Alex; the minute she does that then I am opposed. If shedve
been smart, Donna couldve looked as if she didnt care, but even
that Idve been suspicious of, because Donna wouldnt look natural
that way. It was natural, all right, how crazy in the open she is for
Alex. But is that healthy I ask you? Is that the way for a Jewish
daughter to behave? Did I behave in such a fashion before
I married Sidney? In the first place Sidney everybody knows is a
little womanish, so how could I behave so feverish with him?
Believe me, its all right for a man to be a little womanish, its good
for him, a leaven, and it isnt because I wanted to be such a man,
I didnt, Im not. No. Sidney is a secret, he is a little of a sly one,
Bella pokes her finger at the air, shaking her grayblond locks up
and down, and thats a kind of man that isnt so bad, and isnt, let
me tell you, isnt so usual in this world. You see Sidney walk around
with that face of his, not smiling but he looks sly, as if he knows
something about me Ill never know. I like that. Maybe I
dont love that but I like it, Im fond, its very dear to me. Is there
a chance maybe Donna will feel in the same way toward Roy?
Maybe. A chance. Because love him she wont. Thats a good start.
Yes, yes, I know how she loathes him. I never loathed my Sidney.
Pitied him a little, yes, but he never made me sick. Roy makes
Donna sick, not to her stomach, mind you, to her skin. But Alex,
Alex makes her sick to her stomach, he turns her inside out—is
that a way for a Jewish daughter to behave, to walk around in
this world with her stomach turned inside out? I dont think so.
Its disgusting, that is one of the reasons I discourage the whole
affair between my daughter and Alex. He makes her look like a
fool, like a nothing, with no control. Thats not the law, for
a human being to go around without control. She loves him, she
says, she cries, she hiccups like a mad one, she goes down on her
knees to me, pleading let her marry him, give him the dowry.
When shes acting like that I should give her away to a man? This
would be a great shame, and that is not the law, that is—I can

247

only use the Yiddish word—that is a fatumult—a crazy confusion. I know, I know, I know, once shed be married to him she says and he says and a lot of people say my daughter Donna would calm down. But from that kind of craziness what is the good of her calming down? Its a long fall from such a craziness, and I dont want my daughter to go through that, shes not so balanced in the head as it is. From the craziness of socalled love shell go to a calm craziness, believe me, I know her, shell take quiet crazy pleasure in Alex becoming a famous successful lawyer, she wont be Donna, shell be all Alex. But not with Roy. With Roy she stays Donna. Because her scorn for him will protect her. My daughter needs to have scorn for somebody close to her so she can protect herself. When shes born shes got a cleft palate, a split. It has to be operated on, to close it. But she still walks around with that opening in the palate—in her head. Funny, hah? Thats why she talks like she has snot in her throat and nose, the snot filling up the cleft palate. You ought to hear her when she talks how beautiful how wonderful how brilliant her Alex is; you can hardly understand her, her words are so thick, everything clogs up in her nose and throat, she sounds like someone behind a solid cage. Noises she makes, noises! thats all anybody knows listening to her. Thick noises she makes about a man! And it would get worse if she marries Alex, because then shed never have to make herself clear. Alex would praise her cleft palate, tell her not to care, show it to everybody, parade it before the world, yes, he would in the stupidity of his brilliance—he wont be a good lawyer, take my word for it, a brief lawyer he might turn out to be, preparing cases for other lawyers to plead in court, always a student in a law library—sure, thats good too, but not for Donna. He would tell her she shouldnt be ashamed of her speech defect, and she should be, she should, yes, to hide it, to push it down, to control it—thats the law in this world, you understand? Who knows how she got the cleft palate in the first place? Maybe its my fault, maybe Sidney's, maybe both our faults because maybe we never did get together, and as badly as Donna talks my son talks so smooth, like a flow of water. Russell agrees with me she shouldnt marry Alex, Sidney says nothing, slyly. But married she should be, soon. Already shes graduated

Beaver College, cum laude it says, a smart girl. Shes twentyone, shes not getting any younger, isnt that right, Rachel? Whats true is true, Rachel agrees. So, Bella says, whats the answer? The law is the law, I tell you. Dont you think my daughter could run off and elope with Alex? Do I lock her in? do I put chains on her? No. Out the front door or back door she can go any time. Does she? Of course not. I give Alex credit, hes willing to elope, he pleads with her to elope. So? Does she? Does she sneak out at night from the house and run away with him? No. Shes afraid to, maybe? Donna afraid? Dont make me laugh. That kind of fear she doesnt have—I mean to run. But a fear I might be right? that kind of fear she has. And as long as she has that kind of fear, I stand right by its side. I put my fear right by her fear, a fear she and Alex would turn out badly. She pleads with me to get rid of her fear, but why should I? Why should I kill fear in her? Its hers, she has a right to it, its honest. I dont love Alex, she does. So, a love I cant put by her side. But her fear I can match. I only give her what I can match. I cant give her what I dont have, she wouldnt really want me to, so she takes that fear from me and tells me to stop giving it to her, she fights herself, and yet she wants everything from me I can give. I should deny her that fear? She begs me to deny it, she challenges me to deny it and I understand that. She challenges me to take back what Im giving her because shes asking me to prove my motherness to her, yes, yes, I know what shes doing, shes testing me by her love for Alex. She wants to know if she can ruin me with her by loving Alex, ruin the daughtermother between us, ruin and ruin and ruin—thats why she wont run away. Shes a brave one, my daughter, let nobody say different. She could desert me, be herself in what is conventionally regarded as self, but she doesnt know, really, the truth of that—the self of self, because she thinks maybe she doesnt have to kill me, that Im self of herself. Must she kill me by loving a man? So, I fight for Donna, my daughter, and that she knows too, and thats why she beats her head against the floor sometimes, thats how awful it is, because she wants to take me with her wherever she goes, at the bottom of her, and why not? Again, children, children, you see the conventional of the separation, what we call

249

mature, grown up, to be severed from the mother and father. Thats not true, thats not the law. Still Bella does not stand up. Still she sits in the chair, leaning back, tiredly, tired at the beginning and weary at the middle and tired at nearing the end. So I fight against her love for Alex, fight with her against it, thats all Im doing, children, children—her long oval face drags with its whiteness, her hands drag whiteness down her lap, she has been deadly, deadly pale ever since Lee, as an infant, has first seen her, deadly, deadly pale, never a streak of color in her face, never a patch of pink, never a touch of brown from the sun, and he loves her utterly because she tells him not to be afraid, that hes as good as the next one, and that hes handsome, and that she loves him, and that forever and ever she speaks softly to him, never shouts at him, never criticizes him, never upbraids him, the softest of the soft of any of his relatives, her voice never rising when she speaks to him, always gently and serenely praising him and never at any time touching him if he does not first go to her to be touched. Never. She never breaks that law. Yes, he has heard her voice in anger, but whenever he enters her presence, she instantly changes her tone, my handsome and intelligent nephew she says with quiet and infinite pride. Infinite. Unchanging. But he must hate her for killing the relationship between her daughter and Alex, but it is not a supreme hate that he can muster up, nor ever a violent one. It is regretting hate, a sorry that I must so smally hate her in his boundless love for his Aunt Bella.

But, law or no law, Lee has absolutely got to shit. There is, after all, too much of a load hes bearing in his bowel. Theres the load hes carrying walking east on 71st Street toward Central Park West; creeping down the hallway on the second floor of the Emanuel house on the Boulevard; down the corridor of the Union Pacific Domeliner dieseling across the continent toward Philadelphia; descending the ramp of the Constellation toward a funeral; riding the A bus toward his Boulevard home with Red and carrying his virginity; walking with Celia Renn across the Girard Avenue Bridge; ascending the steps of the apartment house on 16th Street between Locust and Walnut to the apartment of Rosa Caby; walking across the floor of the basement of Rhona Lyrian's sister's home where a party takes place for the raising of funds for a new Philadelphia theatre in which the works of new and unknown playwrights may be produced in the tow of Rhona leading him to Diane Valin who has informed Rhona that she loves Lee and must be introduced to him; the load of his mother isolating herself from her friends and acquaintances because of the death of his Uncle Victor Nathanson in a Moyamensing Prison cell awaiting trial for the murder of his wife's mother; ascending the allweather steps of the Wildwood boardinghouse toward the baseball team his brother manages; the imagining of his brother's flight in a car toward Texas; the superior wit of Barry Handler; Gail Greene; the erection on the police dog Rena tells him of; the experience of a sensation of distant hate he bears toward Aunt Bella, Donna, Alex Bradlow and Russ, a surreptitious, eyecorner-crouching hate, a sort of wagging finger at Lee's lovesystem. The boy is undeniably constipated. Law or no law, Lee has absolutely got to shit. Farting is scant relief. You know where the bathroom is, Danny Naroyan details once again how it is reached in the dilapidated Naroyan mansion at Lindley Avenue and Old York Road, you ascend the gloomguttering staircase, please dont make too much noise, Lee, the familys asleep. At eleven oclock, Lee says incredulously. What do you mean eleven oclock, Danny nags, you know people have to get up early to go to work. Danny yawns voluminously and loudly, Dont mind me, Lee, Im listening, stay as long as you like, you want some more cake? On the second floor landing you turn left and its the first door to the right. Be sure and lock the door, I wouldnt want my mother to be surprised, shes a light sleeper. I never worry about my father, hes dead to the world, he never uses his brain anyway, isnt it incredible, Lee, I should come of such parents, the only music my mother ever listens to is Armenian dances and folksongs, my father cant stand music at all, my carloving brother only listens to jazz and then only for fuckmusic, and my oldest brother the engineer cant even carry a tune, Jesus what a family, yknow, I cant stand them, I hate them passionately, I could kill them a thousand times a day, they have absolutely no conception of the outside world, none. Well, he amends grudgingly, its true my fathers antiwar, and so

251

is my mother, but thats only because of the Turks. But my two brothers? My god, uh! They only know from cars and women and bridgebuilding, and my oldest brother is antiArmenian yet, you know he changed his last name, he doesnt want anybody in New York to know, thats where he is now, with an advertising agency, after graduating as an engineer. But they wouldnt let me starve, and I wouldnt let them starve. You want two bucks? Thats all I can give you, Lee, thats all in my pocket. Nobody in the familys got money, it all goes into the communal pot and the clothes I wear come from my older brother who gets them from the oldest brother. Honestly, Lee, Ive just got to get out of here, away from them and Philadelphia, Im stifling, Im withering on the vine, you just dont know what its like, Lee, you just dont know, Im exhausted exhausted exhausted Pinky Pinky PINKEEEEEEE he squeals at the Pomeranian, come back here right this minute at the scooting yipping creature finally digging its paws in the rug in front of the wheezing grandfathers clock, listen Lee when you come down lets sit in the dining room its getting cold in the kitchen and besides you never saw the priceless pieces of furniture we have there, ahaaaaaah, you never did, did you, priceless antiques you just cant buy them in America, theyre all imported, anyhow dont forget to pull the chain above the toilet thats how it works, its oldfashioned I know, Danny giggles contritely, but thats how it is with us Naroyans, Pinky Pinky Pinky come here you nasty little beast dont you DARE follow Lee up the stairs;

the shadows in deep valences from the ceiling as Lee ascends are buzzards swooping in slow circles but he cannot run : his accumulated faeces heavily slag his rump. His feet in the ponderous carpeting can sense that the mansion must be razed; it is already a ludicrous anomaly with its eaves and gabling; a FOR SALE sign perches on the lawn outside; the Naroyans merely rent the house till the owner finds a buyer; a mansion, a friend, a pomeranian and constipation; a viaduct across Broad Street for the Pennsylvania trains, a General Outdoor Advertising billboard about automobile tires, and a winter night; a young man desperately wanting to take a shit; a ponderous carpet, a grandfathers clock chiming a half hour late, an unknown composer of Armenian extraction who beats rugs and fondles a yipping dog; and the buzzard shadows at the ceiling. A toilet, a hooting and rumbling train, and a scarlet neon cross bearing the words CHRIST NEVER FAILS. A looming bathroom with a brokentiled floor, walls tiled halfway to the ceiling, a tiny stained glass toilet window half open to ventilate the stenches. A toilet whose tank perches above, from which hangs a rusty chain. A clawfooted bathtub of generous proportions, a cracked toilet seat. Mrs Emanuel cannot sleep; Levi snores on the Boulevard. Lee at last must go home. Not now, not yet. In an hour, perhaps; at most, in two. Now his brain crouches on the toilet seat. He expands the sphincter. A pomeranian fart yips, and nothing more. An expresstrain rumbles across his bowel; the mansion hums, emits a faint quiver; CHRIST NEVER FAILS makes two revolutions; shall he and Danny eat raw clams at the oysterhouse tomorrow night; when will the mansion be razed; a FOR SALE sign ruthlessly scars the time of the mansion on the lawn, MICHIGAN 7-3205 the owner's phone, and the shit does not emerge, not a droplet, not a pellet, not a maculate tithe, a buzzard shadow is caught in a cobweb in the far corner of the bathroom, what is the law, Russell of Zion, what is the law of the stained glass toiletwindow. Lee hates the condition of his emotions in which he feels affection for Roy Lindauer, fiance of Donna Zion; Lee would prefer to detest Roy, and has a distinct desire to so do, but the desire never reaches the level of an operating hate; what he does do is hate his own affection, but not Roy—what is the law, Russell of Zion, what is the law. Lee must abhor Donna in a real and roiling scorn because she yields to her mother in the case of Alex Bradlow; despises Donna and her yielding; despises her for not running off with Alex whom Lee hates for his dark handsomeness and for his false capture of Donna's love; at least Roy cannot involve Donna's love in any fashion whatsoever, a negative condition that generates Lee's affection for the man while he entertains contempt for him as well because of the niggardly whine of his voice so much, in fact, it suddenly strikes Lee, so much like Donna's; but Lee's contempt is not hatred, it is a condescension to the fool of the fiance in that Donna can never love him. The one instance on the Atlantic City beach in which Lee does meet Alex Bradlow, the boy registers the impression that Alex is practising a deception in his role of the poor but brilliant scholar, true to the facts though that role is; what rankles Lee is that Alex flaunts this truth, wears it as a badge, so that actually Alex cannot really care that he is poor or brilliant, that his sparkling thin black eyes are aloof to his own condition that he so assiduously burnishes for the benefit of Donna Zion and, possibly, for others, though the latter Lee cannot determine; what further rankles, and delights, in this brief meeting, is that Alex sparkles those black eyes at Lee in a most conspiratorial manner, male to male the communication goes, so that Lee must bravo the man while he would knife him if he only had the courage and the years to do so; that black sparkling glance tells Lee that Alex knows how Donna leans her breasts over the boy Lee, showing him the cleft palate of her teats, the thick speech of the valley between her breasts; Alex knows, salutes the boy for the capacity of the boy's attractiveness as he moves Donna away across the sand toward the brilliant green sea; Alex enjoys the conflict he engenders in Donna and cares not a whit for the outcome; he is a pirate of pain, a corsair plying another's agony—for the youth of it, the white mother of the girl of it, the cleft palate of it, I will have her in these spaces he says, I will fuck her in the meanwhile while I know that Bella Zion is aware of it. Have your pleasure, Bella Zion pronounces inexorably, have it but do not marry it, that is the law, toilet seat or no toilet seat, buzzardshadows or none, FOR SALE sign or no, that is the law, Lee, law or no law, and Lee can see Alex actually retreating with Donna across the sand while Aunt Bella watches in the bright sunlight from the pavilion at the foot of Virginia Avenue, Alex's black eyes sparkling at the mother as he recedes, I am of the species that recedes from mothers he quietly addresses her from the distances, let that momentarily bind your bowel he rockets at her, let that for a moment constrict you and make of you a transitory poisonous snake biting at your daughter, you take the poison from your daughter because Ive provided it to her from my own black sinuous mouth

NOW SHIT

254

NOW BELT OUT A TURD

NOW PLOP IN THE TOILETBOWL

Alex challenges the boy and the boy indeed extrudes three rich blackbrown turds but not at the Naroyan FOR SALE

FOR THE PAST DOES NOT WORK IN THE BOWEL

NOR CAN AUNT BELLA SHIT on the second floor of the rented Atlantic City house because her whole body is shitting in a slow slide away from cancer toward the evergreen sea

its nice you should come to see your favorite aunt she says to Lee, the pillows propping her in the white wicker armchair floating out to sea)

queer : all the lines on her face are gone (I
guess I wont see you again, nephew/

EH ?/Donna
giggles, now Mother

EH ?

now, Mother youre not to excite yourself;

ah, Donna, Bella curls a disdainful lip, ah

WAIT WAIT WAIT WAIT NOT A BUZZARD SHADOW IN THE EARLY AFTERNOON NOT A STAINEDGLASS WINDOW NOT A WINTER TIME BUT SUMMER AND CLEAN AS A LOVELY DRAUGHT OF YELLOW SUNLIGHT/

i must see about the boys Donna ha ha has theyre racing around on the porch the noise

i cant hear anything Donna, Bella sneers, ah
my nephew,
my

to see your old aunt Im sorry I cant get up for you/
theres a sparkling
blackeyed young
lawstudent receding
from Bella on the
white sand :

Nu, Levi, Bella soursweetly smiles at Lees father but Lee is supposed to hate her for not having helped his father study the law the law the law

255

ah, well : theres a sparkling blackeyed young law student who
runs with my daughter across the sand,
theres your law, LEVI
THERE
THERE
NOW YOU WONDER I DIDNT HELP YOU;
all right,
quiet.
all right,
quiet,
silence,
Lee strains to present his aunt with a turd. Silence, a majestic
moment.
Give her a goingaway
present,
a real
gift
SHIT SHIT SHIT.
Lee sweats.
Lee groans,
grunts,
bulges his arteries that they beat the bowel with blood for AUNT
BELLA,
but only a fart, razzzzzzzzzzzing,
results.
Well, now, what the hell kind of world is it that I have with my
aunt, my cousins Donna and Russ, Alex Bradlow and Roy
Lindauer.
Tell me, Russ, the law of that world,
and maybe, then, Ill shit.
motherofpearl
Youve an unfortunate tendency toward civilization, Lee, that
has absolutely nothing to do with the law, Russell Zion tranquilly
and urbanely points out, his white smiles crinkling his pale blue
eyeflesh and becoming entangled in his blond frownlines. I advise
my sister not to marry Alex Bradlow on very simple primitive
grounds, namely, that Alex Bradlow is swarthy, blackeyed, black-

haired, whereas my sister's immediate genetic foreground and background is blond—my mother, father and myself. Roy Lindauer passes muster : blond verging on gray, blue verging on green, in short the presence of light, of bleach, of the clean and the fair. Recessive and—my dear cousin, Russ goes on, rubbing his nose lightly against a massive volume on torts, after all, there has been no breach of contract—inhibitory. To admix the strain dominantly of the presence of light with the black, the absence of light, is to run the danger of evolving the hidden chamber of the nonhorrors. I cannot abide my sister thus jeopardizing herself. And the usual banalities should be added : I do not, personally, wish a lawyer who is my brotherinlaw, who is in addition poverty stricken : I would have explanations and obligations; Id run the risk of having to involve myself with such a brotherinlaw in the most trivial circumstances. Yes, Alex Bradlow would be a distinct weight; and while, indeed, I should never for a moment entertain the reality of having sexual relations with Donna, I want the sense of their potential to remain, a vanity that Alex Bradlow would most certainly remove; he would uproot that whole area of delicate interplay between Donna and myself that depends on the sex relation potential, and I might detest both of them for its subsequent absence. Frankly, I dont want to detest either my sister or Alex Bradlow; Ive no desire to contribute further to the hatreds already existent in society. And, for as long as she is alive, I wish to buttress the role of my mother as the presiding officer, if you will, a Great White Mother. She is the only woman whom Ive been able to respect in this world, and I wish to preserve her authority as long as possible. Do not mistake me in the obvious sense, Lee. It is not that my mother has made it impossible for me to respect other women; it is my father who made that impossible because he singles out one woman and one alone, my mother, thus eliminating all other females for me—by his weakness. I despise, Lee, I despise his weakness, you follow me? But properly to rebel against that weakness I should have to subordinate myself to all females without exception, which I realize, and which has me further abhor him, since he requests of me the fantastic, the impossible, and he knows that, too, leading me to understand that he therefore expects me to turn my back upon challenging the impossible, that I reject the challenge, and that, in its amusing him, as I see his amusement, infuriates me. Oh, he is a subtle man, my father, let him not deceive you with his reticence, his verbal inexpressiveness. He has revenged himself for having eliminated all other females in having singled out my mother for his one male to female relationship—but the revenge is done upon his son, Russell of Zion, for, for me to fight him, would be for me to destroy myself, become a whimsy for each and every woman with whom I come in contact, the urge for which, Lee, is constantly present in me, to be their little boy

    EVERYBOY (you are familiar with the concept)

    their sweet petite blond toy;

so, I stand up for opposition to Alex Bradlow the better to invigorate myself, to sustain myself. When she dies, she will have so ingrained herself within me that I shall not surrender to Everyboy. Even, mind you—and this is most important, against which I must keep up my guard since my entire future is caught up within it—even after I marry Juliana Melamed, whose father is a distinguished practitioner at the Philadelphia Bar, who owns an enormous practice, who takes me into his firm upon my marriage to Juliana and who, upon his demise, descants me his entire law practice. Juliana is very lovely, very intelligent, surpassingly cultured, surpassingly blonde, deeply respects me and is healthily financed. I could never have selected Juliana for marriage had I joined my sister in opposition to my mother. You can understand, Lee, how critical a point in my life the rebellion of my sister is; my sister, older than I by five years; shall she be older than I in wisdom? shall she be a successful rebel against my mother while I shall not be? How can I possibly permit her to steal a permanent march on me? Of course I hurt her by siding with my mother, but at bottom she respects me for it, at bottom she admires me for it, because for one thing she knows that the destruction of her relationship with Alex will insure hers with me: she, too, enjoys the idea of potential incest; and, for another, the destruction of Alex means the maintenance of her hatred toward her mother—for to marry Alex signifies the danger of loving her mother. The enormity of it, Lee! She might love a monster! Of course, its comic—but a real danger, that she could forgive her mother for having been a mother; why, if she does, she will not be able to lash out at men, she will have forgone the only real individuality she possesses. Hating her mother insures her—Donna's—individuality. Why risk that with Alex? And, you see, to go off with Alex might mean that eventually she might be able, actually, to seduce me into bed, and that would totally destroy the delicate interplay between she and I—that, too, quite comic, but—infinitely more safe. To let her mother have her way is the supreme safety measure for the whole damned family! This, Lee, is civilized society at its highest—at its most primitive, that which you have scant notion of. The law, you see, is founded upon the family power interplay, and herein is the law's endless and maddening and pacifying subtlety. We complain of the law's delay: it is the family's; we complain of the law's prolix disputatiousness: it is the family's; we complain of the law's injustice: it is the family's; we complain of the law's preoccupation with trivia: it is the family's; we complain of the maze and the fine points of the law: they are the family's. But the laity does not enjoy the projection of the familial construction on to a purely formal screen; but, while it does not enjoy, it accepts. When the law is rejected, the family is priorly rejected. We in the law attempt to insure the properly discriminatory practices of family rights.

Who, Lee inquires, is the plaintiff in the action against your mother?

Quite sweetly, Russell of Zion replies, Why, I am, of course. There has to be a test case. I am not yet admitted into the bar. In private counsel to my sister I provide her with arguments to oppose my mother while I quite candidly espouse my mother's cause. I must see what kind of case I can put up without yet being a duly registered member of the bar. Donna calls me a bastard while she crookedly smiles and pillows my head, as she knows all the time that Im not a bastard at all and could never even dream of acting out of evil motives. I am an eminently practical human being—the reason, by the way, for your detesting me, Lee, while you adore me and

259

cannot now shit.

Disgustedly, Lee pulls the overhead chain and flushes down a bountiful accumulation of farts after which he joins Danny downstairs in the living room. Imagine, Danny says in awe, bidding Lee examine the sandalwood highboy, imagine the endless hours the Persian craftsmen expended in fashioning these minuscule motherofpearl inlays and who the fuck now appreciates it. Jeez dats oldfashion some jerk says. Eeeeee, what stupidity—tell me, Lee, what can you do in the world against such stupidity, Im willing to learn, hear arguments, eh?

Danny all I want to do is shit. Im coughing more and more, Im more and more constipated, even Renas getting impatient. Really, what do you advise?

My mother knows a lot about that kind of thing, Lee. Let me talk to her and the next time you come over Ill have some good practical advice. Thats the only thing my mothers good for, ach, shes so stupid, so narrow, so provincial youve no idea. Well its not all her fault I guess, what could she know? She never even saw my father until the day they were married, you know the old country customs. And she was sensitive yet, I mean she had some sensitivity that got totally submerged in my father, hes a peasant, a clod, Lee, dumb, just dumb. But things like cures for conspitation, this she knows. Goddamn trains, Danny mutters, the rumble of the PhiladelphiaNew York express vibrating the faience. Sonofbitch civilization. Oooh do I hate this country, Ill be glad to get out of it, I dont feel its my country at all, Lee, I feel foreign here, I always did. Bastard Americans, both my brothers are at home, moneygrubbing, cars, women, christ I hate them. And they look on me with contempt yet, little brother Danny, let him have his fun with his music, but only after the day's work is done, the pricks. My older brother is running after a married woman yet, hell get his balls cut off, mark my word, but what does he care, that stupid greaseball, he has such faith in America itll manufacture him new balls, better than the old ones

he stands at the front door slightly ajar Its so cold, Lee, its so cold, cuddling the highgrowling Pinky in his folded arms, say goodnight already, Im more Jewish than you are, you sure you shouldnt take the subway

No Ill walk

Youre crazy

Im crazy

You know you can come over whenever you like

Yes

Its cold Pinkys going to freeze to death arent you Pinky Pinky Pinky Danny squeals in the dogs ear

Goodnight Danny

Take care

Ill be fine

Ill be sure and get the constipation recipe

Good

Dont worry about it

All right

Sure you dont want an extra muffler

No

My god I could never stand the cold Im always cold in the wintertime I can never get warm

I prefer the cold

Youre crazy

Sure

We had a good talk, Lee

Yes

We always have

Yes

Its the only thing in this fucking society to talk about ideas

Yes

My god where do you think well all be in twenty years youre twentyone and Im twentythree were old already

Dont w

Dont worry about it Im always worrying about it there are some conductors already famous at my age and what the fuck did I conduct the NYA Symphony Orchestra and Brahms was hailed by Schumann when he was twentyone Im twentythree, Lee, its no joking matter Im freezing Ill catch my death of cold wont I Pinky

Pinky Pinky Im not worried about you Lee youll be famous in due time but me me Im not so sure any more

Goodnight Danny

Yeh goodnight itll soon be dawn christ I got to deliver those fucking rugs in the morning

his rounding square face squaring into roundness under the brittle brief blond hairs on the balding head squintstruck through the spectacles by the full moon on the icy night, huddling Danny Naroyan, his stockiness squeezed into cuddling the pomeranian bitch, I got to get some sleep, Lee, say hello to your mother and father

Yes

descending FOR SALE

GOODRICH RUBBER TIRES

a moon sashaying silver through the bluewhite night exactly twentyone years of age

CHRIST NEVER FAILS

LETS CHANGE P

MILKBOTTLE H

pigeonbreasted Anne Kanovsky in cotton housecoat that exposes her projecting sternum with rankling harshness, let him see it, awaits her husband in the closefisted sodden Philadelphia summer night on the roofporch of their house, from which can be descried a fragment of the Fairmount Park reservoir paralleling 33rd Street. Kanovsky undresses in the bedroom dark and gnarling a can of beer joins her. Blubberbodied, purplehaired, purple pimples encysted in the faceflesh, teatbelled lips squashing a mashed dead cigar, he sighs himself down into the pillowed summer wickerchair Want I should get you a can Anne?

No, Kanovsky. How did the rehearsal go?

It was lousy. Actors, shit.

The actresses?

Also.

Well, an industrial film, Kanovsky.

So? he growls. Industrial, it should be good. Its no excuse.

Still, its a start.

All right, Anne, its a start. Cover yourself, will you. Youre not that young any more.

Its very hot.

Yeh, with the Strawberry Mansion delicate odors, steamed piss. Lately its hard to sleep.

The heart again. He gurgles the beer. This beer is good for a toothbrush. Christ. Anne, let me tell you.

Yes, tell me.

Dont worry about the heart, he waves a flaccidskinned arm expansively and brings it back to wrench the cigar from his mouth and grandly toss it to the street below. Her breastbone sticks out of his mouth : what does he need with a cigar.

Its not my heart Im worrying about, Kanovsky.

Im glad to hear it.

Its you Im worrying about.

The doctors told you not to worry, Anne, am I correct? Anne Kanovsky is chickenbreasted and grayeyed. The gray eyes are grave, widely spaced and unclouded. They are cool, gray and grave in a rednosed pinksplotched and whitepimpled slipperon-tiptoe face.

Thats true. Anne puts a knuckle to her mouth and gnaws on her chicken breastbone but Kanovsky has already chewed off all the meat. The sky is overcast with overcast, black billowed by purple, the air heavy rustling blackblue taffeta. The eyes of Kanovsky and Anne flash momentarily with heat lightning, at which they gape their mouths, a gold tooth of Kanovsky's hovering above them, a plump gold ghost, the nerve extracted, the gum the ridge of the Fairmount Park reservoir, and then the goldtooth ghost strangles on the twisting telephone wires, a telephone pole abruptly grounding a forked bent corkscrew of bolt lightning

its got to rain, Kanovsky rumbles from the belly in the striped shorts, beer and piss itll rain in foaming yellow drops, and nobody relieved. Jesus. Bruno Kanovsky, porcupine the quills removed

But in spite of the doctors I cant help worrying about you.

Whats to worry about me he bites off his lower lip and jams it between his teeth, lighting it with the yellowgreen flare of a tele-

263

phone pole match. Better than a Havana, the Kanovsky pana-bella. Rolled in my own mouth.

Against my better judgment I love you, Anne whispers.

Nobody has a better judgment for Christ's sake, he protrudes a thick growl, tilting back the wicker chair and propping his stubby feet on the porch rail its so goddamn dark I cant even smell my feet. Aint I what you want, Anne? In the long run? The short run but I can see her appalachian breastbone, thats clear in any dark, beat them to death with the breastbone of your woman, thatll silence all enemies, Samson Kanovsky, blind with his own blubber and feeling his way through the worlds torrid fat. He jabs and picks at a purple pimple just under the aperture of his left nostril; if it bursts he may be able to see his way whitely clear. Get this through your head, Anne

I dont want to get anything through my head, Kanovsky. She giggles as a parrot might, shrill, giving directiongiggles, giggles taught by a master. Thats very frightening, she says, drawing her legs up on the hammock swing, the iron poles creaking, her chickenbreastedness leaning out of her cotton housecoat, a bony pole seeking support on the porch floor. Thats not what a person's head is for. A head should stop things, I know youre not talking literally, Kanovsky, but your soul, your soul talks literally, your soul is all body, your soul is real, your soul can be felt, youre the only human being I know with a real soul and believe me thats hard to live with.

Dont you know, Anne, I dont want anything from you?

Yes, I know that, her breath wiggling.

So. That should make you feel secure.

No, on the contrary, thats worse. Im afraid of a man who doesnt want anything from me.

Swinging. You got to swing? That creaking.

Im sorry, Im trying to keep still. She would roll herself into a ball but that damned chickenbreast, that wouldnt curve. Did you remember to mail the premium payment?

I forgot. Its still in my pocket. Tomorrow I'll mail it.

You already mailed it.

I told you I forg

No.

What do you mean no? How do you know I didnt mail it, I mean what makes you say that?

She giggles. The tone of your voice, Kanovsky.

So maybe I didnt forget to mail it. Maybe I mailed it. What difference could it make? I could swear I forgot. Why are you bugging me with such trivia? Whats the matter with you?

Its not trivia, Anne says, her voice twanging with the swings springs. Its very important, its for you, you know its for you but you say you dont want to know its for you and youre lying. Its all right, Kanovsky, you can say my insurance policy is important, its all right for you to say thank god Anne has a policy on her life for ten thousand dollars I wont have to worry if she suddenly dies I wont be thrown out on the street Ill have that money and the money I can get from the sale of the house. You can say that, Kanovsky, I wont mind, I took out the policy for you

But you took it out before you or any doctor knew you had a heart condition or else you couldntve got a policy, aint that right? I never asked you to take out a policy in the first place

I know you didnt

I didnt even know you had a heart condition till you told me. You didnt have to tell me

But I had to, Kanovsky. I was frightened.

It made you feel better to tell me

Yes.

It didnt make me feel better.

Thats why Im even more frightened. Because for you to know there was a good chance for me to die soon and youd have twenty thousand dollars so you could be independent and wait till you could really choose a good film to direct—that would make a real man feel good, I mean a real man who doesnt love the woman who loves him. I dont understand. You should want me to die, Kanovsky. You should hope for it. I know you do hope for it so you must be lying. Its your lying that frightens me more than anything else, Anne lets her legs swing freely now from the swing, the short lumpybodied woman, Im lumpy, she jokes to herself, Ill dissolve easy. Her chickenbreast scratches at her throat. She can hear a lump of thunder dissolving in the distance. It will drift closer. For a moment she presses the palms of her hands against her ears, nothing must dissolve, nothing. Her lumps harden. She can hardly move. What are her babylumps made of in the ancient rhyme. Hearts? Her heart is on her hip, she walks with a limp, the curious cripple. Then, taking her hands from her ears, the night-heat hisses in with mustaches of lightning. Her brain will pop out with little pops, like babythunders, as a reservoir of heavy water rushes in from Fairmount Park, sloshing about in her skull, making it waver from side to side, let it rain outside, outside,

outside

Put on your rubbers, she says in a flat dry voice to her husband.

He bulges toward her. What the fucks the matter with you Anne

Dont come any closer, she pleads. She giggles. Cage-direction : stay where you are, dont cross, youll obscure the other actor, if you come any closer Ill stab you with me breastbone, she twirls her mustaches, her upperlip quite heavy with hair, disgusting Kanovsky, why dont you get it plucked

its painful

Shit, his voice greases off.

Ah. Ah, she pleads with him. Why dont you tell me you want me dead? Ill feel a lot safer. I might live, then. I might want very much to live.

Dont be stupid. I want you to live.

But thats not enough, not nearly enough. Because if you want me to die Ill know if you mean that that you want me to live.

Im telling you, Anne, you should drink some beer. Ill go get you a

No, she reaches out with her chickenbreast, a batonwand, gates at a traincrossing, stopping him, the man with the purplebarreled torso and the bludgeonlegs, the purplehaired thighs, the purple pimples more expansive and fullbodied on his back and chest, he flings the crust of the one under his nose down at the porchfloor, Good, good, a snip of pain making him sneeze, but the white clear streamway of pus in a moment followed by blood, obscuring, Goddamn it. You got a cigarette, Anne?

Tickling her housecoat, she proffers a corktip. In the match-light his eyes are ponderous brown slabs of meat in the sockets. The lightning does a spasmwrench in the blindboys sky shinnying up and down Kanovsky's spine, up and down

four thousand three hundred and eighty three the whole Straw-berry Mansion California beach of Georgian Victorian three-storyed houses counts as the hoops, the iron rings, the quoits, the brass rings of the African negresses, the Victorian dresshoops, the midVictorian bicycle wheels spin round Annes girlbody on the continental porch, somebody has my husband by his hands, I thought he had himself by his own hands, oh my god, my god, what a terrible error Ive made, but Ill establish a world's record before my heart gives out, my husband is my protruding chicken-breast, he is my cripple

You want me to kill you with my bare hands Kanovsky says, but I dont have bare hands, I cant get them bare, I can keep on stripping and stripping them but theyll never be bare My fathers name is Bruno Canova. My name is Anne Canova Kanovsky. Any husband of mine I have, well, I must prove hes a man, otherwise Im terrified. I dont want to live in terror, Kanovsky, do you understand? So: tell me about the actresses.

Theres nothing to tell you without a full payment of ten thou-sand dollars.

Youll get the money, have no doubts.

Look here, Anne, he pats her arm with ponderous gentleness, all this is so much theatrical mumbojumbo. Believe me, whether you know it or not, Im faithful to you.

You dont love me, Kanovsky, her wide gray eyes stray distantly from each other, creating spaces between of expansive beauty, of stupefying serenity, pearlgray stretches in the dark night, cool in the heat. You cant betray me by loving me now.

Youre very excited, I would advise you to lie down, you should remember your heart

Thats not very·kind of you to ask me to remember that, she softly remonstrates. If I forget my heart, Kanovsky, it might im-prove, for it wouldnt be tortured by my solicitude. The heart, my husband, only wants to be let alone, it does not wish to be re-

minded of me. I alone am the culprit. You must let me be excited
To kill yourself?

Ive got rights. Would you yourself rather kill me? Take over,
Kanovsky, take over now obliterate my rights.

He regards her quite steadily through a feign of cigarette smoke
in the sodden night. His sweat forms crystal pustules on his un-
shaven wavyfleshed face, his blundering nose, his forehead with
its lowlying muscles, his purplepomaded clusterwaves of black
hair, his churnchunk of neck, his teats swinging under his ribs. His
purplestriped shorts are threaded with soaked belly hair and abdomen hair and groin hair and thigh hair. His testicles, puffed
and itching, he would like to air out by hanging them over the
porch railing. They can hear the sound of faraway locustdroning
that the rain makes falling over Central Philadelphia, a sound
modified by the hair growing in Anne's ears and in Kanovsky's, a
hundred thousand Constellations approaching Philadelphia, the
terminus of the nonstop flight from Los Angeles bearing a father-
deprived young man, Lee Emanuel, flying toward a gravestone,
the flight of a highly modified mourning high over the heads of
Anne and Kanovsky on the Strawberry Mansion porch, the flight
of a buoyant epitaph, of stone hollowed out till it is airborne and
met by the incredibly thinnedout remains of airborne cigarette
smoke, all graves meeting above the head and beneath the feet

There are many women, Anne says quietly, beginning with the
time that I told you my doctor said I have a bad heart. Isnt that
so, Kanovsky?

He abruptly shakes an admonitory finger at his wife. You know
something, Anne, I have some good advice for you. Its like something I told Lee Emanuel who is a very stubborn young man, I
have so many ideas for him, oh that boy, that boy, if he would
take only one of my ideas—well, what can you do? Everybodys
got to roll his own spitball. Kanovsky laughs heartily. I told Lee
like Im telling you in Russia with the Moscow Art Theater and
in Israel with the Habima you got months and months for rehearsal, you can rehearse till you get a perfect performance, and
you dont have to put the play on till youre satisfied. But the United
States—ah, Kanovsky leers grandly, you got a few weeks maxi-

268

mum to rehearse and then the shows got to go on, ready or not regardless. In the United States always its a deadline you cant go over. But I told Lee hes got to take his time, what do I care how long it takes him to write the play so long its right. Im a very patient man, Kanovsky is. After all, Im European. The oss didnt hire me for nothing, Anne, I mean not just because I speak Russian. You want to know what my point is, heh? My point is just because were in America you dont have to hurry to do anything, because—he pounds the railing—because youre living with Kanovsky the European only it should rain in a hurry, why isnt the rain American he shrugs at the sky. My dear Anne, suppose I did marry you without loving you, theres still plenty of time, dont rush me. After all, when I married you all I knew was your parents were dead but you owned this house clear, and your eyes were a beautiful gray and you adored me for being an oss hushhush hero. Already its different from Othello and Desdemona, aint I right, hah? You were a mature woman when you married me, and Im a white Caucasian, and wheres a Iago Im asking you? Im telling you in the oss I couldnt even kill a man, you think I was crazy?

Anne cries softly, her chin resting comfortably on her chicken-breast.

My gray dove, he says thickly, grunting his chair down on all fours and cradling the back of his wife's neck with a calloused throatpalm, cry, cry, its good for us both. That could be why I married you in the first place, I knew all of a sudden here was a woman who could cry for both of us and that was enough because Kanovsky could never again bring up a tear because his eyes would never again get seasick. Forever dry land eyes Kanovsky. Yes. For a Kanovsky to know that, to marry a woman for that, is better than love

I love your Russian accent, Anne says softly, I love your hush-hush oss heroism, I love you being a director, I love you being born a Russian, I love you because you have pimples, too, bigger than mine, because you speak five languages, because you saw me with gray eyes, because you were charming to me out of habit to all women but why should I so ugly be included I thought be-

269

cause my gray eyes couldnt be everything what did they tell you about me? They told you I had a house in the clear, no mortgages. All right, but that a gifted director could bow to me, court me because I had no mortgages wasnt that wonderful? Could a man's need be so great he could court a woman only for her lack of mortgages? Some women have beauty, youth. So it was all right for me to have a house clear because what does a man see in a woman after the vagina? I had a right to be taken by a moneyless man, I have a right to love you even if you are not gifted. More so if neither moneyed nor gifted. But they told you also my mother and father both died of heart attacks.

They told me, Kanovsky states heavily.

And they told you I was a virgin.

That too they told me.

Piquant, eh Kanovsky? Dead heartattacked parents and a virgin fortyyearold daughter. Piquant, with the relish of a house in the clear added. I was saucy.

I have no complaints about you in bed, he fumbles deeply in his throat. He sighs. He tilts back the wickerchair once again, groaningly raises his feet to the porch rail once again.

Would you like me to be silent?

He shovels up his shoulders. Be quiet, be talkative, either way.

Im good in bed, Kanovsky.

Yes youre good in bed he all but roars, except your breastbone hurts me.

You dont have to lean so heavy.

I get tired, what the hell do you want I should do, be an angel, be a queer? I got to lay on you, Im not so young anymore, I dont feel like I should fracture my elbows

I could get on top

No. No. Im not a woman yet, you got to lay underneath is that clear Anne? He squats under his anger, an aged and castrated bull using the bullfighter for his penis.

Nothing is clear, Kanovsky. Nothing.

Thats a lie, youre lying, you got to thrash around in confusion you think, you got to be desperate goddamn you he smashes down the chair and stands, roundshouldered, goddamn you youre making me angry I dont want I should get angry its too fucking hot you understand me? You got no right to make a man angry on such a hot night after I wrestle with those fucking actors and actresses.

She huddles, dryeyed. Im not crying, Kanovsky, she says sharply.

Jesus I got to think of your heart.

Yes. It beats slower.

You sure?

Yes. Thats when its worse, when it beats slower. When youre angry, that happens. When you fuck me, that happens. But you think it beats faster

I can feel it

Thats your heart you feel. So you better not fuck me or be angry. Either way you take a chance of killing me. You better start having affairs with other women and getting angry with them. I give you permission

I dont need anybodys permission, Anne, I tell you.

Then what are you going to do?

Doing is out of all proportion to whats necessary, he slyly remarks. Like what youre doing in a field of Kanovsky. You have more than one name, it is Anne Kanovsky, not merely Kanovsky. Youre envying me, you assume you can be Kanovsky as all women assume they can be anything they like at any time so that they say it doesnt matter if theyre women. Youre the hero in marrying me, what could be a more heroic act? My mother and father died when I was very young and Anne Kanovsky conveniently becomes the Kanovsky orphan, for a woman by definition is always born an orphan. Once I surprised you smoking a cigar, you giggled, said you wanted to see what it was like. You started dressing in mannish clothing not long after we were married, and yet when I met you you wore the most feminine of garments

I decided mannish clothing hides my chickenbreastedness better

What? You got your genitals on your breast? But even I dont put my prick up on my chest, it would be too vulnerable—with any kind of clothing

271

I could be the vulnerable man, eh? What man can be so brave as to be a vulnerable one?

So you make yourself out to be a better Kanovsky than the real one?

Whats left for me but for me to do that? I have to make up for you.

Did I ask you to make up for me?

For myself I had to.

Are you one of my actresses?

I want to be, Kanovsky, I want to be.

I couldnt cast you, Anne, do you understand that? Because you cant be any more or less than Anne Kanovsky.

But you never tried me.

Your heart couldnt take it. I couldnt take a chance you should drop dead on the stage.

But now, here, you can take a chance, isnt that so?

I admit nothing.

All I ask is you should admit. I wont hate you, I wont drop dead. She squints her mouth.

You sound childish, he waves her away.

Let me sound childish, let me sound like a baby

Maybe I should offer you one of my teats? But Im telling you milk out of a man you couldnt get. Spit, maybe. Sweat, maybe. But thats all from the outside because of the weather. Inside weather I dont have. A weather forecaster would go crazy locked up in me.

I could make weather in you.

The crying for the both of us.

Yes.

Very feminine Im sure. My weathercock, my weathervane, my seasons are Anne Kanovsky. Volcanos, snow, lightning—the effects in Kanovsky all by Anne. Some credits all right. Direction by Anne Kanovsky. Lights by, staging by, costumes by, produced by Anne Kanovsky in association with her husband. Maybe you once said you had no ego?

My loving you is my ego. You have a thousand egos, Kanovsky. You love many beautiful women, all your actresses. My heart is

272

beautiful, Kanovsky. Cant you love my heart?

It has no face. I need a face to make up a world. But that doesnt mean I love many women. It doesnt mean Im unfaithful to you Unfaceful

Yeh. Yeh. You got plenty humor, all right.

Anne Kanovsky's face loses weight by the minute. It is all eye and pimple balanced on a chickenbreast. One of her legs is shorter than the other and keeps receding on the swing so that she must use an arm in its place. Whom have they been, she asks him with a bright tiredness.

What are you talking a

The girls, Kanovsky. The girls. You know, by holding back youre affecting my heart. By your not telling me, I can feel my heart getting weaker. Only the truth can save me

And Noah was commanded by God to take two of all things on heaven and earth, Kanovsky intones. Two lies and two truths

I dont joke, Anne says.

Before you didnt want to be saved, may I remind you.

Im changing because Im not so sure any more youre a man. So maybe I now dont want you to have ten thousand dollars insurance and ten thousand more from the sale of the house. Theres no weather, Kanovsky. Feel for yourself. Were out in the open and its neither hot nor cold. A moment ago it was hot. Three months ago it was cold. Now its impossible to tell. We cant see if the sky is clouded or clear, light or dark. Look for yourself. Youre neither sweated nor chilled. In short, the atmosphere is ideal, altogether. How fortunate for you, Kanovsky, that youre married to such an ideal. As much as you may not be a man, I may not be a woman. Confess: is this not what you wanted all along

It is a quiet fire, a subtle crackling that does not disturb·Mrs Sherman. It is an aromatic thinly veiled smokesmoke that the fire exudes from the sheets and the mattress on which she reposes, asleep. Mrs Sherman inhales the aroma with something akin to the appreciation of a connoisseur.

Levi I dont want Hertzog to have powerofattorney. I dont trust him, nephew Donald Schwartz tells him worriedly.

Rena mounts the steps of the Emanuel house at 236 East Roosevelt Boulevard, her lower eyelids slackjawed, and insistently rings the doorbell at four in the afternoon.

I heard the funniest goddamn joke the other day, Celia Renn leans against the stone balustrade of the Girard Avenue Bridge in the honeysuckled summer night.

Listen Lee I guess the best place for you to sleep is in my room, Dave worriedly counsels his brother in the Wildwood boarding house. Come on Ill introduce you to some of the team.

The boy wishes to creep no further down the hallway.

He knows damned well theres a trafficlight at the corner of 71st Street and Central Park West. Because he can see the red light in the distance.

Im so glad you could come tonight, Rosa Caby trills at Lee. You must forgive my apartment, I really get so little chance to clean. Except the ballet slippers under glass, she mimics the start of a pirouette. Youve met my good friends, of course, Fiona and Cornelius Nuri.

Youve never before dressed so formally, Lee, but then Ive seen you altogether in so few circumstances. You do look so well in your white jacket, Diane Valin commends him.

What my mother recommends for your constipation, Lee, Danny confides quite seriously, is that you give up eating meat and become a vegetarian.

Now: Lee has scrubbed every inch of his body in the bath. Bloated sweat flickeringly thrills his face and neck. The rest of his body remains immersed in the tubful of scummy water. But the scum, he is convinced, lies entirely on the surface. The problem now is to raise himself out of the water without contaminating himself by the scum. He will permit only his hands to be dirtied, for they, in a few minutes, can be rewashed in the bathroom sink.

But I cant dance, Red. Id only make myself a fool and you as well by going to the Adelphia.

Diane Id enjoy taking you to Wildwood of a Sunday but wed have to go dutch.

The boat owned by the Delaware River Dayline, a three-decked ferryshaped sightseeing vessel, reverses engines to move

274

from the dock toward the river channel bearing the entire senior graduating class of the Kensington Highschool For Girls.

Theres another dance Id like you to go with me on, Lee. Itll be at country club for the graduating class.

The marriage dinner for Rena and Lee takes place at Uhr's, on South 5th Street, an orthodox Jewish restaurant.

The formal dinner following the marriage of Juliana Melamed to Russell Zion takes place at the unobtrusively Tudor home of the Melamed's in Cynwyd, a Philadelphia suburb. Pink champagne is the drink of the evening.

Norma and her girlfriend, Claudette Tahl, having twice rung Lee's bell several hours apart during the day at 119 West 75th Street without finding him in, write a note stating they have attempted to contact him without success and that if he reads this note before morning would he please phone them at the following number.

About that huge German policedog the girl next door had, St Red continues. Well, you know, shed feed the huge animal regularly during the day but before she put down his food—great hunks of steak—shed take a longhandled mop and start exciting his genitals. Hed whine and then scream in a faraway sort of scream and then when his erectiond slide out of its hairy cylinder like a shiny red pole, tubular yet tender but yet like steel coated with crimson slime—Id get hot flushes myself watching the thing slide out like a ramrod thickbodied scarlet boaconstrictor from a tunnel, I could imagine myself a sort of Promethea Bound, punished by the Gods for having stolen sex from them and given it to man, spreadeagled on a rock for all eternity so that a dragon's penis like that policedog's would be sliding in and out of me forever and ever but equally for all eternity Id be prevented from coming to an orgasm—shed suddenly withdraw the mop and back away and hed leap for her with a howl that made my nipples ring. But his collar and chain held and hed be jerked short, all but choking. It was then that shed set down a panful of steak chunks. This went on for about a year, Lee, and all during that time I swear I never saw any kind of expression on her face. She was pretty, blond girl, rather thick of leg and thigh, and flatchested, but her features were slight and sniffy, you know? Youd think shed do the whole act tensely, or at least have a sort of compression to her face, but no, nothing; not a smile, not a frown; not happy, not sad. Relaxed. Not dreamy, though. Just sort of—mildly interested as she went about extruding his penis; her eyes were focussed on that member, at any rate.

Why didnt her mother or father intervene?

I dont think they cared, Lee. As far as they were concerned, she was the dog's mistress and responsible for him. Shed wanted the dog in the first place, not they. I think I remember her telling me once her parents hated all kinds of animals.

Anyhow, the worst of it at the Stanley Theater during the film showing of Frankenstein are the final frames. Lees scalp becomes a nest of bites. He is convinced that the Monster will—must, absolutely must—spring from the screen itself and lay those brutal automaton arms on the boy to crush him to death. But both an odd relief and an intolerable tension seize the lad when the citizens of the town in that distant land corner the Monster in the towering gloom of the pendulous castle and then proceed to put that accursed pile to the torch. Fire, fire, fire. It is the one element before which the Monster must cower and retreat in a monumental and bellowing terror. So that, as the flames ascend from one level to the next, and the Monster himself climbs in nauseating apprehension from one level to the next in a crouching mortifying attempt to escape, Lee senses himself stretched on a rack while he watches the Monster's frantic flight; he feels his torso, still in the sitting position, rising up within itself;

as the flames spread, Lees ringworm infection on the upper inside section of his left thigh and in the crease of the groin itself starts to subside;

the Germans annex Czechoslovakia

Will you, Lee, will you, Rena asks rather pitifully

Rachel Emanuel conducts an intensive survey of the Emanuel house from top to bottom to check how inadequately the maid Georgiana has rid crevice and cranny of dust. Rachel wets the tip of her finger and runs it along doorjamb and windowsill, meanwhile chattering to nobody in particular since she is quite alone,

276

but the chatter is accusatory, the gist of it that she is currently intimate with only a single male, her husband. Lee inducted at Camp Meade, her brother Victor Nathanson is dead, David is umpiring somewhere in California, and her first Lee has been dead many many years. How dark the house is, but she can see the dust on her fingertip she nods to herself with chortling satisfaction. Ah, the top of the medicine cabinet in the bathroom; surely Georgiana avoided dusting there, because she is in such a hurry on the winter afternoon to leave for her home in West Philadelphia, a long trip from the Boulevard. And—dust Rachel finds. She will bawl out Georgiana in the morning, not that it will do any good she complains to Gertrude Forsten next door over the backyard fence, the colored girls just dont listen to you. Where else is there dust? The bedrooms of her two sons, who are gone. No, I wont throw out Dave's old clothes, you never know when he might be here and could wear them; of course, he's dead too, having run away like a thief, deserting his two beautiful children, you couldnt want them more beautiful, and marrying a shicksa yet in the bargain Lee whats her name

Sue

Thats a Jewish name?

It could be Jewish, mom.

No, Sue is not a Jewish name, I can smell

Its possible

Im telling you shes a gentile and Daves as good as dead Dont you dare marry a gentile Lee

Whos marryi

Im warning you

stiff, staring straight at the back of the man ahead of him in the line, Lee moves slowly around the corner to Arch Street. With a gleeful tightening to his throat in the russet and opal springtime dusk, it is seven oclock in the early evening, he swiftly pinches a glance from the mockups under the marquee of the Troc Theater

I could tell you, if you want to know, Kanovsky counters, that its starting to rain. I believe this so strong, he thrusts at Anne, that Im going to let down the awning. And, unlooping the S-wound cord, he lowers the redandgreen striped canvas.

277

If youre such a magician, Kanovsky, Anne magnificently presents the choice to her husband, gesturing regally at him with her breastbone, and if indeed it is raining, why do you take your murdering of me so seriously? Anne smiles not, but an exaltedness raises the sorry imbalance of her skull, and she rises to take a few paces beyond the covering of the awning. She is immediately drenched by the downpour. A flashing flood of black rain runnels her hair, turbules the pimples of her face, whirlpools her eyes, breaks nose and chin, sheets blackfoam from her shoulders and cascades ebony over her body, bifurcating twin seething falls to either side of her white chickenbreast. My breastbone, she calls out to him, in the rift in the Black Sea, a dry bridge over which the Jew Kanovsky can pass in utter safety. The Mediocrities who pursue him will all be drowned. Your Mediocrities, Kanovsky. You have only to pass over me, and then I shall close over myself and engulf your Pursuing Inequities. Will you not look upon them comically so that you can look upon your murdering of me equally so?

The water is very cold, Kanovsky says stupidly. Its true I am very hot, Anne, but that water will give you pneumonia

Oh, she says pathetically, you will kill me for no reason in yourself. It is very sad. She bows her head and slowly leaves the downpour to huddle, shivering, on the porch swing. Youre a run of the mill murderer, Kanovsky

the downpour switches off as abruptly as it begins

Summer storms are like that, he continues to talk stupidly.

Youre not worthy of your frailties, my husband, Anne speaks covertly, her voice issuing from a tiny cleft in her clasped fingers. You buy a fast car with the insurance money and drive at high speeds with and without passengers, endangering your life and sometimes the lives of others. You make hundreds of industrial films, you live in a hotel

It is as hot as it is before, he says stupidly

The awfulness is, Anne Kanovsky says, that I am not specific to your guilt after you kill me. I am effaced. Your guilt is nothing more than dutiful, prearranged, traditional, hackneyed, something generalized you pick up through the years, having it before

278

you meet me, and you kill me, my darling, as you ride a fast car, no differently, so I give you nothing specialised. How stupid of you, Kanovsky, you can learn no new fresh unique guilt. Save yourself by killing me now,

now,

now Who are the girls youre sleeping with

Miriam, Astrid, Neva, Barbara he says, stupidly, as he veers his eye away from her, as if he fears one of these he mentions will suddenly appear behind him to accuse him of falsehood

But I cant believe you, Anne says. Is it possible youre really being faithful

Its not possible. Im philandering, he says with a grand stupidity. Philandering, he rolls the word off his tongue thickly, the broad a stuffed with the Russian accent

But you must be lying because you still dont want me to die, Anne cries, throwing out her teeth like a pair of shears whitely cleaving the dark and then gaping in disembodied laughter. Cant I make you want anything, Kanovsky? Cant I even make you want my death? Cant you for gods sake convince Miriam and Astrid and Neva and Barbara to go to bed with you? Are they so repelled by your lack of desire to see them die in sexual embrace? Do each of them know how taken aback you are by the prospect of a woman resembling a fresh corpse after the sexual act? Did you tell them that? Did you discourage them? Did you allow me to discourage you to discourage them? What can I get from you? she beats on his chest with balledup fists. Fight me, fight me

FIGHT ME

Anne, my darling, I got to get up in the morning, theres a nine oclock call for the cast

Suppose I found a man to sleep with, what would you do?

Ah, but Anne, Anne, no man could dissociate your lovely gray eyes from the rest of your body. It is only I, Kanovsky, who can do this. Let me show you

The naked Lee before the mirror slowly inserts two fingers each at the top of each of his eyeballs and a thumb apiece under each eyeball and then starts to push. A throbbing commences. A dizzi-

279

ness descends from the eyeballs to the belly. He starts to vomit but not for a moment does he relieve the increasing pressure of his fingers and thumbs. The eyeballs begin to protrude. A spicule of blood spits at the mirror and trickles down. He snorts in the coagulated hunks of blood from his sheared nostrils and hiccups from the still wet blood of his truncated tongue. His temples thump mightily, the thoughts of Samson Kanovsky beat upon them steadily with tiny balledup fists. Lees protruding eyeballs bulge with hate If I can do this Kanovsky why cant you to your wife

Show me, Kanovsky, Anne challenges

Raising his hairy purple hands, Kanovsky is about to bring them down on his wife's eyes when his fingernails rear up in horror and break off at their moons

Dismember you cannot, she bawls at him, but kill me in entirety you can, is that not remarkable? You see, youve discovered something unique in yourself

He stares in slavering disbelief at the bleeding issuing from the flesh covering the third row of the phalanges of his hand. Youve no faith in my stupidity, he says.

Thats correct, she says calmly. I cant stand your not being attractive to other women.

Oh, but Anne, I cannot tell you how wrong you

Im not wrong at all. You repel other women, and that is an insult to me

It is impossible for you to be insulted, my darling. You simply do not have it in you to be insulted

put it in me

eh

put the susceptibility to insult in me, Kanovsky. Give me that

but that would be to remove one of your finest qualities

i want no fine qualities, not from you

from a lover, then

i want no lover. Just give me vulnerability to insult

but you just said i repel other women and that insults you

ah but you dont repel them far enough, Kanovsky, you still stay near them, they still are within inches of you, so it is but a half repulsion then you should be half insulted

no, the one does not follow the other. Thats an error in logic. You admit that

all right

can you repel them altogether

but i cannot be responsible if they do not respond, if they still persist in being close to me

then take them altogether

i really cannot be unfaithful to you

that means you cannot slap my face

that is correct

you cannot render me so close to you as to be hurt by you

not at that cost

it would cost you nothing

you might die

yes

I cannot take that chance

it is the chance I ask you to take. Death, after all, is an unmistakable demonstration of contact

you are a foolish foolish woman, Anne Kanovsky, an impossible woman, I did not suspect

no, you did not suspect, really, what it would mean to kill me, did you

no

and now that you do suspect, you are no longer willing to go through with it, is that right

yes

but the knowing should give you dignity. The knowledge that death is an unmistakeable contact, your discovering that knowledge, should give you enormous pride. You can now murder pridefully, and pridefully collect twenty thousand dollars. What an enormous triumph

but i drive my car rapidly, i endanger my life and the lives of others

yes, but you can do that with great pride, Kanovsky, with perfect insanity and not with that imperfect neuroticism

i cannot accept such knowledge

it is true then you want nothing from me that you must know, but you will take anything from me that you do not have to know
yes
are you certain
yes
good. You are killing me, now. She leans back, gasping. A faint bluish discoloration begins to diffuse her face flesh
but I know nothing, Anne. Nothing.
watch out, youre saving my life, youre resuscitating me, its easier for me to breathe but wheres the twenty thousand dollars, you can certainly and absolutely pull me back to unconditional life by my chickenbreast. Grab it and pull
no
just grab it, it isnt slippery, its protruding enough from my chest
She lies flat on her back on the swing that sways gently. Kanovsky stands over her, this chunk of lavender meat. Grab it, she says
no
Lee squeezes out his eyeballs, they sound as two soft farts vented by his anus plopping to the carpet, why cant you seize my breastbone
but hes only a dramatist, his two eyeballs are stage directions
then youve nothing to be afraid of
but hes naked
take off your clothes, Kanovsky, do a striptease
but thats for no money, i wont get a twenty thousand dollar fee for the performance
thats correct, but youll excite me back to life
i dont want to excite you, Anne
true. Is there anyone at all whom you want to excite
yes
the truth, Kanovsky, the truth. Whom do you wish to excite
I cant tell you
liar. You dont know. There isnt anyone. Dont you want the twenty thousand dollars and your wife alive at the same time?
no, no

which, then, do you prefer—the money or my staying alive
but youre directing me, Anne
of course. Dont you want me to
but that very question is a direction
of course. Dont you want me to
Absolutely not, Kanovsky thunders selfrighteously. If I surrender my directing you, youll give up wanting to live
yes. But you said you cant cast me. Remember
Ill cast you, Ill cast you
better and better, Kanovsky my darling. Tell me what you want
me to play
I havent given it too much thought, Ill have to reflect
you havent given me very much thought, is that right
well, not in terms of casting you
But those are your whole terms of being in relationship to me
no, I did not say that
oh. Then you can partly direct me, and I can partly direct you.
Is that a more reasonable description
more reasonable, maybe. But the direction should be only the
man's
then you havent been living with me. Theres nothing much you
can realize from me. Thats good. You are interested only in realizing yourself
that is the distinctive male quality, my dear
then it really makes very little difference to you if I live or die
since you put it that way, Anne, if you must put it that way, yes,
yes
then I choose to die
but that escapes my direction. The choice is not yours
then you tell me, my husband. Shall I live or die
this is not a play
certainly it is. The best of life is the essence of a play. Have not
you yourself said that
you must, after all, permit a man to speak theoretically
a man permits himself to do so. A woman does not thus permit
a man

283

youre not a woman, Anne, youre a terribly sick human being
that can no longer be said to possess sex
  you speak of my heart, I take it
  what else is there left in you
  ah, ah. Very good, Kanovsky. Youve finally hit on my sexlessness. Does that not frighten you
  it relieves me, you goddamn bitch
  it enables you to call me a goddamn bitch
  with pleasure
  with murderous pleasure
  yes, yes
  Anne Kanovsky stands in her wretched impressive crippledom,
one leg shorter than the other, leaning on the chickenbreastedness
she has extracted, her face mottled in the dark by jagged pink and
white sores, her cool opalescent gray eyes as far apart as the whirling poles, the night with its nowstars hooping about her in constel-
lative rings, one of her jaws shorter than the other, the woman
wrenched, one side of her body slipping away from the other and
still she maintains her wretched and miserable serenity, her housecoat gaping, her breasts balledup sacks as two tiny fists on her
chest, the nipples pulsing as with a rosy jagged starlight, her groin
something like an oinking pig at a trough since a steady stream of
piss, amber streaked by red, courses from between her bowed legs
on the roofporch floor
  Anne, Anne, he says in a giggling embarrassment, do you know
what youre doing
  in the elemental matters, she answers dryly, I know all the time
  is there something I can do to help you stop it
  you can stanch it if you like
  how
  She grins. By sticking your finger in the dike. You remember
the old story of the Dutch boy and
  oh for christ's sake, cer
  go ahead, then. Lets see if you can deal with elemental matters.
Otherwise, my darling husband, what will occur will be that I
will literally piss my life away. She throws back her slipshod skull
in a hawking, screeching laughter. Literally. Oh, I feel so happy.

284

Im doing something literally, you dont know what that means to me, trala, trala, Anne Kanovsky literally pisses her life away. You see, my husband, the heart controls the bladder, which very few people realize. Now, since my heart grows weaker and weaker, my bladder is running amok. And, wonderfully, it doesnt stink. Remarkable, no? It is innocent, uncorrupted, nonputrefying piss. Do you think you can stanch that kind of piss, Kanovsky? Oh, I daresay you could easily stop the flow of the ranker kind by an act of desperation, so that your nose would not continue to be assaulted by the stench. But here, no stench. The odorless piss of Anne Kanovsky. How will you treat it?

you better let me call the doctor

She bars his way. Watch out, she says. Come any closer and youll be drenched. You cant get off that easily, my husband. This time—no doctor. You alone hold the therapy

youre committing suicide

ah, is that your interpretation? I was waiting for such a statement. You feel yourself justified in earning twenty thousand dollars if I commit suicide? Youd better hurry if youre going to do anything. Im getting weaker as my stream of piss grows stronger. The flow of her urine is a thick muscular fullbodied column of liquid amber striated by scarlet spicules of blood. In this tremendous operation of hydraulic engineering bits of bone emerge, a swirl of intestine flaps out, some foam rubber lung tissue jounces forth, there goes a pearshaped gland bouncing a few times on the roofporch floor, a glistening shivering nerve plexus that shoots far enough toward Kanovsky to tickle his bare toes so that he yelps both in horror and pleasure and does a brief dancestep sideways to avoid further contact and the bloated culdesac of Anne Kanovsky's stomach that very nearly wraps itself around Kanovsky's ankle and continues to puff with the effort as it huffs grayly against the porch railing

Dont let my heart come out, Anne Kanovsky cries, her voice in the hooping distance—please please please stop my heart from being pissed out, she falls to her knees, the vast column of coursing piss, now forced directly against the porch floor, developing a counterthrusting fountain against the woman's thighs so that

285

Anne is buoyed upward, tossed and floating on top of her own fountain of urine as she extends her arms toward her husband—

YOUR FIST, SHE YELLS AT KANOVSKY, THRUST YOUR FIST BETWEEN MY THIGHS, NO LONGER CAN THE FINGER OF THE BOY AT THE DIKE DO ANNE KANOVSKY JUSTICE

ONLY A MAN WITH HIS FIST UP A WOMANS URETHRA CAN SAVE HER LIFE CAN SAVE HER HEART OTHERWISE MY HEART WILL STRIKE YOU IN THE FACE CAN YOU STAND THAT KANOVSKY

CAN YOU STAND MY HEART STRIKING YOU IN THE FACE

FOR IF YOU CAN IT IS WORTH TEN TIMES TWENTY THOUSAND DOLLARS

OTHERWISE, KANOVSKY, YOU WILL BE CHEATED, YOU WILL CHEAT YOURSELF, YOU WILL HAVE TO BE SATISFIED WITH THE MINIMAL AMOUNT

FOR NOW I DIE KANOVSKY LET US SEE IF YOU WILL CHEAT YOURSELF OR NO

and Anne Kanovsky's heart, whanging out in snarling systole and diastole, in savage bright red and lustrous black spurting bellows from between her legs, scoots out from one curve of the climactic foaming yellowred urinary fountain straight toward Kanovsky's face, vena and artery torn mouth superbly and bloodily cursing

BUT ITS NOT A WEAK HEART AT ALL, KANOVSKY SCREAMS, YOUVE MISLED ME ALL ALONG, YOUVE LIED TO ME ALL ALONG, YOUVE MISREPRESENTED YOURSELF ANNE KANOVSKY AND A STRONG HEART CAN DO ME IRREPARABLE DAMAGE

So saying, Kanovsky plummets prostrate to the roofporch floor as Anne's heart curses and whistles and cheers derisively as it arcs directly over Kanovsky's blubbering body and goes careening toward the Fairmount Park reservoir, sirens screeching as Anne Kanovsky herself, holding her chicken breastbone aloft as the one component of her body she has magically saved, gently then snuffs out the soft tranquil serene glow of her gray eyes with the bone even as she would two gray candleflames and, like a sadly crippled Aphrodite who has risen in birth from the waters only to find that they are, after all, only the purest piss, settles down once again, having blinded herself, into her rapidly drying pool of urine, for

286

the night, now, rid of its moisture, is passing itself off in a hot dry wind. A limp, hollow Anne Kanovsky lies quite dead on the roof-porch floor : heartless.

Rising, Kanovsky skirts his wife's lifeless body. His whole thick squat purpleblubbered lavenderpimpled organism feels quite cheated. He must phone the physician, he must obtain a death certificate. He very nearly trips over an empty beercan. A curse suggests itself to Kanovsky, but he finds himself incapable of it. Instead, as if to rid the scene of incriminating evidence, he bends, snatches up the empty beercan and throws it over the porch railing. Only one odd thought strikes him as he lifts the phone in the dark bedroom : the empty tin beercan has made absolutely no sound in presumably striking the surface of the street beneath. But Kanovsky dismisses that with the word

Shit

and the thought that empty beer cans can be heartless, too.

but youve got to hand it jaredlee to the hand that hands down the decree

THE LORD GOD ALMIGHTY IS ANGRY WITH ESTHER GOLDSTEIN; dont you think lee my mothers attracted to your father BUT THE SEX

shoes are far too large, sexJEWS

Aaron Emanuel as Lot is my Judge THROW the

Salt. Penis. Over. My. Shoulder listen you bastard Marcus Kronthal you handsome blackkinky movieowner from next door I know youve been after my wife Esther for

Solomon, Solomon so hows your daughters husbandtobes mother and father with AWESPECIAL RUTHREFERENCE TO LEVI EMANUEL does Lot have one daughter or two one daughterinlaw or

IM GOING TO START THE WHOLE HUMAN RACE ALL OVER
AGAIN ARE YOU OUT OF YOUR RIND oh,

Levi, deaddrunk in Philadelphia send your brother Aaron in his flopping army overcoat to Esther Goldstein and the two perform a dance both in the same pair of shoes large enough for both of them

my daughters too young for you, Levi, however if you

287

will permit your younger brother Aaron who has magic bulletless cannon to go BOOMBOOMBOOM into my little Renale what harm can be done WHAT LORD GOD JEHOVAH COULD POSSIBLY BECOME ENRAGED

on the choppingblock with your hand, jaredlee
my surgical hand?
aye
to deflower Rena?
in a manner of spoking, aye
Levi Emanuel looks back and the Nurse is turned to salt
and the chandelier above him glitters salt
his eyes burn with Atlantic City
OUT IN THE SUN TOO LONG Rachel whispers behind him.

He turns. Out in the sun too CANCER OF THE EYES the visions multiply out of hand

MY HAND twitches on the bedrail,

the cold saltwet Atlantic City rail in the spraysmitten night and the sea coming in to smite his forehead with the suns Aaron

dances with Esther Goldstein, a MADMAN

YOU SEE

CAN

TAKE

OFF

HIS

SHOES

HAND ME MY SHOES LEE
Ive lost my hand
Lee hand me my
hand

As the cleaver of his nephewson poises above his wrist but I dont really think I can have Esther, Marcus, we change places, now you in front, now I, now you, now I Rachel, what do you see

I dont have to visit the Goldsteins Rachel says it enough you should

But its not right
You go

But Im not a representative

Ah, Levi, your son

Ah, Esther, your daughter

Ah, theres a customer in the store, Solomon stumbles looking neither to right nor to left of their merriment

SLICE OFF YOUR HAND Solomon Goldstein stumbleshuffles into the store the customer in a sleepy voice requests a half pound of swiss cheese

coming up halfpound swiss cheese Solomon arranges the cheese in the tilted slicer a circular steel and white sailboat anchored to a sliding white dock the question is what do you do to prevent what you cannot prevent that isnt going to be prevented because theres nothing to prevent I mean Im talking about Esther and Levi what can you do to stop from happening what is bound to happen in the circumstance that cannot happen at all after all she isnt that old and after all no beard is growing from its testicles either and yet its commonsense theyre laughing about the same thing Im slicing cheese about namely and to wit why should they prevent what cannot be prevented when theres nothing to prevent because they know I cannot prevent what they dont want to prevent because I cannot find anything to prevent what has already been prevented because it is unpreventable but why should they be laughing while Im sadly slicing cheese if theres nothing to prevent I cant even go in there to stop what doesnt have to be stopped I think maybe if I would be slicing red meat instead of cheese I could see better what Im slicing because this cheese shes looking whiter and whiter of course I know why its because the red meat is in the livingroom being Esther and Levi while Solomon is the white cheese in the store I dont want to get angry because while theres something to be angry about my anger cant stop what isnt going on when it should be going on. Oh, is that a dirty trick. Now at the trick I can get angry all right. But where do I put the dirty trick when Esther and Levi cant look at the dirty trick seriously. If I show them how dirty the trick is right away theyll volunteer the two of them to clean it up, laughing. And Ill laugh, too, a dirtier trick. Here I am already laughing in the dirtier trick while it makes me angrier and angrier, Solomon Goldstein my wife and Levi

289

have in common, me. Do I have Rachel Emanuel in common with Levi? No I do not, because she doesnt show up here. She doesnt show up here because she doesnt want to be where I am, we could joke with each other seeing ourselves the same person, one male and one female, playing with the cheese slicer. I hope the customer chokes on the cheese but unfortunately it has holes in it

mein kint

Yes, mother, Rena critically altering a skirt, her mouth skimped with pins. Esther bends and straightens at the diningroom table, deftly placesetting, her redglinting black hair in oriental piles atop her skull, her cotton housedress slopping over with breast. Silver and porcelain take fragile breaths and pinch them in. Behind the alleyway fence next door the policedog wobbles small sounds in his throat

Mein kint, Esther trickles out a chuckling tolerance. Youre not yet eleven years old, am I right?

Yes, mother.

But already youre bigger than I am, isnt that right? Esther's voice is positively frivolous, wobbling in her throat something may be tickling her with a longhandled mop Rena thinks, but no thats impossible. Tickling him, yes. My mother does have a deep contralto voice though doesnt she. It would be interesting to attach a chain to her and tantalize her she slides a pin into the hem of the skirt

If I lower it an inch thatll be enough wont it mother?

An inch is plenty mein kint

Maybe two inches

No an inch is enough

Remember how almost to a year ago you made me go around in baby skirts so half my thighs were showing

Because you were still a baby mein kint

Yeh but everybody was pinching me

Oh mein kint such ideas Esther trills

Mother look dont you remember my blackandblue marks

Of course I remember them

So how can you

But children do such funny things, dont they mein kint? Esther
Goldstein takes a towel and rewipes an already spotless plate
Mother you washed that plate yourself, I know, So why are you
cleaning it again, I just handled it didnt I, But your hands are
perfectly clean, Who knows how long they stay clean, Your hands
are the cleanest I know, Thank you mein kint, Then why should
you, Just to make sure, Every night you have to make sure, Every
night they can get a little dirty, But its not even summer its
autumn the airs crisp and, Ill take care of my hands and you should
take care of yours, But I do mother you know I do my hands are
my most valuable, Be careful you dont stick yourself

What funny things

Rena, Rena my child dont you think I know you pinched yourself down there yourself just to give yourself blackandblue marks
so you could argue with me to lower your skirt

Mother that just isnt true I did not pinch myself. There, Rena
carefully folds the skirt in the livingroom and places it on the
piano stool in front of the old upright. Its ready to sew. Ill help you
finish setting the table. Its a shame she thinks what that girl next
door is doing to that poor dog, I really wouldnt do it to my own
mother

No no mein kint Im nearly done sit down and nash a little youre
a good girl in lots of ways but you shouldnt say you didnt pinch
yourself because you should be afraid your tongue will get blackandblue from the little lies pinching it

I dont want to spoil my appetite

What are you talking about you got the appetite of a little horse,
Esther Goldstein merrily shrills

And I look like a little horse

That I didnt say

Youve said it plenty times, mother. Pl

There goes your tongue again, pinching, pinching

Im sorry mother I did not lie about those blackandblue marks,
I did not make them myself BOOM BOOM BOOM

LETS CHANGE P

MILKBOTTLE H

Oh its so high at the top of the silo of the Levi Coal Company

291

the elevenyearold Rena in the pinched black sweater shrills, her blackred brassgold wavulant burnishes in the autoglumnal wind to the face of the oversized overshoed Aaron, her pendulum breasts telling hightime time at the crotch of the arch to boom-boom-boom Aaron.

ICE NEVER F

CHRIST NEVER F

KENSINGTON EL

STETSON HATS

dusk. A giant policedog rears at the top of the silo and Rena throws herself into the arms of her unprotector, Aaronee Fiona Nuri gazes adogingly at the six feet seven Cornelius my policedog she breathes she babytalks you dont mind if I tantooloize you a teensy weensy bit because you gots such a gweat bwig shaggy chute the shoot Im a woman why should I need women Aaronee shwugs at Renele

VACANT the newphew Laaron confides to the girl, tapping at his empty feet, some of my organs are far too small for their sheathes WATCH

out the SILO DOG SPRINGS AT THE LITTLE GIRL

will you believe me aaron

oh yes because i cant hear you

will you believe me laaron

oh yes because your words make no sense

estherlee estherlee estherlee

WHERE SHALL I TURN when the dogs are rearing at me in baby-talk WHERE SHALL I TURN when the faces are off and a white silo rears at me HELP ME LEVI the little girl calls

Five silos my coalyard boasts, Levi answers. Concrete. The most modern coalyard in Philadelphia, modern

help

Not at seventyseven. Think yourself seventyseven, Rena my once daughterinlaw

but your brotherson has a great overcoat many sizes too large for him

but he gives things away, his stock, he gives you a vacancy, the

292

world forever goes boomboomboom to him Im warning you. See Nina Tarassoff see Terry Shannon

Yes theres an old man spinning a top but you dont have Aunt Lilly and Aunt Harriet and Esther successively for mothers coming into the dress store across from the Bijou Theater in the Philadelphia Tenderloin you dont have to sort out your mothers you don't have to say when Aunt Lilly visits heres a whore whos your mother you dont have to say when Aunt Harriet visits you heres a slave whos your mother you dont have to say when mother Esther is with you heres a sonfucker whos your mother you dont have to think when all three are in the same house with you whom you address as mother I mean think of the protocol arrangements in their own minds and your own bloodmother waiting for a slip watching you narrowly as she herself thinks shes talking to her son-husband Nate look Nate please Nate you mind if I bring Rena along shes my daughter you wont be jealous of her now will you because its you I really love as a man I just love Rena as a daughter I never even think of you as a son please dont condemn your little sisterdaughter just dont think of her as your sister but as your little girl but just remember she isnt going to grow up for you Nate

so that you can commit doubly inverted incest THATS IN YOUR MIND ISNT IT NATE YOU WANT TO SCREW RENA BOTH AS YOUR SISTER AND DAUGHTER AND IM JEALOUS OF HER ON THAT ACCOUNT

so, Rena admits openly to Terry Shannon, you can see the real problem : WHOM DO I ADDRESS AS FATHER

my brother Nate

or my father Solomon

isnt it a merry mixup? she giggles wantonly

and youre about to marry Lee, Terry says sternly.

Yes.

With that family brawl going on in you?

Yes, Ive got to be brave, Rena says, her black eyes glinting sorrel. Lees going to help me sort out my family just as Im going to help him sort out his, because his family flaps around him like a loose oversize army overcoat hes got World War One guns booming in him. Isnt that brave of both of us?

293

May the Saints preserve my sanity, Terry says, by binding my head with a halo, I thought the Irish were a lunatic kind but the Jews have outstripped them

Oh yes, Rena says, because the Jews gave birth to the Irish through the Scots many long years ago, and the Little Men you Irish see in the glen are nothing more than one of the Lost Tribes of Israel did ye ken that, Terry, as she takes her place by the alleyway window her back to the dusk because the tall precocious hightitted eleven year old Rena just now witnesses one of the Little Men racing through the alleyway his manycolored wool scarf tallis knotted around his neck and hightailing in the rising wind and the rising whine of the dog next door, who has seen the Little Man too even as his dogprick lets loose a scarlet torpedo at the blond flatchested girl nagging it I love dummies I love Lee hes dumb for all his white silo mind far taller than mine but Im really much more intelligent because I dont believe in anything and he,

oh, he

he believes anything at all when hes happy and believes nothing when hes unhappy and thats rather commonplace

whereas Ive no beliefs at all whatever my mood

oh yes I know he believes he doesnt believe and you see theres an illusion right there, theres a belief

whereas I cannot even believe I dont believe I keep going back to a spinning top, and beyond the spinning top to a girl searching for a spinning top, and beyond the girl lost who searches for a spinning top to a girl who isnt lost but wants to be lost and beyond many mothers to the question of who my father is and I go to a primitive tribe where the oldest brother is the titular father and it becomes then a question of sex because Ive no desire either for male or female not because I have both hermaphroditically but because some humans are born without sexual impulse at all though they own the characteristics of one sex or the other; what I mean by sexual impulse is the desire for femaleness or maleness, not the enjoyment of the organs which I certainly confess I have. My desire is to be human. It seems to me all other people who re-

294

semble humans actually are, but that I am not, so that I want to be lost, I dont feel Ive any right at all to be human, so that when I am so close to Lee and tell him I love him what Im actually doing is trying to be human through mimicry oh dont hate me for my mimicry Lee darling dont hate me

because when I tell everyone that what I really want is babies they signify to me that my mimicry is successful at least in one respect, that while I myself cannot be human I can give birth to children who are

believe when I say I am not human because from the start to the finish of my consciousness I am altogether a mimic

not a monkey not a parrot not a mockingbird but

a side issue

not a throwback but a

side issue, an evolutionary byway so that I know all bets are off when I encounter the spinning top

mein kint

My poor, poor mother. Shes frightened of me. She wants to kill me. I understand but I really didnt lie about those blackandblue marks

A HOOP SPINNING AND A TOP Norma sits suddenly upright on the coarse sand She never loves you, Lee. Rena never

Thats simply not true, Lee cups the sand

She cant. I wish I could explain it to you. Shes like the blind boy jumping up and down in the girls spinning hoop. Rena is blind Lee, quite quite blind. She really doesnt see any of us. She cant. She never really sees you. She mimics you, Lee, but she never

lies about those blackandblue

All right, mein kint

I DONT BELIEVE THAT, NORMA

No, no of course you dont, Norma says a little sadly, because theres a little of the blind in you, too, a little of the mimic in you, too

so why was it you got in so late last night

But I called you, mother, you said it was all right

I changed my mind

Yes, you changed your mind. Renas hands tingle. The long

295

chain beyond the alleyway next door wrangles its links in curdling embroilment and then a snap is heard and then a dog's long rising sling of a whimperwail

The Little Man severed the dog's chain, Rena says. And a hard crumple, the clearing in silence a soft bone makes flung against pavement. Then she hears a series of staccato yelps, littledog yips

She torments him, Rena says in an undertone

What are you talking about now, mein kint

The girl next door and her dog. She torments him, she

She gives him blackandblue marks, yes?

The chain just broke, I ought to go and

Were having supper in a minute, Esther forbids

But she might

You are staying here, Renele

Mother, she

Here, I said. Here. Because of last night you stay here. Youre not such an age you can be with older boys

Mother I was not with boys I was with Carla Coffman I phoned you she developed a bad headache and Id be staying with her awhile whats the matter with you. You want to torment me, yes, you want to tor

Like the dog

Rena wants to take a hatchet and chop up the dogs prick into little pieces and mince them and throw them to the dogs winds, more than four of dogwinds, a thousand winds for the dogs chop chop chop REVENGE ON ALL PROCREATION HUMAN AND LOWER ANIMAL AND VEGETABLE AND ELECTRICAL

REVENGE REVENGE RE. Mother

Esther's fury gives her baldspots. The white patches on her face rash through her scalp with such brilliancy that they show through the black redglinted piledup hair.

Rena's arms shake. She folds them over her breasts. She presses herself against the window. She doesnt want her mother to see the Little Hebrew Man running down the alleyway because then her mother would be frightened out of her wits and perhaps actually attempt to kill Rena while accusing her daughter of knowing the Little Hebrew Man and hiding him. How do you handle a non-mother? How do you cope with an unidentified woman? I have to practice, Rena says

Theres no time now, Esther says. Maybe after supper

Its time for my practice, Rena hears herself saying. Something must be cut off to stop her mother from cutting off Rena. Something must be cut off to put Esther in Renas service

You can tell me, mein kint, you can tell your mother anything

No, thats impossible, Rena giggles

Why are you laughing

To tell my mother

Yes, your mother

Yes, my mother, Rena mimics

Dont make fun of me

Dont make fun of me, Rena echoes helplessly, controllingly, helplessly, controllingly, helplessly, contr

Her mother is completely bald, her fury blindingly white through her black hair and throwing it into tons of shadow

Levi Emanuels hand roulades within itself on the bedrail. His eyes are shut, but beggars run through his brain, Little Hebrew Men, their tallisimscarves, knotted wools about their throats, high-titted in the Emanuel alleyway wind, handout, handout, a handout Levi mutters. He whistles. He hums a tune. Yes, one of the Lost Ten Tribes of Israel, he mockingly agrees with Rena.

I saw them first, she says, in the hope I mightve been related to them, because I thought that, not being human, I might be divine, the mistress of the One God

Oh, Lee, darling, darling Lee, Im the mistress of the One True God, Aphrodite rising from a fountain of urine, Anne Kanovsky, I stink I stink I stink

I STINK I STINK I STINK CLEANSE ME Levi Emanuel roars from the deathbed, Ive slept with the mistress of the one true god

Lee is about to grab him by the throat. Not Rena

Hes quite delirious Mr Emanuel the Nurse touches him

Delirious? Yes, with

Youre the one true god, arent you Lee, his father says, so Ive revenged myself. It shouldn't hurt the One True God

It cannot hurt him who conceives himself omnipotent

all
I
asked
from
her
was
a
handout she had so much to give with her hands
NO YOURE A LIAR SHE COULD NOT HAVE NOT WITH HER HANDS
I KNOW I KNOW I BECAUSE SHE

who were the young men mein kint

Carla, Rena says, not a smile on her face but the curve of
breathlessness

Stop, Levi says to Rena, youve got to give me a handout. Stop.
Agree with your mother. Dont cross your mother. If you dont cross
your mother theres a chance I can fuck you when Lees not there

But Lees the one true God. I couldnt, Levi, I couldnt

Hes not that. Hes my son

I dont marry sons

You marry men

No I dont marry men

But you admitted you were nonhuman, not Lee

I gave him some of my nonhumanness, Levi, I COULDNT RE-
MAIN ALONE

But no son of a father is god

Youre behind the times, Levi

I am a Jew

Thats why you die

But Im a son

Are you?

I am a son

Tell me about your father

Nay, girl. Nay. Dying sons talk not of fathers. Levi waves his
hand in defeat. You may

So who were the young men, mein kint

DOGS, Rena throws her hand up in front of her projecting teeth

Shame me not, daughter

Carla, then. Carla Coffman. Do you want proof

I need no proof. I just want the truth from my daughter. You will give me the truth

I can phone her

You are not permitted to phone, my daughter

She will tell you

She will tell anything you want her to tell, you arranged it

Let me call her, Rena closes her hand on the phone, lifts it out of the cradle, cleaves it to her ear as her other hand rests in the cradle preparing to dial

Teeth crushing back her mouth, in little yelps and titters of rage, Esther Goldstein locks her fingers round the telephone handset Rena sucks to her ear and, sucking it from her daughter, she plunges the piece down directly on the hand Rena rests in the cradle

NO CALLS MEIN KINT NO CALLS YOU UNDERSTAND

But. My hand. Rena

whispers. Then shrieks one word only:

MY.

Then

whispers. Its crushed

No mein kint, your tongue is pinching you again

I cant move it, I, the bones

Ill show you your bones, Esther Goldstein seizes the hand as Rena screams, and

screams, and

screams

See, each bone, bone bone

Esther screams with her, nothing is broken, nothing, nothing you pinching pinching blackandblue daughtertongue, feel,

feel,

feel

as she enragedly kneads each finger of Renas hand,

her daughter sinking to her knees, the hand

limp be

wildered Solomon bundles himself through the churchcurved doorway holding his thumb ten thousand miles into the air wheres

299

Levi Emanuel I thought he was in here with you my
thumb is bleeding I
cut it on the slicer, heres the part I cut
off Esther
waves him backstage ITS
YOUR DAUGHTER'S HAND NOW NOT
YOUR
THUMB

EVERYBOY

EVERYBOY

EVERYBOY

    potatochipfaced Celia Renn, actress at the political left of left
New Theater, located on 17th Street between Race and Vine,
presently rehearsing a Kentucky coalmining drama, the Depres-
sion sidling clandestinely past Lee in titles such as Coxy's Army,
Bonus Marchers, Herbert Hoover, Unemployed Figures Reach A
Boy On A Bellycycle, General Douglas MacArthur Leads Troops
Against A Child's Kitchenmunching Eyes

    where IS that breadline. But Nearly Everybody Reads The
Philadelphia Evening Bulletin expertly flung end over end on a
sharply rising plane against the top stone step of the Emanuel
home

    Lee see if the paper is here yet Rachel peremptorily directs her
son who jerks open the front door on the porch and stoops to pick
up the folded sodden newspaper. Let it dry out on the radiator its
still raining?

    Yeh

    Shut the door Lee youre letting all the cold and damp in pop
dont have money to burn moneys scarce

    Pick a face Lee scans the photograph of a breadline, pick a its
raining. The newsboy under a yellow slicker pumps down on the
pedals and the tires slickfoam behind a little boy on the step gingerly scooping up the saturated newspaper a portly blackhaired
woman behind him chiding him about the heat running out into
the cold. Well, shovel the shuffling faces on a warm geraniumlined
porch, the gray rain spasming down the windows, a body jerking
down the twilight glass

clandestine are the poor

what do the men have under their trousers. What do the women they all look like tall white Aunt Bella in borrowed faraways have under their skirts. Theyre deaf, they cant hear me, a saturated face is expertly tossed against the Emanuel top step, neatly folded. The face sighs with the radiator as it dries out, its all right Lee. Dont worry. Celia Renn's face frowns out of the depression under the summer orangered moon as she watches an invisible spinning top. An old man and a baby. Im surrounded by old men and babies, Celia Renn the top spins furiously against the stone rail of the Girard Avenue Bridge, the wind abruptly belching out of her Im going to audition at Hedgerow with Joan's speech before her accusers would you like to hear it Lee she flings her summer-saturated face against him. His fingers through his pants pocket scratch savagely at the ringworm infesting his inner thigh No shit this is no time to rehearse an audition is it Lee she links her arm in his, her motherly straining body bouncing on his hip Come on and kiss me for christs sake she demands.

He kisses her, his lips deflating as he draws them

No jesuschrist thats not the way I know Im not beautiful for christ's sake but look at the body. Her potatochip face serious, sad, Its a magnificent body. Isnt it?

Yes

ICE NEVER FAILS

CHRIST NEVER FAILS

JESUS CHRIST I WANT A MAN I NEED A MAN Celia thrusts her jaw at the boy, crossing him out. Her words are a furious moan, an ejaculated savagery Her neck cords spiral off the top of her head. Then, immediately, squatting into the motherly before the boy, her tones a croon I didnt mean to hurt you

You didnt hurt me, I understand

No you dont understand. Admit I hurt you

I cant admit that, its all right

No. No, Lee. She pleads. Im very sorry. I didnt mean to

I assure you

Oh dont assure for christ's sake. Its all right for you to be hurt and for me to be sorry

I dont know what to say.

Dont you want me, Lee? she says, crooning.

Yes, I want you.

But you cant do it, is that right?

Yes.

Is it my funny face?

No.

It must be my comic face.

No.

Sure, sure it is, she grins a guttersnipe. Ill be a character actress before my time, she shrugs, chuckling. How old do you think I am?

Not very.

Go on, go on. Im close to thirty. You musnt tell anybody. You wont, will you?

He shakes his head no.

But Im awfully good in bed, she assures him with a sweet swollen smile. And I am a blonde. Ah, shit, she says, Im too aggressive. That frightens you, its frightens a lot of males.

Im not fr

Yes, you are. Im rough and Im tough and I WANT A M she grimaces at the stone rail, her fingers contortedly inventorying her face and then pushing it up over the rail, her elbows lacerated by the stone, Why do you have to make me come right out with it goddamn it. Ah, shit. Ive got to cry. Dont mind me while I cry. Ill get over it, turning her back she whispers to the stone and the river below I want a m I want a for the girl of the Ark, Jeanne d'Month, whom I study, to flaunt at my executioners from the apex of the fire. To study the role of Joan, a woman requires a man, for the role, played now, must needs have revenge. Did Joan believe that anyone who would enact her could possibly do it without relatedness to a male? Surely she must have known she would be portrayed; personages enamored of history must be aware that they and their deeds will be staged; but if they in their experiences do not include the commonnesses of men's behavior, we portrayers will provide what was missing, in a multiplicity of revenge, betraying the historical personage herself, taunting those who deprived her and we ourselves insulting the memory of the historical figure. We will insult the males in our audiences now by playing Joan as if she had not needed a man. We will tell them how extensively the female can lie—in the very flames of the fire. I will tell them how much I myself can lie, enacting Joan, and yet convey to them that in the wings there is a man, Celia Renn's man, and Joan finally will satisfy me. She must satisfy me in order that I portray her. Did she not satisfy herself in the knowledge that I, or someone, would portray her in her need for the male? If it is not Lee whom I will fuck, it will be another male. If there will be no male as I study Joan and as I finally enact her, then there will have been a double betrayal, in that I did not carry out Joan's major desire, and in that I will have been frustrated. My acting then will be overwhelming : for I will have put into Joan the element of her need for a male, and my inadequacy of obtaining for her the contemporary satisfaction, which will make men stand in their seats at curtain and implore the actress who did Joan to grant them the favor. Having become Joan, I shall have the male. By God she shall have some use in the present. We do not portray simply for the formal stage. I do not, at any rate, making me, perhaps, a lesser actress. All right. Lets grant my lesserness. In that very lesserness, in my very use of the portraying of Joan to gain my sexual end, I reduce the Girl of the Ark to dimensions palatable to understanding. Was this not her desire as well? Did she not exceed herself in order for us to fall short and thus comprehend her? Otherwise, we should not and do not make the attempt at understanding. Her grandeur can be understood only by the meaner. She was a damnable sadist, as are all historical personages. Does she not, in the time that I study her, delimit my sexual attractiveness? Christ, I cant even give myself away, to this child, this boy, this Lee, and hes one of many who turn aside. Joan bulges at my eyes, she puts sacks in my cheeks, she dulls the luster of my mouth, she brings on my menstruation too early, she gives me a stink I do not otherwise have—from leading her goddamned troops of men, from her battles and her exertions at the van of regiments of men—Im ahead of them, Im their leader, and if I offer myself to them they

303

must turn away. Who shall lead them from a position under their bellies? Michelet reports some damned duke felt her breasts, and they were good breasts, solid, as the duke relates, even as Celia Renn's; but that he could go no further because Jeanne clouts him. My very offer to a male is of course a clout at their balls: they think they might fall into an obscure homosexuality by yielding to my aggressiveness. Was Joan an obscure homosexual? Obscure, indeed; homosexuality lost in God; sex lost altogether, Rena; Joan seeks to find out what the hell her sex actually is, and I suppose the French would have it that she yearns toward a national sex, sex transcendental, sex Gallic, the thrust of nationalism, nationalistic Celia Renn and Lee hasnt the faintest idea of what I am sexually, naturally he turns aside, naturally men turn aside from me since my puberty when I come of nationalistic sex, JudaeoAmerican sex, Sex Assimilitave, a helluva method to exonerate my ugliness. Was Joan fair? Was she a girl of great beauty? Not that farmgirl, that consorter with swill and animals, who may have tumbled in the hay with dogs and pigs—ah, she heard the animal voices of God and the angels, she heard the high cries of the lower animals as they were left behind; and the Almighty, guilty, gives vent to pigvoice and horsewhinny: these voices direct her how to lead men. These animal voices in Lee direct me to lead men, me, the Jewish girl from middleclass Strawberry Mansion: I offer myself to them out of my need to lead them, to pull them around this way and that by their penises. All women play Joan of Ark, then, in diminuendo, in their sexual nationalisms. The women would lead armies of the unsexed, nonsexed, transsexed, that they later be enshrined, made Saints, their vaginas, a beatification, made grottos of Beauty Worshipped, unentered, to be gone into only with shoes off and penises strapped down, a holy of holies, Mary Mother of God. Mother. There it is. Mother. Look, all you bastards, I was the Mother of the Penis. Youd better bow down before mother, you pricks. Wipe my ass and dry my piss. Youre here, you bastards, give thanks. Im made ugly, to be given thanks. Im rejected, to be given thanks. Im scorned, to play Mary, Mother of God, St Joan of the Stark Ark, what the fuck, what more could I ask for, a rude Mary was Joan.

304

Rude Celia, thats the role, thats how shes to be played, but ingenuously, yet. The naive pussy. Sophisticated innocence, Celia Renn all over, the American Destiny, Sex out the window, we go down without sons, as France, Joan of Ark castrating the French male multitude—no wonder she was burned. Theyll burn all the mothers, but itll be too late in America, well find we wont get our balls back by eating charred pussy, which is what Ill be munching on as I go onstage, betraying whole armies, betraying Joan, betraying myself, Mrs Sherman burning at the stake I want to be here when my husband calls I NEED A MAN I NEED A MAN the whole lot of them Mark Fahn included. Do we Joans ever have enough of the sublimity of the nomen in our cunts? Will I really enjoy playing the cunt burning at the stake for the noman in it? Ill be sweating that cunt from the roots of my hair, and be celebrated for what I am not, as the French celebrate Joan, the French, that mass of male erectile tissue apotheosizing Joan the Virgin, they cant even see their own damned jest, and expire for lack of wit even as they extol their supremacy at it, as we expire for the lack of the engine to control the engines, the mastery of which we proclaim ourselves undisputed, that witty engine Joan of Ark we burn every day at the stake. Oh, Im dirtypure, thats Celia the Renn, and the whole playing of Joan will fall into dullness as the men wait for me at the stagedoor, as the men go through me to make Joan a sensual idiot. Who raped her? eh Terry Shannon? Joan of Ark Shannon, the Irish farmgirl. Joan Goldstein. Joan Emanuel. Joan Gratz. Joan Lee. Joan Caby. Joan Levi. Joan of Fart WHO RAPED HER? Thats how Ill play her, thats the clue, whos going to rape her, thatll drive all the nations wild, wholl be the first country to rape Joan of Ark? The first country to do it will be Master of the World, and its God, as the triumphal·rapist Nation burns the ravished girl, will be Mary the Ravished, MOTHER OF ALL MEN, for thats what Joan wanted to be, in the argot of the American adolescent, SUPERCUNT, which is precisely why so many men followed her, they smelled that, they followed supercunt's trail, they knew they were on to something extraordinary in the way of pussy, a pussy who saw visions and heard voices—right out of the thigh junctures, what a revelation, for

what female had ever had hallucinations in the cunt before? Christ
WILL I PROJECT ONCE I GET ON STAGE the bridge over the Schuylkill a black and buff arch at two in the morning, the auto traffic
fanning headlights over the boy and the woman on the sidewalk

You know, Lee, her face drying on the dark radiator as once
again they walk GENERAL LEE TIRES what do the women have
under their skirts theyre deaf they cant hear me the breadline waiting patiently for my penis

HOLY JESUS Barry Handler squeals thatd really plunge the
country into a depression, Everyboy, where the hell dya get the
conceit

I never did ask you how old you are darling, Celia mistily looks
up at Lee.

Ah, sixteen

Oh, come on

Yes, sixtee

Seriously?

Uhhuh

Oh, well, then I really cant blame myself, can I? she says,
archly, starchly

little Mrs Naroyan accuses both Danny and Lee Boys boys
youre all like each other you cant take care yourselves all the time
you need a mamma, she puckereye regards them on the grounds
of the second Naroyan mansion, once a nunnery, far out on Ridge
Avenue, laughing at them Come out of the dirt she commands
the crouching Mr Naroyan who has his hands plunged into the
soft black loam of his vegetable patch, How you like the tomatoes
eh Lee he gleefully palms a plushly scarlet tomato. Eeeh, its good,
the vegetable, eeeh Danl?

My father. My father, Danny apologises and yet with pride,
You cant keep him away from the earth, theres nothing better he
likes doing than scrounging around in the dirt with growing
things.

Things grow, Mr Naroyan painfully pulls out the words, his
sunburnt brow painfully furrowing, eeeeh, thats eeeeh the best

Shut up shut up Mrs Naroyan snaps

306

Oh mother let him talk if he wants to, Danny chides in swift annoyance.

Talk talk, she shrugs. Ah. Talk.

People eeeh, Mr Naroyan counsels Lee, if people they grow, slow, then all right, the people all right, eeeeh Danl? But, trouble, trouble, Mr Naroyan fiercely shakes his head, they grow too fast, eeeeh, they got each others way. No good, no good, his red round face sweats prodigiously, his hand gropes in the soil.

You cant teach him anything, Danny sighs to Lee. Imagine, in the country thirty years and he still cant speak decently. My mother at least is intelligible

Lee. The blackhaired Mrs Naroyan addresses him balefully. You eating meat?

No Mrs Naroyan I took your advice.

Danny snickers So tell us, tell us, hows it working out.

Well my bowel movements seem to be regular again even though my mother thinks Im crazy. But Im still coughing badly

Yeh I noticed Danny says, worrying.

Vegetables best diet, Mrs Naroyan nods fiercely, good for everybody. You stay for supper Lee, she speaks in adamant tones. Plenty vegetables

Eeeeh, eat my tomatoes, Danl you tell him, eeeeh. Special.

Hell eat your tomatoes, pop, stop worrying for pitys sake.

Who? Eecc, me. I dont, eeeh, worry. Worry, eeeeh, worry she for people not grow.

Im going to be totally bald like my father, Danny suddenly blurts to Lee. What a blow to my vanity. Listen, you can see the center of the city from the top of our ridge up there. Come on, Ill show you. Mother, well be right in

And he starts off in his bouncelegged sprinttrot toward the empty caretaker's cottage, the tall young man loping after the short stubby one.

Id offer you some whiskey, Lee, but mother holds the key to the liquor cabinet. He soprano laughs. I guess you think thats absurd. Isnt nature magnificent he stops short at the top of the ridge oh by the way were organizing the Gail Greene Foundation, I think its utterly stupid of course believe I had absolutely nothing to do

307

with it its a friend of hers, in her memory, prizes for the best piece of music written by a Philadelphian, annually, and for the best virtuosi in piano and violin you remember Ga

I was at the Jewish Hospital the day she

So young, I still get over, of course you never knew her as well as I did, Im jealous of the knowledge of her life, the treasure of nobody knows her as well as I did

Is that a treasure, Danny

Well of course it

It offers you sustenance

In a way. I can guard her fizzes of minuscule flies tingle the eye Fucking insects perforate the aquamarine predusking the crimson acoustical shell of the semisun light falling on the eyedrum crepesoled my father sinks in the west now hear oh israel the lord our god the lord sinks in the east, in the south and in the north in reverse mortality, turnabout is fair fey. Black and stalwart the broadbrimhatted Billy Penn walks in statuary pace atop the Philadelphia City Hall psfs the Philadelphia Saving Fund Society banks to the east, and the Lincoln Liberty Building to the south. Two horizons: the curve in the distance we see, and the curve we stand on we do not see what of Gail do you guard

Lee Im not so stupid, the balding fizzskinned Danny tartly remarks, as not to realize there could have been a Gail Greene Foundation during her lifetime to help talented artists. He barks.

I think you guard the lateness of the hour. Was she a great performer?

Oh for godssake Lee we all know she wasnt

Isnt it somewhat arrogant of your friend to organize a Foundation? Who the hell was Gail Greene?

Well I dont see why only famous dead people should have Foundations organized in their memory. Whats the matter with you, Lee? Im surprised. Im really

Then I suggest Foundations for each of our friends who die young, famous or no.

Danny is uneasy. Well I didnt mean to imply it should be carried that far goddamn mosquitoes at the stroke of the nosun they bare their penis stilettos ever hear of a bloodsucking prick

308

Lee, really. Danny blushes

So you begin and end with Gail Greene. What a long time her friends take to bury her. I call it a sporting kind of grief. I call it a dab of grief, the sort perennially negotiable, that can be handled without one going mad, or dying oneself. A polite grief that one can quite humanitarianly carry about with one, a sort of identification card in addition to one's drivers license, I am the recording secretary of the Gail Greene Foundation, we hold wakes for her memory once every two months—with a suitable musical program, of course, coffee, tea and macaroons served on the memorial premises. A grief one can possess with impunity, displayed with one's other possessions, and owning a certain enviable distinction. A grief—better yet—to guard one against deeper griefs, the kind one can use as a shield, with appropriate dialog to the effect oh I cant mourn that one's death so severely because I already have one Ive been in mourning over for years, it has precedence, you understand then why Im not prostrate now, I already own a corpse, my dears, the Gail Greene Foundation —would you have it molested and competed by another cadaver? Why, uncivilized, sirs. An old grief, properly tended, helps one defy lapses into the savagery and primitivism of a profoundly close grief. You simply must go elsewhere, sir and lady, find a human who has not yet grieved over anyone—and give such an innocent a chance at your particular prize. As for us, why, we have ours, thank you very much, get thee to a gunnery and shoot down your own. Yes, we admit it, it was very fortunate we could experience a rehearsal grief, so to speak, one that did not affect us too deeply, so that when our father dies, or mother, or anyone so relationally close, we have Gail to fall back upon, we have the dead to protect us from the dead—of what other earthly use could they possibly be? In short, we have a fashionable sadness to aid us in combatting an unfashionable sorrow, particularly American, dont you think? Oh, we Americans have our refinements, you know. Instead of building the Pyramids, we erect trustfunds and establish Good Works. The archaeologists will discover no mummified Pharaohs in the United States, no solar barques, no exquisite artifacts, but, rather, time—in capsule form, a microfilm of the masses in action—walking down Broadway, for example—true, this does remind one of Egyptian and Greek friezes, but we cant jettison the Ancients entirely, can we? and the diggers will unearth the records of Foundations, so much paid to this one, to that one—the assets and liabilities of mortality, the remorseless accumulations of the Dead Hand, Mortmain, Incorporated—all Dead Hands on deck, blacken the mainsl, nigrify the topsl, because we are going down, Danl, we are going down to perpetuate the Gail Greene Foundation

TAKE YOUR FUCKING HAND OFF ME DANNY

TAKE YOUR FUCKING HAND OFF OF ME LEVI

TAKE YOUR FUCKING HAND OFF OF ME GAIL

TAKE YOUR FUCKING HAND OFF OF ME RENA

But I like to show how I love you in public, darling

I know. Im sorry

It cant hurt to embrace you in the open, Lee

I know. Im sorry. But I rather you wouldnt. Tight, he touches his chin, rattles his upperlip with a forefinger. Lets walk, Red

It was just that when I saw you I was so happy you were here, so happy you were about to be with me, I wanted to show everybody how joyful I was

I know. Im not blaming you

But you are

Not really. The words issue on straight hard rails, chainmailed. Its simply Im not used to being touched, openly, that is.

But my family is full of that, the open touching

Yes. Its very wonderful Danny never touches me he understands oh does he, does he, Danny what do you understand; I understand I must never touch Lee; why not; it would damage us; why; hes simply not to be touched except at his own request; why; I just dont think of it otherwise; why; hes my closest friend and I respect his feelings; dont you respect your own feelings; no; why not; theyre ungovernable; dont you think if a person does respect his own feelings they can be equally ungovernable, perhaps even more riotous, perhaps perfectly chaotic; I dont believe in the perfection of chaos because then one's feelings may not be mitigable at all; are your feelings visavis Lee mitigable; yes, by

310

my being his closest friend; friendship, then, permits you to tolerate your feeings toward him; yes; friendship is a buffer, then; yes; friendship, then, is a form of hatred which permits you to continue to love a man;

yes;

you could hurt him, then, and still love him;

yes;

you could think of murdering him, then, and still love him;

ves;

you could think of his being in bed with a woman and still love him;

yes, yes;

you can think of him rejecting you as a friend and hate him for that and yet continue to love him;

yes, because I would still insist on my being his friend even though he disavows his friendship for me;

a monstrous friendship;

no, quite ordinary;

you detest its commonplaceness;

no, I love it, theres indescribable pleasure in the commonplace;

but the indescribable is a luxury;

which is why we stop short of description quite often;

you stop short of Lee;

yes, he is a luxury, a man I may not physically and describably love, a man who because of his own limitations enables me to curtail my physical love for him and control it, and I glory in the abomination of a single control

I am, after all, Rena, quite uninhibited in bed.

Her smile is rigid. Danny is rigid. I think we better go back to the house. Supper should be ready.

The two young men trail toward the quondam nunnery in the dark.

Did I tell you, Danny says quietly, I got a letter from a symphony orchestra in the south through the recommendation of Curtis Institute. They ask me to come down as assistant conductor.

And?

Well, they dont pay.

But its an opening, Danny

I insist on being paid a living wage, Lee. I insist that I, as an artist, have got to be recompensed. Thats all there is to it.

And youre not going.

No.

There is a short silence. The mosquitoes suck blood with their dagger penises. It rains over Central Philadelphia. I want a man, I need a

Little flames tickle the soles of Mrs Shermans feet, warmly tickle, and she grins, lopsidedly, one shouldermouth higher than the other. What a shame, she thinks, that she is asleep. But she will awaken, she contents herself, when Mr Sherman phones from out of town I want a man

The dry grass cracks under Dannys shoes like the backs of insects being crushed. You know Dr Schweitzer wouldnt approve, Danny attempts a chortle. A stuporously bodied moth collides with Lees forehead and he frantically sweeps it away

JEANNE D'MOTH

LEE AT THE STAKE

RENA SETTING FIRE TO THE BUNDLES OF WOOD

HIS FATHER'S MUSCLES ARE MOTHS UNDER THE SKIN FRAN-
TICALLY WANTING TO HATCH OUT INTO THE AIR THE BIGBODIED
MOTHS OF MY FATHER LEVI EMANUEL MY GOD SUPPOSE HIS
MOTHS FLY DIRECTLY INTO MY OPEN MOUTH I WILL SCREAM HE
CLAMPS HIS JAWS BY HIS FATHER'S DEATHBED BECAUSE IF THE
MOTHS GO DOWN INTO LEE THEY WILL HATCH A BILLION FATHERS
IN HIM ALL UNCONTROLLABLE ALL TALKING TO THE SON FLYING
AT THE SON BEATING AT THE SON THE SOURCE OF THE FATHER'S
UNDIMMING LIGHT

KEEP YOUR MOUTH SHUT AT YOUR FATHER DYING

KEEP YOUR MOUTH SHUT

RENA IS A MOTH CURVEBODIED AND FLYING DIRECTLY AT HIM
DIRECTLY

DEAD AHEAD COURSE

FRANTICALLY BEATING AT HIM

312

Lets get in out of the moths he growls at Danny, LETS GET IN OUT OF THE

youll have to pass directly through them to open the screendoor

worms

flying

spring. Ah.

If he is a child, his father wont die. If he can sit on the pavement as a threeyearold, his father wont die. Lee looks down at Levi. He wants to look up at him. If he squats on the floor, he will. But then he will see the pissbottle and its tube leading to Levis prick. I am a child.

Ah.

Then if necessary he can stuff the moths into the pissbottle and drown them, drown them in his father's own deadly poisonous piss.

That will kill death.

That will kill age.

Then, under the bed, he can wait for the worms. In the cold. As long as its cold, Levi wont be a moth.

The child peers down at Levi. My father is holding me aloft. He tosses me up. He plays with me.

But thats not true. He never plays with me. Thats why hes going to die BECAUSE HE NEVER PLAYS WITH ME AND THE GAMES GOING TO PUNISH HIM. Oh?

Is it part of a game?

The moths whirl and crash against the light warming the screendoor.

Wait a moment, Lee says.

For chrissake we cant stay here all night, mothers got supper rea

DANL, his mother calls

Just a moment, Danny calls back irritatedly

Danl, Danl, eeeh, his father grunts

Lee for chrissake

I can feel the moths on my tongue, my tongues their white

313

underbody, Ive bedsores on my tongue its been lying on its back too long it wants to stand up give a moment Danny. Lee starts to cough, deep, mucus-splattered coughs. Then he laughs. Gail's coughing is dry

Oh shut up Danny curses

If its part of a game then my father cant really be punished. Then he wont die

daddy play with me

daddy play

with me

daddy

play

with

MEEEEEEEEEEEEEEEEEEEEEEEEEEEEEEEEEEEEEEEEEEEEEE; the cry drowns in Rocky River

Ive got to rescue my father, hes drowning in a pissbottle

He plunges his palms under his father's shoulders. Levi momentarily awakens. What are you doing here Lee?

I want you to live. If you yourself have the want to live youll live.

Thats not true Lee. Be honest.

Lets, yes, lets play the honest game. Lets play any game. I dont care what the game is. Honest game? All right. I play honest. But you got to lift me up, pop

But I cant Lee I dont have the strength

THEN ITS NO FAIR BEING HONEST DADDY ITS NO FAIR PLEASE PLAY WITH ME PLEASE PLEEEEASE PLEEEEEEEEEEEEEEEEEEEEEEE

see theres nothing to it Danny dashes through the open screendoor now staring at Lee through the circling dashing plunging splashdying moths.

Im sorry you dont have the keys to your mother's liquor cabinet

I feel so much better Lee Celia laughs Im going to tell you the latest joke I heard. Youll excuse me if I do it in the Yiddish accent, because otherwise it just wont have the flavor.

Once upon a time, kiddies, on a low stab from a sticky knifenight in the Strawberry Mansion back, no different not a pig's

eye in a trough different Im telling you from this one, absolutely
a nonKosher night, when the moonlight could only be a smear of
baconfat and the smells are strictly from Christian pork melting
in a persecuted Jewish hell, theres living a peculiar triangle in a
oneroom apartment because population conditions in Strawberry
Mansion its an electronic paradise : yes, who else but Jews could
make a case already theyre meant for a Chosen Molecule? Already
theyre saying were living in the Atomic Ark because God is loos-
ing upon the world a Flood from Hamgrease. So, were a Tight
Little Moil circumsized from the Body of the Sinning Generations. The husband's name is D'Oily Carte Moyra, the wife's
name is Misericordia Moyra, and the son's name is Gaylord
Moyra. If youre looking out the window from the apartment you
could see what youre seeing as of like now : bushes like Nazis
skulking in the park, a Concentration Camp moon—where Im
telling all the Jews in the next war theyll be sent, colonize the
barren New Israel, look what a fine job you did in Palestine, the
moon isnt a challenge maybe? and look how bright it is on one
side yet so you could go to work on the bright side (symbolic,
hah?) and go to sleep on the dark side—and a boy and a woman
walking just like Celele Renn and Leeele Emanuel, shes dying
from hard undigestible sexpits from the fruit of the womb, and
hes laughing yet from watching her trying to spit them out—spit
out the parables hes thinking in his mind already, you got parables in the mouth. Whats the matter shes thinking, you want
Jesus Christ he should be a shining young girl name of Celele
Renn? and not Joan from Ark at all. Dont be bitter hes thinking.
Whos got better right to be bitter from sexpits in the belly shes
thinking. Anyhow, whats happening to Misericordia Moyra and
D'Oily Carte Moyra and Gaylord Moyra? Because of the electronic conditions theyre all sleeping in the same bed, D'Oily
Carte and Misericordia side by side parallel like they say, and
down from the bottom of the bed, sleeping as it were at the foot,
is their little son, fourteenyearold Gaylord Moyra, perpendicular. Well, D'Oily Carte is having a very hard day it is true at the
Diaper Service Foundry where more clinkers than usual are
coming from the infants they also serve; its all right the clinkers

315

should be hardhearted but when theyre cleaving like infant ten-
tacles to the diapers you just got to roll up your nose and go in
to help the Machine—its only human a Jew should help out a
Machine, and who else but a Jew would bleed for a Machine Im
asking you? because a good Jew prays that some day the
Machine will make things by hand. So D'Oily Carte Moyra let
me telling you is exhausted from the word Stop. Even so and
nevertheless, as a bonaschmate chosen one from the Atomic Ark
he is feeling little by little the Rhythmic Pulsations from the Universe with the Yammeke on top. He feels a hamische harmony.
He experiences, as it were, a voluminous flow, a wordless Cosmic
Chant issuing from the pores of an Infinite Salami a section from
which he could swear is making him to gird his loins. In consequence from which D'Oily Carte Moyra like its a signal from
On High makes from his elbow a shape like a regular goy goad
and lo and behold what does he do but give a gentile lovetap to
his schmearly beloved wife Misericordia and follows up yet with
a stentorian whisper the word Lets. Upon which what does
strudelshaped Misericordia say? She says, also the same stentorian whisper only with a female shriek in the middle, she says,
Sha, sha, D'Oily, youll wake up little Gaylord. D'Oily, as it were,
like we say in Gentile, he subsides. But its temporary only. He
subsides, you should forgive the expression, like a surly dog. His
one good heart thumps, his brain is in a fever from visions from
all kinds spiced meats like rolled beef, like hot pastrami. His sexu-
ality, he is feeling, is in danger of being cornered like a wild beast
in the middle of a throbbing bagel. But—a Jewish gentle-
man must subside at least a minute. He moves an itch closer to
Miscricordia because the pores from that Infinite Salami are
eppis beginning to sweat a little. D'Oily says, a little louder, Look,
my dahlink Misericordia, Im promising you Ill be very very quiet
trust me, lets. No no no, Misericordia objects, her strudels shaking like dough in very nervous fingers, Im telling you we would
wake little Gaylord, hes got to go to school tomorra, he needs his
sleep hes a growing boy. Absolutely not, D'Oily, absolutely not.
Repulsed, D'Oily Carte Moyra clenches his thighs. He makes
control from all quarters. He tries to think already hes got

frozen testicles and an anonymous Gentile is going chop chop chop. He tries to think already hes an icicle and lousy goyim children are throwing snowballs at it. What doesnt he think? He thinks hes a statue. He thinks he has an operation. He thinks god forbid hes a fairy in a straightjacket. He thinks already hes the Lord God Jehovah and what does he want with a woman? But thats sacriligeous and quick he changes and thinks already hes such an old man hes got one testicle in the coffin and the other testicle on a Jewish pickle and his penis a gold toothpick maybe for picking crumbs from his false teeth for eunuchs. But all D'Oily's imaginations are absolutely you sonofabitch Lee Celia hiccups slightly no consequential. No use. His groins he feels they are like a swollen humentash, a jelly one in the bargain. Misericordia, he says, his whisper like the Infinite Salomi already is going around and around him like the whirlwind did to Job and all D'Oily can do is smelling spices from the East, spices from the West, spices from the North, spices from the South, his head is a Running Nose and the sweat let me telling you is coming out of him like chicken soup. Misericordia, he whispers in a Cosmic Urgency, I give the word from a Jewish Cavalier yet Ill be so quiet so silent Im promising you could hear a shtickele futzarussl drop. Im pleading with you, Im begging with you have mercy, Im asking your compassion on bended prick—Misericordia, LETS! This once, she says, this one, D'Oily, okay. So, like Im telling you, theyre having a Harmony, a Voluminous Flow, a double Cosmic Chant this Misericordia and D'Oily Carte Moyra, husband and wife, reversed, naturally. It goes beautiful. Its positively a lyric on a loop. Its enchantment from—from—from Hollywood in Jerusalem! Well, to make a long story short, kiddies, when its all over and Misericordia Moyra is laying back content like a Hebrew Aphrodite, her strudel a little deflated but still tasting, its been apples in Paradise all the way down to a Jewish Serpent who is okay in the hands of the right barmitzvahd man, and D'Oily Carte Moyra himself no other is also laying back, a smile on his punim like a duly circumcized Yascha the Ripper, it happens that D'Oily, so overcome he is with a jubilance and a Jewish Whale of a Oneness with the Universe that in his absolute and

317

unconditional and Old and New Testament combined hallelujah abandon it comes into his whole body all of a sudden he should express his joy and suiting action to impulse with his left leg he gives a violent kick—such a kick, children, such a kick D'Oily is giving that poor little Gaylord Moyra is knocked off from the foot of the bed where? Im telling you, Im telling you, Gaylord is aflying four feet in the air and landing on the hardwood floor. oi oi oi Misericordia sets up a howl, look, D'Oily, look what you did to my little Gaylord, look, look already. What will happen to him now? You hit him in the head, D'Oily, in the brains you hit him. She wails, she carries on, its a regular wailing wall from Misericordia. Look what you did to my son, he wont go to school tomorra, hell be an idiot the rest of his life, oi oi oi, in an institution yet well have to put him. On and on she goes. D'Oily Carte Moyra is stricken on the spot in the bed. White, he turns. Red. Yellow he turns. Speckled salami color he turns. What color doesnt he turn? And, kiddies, would you believe it, in all this time Misericordia is weeping and wailing, Gaylord Moyra dont say a word from the floor where hes still laying. But at last, when Misericordia Moyra is already turning down her voice to a scratch, at last little Gaylord looks up at his tate from the floor and he says,

OI, PAPA, PAPA, YOULL KILL ME YET WITH YOUR FENCY FOCKING

pop music, Rena says, thats all I can play now. MILKBOTTLE H decants a jetcream milktrail against the eastern blueing, a noplane high over blackening Kensington, high over St Red's hazeleyes

Lee Sy and me are getting a divorce Nina says I want you to meet my analyst Jeffrey Adams six feet six inches in Nina's stocking feet dazzling in a red and whiteblocked lumbermans wool shirt his logging nose resting comfortably on the top of Lees skull, his hair the color of the lowkey red of a distant morningfire, his muscular mustache the autumnal yellowred spiked with saffron Hell youre not a psychoanalyst youre a goddamn lumberjack, his frame a bulging timber, his saffron hands a jagged logjam, redbrown eyes, the slope of the redwood giants to his shoulders. Her

analyst. Her eyes. Renas eyes, the Negro jazz pianist Roko except
that Jeffrey's fingernails can be peeled off by a sucking mouth
resting on Jeffrey's analytic desk oh sure I know Sy never feels
hes in competition with me Nina slurps the words over his lips
but I never get rid of the sensation Im in competition with him
Jeffrey very kindly, halting rather than aloof, tentative rather
than showing his ten bankbooks and two grown daughters and one
wife from whom hes separated, from an old American family at
last receding into the savage democratization of European psycho-
analysis

EVERYBOY EVERYBOY EVERYBOY

LETS CHANGE PARTNERS LETS CHANGE PARTNERS LETS CHANGE
PARTNERS Ninas rallying demand

CHRIST SCIENTIST NEVER FAILS

but I really cant tell you who the man is Im in love with Nina
says secretly hes my little organgrinder monkey who brings me
my MILKBOTTLE H

When am I going to meet him, Lee says pleasantly.

I dont know, she says worriedly. I really dont Coffee Lee?

Whatll I do with the scholarship to Curtis Institute now Rena
inquires carefully of her mother. My left hand just wont work I
cant play Bach or Mozart or any of the

The doctor examined your hand mein kint theres nothing
wrong with it

But your jazz pianos very good, Lee says.

No, no it isnt, Red shakes her head impatiently. If you knew
music youd know it really isnt. I fake, specially my left hand f

BUT ICE NEVER F

But dont worry, she reassures Lee. Please dont worry. I dont
like to see you so concerned the giant presses of BUDD'S LOCO-
MOTIVE ENGINES GENERAL MOTORS BODIES Hunting Park Avenue
the A Bus hulkwheels by the greasechapped foreheads of the
factorymen leaning out of the whangshranging windows the dies
behind them stamping out the carframes in steel Esther Goldstein Budd the mother of the giant presses dont stick your finger-
tongue in a telephone die your voicefingers might come steel-
clanking out Esther Goldstein Budd the die press magnate, well,

319

now, the issue is can Rena apply for workmen's compensation due to the error in production of a psychosomatic hand not called for under contract

All right, Lee, Red says. Thats really quite enough

No it isnt enough. Nothing is enough, you understand? Jazz is not enough for you.

What do you think would be enough for me, Red applies the warm hazel of her leafy eyes to Lee's sweating arm, the sun stumblered behind them down the westerning of Hunting Park Avenue, a cool glow on the black macadam, blue cenotaphs of shadow rising ahead crossing Ridge Avenue and the afterthought Gothic of the prowing highschool on the corner, a sandlot baseball team warming up on the athletic grounds across the street, a flyball ascending north and south and the center outfielder running with his chin over his shoulder

Mozart, Beethoven

No, Lee, youre wrong.

What would be enough, then?

The Saint Red pushes curves up her throat as she dots the knuckles of Lee's fingers with her own tips. I dont know, she says, her eyes light succeeded by oncoming nocturnal brilliance. But youve got to promise me you wont worry about it.

Youre sure you dont want me to be concerned.

Oh, yes. Very sure, she nods happily, a hankering humble on her face : but tread on me lightly, prithee. Will it be all right in the house, Lee?

Yes

Youre very sure

Very. And she pushes the curves down her throat now. I dont understand, Saint. I know you hate her

Oh what daughter doesnt darling, she tickles him on the neck

All right, thats e

Enough, I think, that I sing

Dont, Im tickl

Lee, Lee, I only want to

Yes, but were in

Just to sing will be enough.

320

Youre absolutely sure.

Yes

But your mother doesnt want you to

You wont mind if we dont talk about it now, huh? Especially
si

All right. I heard a joke. A Mister Haimowitz meets a Mister
Feingold in the famous New York garment district. You heard?
Haimowitz prods Feingold. Heard? What heard? Feingold responds. Weinstein died, Haimowitz informs him. What? Feingold
says, in the middle of the season?

The Will Rogers Memorial Park Beach in Santa Monica California projects not so much an air of betrayal as a mood of marvellous consternation for as the sinuous Constellation circles the
area Lee can see quite clearly from above that the little girl

IS REVERSING THE DIRECTION OF THE HOOP THAT HER HIPS
THROW ROUND AND ROUND HER BODY WHEREAS BEFORE THE
MOVEMENT IS CLOCKWISE THE MOVEMENT NOW IS COUNTER-
CLOCKWISE AND THAT INSTEAD OF THE REVOLUTIONS COUNTED
IN TERMS OF ADDITION THEY ARE NOW COUNTED IN TERMS OF
SUBTRACTION WITH THE RESULT THAT THE LITTLE BLIND BOY
WHO HAS BEEN JUMPING UP AND DOWN BETWEEN THE MAN AND
THE WOMAN WHILE HOLDING ON TO THEIR HANDS NOW COM-
MENCES TO ROCK BACK AND FORTH WHILE HIS FEET ARE
FIRMLY PLANTED IN THE SAND HE RESEMBLES A NEEDLE ON A
METER OR A DUMB DOLL ON A SPHERICAL BASE ROCKING BACK
AND FORTH OR AN OLD MAN OR AN OLD WOMAN OR OLD SHATSKY
THE DEMOCRATIC WARDLEADER ROCKING BACK ON FORTH
ON THE PORCH OR THE OSCILLATIONS OF AN UNCONTROLLABLE
HAND

MY FINGERTIPS ARE BLIND IN THE MIDDLE OF THE SEASON

the afternoon game between the Wildwood Wildcats, the baseball outfit Clancy Mann, Lee's brother, manages, and the Haddonfield Hubbas, the visiting team, draws stubstumblingly to a
close on the New Jersey shore. In the slowjawing heat of
the blackening distance may be descried the planking of the Atlantic Ocean, across which is flung the haphazard buzzes of a
glitter, the barbed wire of twinkleglints that Lees eyelids gorge-

ously chew from his buttocks high in the bare crouches of the bleachers at some remove from the meagre group of spectators squeaking the stands close to home plate. Clancy mugs near the dugout with the captain of the Wildcats who are behind in this game in the top of the eighth, and who occupy the league's cellar. The captain's name is Vince Harrison; he plays shortstop and is constructed in a series of choppy squats, tub legs, tank torso and a low watertower skull slugged down on a hogneck; but his whiteblue eyes flake squirrelling scales of teetering jabberice down to thinfisted lips that barely make known a mouth by a pale pink hardly distinguishable from a raw red face jesus is that guy hung the teams sardonics have it, that poor fuckin wife of his with three kids and another one comin how the hell she takes it is one for the nookiebooks but shit he just bangs her to make another and then hes off again to a high flyball

deep in right field

jesus what the fucks the matter with that Mariello Clancy curses for once in the goddamn ballgame we get two men on and Mariellos gotta pop out youd think the sonofabitchs got the idea his adamsapples got a date to come up for air off the top of his head shit Vince youre the captain of this goddamn flealeague outfit why the fuck didnt you shift the batting order Why you miserable prick Clancy they tell me youre the manager of this shithouse brigade well unplug your asshole and take some responsibility digging out your own turds you signed up yourself Well goddamn it I didnt sign up my kid brother for two weeks deep

and high into rightfield the ball jots up and

Lee is older than action at fifteen years of age his hands grabbing at the coarse splinters of the pinewood bleacher plank. He leans back only to lean forward. He leans to one side only to lean to the other. The Haddonfield Hubba outfielder trots in a leisurely fashion toward the rightfield fence, occasionally glancing over his shoulder at the still ascending ball

deep and high into rightfield but Levi Emanuel himself is running for the ball over tawny bedsheets the flyball struck by Lees cousin Charlotte Nathanson the girl being a girl dares to run toward the firstbase sack even though everybody knows she hasnt

322

possibly got the chance of a flyball bubbling up through a jar of blue jelly Take off the lid Lee yells Take off the lid

Get back Levi Clancy roars goddamn it youre not in N'muxt now the Lithuanians dont know their rear end from Jack and the Prickstalk when it comes to American baseball theres already a man running to catch the ball from the opposing team;

his eyes will catch the ball, Lee thinks. The Haddonfield man cant catch it. My father cant catch it. But my eyes will catch it and then split

He splits the ascending white ball into two halves, Lee does, and jams them into his eyesockets. The white sand of the Wildwood beach lurches up like a helicopter. The Lee rotorblades surreptitiously slice off the teats of the handsome brunette lass squatting no more than ten feet away from the boy and then roll them up to him and he quickly buries them between his legs in the sand so that at any time he can jab a finger down and touch them still pulsing their nipples waggling like antennae under his fingers youre the man for me Lee youre the a wave lurches up on the shore like a helicopter landing in teeterfoam and cackles whitely down Lees face to hide the pimples on his chin while a herd of oilyskinned black ants giving birth to themselves squirm slidingly in a rough triangle underneath the swimsuit of the handsome brunette lass directly on the crotch of the girl whose breasts Lee now cunningly owns. Naturally the boy cant see the entire herd; he discerns only the straggler oilyskinned black ants on the inner thighflesh of the squatting handsome brunette lass who boldly though breastless stares directly at Lee while she slowly flutters her fingers down to her crotch and

scratches

slowly scratches and

every now and then takes a straggler black ant and squeezes him between thumb and forefinger so that his oily blackblood smears down her thigh like huckleberry juice. Lee itches. He wants to take a bath from Charlotte for thousands of years under the bluewhite sun of Vince Harrison ogling the handsome brunette lass. I think I ought to shave the ants off my thighs St Red murmurs on the Ocean City beach in Maryland otherwise I dont feel quite right sitting down crosslegged a towering lifeguard of a figure slams his torso in front of Red and Lee she slings up her great slopes of teat at the man Oh Grant, she says, Grant, I want you to meet my husband she grins sloptitted at the man her black swimsuit slicing her mochabrown flesh Lees eyegums sink a thousand fathoms deep into her this is my husband Lee who glints up slacksocksmiling at the bronze atlas stalwart yeh Lee shes told me a lot about you you decided yet he juts his jock at Red the bluejock boy that is Grant the Jantzen stuporman his shoulders wide as a screaming gullballs flight high into the deep righttitfield of Rena, blue mocha and greenwave over the Nathanson grass catch my brown nipple batted high into the afternoon nip sky bite it with your palming fist If your boss give me a two week contract, swiftly she kneels to Lee thats what you wanted isnt it you wanted to stay two more weeks at the beach THATS WHAT YOU WANTED THATS WHAT YOU

WANTED husband WANTED DEAD OR AFIFE

OF THE DANCING BLACK ANT ON MY WIFES CROTCH; I want her,

yes,

DEAD OR ALIVE

bluejock screams in a bigbirded triumph down at the boy Youll get your contract Rena his jock half of the

KNOWN WORLD Lee turns it into

shadow instantly

Im a magician the little boy tells himself; Im a magician with the woman I love; I need know nothing of the other half of the world because Im

EVERYBOY EVERYBOY EVERYBOY

See you when sign the contract, Rena, bluejock says. Glad to have met you he rams Lees hand into his own bluefist.

So long, Grant, Rena slurs her mouth at him SUPERJOCK jesus she plays with the sand granules theres the needlepenised Lonnie Mahan and now the blockbusterpricked Grant

PUT THEM TOGETHER AND THEY SPELL LEE ABSTRACT THATS WHAT YOU WANTED LEE ISNT IT TWO WEEKS IN THE SUN-

DRENCHED GROTTO OF RENA WITHOUT HAVING TO TOUCH THE
WALLS watching

the handsome brunette lass murdering the oilyskinned black
ant on her inner thigh but you have

her breasts, dont you

you have her money, dont

you, you I dont want to catch the ball itll hurt my slicedoff
fingertips itll hurt the hands of my dying father : NO WOMAN :

NO DEATH youll collide with the Haddonfield Hubba outfielder : NO DEATH :

NO WOMAN pokes her finger slyly into the crease of her swimsuit : BURY THE BREASTS DEEPER : KILL

YOUR MOTHER : IF YOU KILL YOUR MOTHER YOUR FATHER
WILL

LIVE

I WANT MY FATHER DEAD OR ALIVE

but how can I kill my mother to accomplish this? Now she
lives alone in that apartment complex for old people near the
Jewish Hospital in Philadelphia. How can I kill her? True, my
fathers already dead, but I dont have him. I can have him, Levi
Emanuel, dead or alive, if I kill my mother. Keep asking her for
money. Keep telling her how girlish her voice sounds. These
things will prepare her. She wont know the difference between
being dead or alive if she has to keep worrying about her son in
New York and the older son in Redondo Beach in California,
Clancy Mann alias David Emanuel. Write Dave shes got plenty
of money left to her by Levi. What the fuck, Dave ought to get
some of it. Tell him to borrow. You yourself borrow. But this is
childsplay, isnt it? You think you want to murder her, but you
want her dead or alive too. Tell her youre going to visit her in her
old age but put off the visits. Make her cry for you. Make her
want you endlessly. That will kill her, that will put her in the same
state with Levi, and then youll have him. And hope, Lee, hope
that her arthritis will proceed apace, that it will make a creaking
rockingchair out of her arteries, so that on one creak too many
the rockers will split and her arteries will come crackling and

splitting out of her body. Kill her. She kills Levi, clearly and indisputably, by. But how can you have Levi dead or alive. How is this magic possible. Childsplay, childsplay. You want them dead or alive in childhood. You want to have them both without their life or death in your childhood and yet quite alive, quite voiceful, quite moving around you in an endlessly circular hoop. How does a child accomplish this without grief? How do you accomplish it with grief? How do you accomplish your parents sexlessness that can permit you to have them DEAD OR ALIVE? How can you make Levi nonman and Rachel nonwoman that will permit you to have them DEAD OR ALIVE. How can you bury womb and testicles on the beach, yours and that of your wife's when its a FLY-BALL HIGH AND DEEP IN RIGHTFIELD Lee brings his fifteenyear-old fist down on the sand the sand spurting into his eye Rhona Lyrian throwing it in a fit of frustration directly at his eyes on the Coney Island beach

What the fucks the matter with you Rhona Danny Naroyan rises to a half crouch dont you know you can blind a man that way.

The ferriswheel turns behind the boardwalk brown fife.

WELL I CANT ANSWER HIM I CANT ANSWER HIM RHONA NASALSHRIEKS I GOT TO DO SOMETHING SO I THROW SAND AT HIM I GOT TO STOP HIM

STOP HIM STOP LEE THAT WILL TEACH HIM A PERSON CAN ANSWER HIM WITH THINGS OTHER THAN WORDS THATLL TEACH HIM A GOOD LESSON

BUT YOU CAN BLIND A MAN THAT WAY WHAT THE FUCKS THE MATTER WITH YOU YOU GONE NUTS RHONA I DIDNT SUSPECT THAT OF YOU YOURE SO BRILLIANT

BUT HES BRILLIANT TOO AND HES GOT TO BE TAUGHT A LESSON Rhona shrills, her juttitted bathingbeauty body topped by the philosopher skull, the high spinoza balding forehead, the thicklensed spectacles through which the eyes nick the glass malevolently, the balding bathingbeauty you want to fuck as you look at the body and become impotent as you watch it evolve into the balding philosophers stone on top of the graceful neck and listen to the balding voice sneerpitched and sarcastic IT WOULD DO THE

326

BASTARD GOOD IF I HAD BLINDED HIM she cackles, THE BLIND
BEAUTY LEE EMANUEL ITD DO HIM GOOD YOU GONNA FUCK
DIANE VALIN she nasalgiggles at Lee SHE LOOKS LIKE A GOOD
SCREW SHES GOT NO MIND YOU KNOW SHES A MODEL YOU
KNOW SHES INFATUATED WITH YOU YOU KNOW SHE LIKES TO
BE SCREWED LEE YOU KNOW THAT she sandseethegiggles at him
WHY SHE WAS ONLY TELLING ME THE OTHER DAY IN THAT DEAD
VOICE OF HERS SHE HAD A MAN WHO DID IT TO HER TEN TIMES
IN ONE NIGHT

Danny is aghast. Whats got into you Rhona

Nothing, stupid. Nothings got into me, you understand?
Nothing. I grind men on my philosophers stone, I transmute
their baser metals LEE KNOWS WHAT IM TALKING ABOUT DONT
YOU LEE the ferriswheel turns but half on the brown fife of the
boardwalk YOU CAN ONLY SEE HALF

But you dont throw sand thats not civilised behavior

You havent the faintest inkling of whats civilised and what isnt,
Danny. You beat rugs. Look at the great composer beating rugs,
she shares the comic secret with Lee, theres a parable, what with
Spinoza polishing lenses, my lenses, he did a personal job on them
her breasts tilt up at Lee, he doesnt want me she turns to Danny,
I could do plenty for him but he doesnt want me, he wants Diane
Valin Can you do it ten times in one night to her Lee eh? Of
course she said she couldnt feel a thing after the fifth time AFTER
THE FIFTH TIME

NINETEEN BILLION SIX HUNDRED AND FOUR

NINETEEN BILLION SIX HUNDRED AND THREE

NINETEEN BILLION SIX HUNDRED AND TWO

NINETEEN BILLION SIX HUNDRED AND ONE

what do you think you can do, Lee, subtract life from death?
Is that what you think you can do

NINETEEN BILLION SIX HUNDRED

NINETEEN BILLION FIVE HUNDRED AND NINETYNINE

NINETEEN BILLION FIVE HUNDRED AND NINETYEIGHT the ponderous ferriswheel turns around the little girls body on the beach

Half the ball. Half life. Half death. Half of Rachel, half of
Levi, be they as frontlets upon thine eyes

Murder your mother as she kills your father, son. But slowly, you fucking coward. Slowly,
ah,
ah,
but in the very slowness of the murder might be the secret of gaining Levi and Rachel neither alive nor dead. Slow, EVERY-BOY,
slow the flyball down. Slow the brunette lass down. Slow Rena down. Slow Norma down. Slow down all mankind. Slow the breaks of the ocean down, stretch all processes out
even as the hands of thy father tremble slowly down the death-bed, and the comber of thy tears break
GREENLY OVER THE MAN
GREENLY
and thy mother yellowly withers into age, yellow as
the dun sand Lee races, throwing cautiontits to the wind
NINETEEN BILLION FIVE HUNDRED AND NINETYTWO TIMES YOUVE GOT TO DO IT TO A FEMALE IN ONE NIGHT TO PROVE YOURE NEITHER
ALIVE NOR DEAD
My father wears hornrimmed glasses.
races across the Wildwood Coney Island Ocean City Will Rogers Atlantic City beach to smash slablike, blinded, rocked, oscillated into the sea, coldbrained watch out. Watch out. If youre killing your mother shes killing you : parimutual process of adoration.
Rhona haglaughs. When you leaving your peasant father and your possessive mother, Daniel?
The sea snaps Lee in two. A riptide bowels him inside out, acrobats him to fling him face downward deep against the coldgrit undersand, gasping with the sandcrabs and the seaworms tickling his ears and then ferriswheels him toes up to smash into the shallow strand, arms akimbo, legs cranelike in the air, the handsome brunette lass standing before him, the
high flyball between her teeth, a moon, a night, and Lee prone on the black beach, solus. There is nothing to do but to go to sleep. Charlottes in Philadelphia with her idiot brother. Lee does

328

not fuck her in the Emanuel bathtub, theres no water for the nineyearold Lee and the sevenyearold Charlotte, and grandma calls from downstairs that Lee has absolutely no idea of what to do with his penis. Grandma Hilda Nathanson, prickless, is wiser than anybody suspects. A prickless woman usually is

I just became a grandmother, Rhona Lyrian says sadly. Im going to marry a barrelchested novelist, poor thing, who believes hes an American combination of Chekhov and Dostoyevsky. Thats what he says, and I cant resist the big athletic thing, so when were with people I will nod yes yes yes when he says hes a combination of Dostoyevsky and Chekhov in America. How can I resist an immigrant, Rhona the philosophers stone says very sadly. Yes yes yes. Oh, the poor thing, she says, as strokes the back of the sand over which Lee trudges, slowly, stretch it out, experience is thus more palatable, he cant pick up a girl handsome as he is, so hell go to his room, the one he shares two weeks with his brother, in the boardinghouse, and undress, and hold his penis and think of a girl, any girl, and masturbate, because hell be alone this early in the evening, its only tenthirty and the sand is heavy in his summershoes. Warm night. The seas behind him, stroking quietly. THIRTEEN MILLION NINE HUNDRED AND SIXTY-EIGHT. A ferriswheel turns halfway in creamcolored tights. The whole beach is loaded in Lee's summershoes, he trudges with sandbags toward the boardwalk and reaches the steps where he unlaces his shoes and empties them of the sand. Rachel: Take off your shoes and. Rena: Lets sit on the bench and take the sand out of our shoes. Diane: Lets sit on the. Tess Rubens: Lets sit on and. The days sunburn is a pair of stiff leather shoes on his skin. Lee would like to unlace his flesh and ease his bones. He supposes his father would, too. Does his father, dying, feel sunburned, hot, stiffskinned? Would his father like a panama hat to be placed over his face while he takes a nap on the bench on the Atlantic City boardwalk on Saturday, the first day of his weekend there at the Maryland Avenue Hotel as he unloads the charcoal bags from his belly? Its only a nap, pop, Lee whispers to his father, and you like Nature so much, so very much, you want a house in the country, A couple cows, Levi smiles, a horse, I guess

329

though I couldnt ride bareback now to see the Devil in the late afternoon sun flashing from the windows of the only church in N'muxt. No Devil, for He is of the life. The flowers. Smell, Rachel, smell. Levi in the summer wears a shirtcollar of rounded corners, rounded as the corners of his jaws, of his temples, of the back of his skull, rounded as his shoulders are the corners of his summer shirtcollar, and a loudly striped tie that Rachel picks for him. And a panama hat. The summers for his two boys and his wife in Atlantic City, three full months while he places one charcoal bag on top of another in the Levi Coal Company yard in Philadelphia, one year after another, THIRTEEN MILLION SIX HUNDRED AND FORTYSEVEN. My son, I will not be here forever. It would be good, he ever so gently adjures Lee, it would be good if you could learn a trade if youre not interested in becoming a professional, subtracting. Empty the shoes of the sand. There are no shoes by his bedside now. Slippers, yes.

Slippers for a dying man.

The boy walks in his bare feet down the hallway, crouching.

He walks in his stockings up the steps to the boardwalk where he puts on his sandless shoes. People stroll. The flesh strolls, the bones saunter, the night warmly lags behind. His brother wont be in the boardinghouse room. Clancys getting drunk somewhere with a wench. Lee wants his brothers wench but he will have her only by himself in the dark room crossing the boardwalk, down the concrete ramp past COCOANUT COVE Louis Armstrongs featured in beercolored neon, Lee brings on a kind of sleepy crying in himself, everyboy should have a girl, even his father should have the girl Christine Novak. Its all right, mother, pops got to have a girl because he wont able to piss on his own grave to keep it green. Its allright, mother, because nobody expects you to straddle his grave to keep it green. And Christine dies of pneumonia, and pop cant piss on her grave to keep it green. Its all right, mother, because pissless time has sand in its shoes, and everybody should have a girl. Paradise she says, the Fundamentalist says Paradise in a cotton dress, sixtyeight years of age, five feet six and half inches, name of Hanora Runnymede, wife of the deceased Rufus Runnymede, Paradise Honora pronounces in her perpendicular voice straight and clear from her severely laced breastless body, ironspectacled and clipeyed as she stands off the shoulder of the Coast Highway and looks the horizon of the Pacific Ocean straight in the eye, Honora Runnymede of Garden City, Kansas, lean of form and face, arms stiff at her sides for her first visit to California, Fundamentalist Honora Runnymede nods her head and says Yes, Paradise, this farmwoman who gives birth to her first child in an isolated farmhouse in the snowdocked wheatfields of Kansas while Rufus trudges to fetch the doctor, her baby comes as she lies on the open sheets of a fresh newspaper and with her ponderous black and silversteel scissors calmly cuts the umbilical cord Paradise, yessir and Levi overhearing irritatingly hums a tune as he crouches with redheaded Terry Shannon on a Pacific palisade TEN MILLION THREE HUNDRED AND EIGHTYSIX :

The sole human on the beach is the little girl twirling her hoop counterclockwise around her waist; doggedly. She is motherless and fatherless on the sand. She is now undoing the record number of revolutions she has made : as an example of classic courage.

A gull nips at a plummet and bulls at a straightaway. A pelican slams the waters to mug a fish. Telephones no longer ring in the old lighthouse converted into a lifeguard lookout station; the brief breakwater extending from the lighthouse stumbles its boulders in dim white chops to the wateredge. Twilight toils up from the night

The tune dont irritate you Levi inquires of the Red Ashfreckled woman, Terry Shannon.

She hums back a no. Hum, Levi, hum.

You hear that woman underneath us? You hear her paradise, Miss Shannon?

She is a long way from home, Levi, for the first time, and paradise is both her refusal and her distillation of nostalgia. I am very ugly, Levi, I wish you would not look at me. I cannot remand you to the custody of your youngest son. Besides, though I do not wish to wound you, your son is alone down there on the beach in the person of that little girl twirling her hoop. Her name is Lee.

331

His rounded shirtcollar face yields a photograph of considerable dignity. He holds a trowel as he stands next to the cornerstone erected for the new Brith Mikveh Synagogue; Levi Emanuel, chairman of the Building Committee, chairman of the School Committee. In the cornerstone are the minutes of the most recent meeting of the assembled Brith Mikveh Congregation, Mr Wohl, President; the minutes of the last meeting of the assembled Brith Mikveh Sisterhood, Mrs Levi Emanuel, Chairlady; the immediately preceding Friday night sermon read by Dr Jonah Silver, Rabbi of Brith Mikveh, whose theme is the radical nature of monotheism, Thou Shalt Have No Other Gods Before Me, and the notation in cipher at the end of the sermon that Mrs Jonah Silver, the Rebbitsen, looks up at her husband with sour contempt and a tremulous longnosed smile; the most recent financial statement audited on Brith Mikveh Synagogue, and the very first; a list of the founders of the synagogue, and its current roster of officers, not omitting the name of its present cantor; a miniature Torah; a Hebrew prayerbook of the Conservative denomination; the minutes of the most recent meeting of the Brith Mikveh Mens Club, and the profane entertainment provided; the score of the most recent game played by the Brith Mikveh Baseball Club, and a list of the players, not omitting the manager's name; a necrology of the past year, not omitting the blindness and death of the optometrist's son, a contemporary of Lee Emanuel, the girl with the hoop, who mocks Lee at a teenage party in Logan for wearing an open byronic collar while the rest of the boys are correctly attired in starched shirt and tie (you understand, of course, that Lee brings about both the blindness and death of the optometrist's son not only in retaliation for the indignity at the party but also in revenge, after Lee has caused the boy's blindness, for the blind young man's nauseous sarcasm when he encounters Rena and Lee on the Atlantic City boardwalk in front of the Ritz Carlton Hotel, upon the blind one remarking in a laughing snarl that if it is true a play of Lee's is about to be produced then he, the optometrist's blind son, will surely be in the audience to listen to the lines and to tell Lee afterwards the value of the play

STRIKE HIM BLIND

332

AND STRIKE HIM DEAD GOD OF MY FATHERS AND GOD OF MY
FOREFATHERS LET THIS OBESE CHURL, THIS HOGLIPPED SON OF
AN OPTOMETRIST ALREADY UNCLEAN, KILL HIM
  KILL HIM
  KILL HIM
in the revolutionary doctrine that Lee Emanuel shall have no
other gods before him); a prayer shawl;
  tvillim;
  a photograph of the Brith Mikveh Congregation assembled on
the lot acquired for the new synagogue; and a photograph of the
children of the members. Levi Emanuel lays the cornerstone. My
fingers, he tells Miss Shannon, are still a little wet and gray from
the mortar. But Lee Secundus doesnt dismay me, Miss Shannon.
Im here to remember the son after whom he is named, the first
Lee, killed by a batted ball. The first Lee, you see, strongly resembles me. Of the three sons of my loins, he is my sole replica,
and he is killed by the god of my fathers and the god of my forefathers. He is my only son, Miss Shannon; consequently, David,
my eldest, flees to Texas, thence to California, thence to Alaska,
and back to California; my youngest, consequently, Lee the
second, retreats into hooped girlhood. I SHALL HAVE NO OTHER
CHILDREN BEFORE ME, LEVI EMANUEL TRUMPETS and adjures the
cantor to make that sound through the shofar, the rams horn, on
Yom Kippur, Day of Atonement; for I have sinned, Levi blows
through the shofar, I have sinned in having no other children before me, because Lee the First is Levi Emanuel, the blond child,
the favored Jew, fair of skin and blue of eye, torn in victorious
challenge from the womb of Rachel, my wife, swarthy of skin and
black of eye, Lee Emanuel the First, Christian Jew, with many
gods before him, not one Jealous One, not Arrogant Prime Mover,
evolved even beyond Christianity to no gods for Lee Secundus
returns one step, he must have at least one god though he mocks
that god, though he shreds him, though he wittily satirises and
curses him, yea, he must have his Father, his God, he must have
me to pillory and to adore, he must have me to pulverize and
to reconstitute, he is an Orthodox Ironic that poor noson of mine,
in his nosonness he must have one god in double strength, whilst

333

Lee the First neither flees from me nor wrestles with me, my godless tenyearold beauty, thus, thus,

Miss Shannon, Levi turns his fetid breath upon her, thus, Miss Shannon, we are here at the end under similar auspices: childless. In Philadelphia neither Ice nor Christ ever fail he hums.

Im the American Victory, myself, Terry Shannon replies, with a head this time, however, thus quite idealistic. The American Victory should really be as headless as the Greeks, and, I suppose, eventually will be when it is exhumed. It will gain decapitation in the inhuman. The unruly redheaded American skull will roll off to leave the orthodox proportions of traditional bodily beauty, and I shall be adored without my ugly Irish head. But now, you see, we pose for ourselves, the most difficult art of all, transitory to be sure, but incomparably exacting, and whelpless. Do not regret the death of your duplicate, Levi; he would not have regretted yours.

Exactly, and I would not have been demeaned. It is in the morning of a man that he is demeaned. My two living sons come at me with lavish hands, David from afar, Lee Secundus at my deathbed. At his majority, Lee Primus would have utterly forgotten me. Had I been wiped out, I would have gained pride. As it is, I die without pride. The crime is that Lee Primus reaches the age of ten and is killed while he only half duplicates me, so I must die only halfforgotten by him, I must die at ten years of age, I must go back to my own ten years of age to expire with any dignity at all, and it is no more than a child's dignity, not a man's. Lee Primus did not grow up for me. Therefore, I die hating the son who is my beloved, that is to say, I die halfhating him, halfloving him, a halfass way to die. He goes abstractedly past the park that day; abstractedly; the very quality that would have erased me from him totally has him killed. I know what that means, Miss Shannon. It means I could not have absorbed the pride he would have conferred upon me; it means that I gave him the quality that, in having me utterly prideful, had to kill him. I could not tolerate the expectation of my total oblivion in him, though this is what I wished for; my giving him that abstractedness was a gamble that I could only halfwin—till he is

334

ten years of age—at which point I strike him down in his mercilessness upon himself. It means I have not the largeness of him in me and that I literally exploded him by injecting that largeness in him. I blew up my boy, I set a dynamite charge, knowing, really, I am capable of but halfpride. Levis roundedcollarcorner cheeks sink into soft smiles of soft pain. On the promise that he could continue his studies in oblivion, Levi whispers, his father persuades him to emigrate from life to death, to join him, join Levi. He had a scholarship in oblivion at ten years of age, which he could have taken advantage of, but I could not bear him away from me; so, abstractedly, he crosses the park and is struck. In the hospital, Miss Shannon,

in the hospital, though the doctors tell me he cannot regain consciousness, that he has sustained a brain concussion,

in the hospital, at his bedside, Miss Shannon, the blond tenyearold boy, half my replica is not better than none,

in the hospital, as the tenyearold blond boy with his face having the rounded collarcorners, and his small form rounded under the white covers, this Lee Emanuel the First, Lee Emanuel the Only, Lee, Lee my only son, his mouth like my rounded colarcorners

THE JOKE

THE JOKE

THE JOKE LOOK WHAT YOU DID TO OUR LITTLE GAYLORD OI OI OI LOOK WHAT YOU DID LEVI TO LITTLE LEE GAYLORD HELL GROW UP TO BE

HELL GROW UP TO BE

HELL GROW UP TO BE DEAD HE WONT GO TO SCHOOL TOMORRA Misericordia Rachel whimpers and carries on

and WHAT DOES LITTLE GAYLORD LEE SAY AT LAST FROM UNDER THE WHITE HOSPITAL COVERS ON THE FLOOR OF THE CROWDED APARTMENT

WHAT DOES HE SAY WITHOUT OPENING HIS EYES

ILL TELL YOU WHAT HE SAYS HE SAYS

OI POPPA YOULL KILL ME YET WITH YOUR FENCY FOCKING

and you promised me, he says, without opening his eyes, you promised me.

335

Did he die, Terry asks, in the middle of the season?

Yes.

You Jews, Terry shakes her head. You Jews, you die most inconveniently, do you not?

On occasion, Lee Secundus wryly replies, that is not so. Even at my tender age I can go into any saloon and order a drink. If the bartender demurs, I merely produce my death certificate;

wily of you, Lee, wily, Terry concedes; but, actually, you abominate saloons; each time you enter the Rendezvous to pick up Rena, your head is lowered, you glance neither right nor left, you choose the farthest table in the farthest corner; that men and women are openly quaffing hard liquor gives your skin a southern drawl, and you must avert your face FIVE HUNDRED AND THIRTY-THREE THOUSAND observe, Levi, how theatrical your little girl becomes at nightfall

MILKBOTTLE H :

as in pretentious musical spectacles, the little girl's body is luminescently limned, and her hoop turns phosphorescently

FIVE HUNDRED AND THIRTYTWO THOUSAND NINETYSEVEN

ON the ebon beach, milkcolored against the black

CANT THE LITTLE GIRL NINA TALK FOR CHRISTS SAKE

It is nothing that we say, Miss Shannon, Levi explains. I am sixtytwo years of age, and Esther Goldstein, Rena's mother, is fiftyone years of age. Solomon, her husband, is busy in the store. Rena and Lee are in the livingroom where a long mirror, above the sofa and paralleling it, both sofa and mirror shaped into some Arabic emblem, hangs tentatively from the wall striped cream and magenta, alternately. Esther and I are in the diningroom, seated at the long table covered by creamtoned damask. It is evening. Next door there must be a dog; I hear him cry, peculiarly: he makes the sound not for another dog; it is a lascivious lament, a sensual dirge. Ruddyfaced, ruddywristed, my irongray hair carefully combed, parted on the side (once it is parted in the center, when I am a young man, so that I am truly softcollarcornerrounded), I lean forward, my elbows on the damask. The sensual body of Rena Goldstein, twisting to my son from the piano stool, makes light of a popular sentimental tune, but

even as she mocks it, Miss Shannon, aye, even as she mocks it it
reacts with pain beneath itself; not in protest, you understand,
but with some shame; and it is that shame, as my son stands at one
end of the piano, his body tousled, his arms folded on top of the
upright and his fingers pouting and his ears frowning, it is that
shame, combining with the dog's concupiscent mourning, that
wanders into us, to Esther and myself, Esther though she is mira-
culously smiling nevertheless wringing her hands, the red glints
of her black hair spotting the dull yellow lustre shed by the cluster
of masked bulbs above the table. She calls me Mr Emanuel; I
call her Mrs Goldstein. She wishes me to bring my wife the next
time; I inquire when Mr Goldstein will be finished his chores in
the store; and we agree that Rena and Lee are startlingly handsome together though the dog next door cries and the sentimental
tune is ashamed. Esther, I see, has that kind of firm, large bosom
that her redglinted black hair and Spanish features demand; her
hips are modest, her legs are slim but rapaciously curved; there is
a girlish greed that erotically splits her into a thousand rapid invitations, and the faint black down on her upper lip is enough
for my testicles to curl up my prick into a bristling mustache; the
roseate creaminess of her complexion is rough enough and lined
enough for an older mouth. I itch redly, I itch mournfully, I
itch mockingly, I itch ashamedly,

I am eating, in brief, at The Last Mirror;

and there is a scheme of

erotically senile incompletion, Lee ejaculates at his father, precisely what I inherit from you and expressed in the numerous
flirtations I have with women that I do not press toward fulfill-
ment, as if in too many instances I am preaged, a JudasChrist,
betraying and betrayed, with numerous itching corpuscles òf senility floating through, the Levi antibodies to the erotic infections,
eating at a succession of Last Mirrors

;and there is a scheme of urbane and charming betrayal. We
have nothing to give to each other, I in my ruddy aging handsomeness, she in her sensual display of Southern Lights. She hardly
dares glance at me while I take my repast in The Last
Mirror. The Magdelene of Esther Goldstein regards me as a full-

balled Christ in softly crucified erection. She smiles softly, she bathes my feet, and we come round to each other through her daughter and my son. I am the Second Man, and the Third Man, and the Thousandth Man she has never had a hundred thousand times over; and she is the Second Woman, and the Third Woman, and the Thousandth Woman I have never had a hundred thousand times over (Christine Novak is my inferior, and I cannot speak of her, not yet, not yet) while a dog erotically keens and a popular sentimental tune is ashamed of the masses of men. Esther has passion and contempt for me; I have passion and scorn for Esther; and both of us are delighted and blushing. She silently apologises for Solomon Goldstein, while I do exactly the same for Rachel Emanuel. Neither of us are identified; we cannot identify each other, for to do so would strain both our hearts in erotic spectacle; oh, not that we do not strain our weakened hearts in many another direction, with work, with anger, with cunning, with dissimulation—yes; but we will not strain our weakened hearts with love. We will not strain our weakened hearts with love for one overpowering and overriding reason, and that is our memory of our youth. We choose in the repast at The Last Mirror not to cast ourselves loose from the sound of troika bells on the outskirts of Odessa, that erminewrapped count and countess flurrying by in the snow of Esther's winter night; I am a virgin at my window, Mr Emanuel, and I have a white moon from the sky she flurries her fingers along the damask tablecloth as the dog floats his mouth toward the Old Testament heavens. And my eyes, Miss Shannon, are wet from Esther's snow; while I refuse to cast myself loose from the Devil flashing from the churchwindows in N'muxt in Lithuania towards which I ride in the setting sun bareback on my horse; I am a boy, Mrs Goldstein, with the Torah in my skull that Satan smites with brilliant laughter. Thus, with painful grins, we betray our age, and we will not love because we insist on our youth. An odd meal, Miss Shannon, at The Last Mirror. So, Esther and I pick at a popular sentimental tune mockingly played by her daughter and loosely listened to by my son, my youngest, my baby, who knows I fall asleep, now, as I read Art, or listen to it, or see it in a painting, but I give him money to keep him alive for it, alive without struggle, for I want no son of mine to be in want as long as I can prevent it. But his Art and any art has me doze; art is very sweet, but sleep is sweeter, and the scenes of childhood sweeter still. For all I know, Miss Shannon, we may live only for Childhood in ourselves; for all I know, we may live only to keep within ourselves as long as we can the First Snow, the First Rain, the First Fire, the First Girl, the First Dance and the First Pride I have before the Chassid as I recite for a full hour from the Five Books of Moses, knowing, as I finish, that I can go on and on and on, and knowing that the Chassid knows this too

but some children may inherit the awful sense of these Firsts of his Father with his own Firsts, Lee protrudes at Levi, so that the Last Mirror breaks in the Son and strews within him little rotting pieces of the Father's childhood; I am very different from you, my son, Levi gently chides him, for I rid myself of my father at a very early age : that was one of my most glorious Firsts. You, on the other hand, Levi goes on grimly, are at your

penis)

;and Esther and I exchange dehydrated drolleries, our hearts quite calm now, for we put all our ecstasies and agonies upon our faces where they may be gratified by a shallow shame. Solomon Goldstein need not be jealous when he enters, nor Rachel spiteful when I return. So. Down there is my little girl Leeboy, the little artist subtracting with his hoop from paradise. Shall we go down and count, Levi courteously inquires of Terry Shannon, so that, as they stroll toward the ocean, Lee selfconsciously strides away from the ocean, the shushcrashing sound of the Atlantic breakers now humming in his ear my hum dont irritate you does it my hum dont irritate you does

it my hum

tuneless, irritating as the sagging, black, naked, angled, open outside stairs that lead up to the boardinghouse proper where the Wildwood Wildcats live for the duration of the summer baseball season. Everyboy mounts them as he holds on to Everyboy's wooden jagged splintered handrail. He mounts to a darkened house and an empty one, the moths and furbodied insects brushing by, ignoring Everyboy. A faint saltwet down sprinkles Everyboy's face. He reaches the deserted porch, his spine an odd rockingchair on its side, his skullhair sprung by errant steelsprings tufting from the gapes of a derelict sofa. Everyboy pauses, clenches hands on the saltwet porchrail. A ferriswheel rockets into the nightsky; the ghost of a tidal wave shudders over Everyboy; boys and girls on the boardwalk cry in dirging lust; there is a dog, there is a cat, there is a big furbodied moth; the night is four-footed and winged; a chilling jazz motif picks at Everyboy's ear-lobe; a spew of curses, fourfooted, spicules down the street; there is a whiff of smoke from Philadelphia, from Mrs Sherman who may very soon catch fire, and Everyboy angrily sneezes; there is a dog and a cat and a moth curdling Everyboys blood STOP HUM-MING THE TUNELESS TUNE, LEVI

and Everyboy rushes, stumbling, into the boardinghouse, bumping into chairs and beds till he reaches the room he shares with his brother Clancy. His father's tuneless tune tyrannizing his ear, Lee lopsidedly undresses, his abstracted smile on a shake-down cruise, the smile ploughing through high seas, his mouth open and his teeth breasting the spumy waters, a rolling in his loins, the Everyboy craft vibrating with remote and sickening shudders he no sooner pulls the single clammy sheet over him than with a tuneless grunt he shuts his eyes and with his left hand clamps over his penis as he encounters the handsome brunette girl first lightly squatting on his chest, her oily black hairs on her inner thighs, the girl faceless now but extraordinarily beautiful, her open thighs directly under Everyboys nose

he sneezes, allergic to oily black hair

with thumb and two fingers Lee nips his penis. Lengthening, the penis dispatches long envoys into Everyboy's bowels and deli-cately prods at his anus while a thick salty white sweetness deli-cately overflows the brunette girls oily black hairs. She squats directly and lightly over the boy's mouth but though he moves an electric light bulb so that it shines harshly on her mount he can-not see the brunette triangle itself, nor can he, widening his eyes though he does to their fullest, manage to see the girlslit, the girl-slit, the magical girlslit. But his prick is rubberystoney now and he

340

encircles it with his fist to ride the skin up and down, up and down, beseeching the handsome brunette lass to sit on top of it and, in a disappointingly invisible twitch of motion she hitches over her swimsuit and soothes down on Lees blushing icepick his fist compressing and decompressing the rigidly molten member, Everyboy's breath grunting at the unseen clamwarm trough of her, he sneezes violently once, twice, three times, the mucus snoring on his upper lip, the girl enigmatically beautiful, her torso thrown this way and that by the elongated icepick plunging at her transparent plastic cunt that Lee is blind to though he snorts his eyeballs to see to see, to see, the snot dribbling down his own thighs, he jabs till he hears the soundless crunch of her, the plastic vagina shattering, his fingers pounding in his nose, his temples congested and his prick abruptly sliced

sliced from top to root

a larval gelatinous mass of luminescently white blood :

bolting its pigs;

swallowing fat bellies

to vomit without nausea, clashingly lapping; having eaten without satiety, having gulped without volume, the whole side of the room slides off the bed and down the street and over the beach and, in a brief screeching spasm, enters the mild lukewarm dimensionless billows of the sea, the whole Lee Everyboy contracted into his penis, itself reduced to a slab of idly bleeding seaweed, rocking,

rocking,

nudged slowly back to the shore where, slowly, Lee gradually regains size so that he can crawl back to the hot sand, the brunette lass unable to observe him but nevertheless reiterating BUT THEYLL BE BACK

BUT THEYLL BE BACK; and Lee reassuringly replying

NOT FOR A COUPLA HOURS

NOT FOR A COUPLA HOURS

The music is lovely, isnt it?

His father helps all the time. He provides the background of a tuneless tune but now Everyboy is in the enviable position of lying flat on the hot hot sand directly in front of the handsome

brunette lass while she gazes out to sea and not for a moment
suspects that Everyboy stares uncompromisingly and joyously at
her now naked black mat of crotch

BUT THEYLL BE BACK I TELL YOU

NOT FOR A COUPLA HOURS; incredible the manner in which
Leeboy and the brunette lass communicate with each other without the girl being aware of Everyboy, a species of the circum-
adoration of the globe, a condition of Satan and his tuneless tun-
ing fork, of course it could be as marvellously simple as a baby
crawling to a grownup girl to observe at first hand the curious
black twitching creatures on the girl's genitals

JESUS CHRIST I CANT I CANT I HAD NO IDEA YOU WERE SO BIG
IT SCARES THE SHIT OUTA ME

YOU DONT HAFTA BE SCARED ONCE ITS INYA NOTHINLL HURT

BUT JESUS I NEVER SAW ONE THAT BIG ITS PRETTY GODDAMN
BIG

AW COME ON I WONT HURTYA

WELL GO AHEAD BUT FOR CHRISSAKE TAKE IT EASY

SURE SURE

DONT DONT DONT THAT HURTS I TOLD YOU ITD HURT YOURE
TOO GODDAMN BIG FOR ME IM SCARED IM SCARED

imagine a grown girl being scared of a little baby, Everyboy
snorts to himself, but the marvellousness of it that the brunette
lass continues to gaze wideeyed and expressionless at the Atlantic
Ocean as she keeps her thighs wide open and continues to insist
that EVERYBABY's little prick is too gigantic and the baby gurgles
his words to allay her fears meanwhile his eyes now but an inch
away from her black crotch so he can observe minutely the crawling black creatures thereon, Besides theres tuneless background
music he murmurs goddamn his father whats he doing here on
the beach with his ruddy thick blond wrists and kindly face I
dont need you EVERYBABY informs him I can see for myself I
CAN PUT IT IN ALL BY MYSELF YOU THINK BABIES DONT KNOW
ANYTHING WELL YOU JUST WAIT AND SEE Dr Newman would you
as a favor to Rena and me because you know Im entering the
army and we wont be able to get married for a while and we want
very much to have sexual intercourse and you see Renas a virgin

and I dont want her to be hurt so would you I understand this sort of thing is done you know so itll make it easier for us and could you also at the same time fit her for a diaphragm

Of course, Lee, its no favor at all, theres nothing to it, send her into me.

Thank you very very much

No, no, no thanks due, Lee, just drop in to see me whenever you like, Dr Newman's oriental yiddishness crumpled in plastic yellow glints, I like talking with you, his feet not quite reaching the floor as he sits at his desk, bubblethighed, his lips lapping at some secret MILKBOTTLE H while he studies for his medical exams under the Atlantic City sun on the beach, permanently burned, falling asleep into the yellow sun, I will make sure, he brutally reassures himself, that virgins are no longer virgins, that violation after all is the most silken of crudities, the softest of horrors, that politics is mans noblest calling, the cruciform Recipe, the prescription of God, the stigmata on the crotch that the female bears, here we go nailing ecstasy to the cross Dr Newman turns to go from the office, youll have to excuse me, Lee, Im expected at the hospital, and if there be vinegar to wash her vagina I shall bathe it myself, poor female, the hot and dusty clitoris come a long journey from the City of God, come to announce to Abraham and Isaac and Jacob and Moses I will lead thy people out of bondage, for I am the one angel that sits between God's feet, Angel Clitoris, and I am forever dispatched by God to succour Man, Recipe, Recipe, yes, Lee, have Rena come in her groin is solidly covered by crawling black ants that are so numerous that they even bridge across the crack in EVERYBABYS pavement,

Oh, oh Im telling you it wont hurt

Im not afraid itll hurt Dr Newman

Youre a brave one, Rena

No, not really, not but a monstrous giant of a black ant with a cracked white plaster face and a gigantic white ball between its jaw starts running across blowing a tuneless tune on a scarlet fife

You gotta let me try

No no

the Frankenstein monster of a black ant dancing across the pulsating black crotch the monster differentiated from the others by his plaster white face the crack sizzling like lightning across it

THE FIFE OF THE DANCING ANT AXES OFF THE SURF

ICE NEVER F

CHRIST NEVER F

MILKBOTTLE H

takes a running leap from his own cracked whiteblack face, the white puffball beteen his jaws, and flies

HIGH INTO RIGHTFIELD, leeboy's cousin Charlotte whitely dripping from his saffron oriental jaws in the late aquamarine sky palely ripped by MILKBOTTLE H'S LIGHTNING BUT I DONT WANT THE BALL AND I DONT WANT TO CATCH IT EVERYBABY WHIMPERS

THE BLACK MOON IS BLINDING MY WHITE EYE

IM TELLING YOU IM GOING TO SCREAM IF YOU STICK IT IN

I CANT CATCH IT WITH MY BARE HANDS CHARLOTTE I CANT CATCH ANYTHING WITH MY BARE ITS SO LONG AND THICK YOURE A MONSTER YOURE A MON ALL BALLS ARE TOO HEAVY FOR ME A BABY TO CATCH CHARLOTTE

WHANGO AND WHANGO RENA PUMPS UP AND DOWN ON DR NEWMAN RINGS PRICK MY GRANDFATHER HARRY RING HE COMES AT ME WITH A KNIFE YOURE A LIAR CHARLOTTE YOURE A LIAR GRAMPA HARRY RING IS DEAD I GOT TO CHANGE MY SHIRT ITS SOAKING WET I DONT HAVE THE PERSPECTIVE TO CATCH A HEAVY BALL JESUS CHRIST EVEN LOOK AT YOUR TESTICLES THEYRE LIKE WASPNESTS HANG ON TO YOUR TITS BABY HELEN NATHANSONS ARE SOMETHING TO GRAB AT

THE BALLS COMING DOWN

CATCH IT

NO

THE BALLS COMING DOWN

CATCH IT

SAVE THE GIRL DOCTOR AND

LET

THE

BABY

D

LET

THE
BABY
D
ie..
.... let
wheres lee
were calling for him mrs emanuel
shit my names rena call me rena
were calling for him
where is he
we dont know
didnt he leave word
were trying to find out
he mustve left word
calm yourself mrs e
the names rena what did i have
rest
what did i have why dont you tell me wheres my husband
were trying to locate him
but i felt the
here take this
i dont want it
im afraid youll have to
wheres lee wheres lee wheres lee wheres lee wheres lee wheres
lee wheres leeeeeeeeeeeeeeeeeeeeeeeeeeeeeeeeeeeeeeeeeeeeeeeeeeeeeeee
LEES DROWNING GODDAMN YOU YOU BITCH RENA LEES
UNDERSTAND
DROWNING IN ROCKY RIVER IN THE FUCKING UNITED STATES
ARMY DROWNING YOULL RIP ME APART

Lee jolts upright in the bed, jaws aching. A scream is smashing, smashing, smashing against the jaws of his ears, then abruptly muffled

SHUT UP you bitch, Ill kill you make another sound.

Dont hurt me, Vince, please. Its just youre too big

SHUT up or Ill smash your cunt in, now spread your fuckin legs as wide as theyll go, hear me?

Lee, stiffly upright in the bed, wants his brother Clancy never

345

to come. Nobody. Let whats going on the next room do so without interruption. Everyboy clenches his prick, erects it in a moment. Fuck her, Vince. Terror sweats the boys prick up while he muffles it with his fist, the prick wont cry out. Rip her apart, rip the girl apart, Vince, jab her, jab her, jab her, maybe there'll be a murder, MURDER WITH THE WEAPON OF A PRICK

VAGINACIDE like the murder of small business in the united states of america Levi he talks to himself in the deathbed;

where is the wonder of the flying black ant now, Lee grips the bedrail by his father;

like the murder of all the middlemen in the united states of america on American Street in Philadelphia, cobblestoned and grasstufted because so few drive their cars parallel to the PennsylvaniaReading Railroad freight tracks, the warehouses and the silos and the courtyard urinals of Kensington. The plants with their RECEIVING platforms paralleling the tracks. RECEIVING MILKBOTTLE H nothing like cold milk sveetest there is Levi nods to Lee who sees his father endlessly tilting MILKBOTTLE H to his ruddy lips. In the wheelchair on the puffily hot June day Levi Emanuel sits upright, his spiculethin forearms resting on the black metal arm supports, his once bulging biceps no longer in evidence, his upper arms mere slim tubular shafts. Levi sits upright by virtue of a pillow propped behind his back; even so, after a few moments, his torso tends to falter to one side, and the nurse rights it, rights not Levi but his torso since his head remains perfectly perpendicular to the stone porch step on which the huge rubbertired front hoopwheels of the wheelchair are braked. Levi himself needs no righting: this is clear from the insistence of his skull as his torso tilts, the angle made by the latter to the former resembling a phase of Hindu dance, but the human rights the god even as the nurse does Levi, so that no banal symbols come to rescue Lee from the real sight, and the temple bells desist before the son can issue the order for them to be struck; however, expectation of symbol and bell tattle a niche at the corner of Lees mouth, which faintly wags, the puppy of Everyboy. The color of Levis eyes is very nearly that of the stagnant green of the little pond on the farm of Joshua Nathanson, Lee's maternal grandfather—on whose bank stands the abandoned outhouse; very nearly, the difference being that while the pond's water is scumgreen, Levi's eyes are a green roughly opaque, a green ridged and ragged, and in the process of being deepened rather than polished by stone; and Levis outhouse, not yet abandoned, is contained in the pissbottle underneath the wheelchair and concealed by the fall of his robe, an outhouse in which Lee cannot possibly hide to flick varicolored snotballs on shimmering cobwebs. The cobwebs are cleared, and Lee's sinuses are not stuffed; nor can he hear his mother calling that it is time to go; the young man does not even feel, as a matter of plain fact, an urge to cry, nor any urge on this pollenheavy day to sneeze; he breathes quietly and unperturbedly through his nose. Nobody looks at Lee, not the nurse, not the mother, not Norma, his wife; everybody regards Levi, who pays none of them heed, for Levi gazes outside, looms his eye through the long pane of glass set in the outer porch door, across the Roosevelt Boulevard through the house once owned by his sister, Bella Zion, and his sister's husband, Sidney, who dies one year after his wife despite a prefrontal lobotomy performed upon him as an emergency measure to relieve his constantly increasing pathological melancholia; Levi focuses, beyond the house of his sister, on the Outside. It is a very simple Outside consisting of three persons, his grandson Richard Emanuel, his office manager and chief weigher at the Levi Coal Company, Henry Feinstein, and his principal distributor of bagged coal and charcoal, Gene Hertzog; these three form a partnership offering to buy from Levi the Levi Coal Company; they comprise the Outside that Levi, dying, visions on the puffily hot June day in the wheelchair on the stone porch step, the Receiving Platform that grows from three to many times three, the Outside that either will efface the Levi Coal Company entirely or incorporate it as a unit in a larger organization, a process that suggests to Levi a positively jaunty skip over his immediate issue, David and Lee, who expedite the process by default, who are themselves, Levi recognizes, surreptitiously jaunty in the default. Nor would it have mattered at all had Levi studied the Law after having immigrated to the United States, for the same process would have taken effect, with the one difference that Levi's rancor might have been deeper in that his devotion to a metaphysical Idea would have gradually assumed the shape of a fealty to the philosophy of corporate enterprise. It is a curious victory that Levi relishes in the stainless steel wheelchair, the hoop for the moment relinquishing both addition and subtraction on the tawny sandy beach of the eye; his victory is that his rancor is a shallow one;

it is no small matter that a man for the time of sixtyone years rise in the morning at five oclock to labor through the day and return to his home at eight in the evening

to achieve at the age of seventyseven, dying, a shallow rancor at weighing the substance of his life.

But the shallow rancor is short of perfectability, for Levi must concede the existence of a grim fury caused by the getting of the shallow rancor. But it is a special grim fury, all the more frightening by virtue of its specialness: for the fury is a jaunty one; it lurches for joy in Levi's heart, a heart that revolves hooplike around a girlboy's hips, and that girlboy is Levi himself at seventyseven, dying. And it is the Outside, the three males, Richard Emanuel, Henry Feinstein and Gene Hertzog, who count now the subtracting revolutions of the Levi Coal Company hoop. Levi Emanuel's heart whirls in a happy fury, and this he knows he will at last find impossible to tolerate, for he condemns it. It is for this very condemnation, Levi further knows, that he surrenders his desire to study the Law in order to go into business. A happy fury toasts the beginning of his life in the United States, a happy fury passed on to his sons who can only condemn it as he himself does. If he could but return to his sensation of the shallow rancor, he would take his last breath now; but that shallow rancor now is merely an idea and rapidly becoming a misty fantasy. Levi tries to peer through and beyond the Outside in order to retain at least the idea of shallow rancor, but the three males persist in seeing him the girlboy, and he cannot break their counting; the Outside will not grant him his shallow rancor; the Corporation will not even allow Levi Emanuel a sense of regret, for in the very process of subtracting from him, the Corporation

348

justifies him, justifies his Small Business, certifies and approves it, so that his sixtyone years of unremitting labor lead crowningly to the Outside, and his happy fury can have no bounds. Boundless in itself, the man himself must limit it by condemnation. And what measure of satisfaction the condemnation itself has in Levi is itself spoiled by the gradual reduction of his energy to condemn. He must hand over his condemnation to his sons; his must redouble theirs, for theirs alone is inadequate to nullify totally his substance for them; but he finds he loses the energy to hand his condemnation to them; and he hears a little chirp in his heart, a little tuneless chirp to the effect that the United States of America certifies and approves Levi Emanuel and the whole of his seventy-seven years.

Chirp. Chirp.

Emotionless, Levi Emanuel listens to the chirping. His head lolls. The nurse advises Lee that the old man be wheeled back to his bed, it is obvious he is tired and sleepy. Theres nothing to be concerned about, the nurse reassures Lee. You can see a little smile treads his lips,

chirp. Chirp.

ICE NEVER F

CHRIST NEVER F

MILKBOTTLE H

LETS CHANGE P

LETS CHANGE ORGANGRINDERS RED ASH WHITE ASH RED ASH WHITE ASH RED WHITE RED WHITE

RED WHITE AND GREEN

CLANCY MANN HORSES HORSES CRAZY OVER HORSES

HYMIE KRAUSE HIT IN THE HEAD BY A HORSE HOOF

POW

I TOLD YOU CARLA COFFMAN

HORSES HORSES CRAZY OVER

SCRATCH CLANCY MANN

LEVI SCRATCHES LEE

SCRATCHES

HORSES HORSES CRAZY

349

HOME STRETCH

dont you think if a thief wants to come in, a locked door wont make any difference :

he takes a walk :

he goes flying :

he crouches and he creeps :

a small moth : Levi Emanuel; Lee One; Lee Two; Gail Greene; St Red; Jeanne d'Moth :

CHIRP CHIRP

MILKBOTTLE H

TILT

HORSES HORSES

THEYRE OFF :

Through the revolving door of Thompsons Cafeteria located at 16th and Chestnut Streets Rena Emanuel precedes the young man Clement Lichtenstein, childhood acquaintance of Norma Emanuel. It is midnight. Through the wimpled plateglass window of the cafeteria may be seen, sitting alone on a scarlet leatheretted tubular steel chair drawn up to a green formicatop table, the long stoopbowed convexity of Lee Emanuel roundshouldered over a tall white coffee mug. The plateglass window is a bright brownish orange wash to Clement Lichtenstein just before he enters the cafeteria; once inside, the window is black, in which is reflected a dim bright brownish orange, green wimples, lustreless scarlet, a white tip, a lustreless t-shirted convexity in the lower right hand corner of the cafeteria near the window as Clement slips in so as not to be nudged by the revolving wing of the door. Lee, Red grins to Clement. Of course, Clement indulges. A great dim scarlet block is reflected on the window behind Lee; then a lustreless threerunner chromium tray rail scales on the window to the ceiling; a coffee urn in muffled chrome; unidentifiable foods in dimmed white plates behind glass on glass; two widely separated attendants in grayed white uniforms; eightyseven empty tables; three hundred and fortyeight empty chairs at the tables; restrooms : ladies, mens; a dark red wall; dim steel antlers screwed to the wall for coats, hats; dimmer brownish orange lighting fixtures. Through the plateglass window, from the inside, may be descried a receding highspeed trolley; dark gray pavement; lighter gray cobblestones; and the glass on glass of Bonds Clothes across the street. I cant seem to get the Adelphia Hotel Copper Bar out of mind, Lee stands Id like you to meet Clement Lichtenstein hes been wanting to meet you for some t

Very glad to

Shes been talking about y

Where we had the Kensington High School dance

Yes.

Seemed copperchromed, the Copper Bar, Lees faceflesh, coppersquared and wimpled, lustrous bronze I dont dance very well at all, he apologizes to Clement, the Assyrianskulled lad and St Red having walked together from their ballet classes where I met Clement she reminds her husband on the east side of City Hall Clement says to Lee lets go into Lintons theres something youve got to understand of course its entirely theoretical

TEORY Levi mumbles.

Is it about Red

Theoretically

Each with a cup of coffee are three people in Thompsons Cafeteria : Clement Lichtenstein, Red Emanuel, Lee Emanuel on scarlettopped tubular steel chairs, their elbows on green formica in the lower right hand corner of the wimpled plateglass window bright brownish orange, Lees face in bronze copperchrome, a Copper Bar on his face never entered out of a black curly night hairing his head. Lee is new; Rena is twentyone years of age; Clement is a sandyhaired Assyrian of kinkyhaired age in angular sandstone, kinked angles clawing kinked sandwashed eyes, one basreliefed sandstone side of his skull setting off the smaller sandstone wing of the opposite side; Lee black copperchromed, Rena mochacreamed and orange, Clement gray and picking and pecking and poking from a longexposed sandstone tablet, a smile kinked on his tawny lips, his fingers delicate in stone, briefbodied as a preserved gray moth in the lightest of sandstones, barely to be discerned but kinkvoiced, commandingly urbane, resonantly scratching in basso profundo the Clement Lichtenstein of the Assyrian Ballet Company in sandstone tights through the brown

351

orangebright plateglass window, his body scratching on glass while a midnight cafeteria empties behind him, empties on a sweat-pimpled Philadelphia summer night black coffee into a white mug. A navyblueshirted policeman on the beat peers suspiciously into the Bond Clothes plateglass window; homosexual male mannikins, weightlessly dacroned and archstarchly lisplipped, bronzed and greened, make dummy faces at the uniformed man weighted by the gleaming brass circles of cartridges, the black revolver and the black nightstick he swings menacingly only to pass on quickly to Nan Duskins next door where, relieved, he gazes on the lesbian mannikins who shyly cast down their dummyeyes and severely flatten their breasts under ivory frock and pale mauve. Grinning tightly, the cop loglags across Chestnut Street, the pale gleam of mauve steel cartracks in sweptback wings west and east toward the stolid squat ponderous massive MILKBOTTLE H lit ivorily to enhance the gigantic H in cursive Tudor black, a scarlet police squadcar slowly idling west, a hail to the cop on the beat who taps his nightstick against the Thompsons Cafeteria plateglass window to attract the two whiteuniformed attendants who remain as distant to each other as ever, one smoking under an electric clock, the other smoking under none, the white crumpled stovepiped head of the shortorder cook in profile at the order unglassed window as, through lowered spectacles, he runs index finger down the morning newspaper niched columns. Duke Montaigne, six feet seven inches tall, tilted at the neck, tilted at the waist, tilted at the knee, a curved obeisant knee mustache, wash brown, stumbling from upper lip, pauses tiltedly in front of Thompsons Cafeteria pale mauve plateglass window, his six feet seven inches a childs elongated crayon stick, black. He rubs his own pale brown crayon skull against the glass and cups his blue-tinted pinknotveined eyes, the blue staining his clipped cheekbones, to peer within for far friend or hazy acquaintance to lap a kinked arm about and bring to his apartment of thirtyseven cats to share a glass of sherry and crook a peek at the most voluminous collection of pornographia in Philadelphia if hazy friend or far acquaintance can find restingplace among the thirtyseven cats and flip aside catturd or blot away catpiss to enjoy a tilt at sher-

352

pornograph and the brokenboned wrist of Duke Montaigne who commences at his wine at lunch in the section of Philadelphia known as Frankford in fury and fear Lee accompanies St Red up the wooden stepboards of the Number 5 trolley at Frankford Avenue and Orthodox heading south where he works respectably at a respectable jewellers never losing a day's work at the repairing of watches, the small hand of his arm and the big hand of his leg working clockcounterwise round the square dial of Duke Montaignes face, a bluetinted ivory. By five on whatever timepiece Duke is drunk, a tiny tremble tickling his control but insufficiently startling to notify his employer for whom he has worked a quarter of a century of his condition. Duke leaves. Duke enters a saloon, shivering with sherry. By midnight he is broken in three places, neck, waist and knee unacquainted with Clement Lichtenstein or Rena Emanuel. Duke Montaigne believes, however, that he recognizes a Lee Emanuel and forthwith he waves thirtyseven cattongues at him through the window in whining glee. A Lee Emanuel. A Lee Emanuel. A shape out of Horn and Hardart acquaintances, a lawyer Silas Klein, a composer Mark Fahn, a block of clock a stained felt snapbrimmed hat tugged down over its dial, one never sees the top of the block of the clock though milkbottle h silas klein is lit with an infernally red radiance and infernally pouring white so Duke Montaigne for one quarter of a century dares not raise his eye, broken in a fourth place, one two three four NINE THOUSAND THREE HUNDRED AND SIXTYTWO THE HOOP AROUND THE GIRL ON WILL ROGERS BEACH IN CALIFORNIA CLOCKWISE NOW COUNTERCLOCKWISE NO SOONER ADDED THAN SUBTRACTED AND NO SOONER SUBTRACTED THAN ADDED SO THAT THE COUNT GOES BACK AND FORTH BACK AND FORTH BECAUSE

LITTLE GIRLS MUST LOSE CONTROL

BUT TICKINGLY SO

SO THAT HER EMPLOYER SEES NO STARTLING DIFFERENCE

SHE REMAINS EMINENTLY RESPECTABLE THIRTYSEVEN CATS REMAIN EMINENTLY RESPECTABLE NOBODY SUSPECTS THE GIRLS COLLECTION OF PORNOGRAPHIA EIGHT HUNDRED AND NINETYONE

TWENTYSEVEN

SIX MILLION FIVE HUNDRED THOUSAND AND THREE NORMA AND
LEE DARE NOT RAISE AN EYE AS THE GIRL FIGHTS A LOSING BATTLE
FOR CONTROL HOW MUCH CAN ONE EXPECT OF A LITTLE GIRL IT IS
THE CRIME OF THE PEOPLE ON THE BEACH TO HAVE EXPECTED
PERFECT CONTROL;

no, Duke Montaigne for twentyfive years dares not glance
above the level of his own eyes

fortunately he is six feet seven inches;

it may be assumed he is born never to look above the level of
his own eyes;

it may be assumed he is born at the level of his own eyes;

Silas Klein informs Lee Emanuel that Duke Montaigne is dead
at fortyfive years of age;

we may deem ourselves fortunate, Lee intones, if we too can
die at the level of our own eyes

but Lee's eyes hiss as they scratch across Thompsons Cafeteria
plateglass window recognizing the drunken Duke Montaigne, so
that the Duke's eyelids break off at their tops. Broken in six places,
sherry pornocatman Duke Montaigne uncups his eyes and peers
down at his fingernails, dirty, ridged, clenched corrugations. A
Lee Emanuel does not know him, Duke knows, because the Lee
already has two unknowns sitting with him in a clocklessly clocked
cafeteria. Duke dares no longer look at the Leeclockless, but if
Duke can follow the sandals at his feet, he will find the way home
to cats and pornographia and sherry. Perhaps that other owner
of cats, the toothless blond painter Sam Abrams, waits for Duke
patiently; tomorrow a clock awaits Duke's repair, a clock he may
look down upon, so Duke Montaigne begins to weep. He thinks
of a clock he can look down upon, and to which he may lovingly
attach a little hand and a big hand and perhaps a very little hand,
the kind that ticks the seconds. So he takes his hand and lightly
steadies the wobbling adamsapple in his throat. There isnt a pornographic clock in the whole universe, he happily confides to himself, commencing to follow the sandals at his feet. Time, being
sexless, Duke Montaigne thinks, has emptied Thompson's Cafeteria absolutely; no wonder there isnt anybody inside. And Lee
Emanuel knows that the brown orange wash that is the cafeteria

354

is absolutely empty at 16th and Chestnut Streets in Philadelphia midnight of the Philadelphia summer evening, Rena Emanuel and Assyrian Clement Lichtenstein notwithstanding, because Duke Montaigne crawls back and forth, all six feet seven inches of him, back and forth through Lee Emanuels intestines, clocks and sherry bottles tied to the catintestines tail as the grossly fat Rena Emanuel and the grossly thin Lee Emanuel, married yesterday on Lees furlough, board the westbound train at the Pennsylvania North Philadelphia station, the train stockblocked to the couplings with travelling servicemen so that Rena and Lee must sit gingerly on their valises in the aisle till an empty seat happens at Pittsburg the American Legion convention, state, and Rena singing at the Sunset Crowbar where a bounceeyed bouncer draws Lee aside to tell him about lizzies and a murder

GARDEN CITY, KANSAS

the sign on the clapboard snowdrifted depot informs at two in the morning, Rena and Lee the sole survivors of the westbound train who put down their twisted limbs on the wooden platform blackened out of the snow by the horizontally plunging fiftymile anhour wind careening off the stupendous slopes of the Rockies, the blizzarding stony shot of snow high, kilted and flaring in swatches of swirl in the Kansas nightsky;

About all I can manage is a slow waltz Lee grimly apologises to Rena as he stumblingly accompanies the girl from the dancefloor to the flagstoned terraces circling the countryclub. It doesnt matter, Rena assures him. Grimly Lee touches the girl to a halt so he can turn for a moment to the graduating class of the Kensington Highschool For Girls. The maidens and their escorts, whitejacketed and blacktrousered, swirlgowned and flowered, dance high above the polished ballroom floor. Oh theres Carla and her fiance Rena points, it was awfully sweet of them to drive us here wasnt it. Lee grunts assent. Theyre going to be married next week, Sonny Bond is the one person who really understands her, and he doesnt mind her headaches. He owns a recording company, Lee. He loves whatever she does. Mostly, she reads. You saw her library, didnt you? Shes read so much more than I have. She wants to act but she hasnt been able to do much about it

355

because shes in bed so much from her headaches. How small and dark she is, isnt she Lee? but so lovely, so exquisite, and Sonnys heights just right for her. Hes very tender to her, all the time. I think theyll be very happy, dont you? Lee nods, whitejacketed. I love my corsage, Lee, and Im glad you could take me tonight, do you know that? because I do know how you hate these affairs and I think its very sweet of you and it really doesnt matter that you cant dance I really dont care, all that matters is that youre here with me you know I couldve graduated when I was fifteen if Idve kept up with my studies I had a secret look at my IQ and it was a hundred and sixty but I practically stopped going to classes when I was fourteen and then when I met you oh, Lee, Lee. Is my gown all right? Im so big, Im glad youre so tall, darling. I just want to look at the dancers a moment longer, Lee says softly. Thats all right, Lee, as long as you like. As long as you likes, the children, sixteens and seventeens and eighteens, serrating through the chandeliers hoop from which clinktingle lozenged crystals to the clutchup and the brakeless flushdown of the dancers breathaphragm, though a crinklecrystal here and a kinklecrystal there stutterstrikes in contrastroke from a breezebrittle and a windloop lackeying or lolloping from the bellowsdark without, here a chicklelight and there a flickalight tanglesmocking a dancechilds lock of hair shaken to reflector floor to leap at and miss the taken toss of organdy, to fall again and restore, reblaze the ivory curls from oaken parquet, so do the ligament steps littercollide and parry, liftlock and lip a linger, churn some and hang a rest, the chin deftdaft under a whirlaneye, slickducting and swirlaflood toward and uptoward the center of the shudder of the chandelier as long as you likes, as long as you likes by collarclip to the begabeard for the night, broaden a shoulder for the ancient chandelier of the world scraped to a burn, chafed to a chaste incandescence, made moistly cold for boys and girls in archfoot and tearducts of cheekdowned toes as long as you likes, as long as you likes the sixteens and the seventeens and the eighteens to the chattertungstens of the chandeliers wishingwellhoop, cast up thy hearts to the electric, lord, as long as I like tell me, lord, as long

356

as I like, Carla, for the plumsized embryo in thy skull, give it a name but give no names to the long as you likes on the oaken pulses of the calfroom floor, give the sixteens and seventeens and eighteens no names, their most wish flung highest and throughest but crestcaught and faceted, refaceted and shyfracted by their own breaths on lozenged crystal clockwise and counterclockwise, and the stooping, sudden sneer updrafting of the bitbreeze and clipwind from the brittle bellows of the wind outside, so that the as long as you likes must trough a beat, must dip their maying in a flip of crystalmissed mist glimpsed beneath bouffant and loosened cummerbund though they lord a snort at the bottom prism

that bottom prism the apple of adam and eve dropped evolutions ago far down into the earth where, subjected to the endless and incessant pressures of the stomping feet of the sixteen and seventeen and eighteen year old dancers, generation upon generation,

is slowly transformed into the purest crystal prism and dug out by the sixteens and the seventeens and the eighteens

to hang at the bottom, slowly swinging, swinging lowly, of the crystal chandelier,

for the dancing of the sixteens and the seventeens and the eighteens as they bob around, bob under, the orchestra playing the slang of the evolutions,

to try and catch with newnerved neck and plucking jaw and snakesnaring teeth

venom where is thy sting

at the crystal apple of adam and eve

never to drop again, for the sweet succulent substitutions have transpired, the sixteens and the seventeens and the eighteens, who fall themselves from the chandelier hoop, fleshreflections of the crystals, fall away in spurts of spiral, in slings of white net and scold pink bodice, in black metalcreased trouser and sweatbitten patent leather, fall by flattening nipple and dullgraded groin, by tresses tumbling and circled waists secanted, by fingertips nervelessly decanting and the eyes of the sixteens and the seventeens

357

and the eighteens with little bits of earth in their corners as they begin in their dancing to walk, walk, walk toward boysroom and girlsroom, as short as you cans

do you see, Rena, the tang of an apple smarting his throat.

In a way. But you said you had something to tell me, the mochacreamcolored girl subtends Lee toward the curving stone balustrade that bounds the terraced flagstones, dim pink, mauve and aquamarine beneath their feet, the moon crabveined, runningsored and the color of a rotten orange bulgeteated above the orangemilking evergreens. The cleft broadens between Renas breasts; her brow broadens in shadowed ivory above the thickened frontal bone; her breasts milk the shadowed rottenorange brasses of her hair slurring down her temples to blunder on the great mochaflamed slopes of her shoulders; her fleshpores suck slickly at the mucid nightair to amplify her ugly magnificence, her lips verging on the negroid, her nose slumbrously semitic, the girl highhipped and longlegged and engined by the vacuous virginity of her eyes taunting the mortar and pestle of her loins.

Have a sliver of apple, Lee lightly offers, leaning alackanight against the warm stone balustrade.

Never mind the dancers, Rena says.

I do mind them.

I dont. You have something to tell me. Im a slim girl, she says. And slim she is, profiling to Lee, her breasts flocking to the air, her arm a slender span to his bicep, her smile the most aerial truss the woods and the dimming orange of the night can scentingly trust to devise for the dipping cantilever of her Lee, farpained she is awaiting the testweight of his leaststress borne on single accent is the girls giveyield : but she is a springback and peasantdocked.

Yes, Lee twists his eyelashes. No ringworm. But its very difficult, prepare thy stutter, mix of intent and compel. Ive never said this before because I dont want to hurt.

The reverse is the truth, Rena knows : youve never said this before because you never before wanted to hurt, but we will not make Lee privy to the truth because he will not know how to keep it so. Besides, he has hurt the female all along by not saying it, the I love you; he is more cavalier than cavalier by not having

358

said it, surarrogant. It is an enormous contempt that he does me by informing me he has never said it, he makes me more afraid than ever, he has not learned how to make a promise and renege, he has not learned how to commit and to withdraw from the commitment, but I must allow this for he wishes me to, and to his wishing of it is a fleshly cast. The complete truth of the matter is that he has never wanted to hurt so much so clearly. He hurts a female more deeply by not saying it, but he does not get to the female, he does not even recognize the fact that he deals with a female; he has not dared to sex the person he dealt with. But he sexes me, or at least believes he does, in which may repose an even greater hurt in that he does not sex me as I am sexed; he may sex me as he is sexed, in which case I remain yet one step off, one person off; if he gets to himself in this Rena instance, I shall have a hurt I shall never have experienced, for there shall be years in which I am Leesexed; but it may be I am already Leesexed, in which case we are already married, we are already identical, and he feels free to say he is himself, knowing I am not myself bound to betray him, but that as soon as he comes to me as I will be he will urge me toward betraying him : he has a solution to remain Lee, by my thrusting him back upon himself, he recognizes the potential thrust of him toward himself to be accomplished by me, as if he would be pounded by himself, as if I have that within me to better bolt himself upon himself, never to realize what the wounds would be within me when those Rena-bolts go home in him for their very locking to him will prevent his sight of their origin. This is what possibly makes it so difficult for him to tell me he loves me, his sense of the fact that I will rid myself of what is not me and give it to him, and he is afraid of my bolts bolting him, afraid of his being what he really is so that then he must really contend with me without being able to see me hurt, to bleed, to embrace me without hearing my agony, to hold me while I scream and shrug off the scream, that it is but a sound and not an agony, for who can know my agony but myself, therefore do not feel it; to feel my agony is to be a liar to oneself. Lee has the fear that, while he will not in fact hear my agony, not really, he will nevertheless interpret the shape of my lips as such,

359

insist to himself that he actually hears it and feels and must react to it, and he is fearful now in understanding that that may not be love—the interpretation of me. Love is not interpretation; love is not sensing another's agony, nor feeling it; love is compelling the object of one's love to do as he wants that object to do whether that object be agonized or gratified; love is not caring for the object of one's love's agony or gratification, an utterness of notcaring; to love is to get one's pleasure out of the loveobject; love is ruthlessness. What is it, then, that Lee feels for me, and why should I at this point welcome it? I think what he feels is a taste of the ruthless, and my own taste of it. The truth finally is that we are about tentatively to taste, and that we are afraid of not recognizing what the taste is. But Lee is fleshly in his white jacket, and I want to divest him of the jacket; I want to grip him so that he will break my grip; I want to lacerate him so that he will rack my jaw with his knuckles; I want him, in brief, to make me unconscious because I dont want to recognize anything, I dont want to know anything's name, not even my own. I hate names. I want to live in a world that has not been named nor ever will be, where nothing recognizes anything else so that there are no bills, no invoices, no promissories, no lists. If Lee knew, St Red abruptly has a long laughter in herself, if Lee knew he is entering a girl with no lists and no names, he would swiftly fly fly fly and write me a long letter telling me I am this and that and the other and that I really am full of known things and that I had better get to know each one by its name and then he will see me and we will go over each name together till I am very sure of each one and then he will have me recite each one till I am a very litany of the known to him, and then he will stay and make me write a long list about him and name everything in him and say See, see, we are all known. The truth of the matter is—thank God Im finally forgetting Im a girl, for a moment, with the dancers, with the graduation, I become for a while deluded, the ages of the dancers sloughing off on me, but I can throw it off now because Im outside with him under a moon the color of my own hair that makes the moon not a moon nor the hair my hair and we are altogether unnamed, unnamed, unnamed—the truth of the matter is that love in its essence is not love at all, for love has no name, do you understand that, Lee? No, of course not, he hasnt the slightest intimation. The truth of the matter is that hes fearful of entering the unnameable, and that he has the sense that hes about to pronounce the phrase I love you that has no love to it, that hes about to commit himself to the uncommittable, to loose himself upon the uncharted and unchartable. No wonder hes shy about the truth of the matter, because he senses I know he has no name, that I merely mouth the phoneme to make him, the unnameable, more comfortable with me, and more comfortable to myself at seventeen. For a moment, sires, I am seventeen. For a moment Im comfortable, I have a language; but beneath me he senses Ive no words at all. Jesus, for a moment Im agonized between expression and non-expression. But if—if there is ever a time I might want a name, if there is ever a second in the clock that I wish a male call me Rena, now, now is the moment,

now is the moment,

for the truth of the matter, sires, is that love is the doubt whether the world has name or no name; love is the wondering if world has name or none; love is that supreme hesitation before one makes the decision :

that, lords and masters of the orangeblooded summer nightsky, that alone is love if love there is;

and I want in my supreme hesitation for Lee to be in the same supreme hesitation, in that doubt and wondering if name be or none

87 empty tables/348 empty chairs/

Rena St Red no matter how many names I give her has no name though I continue naming her, though I never end naming her for the very fact that I know she has no name

CHIRP, CHIRP :

BUT Rosa Caby is named Rosa Caby and Diane Valin is named Diane Valin and on the stage of the Troc burlesque theater the stripper has a name JUBILEE JORDAN is the long blonde's name, six feet two and a half inches as advertised AND NOW LADIES AND GENTLEMEN THE STAR OF THE EVENING THE GIRL YOUVE ALL BEEN WAITING FOR WHO HAS SMASHED ATTENDANCE RECORDS IN

EVERY CITY OF THE NATION AND WHO HAS PERFORMED BEFORE
HINDU POTENTATES AND THE CROWNED KINGS OF MANY LANDS
TOO NUMEROUS TO MENTION AND WHO TONIGHT WILL DANCE
FOR YOU AS SHE HAS NEVER DANCED BEFORE WE WILL NOT IN-
SULT YOU BY HOLDING THIS FABULOUS FEMALE BACK ANOTHER
MOMENT OF YOUR PRECIOUS TIME AND HERS IT IS OUR BREATH-
TAKING HONOR TO INTRODUCE TO YOU

   J U B I L E E   JORDAN   THE   ALLAMERICAN   GIRL   YOULL   ALL
RECOGNIZE FROM YOUR HOME TOWN AND MINE

   AS UNSPOILED AS EVER FOR YOUR DELECTATION

   HERE SHE IS

   MISS PATRIOT HERSELF :

The long roll on the drums abruptly stops. The musicians in
the orchestra pit flick a hard eyelick at the wings and then a
softer sashay at the men in the front row of the audience and
then dolce, very dolce, after casually picking up their instruments,
begin to play The Girl That I Marry Will Have To Be As Soft
And Pink As A Nursery. Jaredlee, having no time left at all, pays
no heed to his efficiently sharp surgical instruments and he proceeds to rip himself apart by main strength. He seizes his testiclepenis complex in both his hands and uproots it as he would
radishes from soft dirt, and a foreshortened scream knocks back
and forth in his maimed mouth; since Jaredlee has already
plopped forth his eyeballs, he can only feel the glutinous testiclepenis mass in his palms as his legs buckle in crawling crabs of
cramps; he staggers, an acceptably Biblical vision, as with a
boundless weight in his hands, a leadenness unaccommodatable
on any scale, a tangled shallow chasm at his groin, a rubbled diver-
tissement of bloodied black curling hair, flaccid flaps of em-
purpled skin, a slow whirlpool of crimson and purple and ivory
making soft belches under his abdomen; then he remembers to
transfer the whole mass into one hand while with the other he
makes a fist and gouges it into the slimy evacuole he has just
effected for a modicum of sardonic coagulation to ensue; and,
to reassure himself of the authenticity of the organs, he knocks
the testicles together to hear their soft sodden gulps, and with a
finger he strokes the penis, now an independent member,

an independent member at last he gurgles out the announcement with as much amputated laughter as he can summon forth,

and without so much as a flicker of astonishment, JaredLee feels the member beginning to rectify its hump,

the member altogether at last in the palm of his hand, the blind Jaredlee exults,

for he can whip it into submission or elongate it at his pleasure, at Jaredlees pleasure exclusively, and not at the penis's.

or he can send it on its way into total independence if he wishes. But now he must really hurry. He flings down the testiclepenis complex. He immediately forgets what he can or cannot do with the mass. He must complete his program by the moment Jubilee Jordan enters onstage, Miss Patriot herself. To this end, Jaredlee squats on the floor of his bedroom at 236 East Roosevelt Boulevard and with the butchers chopper he amputates both his legs at the thigh. His throat forms small, cluttered, highspeed reverse-recording sounds. The crib is untenable. He seeks to raise himself to the top of the wooden rail surrounding the crib by his hands, but because of his curtailed torso the act is impossible to consummate. What has he done? He has besmirched and befouled the crib. The toys of his dismembered body lie all about him, beshitted, bloodied, pissed on and wrenched out of all recognition. But the program is meritorious, because the object is total dismemberment in order to be ready for Miss Patriot, Jubilee Jordan. Gleefully he grasps the icepick and punches holes in his eardrums

BANG

BANG,

BANG

BANG. Two holes apiece. Then Jaredlee reached round to the cleft of his buttocks, plunges in his fist, expands it and then plunges it further to grab rectum, bladder and intestinal tract, a blizzard of vomit spewing forth from his mouth, vomit in gray, green, maroon and mottled blue when he wrenches forth the voluminous kelp of the viscera from his asshole, asshole and all as his belly collapses, his navel instantly submerged in a quicksand of displaced organs, each sucking at the other, hissing at

363

each other like snakes in a squashed bag, striking baffledly at each other, their functions a farrago of the nonobjective, each organ desperately striving now to sink its orifice into the heart of another, the object only, now, to connect, each organ stumbling one after the other, thrashing, squirming, the heart letching after the liver, the liver lusting after the prostate, the prostate slavering at the mouth after the kidney, the kidney screeching for the appendix, the appendix wriggling after the diaphragm, each completely discomprehending of essentiality, the while Jaredlee holds aloft the whole visceral seaweed, the whole oceanlife of the human gut, crooning over it, Gus Nathanson Emanuel, look at the goddamn slop youve made Helen Nathanson Emanuel squeals at him, the quartertones and the eighthtones and the sixteenthtones and the thirtysecond tones and the sixtyfourth tones of the sound of the tornup human gut, Jaredlee crooning in all these tones as he drapes them around his neck, singing THE GIRL THAT I MARRY WILL HAVE TO BE AS SOFT AND PINK AS A NURSERY

87 empty tables/348 empty chairs/;

the saltblood spumespray of the internal human sea crashing over Jaredlee in the crib at 236 East Roosevelt Boulevard, drowning, drowning, drowning in the Rocky River of birth itself. But at the last moment Jaredlee effects a rescue.

At the last moment, summoning up the last ounce of his crooning energy, he lays himself prostrate on the floor of the crib, the river sliding by, old familiar marine haunts of Rena Goldstein sliding by, Rachel Nathanson, Levi Goldstein, Dave Ring sliding by, and, tossing aside the gutmass contemptuously, he seizes the butchers cleaver

because a blonde girl in diaphanous red white and blue, six feet two and half inches in height, can be descried tensing in the wings by the Jaredlee scrotum in the left balcony.

by the Jaredlee eyeballs in the rear of the orchestra,

by the Jaredlee peritoneum in the box seat,

by the Jaredlee left leg in the dress circle and the Jaredlee right leg in the gallery,

by the right and left ears of Jaredlee front row center

TIME TIME TIME (chirp, chirp)

364

and he brings down the cleaver true and straight and magnificently perpendicular

ON THE SINGLE HERETOFORE UNMENTIONED

(displaced, you see, congenitally)

THIRD TESTICLE THAT HAS BEEN MASKING AS JAREDLEE'S ADAMSAPPLE IN HIS THROAT

THE BLADE SLICES SUPERBLY THROUGH THE TESTICULAR ADAMSAPPLE

THROUGH THE JUGULAR

THROUGH THE SPINE

SO THAT, BY GOD, AS MISS PATRIOT HERSELF SWINGS ONSTAGE IN RED WHITE AND BLUE

JAREDLEE'S HEAD ROLLS TO JUBILEE JORDAN'S NAKED FEET.

Oh, Rena says, I didnt

know

it

was

that

hard

to

talk. Yes, you see,

Lee says,

its my special

adamsapple. Its actually a third

(what Ive been finding it terribly difficult to say to you)

test youre tickling me, Diane.

Or is it that youve got that appleprism of the sixteenseventeeneighteen year olds sticking in your throat. Come on, tell me

Its taken me some time

I know

Ive wanted to say it before but Ive had to make certain

Certain

lee

Darling Rena, perhaps I shouldnt

Perhaps wraps

My adamsapple, bites off more than it can chew

Did anyone ever squeeze out your blackheads

No, Diane
Blackheads in the night. Squeezing out moons. But theyre
orange. From backheads are white. But moons change in choler
Lee what is it you
Worried?
Do I
I dont want to see you wor
Dianes face looks pinched in the sun, the sunlight squeezing out
grayheads lying on his chest
I
Yes
I
Yes
I
Yes
In a minute give me a (theyre really quite
Minute, Lee. Does that hurt?
Yes, but I still cant
But its such a small pain, rather thrilling dont you
Think. Dont fight it
All right, Diane, what are you worried about you look wor
Do I? Pinched? Yes. But Im doing the. Both of us look wor-
ried. What are you worried about, Lee the redhead Diane Valin
props herself on her elbow.
Nothing. The Girl That I Marry close to the lowlying Wild-
wood boardwalk Diane and Lee lie lingerlooselimbed in the sand.
Lee, fluently dismembered, his parts strewn magnanimously
and illogically all over himself, inside and out, smiles down the
entire left side of his body, and Diane curves herself over his belly
in the sun to open her mouth at his hip for Lee's smile to flood
her throat where it strikes rich rapids so that she laughs the bucking, spraying, spuming turbulence of his smile in her aloud loudly
in a great brayspray into his face I think Im enormously fond
of you Lee, she laughs, yes, I admit it openly her russetroan waist-
length hair peacockeagled across the boys loins.
Dont you know shes after your blackheads Rhona Lyrian sour-
nasals. Shit. Diane Valins the type of woman whos after every

366

mans blackheads. Thats the sort of thing I find it impossible to compete with, Rhona complains, whining, highsurprised her voice, as if caught redhanded in the act of stealing from her own voice. Rhona jerks her head, darting a glance behind her, an incessant action. But shit on that. We'll put on our own plays, dont think I havent got connections, my uncle is a state senator. And as for your Rena Emanuel, Rhona writes to Lee while he undergoes flight training at Randolph Field, why, what she has between her thighs is a sliced peach, I cant compete with that, either especially when the peach lacks a pit. And that peach has been seen with mouths, I think this is something you ought to know, Lee, for your own good that boys for every womans own good

now why dont you consider my body especially if you cover my face with the flag of the United Nations, Rhona urges, I can be considered as a sort of international makeshift for Lee Emanuel. Go on have a piece of cake, have an apple, have a rolled beef sandwich, have another cup of coffee, have you thought of casting your play Ive just the girl youll love her, Lee, shes one of the stars in Pins And Needles, the ILGWU revue, I know her personally, can you imagine she used to be a pieceworker in a dress factory, I tell you we cant fail, Philadelphias ripe for a repertory theater featuring original plays Rhona's eyes are magnified tenfold behind the thicklensed spectacles, the eyes themselves lodged in their sockets with mascara paste, the spectacles featuring cathedral glass overlaid by frosted glass, have some orange marmalade, have the truth for your own good

THE TRUTH IS FOR YOUR OWN GOOD

Oh dont misunderstand me, Danny Naroyan irascibly insists, its not that I dont love Rhona, because I do, I do, Lee, its simply that Im afraid of her, too, why, you dont know what the womans going to say next, especially if there are other people around. She has a terrifying candor, she says whatever comes into her head;

She may even say what comes into your head

(because Rhona Lyrian's skull is constructed out of a hodgepodge of many ugly skulls, and when shes growing in the womb she grows by fits and starts. Her speech, therefore, is spasmodic; she looks behind her constantly:

367

Am I going to grow now? she inquires of the invisible architect.

Are you going to grow now she inquires of Danny, because I dont see it as of this moment.

I am dissatisfied with my ugliness, she says, because its really unconcentrated. I have beautiful skin, for example, so my ugliness is a soft one; but theres too much of it on my enormous forehead; Ive the illusion Im growing bald. My lips would become a negro, my nose enhance a man, my squinting eye an explorer, but Im none of these. Dont stare at me too long, youll become a philosopher, she nasals disdainfully. Stare at anything too long and youll become a gravedigger.

My eyes are glass coffins, Rhona Lyrian remarks. Let me bury Diane Valin for you, Lee, she urges. Shes a model, right? Well, Id like to model for her myself, for that pinchnosed redhead with her perfect spitshaped tits, but Id have to throw myself across my own grave to do so. I want her to want me. But shed have to be a fly crawling over my glass coffin, wouldnt you my dear she suddenly grins at Diane.

Youre absolutely adorable, Diane chuckles richly and throws her arms around Rhona.

Stop that, Rhona commands, Lee doesnt understand. Youre not looking at two women, Lee, but at models for them. There are no women anyhow, anywhere; only models for them. Men are the only live creatures, she says in a totally startled register, I never realized that before. Which is why Diane and I find it impossible to live; we can only model; we can only tell the truth but we can never be the truth. Which is why men fall in love with us : with models. That is why homosexuals tell you the truth for your own good : theyre imitating models. Now, when women fall in love with each other, that means theyre making a desperate attempt to reach aliveness, to stop being models

Rhona screeches in abrupt laughter

Youre absolutely adorable, Diane chuckles slickly I cant stand it anymore Diane whispers to Lee in Fairmount Park I CANT STAND Lee uncovers a breast and jackintheboxes a nipple Im going to arrange for us to be alone in a friend's apartment this weekend she promises. All right?

368

Theres something youve got to understand of course its entirely theoretical

BIRDS ARE MADE OF ELECTRICITY

I NEED A MAN

I BELIEVE IN ABSOLUTE FIDELITY

MILKBOTTLE H TILTS OF COURSE ITS QUITE IMPOSSIBLE
THAT IT WILL SPILL IF IT REACHES A CERTAIN ANGLE ALTHOUGH
ITS AMUSING THEORETICALLY TO DISCUSS WHETHER ITS CON
TENT BE MILK OR WATER

CHIRP CHIRP BIRDS ARE MADE OF ELECTRICITY although on the
last few miles of White Horse Pike before Atlantic City the New
Jersey landscape comes milk and water in the dusk of the Buick
sedan whose rear seat is as highstuffed with valises as is practicable without Levi, driving, prevented from hindsight in the rearview mirror bulging summersuits and dresses on hangers clogging the hook between the door and the rear side window, Lee
hunching with birds made of electricity stuffed underneath his
shortsleeved rayon shirt, blue, both the rayon and the electricity,
Nina Tarassoff using him as a model for her Picasso boy whose
purple electric bird perches on his shoulder, now I want you to
take those birds out of your shirt, she says, and have them fly
electrically over the New Jersey landscape in the dusk, shes quite
peremptory, quite businesslike, Ive got a right, she continues, because Rachel and Levi are my mother and father as well, and
theyve got a whole stable of organgrinders and their monkeys organized into a corporation whom they send out each morning
and they've already become millionaires from the organgrinder-
monkey industry, because snow falls in copper pennies, copper
crystals blurrily fan out over the whole New Jersey landscape,
SANTA REDCHEEYA, SANTA RETCHEEYA. Little boys and their electric birds are my models, Nina fiercely avers. No, Jeffery Adams
does not make me pregnant, hes my psychoanalyst, and it
wouldnt be ethical, to clear up my neurosis by implanting me
with seed. Lumberjacket colors, nonetheless, not milk and water,
she throws a palette into Lees eyes youre blinding me youre blin
no Im not Rhona Tarassoff denies, Im simply making you see,
the clue a muted rainbow, the clue the visions in muted rainbows,

369

the clue Jeanne d'Moth and her Electric Bird, watch out, Levi is choking the bird. Thats not so, Lee says, for he says it is true my son that birds are made of electricity. Sit still, Nina cries. You boys, you boys—sit still for my analyst's sake, he cant see them in their muted rainbows otherwise. Its cold, Lee knows, cold this summerdusk, July First, and I wish I were munching on a hot-dog on the snowsmeared corner. He shivers in the back of the Buick, knowing Nina Goldstein summer and winter though Im going on vacation, and the electric birds bounce up and down on the rear seat stop it stop it youre shaking the car Rachel complains up front Dont be ridiculous Levi countermands her plump shoulders Levi Im sure I left something You didnt leave anything

SMELL THE SALT AIR her plump shoulders fatten with her looming sniff Im sure I left something you were in such a hurry to go Levi I cant understand why youre always in such a hurry a few minutes more what would it matter

We want to get there before dark am I right Rachel

So a few minutes after dark who cares

I want to get a few minutes in the water

You and your water

milk

I want to cool

plenty time to cool off in the morning whats such a hurry you made me forget half what I should bring along

every year its the same thing

no its not and would you believe it its true I always find something when i start looking in the trunk I forgot something

so Ill bring it with me next week youll write youll t

who can remember i wont remember looking in the trunk

so forget it

youre in such a hurry levi did you turn out all the lights for godsake

the gas the gas i think maybe i left on a burner

i checked all the

and the water upstairs

that too

the back door youll see youll see is unlocked

370

im telling you rachel i tried it five times its locked besides dont
you think if a thief wants to come in a locked door wont make
any difference
never mind there are all kinds of thieves
no only one kind
whats one k
the kind that steals
its not for jokes levi
shut up already the traffics heavy and whos driving
the electric birds are driving
we shouldnt go this summer anyhow
what all of a sudden
victor
you cant do nothing for him
sha sha
you think because hes a boy he dont know
all right'already you have to shout all over Atlantic City
were not yet in Atla
i could swear i can hear water dripping youll see when you
get back therell be a flo his breath in electric birds starts and
stutters over the flatlands, the saltlands, the oceanbitten marsh-
lands, the sea sneezing high up in his nose to spray forth through
the open car window and through the summersnowing winter-
ovened twilight. A chill coughs from his skin and skitters the least-
light and is lost in the worlddark summing up over the hotel tips
fraily marking the distant coastal town, flickering brittles that
snap off in the Leethroat, his cheeks leatherretted from the tack-
tacking wind smartsoftening off in delicate blisters at eyepouch
and tattletonguetip, the Martian canals on the Jersey backshore,
rectangles of waters quickslackslow, bluesmudged green marsh-
weed I got a racing catcloud whose hair, slicked back, makes the
last of a ninth purplelife across aquamarine turrets tattling golden
smokeeagles after. A pool of waterblack is smashed in the eye by
a bulging silver shower that, gulping, cuts itself off at a sudden
swarm of tepid clarity. Rose ice gives off a banked mist, touching
the nightfrosted cables on either side of White Hose Pike with
the exhalations of blue moths. And all around the spasms of the

371

electric birds in the boy courses a hidden green waterway, a speckle of wings thinly arched, a small white beast of bridge over toyboat and skinny bungalow ankles in the meanderstream to the approaching bay CLAMS CLAMS CLAMS LIVE BAIT LIVE, a bearded face smoking a red pipe that fishes for blue smoke in the pickled wavelets, a grizzled ancient sun lowering his heavily bemedaled chest behind the whinewinded car, my old father and my old mother the boy kills them with the immortal secrecy of his sight, sight belonging only to him in all the brightleft world of the whiffs of sandy rain waving their stalks from the surreptitious sea, of the salt blinking pale glass prickles at forehead and exposed boygums, and topaz seriatims in echoic echelons north and south from the rising black horizons. The air, spoken in husky trebles, moves now in dim transparencies. A gull haggles coarsely. Two gulls, three, and a maiden fourth sling widening mauve hoops round a mosquitoripped bog. The flaw of a far wave slashes a sting of tobacco bitters at the roaring windshield, a boynose distending, rending, the nose scooping at the throat and lung, throwing up the ammoniacal stench of the navel reservoirs to precipitate brackish brown currents from the thickening surge of the salted silts LIVE BAIT LIFE CLAMS CLAMS CLAMS, the species of the ticklebirds ticktock scratching at the dark, the sea cumulus in the boy, the tides twisting up his breastbone, he struggles, seethe over seethe, to take himself to crackleflight far out over and above the Emanuels, over Levi and Rachel and Lee, boasting of his biting insects on the leash, boasting of his comber fought into his controlled sinuosity, seizing the affrighted ghosts of the oceans backlashlands, pearlhandled weapons now his under the halfstorm moon, he swings in pinions of sweat and flares his electric birds of nostrils over the fishermen fumbling up their tackle, the fisherman pulling oar over the sunslumping baywaters, the glitters slidesinking into long ray troughs, as the boy ascends through the fishsplashing window over the long white causeway to the sea,

so that, fucking her, somebodys father dying downstairs, sneezing, pricked by allergy testshots from the root of the prick to its tip, the member swelling to three times its size and inordinately

372

sensitive, sneezing a urinal spray each time the left testicle death-rattles its last brew,

thats mine, mine Levi declares

Lee and Levi grappling over the ownership of the left testicle

Ill stuff both man and boy with cotton Dr Newman prescribes its the left ball over the rightfield fence Clancy Mann shouts so its mine

three males battling over a single ball

but I wont be able to hear a thing if you stuff my left testicle with cotton Levi objects

ILL BE DEAF IN ONE BALL

never mind youve got to eat

Dr Newman Ive been losing weight and coughing.

Im glad you came, one more month and you mightve contracted tuberculosis never mind the constipation I want you to start eating, bananas, cream, steaks, everything her groinhair a slate cloud floating lazily around the prick as electric birds dart in and out Red your thighs are like bananas the doctor told me to eat everything, cinnamon and ebonystreaked her thighs, lemon-tinted and faintly sour to the squeeze, blackpipers the dartbirds snapping at the sandy cloud, gulls gritting their wings;

one million three hundred and four the hoop revolves about the hips of the oneeyed prick, swivelling

TWO

NINETEEN

FOUR THOUSAND cockwise and countercockwise with ticktock delicacy he palmprods the bath's surface scum toward the foot of the tub and with the other hand, his pores in steaming hoops, he gouges the bathbrush bristles into his grimy ankle fretted with Rachels veins fritterbitten by blue knots now you make three and half turns of a figure 8 he chattersweats over his body, and then reverse the bristles procedure, etching the white soap into the ankleflesh so that he is paradisaically pristine, the very blush of itching purity over each square inch of his flesh, but he must work quickly else the newflushness be polluted once again by the very liquid cleansing it)

He lowers her last leg into the black bathwater so that Rena

373

may take a breath, mochamarbled breasts shushed by red mouth-prints she looms over the boy pinioning his arms to the bottom of the tub

LET ME UP LET ME UP he cries a tragedy might occur the drain-stopper might be dislodged, the water flow out and in so doing deposit a dense layer of supercontaminated filth atop his roseate skin condensing to the strains of the liebestod from tristan, the most wonderful music to accompany one making love Rosa argues, doesnt it perfectly match what were doing, mom, mom he stutters into the phone from Bermuda on his honeymoon with Hannah

what is it mein kint

its Rosa he yips in a steaming stammer, the furriers daughter catching little animals and stripping them of their skins shes coming after me with a knife and its not time for her change of life the gold snow hurtles through the window at 236 East Roosevelt Boulevard and stinging his ass just as he reaches the bathroom down the hallway

SHUT UP WHAT DO YOU WANT FROM ME LEVI SNORES the MONSTER GESTICULATING from the parapet of the ancient castle that he WILL NOT PERMIT HIS DAUGHTER TO SING IN NITECLUBS youve got to promise me, lee, youve g

but my draft board says Im 1A Ill have to go into the Army I might be killed what I can promise you is the moment Im discharged well be mar

say it Diane say it

its very difficult Ive never said it to the room in the yellow box Diane's face is exposed in red splotches under the yellow light red and yellow splo

Rhona, excitedly, heeheehees its because youre yellow Lee not Diane youre y

Lee shakes. A liver springs at St Red from across the room, a heart, a brain, a ligament slashes across her throat youll take it very easily wont you but what about Dr Newman and his hymenectomy and Mrs Sherman's whole body turning gray, now black, now gray my husbands on the phone her charred voice curling

374

round the instrument while Mark Fahn gravely seats himself at the piano, the gilt mirror slinging slaloming excoriating quicksilver flakes around the bedroom, the magenta stripes hooping about the girl and the boy on the bed

thirteen thousand and one

sixtyfour

nine

one billion

TAKE OFF YOUR GODDAMNED HAT SILAS KLEIN AND LETS SEE WHATS I will play my composition in sounds interspersed by silences Mark explains because I am a pederast I need a boy I NEED A

BOY patting the water Lee dams back his breath patpaddles back the dirty waters and when bubbling seams of anthracite scum convolute at the foot of the tub he turns his arms into pillars of stone and quarterinch by quarterinch he pushes his neck, shoulders, chest up the slanting chilled porcelain, continuing to pat-push the water away from his body periodically by stiffening a leg and balancing on his hip so that he can bend one arm to do so while maintaining his yardage up the rear of the tub I tell you

she pursues me with a knife,

the leash a knife,

the monstrous german police dog tied to the leash of the knife when he SPRINGS make them shut up in the bedroom Levi bellows I dont want them fucking while Im dying;

besides, what shall I do about the business do you want it does Dave want it I want an honest answer

no I screaming BUT ITS TOO BIG ITLL HURT ME LEE IM FRIGHTENED

LISSEN ONCE ITS INSIDE ITLL BE ALL RIGHT

EVERYTHINGS ALL RIGHT ONCE ITS INSIDE VINCE HARRISON SNARLS AT THE MULTITUDE OF WOMEN ON STRIKE : VAGINAS OF THE WORLD UNITE YOU HAVE NOTHING TO LOSE BUT YOUR STAINS MISS JUBILEE JORDAN MISS PATRIOT HERSELF PLUNGES HER NAILS INTO THE VELVET CURTAINS AND STARTS TO HEAVE THE SHOTPUT FROM SIDE TO SIDE, Joan of Ark dashing against the windowscreen Look tonight youve just got to stay over and not go to The Heel Rosa contorts her ultimatum or I dont want you here again.

say it say it Rena lowers her crushing graystone balustrade flagstone weight on Lee.

The. Champagne. Glass. Orgasm. Smashes. Against. The Linton's Restaurant on the north side of Market Street between Thirteenth Street and Broad contains 87 long tables and 348 chairs, filled to capacity at one in the morning. The Assyrian Jew Clement Lichtenstein turns his head sculptured in sandy kinks to Lee sitting at his side and sounding his cup of coffee with an aluminum outboard motor. Clement smiles hard dry sandstone tablets, dissolving them on his forehead Well Ive made my proper valedictories to Rena. The summer heat branches out under Lee's shirt

You saw her between sets.

Yes.

How was Lonnie tonight.

Hes added a few very funny ditties to his psychoanalytic repertoire.

Hes very witty.

Oh, ve

god and moses quirk in the leemind, the divine homosexual as Lee tickles an errant eyebrow toward the Lichtenstein handing down the decalogue to the human fag, except that Clements position and mine are reversed, he taps fingers to my forehead, hes short and extends to the summer ceiling the plateglass window looks out on Market Street the moviegoers flattening out from the Family Theater next door, a sailor grinning his sealips across the window smearing in his bandana eyes. Clement touches me from on high but divinely resists, properly deferential to Red and me, flicking us both nonetheless, he draws up the Leemountain to receive the giving of the Law, does he believe I will receive her blessing to sacrifice my golden calf to Clement Adonai. Seerdonic, I like my coffee very sweet, Lee shrugs. No crime.

Oh, no, not at all.

Im wanted by man through a woman, I daresay, the approach

is a problematic one. Whatever he might say is a category of courtship the conveyor belt behind the counter gently bearing trays carrying culinary varieties, frailly bumping, nudging counter and passing spigot, a waitress scoops up an order of bacon and

An extremely handsome woman your wife, Lee.

Nods, dimpling the coffee. God keeps his chin high. Lee scrapes the bottom of the cup with morose savagery, a conveyorbelt in his throat gently scraping against his windpipe leftover multiplicities of devoured food staples.

Im sorry to see you go, Clement

Oh I understand Washingtons alive with foreign cultures, and as a government chemist I should have invitations galore. After all, Ive never been an eremite and Ive cast my flies indiscriminately upon the waters. Im not one for the absolutes in any category, not of the power absolute, not the money absolute, not the fidelity absolute

But youre saying goodby.

Not permanently, Ill be looking in on Philadelphia weekends, I expect the three of us will be seeing each other. By the way, Lee, do I remember you correctly in dimly recalling youre prey to a few absolutes here and there the men and the men and the women and the women and the men and the women and the men at the counter engage linked elbows, the summerheat from the million-watted ceiling bulbs dropping great lightsome limeturds upon the ingesting customers at counter and table, limewhites glistening milkily down cheek and chinpoint, the revolving door entrance dispersing an occasional shadow from open mouth to mouth

Lee laughs. The epigram, Clement, is that he was the sort of individual gifted with total dim recall.

Ah. The Lichtenstein pats his mouth with a soft buttered roll.

A man with peacock muscles tatooes his spread up the aisle, a sandstone Lichtenstein sandblasting his own exterior to provide the proper backforeground. Folding his peacock into a crouch, the man slugs his jaw into the Daily News and pudges a fist into franks and baked beans. A tiny ball of hot grease pellets at Clement's thin breast, and he smarts. My rape is a distant thing, he quickly obliterates one of the languages from the Rosetta Stone,

377

the demotic. Im as distant from myself as a dilettante. My birth is a piece of dilettantism, I am conceived dilettantically. I dabble at my own sperm that disgust itself be dilettantish. I play piano with winkdeep elegance, and I must be, really, aghast at Couperin : he couldve been my brother, but he insisted on the Gallic shallows, in which an American dilettante cannot get his fetish wet. Clement Lichtenstein shrugs a kink in his hair Well I do remember something of the sort he applies the palest of huffs to his lips, his eyecorners refusing to pare their callouses

solute fidelity

Quite.

Do you have St Red and me in mind an electric bird of glass skims just beneath Lees first layer of skin, Clement watching it, it needs polishing, an early battle, two glass birds in a tinkling struggle before the note of puberty. Ive retired mine, it grazes on blades of glass, Clement thoughtfully feeds it glitters, while Lees remains pseudowild, cryptoliberated, he would like to seize Lee's wrist, the man's

One can make no promises to oneself, Lichtenstein temperately taps his forehead, but he forgets to wipe off the pain at either corner of mouthcurl

Youre forgetting yourself

We dont constantly gather in the crop, Lee

I believe in absolute fidelity.

But youve absolutes in no other area Clement practises his fingers at the bar mimicking lower limb ballet extensions Ive never toyed with the idea that my freckles are the external sign of my internal colloidal structure

The dazzling display of the Lichtenstein Lights

Heavens, Clement grins

I realize Im being arbitrary, but I expect my wife to be absolutely faithful to me, as I am absolutely faithful to her

Im not referring to Lee and Rena peacock muscles wipes his face with his newspaper

Colloid or no, then, youve no reference to make ambiguity ambiguous the nettles buzz around Lichtenstein's outhouse by the Nathanson pond in Lansdale. A cow moos. Mrs Lichtenstein calls for the boy and Lee's insects sting Lichtenstein on each damned freckle my suspension is becoming disturbed my suspension is bec. Resolution on my part, Clement thinks, would disturb my essentiality. I would trickle forth. I had better recall my electric bird from retirement, but its infamous of Lee to demand I return to childhood, that I wrestle with him on the pavement, that he not see me, that he seek to throttle me, that I be beneath him immobile as he is, but he forces me by my species of adultery, he compels me to pose Rena as he poses her, and I yield, yield, though my lineage be aristocratic, theres a brutish peasantry to the lad. My succumbing, at bottom, however, is for my colloidal state. But the question might be, What do I want of Rena? How peculiar, that I should want Rena strained through Lee, that I can embark upon the female only through the male, a scent of her upon him, an expression of hers on his face, a mellifluity of her mood through his capriciousness, summed up, my god, summed up in his sexual absolutism. The whimsical, grabbed at through the perfectly rigid

I adore your wife, as you know

I know.

Shes fantastically entertaining

I know

I did not mean to talk of her

I know

Youre very difficult

Yes. And I shall meet her at the Rendezvous, and we shall take a cab to our home on Marley Road, and she will open her pocketbook to give me two dollars to pay the hackie, and we shall mount the high stone steps and enter our apartment, and she will insist on immediately taking a shower, Terry

so that, fucking her, Clement Lichtenstein looking on, what can Clement know? Theres a band of Lichtenstein lights surrounding Rena and me, the disperser Lichtenstein, the ballet dilettante exercizing his extensions, pirouettes, en pointes, who can know nothing of absolutes as they occur, that I may effect absolutes link for link, in a chain, as they occur to me and which I keep recurring so that there exists no lacunae, and that Rena St Red in participating in my chain of absolute is herself precisely that, and would find it impossible to be otherwise, to be both faithful and unfaithful I will absolutely insist, though my insistence on absolute fidelity should not in itself be absolute, the insistence, that is, I do admit; but when I do not insist, then fidelity itself is not in question, does not breathe on the scene, is not, in short, alive, and when it is not alive, not pertinent, then I cannot question it, cannot doubt it, nor can Red, so that we are perfectly faithful to each other, for she certainly cannot cancel herself out by being absolutely faithful to me one day and cuckold me the next. After all, she does not collect postage stamps; if she does, she sends herself to odd places indeed, herself in multiple sections, but, but, but since I do not insist on absolute fidelity when absolute fidelity is not animate, is not germane, she does not have to accommodate herself to the antinomy. Poor Clement is far too colloidal to comprehend this matter; the poor boy is in a solution; Red and I are crystallized. He would immerse us in his solution, this is his characterological approach, he must impute doubt to the position of absolute fidelity, he cannot see that there may be exceptions to his fluidity; and to the extent that I am as fluid as he, he cannot understand my point of solidification. He would claim me, claim Red, the two of us, for his Lichtenstein Lights; he bubbles at the mouth, his freckles bubble, he makes stony bubbles, he froths at his kinks; the colloid is a lonely solution indeed, and we establish points of contact only when we solidify into positions of absolute fidelity, the prime definition of love. If we did not possess such positions of perfection, we should not know each other at all, we should have no names, we should give up all effort at substance. In giving up his effort at substance, Clement Lichtenstein laps at my wife and I, very aristocratically, yes, prophylaxis having been donned, so to speak, an error right there, for the prophylaxis cannot contain Clement's liquescence, and his very aristocracy is jeopardized. We threaten him, put his relatively-dilettantism in danger

Do you really think that, Lee? Do you endanger me?

Possibly.

I like that. I wish to be endangered. If he possessed a lipstick, he would at this point proceed to carmine his lips Did you know that?

Yes

But theres no person in this world who can be absolutely faithful

A statement to the effect that both Rena and I are unfaithful to each other

There are exceptions, of course

I dont believe you admit the weakness in you of a possible exception

Really, Lee, Im not making accusations of any kind. Im certain that the two of you are thoroughly faithful to each other, drumming his teeth against each other. Im simply terribly concerned that you of all people should entertain the notion of an absolute. I dont want you risking being hurt at any time in the future

You accuse me of the possibility of such a risk

Id accuse anyone

Including Lee Emanuel

Well, yes. And, Rena. Who could be terribly hurt by you. What the hell after all is absolute fidelity? Is this the capacity of the total organism?

Did you know youre being quite tough now? Quite hard?

Its not that I want to be.

Youre reaching substance. Yours is scarcely a fluid position.

Youre two of my very best friends.

That sounds quite rigid

Oh I can back off at any time

Enmitously.

Enmitously.

Another rigid position. Perhaps youre not fluid at all, Lichtenstein. Simply that you occupy a series of absolutes

And that youre actually the fluid one in your uncompromising position of single rigidity in which you can afford to turn in the complete circle of the compass, which makes you capable of inflicting enormous pain, both on others and yourself.

That, Clement, is your absolute conception

I did not want to become abstract

But you pose the abstract of why I should insist on absolute fidelity

Then you concede absolute fidelity as abstract

Lees electric birds are immobile, having pierced the layer of his skin. Their beaks protrude barnacles up and down his forearm, the allergy tests, the Provincetown wharf, Jennifer Hazlitt and Laura Ingersoll. His nose swells. He sneezes uncontrollably for the space of about five minutes. My answer to that is that I do so concede.

Then you must concede also that a person can love you without being absolutely faithful. You must concede that a person loving you can forgive you for an act of infidelity.

87 full tables. 348 occupied chairs But I tell you Anne Kanovskys dead, you can smell her remains through the open door of the womens urinal you are executing me Lichtenstein in the sweet odor of piss, sugar in the fathers toiletbowl, would you care to drink my yellow coffee your insistence has the sweet dead smell of my father the

bribe to the son from any mans father

executing his will

But I could spread a peacock screen the burning jet in Schulte's on the northwest corner of 13th and Market Streets for the lighting of cigars a fat woman ponderously blows on hot soup

Im protectively constituted, Clement remarks, petite though I be. Im capable of the impersonally personal charming, eh? In Rochester AMNESIA we walk over the bridge the opalescent scum on the river surface what are the chemical constituents Clement the dross the St Red oh I dont know really there are all sorts TELEGRAM AUNT BELLA DIED THIS MORNING AT IF YOU WISH TO ATTO THE FUNERAL I WILL WIRE YOU MONEY FOR RENA AND YOU TO FLY IN

no i dont want to go

no i dont want to go

no i dont want to return to Philadelphia I abominate Philadelphia I wont return for a funeral for any goddamned reason AMNESIA what are you talking about Rena

I could remember where I was I couldnt remember my name
thats why Im late

darling

but Im all right now

are you

yes I am; featherdusters of her faces brush Lees face, her pupils
dilated, the wild excitement of the memoryless provocative over
her entire body over the peacock train of her eyes Nate Goldstein
she tells you she has amnesia

she tells me she

for an afternoon

yes y shes abso the fat woman blows ponderously on hot soup
we males will say darling to this man

darli

I love Aunt Bella

fly in to the funeral

no

you love Aunt B

yes

then fly

Ive amnesia

but your father. Its your fathers sister

I wont fly in without Rena and shes working in Rochester

darling Ill fly in with

no you cant leave your job

then go in by yourself

i abominate Philadel

i cant remember Philadel

amnesia

you grow up in the city

i do not grow up in St Red she cant remember what she grows
up in for a whole afternoon what are the chemical constituents

oh, various elements of dross you wouldnt identify

i know waste

good, good, Lee then you can forgive a person of an act of infidelity

I do not demand absolute fidelity from any individual except my wife and myself identify the waste for me youre a chemist

Im a musician, really, so is Rena Kanovsky lowers his cigar to the brass jet and lights it, his massive purple pimples two bedsores just above his buttocks

the particular moral stricture is for Rena and I alone

THEORETICALLY THE CONGREGATION BRITH MIKVEH STANDS IN JUDGMENT ESPECIALLY THE IRONJOWLED MELINKOFF WITH HIS EIGHT SONS i like fat women blowing on hot soup Lichtenstein is prone to admit THEORETICALLY IF ST RED WERE UNFAITHFUL WOULD YOU LEAVE HER

I CANNOT CONCEIVE HER AS BEING UNFAITHFUL

BUT SUPPOSE

I CANNOT SUPPOSE

I UNDERSTAND THE INTENSITY OF YOUR LOVE FOR HER BUT CERTAINLY FOR THE PURPOSES OF ARGUMENT YOU CAN SUPPO

no;

yourself, then. You. Can you su

No. N that sweet urinal stench in my nostrils

Were not that close to the womens

On hot summer nights the

The doors closed

Yes, I suppo, its these damned purple pimples of mine, Lichtenstein

Would you like me to lance them, darling

No, Anne, n

itd only take a moment

no, i dont care for the pus

you dont have to see, Ill drain it without your seei

no, take your drumming fingers away fr

Darling, your purple pimples have muscles I wash christlees pimples in dont you think I'dve made a lovely Jesus, assyrian type, Kanovsky, worn sandstone THE EMULSION OF THE TRINITY

You dont mind if I put more sugar in my piss do you

Do you think a woman who loves a man will cease loving him if he commits an act of infidelity opalescent scum. Identify, identi

384

Im not that brilliant a chemist youre underrating yourself why the sudden unbecoming modesty

Im not an expert on waste materials

Who are you setting up then as an expert? Lee Emanuel? Rena Emanuel? Why do we suddenly qualify

Will a woman who loves a man stop loving him if he commits an act of infidel

whos the woman

Im talking theoret Lichtenstein softly rubs gentleness into the long basreliefs of his face. An act of supreme horror, your rubbing gentleness into your. Why. Theres no color, the gentle rubbing of the waxen into your stone, compassion created out of decomposition. Are there prayers to be said for wax melting on a warm night; Im wan; the bloods gone to you, the energetic dracula, why do you want our blood, look at the two clownspots of rouge on your cheekbones, lee; by your very feverishness, I whiten, appalled at your hatred of my cosmeticized compassion, I do you no inverse ill. But, Lichtenstein, your colloidal collage, your suspension, insults; the intellectuality of your mortification; sly sublimity; the hermaphroditical supramundane, yours, incurs my outrage; merely the act of suspension infuriates; the lofty smirk that shrinks, then shrinks me; the downdip of the two-sexed predator upon one male and one female, quite differentiated; the politics of the colloid; Ive not drawn any blood from you at all; yours is the accusation, automatic, against any of the blooded; that we have wide sucking mouths; yours purses, smalls, disappears altogether;

true: Clement Lichtenstein, Aunt Bella Zions unrelated son, and nonconsanguineous brother to Russell Zion, the three blanched by the same vampired pallor, and the two males adroitly, trimly, tidily made, both of modest height I sculpture Lichtensteins once a week Russell notes, true: Clement sits high in his chair in smileless formality, his lips smoothed in to eliminate aperture, mouthless, he speaks as the dread, expressionless, tongueless oracle)

You would not forgive your beloved for an act of infidelity.

No.

You would eliminate her.

Yes.

You would kill the whole relationship.

Yes.

And you would expect her to do the same were you to act similarly.

Yes.

And if she did not.

I cannot conceive that condition.

You cannot imagine it at all.

I cannot.

Possibly out of fear.

Possi

Possible you might fear forgiveness.

Is it not healthy for us to do so. Forgiveness poses the static position, a return, specifically, to what we are not. This forbids consequence, nullifies logic, I am then the woman's sister, the two of us competing for the ruined male within me. We haunt graves, we become prey to species of prayer, to ceremonies of understanding, and we sweetly foresee each other. An impossible sitution between a man and a woman. Forgiveness is the fundamental attitude of the child, Christ is fixed at infancy, and that Jehovah knows in the canniness of his control. Forgiveness, then, is an act of superiority in order to gain control, which Jehovah implanted to manipulate his mannikin

Why does a Jehovah have to make certain. Why should a goddess have to

Because of her absolutism. Anyone who forgives is inhuman, has forfeited the variable

And you in not forgiving maintain the variable.

Yes.

But we are not all capable of the variable.

True.

But are you absolutely certain that you are.

No, but I am certain that I would forgive forgiveness, so that, regressing to the nonhuman, I would be behind the forgivor.

which would make her position, the forgivor's, untenable. She would be terrorstricken at the dimensions of the yield behind her. She would fear falling backward. She would fear losing her voice, all articulation; she would fear an endless endoverend plunging, with the forgivor of the forgivor never catching her, never stopping her. To forgive, you understand, invites the possibility of the limitless. For a female, this is patently impossible. Once the forgivor is forgiven, I assure you she runs.

Then there is either absolute fidelity or no relationship.

Amend that to the relationship of no relationship, even more formidable

And that you would not risk.

There is no risk, the greatest danger of all. Such a riskless related nonrelationship involves the non-annihilative. Imagine it, Clement Lichtenstein. Imagine it

No. Clement snaps shut his pale gold cigarette case, and reclaims his mouth He does not wish to glance at Lee at all. The Assyrian sees Jews in dense columns advancing.

Give me a cigarette.

Id rather not.

I would like one.

I must go.

Do you deny me the condition of mouthlessness? Is it a conditon we should not employ with the female? Does it castrate their buried balls? Do you ask of me that I forgive the condition of buried balls? And if my mouthlessness castrates the woman's buried balls, am I to be forgiven, Lichtenstein?

I will not look at you. I will not look at the blood on your mouthlessness

Ah, very beautiful, Lichtenstein

I will not forgive you my urgency in having had to say that. I have never for a moment implied that Red has been unfaithful to you. I have simply wanted to make you aware of the possibilities of love without absolute fidelity.

How unforgiving of you to have wanted to make me so aware. Why have you not been able to forgive my position of absolute fidelity?

387

I must smile.

Please do.

My eyes are a bit moist. I must smile.

You are a little oversensitive tonight, what with leaving Philadelphia. Yes. You shant be coming back. Im not sure. You shant be coming back. Im not sure.

You wont be coming back.

Im not sure, Lee.

Mister Lichtenstein

I may not make Washington my permanent abode

But you shant be coming back to Philadelphia.

He offers Lee a cigarette. No, Clement says. But I wish you might entertain the faint notion of love existing without absolute fidelity

But you no longer know what absolute fidelity is. Are you being faithful to me in any sense? How could you know what any sort of fidelity is?

Clement's pale urinal eyes widen. He shaves his fingernails, as some primitives their teeth, into triangles, and he slowly scratches at the table surface.

Lee asks him: Whom do you love? My wife or me?

I love the two of you. You both know that.

Equally.

Equally.

So that we can both forgive you your loving us equally? Forgive you your presumptuous enormity? Do you warn the two of us? Do you want me to forgive you your warning? Can you not warn me without getting my forgiveness—because you are about to run from the city. Cant you run without forgiveness? Can you not escape without it?

And do you stay in this city without possessing the quality of forgiveness?

So?

I love both of you. I want the two of you to remain together. I want nothing to separate you.

You mean you cant love either of us singly.

Lee, Lee

Come, come, Clement. I cant envisage the two stone tablets of the decalogue of your heart breaking. Cant you love us singly?

I dont think I can love anybody singly. I think I can only love an individual when he's related to someone, so that I must love the two

Thou shalt love thy father and thy mother. Is that as far as you go? Is it that for which you wish to be forgiven? Are Rena and I so parental that you must shake an admonitory finger at us? Would our not remaining together punish you? punish you for the presumption of loving both of us?

I will be absolutely faithful to the two of you together.

Adultery esthetically wrought. Let me be, after Rena, the second to congratulate you

You cannot be spoken with.

True. Ive no mouth.

There are peacocks in muscles, Clement says, distantly, watching their display mount to the revolving doors and flex through. Youve made yours all black and white. Im sorry, Im really s

Forgive me, Clement.

Ive packing to do, Lee, the sandstone rubs vaguely away at his sandstone. A light dust falls on the restaurant floor.

You have to pick up after them Rachel Emanuel says. The men, always you have to pick up after th

Yeh, Gertrude Forsten says. Even when theyre grown up

They never wipe their shoes

Yeh

My Lee would you believe it he tramped in dust on the living-room floor last night. Dont you think it left marks

Let me tell you I thank the Lord for the vacuum cleaner. I could never get through the day without it. I'd be lost

/the fife of the dancing ant axes off the surf

/surfife : if only in parts ive packing to do miss jubilee jordan dr jared emanuel ive packing to do at the goldsteins dining room table and at lee emanuel's bedroom at 236 east roosevelt boulevard a light dust falling by snowflake and desert hotwind the slow circling of the boys hoopworld cockwise and countercockwise packing in parts if only to seervive the computer wise beyond computerdom neither adding nor subtracting neither multiplying nor dividing but mollifyingly in motion surely that most aptly characterises the whitehaired Walter Bergstrom who preempts the hoop from both boy and girl, saying indeed my belly is blind but fat and revolves independently around my body. It is my notion, he says, that we grownups must wrest the games from the children, permanently. Lilly, he turns to his gigglebreasted wife at the Goldstein's midnight dinner table, pass me the salt. The whitehaired Walter Bergstrom

pass me the dust

sits resembling a pioneering Covered Wagon upended as a memento of brave Americans in the grocerystore diningroom of lower middleclass Jewish immigrants. A native of Baltimore, he speaks out of the lightest touch of a Southern accent stubbornly maintained after many years in his adopted city of New Orleans where he manages a gambling establishment for a Mr Kream, whose principal diversion is a string of racing horses Howd Babysitter do Walter Nate Goldstein stammers knowingly. Why hes comin along Nathan Walter Bergstrom nods slowly gravely salting the roast poultry on the plate before him. Think hell place at the sixth at Hialeah tomorrow Nate is a nervous Jubilee Jordan blinking his thin hips, his eyelids twitching at the brown heavy velvet draperies of his eyeballs. Im expectin a phonecall in the mornin Nathan, Walter Bergstroms suede blue eyes never dispatch themselves from the gravyladen poultry. Well you know how it is with us podiatrists Walt

Walter, Walter Bergstrom gravely recollects

You know how it is with my stammer, sometimes I

I surely understand, Nathan, Walter prettily clips the leg from the duckthigh Lilly pass me the bread but she already has put the slice of ryebread in position approximately three inches from his brightred lips so that his buffalobacked fingers, having delicately lunged from the tablecloth, merely continue their incepted motion without pause to grasp the wifely anticipation and thrust the whole slice into the billowing mouth

with us podiatrists were constantly putting our foot in, Nate laughs up one cheek

390

Shit Herb Goldstein ejects thickly through his girlpout around a Coke bottle you can

Ill hit you I can still hit you Esther Goldstein kickshrills at her son because that kind of language

I didn't hear you, Herb, Nate abruptly hugs his ear

Ah balls go screw in your ear Herb hoarsely tugs at his underbreath

Anyhow Walter you wont mind if I phone you late in the morning so I can get

Lilly if Ive told you once Ive told you I dont know how many times I can count one hundred thirtyfour billion and three

twentyeight

fourteen

eighty thousand to stop sinkin that manicured bit of yours into your ear youre going to have an infection the size of an airraid warnin Walter Bergstrom remarks aggrievedly.

Can I have a drink Walter it might stop the itching

I told you you can drink as much as you like when your poor little ears itchin, now pass the butter the whitehaired upended Covered Wagon quietly commands, his pink canvasses smoothly curving over his hippohulk, his belly softly booming its buttery belches Aaron Emanuel quietly dreaming BOOMBOOMBOOM in Lithuania if I had a big strong hippobelly like Walter Bergstrom's Idve been able to bounce the BOOMBOOMBOOMS of the cannon right back, his whitehaired hogshead pulsing great hydraulic jets through his distended spigotnose, his softblue suedeeyes always one softstep ahead of his croupiers pass me the milk Lilly before you pour yourself the bourbon

I always say a man should have his milk before his wife has her bourbon Lilly tilts her blacklacquered hairwaves in their tightfitting patentleather pumps in genuflection before Bergstrom

Now Lilly theres no cause exaggeratin in front of company Walter gently boomchides his wife

Chuck still have a temperature Rena inquires of Hannah, Nate's wife, whose bourboncolored tresses trip awkwardly over each other in front of her eyes. Hannah's lips snatch at her grin, pluck off pieces, Dont worry about my husbands skoalamerican

391

boy, Gonnas with him, he only has a temperature of a hundred and four, I just had to be at the synagogue tonight, the ladies auxiliary

Shes vicepresident, Mrs Ackman, Hannahs mother gamingutturals, tucks in her pride between her plump cheeks, my daughters always essential Esther isnt that the phone gracefully lowering the potato salad Esther stumps the instrument to her ear Everybody quiet, quiet its long distance Nates on the phone from Bermuda

Mr Ackman the furrier smiles benignly through his heavily granulated eyes. His narrow roundshoulders squint through his expensive suit, and his high starched collar squeezes out a head many times too large for the opening, his features pallidly oriental in their cast, he nods his head and jubilantly for all answers pronounces Yes Yes Yes

Yes yes

Yes yes

Thats right, Yes, Mr Ackman the furrier agrees

Youre right, Yes, YES, Mr Ackman quickly nods the head many times too large for the starched highcollar opening, YES YES

Pop whens the frozen food counter due in Nate wings his chin at Solomon Goldstein whose bald satyrskull skids up a gleam from the plate of gefullte fish Not till next week

At least youll be able to compete a little with the supermarket when you have the fr

What with, Herb interrupts, a frozen turd

Shut up Nates on the phone from Bermuda hes telling me something about his honeymoon

We never had our little blissful issful ittle mooneymoon Fiona Nuri chirpchirps up at her commonlaw husband Cornelius, five feet taller than she, his gigantic Easter Island skull bobbing unsteadily on a pitcher of beer, eightyeight pianokeys his adamsapple, No but listen to this passage from Walt Whitman he urges Lee you like Walt

N

Fionas my little easterisland girl arent you darling his sunstricken blue eyes themselves wobbling on billowing white kegs of creamy beer, the Lithuanian Christian Golem bearing tower-

392

high vats of beer in either hand to the thirsty populace By God
how can anybody not love the Good Gray Walt, this wobbling
granitic slop whose skull rolls down the mountainside guzzling at
his own sheep leaping from Cornelius crags, his lean railway track
hands slopping over with steel, the vaulting torso reeling from hip
to hip, the lowered drawbridge chin hunching down to admit the
filthcaked princess Fiona a tenth his size rocked in Walt Whitman Nuri's skyscraping cradle, her crotch diapered by his
blanched tongue as he croons with his prick to her, her bland blue
eyes blinking itchdiapered babytalk at him ooh give me that itsybitsy hunk of Rexy Rection oooh it fills my whole wittle cwadle
up ooooh now you can go to the pwiano and mwake your great
bwig pwowuhful mwoosic while I paint my wittle cewamics her
hips widening to the length of a musical comedy stage flaring to
Miss Jubilee Jordans urging Cornelius you gweat big circus dway-
horse on top of the Atlantic City Steel Pier pwatform you can
dwive into my itsybitsy pool PWUNGEPWUNGEPWUNGE but you
just make sure you get up in the morning and make our wittle
mwuney for the day wont you Cornelius the pwoor gweat bwig
things gotta bwe a mwoosical cwopyist he cwopies ten million
mwoosical notes a day to mwake us a living dont you Cawnelius

Yeh well you know Lee he heaves apologetic belches some day
Fiona's ceramics will be phenomenally successful in the market-
place

and then well just be wolling in mwuney wont we Cawnelius

Isnt she adorable Lee isnt my little

Oh Lee just doesnt know how much, does he

But if hed read Walt Whitman hed

Now now children, the flushing Esther Goldstein interrupts, no
poetry tonight. Lee

Yes

Cant you please talk with Mrs Sherman to sit somewhere else
because I cant talk with my son from Bermuda.

She's waiting for a phonecall from her husband outoftown,
mother.

Its sweet you should call me mother but if you could only get
Mrs Sherman to

You can ask her to move, mother.

But shes so burnt and they havent put out the fire yet.

I wouldnt worry about that because her diamond rings are still intact and Id certainly respect her loyalty. Anyhow, let me warn you if you do move her shell probably cwumble. As it is, she appears sootily sunburnt. Shes just about to answer the telephone. She has arisen from the bed, burning though she is, to answer the telephone, hobbling on her spiculed high heels, her hair dyed an even deeper orange from the fire, her smile crack-crackling, the phones ringing, she wants to assure her husband that shes perfectly all right and that he shouldnt worry. You just cant move her, mother. Itd be an act of treachery.

Get that fuckin corpse away from the phone for christs sake, Herb yells, his tongues stirrupped by the nose into slabbed tones.

Oh yes yes I can well understand her loyalty, Lionel Shafkin presses something at the bottom of his throat in order to speak by a hiccupping process, masticating and ingesting air, enunciating a syllable each time he inhales since the excision of his cancer-polluted larynx, a small stooped blubber of a man whose wife, Harriet, is Esther's older sister, whose movements proceed, according to Jared Emanuel, on the dotted line, a dottedline of a woman snipping away at her own flesh dotted lines to replace whatever is removed by another dottedline fleshsection, a minuscule juggler, forever poised and forever dotting, dotting her grayed skull vigorously at her husband Lionel who has approximately six months of hiccuping life left to him because part of his cancer escapes the voicebox before an operation tosses the larynx into the hospital's alcohol garbagecan, escapes and runs into every nook and cranny of the rest of body and revenges on the man who in his youth mounts the Baltimore soapbox and preaches socialism, preaches anywhere, preaches to Harriet, to his son Reuben, to Reuben's wife Shirley who in her social work accepts wayward girls from the juvenile authorities to live in her house so that she can pay said girl five dollars a week since shes performing an act of rehabilitative mercy, Lionel preaches, preaches in bed before and after and during the fuck while Harriet fucks him vigorously, dotting her skull, dotting her hips, dotting her vagina, yes yes yes she agrees, no no no pop Reuben disagrees, I dont know I dont know pop Shirley shakes her head, dotdotdot, but the cancers revenging itself for having been hurt in the voicebox, for having bled, for having been scalped out of the voicebox of this blubberstooped little man, this kindly and gifted cabinetmaker, one of the last of his craft, the cabinets machined out of his hands, his little blubberhands, his little stoopknuckled blubberfingers peempom, peempeem pom pom peempom he imitates the famed radio star The Streetsinger as he lies abed refusing many a day to go into work because he would rather stroll through the Baltimore parks and preach socialism to anybody who will listen, preach to himself if nobodys around but Harriet dotdotdots his every word if she walks with him, any time shes near him, hes her benignest, her stoopblubbered lover, the cabinetmaker who dots her womb, my love my Lionel, the jovial socialist dont you dare criticize him because i love him for singing about roses and violets and the Streetsinger's Fragrance Divine I love him because he wants everybody shouldnt slave, they should have time to enjoy themselves and hell lay late in bed singing in the morning all morning and what little blubberman in the world does that besides my Lionel, my jewel, my dancing socialist yes we go dancing, yes, in our forties and fifties we go dancing he says late in the morning in the middle of his singing Harriet lets go dancing tonight because all good socialists should dance once a week thats my Lionel, hes no slave, hes a craftsman, he signs his name in the wood LIONEL SHAFKIN, made by, but the cancer too is made by LIONEL SHAFKIN, made craftily, and its taking revenge, the worst kind, by talking, by talking because it escapes from the voicebox, and it talks clearly, it blabs in every part of his body, it preaches to all the other cells they should be cancers too, join us because were socialist cancers, the best kind, the noblest, the most advanced, the most humane, theyre true to me at least Lionel Shafkin smiles ruefully, theirs is a loyal revenge, so its all right Mrs Sherman you should keep sitting there at the phone waiting for your husband to call, let her stay his eye flashes noble fire at Herb Goldstein

Ah you fuckin red, Herb grumps, his spectacles nevertheless crinkling sprites at his uncle.

Listen, Wally, Nate stammers to L Wallace Mathews, the bald-headed Kensington councilman whose potbelly supports a spoke-chest, a spokeneck, and is supported by spokelegs and pinpointed flatfeet, whose redmottled face is varied by gray mottles, a masonic emblem joggling along his potbelly, his wife Gladys sitting in il-lustrated white grins beside him, once Gladys Jubilee Jordan Miss Patriot herself on the Scandals chorusline, now nestling two sluggish hogtits on her chest whose creased greasenecks are buried in her troughthroat, her brunette tresses in iron marcels, suspi-ciously, Marcus Kronthal the handsome nextdoor movieowner lotharioing by her side, fancying himself the Sheik of Israel astride the black stallions of his kinky hair galloping down the cobble-stone dunes of Philadelphia away from his wheelchaired wife, the Infidel Invalid, the Crippled Witch refusing to die, every fuck-ing things in her name, the moviehouse, the car, the home, the Sheik of Israel himself is in her name he twirls his nonexistent mustachios by curling his crimson lips, by curling his black eye-lashes, by curling his black eyebrows, the Lanolin Villain gallop-ing down the cobblestone sanddunes Gladys youre more beauti-ful than ever

Oh, Marcus she wiggles

stammering, I got a ticket for illegal parking is it possible I might drop in your office tomorrow to have it

Sure, sure, Nate, any time, any time at all, Im always avail-able and accessible, L Wallace Mathews pontificates.

Pass the marmalade Lilly, Walter Bergstrom issues the ukase in his melodious basso.

I guess I better undress now, huh Lee, Red winkthroats a whis-per and youre going to stay all night Rosa insists

Yes.

Youre not going home to mamma.

No whyd you give up ballet.

Theres a mysterious reason Rosa tiptoes to the ballet slippers under glass.

Tell me.

I cant. I just cant. Its a secret. Its an awful reason. I cant tell anybody. Nobody knows but me, Rosa Caby winkthroat whispers. Theres nothing you have to fear Silas Klein assures her. Im your lawyer

Lawyers represent, representational, Rosa casts down her voice, the eyelash shadows in her throat fluttering over it, I darent tell anyone she toedances around the glassedin balletslippers, her spiculetipped breasts high in her bodice, but Im never going back to my husband, not that he doesnt befriend me as soon as I reach America from Istanbul, Im a Carmen in his cigar factory, a poor defenseless little Carmen wrapping cigars

Cigarettes, Rosa.

Oh you musnt be so literal, Mark, she flounces away from the baldheaded boy, who turns from the piano during one of his composed Silences Would you mind if I played one of my Etudes during one of your Silences Cornelius politely staggers toward him.

I would, Cornelius

I just cant dance anymore, Lee, Rosa twitteringly complains. For an awful season

He doesnt own the cigar factory, Silas feels constrained to enter the clarification. Hes a foreman there. Lets keep the record straight, Rosa. Its unbecoming of so beautiful a girl

Woman, redheaded Hoppy Zitin insists

Girl, goddamn it

Im so much older than you, Lee Would you rather undress in the bathroom Red

No. I must do everything before you except you wont like my breasts

But Ive seen

But not when Im altogether naked then its different youll see how awful they but I wish youd take back your eyes and your genitals and your bowels and your heart and your shoulders I wish youd take back your whole body but I cant because after my husband fucks me he rolls over and snores and I wont be able to live if he isnt in pieces, the pieces can snore, I dont mind that TAKE BACK YOUR WHOLE BODY LEE I cant theres a mysterious

397

reason an awful reason I cant Rena but if you wish you can see my whole body under glass do you think Sy could paint my vagina if it its under glass

Now theres the perfect solution for you Lee Dr Clifford Gratz instantly takes up a collection.

BY THE PATRIOTIC GRACE OF GOD ALL THE MEN ARE HERE MISS JUBILEE JORDAN ANNOUNCES OVER THE PHILADELPHIA INTERNATIONAL AIRPORT LOUDSPEAKER SYSTEM HER BICEPTITS WRENCHING AT AND SHAKING THE GRAY VELVET CURTAINS OF THE PHILADELPHIA DAWN MILKBOTTLE H TILTING PRECARIOUSLY ICECOLD IM NOT SURE THIS IS THE TIME FOR ME TO DRINK SWEET MILK LEVI ANNOUNCES OVER THE LOUDSPEAKER SYSTEM LEVI EMANUEL IMMOBILE AND SHATSKYPARALYSED ON THE WHITE SHEETS FOR THE FIRST TIME IN MY LIFE I DONT WANT TO DRINK ANY MILK THE WHOLE GODDAMNED MILKBOTTLE IS ABOUT TO TOPPLE LEE PROP IT UP DAVID PROP IT UP LEE THE FIRST PROP IT UP SY TARASSOFF YOURE A PAINTER FOR GODS SAKE PROP IT UP ON A CANVAS NOW IS THE TIME FOR MY STRIPTEASE YOU NEVER HAVE SEEN DEATH DO A STRIPTEASE HAVE YOU LEE EMANUEL HERE IT IS EVERYBOY FOR ALL YOUR PARTS JARED EMANUEL SAYS WHOSE HOUSE ARE YOU STAYING AT WELL WERE STAYING AT MOTHERS YOU KNOW YOURE WELCOME TO STAY AT OURS BY THE WAY THIS IS MY SON RANDY HOW OLD ARE YOU RANDY IM FOUR YEARS OLD DAVID CLANCY MANN EMANUEL SAYS I HAVE A JAW LIKE A TOOTHPICK AND IM PICKING AT MY SLOPING SHOULDERS IM HUNGRY AS HELL LETS GO INTO THE AIRPORT RESTAURANT AND HAVE BREAKFAST WHERE YOU STAYING TONIGHT LEE OH IM FLYING RIGHT BACK NORMAS WORRIED AND I THINK I SHOULD JESUSCHRIST LETS GET SOME BACON AND EGGS WHOS DRIVING YOU TO YOUR MOTHERS RICHARD IS CHRIST JARED DAVID SAYS I HAVENT SEEN YOU IN SEVENTEEN YEARS YOURE LOOKIN GREAT THANKS JARED CHUCKLES THATS A GREAT LITTLE SON YOU HAVE THERE IN RANDY HEY RANDY YOU GONNA PLAY SOME BALL WHEN YOU GROW UP RANDY TELL HIM WHAT YOURE GOING TO DO IM GONNA BE A DOCTOR LIKE MY DADDY JARED CHUCKLES THE AIRPORT LOUDSPEAKER CHUCKLES THE PHILADELPHIA SUN BREAKS

398

THROUGH IN GOLDEN CHUCKLES HEY THERES RICHARD WADDYA
SAY DICK CHRIST I HAVENT SEEN YOU SINCE YOU WERE OUT ON
THE COAST WADDYA SAY DAD CHRIST WOULDYA BELIEVE IT
CLANCY SAYS I GOTTA GROWN SON TWENTYTWO YEARS OLD JESUS
CHRIST HERE WE ARE LAUGHIN AND POPS GONNA BE PUT IN THE
GRAVE WHAT KINDA CAR YOU DRIVIN DICK OH I GOT MY
THUNDERBIRD JESUSCHRIST WADDYA KNOW A THUNDERBIRD
WOULDNTYA KNOW IT TAKES SOMEBODY TO KICK THE CROCK
SO WE CAN ALL HAVE A FUCKIN REUNION CHRIST I NEED A SHAVE
AND SOMETHIN IN MY BELLY JUBILEE JUBILEE JUBILEE AN-
NOUNCES I TOLD YOU ID BRING OUT THE SUN FOR YOU THE SUN ON
MY PHILADELPHIA BELLY AND THE SUN ON MY PHILADELPHIA
CROTCH THE JAREDDOTTED LINE JOY OF THE GOLDENDOTTING
SUN JESUSCHRIST DICK IM SORRY I COULDNT FLY TO YOUR WED-
DING WHAT THE HELLS HER NAME AGAIN HER NAMES NORMA
SAME AS LEE'S WIFE CHRIST IM SORRY I COULDNT SEE THE OLD
MAN BEFORE HE DIED BUT I JUST DIDNT HAVE THE SCRATCH YOU
UNDERSTAND JARED SURE SURE I DO WELL WHAT THE HELL ARE WE
WAITIN FOR LETS GET SOME EGGS AND TOAST AND COFFEE AND
INTO THE THUNDERBIRD FLIGHT SEVENTYNINE FOR CHICAGO
FLIGHT NINETEEN FOR WASHINGTON DC NONSTOP FLIGHT THIRTY-
ONE FOR LOS ANGELES SAME OLD CRUMMY TOWN CLANCY SAYS I
USED TO DRIVE A CHARCOAL ROUTE DOWN DELAWARE AVENUE FOR
POP AND THERES THAT GODDAMN DIRTYWHITE HARBISONS MILK-
BOTTLE YOU CAN SEE ALL THE HELL DOWN HERE FROM KENSING-
TON DRINK THE MILK LEVI MISS JUBILEE JORDAN THE NURSE
LEANS OVER HIM HER TROCADERO TITS IN MULTICOLORED CARD-
BOARD FLATTENING OUT OVER HIS EYES OUR SON LEES ASHAMED
TO BE HERE HES NEVER SEEN A WOMAN DO A STRIPTEASE HES
AFRAID SOMEBODY HE KNOWS MIGHT CATCH HIM HERE TELL
HIM ITS ALL RIGHT LEVI TELL HIM ITS ALL RIGHT HE DOESNT
HAVE TO FEEL GUILTY OR ASHAMED WATCHING DEATH DO A
STRIPTEASE I WONT DRINK ANY OF YOUR MILK JUBILEE IM NOT
THIRSTY FOR THE FIRST TIME IN MY LIFE LEVI TRUMPETS TELL
HIM JUBILEE TRUMPETS TELL HIM ITS ALL RIGHT FOR HIM TO
SEE ME NAKED AND FOR EVERYBODY TO WATCH HIM WHO KNOWS
HIM THEY WONT BLAME HIM I TELL YOU I WONT BE HERE TO

WATCH YOU REMOVE YOUR GSTRING LEE PROMISES BECAUSE IM
TAKING THE TRAIN RIGHT BACK TO LOS ANGELES WITH NORMA
SEE I TOLD YOU LEVI EVERYBOYS ASHAMED REASSURE HIM
THAT ITS ALL RIGHT TO STAY I CANT I CANT I CANT STOP MILK-
BOTTLE H FROM TOPPLING BESIDES NORMAS PREGNANT I CANT
TAKE A CHANCE HER GIVING BIRTH THE SAME DAY THE PHYSIO-
THERAPIST WALKS POP AROUND THE HOSPITAL BED NOW MISTER
EMANUEL WHEN YOU MAKE THE LAST LAP WHICH IS THE FIRST
LAP THERES A SAUCER OF MILK WAITING FOR YOU THAT RACHEL
EMANUEL HAS PREPARED HOW DO YOU TAKE YOUR COFFEE SIR
THE WAITRESS SAYS WITH MILK LEE

black. Give it to me black, mother, he says to Esther Goldstein
But youve never taken it that way bef
Black.
Why are you so angry my son.
You know why Im angry.
No I dont kn
you know you chase Rena with a knife this afternoon down
the grass slopes of the stairs.
Is that what she tells
Theres no point denying Frankensteins Monster the Golem in
a flowered yellow housecoat in the yellow room climbing the
yellow grass slope toward him Diane I cant. The Golem is female
and will contaminate her fingers in the white greasy salve rubbed
into the ringworm infection on the inner part of his thigh brushed
by the left testicle. Underneath the white greasy salve is the suppurating ringworm in crimson slick patches occasionally granulated Dr Newman doesnt rupture the ringworms hymen a grease-
less white salve cakes Aunt Bella Zions face Uncle Sidney Zion
sitting patiently by her side in the upstairs bedroom at the window from which may be seen the high white flyball of the sun
batted far out to sea Sidney Zion is voiceless watching wife Bella
die so wheres Lee Bella asks her brother with Rena in Rochester,
where she sings. Good shes singing. He dont want to see me, its
all right Levi thats why I cant look at your father Russell Zion
tells Lee walking toward Market Street it has nothing to do with
that its simply that Im forgetting to return to Philadelphia I dont

know where Philadelphia is Ive got amnesia, Ive a right to the same things as Rena, I too can forget a whole death, I too dont know my name I abominate you, Russ says, for not knowing your name with respect to my mother. But you dont know, Lee says, your mothers dying of ringworm under the white salve why doesnt your father say anything why is he voiceless. Because he has a prefrontal lobotomy done on his throat, a historymaking piece of surgery, Jared has never before realized that the brain can lodge in the throat. No, no thats not the reason, your fathers a socialist, and hes been preaching immortality the same as Lionel Shafkin, and Bellas taking revenge on him, thats why hes so silent in the yellow room. Why do you want the lights off Rosa. Because the reason for my giving up the ballet is a terrible secret I wish you wouldnt come any closer to me Diane Im a

virgin, Lee.

Oh no. Rena is.

Not after Dr Newman.

All right technically shes not a virgin, he

Youre splitting hairs

No he spl

Itll be easier Rena if I lay flat and youre above me that way as soon as it hurts you can lift yourself off

But it shouldnt hurt because Dr Newman

Its always possible

My daughters a virgin she does it ten times in one night with an actor Diane, well, really, after the second time I dont really feel Newman is a doctor not an actor. Didnt you know hes interested in the stage, the hymeneal proscenium Clifford Gratz points out Id know that and Im only a dentist, as Labia Majora equals minus M, the Minotaur at the center of Renas labyrinth Jay Grays didactically interjects. Milkbottle H slips, quite slightly. Burnredfaced Gene Hertzog says Ill be goddamned if I want Donald Schwartz to have powerofattorney thats bullshit to hell with the Levi Coal Company I can do without it who needs it who wants it its a headache Ill be fucked If I got into partnership Levi if your newphew Schwartz has powerofattorney thats what he tells me on the phone Russ, Lee reports. Hes full of shit, he isnt going to throw up that business simply because he doesnt have power of attor dont let him bullshit you dont promise him a goddamn thing.

Im cold

Diane frowns her disraeli nose, Hymie Krause the Levi Coal Company truckman

Youre dead of cancer of the nose. Look at all the holes around the room, the nostrils are spreading around the yellow arclight at the opposite end of the room.

Dianes red hair narrows her forehead. Its summer, you cant be co

Your hair. Red Ash. The clinkers in my bowel

Clancy

Is that the actors name

Yes

My brothers an actor. I direct him, in tribute

Ill put out the light

No

Dont you want to

Look, Hymie, go to your horse

But I squeeze your blackheads on the beach Diane pleads. There must be some recompense. You feel shivers of compressed delight

Too exotic. You cant squeeze the blackheads out of my ringworm, whichd be universal, something everybody could recognize, be familiar with. You squeeze my nose, Hymie, trying to keep the cancer horse from kicking out my brain

Operate, Mrs Coffman

Operate, Mr Coffman

Operate, Carla

Theres nothing to operate, shes got the simple headaches of adolescence

Ive got a headache, Diane says

Nothing, Lee says. Merely the blackhead in your brain

Operate, Rena says, even though shes my dearest friend

Jareds opinion: a delicate procedure, to excise the blackhead from your vagina, Rena

Operate, Rena says, Im cold

Lee sits bunched up at the head of Dianes bed, Im yellow, Im cold

I want to be operated on, Carla says

Youre not cold, her fiance Sonny Bond says

No, its nothing more than simple adolescence that has to be removed, Rena says so, Renas my friend, Im tired of lying in bed, take the adolescent blackhead out of my brain

Its going to be a tight squeeze Jared gives his considered opinion. Its a case of simple adolescence, Diane tells Lee

Im cold, Ive got to put on my clothes. Forgive me

I understand

Liar. Stop understanding, Diane

Understanding flows out of me each time I pincer my sharp fingernails around a boys blackheads

But you wont chance the ringworm will you look at that poor young girl in the Jewish Hospital bed right next to Renas miscarriage her ringworm lodges in her hipbone because she scratches between her toes and the parasitical fungus enters her blood and nestles in her hipbone theyre treating her with xray

Ill roll out the ringworm by a roll of my hip Jubilee Jordan offers

Ive got ringworm of the eyball Lee says and a thick greasy paste is smeared over it and Achille Volpe comes to sculpture it using his own blind white left eye to mold it

I understand. Let me lie next to you

The cancer of the heart is the size of a peach in Carla Coffman's brain

This is not what I expected to discover, Jared says. Im confronted by a severe problem. If I remove the cancer of the heart in her brain Carla will die. If I permit the cancer of the heart to remain in the brain, Carla will die. What is it that you prefer, Carla

Thats unfair. Im under anesthetic

It is one of the conditions of life that one must come to decisions while drugged

But if the cancer of the heart is in the brain, what lies in my chest cavity

It is not necessary to know that to come to a decision but since

403

you ask I will tell you : your close friend Rena lies in your chest cavity

What is she doing there

Shes running

From whom

Her mother

Why

Her mother unfairly uses a rib for a knife

But youre using a rib for a knife

Yes

Why

Its the only congruency I can summon up to remove the cancer of the heart in the brain. Of course, I could reinsert that cancer into your chest cavity

But that would deny Rena a home. Her mother would find her

Yes

Or my mother would find her

Yes

And her adolescence would be discovered. This way, Doctor, she can hide in my death. Oh, its true Im her friend, but shes no friend to me

But, either way, Carla, you cannot function without the cancer of the brain in your heart

Thats not the way you put it

Its the only way Lee can discover how to blow his nose

Stop blowing your nose

Ive got to. Renas in there, Carlas in there

Suppose I dont come to a decision Dr Emanuel. The anesthetic says I dont have to. The anesthetic says Im small and dark and sad. The anesthetic says Im very young

Twenty years of age

NINETEEN

ONE BILLION AND THREE

FOUR

The anesthetic circles in hoops around my head Im too young to have to come to such major decisions AS TO WHETHER I SHALL DIE ONE WAY OR DIE ANOTHER why does Rena have to hurt me so

Because youre small and dark and sad and she is big and the color of rotten oranges and jubilant and she lives in you. She invades your small, dark and sad room with jubilance. She injects herself into you and bursts within you and the cancer of your heart runs frantically to hide in your brain. Youre pale, small
dark
sad
on the operating table. What do you want me to do
Just sit on the bed.
Yes, Lee
Youre a model, youll have my brother Clancy ten times in one night. Theres no room for me. Youre all stuffed up, theres a flood from MILKBOTTLE H damned up in you why shouldnt my father want a drink of cold milk now hes always loved cold milk at midnight why do we have to pose for him Rena youre not to undress before my father Im cold. Im afraid
I wont hurt you Diane says with her pinchedin disraeli nose, her pinched in convex breasts, those small delicate mammillary noses
its not that its that Im afraid of discovering the comparative weights of three elements, the element of my father's body, the element of Gail Greene's body, the element of my penis
GODDAMN IT IM NOT DYING, Diane yells
NO NEITHER IS MY PENIS
then lift him
who
your father
wait
no. Lift him, then Gail
You goddamn nurse
Ill nurse you after you lift them
And Carla reminds him : and lift Rena, lift Rosa, lift Diane
Is that your decision, Miss Coffman
Yes, Dr Emanuel
In unison the various parts of Lee stationed around the Troc Theater agree with Carla Coffman I didnt expect that I could be stirred by a stripteaser on the operating table Doctor. In uni-

son Harry Ring Achille Volpe Cornelius and Fiona Nuri Hoppy
Zitin Mark Fahn Sy and Nina Tarassoff Dr Newman Rachel
Emanuel David Emanuel Maurie Tarassoff Bettie Emanuel Sue
Emanuel Aaron Emanuel Bella and Sidney and Russell and
Donna Zion Terry Shannon Norma Celia Renn Daniel Naroyan
and Silas Klein Herb and Frances and Nate and Hannah Gold-
stein Christine Novak and Gene Hertzog Clifford and Nadine
Gratz and Milkbottle H Charlotte and Gus Nathanson and Bruno
Canova Duke Montaigne Mike and Myra Burroughs Lloyd
Engle Noah Hudsen Clement Lichtenstein Kanovsky and Anne
Kanovsky Jubilee Jordan Frankensteins Monster : lift

LIFT

LIFT BELLOWS VINCE HARRISON WHOSE PRICK IS AS LONG
AND BIG AND BROAD AS MILKBOTTLE H AND SWOLLEN WITH
HOMOGENIZED MILK

youre responsible for murdering mother because you insist on
moving to new york with nina, Maurie Tarassoff accuses Sy

lift

you cant paint because i murder mother, sy puffs his pipe.
Your eyes are red

from rubbing off the paint i cant see through color

lift

you cant see through the mothers color i use

you paint mother with nina's color

lift

one should paint mother with wifes color to obscure mother
whos underneath/you or mother

lift

shes going to die one way or another like carla coffman
mothers in carla's adolescence

callous

no, paint

you paint callouses

to peel them, theres white tenderness beneath

you paint callouses on mother

to peel her

you paint mother to peel yourself. Does Nina save the peelings

406

she uses them on her own canvasses. She paints my mother all the time because her mothers alive. Would you have me withdraw my compassion from Nina

to keep our mother alive, yes

shes not ours. Shes mine, shes yours. Not ours

youre puffing paint from your pipe, brother

lift

that gives the paint a smokey quality, it gives mother a smokey quality

its gives mrs sherman a smokey quality

yes. Mothers waiting for fathers phonecall and we all know fathers dead and thats the reason i move to New York

lift lift lift

to be away from father

yes. She wants me to answer the phone. She wants you to answer the phone. She wants us to be in communication with father. She doesnt want to. Consequently I break communication between myself and mother. She wants her oldest son to lift him out of the grave, out of the dead. Thats what oldest sons are for, she says. Go talk to him yourself I tell her. Dont give me your responsibility. But she says that responsibilitys for oldest sons, to raise fathers from the dead and take them away from their wives

lift lift lift

and?

and have the fathers live with the oldest sons in new york so she can scream at me from Philadelphia that I robbed her of her husband. She begs me to move out of Philadelphia

stop it

you want to know the reasons

stop it

ive got fathers body with me in new york. She kills herself, Maurie Tarassoff. Now go ahead and paint. Ill take care of father. Youre too young

to take care of Mr and Mrs Coffman. Youre better off dead, Carla Marcus Kronthal Harriet and Lionel Shafkin Mr and Mrs Ackman Gladys and L Wallace Mathews chorus to Lee:

LIFT Dr Arthur Shumway Mr and Mrs Wohl Zusserman

Melinkoff Degen Dr Jonah Silver Barry and Selma Handler
LIFT Lily and Walter Bergstrom and Donald Schwartz LIFT
Hymie Krause
I KNEW IT I KNEW IT I KNEW IT LEE EMANUEL SCREAMS IVE
GOT RINGWORM IN THE AFRICAN INTERIOR OF MY HIPBONE
AND
THIS
IS
THE
WAY
IT
MAKES
ME
FUCK
he doesnt want to lift whispers Rhona Lyrian Flikker Hedda
Myers Xena Ritchie Joshua Nathanson Mister MacLennihan so
he contracts
RINGWORM OF THE HIPBONE FUNDAMENTALLY ALTERING THE
INTERIOR OF THE VISCERAL CONGO PYGMIES BLOWING BLACK-
HEAD GUNS THOU MAKEST A PYGMY IN THINE IMAGE OH LORD.
And pygmy ants the life of the prancing pygmy lances off the
earth. Where dyest thy itch oh lord, this ringworm of cloud, this
girlgust honeysuckling, the white snowsalve greasing off in tire
blowout patches. I prickle in my homeanness, I come off in
thrashes of angel, the Lord itcheth with small boys, my son.
Threeist out thy hip in femalies, virgin god, the hospital sheet of
owlectrons over thee, that the heavyside liar that stomps Hymie
Krause, horses kicking my brother three thousand miles to California. What oxray profails, Carla, what clocksray chimpanzee-
ing through the brainvines. Ah, do I itch bedrails, the nurses of
serpents under the coils of the chinese buddha, the shafkin cabinet signed Leeonel priestrate on my chest, the Devil impaled on
my N'muxt penis minarets, flashing
pissbottles and
rubbers
I leave I leave o
my milkbottle too rich with leviblood. When doth the Lord

stride with the chandelier through the hipnight. Mustardbation, the genitals yellowshit, the lurid canarykite. We are less divine when ringworms will not jingle. What will you tell Aaron Emanuel salaaming with his people before the Golden Phallus

WEARING GOLDEN PROPHYLAXES THREE TIMES TOO LARGE FOR HIM NO JEHOVAH WILL PERMIT HIMSELF TO BE FUCKED BY SUCH A MAN; he doesnt want to lift he doesnt w

men have masscarriages through the hipbone, the ringworm itching out all ambryosias, smell the hospital honeysuckle smell, rachel smell thee all thy shilldren as you go riding in the congo, riding in the congo on christinasuckles spilt for two. My bunions squeal. The squalling ceilings, yellowwhite, mothers magenta this year. Itch: how then will she touch. Itch: how then will she douche her makeup one flinch deep

thirty trillion flinches deep AH. aw. yes

THE LITTLE GOLEM ON THE BEACH THE PYGMY FRANKENSTEIN MONSTER HATH RINGWORM OF THE HOOPHIP

    RED

      RED

        RED

        IS

          THE

            CHOLER

            OF

              MY

              SHOETIMES TOO LARGE

OF MY SHELOVES HER.

worms;are;gristly chew

LIFTletherchewonmyfathersprickspittingoutthenonediblRED ASH RENA; i itch with blinkers, i watch the oceans on their rolling hipbones, the oceans in the hospital suffering from hordes of ringworm, thrashing under my eyelid diane hashing under my leyelid rosa the crimson ringworm of the setting sun against the opalescent scales

SMELL

sweet sugared piss of my life

SMELL

oh walt shitman of the isolated cornelius nuri skulls

It ith not caththrathun that he fearth buth the theecapittha-thun of hith thkull; fie, feeonah

what ith thy theramical fee;

pewter death go thracking in KILNWORMS :

They who do bake me in unseen rays; they who do hold me sovereign in my spartan draconism; they who do filch from me my unquivers; they who do roll me from the motherbodies to the girls; they who do say come thou enter; they who do bid me clasp; they who do hold with anastoMoses and the Promised Land; they are Third Bibles in the room.

Third Bibles, this Rue Testament. The Gospel of the Bord According to St Fled. The Gospel of the Whord According to St Shed. The Gospel of the Gord According to St Bull. The Gospel of the Floord According to St Softshoe. The Gospel of the Cord According to St Jonah Silver. The Yom Caper Kenosis of the Shamused Land Hempty Empty Sat On A Wall Hempty Empty Had A Great Fall And All Clementkinks Horses And All Clementkinks Men Couldnt Foot Hempty Empty Together Again;

Because Hempty Empty wears a shell forty trillion sizes too large for him,

Oh darling Cinderella has three evil mothers and they are Esther and Harriet and Lilly thats why I dont want to say

it SAY it Lillys married before yes shes married to a Philadel-phia gambler yes and when he doesnt have any money during the depression he sends Lilly out to whore

thats my mother lilly

and my mother esther well she dont know who she is so she has mother lilly take care of me and then i go to baltimore where she has mother harriet take care of me and theres a great big fire and im saved but i contract cancer of the mother

as achilles had his heel so doth Volpe have his eye and

WHEN THE ARROW OF SIGHT SHALL ENTER INTO HIS MILKY BLINDNESS THEN SHALL HE SEE DEATH

You got cancer of the mother, Diane says.

You got cancer of the mother, Rosa says.

410

But Prince Charming, Rena says, can CURE CANCER OF THE
MOTHER tell me you l
and the greatest of these three mothers, Faith Lilly and Hope
Harriet
is Esther Charity lift
Lift up thy hands in charity, Lee
AM I MY FATHERS WEEPERSLEEPERSHEEPERPEEPERDEEPER;
aye;
reaper
Lift up thy itching hands oh Lord Lee, that the Sling of Glory
may come in;
Bermuda.
Rosa.
Hannah.
Nate.
Gail.
Levi
cataclimbs of names. Catasuckles. Opposed to the boy anafalls
in the bathtub and his nonames. Catanames. A dog lunges a
length of chain, and a blond girl falls, dumbing her skull, her
thighs gothic. Gargoyle the Dog is his name, seeketh he pussy-
cataname, for no dogs pussy hath been put by men on the cathedral, nay, son; nay, Jubilee; for tis Jubilee Jordan, Miss Patriot
herself, who dislodges Gargoyle the Dog and is herself thrown
to the pavement, her head cracked in the pussycombs, and her
thighs all gothic to the dark, that the Scarlet Phallus Crow From
The Crown Of The God Of Men
Oh, Lee, I hear thy cock crow in gargoyles. The boys and girls
of the Graduating Class ponder this in the simple churches of
America, for they have no gothic here in the Rue Testament I
am such a boy and I am such a girl Lee professes in the simple
synagogues of America. The Golem comes not to me from
Prague but from a comicbook Frankenstein Monster, see: terror
is made godless in these cities:
Then you must lift.
The reluctance to lift is directly associated with Lee's anticipation of making an error. But two bodies wait, living. Gail

Greene's body, lightly flushed under the white sheet in the hospital room; lightly pulsed, nevertheless, even; her eyelids folded over the six foot length of her body; the long equine face resting its sleep no further down beyond the upper thigh of one leg amputated; the black shoulderlength hair in lustrously yielding tensions under the soaping sun as thin as you are, Betty Emanuel, before you marry Dave but you will never lift me now because I register over three hundred pounds but theres one you can lift, and the living body of your father though he be three times Gail Greene's heft but then she has three four five hours to live while Levi has three four five days. In deference to Gail's imminent insubtantiality the lifting must be done now and the error made standing under the canopy at Dr Joan Silvers Lee marries Rena who weighs two hundred and sixty pounds Im too fat why should you want to marry me. It is a reverse brotherhood. After you have your first miscarriage in Kansas you rapidly lose weight after Betty has her first child by Dave she rapidly gains weight it is the redistribution of fate; besides, Dave wants you, Rena. Gene Hertzog the wholesale charcoal trucker, Henry Feinstein the chief weigher and office manager and leader of the boyscout troup that in unison divorces him from his wife in the supreme example of American adolescent efficiency, and Richard Emanuel Daves son by Betty form a partnership to purchase the Levi Coal Company over a period of ten years I dont trust Hertzog the worried beak of Donald Schwartz, Levi's lawyer nephew, proclaims, hes sneaky thats what he is hes just plain sneaky when I hear Levi is giving him the Buick out of gratitude

Hertzog buys a hospital bed

Hertzog purchases an airconditioner for the dying room

Hertzog visits Levi each day now Mrs Emanuel theres anything I can do for you you let me know dont you worry about a thing

you need a nurse Ill get a nurse

Lee the whole time youre in Philadelphia I want you to use the Buick

just call on me my time is yours

you want to see the vouchers for payment of the electric bill the gas bill the doctors bill I got them all here I want you should feel secure you shouldnt think anythings done under the counter

theres nobody else Rachel says who else is there to do all these things nobody else wants to nobody else does whats true is true so dad gives him the Buick a small return for his favors

just the same, Donald says, hes sneaky, he could pay Levi a token sum and even that he doesnt do, he could at least pay the depreciation value and what does he do oh hes a smart one that Hertzog as soon as Levi gives him the owners license right away Hertzog has it transferred to his wife's name the same day I hear about it I go into the Emanuel garage to obtain the keys I dont think its right Hertzog should have the car at least give it to Lee so I go in the garage to get the keys and right away I see the keys are gone the ownership license is gone I tell you I dont trust him

DONT MAKE AN ERROR NOW LEE his father grunts at him you got to weigh you and Dave want the business or not because Im in no condition to think clearly Lee Im in no condition LIFT LIFT LIFT

All you have to do is put your arms under his armpits the nurse quietly explains. All you have to do is put your arms under her hips the nurse quietly explains. Nothing more.

Nothing m

Thats all.

But she doesnt appear to be sick. Levi does. There is a difference of five, six days between their respective deaths. Why must I be compelled to make an error. Gail Greene is simply an acquaintance of long standing. Levi Emanuel is my father for thirty-nine of my years. These two simply cannot be equated. Levi is fully conscious. Gail is under sedation and feels no pain the doctors say. Levi feels pain. A wan summer light enters the windows from the alleyway separating the Forstens and the Emanuels; we burn a light in the breakfast dying room; the airconditioner hums low. In Gail's hospital room the strong afternoon sun numbers the motes of dust by gold; through the window may be descried the long rolling green lawns of the Jewish Hospital grounds, some picture postcard illustrations, not usually having stamps affixed,

413

of old men and old women in wheelchairs under the swollen green
trees

I want Lee where is he

Were trying to reach him

Why isnt he here why isnt he

Were trying to reach him as fa Dr Arthur Shumway says paci-
fyingly

Art

Yes, Rena

I felt his hand I tell you I felt his

That impos

I tell you I Lee Lee Lee his hand why could I feel his h

in the fucking, the first time, with Lee, the first time, but this
is imposs, as Art Shumway, his hand cant be fractured, theres
something wrong in this sexual intercourse

something wr

lee im not saying this you understand im not accusing you i
dont mean to accu but your hand

what of

your h

cant be that of a

hand its

only inter

course, not with a

ch you cant

Rena what are you try

a prick is

nt a

CHILDS HAND FUCKING ME NO THAT CANT no

Were not in a hospital room Lee are we

No

Im not giving birth am I

No

Then why is it I can feel childs brokenknuckled penis youre
weighing youre weighing youre getting even taking revenge your
fathers lift that gail

mein kint WHAT KNIFE

414

my mother kills the child with her knife she sticks it up my
cunt she chases it all the way up vulva up the stairs down the
thighs im running from her all the time running from birth shes
bringing the phone down on your hand

on your prick

rena youre getting hyster

doctor arthur goldstein you sonofabitch thats not the way i
want to have intercourse LIFT while all one sees

dr newman tell lee im a virgin because i ·want him here

but he is. On the bed

he doesnt believe me the cement wall of the Forstens, gray,
patched, seen through the dying room of Levi Emanuel. Under
the armpits. Under the hips. One young girl. One old man;

that, lifting, Lees arms under the armpits hips, the one heavy,
the one light, one unconscious, one awake, one old,

one young.

Impossible.

that, lifting, the refrains of flesh at his fingertips, there is this
probe. What yields. They are naked under the sheet, Levi's bare
flesh, Gail's. His breath comes in wasps. His breath comes in peek-
ings. He looks through a crack in the door. But one is debarred
from doing so : an injunction against the lifting of the flesh; and,
injunctions in the process of transformation motivate one to
spread one's refusal to accept; one pushes oneself aside; one
spreads one's legs; thighs become hands; Lees muscles cry into
sensuousness; one does not feel the woman in the man; one does
not feel the man in the woman; they are at crosspurposes; but in
the dying, one bends one's knees at an altar; one makes a sacrifice,
hands ripple sacrifices under the sheet, hands ripple sweated foreheads under the sheet; she is nothing more than someone of long
acquaintance, and a virgin; his father is a man of long years with
Lee, and no virgin. But Lee is a virgin to his father, and no virgin
to Gail. In the presentation of Gail to Levi, and of Levi to Gail,
the courtesy is done by hand, the introduction of the nakednesses
under the sheet that one is not supposed to witness. But in the
witnessing is the heat. Lee averts his eyes from Gail, from Levi,
and the eyes enter the thighed hands in that in this instant of

415

the lifting the friending to Gail must be more than so, the sonning to Levi must be more than so, in that death do us part. In the lightness and the heaviness of the dying we are seduced : the naked bodies coming in as combers from the sea upon the prostrate handthigh sands of Lee so that, all but losing his balance, all but breaking his throat in two to regain air from the towering descent of the green flushed lightness of Gail and the green flushed heaviness of Levi, he grimaces his abdomen into a pyramid. Ugly. He must throw them off. But he must throw them off courteously; be ugly in compassion; come to life out of this dying tenderness; and in so doing is thrust into error, but it is the horror of a half error, of unconsummated seminecrophilia, of half error monstrously compounded, a tending to masturbating seminecrophilia, and that, too, condemned to further removal. It is a sensual removal in the concourse of contact, the gasping for air in two beings windpipes, a surgical operation done over immeasurable distances as his thighhands probe into the bubbling delicacies of Gail Greene's naked hipflesh, Lee's fingernails tickled by the bubbles growing under the nails, his father's hairy armpits honeysuckling into Lee's fingerjoints, the odor trellising about Gail's hips. What shall he do with these weights. The young girl and the old man seek him; he is their sole object, and their object, without either girl or old man aware, is error upon Lee, to which they must commit him. It is as if they will commit him to an asylum for an instant. It is as if in this instant they tell him how much an inundated lunatic he is in the legion of the temporarily insane. The old man glares at him; the young girl lolls her drugged head at him; the young girl and the old man are shadowily fragrant, witheringly warm, they offer Lee the question of where, where precisely, where vaguely, where anywhere Lee Emanuel is the dying, where, where, where. Either glaring or asleep, where? In the lifting it is your responsibility to tell us where; in the lifting is your responsibility to locate us as we are. Lee's pyramid has many slaves; there are untold generations of slaves erecting my pyramid that will cast you off, that will have you sacrifices to the pyramid god. The slaves lift up great ponderous blocks of stone, lift up my muscles, lift you up, old man

416

and young girl. Generations raise you. You understand I do not
have to answer your challenge of where your dying as if I know
exactly where the death is. But theres a cowardice in the incom-
petence of being unable to assess the penultimate. I may say there
is no dying, and I know precisely where your living is. And, again,
the error presents itself, hard, unyielding, penetrative, and erring
in each of these attributes in that there can be no penetration,
so that it must lose its potency. The error, losing potency, is no
error at all. But Lee, really, does not want to find the errorless-
ness. He prefers the error, and the old man and the young girl
have him, take him at the height of his tension as a sighing swirls
inside his mouth, shut mouth, no sound issuing in the breakfast
chamber of the Jewish Hospital, gold and gray commingling on
the green rolling lawns of the alleyway wall. We want you, we
want you, we want you the old man and the young girl utter together, in that it does not matter who you are. In our dying you
are condemned to anonymity. And it is precisely Lee's erection
that would dispel that anonymity and become an even more in-
dubitable anonymity, so that, straining to lift the two, the girl
and the old man, he would shift their weight to his erection, by
god that would tell them who he is, that few men could so lift
and so support—and they have him unerringly and masterfully
in error, in that his penis swells to them both undifferentiatedly;
swells, without possibility of recompense; swells, both to female
and male in their coupled dying; his penis derives pleasure from
the contact with their dying. That, then, is their precise location
—between Lee's thighs. And for this, for this he would rend them
in two. He denies their dying in his genitals. He denies the girls
unconsciousness in his genitals as he denies his fathers pain in his
genitals. In this moment he knows, by the visitation upon him
of temporary sanity by their commission that they order an
autopsy upon his genitals. It is only fair, they say, that the cause of
our deaths be exactly known. It is only fair that the record be
clear : we suspect you of murder. And still his erection sustains.
He is accused of murder, and his genitals harden the more; he is
accused of murder, and he wishes to fuck them the more. The
intent is clear, they say; look down at your thighs. We avenge

ourselves by your lifting us. We avenge ourselves for your degrading us. And it is only fair that you undergo full punishment the glaring eyes of Levi phrase, the lolling blackhaired head of Gail moans. For what more of an error can you possibly commit than being stimulated to an erection as you lift two dying human beings. Youve got to pay for your error. For ours, then, is an accidental death. We are between your thighs and we demand to live, but you let us die by not having an orgasm, by letting your member become flaccid by default. You are no primitive, that is clear. You make no effort to save us. You do not spray us with sperm. You withhold, you frustrate us, you do not attempt the slightest bit of magic. And it is magic that we need. All else has failed you goddamned rotten sadistic ruthless rationalist. It is reasonable for us to die you

    reasonable

    reasonable

    reasonable

    is that a truth we ask you?

    It is reasonable to let us die while your loins mock us?

    Another error, part of the same error, your reason. Cast us down, then, it is time, even as Moses dashes down the Tablets of the Law upon the idolatrous multitude. Dash us into fragments and tiny pieces. We come from God and you worship a Golden Phallus. What greater error can you possibly commit. What are you weighing, then, in either hand, an old man Levi as against a young girl Gail Greene. What is the virtue of your lift. We do not need your lift. A stunned Lee holds them aloft. I am asked to lift you.

    Evasion.

    You do not have to respond.

    Get somebody else to lift us.

    Get somebody else who will not favor us with an erection. Now, if you submit to an autopsy, you might be exonerated. Let them slit open your penis

    Gail chuckles.

    Levi roars with laughter.

    One half for me, she says.

One half for me, he says.

Can you do without us, both say. Can you do without the young girl and the old man in your penis?

Obviously it is too much to ask of Lee that he die for this young girl and this old man in the moment of his lifting them. And there, too, he is in error, for he cannot possibly die for them. And they are aware of it. They castigate him by farting. A soft fart from the young girl, a hard fart from the old man. Both issuing through Lee's anus.

He looks around. Nobody sniffs. The combined farts are odorless. Whitejacketed attendants, his mother, Norma, Danny Naroyan. They neither sniff nor glance at the bulge in his trousers. Fortunately, to make himself a better fulcrum, he bends at the knee, which conceals the erection, the whole character of Lee bending at the knee, so that he is absolutely faithful both to his erection and to lifting Gail and Levi, a perfect illustration of his keeping himself sexually intact for Rena while he believes her capable of any act in the whole spectrum of behavior; his absolute fidelity is his stubborn insistence at masking her innate anarchy to himself, for he himself anarchically loves the girl, loves her with the erection toward a dying girl and dying man, an erection pointed away from St Red, simianly, Rhona Lyrianly bent at the knee, for it is the divine genius of the anthropoid ape that sways through the Spinozamugged Rhona and her long, pluckfingered arms that pick out fourlegged blackheads from Diane and Rosa and all females as Rhona lopes through Lee, nagging through his dense hair, bidding him bend at the knee, to be dubbed, Knight Emanuel, made royalty for the contribution of his erection to the dying Rhona swaggers forth her leer, There,

there

The ape Lee Emanuel lifts Gail and Levi, and the error at last is thoroughly clear, that the beast, unable to acknowledge his bestiality, bends at the knee, permitting him his bestiality and at the same time his human aping, in that he is lifting down human Gail and human Levi, an operation that, in its debasing, stimulates the beast to an erection, for he would crow his equality, vaunt his emancipation, that only a beast could do as humans die

419

for he does not recognize their human dignity at all : it is an opportunity for him to raise his bestial dignity, for he will live, passing them, and he shakes his penisfist. The error lies in the assump-
tion that the erection is a consequence of eroticism; actually it ensues from revolutionary scorn, of Marxist ardor rampaging in the
ape's balls, something no human as yet realizes, Lee smirks to
himself : neither Russian nor American cognizant that Marxism
spreads to the lower animal orders Gail stirs Levi trumpets wordlessly at Lee, both touched by Lee's bestiality made royal, and they
know they are leaving the world to the beasts; that one, after all,
dies for the lower animal orders. Lee feels that Gail and Levi
momentarily want to be beasts, that only so may they tolerate
their humanness, forgive their humanness. Lee has smelled their
combined farts, quickly, animally assimilated them before any
human can detect them. Their castigation of him is a warning to
the other humans, but Lee intercepts it, successfully. How else,
then by consulting beast, can he endure their dying? Rhona
knows how superior a beast Lee is; so does Rena. Rhona wants to
blind him for it; Rena believes she can cope with it by virtue of
her nonhumanness, by her offshootedness. They both know he
battens on the waves of the dying so that he can keep up his es-
pionage. Lee is the lookinglikeman who faithfully reports on the
humans he moves among; hence his notion of absolute fidelity to
Rena : she must not suspect his bestiality; and he certainly cannot clue in Clement Lichtenstein, cannot reveal the prime bestial
motivation, the Frankenstein Golem Monster on the movie
screen that Lee instantly concedes kinship to, that beast both
Christian and Jew know, the Christian attempting to exorcize
him by an hallucinatory horror, and the Jew by a benign fal-
sification. The next move by Lee is that he rises in his seat as he
sees the flames leap higher and higher about the Monster; the
boy rushes into the aisle and charges to the rear of the movie house
where, with an erection, he watches the filmed fire consume the
beast, and he cannot but wonder, the beast sweating under his
thickly matted eyes, when the fire, as he lifts Gail and Levi, will
reach out toward him, toward Lee who starts, trembles, revolts.
Levi wordlessly commiserates. Gails eyelids fumble at an opening.

420

In essence, Lee weighs the balance of his bestiality against his humanness, shifting old man and young girl on to the scale of his erect penis, and this is the worst error of all, since it is inequitable to weigh any living thing in the process of dying; for, by the weighing, he would prolong their lives The error seems endless, but everybody is powerless to correct it at any given point, and Lee is embarrassed by their powerlessness to correct his erection. Nobody can cut off his beastprick at the source; nobody can elongate it into unmistakeable humanity. He must put these people down. Not put them down in the places they belong, Levi in the wheelchair and Gail on the rolling table destined for the xray room, but put them down in somebody elses hands before the transfer is effected. Because he is not equipped to handle the dying either as beast or man. He cannot, after all, reach a decision either as beast or man as to whether or no Gail and Levi should die or live. He confesses to himself he has no opinion one way or the other, and he feels he must exact a decision from himself, feels that this is a prime moment for a being to decide if he wishes another being to live or die, whether or no the decision will affect the outcome of Gail and Levi. But with penis erect, Lee is bereft of decision. His penis castrates him, renders him impotent while, itself, remains magnificently virile, a stupefyingly comic reversal, indicating yet another error, which is that Lee deems their dying susceptible of pollution. Do, then, both Gail and Levi provoke Lee's erection in order to mock his bestiality? to cast doubt upon it? to make him bend like a beast under Gail's lightness and Levi's weight? so that they can be amused at the frozen shamble of his gait? the young actor inept at his role? Do they then transform Rena into a figure of monstrousness, showing her to him for what she is? Rena waits in the corridor, heavy with child, waits for Lee with Rick Russo, her husbandtobe, as Norma waits on the porch, heavy with child, for her husband Lee. His erection is panic-stricken, it does not know which way to turn, to point, to give of its sperm, virility without object, virility not even certain that it can turn upon itself and discharge down Lees thighs, and he senses that it completes a circle, he senses that it makes of itself a hoop and begins to revolve about his hips, neither clockwise nor counterclockwise. The dying of Levi and Gail has gotten even with Lee in his lifting of these two figures; he has brought their dyings up to his mouth, to his level, and he is stricken to the earth by the club of an erection that, mercilessly, refuses to touch him and hoops about him instead on the sandy beach of a golden gray afternoon, the gulls CRAWKCRAWKING from the ceiling in a swaying, iridescent chandelier of flight, his skull become a pendant prism bound in crystal facets flashing with fragmented pregnancies:

These are not mine, he says, putting back the bundles of Levi and Gail on their beds.

This is not mine, he says, tucking back his erection.

Alarmed at the vacancy between his thighs, he quits the room
Pass the salt Walter Bergstrom the vertical covered wagon rumbles to Lilly
Yes my love
Pass the
Yes my
Pass
Y

Y

Y i tie his shoes in the morning I untie his shoelaces at night
Pass the Y i make him his chicken each night on the hotplate thats all theyll permit in the hotel room and I absolutely detest Mrs Kream while you know I absolutely adore New Orleans but theres nothin I can do about Mrs Kream after all her husband DOES

employ my little Walter, and if my little Walters got to be at Mister Kreams beck and call why you can understand why I have to be at Mrs Kreams beck and takes me shoppin in her limousine

takes me to the hairdresser in her limousine

takes me to the track in her limousine

but I absolute adore New Orleans absolutely nothin would stir me out of that city Pass m
I dress that big fat man

I love him

in the morning and I undress that big fat man

I love him
at night

I just love him I just do I couldnt get along without my little Walter

Now Nathan you just take this here silver dollar Walter Bergstrom hauls up his breath via the freight elevator to the suede blue penthouse atop the covered wagon, the oxen pawing in phlegmatic fury under his chest and give it to your Founding Fathers boy, plugging up the white tablecloth with the silver coin

Isnt he the most generous little old fat man you ever did see Lilly slides over her mouth to her nephew. She lowers a corkscrew into her ear, intending to impale the parasite therein once and for all

Aunt Lil how do you and Walter

Ice never f

true ice never but how do you and W

Esther Goldstein flakes her fingers across her sons lips. This is a respectable family and I

oh mother Im only k

Sure hes thats why his homerun Chuck Rena dryly observes sleeps in a bedroom whose wallpaper

watch where youre going chignoned ribbonbobbing Hannah Goldstein Nates wife rapidly pecks her freckleface at Rena Hannah grinning like the magic iceskater nonchalantly practising on the desert floor why dont you have a drink here let me pour you some more of this fine vintage allamerican champagne Rena darling now drink up drink

UP drink

THATS right let it spray your nostrils a little Hannah primgrins, the five feet two starched sidleclass gamin young. Young. Of course Ill always be young hopping around the table, hopping around people, hopstop and hop again, hopscotch, observe the chalkskin, she counsels, on which the freckles are overlaid by freckles, freckles made chalkmarks on my skin, the ever veryyoung helicoptering up and down, lift a freckle and set it down, children are forever playing games on my face so Ill always be

423

young, the crowsfeet, naturally, the indian headdress the children wear you paying attention Rena?

whose wallpaper is a design of thousands upon thousands of jetplanes diving chandelling immelmanning the child has been known to wake up at night complaining in a voice loud enough to wake a dead psychiatrist that the jets are flying straight at him as he cowers in a corner of his bed his arms like helicopter blades

thats my youth Hannah angrily interjects not my son

blades trying to hide by their slicing the wholeness of his heart who chose the wallpaper Nate

hes a touchdown american boy Nate puts on a stammering shy those fighting planesll be part of his nature hes at the head of his class

the decapitated head of his class Rena merrily asks a dance of her brother the allamerican decapitated head. The feverish allamerican head

Gonnas with him, she can be trusted Hannah munches a green young salad

Sure, a miserly paid colored maid who despises you

Youre still my kidsister so keep your fuckin

The silver dollar, boy. Thats what you give him, boy. You just take this here silver dollar and put it under his pillow tonight

Gee thanks Uncle Walter

Now Lilly you just pass me the jello. Nothin like the sight of jello to calm a man down. The quiverin texture of it is enough to put a mans ragin thoughts into harmony. Put jello into your system Nathan. Isnt that right Lilly

I make it every night in our hotel room Lilly nod vigorously. Wonderful for the miseries too. You got the miseries, niece Rena?

Of course shes got them, Maurie Tarassoff blinks, her family doesnt want her to sing in niteclubs, his red threshingmachine ears waving at the thrust point of his tiny chin a replica of Sys. His eyes tear, he wipes them, blinking, pimples inside my eyelids he explains, sometimes so bad I can hardly see. Lee could help her if he studied mechanical dentistry like I do and make her a good living, see. Eventually Im going to paint in my leisure time, Sy cant checkmate me forever, oh no. Mechanical dentristy through the GI Bill of Rights will free me, you understand. The Korean War gives me my great opportunity and Im properly grateful to the United States and China and the USSR

Pearl Harbor, Rena. Bombs away

Darling. Right next door theres this couple and they both work in a defense plant only at different shifts and the only time they see each other practically is when he comes home from work to go to bed and she gets up from bed to go to work and he takes a couple drinks before he gets into bed and she takes a couple before she gets out of bed and I can see them right from my window they have exactly one hour to do their fucking in but they both drink for about a half hour very steady and then theyre ready and she says come on and I can hear it all clearly because its summer and they leave the windows open and the lights on

Rena tells the tale excitedly, her teeth sweating

Let me tell you about teeth Maurie says

Yes darling Lee in a minute let me finish

You better pull a sweater over your teeth, though

No. No. So the woman defense plant worker she flops on the bed and she spreads her legs and she says to her husband Make like a divebomber.

Okay. So he gets as high as he drunkenly can and down he comes and as he does he screamwhines as loud as he can :

EEEEEEEEEEEEEEEEEEEEEEEEEEEEEEEEEEEEEEEEEEEEEEEEEEEEEEE

and just as he enters her she bellows :

BOOM. And then she says do it again

EEEEEEEEEEEEEEEEEEEE]EEEEEEEEEEEEEEEEEEEEEEEEEEEEEEEEE :

Boom she yells. But it isnt a bellow. And then she says, sighing, Do it again.

Hes getting weaker now :

eeeeeeeeeeeeeeeeeeeeeeeeeeeeeeeeeeeeeeeeeeeeeeeeeeee : he whimpers.

And shes silent.

He wobbles up his head, the defense plant worker does, looking askance.

Well, he says.

425

And just before she goes out like a light for five minutes because shes got to get up and go to work for the United States of America
she whispers,
boo.
And stops.
He wobbles askance. Well, he says.
She tries again,
boo.
And trails off.
He shakes his head. Come on, he says.
She opens one eye. Did you make like a divebomber she says.
He wobbles yes.
okay she says : boo . . .
m
You like my story Rena says.
I love your story Lee says.
Its true.
I know.
It happens every night.
I know.
Its all true. You believe me dont you.
Yes.
Well my mother pursues me with a knife thats true too her lower lip trembling on the Emanuel glass pane of the front porch door in the middle of the afternoon Rena what are you doing here in the
My mother she
Well folks its all easily solved Maurie Tarassoff says if you study mechanical dentistry. I intend to be a specialist, Im only going to accept impressions of fathers teeth.
Her last Boom is very small you can hardly hear it Rena's lower lip trembles. Its the war
Anybodys father can have teeth Im going to massproduce them Maurie avers, his threshingmachine ears flopping wildly. For fathers dead or alive. Because I cant remember my own father. Im studying mechanical dentistry as a sort of memorial. Sy under-

426

stands. He took pop's mouth so I can make an impression of his teeth. In Washington theyve got a tomb for the Unknown Soldier. In Philadelphia Im going to make a tomb for the Unknown Father in the shape of a pair of false teeth he did me an unwitting service in dying when Im a baby. Im a great patriot for the Unknown Father. Teeth, I say, for him, but Ill paint only Mothers in the shape of American soldiers sitting on their bunks in Korea. The General says well have the boys home for Christmas, but Im a Jew and I want to be home by Chanukah.

But my mothers born on Christmas Day, Lee says.

Then I guess Ill have to wait on my bunk till then, Maurie says wearily. Ill send you some of my drawings. Do you think Mother's toothless mouth will ever forgive him? Her tachycardia heart has a gum condition, she can only circulate babyfood and milk from

MILKBOTTLE H chirpchirp but:

actually, Frances Goldstein, Herbs wife, her face an inverted lute, her eyes behind blackframe spectacles sparkling plectrums, her nose hardly more than a shy clitoris and her shy glossyblack-curled groinhair a scintillant hothouse of black curls cauldroning from her scalp most insolently, the plumpest of married maids, a girl of saucy silences who stumblestrokes under water into the tankbodied Herb at the YMHA swimmingpool, whereby they wreck each others apologetic grins in stricken mimicry, Herb drinking three cokes one after the other on the shining tile of the afterbirth, Frances gravely registering disapproval, Dr Arthur Shumway the family doctor prescribing increasingly massive insulin dosages, I got to, Herb says, when Im a little excited, cokes, cake, and a year before he dies hes drinking a case of coke a day, his once impressive tankbody a boom of bloat, what the fuck, he says, between television and the Goldstein Delicatessen and the upstairs bedroom and Marcus Kronthals Isis movies next door what the hell else is there, pop Im gone to the movies for a couple hours so Ill close out the store tonight

okay?

Solomon Goldstein shrugs. You went to the movies last night. Yeh but the show changed.

427

So watch television.

I wanna get out.

You go next door thats getting out?

I feel like goin.

Go

what the hell else is there between the upstairs bedroom and mom throwin her girlvoice Nate's way

Youre crazy Esther says.

Yeh Im crazy. I like it sweet in my mouth, mom, you got objections?

Lets go downtown Frances says.

No. I gotta clean the store.

You cleaned the store an hour ago.

Its dirty again. The goddamn customers.

Theyre your bread and butter.

You want a dirty store?

Why dont you talk to the customers when you serve them.

I dont feel like it. I wait on them. Thats plenty. I figure out what they owe in a second.

The Navy wants you in their statistics bureau.

The Navy can go fuck itself. Who wants to punch a timeclock? Here I got my cokes, my cakes. You wanna get rid of me Frances?

I wont give you the broom.

Come on, come on, dont be a stup. Ill clean the store and then well watch television and then Ill go up and play with Sari.

I dont want you to wake her.

Shes my little girl aint she? Ill wake her if I wanna. What the hell else is there.

Control yourself mein kint Esther says.

You dont know what youre talkin about, mom. Since when do you control yourself. One heartattack aint enough for you

Who can sit in a chair all day?

Am I telling you?

Youre drinking too many cokes.

Youre making too many fishcakes.

Youre still my baby.

428

Balls. Renas your baby.

Renas a girl. Youre still my baby boy

Balls, mom. The phones ringin.

Let it ring, I got to go upstairs.

Take it on the upstairs extension.

You answer it.

What the fuck do I hafta talk about to my brother Nate.

Hes good to you.

Yeh. Five times a day hes good to me callin you on the phone.

Hes willing to finance you to your own delicatessen again.

I lost one. Once is enough. Tell him to put it on the nose for Babysitter. Tell him to put it out for another xray machine so he can see through and through himself comin and goin.

I dont understand you mein kint. He loves you.

Wait a minute, Ill bust open another coke so Ill love him.

Youre just as much in my heart as Nate.

Make room for Rena.

I dont stint on Rena. Who do you think is responsible for the heart attack.

Is that what Nate said?

Im saying it.

Sure. Let me know when he tells it to Rena.

You think either of us would say such a thing to her?

You can bet your goddamn life I wouldnt. Jesus I need a coke.

Maybe it isnt so much Rena. Maybe its Lee.

Hes okay. The guy talks to me. I hear some respect.

He dont mind Rena should sing in niteclubs.

So he dont mind. Thats his hard luck.

Shes your sister. You want her singing in niteclubs with the drunks looking at her and talking about her. God knows what could happen to her.

Like her good old Aunt Lil.

Lilly is lucky. Walter understands what she had to go through.

Dont be stupid, mom, for christ's sake. Hes fifteen years older than Lil and his fat comes down to his toes and she waits on him hand and foot and she lays for him. For christ's sake

Shes my baby sister.

429

Dont cry for christ's sake.

Your father has such curly hair on his head when I marry him. After the fire there are only the three sisters, Harriet and Lilly and me left and our one brother Milton

I dont want to hear about the fire again. Forget it

And Milton dies from cancer of the skin. From the fire, mein kint, from the fire, everythings from the fire but, actually, Frances Goldstein hasnt a chirp in her voice as she stands in the kitchen door, her voice a melodious mezzo:

Forget the fire)

Its not something you can forget easy)

GIMME A COKE AND ILL PUT OUT THE FIRE:

What does everybody think of the way I redecorated the kitchen everybody Frances flirts glowingly with her apron. I hope everybody likes it because I like it, I like a room all in red.

You couldnt paint it more scarlet, Hannah swapsidedly grins. You couldnt make that red trafficlight on Rena's vagina more scarlet.

Dr Newman turns it on. He stores trafficlights in his office as a hobby. Renas his hob

Whats the matter with you mein kint, why dont you answer me.

Red agonals her clench around the champagne glass. The glass is perfectly steady. A thick scum gently floats on top of the champagne, for Lee takes a bath only in the most expensive of liquids. Rena must hold the glass in perfect equilibrium because Lee is emerging and he doesnt want either to disturb the scum or to take the chance of being touched by it; if hes touched, he'll only have to take another bath. Its bad enough as it is because hes itching furiously; Red, of course, doesnt want to take the chance of the itch infecting her. Thus, she stares steadily at the glass, all her senses focused on it for the sole purpose of Lee issuing forth virginally clean, which he must accomplish with minimal motion because bubbles are already ascending from the bottom of the glass, indicating that the stopper is askew and warning him that the champagne may be suddenly sucked down, which would leave his genitals and lower limbs caked by filth. Everyone revels in

430

suspense and silence, but Harry Ring is heard to mutter that he can well comprehend the boy's tension, in that it is par for the male of the species to undergo a certain anxiety at the possibility of his genitals being abruptly sucked down through the bottom of the female's champagne vagina and disappearing to god knows where, especially when wrinkles, resembling a smocking, have appeared at the top of the girl's breasts connective tissue so that a senile sag may be observed. A woman's aging is hardly the sort of spectacle with which to confront a boy at this stage.

But you must understand that the two homosexuals, Lloyd Engle and Noah Hudsen, when I live at 119 West 75th Street in New York, inform me that Rena Emanuel is unfaithful to me and that therefore it is imperative I reach the changing red trafficlight located at the juncture of 71st Street, Central Park West and Rena's vagina. I want to know who is the first to insert the red, green and amber trafficlight between Rena's thighs. Is she or is she not a virgin as she assumes her elbowed position above my rigid member, her smocked breasts and rubbertinted nipples dangling over my eyes, her own eyes rubbertinted, a smocking of halfsmile at her lips, her shoulderlength brassy hair in stilled undulant avalanche down one side of her face as if there to conceal a paralysis, her rumps ceilinghigh, the hemispheres division a black feline stripe, the cat in a single vertical lash across her ass, the cat crouched in the apes biceped hunchhulk of her mocha waterholing hips, and yet withal the nunchild in the childnun's habit, her dark amber mounthair gorillamatted on her decapitated maidenhead, that : shall I esteem it in that the revolutionary has permitted it to remain in position though it be severed, or shall I scorn it because he has simply neglected to remove the evidence. If the first, the significance is that I may repair the decapitation, which has been done only for my own convenience, and that no revolutionary ardor is to be imputed to the surgeon —indeed, that on the contrary he has simply reaffirmed tradition, underlined it, so to speak, by providing the unerring, exact line by which the maidenhead is to fall, a dotted line, in effect, implying that decapitation has not really as yet taken place; but, if the second, I am to be degraded by assuming the role of the

431

man to whom it is contemptuously given to cart off the evidence : that the surgeon has not cut without the revolutionary's vehement enjoyment of blood. I must continue to walk down the street of the thighs. I must not sit down on the Goldstein's blue velveteen curb beneath the period mirror flashing the headlights' vertical cream stripes alternating with the magenta of the traffic's rear warning and brake lights to await in paralysis for a Bellevue ambulance to pick me up and put me in the mad ward because I insist on clapping my hands to either side of my head to keep it balanced so that, since its decapitation, it will not as a MILKBOTTLE H topple off and roll into the Goldstein diningroom where it is forced to listen to Harry Ring's derisive clarification of the knife incident that what actually occurs while Im on Governors Island awaiting my medical discharge is that Rena chases him around his bedroom with a butcherknife after he attempts to have sexual intercourse with her so that it is clearly obvious that it is not Esther Goldstein, her mother, who runs down the stairs brandishing a butcherknife after the retreating form of St Red, but that it is actually Rena who waves the butcherknife and pursues her mother while Solomon Goldstein lies prone in the bedroom sleeping off his ulcers oh Im sure Rachel Emanuel merrily interposes nobody wants to use a knife I mean after all what kind of mother is it whod want to you dont know my mother Rena fearfully righteously interrupts you see shes going through her change of life. But this is nothing more than Rena trying to enter the change of life experienced by Rachel, a much easier kind of change of life to enter, daughterinlaw to motherinlaw. I let her pursue me so I can come here, Lees mother ought to be complimented and, as a matter of fact, is. I am pursued by my own mother so that I can be accepted here, Rena believes. My mother runs after me so that I can reach here, and Rachel is the more complimented because Esther has gone to the trouble of establishing so close a relationship; but, after, all, Rachel doesnt want to alienate Rena from Esther; consequently, Lee's mother smiles quite girlishly, rejecting Rena's whole concept that she, Rachel, is undergoing a change of life, which causes the girl to turn to Lee, asking him to understand what a change of life really is, that he must comprehend what it means to lose ones capacity for fertility, that he in this moment must himself lose it so that he can see how envious her mother is of her, and that he now embrace her asexually really to comfort her, because if he puts his arms around her lustfully then she, Rena, must come at him with a knife, in that then it must seem to her that he, her lover, envies her her erotic thrust and stimulation of a whole series of males and must be jealous of her. Why should he be jealous of her? To do so would be to cast doubt upon her fidelity to him; he must therefore at this point be sexless; only sexlessness now can she possibly trust, so that if Lee asks her why she did not immediately try to wake up her father in order for him to protect her, she can instantly reply that her father would not asexually protect her, in that he would want to enjoy her trembling tits as he fends off Esther's intended assault. This, of course, insults Lee, while he does not wish to be conscious of the insult; insulted, in that Rena here sees him as kind of father, which is precisely how Lee wants to be regarded, but qualified by his husbandliness within the fatherness, the father behind his loverness, so to speak, without his awareness of the bastion supporting him, and certainly without Rena's awareness; but here she is desiring his fatherness and castrating it so as to be able to endure it; and here his own mother is laughing at him, laughing at the fatherness, which angers him, so that he wants to show it as authentic at least for Rena if not for his mother, saying in effect that with Rena the fatherness is functional, but he cannot boast of it to his mother at all in that he must conceal it from Rena who now drags the fatherness into the open and belabors Rachel with it because Mrs Emanuel is laughing, Rena vaunting here is the father you believe you have while it is I who have him all the time and have him in the pure state that you, Mrs Emanuel, have thought only possible in fantasy, a change of life you never bargained could occur in the male of the species, thinking it only possible in the female. The overwhelming mortification resulting in Lee from this picture Rena has of him moves him to want to be rid of her; he wants to tell her to return home; but such would be a measure of extreme default from his reaction to Rena's predicament that he must convey to her mother and father, for he is in Rena's eyes an adult who moves on a plane equal to those of other adults, with whom she had equated him even though the others do not accept that. It is their very rejection of Rena's equating that must have him essay the role. He is pushed up by her, and he cannot repudiate her support, childlike though it is; for to repudiate it would mean for him to admit not his childlikeness but hers which, playing into the hands of her mother and father, then plays Rena out of his hands, so that he would, in rejecting her manipulation of him, lose his control of her. He harbors her here, then, as he would a criminal, and becomes an accomplice, so that she, as a victim, becomes the individual effecting the depredation, for he is ready for his role of the conspirator, honored, actually, that she has made him one, for he would never have taken this by his own impulses upon himself; and yet at the same time he mentally berates her for having thrown him into such an arena; he seethes with hatred toward her, which she detects, remarking that, after all, she has no right to bring her problems here, that it is an unwarranted imposition, for which he must hate her—her telling him in effect that, if he is to hate her at all, is must be for that, for the unwarranted imposition here at the Emanuels and not for the consequence of having directed him into the arena which, after all, he can decide, if he wishes, not to enter. Which presents a further choice, she understands, and inclines her toward the wish that he make it : that, if he decide not to enter her arena, then he must contrive to keep her here at the Emanuels and resist any Goldstein attempt to retrieve her —a condition she poses that has Lee hate her only the more, because he realizes that to accept such he must doubly widen the area of arena. There is no recourse but to bring her back to her family at the balustrade while all the lesser boys and girls of Releena are continuing to dance within. If that is the easier way out, Red says, then you must not tell me, I dont want to hear it. If you have not kept all the women youve never fucked, then I rather you wouldnt say it because I wont believe you. If youre going to contend with my family in the manner of your retaining the women you havent fucked, then I want to hear you

434

say it, because then you are bringing to bear your accumulated virginity upon my family, against which my family will find it impossible to prevail. I ask you to remember, Harry Ring grimly interposes, who it is who bears the knife : only Rena brandishes it. But it is entirely possible, Clifford Gratz suddenly stands up at the Goldstein table, wiping his mouth of the remains of the corned beef sandwich, while his wife Nadine's nose cowers in her nostrils, and it is only fair to assume that both women are carrying knives, otherwise how can we picture the existence of a mother and daughter? Mrs Sherman sardonically, at the telephone, turns round to comment that nobody here except herself is undergoing a change of life. Im burnt to a crisp waiting for my husband to phone me, she says. What fidelity could possibly be more absolute, she inquires raspingly of the assemblage. It is only when Lee will have me above him, me, charred, about to come apart in his hands, that he will have carnal knowledge. Let me come down upon your rigid member, she cries, her blackened breasts creaking and crunching in their interiors. I cant hear my son for all the static and interference, Esther Goldstein accuses everyone. Hes talking from Bermuda about Rosa. Hannah, Nate corrects her. But it is Rosa whom Lee sleeps with; Im looking out for Rena, she pleads with her eldest to understand; Lee has to tell Rena that he loves her, otherwise Ill have to stop the two from fucking right here, and theyre My god my god my god shes on top of him—is that a position for my daughter to be in with or without a declaration of love? The important thing, Levi growls, is for somebody to prop up MILKBOTTLE H; I dont want to drink any milk now; this is no time for a flood; no more in the world is there time to build an ark, you hear that you homosexual Noah Hudsen? Do you think that when God ordained that two of every kind should seek the protection of the ark He meant to include two inverts as well? And that is why you have committed a crime by entering Lee's ark; he cannot forgive you; he should not; he should forever abominate you. No flood, my son, no flood : that is what I ask of you

I

I dont have the bigness of the mouth

435

not anymore
my mouth isnt big enough to swallow the flood all by myself
so you must keep the milkbottle from toppling

over
N'muxt;
I dont want the Devil to drown:
he must keep flashing on the churchspires:
a good Jew must see to it the Devil glitters on the churchspires/
glittering and flashing in the eyes of Rena is the Devil on the
catchurchspires of her corneas, and Lee tenses the rigid spine of
his prick riding bareback down his body. Rena clenches her
thighs around the champagne glass.

Just a moment, Clifford Gratz leemilkbottletowers tiltmenac-
ingly at the doorway, your parts, all a man's parts, will have to
coalesce, his lean jaw shaved from Sy Tarassoffs watercolor of
Lee. You paint a man, Sy, so that he must live some sort of responsibility to your encounter with him Nina's monkey
puffs on Sy's pipe
LETS CHANGE PARTNERS
thirteen;
ninetyone;
two;
six thousand and eight;
z)
PHILADELPHIA EVENING BULLETIN HEADLINE : THE CORPSE OF
GRANDFATHER JOSHUA NATHANSON TESTIFIES THAT HIS SON
VICTOR NATHANSON ON TRIAL FOR HIS LIFE FOR ARSENIC MUR-
DER OF MOTHERINLAW LENA CHERNY COMMITS SAID HOMICIDE
TO DIVEST LENA CHERNY OF HER FALSE TEETH IN ORDER TO PRO-
VIDE JOSHUA NATHANSON WITH THAT SET OF FALSE TEETH SO
AS TO REPLACE THE SET JOSHUA LOSES WHEN HELEN NATHANSON
VICTORS WIFE TOO VICIOUSLY SWINGS HER TITS THEREBY
WRENCHING FORTH JOSHUA'S SET FOREVER THEREAFTER
CLAMPED TO HER NIPPLES MAKING IT UNFIT FOR HER FATHER-
INLAW'S SERVICE
z)
HERO VICTOR NATHANSON IS ACQUITTED AS JURY ACKNOW-

436

LEDGES THAT THE POVERTY OF THE NATHANSONS BROUGHT ON BY A DEPRESSION AMERICA IS SUFFICIENT JUSTIFICATION FOR HOMICIDE BECAUSE VICTOR CANNOT POSSIBLY BUY A NEW SET OF FALSE TEETH FOR HIS FATHER AND BECAUSE LENA CHERNY DOES NOT WILLINGLY PART WITH HER SET SO THAT VICTOR NATHANSON IS UNDERSTANDABLY FORCED TO

BRUNO CANOVA THE SOUTH PHILADELPHIA ARSENIC MURDER RINGLEADER COMMITS SUICIDE ON LEARNING LENA CHERNY'S INSURANCE POLICY DOES NOT CONSTITUTE SUBSTANTIVE MOTIVATION. HIS DIGNITY PERMANENTLY IMPAIRED MR CANOVA TAKES THE EASY WAY OUT

NEVERTHELESS RACHEL EMANUEL VICTORS COURAGEOUSLY CONSTANT SISTER CANNOT SEEM TO RECOVER FROM THE MEMORY OF HER FATHER'S MISSING FALSE TEETH yes,

I, Clifford Gratz, as a duly qualified dentist, hereby protest I have not reared Gargoyle my Dog for nothing. The blond Rena sustains a number of miscarriages and abortions, Mr Lee Emanuel please note

z) recorded;

/Sue Emanuel, Daves CherokeeGerman secondwife, drunkenly panning for uranium with a prophylactic diaphragm, she of the flatchipped indian arrowhead cheekbones and the green full lips of eyes and the chin a canted moth and the hair the color of ale, a cloudthin crossing a silver sun feels impelled to address the midnight supper Now Ill tell you about abortions here, and miscarriages and whatnot whatnots, oh, yes. I have two boys. You listening, Dave?

Im listening but Im worried about Rena Jordan. Vince is dangling that thing of his above her crotch like a wreckers ball swung at chain's end from a giant crane, and you can see Lee eavesdropping intently his ear at the thin partition of the left testicle.

Theres nothing but human sound at the opposite end of the hallway, Mark Fahn gravely warns the boy. I myself need a boy much more than you need your mother and father. It is my counsel that you return to bed where I shall be waiting with one of my composed Silences. Mark grins wretchedly from the pianoseat, revealing rutted chords and computer tongues filched from

Wall Street, where he earns a living working for a member of the stock exchange. It is enough, then, for Rachel Emanuel to scream at the sleeping Levi that she insists on a fur coat resembling Mrs Sherman's, and that if it isnt for, to cause Lee, his rump falling down his gaping pajamas, to scramble up the broad forehead thighs of St Fahn's hallway, Gargoyle the Dog screeching in the alleyway behind, the vast head of his Cornelius easterisland wagging, the bulging eyes of the bluehound slopping over with Fionababies as he paws at the staring browns of Rena on the rug, his outrigger canoe penis surfacing at a sharp angle, Cower in your Silences, Cower in your Silences, Renamark whispers, and let me do the singing, and after Im finished with the song then you can

Oh let him hear now, Rachel interjects merrily, it wont hurt him, hes big enough, the breeze billowing through the girl's cheeks;

no, thats why hes got to screw me, to stop listening to the Cornelius babytalks. How you women surface your children

I WANT TO STAY WITH RENA I WANT TO STAY WITH RENA the child sobs hysterically and he crouches, and he creeps, and he hobbles back to the Goldstein bedroom.

Youve got him till you divorce him, Sue dryly observes, but only because the Marks of this world have their fingers poised above you to extirpate the peasants;

the girls knuckles blanch around the champagne glass (z;

my brother, my only brother Dave drunkenly undresses, born a year to the day the first Lee is hit on the head by a wild flyball. What are you going to call him, mom. Lee. Thats not right you naming him after the dead one. I dont want to hear you call him dead; thats what good Jews do. The hell with the good Jews, its not right, I dont like it, take it back, think of another name, after all Im three years older than the dead one. Youre still too young to understand Jewish tradition, and its already done, Lee is his name. But hes dark, like me, and the dead ones a blond like pop, its not right. You wont even know him, David, youre thirteen years older, and by the time you do know the second Lee you wont know the first, so its all right. I dont want to know the living Lee; I would know him long before its time to know him if you name him something else. Gayly, Thats why Im naming him Lee

438

But thats not right, Esther Goldstein sharply interposes. Thats somehow crazy, crazy

Let her alone, Levi says heavily. Her boy dies, a woman has a right to be crazy

No, oh no, Esthers fingers chafe her lips. Divorce her.

I cant, Lee says in an undertone;

Rena has a dead boy on her hands, Lee goes on, I cant div

my only brother, Dave stuporously circles the table in his jockey shorts, Gladys Mathews anxiously inclining her head forward as he passes behind her, her marcelled tresses the color of infant bats, L Wallace Mathews smiling benignly, the great red wart on his forehead nodding his bald head vigorously, jesus you shoulda heard Barney Samuels the other day, he was tellin us how he was talkin to his priest

Priest? I thought the mayor was a Jew, Lee stares up at Rena's belly moving back and forth as on a track, her vagina weasel-popping gratification as her slickening cunthairs lick bearded lips mixing fizzing acids at the slit of his penistip, Gargoyle the Dog meowing in babygutturals, Is that the way it should be done she modestvoices above the scummy Nathanson pond, Lee slowly but surely, elbow by elbow, cleansliming himself up the back of the tubbank fearfully regarding his pricknettle buzzing around his ears, they sew up little boys anuses, they sew up little boys anuses Lily Bergstrom and Harriet Shafkin and Fiona Nuri and Hannah Goldstein and Rachel Emanuel chorus, so that the boy senses a rumble in his bowels, suppose he has to shit after the penisnettle sews up his ass. What then? You better take a drink of champagne he advises Rena, to cool down a little. No, I just want to hold the glass. Dont any of you tell me to do anything. But if I have to shit while having intercourse, the boy feebly objects you told me I could eat anything he addresses Dr Newman;

Barry Handler, adolescent otter, remarks that Newton Emanuel discovers the spectrum through the St Red shift in his belly.

Do you object to losing your virginity by solving your constipation, Dr Newman, outraged, inquires of the supine Lee

No, L Wallace Mathews explains, unbuttoning his vest to shift his belly more comfortably to the adjacent chair, Barney Samuels professed the Catholic Church as a youth; of course,

439

quite proudly, let it be noted, he retains his immigrant accent, making him the butt of many an injust jest, not by Jews of course, L Wallace Mathews hastily adds, a vote being a vote, circumcized or no, a gross confusion abruptly reigning when Rosa Caby extinguishes the lights.

Oh, Rosa, the lawyer Silas Klein is heard to exclaim, not while Im just about to remove my snapbrim hat. Please, I beg of you, put on the lights and youll see, then, how much I love you from the top of my head. Sam Abrams, the toothless painter suffering from malnutrition, sniggers hes found a fresh canvas. Duke Montaigne, the pornographic sherry fancier, is delighted to discover another shelf for his stolen watch crystals that will magnify the prurient characters inscribed in the demotic atop Silas Klein's Rosetta skull. From the top of his head Silas Klein shouts through the darkness at Rosa.

BUT I HAVE NO BROTHER the nakedtorsod Clancy Mann smashes down his biceped skull on the dinner table and in so doing scattering Lee's parts all over the locale and thats why, he writes Lee, as god is my judge, youre my only brother and I miss not having one and one day I promise you when I have the money youre going to be my brother so dont despair dont be lonely one of these days Ill gather together all your parts and make, as Golem Monster is my name, the first blond Lee THE MONSTER IS MY BROTHER THE WHITE GOLEM MILKBOTTLE FRANKENSTEINS M H LOSING HIS BALANCE IN THE KENSINGTON BLACKSKY

I dont want you to know that, Levi groans. Thats why I want him three thousand miles away, Lee, from me, from your mother, from you. It is why I give his business absolutely no attention. It is why he goes into bankruptcy. Ill pay all his debts so long as he is no longer with us. But I cannot, directly, tell him to run. But now the Golem Milkbottle is about to spill out over us all. It is the one development, Lee, I cannot prevent. The firstborn must return for my death THE FIRSTBORN MUST PISS MOTHERS MILK ALL OVER ME

    fuck (z

    champagne glass orgasm (z

as Daves secondwife, Sue whinenoses through the dark, let me
warn you about Rena

put light on the top of my head

FLIKKER

but i cant lay you on the top of your head

lee doesnt know that he wants to lay you from the top of his
head

PASS ME THE LIGHTS LILLY I CANT BE A GAMBLIN MAN IN THE
DARK

YOU GODDAMN LIAR WALTER YOU KNOW YOU CAN FEEL YOUR
WAY AROUND A CUNT IN THE DARK

i cant hear nate in the dark hes calling from bermuda

lees calling from rosa caby's

you understand the reason for a woman sustaining a series of
miscarriages is that such is the example of the female terrorstricken at society that condemns the medea situation a woman
murdering her children to avenge herself on her husbands perfidy so that as a consequence she can proceed but part of the way.
Conceive she does, and then kills the foetus; the process gratifies
her in two directions at once, in that she can experience the joys
of pregnancy; the pregnancy once experienced, she can then go
ahead and murder the growth in her womb. There are times
when she will permit herself simply the ecstasy of conception, and
then, to kill, she will miscarry; other times, she will go through
three or four months of pregnancy, and then, to kill, will abort.
This is a societal solution that the female can wholly applaud, for
she does not have to know her children, and will not have to experience grief. Only the husband will grieve, will become sour
from the series of miscarriages and abortions. The female, in
short, can have her embryo and eat it, too;

As the lights go on, the speaker can be seen to be Flikker.

Youve taken the words right out of my vagina, Sue says.

Of course, Flikker responds, munching appreciatively at a
Goldstein pickle, Cant you see how wrinkled I am?

why did you chase Rena with a knife

to cut out her hymen

why did you chase your mother with a knife

441

to restore her hymen

Im after my mother. I see her from the top of the stairs.

No, mein kint, no, she yells, yells in a

small

voice.

But I have to. Im your daughter. Dont you understand I have to put back your hymen. Dont you understand Im shortly going to give my virginity to the doctor and to Lee. To Doctor Lee. If Im going to do that, then you, my mother, must once again be a virgin. Dont you understand the significance of the ceremony? Surely you dont want to experience a heartattack in your vagina. That kind of treachery, mother, you will not practice upon me. Besides, mother, why the hell do you need your vagina? Dads finished with you. Your sons finished with you. The young man who commits suicide over you is finished with you. Youre going through a change of life. You can very well have your hymen put back on. And, certainly, you wouldn't want a man to do it. You need a female. And what better female than your own daughter.

But youre only my daughter in part. Lilly and Harriet are your mothers too.

Is that why you had them bring me up with you, so that you could elude your reinstituted virginity? So you see, Lee, that when my mother pursues me with a knife, she pursues me with her frantic virginity. I have made her pure again, and shes out for revenge. She hates her purity. It

CHAFES

her,

rubs,

the blood of renewed purity runs down her leg

OH GOD MY DARLING LEE

OH GOD GOD GOD DONT YOU SEE I COME TO YOU, EVEN THOUGH IM A JEW, I COME TO YOU FROM A VIRGIN MOTHER

the snow steams. The assemblage sweats in its furs

pass me the icecream

courtesy furrier Mr Ackman Hannah's father the snow granulating from his eyelids not a no in his whole soul

yes mrs ackman i love you yes mrs ackman i will marry you

442

yes mrs ackman lets have a baby yes mrs ackman lets go to florida
yes mrs ackman hannah will get a fine husband in Nathan Goldstein his little florid skull nodding vigorously FURS FOR EVERY-
BODY YES YES YES IN THE SUMMER HEAT
    thats the time you really appreciate furs

                                your
                                cunt
                                is
                                a
                                man frozen to death

lee says to rena BERMUDA COMING THROUGH I CAN HEAR
    mom, stammering
    yes mein kint
    rosas in the bedroom i just left her
    hannah you mean
    hanna rosa thats her middle name
    mom what should i do
    whats the matter mein kint
    its awful
    whats so awful
    hannarosa
    shut up your prick hannah giggleglowers at him, her ponytail
sniffing at a fresh drink of champagne
    but im expecting a call from my husband mrs sherman com-
plains
    the lines dead mrs sherman
    i dont understand
    the lines dead
    please explain
    the wires burnt the metals melted the whole house is going up
in flame yourself included
    but thats not what Im paying the telephone company for rachel
emanuel cuts in
    were very sorry
    mrs shermans entitled to some respect shes a former president
of the brith mikveh synagogue sisterhood what do you mean by
cutting her off shes expecting her husbands

we understand

then let her use the goldstein line

were very sorry but nathan goldstein is speaking to his mother whats more important rachel emanuel yelps for a mother to speak to her son or for a wife to talk to her husband

Sparktears flyfall from Mrs Sherman's eyes Silas Klein peremptorily barks at Mrs Goldstein You should get off the phone, for you can readily observe that fire and water dont mix.

But dont you love Rosa.

Yes.

Dont you want to hear what Lees complaining about?

In the dark, Silas has clapped back his snapbrim hat on his head. Mark is in the middle of one of his composed Silences. Rena's grip tightens about the champagne glass. The wind whips incandescent snow through the room. The sun shivers goldenly. Lees parts cower under the bed, behind the mirrored closets as his cousin Jared wipes off his bloodied instruments. Fiona Nuri regretfully and quietly polishes her newest ceramic prophylactic diaphragm. Cornelius, approvingly, nods in her direction, whispering to Lee you see someday shes going to take care of me with millions of manufactured ceramic diaphragms and Ill be free to compose my music twenty-four hours a day. Rachel Emanuel mutters as she goes about looking for dust the maid has failed to clean My first son, and this is what I dont understand, is killed by a ball struck by an erected penisbat. Paul Moyle, fresh out of the Lincoln Brigade and the Spanish Civil War, shakes his sad brown eyes and comments in eight languages that the fascists are here. Minnie Doyle, her wild brown hair in angular extensions, very much like that of a company of modern dancers, inquires sweetly of her husband Charlie if she should lighten the tension by doing a comic dance. But he replies severely that shes going to have a baby and that if she does a split then the propelled foetus may well cause her to appear quite ridiculous by making her resemble a figure out of Hindu mythology : Do you think you could possibly balance yourself on the head of a newborn child? What sort of Middle Ages Jewish Angel do you think you are, to speculate on how many dancers can balance on the head of a new-

born. And dont you think, Charlie, she gravely replies, that
women give birth for precisely that reason, to see how they can
dance on the heads of their newborn, and that they leave it up to
the male to make the count? never preempting from him his basic
philosophic role. Xena Ritchie, the slip and bra model, remarks
that its time for her to turn into a female homosexual, in order
to experience the joys of making love to a mother who has just
given birth. By a caesarian section, of course, Flikker promptly
suggests, and Xena prettily waves her pocketknife at him, pointing to it and saying Was it by this that you came into the world.
Yes, by the smallest possible incision into morality, Flikker grins.
Nina asks the monkey:
  A penny for your thoughts.
  Sy knocks the ashes from his pipe and carefully smears them
across the tablebed: Theres no need for anyone to be ashshamed,
he says. In the middle of the Cretin Labyrinth, Jay Grays suggests, is a Miniataur HBomb. Hoppy Zitin, the tiny jewelers apprentice of the redrimmed eyes and redrimmed forehead my
brains are nearsighted, rasps that the music escapes him for the
first time: I cannot identify the passage. Diane Valin joins Terry
Shannon underneath the tablebed to collect, meticulously, all the
squeezed blackheads and scraped freckles of their worlds. Harry
Ring, in a thousand incredibly rapid mouthwinks around a mari-
huana cigarette, starts to laugh, slapping his ankles. Levi tries to
tell them that a thin stream of watery milk has appeared under
the door, but he can make no sound. Lionel Shafkin presses the
button at the base of his throat, simultaneously masticating air,
and hoarsely erupts What are we doing about Hitler, at which
Harry Ring, collapsing, beats his palms in helpless laughter
against the floor so that the squeezed blackheads and scraped
freckles fly in all directions, Terry and Diane glowering at him,
Well what do you women expect, Harry shakes with laughter, if
thats the kind of thing you put away in drawers. Dr Newman
slowly twirls a hymeneal hoop

(z
  The ironjowled Melinkoff, he of the eight feet in height, he of
the eight sons, he of the eightynine years of age, growls contemp-

tuously at Levi, Now let us see your Dr Silver, Rabbi Jonah Silver, if he is still of value to the synagogue and to you, Levi Emanuel, let us see him return David Golem to the insubstantial parts from whence he came; let us see him reduce your Firstborn to a man no longer caravanning to this place and to that, from this city and to that upon the earth, so that he will no longer make decisions upon the earth based upon a little white baseball crossing the plate for unknown men in a nonJewish game. Eagerly, sealandotter Barry Handler cries to Lee, Surely now you must concede that the course of true love cannot run smooth under the auspices of Western Capitalism. Lionel Shafkin, masticating his cancer in his final desperate efforts and spewing his breath inward, shakes the soft matzohball of his fist at Barry, But not under Stalinism either, no, you cant bury the axe of hatred in the loveskull of Leon Trotzky. The seared blondness of Mike Burroughs clasps the hand of his wife Myra who, frowning through her dark, one of her dark eyes on its knees, petitioning, If theres only a way we wont have to cross the country again, Mike. But theres possibility of work in Hollywood, my wife. But wintertime, Mike, wintertime, you know crossing Wyoming in winterti, Achille Volpes following us, telling us if were in difficulties we can drink the milk from his one white blind eye, and my own one dark eye wobbles. Myra Burroughs one eye wobbles in its socket, dreadfully : she says my eye is losing

its head my eye is

losing its (z

;behind my jockstrap, Vince Harrison assures the helpless young niteclub singer beneath him, is only a blind bat, and all you have to do is to be agreeable and hell emerge docile, you can stroke his tender little feet so he wont spread his wings too far

HAVE MERCY ON THE BLIND BAT OF MY LOINS Levi Harrison cries;

why dont you teach him how to say the name of Christine Novak, Rachel Emanuel pokes him. Why dont you? Yes, your husband's bat is a parrot, Christine moans at the table, christ I need a drink, Im sooty from the Levi Coal Company, Lee youre smart to stay out of the business, all you get is a sootcaked cunt,

446

the baggers tieing up your thighs and filling your womb with charcoal. Its wrong to give birth to carbon, maybe, Levi retorts. Washington, DC, yes. Clement Lichtenstein smiles a kink, from which the people are governed; truly, we have a lesson here in the functioning of democracy. My heart comes in from the people, Levi whispers. My heart flies over the people, Anne Kanovsky volunteers. I dont think Im committing a crime, Kanovsky smugly remarks, in making an industrial movie on the heart. Lloyd Engle, his hands about his ears, screams at Noah Hudsen to kill Vince Harrison's jockstrap bat flying around the room, My dear, my dear, he says, its just too repulsive for words to see Rena attempting to capture it with her glazed pussyeye. Dont you think it monstrous of your daughter to so indulge, he addresses Mrs Goldstein. If I were you, he continues, Id run after her with a knife and teach her a lesson; theres nothing, after all, like a homosexual truth. Tell her, Noah, tell her doesnt she want her daughter? Dont you want your daughter, Lloyd's voice does a softshoe jingle. I mean, really, those bananacolored thighs, bananas and cream, I just love them for breakfast did you notice Lee a discoloration on her thigh. From a thumbprint, I believe dont you want to hear what Nates complaining about? But Silas Emanuel never wears a hat. Oh youd better, theres a bat flying around the room angrily Dr Newman voices that Lee expressly requests that he perform a hymenectomy which makes me entirely innocent. And a little child shall rape them, I suppose, Rhona Lyrian sneers at the top of her voice as she mounts the diningroom tablebed, her legs akimbo. Sy Tarassoff puffs on a joke as he amusedly regards Lee, It seems like little Sammy had constipation so his mamma says to him Lissen I got to give you castoroil. Sammy looks very stubborn, but mamma takes out the castoroil, pours it in a spoon and approaches little Sammy. Sammy take, she says, No ma I wont take, he says. Her voices rises, Sammy take she says. No ma I wont take. Mamma bellows SAMMY TAKE. Finally little Sammy says ALL RIGHT MA ILL TAKE BUT I WONT MAKE. So, Sammy Emanuel? But Gail Greene's constipated too, its the only thing that gives her any weight as she dies. Im very tall, Gail says puzzledly, Im six feet, but my hands, my hands

447

are extremely tiny, I really cant fend anything off with these hands, dont you see? Apropos, Celia Renn turns to Sy, Ive got one for you, it seems like Mrs Gogol and Mrs Merrivale Cohen are old friends and they got a habit talking to each other in the tenement theyre living in when theyre going to the toilet, Mrs Gogol shouting down from the toilet on the ninth floor to Mrs Merivale Cohen on the toilet in the eighth floor right underneath, You heard about my son

oi, and she gives a grunt

my son Irving

oi,

he just graduated medical school

oi,

with top honors, nshumele cum laude, oi, was I proud Im telling you. Then starts Mrs Merrivale Cohen screaming up from her position on the toilet on the eighth floor MRS GOGOL

I can hear you, I can hear you, you heard from my son Irving. Yes,

oi, oi

I heard, I heard, Mrs Merrivale Cohen shrieks. But lemme telling you from my son Hubert Cohen, oi, oi Mrs Merrivale Cohen groans on the toilet. My son Hubert just graduated Curtis Institute highest honors

oi, oi, oi

playing the Rach

oi

oi

playing the Rachman

oi, oi, oi

playing the Rachmanin

OOOOOOOOOOOOOOOOOOOOOOOOOOOOOOOOOOOOOOOOOOOOOOOOOOOOOOOOO

I

the Rachmaninoff Concerto she bellows triumphantly.

For a moment, absolute silence, Celia nods her head. And then, from the toiletseat on the ninth floor Mrs Gogol shouts down commiseratively

Oi, Mrs Merrivale Cohen, dot was a hard piece

448

/ ; z)

Silas sweats profusely, his head's prognathous cube flushing Frances Goldstein's kitchen crimson. Constipated eroticism, perhaps? Mark inquires softly, his ovoid lips swirling gracefully about his grimy white baldheadedness. The little redhead Hedda Myers sits reverently at his footpedals you need a little girl not a little boy

you need a little girl not a little

boy you

need a little

girl, she whispers, her missing front tooth beckoning to him, because Ive got a little space for you in my mouth where the front tooth is missing she begs him, oh fill the empty place of my toothheart, she entreats, with cockmuscles alive alive

oh

but Ive got six sisters as it is, Mark explains matteroffactly.

A seventh cant do you any harm, Hedda suggests, especially one having a missing front tooth

Pass me the filling, Lilly, Walter grunts. Oi.

No, you just wont do, Mark replies. My sisters are dancers while you on the other hand have aspirations toward the acting profession.

Oh, Mark, but Ill be crawling on my belly to you, Hedda assures him, on my white white belly down the MoylanRose Valley Road singing cockmuscles alive alive oh, and my breasts, while shapely, are quite small, Mark, let me be your boy, oh please let me be your boy Disgusting, disgusting, Danny Naroyan shudders, how women throw themselves at men, oh but I adore cuddling my brothers head in my lap Donna Zion cries playfully, St Russell Zion the Baptist THE DANCE OF THE SEVEN VEILS OF THE WOMEN'S FRENCH REVOLUTIONS, didnt you know? we carry little guillotines in our pocketbooks Donna adds in her cleftpalate caresses, and my brother cleaveth to the roof of my mouth, and my husband Roy Lindauer

Roy Lindauer hunts wild jockstrap bats at the bedroof table of the Mouthsteins. Donna laughs softly at Silas who mutters that Lee must come rescue him from Rosa. Its jolly, really, Russell

Zion says, Ive no head left for anything after my sister: France once again will be stable, and the lawyers govern a nation returned to normalcy. The Daughters of the American Revolution, take note, have all become men. His fathers hips, we allude to Sidney Zion, have lost their head since the death of Bella Zion. I can see him, Bella nods mournfully, down there on the beach, his hips going round and round monotonously, first clockwise and then counterclockwise

(z

oh. My tumor is dizzy, Carla Coffman sighs. Please, Dr Jared, give it something to eat. I can lead my boyscout troop forever, Henry Feinstein, chief weigher and office manager at the Levi Coal Company, says, if I become a partner in the business. Jesuschrist Gene Hertzog thinks looking at Levi Emanuel in the deathbed, how the fuck can a man masturbate with his prick attached to a rubber tube: thats something to learn from, he says sentimentally to Lee, a son should learn from that; you and Dave. Yeh. Me and Henry Feinstein and Dick Emanuel, yeh, we run the business so were entitled to it. You and Dave gonna run it? Tell Esther Goldstein running after Rena with a knife you and Dave are gonna run it and shell stop chasing her daugher. Shes scared for her daughter. Whats Rena gonna marry if she marries you, you got nothin to live on, she wants Rena to get a commitment from you, thats all, thats what shes yelling about, answer her

ANSWER its a black day all around Donald Schwartz Lee's cousin says the great sack of his nose falling over his mouth Franklin Delano Roosevelt is the greatest friend the Jews ever had Im telling you so when he dies his tears spattering hot grease over his face

ANSWER

(z)

(z

z)

z

CHIRP CHIRP CHIRP CHIRP CHIRP CHIRP
chirp chirp chirp chirp
chrp chrp chrp

450

rrrp

rrp aaaaaaaaaaaaaaaaaaaaa aaaaaaaaaaaaaaaaaaaa aaaaaaaaaa aassssssssssssssssssshhhhhhhhhhhhhh

\ ovelling

along the winter pavements on the Roosevelt Boulevard paralleling the highways outer lanes the micaslateslick surfaces of the gray mothwing ice slide along the black rubber slippersoles of the boy in the thick whiteblood of the blanch bloodwhite of the golden summer fireflyglinting new fluffponderous snow sapphiresliced horizontally and by sweatblack trowels of pacedoff maples blackboned vertically to a sun thumping along the schoolboys eye from a prismatic white strap he crouches. He loops a circuit. He jerks a thumb of pain up his calves. He hugs in a hoop of lung and he davidslingshots at a wobblelegblurt along the awkwardthigh lumbering and at the mothslick takeoff iceline, crooked leftleg behind the kneebent rightleg to the fore, his eye fearful at the far end of the micasheen, he abruptclenches the fist of his racegait and seesaws into a plumpboy scorch of a skid a slickandahalffeet wigglewhizz till rightoe lockgrates into the freezerough, his rightleg lugs up a little spring and his left yanks up his tuckbody in a semihoop of gruntjump for an anklesting of a squarefoot clamping in a clump of the snowjamjar his arms at a goggleeye teeterbalance, he swaps sway for sway, sapphire for white, white for sapphire and both for maple sweatblack till, his clenchedback tumble a trickling tremble, he grimthrillsmiles at his nofall and crunches one foot ahead of the other to resume his digskip heartwalk to school, all icy surfaces his, all dangerously sliding mothwings his though he awakens in the morning to the raspseethe scraping up through the open cellardoor of his father thrusting, hands webgrabbed around the polished graygrained polehandle, the longhandled shovel into the grayplush bed of the thick fine ash on the cement bottom of the coal furnace. Winking white honeysuckles of awakening condense on the bedroom window on either side of the sleepswaying intersection arclight outside, the frosted glass lamp still micaaglowgold from the nightwas. You dont have to curse the boy's mother enjoins. But I can swear pops blind. The long low retchrasp of the shovelmetal

451

against the gray ash of the white ash coal, this is the sound of a tongue on all fours, the tongue reversed and shovelling into the mouth, Gargoyle the Blind Dog

did you know that St Red that Gargoyle the Dog leaps the length of his chain, snapping it to arc three feet blindly into the air at the apathetic SeeingEye face of the blond girl, his mistress oh he knows her name mistress mine to strike her, fourfooted, the girl flicked off her balance and falling to the cement pavement, her skull abounce but once, but suffice, concussed stop it Red

stop it a batted ball not

a dog

a batte

d/not a my first dead Lee is a boy

I dont want you FOURFOOTED CATADOG YOURE BLIND AND IM CUSSEDBRAINED gargoyle the dog

is blind his sex is

blind my fathers sex is

blind dog dog dog Levi shovels the metal into the fine plush gray ash. Lifts and lets the ashes slide into the potbellied wooden basket, that in turn lifted and grimacelugged through the outside cellar entrance to the icegargoyled cement steps he sidles up, hoisting one leg after the other, the ponderous plush ash in the basket pendant from his arms pendant from his belly till in gray plush ashbreaths he raspretches down the basket into the snow to snag an iceslivered hiss of air in the backyard, honeysuckled frostings on the black garage window, theres a blind man down there the halfsleeping Lee swears, poundhooping his snowman arms against chest and belly under the gray SeeingEye, a praying mantis Golem rising in hissing breath behind the black hedge, film, the castle disintegrating in a holocaust of icy glitter, run for your life with the basket of ash, run for your life

blind man run for your life blind

boy Levi once again hoists the basket, grunts it through the open garage door and the honeysuckle smells of gasoline and oil and the attar of crushed washboard glass from the trashcan through the massive wooden doubledoors and out into the snowN'Muxt driveway to at last haggle down the burden on the streetcurb,

452

thrice more the bellyash from the cellar, ten times thrice the metal seethe against ash and cement but quiltcomforting to the boy abed his retroedging colornesses slowly tearing off the honeysuckle condensations from the windowpane

LIFT, Levi, LIFT I want to hear my blind fathermen taking out the ash of the coal in the furnace that warms my body,

my father is taking out the ashes

my father is taking out the ashes singsongsingsong ten thousand eight hundred and twentyone Norma ascending through her hoopdress of the bellybasket ashes as Lee shaves off the frosted honeysuckles from the mirror and the thick latherash from his face, stripped to his belt, the blond woman pausing momentarily on the landingway, Lee resting a wet hand on the bannister chinning down, the train from Los Angeles, Chicago, Pittsburg pulling into the Philadelphia Thirtieth Street Station, pregnantwadded Norma preceding the little girl of the hoop, their daughter Stefanie, Lee grinds his teeth following them,

my daughter the girl with the hoop

Norma's family waiting in flurryworry smiles on the train platform

and Norma ascends the stairway through her hoopdress

AND IM THE BLINDBOY JUMPING UP AND DOWN BETWEEN MY MOTHER AND FATHER THE BLIND ACROBAT TRYING TO WRENCH LOOSE TO LEAP THROUGH THE HOOP AND BY THE MAGIC OF PREGNANT GIRLS REGAIN MY SIGHT IN ORDER TO SEE MY DYING FATHER I DONT WANT TO LEAVE THE BEACH, NORMA

I know.

I want to stay right here.

I know.

I dont want to leave Ocean City.

I know. But here comes Grant the Man in the Blue Superjock.

I dont care. I want to stay on the beach of Ocean City, Red.

But Grant.

I dont care. I dont want to go back to Philadelphia.

But he may live if you do.

I know, but I dont want to go.

But Aunt Bellas your favorite aunt.

I know but I dont want to leave Rochester.

Your fathers willing to send the plane fare. You go. Ill stay.

I dont want to leave you.

Ill be all right.

Hell send fare for us both.

Ive got to finish my engagement at the club. Otherwise its a breach of contract. You go. Its the funeral of your favorite aunt. Your father wants you there. The family wants you there. Your cousin Russell, the bereaved son, wants you there. You ought to go. Your Uncle Sidney, your aunt's bereaved husband, wants you there. The whole blood family wants you there in the kinky brightness of the Rochester cafeteria knifeandforked clatterandhummed your father will feel ashamed if youre not there. Carla and Sonny are approaching us from the dancefloor. She probably has a headache. She probably wants Sonny to take her home. That means well probably have to go too.

Itll take them a long time to reach us through the crowd. The dance is over. Its hard to make your way through the crush of youth.

Finish your champagne.

Finish yours. Girls of highschool age arent permitted to drink champagne.

Oh shut up, mother. Im not drinking it. Im squeezing the glass.

If you squeeze too hard your virginity is liable to pop right in my face with all its dirty milkwater and I wont be able to get out of your thightub clean. I itch all over.

Thats because all the parts of you are separated. Once you amalgamate you wont itch a bit.

Dr Clifford G Harrison advises that Lee's itching parts can constitute a Baseball Nine and score simultaneously in St Red the Chanteuse.

Solomon Goldstein warns Marcus Kronthal Stop flirting with my wife or never blacken my door again.

Darken, daddy, darken.

Thats not good enough for him.

Marcus protests, Levi is flirting with Esther, not me.

454

ANSWER ANSWER ANSWER.

LUFTWAFFE OPENS ASSAULT TO SOFTEN THE BRITISH ISLES FOR INVASION.

DANGEROUS TILT OF MILKBOTTLE H THREATENS ENTIRE NEIGHBORHOOD. MAYOR SAMUELS SUMMONS CITY COUNCIL

Hey Wally you dont think that things going to topple over do you, Nate stammers, the noahsark of his adamsapple shuddering above the mouthfish hook, Christ my office is only three blocks away, if that thing fell, why, my patientsd stop sucking off my foot.

Whats that, Nate, L Wallace Mathews sleepily engorges by eyelid his own cinereous blue eyes, Lee enchanted by the scarlet honeysuckle of their veins sinuating up the sloppywet bulgeblue walls, wobblewarted. Councilman Mathews, representing the Kensington constituency, bobs up a waterlogged grin, Never thought you had your heart in your feet, Nate. He thumbs his buffhued vest.

Come on, Wally, Im serious, Nate complains.

Sound financial structure, Milkbottle H, the milk company officials have assured us in official session. Why my family came over on the Ark, and doesnt every middleclass family have one moored in the Atlantic City bay. A man should keep his feet firmly planted on the deck of his Ark is my campaign theme. His wife Gladys struggles to push a breath up her barrel bulkheaded corset; her penciled eyebrows and lashes pump out an already puffed face, the faceflesh the bubbled corset of a fatly aging pantomimist slowly sinking in a vat of dough.

Theres nothing like steaminghot pissmilk straight from the cows udder Levi vows. My cow Joshua Nathanson adds. Helen Nathanson, spouttitted, dolphins beneath the bow of the Ark, wearing a necklace of Joshua's false teeth, her smile composed of crippled horseflies tugging her mouthcorners back and forth and diametric across her milkface, Gus her son whining the sirensong in vacant quarterstones MILKING TIME

ICE NEVER F/MILKBTTLE H/LETS CHANGE P The burial of Aunt Bella is over. You shouldve gone, didnt you love her? Too young a corpse, really, to be loved. I dont care how you say it

455

Lee. What effect does amnesia have on love Saint Red? I tell you
Im in the Rochester shopping section, I want to buy something
for you Lee, and suddenly I find myself within a block of our
hotel and I cant recognize a thing, and Im extremely fortunate
a patron of the supper club Im singing in recognizes me and calls
out my name and just as suddenly I remember who I am, he
takes me back to the hotel, hes a pilot, he flew in Burma, hes had
fabulous experiences. And during that entire period of amnesia
you cant remember you love me. I cant remember anything but
certainly I must keep on loving you. Wouldnt you say its curious
for a man to keep on loving a woman who cant remember loving
him? wouldnt you say its possible that her amnesia affects him
because she cant remember his remembering her. But this is a
different circumstance Lee, you dont have to exercize your
memory on the patio of a country club, youre just beginning with
me. And of course I should be a pilot of fabulous experiences in
Burma and recognize you immediately and bring you back to
RochesterPhiladelphia, recognizing you for the love you bear me,
you love Lee. I didnt say that. But you want me to be quit of
memory and say it; doesnt love require memory? You have five
months now of remembering me Lee. You want me to say I have
five months of remembering an emotion of mine for you, but I
cant take a chance of your having another amnesia of loving me
if I attend the burial of Aunt Bella. I cant remember five months
since I met you of loving you, so were practically at the same
point arent we Lee? we can say we remember five months of
everything with each other except loving, does that make you
more comfortable? But an absence of the memory of an emotion
nullifies one saying anything at all about it. I dont know that
your Aunt Bella is going to be buried. Is it perhaps true Saint
that you have your lapse of memory in Rochester because I forbid my own memory from working at the country club in Philadelphia. You dont have to have your memory lapse now at the
dance in the amnesia of early manhood. But you prevent me from
going to the Aunt Bella funeral; why should I tell you what you
are bound to forget for an entire afternoon? when Diane Valin
and Rosa Caby both tell me they love me, and that without any

456

avowal from me at all; I dont have to remember anything while Im in relationship to them; they accept me as a blank; and, evidently, you accept me as a blank for an entire Rochester afternoon; in that particular amnesia you do not and cannot tell me you love me. Do you want me to tell you I love you now? I cant give you an absolute answer now, Red. I dont want an absolute answer; qualify it any way you like. Thats for a ready amnesia, isnt it? thats for a burial of a corpse. I dont know your Aunt Bella that well. Neither of us know her at all as a corpse; why should you urge me to go to her funeral? for me to indulge in your nonabsolute of love? in your own qualifications? Dont say it, then; please dont say it Lee. Then you want me to negate a specific emotion, you want me to force myself to have an amnesia; did you force yourself to have an amnesia in the Rochester afternoon? But such a force of negation, Lee, would imply the enormous strength of the thing negated. Is that an admission of negation, Saint? But I can ask the same question of you here at the highschool graduating dance. Of course you can, but youve got to tell me that youre urging me to attend the burial of Aunt Bella because I love her; you must insist to me that I should go to a funeral because it is that of my beloved's; because I love Aunt Bella, you want me to participate in her burial. But you have loved her for many years, since childhood. And I know you now for five months; is there some sort of funeral you want to precipitate? I dont know how much longer I can keep this champagne glass intact in my hand, Lee, I warn you, mother, Carla Coffman is pounding inside my head. That dark thin nasaledged Sonny Bond must be a monstrous sort to remain engaged to a girl scheduled to die; as he and Carla approach, hes in her background, terribly solicitous to life just as its about to expire, I envy him, I detest him, I want to lay Carla. And you want to lay Diane and Rosa. And you, Saint; and you. Why? Obviously theres a burial in mind. Is that how you forget love—by burying sex in it? But theres no end to forgetting love, so you keep on burying sex in it. Are you telling me you want to forget your loving me? you love your Aunt Bella but youre not fucking her. It then seems possible Red that you want me to go to Philadelphia

457

so I can screw the corpse of Aunt Bella. Well for christs sake Lee I might as well tell you to go screw the corpses of Diane Valin and Rosa Caby so that you can tell me you love me. I have to kill them first in the nonloving, Saint; I have first to murder them in the impossibility of loving them; besides, I have to see my dead brother, Lee the First, burning at the end of the corridor. Then what is involved is the death of youth before you can tell me of your emotion, and then that you must forget the death of youth. You know its you who stops me from attending my aunt's burial —by your damned amnesia, a terrible piece of jealousy. Am I to understand, Lee, that youre jealous of me at this moment, standing in the patio? If I am, I want to forget it; I do forget it. You have not known me then for five months, is that true, Lee? I cannot know you for any length of time at all if I am to tell you of any emotion I have for you; I must not know you, I forbid myself from knowing you. But that only inexorably implies the inception of love. But how can I tell you about it without any knowledge? when all I know is that I hate you for preventing me from going to Aunt Bella's funeral? when I know you want me to hate you by my forgetting you in your experience of forgetting me; you do not know me at all in your amnesia; one hiatus, and you do not know me at all and cannot know you love me; what I do know is that Rosa and Diane are part of you, Rena St Red, and you want me to be the instrument of obliterating part of you for you, the instrument of striking out female multiples in you, to become the magic of one name and one name only. You keep backing up into Rosa and Diane, your protective devices of surrounding yourself with older females to deny a younger. I do not thus employ Aunt Bella. But I challenge you to, dont I? to go get your buried age and bring it back to me to see if it will do any good for us, seasoned love in the casket, Lee; do you want to be sure of having seasoned casket love in you here at the highschool dance before you can tell me it exists? do you want the damned emotion dead before you can announce its presence to me? let me tell you, Lee, if I crush this champagne glass in my hands then you are forewarned, mother. Im not sure I can tell you anything, Red. Ive no intention of making it difficult for you, Lee.

458

Make it difficult, please, make it difficult for me, Red; make it all but impossible, impossible, impossible, for in the utter impossibility is my utter certainty. I dont want you flying over Burma. The hell you dont. For you to fly over Burma is reserved for my amnesia; forgetting you is to want you at war. If I can have a total amnesia, Red, I can make an avowal of my feeling toward you. Something like a concussion will invite the death of the brother for whom youre named to resuscitate you into relating to me, and you will admit the accident of passion rising from the younger grave. You can strike me on the skull with your amnesia Saint—is that not what a young girl does as she sees a total stranger saunter past?—she uses the secret weapon of depriving him totally of his history, the female being altogether opposed to the processes of history. Go to Aunt Bella if that is what you prefer. Are you trying to persuade me to look upon you as my favorite aunt? Im trying to be as simple as possible, Lee. Simplicity is vicious. Its a summer night and I wait for you, I wait for you, I wait for you; my friends will shortly make their way to us through the crush of youth; I dont want that youth, Lee, so please tell me; Carla has the vicious simplicity of a headache. I dont want my brother here because hes Carla's too : they get together in the head, they become blood relations there as we are becoming blod relations in our own heads, which is mainly what I fear, like Nadine and Clifford Gratz; the idea would be to knock our heads together, making for mutual amnesia, so that we can forget each other only to recover and suddenly know that, without preliminary, we are in. In. Yes, in. In what? Theres no need really to put it in so many words. In my girlhood there is. I dont like to admit your girlhood, which could be still another phase subject to amnesia; are you saving the obliteration of your girlhood for the Rochester amnesia? is it that Im not quite sufficiently advanced to root out your girlhood? and that you really dont want me to be sufficiently advanced because of your gambling instincts? you feel for the subsequent, your lechery for the laterness of things, the luxury of pushing back the schedule; is it that you wish me to retain my boyhood? that youre sorry that I must leave boyhood and that you want me to fix it for as long

459

as possible by my avowal of being committed to the wanting of your girlhood; but I dont have to be committed in order to want you, in order to fuck you; I think perhaps you want me so committed as to return me to childhood; leading me to feel that perhaps utter commitment is a kind of infancy, the infant at your dance, the child, Rena, that you take to your highschool graduation, to be able to say, Look here, Im graduating from highschool and Ive taken my baby with me to participate in the ceremony, see how grownup I am, infinitely superior to all you boys and girls. Are you trying to go all the way back to infancy to prevent yourself from telling me what you actually feel for me? No, Red, no. Do I have to put the words in your mouth as one would into a child's? No, Saint, no,

touching her, then, the saltcream mochacrest of her shoulderfoam wave, I

touching her, then, her stoopshouldered nose, I

touching her, then, in a kind of squinting toy of irretrievability, I

touching her, then, playing with her fever of irretrievability, do you take, then, this fevertoy, Rena Goldstein, as your lawful wedded

for your birthday, what do you want for your birthday

a toy bride, mother, a toy br

well take you down to South Street and buy you a new suit, GGG, the best there, I

touching her, then, perhaps her toyness will come off on him, her skin come off on him, her seriousness come off on him, I

touching her, then, theres a fever she never has thats lodged in her hazeling eyes, the microbes and infections, the diseases and antibodies, the crippling polio dead center in her eyes, the wheelchair look and the whitejacketed attendant Lee pushing the wheel chair, I

touching her, then, her white biceplength evening gloves, do you bite your nails up to your biceps he inquires gravely of her, I

do you, Lee, take me as your

touching her, then, her humpbacked nose, her chin tucking

460

back like Sys, youre posing for him arent you, youve always posed
for him, her cheekbones a muted high glare in the swelling
golden moontime, I
  do I smell, Lee
  no
  I try to put something under my armpits but it doesnt seem
to work Lee, it seems I overcome
  no, but Im going to sneeze
  are you allergic to the moon too
  only when its golden
  are you sure you cant smell me its so important to a girl that a
boy dont sm
  Im sorry Im sneezing
  its all right Lee
  touching her, then, but then one might say Sy paints your chin
in his watercolor of me, Renas chin, I
  Ill be patient, Ill wait till youre finished sneezing
  Aunt Bella says one sneezes the truth
  Rachel Emanuel says one sneezes the truth
  Uncle Ben Emanuel Jareds father says one sneezes the truth
  my fathers dying but Im not sneezing. Its summertime and my
fathers dying but Im not sneezing. The sun is out, its midday, its
June, the month of my birth, my fathers dying but Im not sneezing, I dont want anything to go out of me, no fluids, no breaths,
because perhaps by that I can keep in my father, if I dont sneeze,
if I make a fist of my allergy and clench it back, I must love
him so, so, so, if Im not sneezing, my nasal passages are dry, my
sinusitis has a remission even in the heat and soddenness of the
Philadelphia summer, but then a dying can dry up anything cant
it, dying is a dry climate, dying is the hot southwest, the air clean
and unpolluted, dying is the purest of oxygen, is air thinned out
so that one gulps everything in with enormous breaths, not sneezes
it out, sucks everything in on the highest levels, this is the dying,
Rena, this is, so that, touching her, then, the great hoops of her
breasts, iridescence sweating lizards down their shadowcleft, I
  touching her, then, her hair the color of rotten oranges, a hail
of hummingbirds at the base of her throat in such a rapidity of

pulse that but the beak of bloodshadow can be seen, I
The snowmoth melts against the winterscreen.
The fireflake freezes against the summerscreen.
Mrs Sherman Mrs Sherman
Shes expecting my call
Esther Goldstein, whiteeyed, fingerfollows the dry channels, the
white riverbeds of her flesh between her throatcords, whispering
to her midnight guests unintelligible syllables. When sound, then :
Hannah, its your husband, my son Nate. I cant tell him youre
burnt alive.
Oh no youre not going to tell him that at all, Hannah little-
girls, ponytail flitting, thinmothed tapping the back of her neck.
Youre quite right, mother, because Im your insistent choice for
your son, isnt that so?
Grinning, Esther shakes her head. But you lie to me.
Someones always lying to my mother, Red interposes.
Hannah, Esther smiles, its not that youre an insult to my son
Mrs Sherman. Its not that youre burnt alive
Hannah Sherman tries to swallow. Impossible. No spittle.
Hannah the cracklewoman, Nate puts his ear to her flesh :
crackle, crackle. His fingers to her flesh : little lickpops. Her
laughter, the cereal of snap and brittle
You bastard, Nate, you and your mother, bitch and. Wait till
Milkbottle H topples. Youre afraid hes going to marry whores,
mother Goldstein, so you pick a brittlefuck, Miss Hannah Sher-
man the virgin, active in Jewish community life
Not the insult to my son. The insult to me, Hannah
Stop proving your teats in your oxygen tent mother. Even in
the goddamned oxygen tent
I can tell him youre dead though Esther cries, the least I can
do. Then theres no law with respect to you he has to observe. Yes
I can tell him youre burnt alive
He knows that, mother. And he likes it, ponytail twitches at
Mrs Goldstein. Not having what you want him to have, he likes
my dead burnt aliveness, hes not so damn disappointed as youd
like him to be. So your originally saying you cant tell him Im

burnt alive is a wish not to corroborate me, a wish not to admit
he revels in my state. Thats whats youre horrified at

I always wanted a daughter, Mrs Sherman says at the phone.

Never mind, plump little Mrs Ackman contends, Hannahs
mine. Isnt that right Mr Ackman

Yes, yesyes, whitefuzzed volleyballheaded Mr Ackman nods,
yesyes, Yes.

The Jewish Community, Mrs Ackman, stoutly goes on, always
did need a Joan of Ark, and thats my Hannah Goldstein nee
Ackman

Joan of Ark never goes to bed with a man, Celia Renn takes
centerstage, never.

Youve no idea what happens to her as shes burning at
the stake, Hannah giggles. You ought to see Nate, later, after Ive
been burning at the stake. Not before the flames begin to lick at
me, oh no. Its at that point, before the fire, that he feels me and
then rushes to the Bermuda phone which, if held horizontally,
does appear to be in brief black shorts—and longdistance to his
mother;

lee take off your shorts

but youve got your ballet slippers on

i dont want to take the chance of infecting you with athlete's
foot. Its very cold, please lie down beside me.

all right

the point is, Silas begs Rosa, I will take off my hat for you. I
dont mind admitting Ive got fine thin straight brown hair, easily
combed, presenting no difficulties, and with no danger of babies,
whereas when you marry a blond commercial artist, and have
his child, a little girl, you wilfully neglect her, making difficulties
for me, I cant go to Europe, I must help support the three of you.
Its distinctly unfair, especially when Im willing to keep things
simple, a matter of easy monasticism to you, Rosa, you need not
copulate, there are methods short of such. I do, you understand,
want to preserve your insistence that something fatal halts your
ballet career in midstream, and preserve your insistence that what
it is is unmentionable. I am, in short, in love with your tragic

air, somewhat coarse though it may be—Im not, myself, totally unrelieved of coarseness—my blunt approach, my red skin, my blunt head, my square fingers. I am, you see, quite taken by your blueblack hair your low forehead, your lustreless white skin, your resemblance to a certain moviestar, and I will take off my hat to you, brownhaired, thin, fine, straight, Im easily combed, Rosa

You know my secret now, dont you, Lee

Women shouldnt be gone to bed with, Lee, Silas advises, you then become privy to their bottommost secrets. I dont want to know Rosa's. Please dont lie down beside her

She cant continue with her ballet dancing, Silas, simply because she develops an incurable case of athlete's foot. Her feet itch unbearably as she goes en pointe. She loses control of the simplest steps because of the itching. Her tragic air is an attempt to purify the stench of her feet, and is the more tragic thereby.

I suppose, Silas says, I love her the more for that. But, nevertheless, she marries a commercial artist, and has a child. True, shes divorced once again, but I visit Europe no longer. My hat is off to her. I give her my thin, fine, brown hair. Nevertheless, she works as a cashier in an allnight moviehouse on Market Street. I come for her, I take her to the cafeteria, I bring her to her apartment, I depart, Im bareheaded, I walk six miles to my home, my mother waits for me, I put on my hat, please dont lie down beside her, its not that I dont like you, Lee, you know that, Ive an affection for you, Im a lawyer, but I never argue cases in court, I prepare solid briefs;

but Rosa's mystery, you see, is the case of the ringworm of her feet, that commonplace affliction attracted to her faint coarseness. Silas

Lee takes penis between thumb and forefinger as he lies supine on the Goldstein white tablecloth and directs its head up and down the prim vertical outer lips of Rena St Red's vulva, whose barely moistened but coarse black hair sticks snags of flitpain into the penis's pissslit. While penishead dottedlines the labia majora, Rena St Red takes quartertone lessons from Gus Nathanson, her brassgold rottenorange shoulderlength hair in its vast forward

464

sloping tending to push back the girl's face, making it a background, a flat on the stage of the burlesque theater listing advertisements of places in which to eat, stores in which to buy clothes, establishments for drycleaning, various shops in which to purchase hardware, poultry, fish, sporting goods while Jubilee Jordan, her body all brassgold and rottenorange hair, lunges with her hair while the advertisements for hazelcolored glass eyes, false humpbacked noses, mochacolored skin cosmetics and long loosely affixed putty mouths sustaining a steep hernia at one corner, make up the rigid flat, behind, of St Red's face, the rottenorange brasscolored hair plunging, rocking in front of the stiff advertisements for the putter golfclub nose, the flopping fish of a mouth, the pouter turkey cheeks, the brasscolored curtain rods of the superciliary arches, the bleaching mochacolored flesh, the couturier lines of the passionate fashion of the moment, the roast venison of the irises, those great flat circular slabs of meat slashed by the dilator knives, the hourglass amber spotlight of the hair, a teaktorquing body of striated sheen, is sweatclamped between the enormous griphands of the girls haunches at the start of the transcontinental motion, the hulking broad meatland of the free and the brave at the start of the revolution, its sierra rise to the transcontinental train of Lee's childhood erector set, she towers above him as she unders him, the choochoo penis he has long wanted for a birthday gift, long nagged for to mother, which no sooner bought only baffles the boy, the girders make no sense, the motor incapable of attachment and the transmission of energy, so that the boy must do it by hand, but retaining of course the mechanical penis, the choochoo prick, a very choochoo of an expression on Lee's face under the gigantic slide of the amber wheatlands above him as his shuttlecock goeth up and down with the feather attachment of his groinhair while in the heaving harmonics of her opposition from Los Angeles to Philadelphia her pinions of haunches, her baldeaglespread hips, swoops her vulva back and forth across his choochooprick, back and forth in the Gus Nathanson rockingchair of her hips :

FLYING TO MY FATHER'S DEATH IN THE CONSTELLATION ACROSS ST RED'S GREAT DIVIDE/

465

Helen Nathanson vigorously nods at her son St Red, her milky gobs of teeth in prideful hurrah, what did I tell you imbecilitys got its compensations, Ive been able to teach him the simple tasks Charlotte you see youve got a sister as well as a brother. Hah. As long as he keeps going up and down the scale in those quartertones, as long as idiocy mans her hips, hes got my nephew under control, the two of you are born just about at the same time, Lee, and now youve got your cousin Red for a girl. Things work out, I never did deny Gus Goldstein never had more than a choochoo prick, observe how coarsely his brown hair grows black on his girlmount, observe how incrassate the flesh becomes as the Philadelphia airport orgasm is sighted in the distance, how monstrously stupid Gus's girleye through the farmhouse keyhole as I pump up and down on the firemanpole prick of Joshua Nathanson

IT IS THE BOOK OF LAMINATIONS OH LORD

SIT YE DOWN BY THE WATERS OF LAYERS OH DAUGHTERS OF JERUSALEM

SIT YE UP AND DOWN AND WEEP :

Ive raised my son Red Gus to be Lee's woman, and so revenge myself on my sisterinlaw Rachel Emanuel for being sister to my husband Victor who poisons my mother Lena Cherny with arsenic :

See how Gus Goldstein drools at his vaginal lips.

Listen to his moans of love in quartertone :

PERFORM OH GOD OF VENGEANCE IN COPULATIVE IDIOCY/

My son when only an infant falls out of his carriage in a burlesque skit and is struck on the skull by the batted green ball of the earth OI PAPA YOULL MAKE ME AN IDIOT YET WITH YOUR FENCY FOCKING. Well, Lee Primus, how does it feel to be screwing Lee Secundus's girl? I trust it is not embarrassing because Lee the Second is watching you from his many parts at various strategic points in the Trocadero audience;

of course, Lee is enraged.

Of course.

It is not he whos taking St Red's virginity.

466

The individual taking the virginity of Rena Goldstein is Lee the First, for whom the second is named. Lee the First is taking it because hes on fire at the other end of the hallway of the house of the Emanuels at 236 Roosevelt Boulevard, Jubilee St Red stripping down to her hymen on the stagebed of the Goldsteins at 3892 Frankford Avenue

Pass me the hymen, Lilly.

My dead brother is the one Ive got to kill.

My dead brother fucking my woman is the one Ive got to kill.

Lee Sherman sitting at the telephone waiting for my call out of town is the one Ive got to kill. But how can he hear my murdering him when hes burnt to a crisp? But Levi Emanuel and Rachel Emanuel will hear my murdering him at the end of the hallway.

When I reach there.

But I dont want to reach there because Ill hear them.

Indispensable to the murdering of my dead brother is that my parents and I hear each other.

Ive got to put off the murder.

Im not yet brave enough for the murder.

But I can exact vengeance from my idiot cousin Rena Nathanson in the meantime. Its my mother's fault, Rachel's, yes. Because her brother is Victor, indicted for the murder of his motherinlaw. And Helen Nathanson strikes back at my mother through me via St Red, oh

LORD : IDIOCY DEPRIVES ME OF THE ACT OF TAKING RENA GOLDSTEIN'S VIRGINITY.

Burlesque, burlesque, burlesque

But thats really not so, Dr Newman avers. I perform the hymenectomy on Rena Goldstein, and Im prepared to testify to

Just a moment, Silas Klein interrupts, medical jurisprudence happens to be one of my special fields;

I might add that I myself have pleaded cases in medical jurisprudence, Russell Zion smiles with prim canniness;

I think I might have an opinion or two on the matter, ottersealbeaver Barry Handler volunteers, since my father runs a leather processing factory, and leather hymens are in consider-

467

able demand for women's pocketbooks, women's shoes, men's hunting jackets and handtooled cases for binoculars to be used by either sex.

A perforated babble rises from the Goldstein midnight supper table. Red squeezes her champagne glass more tightly. She addresses her mother, her father, her oldest brother and Lee. Im warning you to stop talking about me, Im warning you to stop screaming at each other, I wont take much more, Im warning you. Im warning you to let me alone,

let me alone/

let me alone but Ive got to get out of her thightub, Lee frantically tells himself, to get out without aught of my own filth contaminating me after Ive scrubbed myself so faithfully in her vagina, Ive got to

COME OUT CLEAN

CLEAN

z

z Silas are you still working on your magnum opus.

The work on rhythm.

Yes.

As being the irreducible, sole and binding factor on all the arts.

Yes.

Well, you see, the square red blockhouse of Silas's skull, with its undiscovered blue eyes, trapdoor mouth, heavy keynose, the unknown brother of Vince Harrison, captain of the Wildwood Wildcats, whose milelong penis is contained in Silas's jockskull, wound round and round in cerebral convolutions, Silas a phenomenon at birth, Jared Emanuel failing to solve the surgical problem

/my only failure, he sneers, due to the fact that such primitive mechanisms are involved/

of prolapsing the skullenclaving penis into the scrotum

COULDNT LET THE FUCKIN AIR GET AT IT COULDYA Vince Harrison bawls from the third base line;

of Silas's squat blockbody, boulderthighed and mincefooted No I guess I dont like taking off my hat. Its not my thin brown fine hair Im worried about, its just that Im afraid of wetting my pate

468

when I least expect to. My red face, you see, comes of doing a handstand over the toiletbowl, since I urinate through my scalp he shakes his head at Rosa; rhythm, Ive found, he says, doing a melancholy handstand, is common to all things, I cant seem to restrict it to the arts, I cant seem to impose any sort of restriction on rhythm at all. Silas barks badly now, Rosa petting his head. You see what women do to men Danny Naroyan shrills at his pomeranian, throwing the tiny animal into the air and catching it to snughuddle its terrified squealyaps, you foolish animal you he accuses it, trying to run away from me while youre falling through the air, Dannys baleful, Silas's second unknown brother, the phenomenon of Danny's birth being that his genitals are contained in his heartsac, and again Jared Emanuel confesses a failure, not really failure number two since it parallels the first, he sneers, the primitive mechanisms involved, Women, says Danny, make men pee through their scalps, Im not going to have anything to do with them, first thing you know Ill be having to wear a bulletproof vest so a girl wouldnt die of shock as my penis would protrude through my own nipple, how can I take a chance PinkyPinkyPinky he squabbles with the pomeranian, Id be put in jail for the indecent exposure of my heart

COULDNT LET THE FUCKIN AIR GET AT IT COULDYA Vince Harrison bawls from the first base line

So youve suspended your work, your magnum opus on rhythm.

Well, Lee, I hope you show some respect for my advancing age, and refuse to slip in beside Rosa. Lets say that I trust rhythm will accept my age, he barks softly, showing the irregular gaps in his dentition; it seems to accept just about everything else. But will it let my age pulse? My scalp begins to suffer from strangury, painful to discharge urine there, and there isnt too much of it any more to discharge Rosa pats his head softly. What curious developments take place in the skull, eh? Literally, my scalp prickles. Silas's tone takes on some hope. Theres some rhythm in that, eh?

NINE HUNDRED TRILLION AND EIGHT
MINUS FOUR

469

Avidly the mammoth idiot of a girl rackwrenches apart her
cracking cartilages, widening her hophips into giant swings of
hoop, vagina and anus in whipsmacking antiphonal broadsides
ATHLETE'S FOOT MY ASS she gobbleguffaws down at Lee ROSA'S
ASSHOLE AND CUNTHOLE MAKE TOO MANY LICKSMACKING
SOUNDS AS SHE BALLETDANCES Red guffawgobbles AS A MATTER
OF FACT AS SHE DOES A PIROUETTE THEY SOUND EXACTLY LIKE
FARTS AND THAT MY DARLING LEE IS WHY SHE HALTS HER
CAREER MIDWAY IN A GISELLEFART THATS AN AWFUL LONG
PRICK YOU GOT THERE VINCE EMANUEL I REALLY DONT KNOW
IF I CAN LOWER MY ADAMSAPPLE DOWN FAR ENOUGH TO GULP UP
YOUR PRICK

THE APPLE OF SEXUAL WISDOM hear hear STICKING IN
ADAM'S THROAT hear hear.

Pass me the apple, Lilly

HANG ON the mammoth idiot of the girl yells as the mammoth
imbecile of the boy clenches his hands around the mighty monoliths of undulancy that are her teats and they swing in great ape
arcs from each other tell me what you want Lee I aint got so
much time Dave dont want the business does he.

No.

Do you want the business Lee yes or no.

No

Then what the fuck are you seeing our daughter for Solomon
Goldstein furiously flushes up from the head of the table here
your fathers licking the bucket and

Kicking the bucket KICKING THE BUCKET KICKING KIC-
KING KICKING NOT LICKING KICKING GODDAMN IT Rena lifts the
champagne glass.

Thats when youre dead you kick the bucket Solomon disdainfully retorts. But when youre still dying you lick it you lick it
theres a lot you got to learn my daughter and you, you, Lee, you

470

listen, what do you think you can support our daughter on Im asking you

ON THE COLUMN OF MY PRICK EXACTLY AS IM DOING NOW Lee backbawls at him YOU KNOW A BETTER WAY FOR A MALE TO SUPPORT A FEMALE MR GOLDSTEIN.

Show, Mr Harrison, Esther Goldstein sweettolerantly interposes, show my daughter what can happen to a girl who sings in niteclubs.

Pass the jockstrap, Lilly, so I can give my niece here thirty lashes, why thats the way we learn wayward girls down south, Esther.

But its Rosa and Hannah who are responsible, Lee defends St Red.

And little me thoo, the orangefleshed Fiona Nuri pipelithsps. Thath why Cawneliuth conthenthrateths on my ath and cunth.

Yah, yah, Cornelius smirks.

Mark Fahn gravely admonishes the entire assemblage, during a pause in one of his Silences, that it had better take care since it seems to be encroaching on his pederastic domain. He rolls back one of his lavender lips and, kneeling on it, pays homage to his tongue.

Well I can tell you, volunteers Flikker the Gargoyle Dog, how I lose my own virginity.

Virginity the chain, the hoop, not necessarily Flikker the Gargoyle Dog's alone, but its length, uncoiled a thousand times, the hoop rounding both subtractively and additively, the sense of the snap at the terminus, the foreclosure of the yield Dr Clifford Harrison poising his foreshortened height above Nadine Goldstein, does it. One never realizes how cold the Roosevelt Boulevard room is capable of becoming if one cannot envisage Rosa Caby drawing the thin coverlet over her, beckoning to Silas, come now, she says, give me your Nadine, the longbeaked girl, the sniffer. Do you smell me, Red insists. There are too many girls here, Lee realizes; it is impossible after all to discern whom one is taking. Thats no excuse Rena objects, virginity doesnt belong to the masses. If you soften up the bones, Timmy Lascar points out

471

sweetly, Marxism can enter anywhere. Dr Newman instantly protests that although he is something of a controlling factor, in that he performs a hymenectomy and administers futile treatment to Levi Emanuel as well, he is not therefore necessarily the transitional chain whereby Levi Emanuel crosses and takes, incarnated in Lee, the virginity of Rena Goldstein. Till death do us part, Flickerlee raises his paw. You simply put your head down here, Rosa guides him, and rub it lightly, oh ever so lightly, theres nothing to be afraid of Rena. No, not if Im an idiot, she grins. So that it can just as well be said that Rosa Caby is responsible for taking Renas virginity, too : actually, it is Lee who does it through Rosa, Dr Clifford Flikker points out, since it is foreordained that, by Lee having himself repelled by Rosa, she repulsing him by her very insistence that he lie beside her, realizing quite well the possibility of shock, but theres a chance shes taking, you see, she must take it, she must be quit of her indeterminate status with respect to Lee, she must know if he is to become her lover or no. If he isnt to become her lover, shes quite aware of how she gambles with anothers virginity, but how can she be held accountable for such if the other is anonymous. Ah, then, but Rosa detests anonymity, she must perforce picture a specific, I see you with Charlotte Nathanson in the Academy of Music gallery for a Stokowski concert, Lee, do you lay her? I dont, shes my cousin. A beautiful girl. Yes, very. You dont have to marry her. Do you love Charlotte, Red asks. You see, how can I make any kind of determination, Rosa defends herself haughtily, as to my responsibility for taking Renas virginity—I dont know the girl till later, after her virginity is gone. But you do know her later, you do, Silas accuses her angrily, so that there is a hymenectomy in a kind of semianonymity. Goddamn it I try my best to prevent Rena Goldstein from losing it. I guide his fingers, I have him play with me. Nothing, nothing results. Christ, she says thickly, I tell him Im sorry as he feels my chest. What more can I tell him. Im sorry I delude him. No, theres nothing th

Silas claps his hands over his own chest, drawing his nipples over his ears

All right so Im flat as a board, I have no tits

472

Nate is stuttering over the phone Mom shes got no
Whats the matter mein kint whats the matter
Hannah Caby
Use her married name arent you proud of your name my son
Rosa Goldstein takes off her tits mom theyre rubber
What do you want me to do about it my son can I give her
what shes
Mom but theyre rubber she aint got any
Theyre all burned off off Hannah Sherman screams vindicti-
vely Ive been at the stake youve got to remember my mother
and father are furriers Ive got to get rid of all my fur to be an
acceptable Jewish girl acceptable for marriage Joan of Ark has
got to be burned in order to be an acceptable female symbol to
French manhood do you think Joan of Ark really had any tits
I WANT A MAN I WANT A MAN YOU CAN HEAR HER YELLING DOWN
THE WHOLE OF FRENCH HISTORY Celia Renn holds out her breasts
from the oxygen tent
    Its not you who are dying St Red savagely puts to her, its my
mother
    The hell you say you big fuckin virgin you. You wont have
any trouble you big cunt you with your massive tits and ugly-
beautiful face. Your virginity is taken not only once, but a hundred times, a thousand times, theres no end to the taking of it,
your hymen grows back each time after a fuck, its absolutely impossible to determine who makes you lose your virginity
    Lee.
    Yes.
    Tell her at once whos responsible. Tell her its Lee Newman
    Yes, its
    Tell her its Dr Gratz
    Yes, its Dr Gratz, he resembles me in many ways, is that the
way Im going to get out of her—by my resemblance to all possibilities?
    The fact that Rosa Caby effects the loss of Rena Goldstein's
virginity by one step removed I want her, want Rosa as I slouch
my hips around the great dogpenis, I want that girl. Fourfooted,
he towers over her, the girl with the orangebrass hair spreading

473

as golden blood over the mattress pavement, the girl unconscious from the batted balling concussing Lee the First, so young is he to be my first fucker that I must lie unconscious, I must not be consciously aware, she laughs, of corrupting the tenyearold boy within Lee, so I must lie here stricken, slavering imbecilically above him, while the great dumb gargoyle dog of him protrudes his crimson firemans pole at my distended thighs, Grandfather Nathanson—oh yes, I must have age, age, seventy years of age

Lee Emanuel I am seventy years old; otherwise it is unjustifiable that I have intercourse with my uncle's wife

/oh no

/oh no

she wont think of me as a boy now

will she

will you Red Nathanson do you take this boy as your lawful wedded husband goddamn it its the dog who takes my wifes virginity, the seventyyearold dog

I can tell you, Lee, we put our hands down on that

Feet, daddy, feet

Its hands down, daughter, I know where I got my feet, but we aint that hard up we should let your daughter marry a seventy-yearold dog.

But then he relinquishes his claim on my virginity and I absolutely refuse to accept that.

But its Doctor Newman.

With rubber gloves

Rubber.

Yes. Rubber, oh no, Lee, you wont

Flat. What did you have.

But you know thats impossible. Youre not dealing with Rosa, or with Hannah, I dont wear a

Rubber gloves. Rubber hoop. Rubber boy. Rubber, Rena. Rubber Rena. Of course, I shouldve. Dr Newman with his rubber gloves removes a rubber—Lee cant continue for his hoops of laughter, a thousand million hoops of laughter going round and round and round him.

Red slaps him.

But Lee feels nothing.

She slaps him again.

Again he feels nothing. Because he is the one who does the slapping. I am the one, Red. I slap. You, never. You cant slap.

She slaps him again.

Dont, dont, dont his hoops of laughter lift him above her, as he points down at her thighs, RUBBER RUBBER RUBBER A

RUBBER HYMEN

WHO TOOK YOUR VIRGINITY RENA GOLDSTEIN

ONE THOUSAND FIVE HUNDRED MILLION AND TWO

SIX QUADRILLION NINETY BILLION AND FOUR

SIX

ONE

MINUS ZERO. You fool Dr Newman too, eh? I SHALL LIFT MY FATHER'S ASHES AND STREW THEM ACROSS THE FOUR WINDS OF THE CUNT THAT SHALL BE HIS MEMORIAL.

Sweating, then, the two of them, sweating and jangling their icicles one upon the sweating other, the polarized equatorial beasts, the one male, and the other female, ICE NEVER F, MILKBOTTLE H, CHIRP CHIRP, LETS CHANGE P, the female holding aloft a crystal champagne glass, what shall I lose that I have not lost, who is my lover that shall not have me lose, who is my woman who is not my gain, I shall make her intact in my mind she who is not intact in her body, whether it is I or no who disintact her, I shall make him intact in my mind who cannot accept his unintacting of me in my body VENGEANCE TOWARD HIM WHO TAKETH HER VIRGINITY

so vows the old Hebrew man.

So voweth he.

Make the vengeance toward yourself, then, the girl thinks, old Hebrew man. You must take it upon yourself if you can find no other.

Who takes her virginity, he whispers.

Not only do you lift Gail Greene about to die of cancer. Not only do you lift Levi Emanuel about to die of coronary thrombosis. But you lift Rena St Red Goldstein as well.

On what?

On a lever.

What kind of lever?

The lever of the penis.

And what is your fulcrum?

Death.

Death is the fulcrum of the penis used to lift the weight of the
hymen in an everincreasing velocity so that at last the rubber hymen is tossed into the blue sky in an unerring arc to strike the
temple of Lee Emanuel the First and kill him by concussion MUR-
DERESS MURDERESS MURDERESS RACHEL EMANUEL SCREECHES
AT SAINT LEE, I

got a girl for a son, I got a

girl for, the

force of Rena's virginity stunning a tenyearold boy

Surely, Lee remarks suavely at the balustrade, you couldnt possibly want a declaration of love from a tenyearold;

now just a moment, Dr Saint Clifford objects, this is getting
out of hand.

Nature snickers. Out of whose hand.

Nature's.

A fire, a blizzard and a milkflood threaten the amphitheater
at the point Jaredlee the burlesque surgeon is about perform the
greatest feat of his career, namely, the construction of Golemlee
out of his many separated parts I mean we cant let the issue of
Reds virginity remain in doubt. But natures not only getting out
of hand, its out of hand completely :

RED

GREEN

ROTTEN ORANGES

RED

ROTTEN ORANGES

GREEN;

THIRTEEN

MINUS THREE HUNDRED AND THREE

WHOS THE MONKEY RIDING THE CHANGING TRAFFIC LIGHTS
ELEVEN FOURTEEN SIX THOUSAND AND TWO GREEN

ROTTEN ORANGES I mean youve got to put a man together in order to define the existence of virginity.

I resist.

You dont want to approach the reality of a girls virginity.

True.

Then by the very act of refusing to approach virginity you must certainly understand that you take it, that you destroy the hymen. It is the Monster growing out of the first tenyearold Lee who deprives Rena of her virginity.

The virtuous citizens in the Goldstein amphitheater rise to an uproar. The vast milkwhite bulk of the covered wagon of Walter Bergstrom freightelevators from his chair, his gambling ethic outraged. Cant you keep the diceballs in the box, boy? he stentors at Lee Esther Goldstein, feverishly changing life, brandishes a breadknife, chanting its good to change life because then you can cut the harnesses of the horses drawing the troika, and the troikabells, like stilled silver blossoms, will lie silent in the moonsilvered snow, let in the snow to the summertime, for gods sake let the snow into my Renasunflesh. Slashing at the windowpane, Esther summons in the full stompsledge of the blizzard. Im a furrier, Im all right Mr Ackman yesyesyesses to himself. God Im glad Im married to a furrier, Mrs Ackman pouts to herself vigorously. A clear demonstration, Lee pulls aside Solomon Goldstein, of your wife pursuing Rena. Pityingly, Solomon regards him, saying, I dont want you should make a fool of yourself, my son—its the blizzard shes running after; you got to calm down, son, if you want to stay angry. My wife uses the knife to cut the season as it goes up and down the stairs. Its natural enough my daughter should think the season is her mother, thats the way a good daughter should feel, who can criticize her. We can only criticize you, Lee, for not being able to understand theres no season at all : youre not too clear about the weather of the world, are you, my son? It is the weather of the season that runs up and down the stairs, and all virgins flee before it. Naturally, I, as a man, I understand how men want to take advantage of virgins fleeing before the season. Our question is, Are you ready to be such a man? Because, if you are not yet a man, we have our doubts if you should take advantage of our virgin Rena.

I got to shit. The pressures mounting.

Certainly Levi Emanuel its no no no to your coal company. What else possibly could my answer be, the Emanuel burning to a fine White Ash at the touch of Rena Sherman, past president of a sisterhood, riding around in Fairmount Park at the age of eleven her udders twin monoliths, twin MILKBOTTLE HS about to topple, the girls breasts the girls own firefighting equipment, the bicycle seat slamming into her virginity, palming it, the bicycle seat reminding us how the intact virgin is virtually a shell-game, at least I can content myself by observing that there is at least the preparation for the subsequent removal of her hymen with such ease by Dr Newman, theres nothing to it he himself admits, no problem whatever, Im presented with a fait accompli that must disarm my rage and, in the disarming, enrage me the more, the rage infecting the girl who then burns me to a crisp so that its impossible for me to answer the phone of the man on the road calling, Levi himself, wanting to make sure that Im quite all right, that Lee Sherman is in bed waiting for his fathers phone-call, no, no, no, youve nothing to be fearful about Levi, not now, because now we know the shipment of coal to Dave is White Ash, as long as Im David Lee burning to a fine white ash that you can quite easily remove from the cellar and in such ease blame your firstborn, Clancy Mann, for playing the ponies and forcing you into bankruptcy, no, no, no I dont want the coal business which is precisely the same as saying yes because you cannot possibly believe a yes coming from someone burning at his older brother's stake, you cannot believe I would preempt my older brother, lifting us as you do out of your cellar, both your sons, you cannot believe a yes or a no from someone who cannot communicate at all in the midst of the blaze, the fire making me sneeze, the convulsive sneeze transmitted to the girl who, allergic to virginity, realizing Dr Newman shoots me full of pollen for the allergy tests, can do no more than to sneeze forth her hymen at the young man even as Anne Kanovsky propels her heart toward her hus-

478

band who a moment before believes she has none at all, pollen, you see, pollen then responsible for disabusing her of virginity, fecundated by the seed of all the plants of the Eastern Seaboard, wherein Betty Emanuel then plays her role, Daves first wife, that authority on the hymens of plants, who now crouches from person to person around the Goldstein midnight supper table asking for a particular kind of alms, that her hymen be watered, after all, the womans in her late forties if I may speak, Mrs Esther Goldstein, of changes of life, here is something you really might exercize some compassion for, this fatted plant moving from one to the other, her skin a waxen milky sheen even as Frances Goldstein Herbs wife, who watches Betty carefully, hoping of course she may learn something of that woman's survival technique once Herb is dead and buried, this seems to be a ready method for obtaining quick sympathy and quicker fluids, everyone apologizing that it is to be hoped that Betty doesnt mind if she is watered by champagne since that is presently the sole drink at the table, Rena herself terribly thirsty in the midst of her burning of Lee, but not quite sure whether she should drink, or water Betty, or crush her champagne glass in her hand because everyone can see straight through her crystal virginity, except that Lee cannot because he hasnt started his bowel movement, all of us realizing that the comprehension of virginity, or its lack, is dependant on a salubrious defecation; the hymen, we establish through Betty, can grow back without any trouble, so that this plant attribute, we immediately discern, is that with which Lee should like to endow Rena, making his whole doubt as to what or who takes Rena's virginity rather academic for, as the fire blazes about him in the dead of winter and communication escapes him altogether in the stench, crackle and smoky devour of sexual intercourse, he cannot help but entertain the notion of having Rena regain her virginity, an appalling development that has Dr Jonah Silver strum his goatee in utter humiliation, for he marries Rena to Lee, and to participate in such an abrogation of normalcy by awarding it official Hebrew license throws his whole Hebrew ethic into utter disorder, that a male should want to reinstitute virginity after once taking it strikes him as a perverted act of Christianity that

479

pollutes the ceremony he conducts under the blue canopy at his home, he is horrified at Rena holding the very champagne glass he knows he has wrapped in paper to be crushed by Lees heel to signify the ceremonys terminus and thus by the sound of shattered glass symbolically frighten away any evil spirits or demons who might have wandered in, so that the marriage would be started with every assurance of success, but now, now, what must he imagine must ensue if Rena herself holds that very glass he believes must be beneath Lee's heel, and will herself crush in her hand, and all that can occur to him, as he hears concurrence from the others around the whitely blazing coitus table, is that Rena herself takes her own virginity in a monstrous act of hymenicide, her virginal intactness committing suicide, as if she herself will relieve herself of Lee in a frenzy of anticipation, in a suicide of purity that Lee himself will refuse even to consider, certainly he will not hear it is his own body begins to babble a crackle, he must interpret the crushing of the glass as his own virginity crushed and spiral out his mind to deliberations upon the matter of the taking of his own virginity, considering that Dr Newman by removing the Saint's hymen removes Lee's virginity as well, so that Lee is not even able to engineer his own ending of virginity in himself, the whole thing taken out of his hands so that at last there is a supreme masturbation involved in lifting himself out of Rena's dirty bathtub, no wonder his flesh prickles, no wonder his father walks the nights in his final years itching with the clean filth he removes from his son with which he cakes his own flesh, his heart sobbing for mercy under the weight of such pollution, not that Rena has as yet broken the glass, no, she holds it aloft, a Golem grin on her face, a magnificently beautiful Dumb One revolving her hips at the thrust of Lee from the supper table, the audience at the Goldstein Trocadero rapt at her gyrations, her brothers licking their own vulvas at the sight of her, Nates lean face fattening, Herbs fat face losing weight with incredible swiftness—the whole family raking out her virginity and feeding on it at the table Lee realizes in a rushing relish, a banquet that all the flatchested male and female whores of the world must want to gorge upon, that Nate hath his sister if he hath not his wife, that

Herb hath his sister if he hath not Frances, Rena challenging her mother who, sick to her change of life, rushes down the stairs with a breadknife in her hand to defend her husband against the onslaught of his daughter, Solomon not having the faintest notion of what his daughter is about to declare before Customs, the truth of the matter being that Esther is intent upon preserving her daughter's virginity by the use of the knife, just as Rena is intent upon preserving it by confronting Harry Ring with a breadknife, Im defending my mother she says in low tones to Harry, you must not know what my vagina is like, I forbid you to have any idea of what it is, because if you should happen to overcome me then you must know my mother, and that is out of the question because I will never let anybody know who my mother is, what my mother is, that must remain a mystery, the mystery of the Renabirth my little Hebrew satyr, oh I know you for what you are, Harry, the GreekHebrew synthesis who would seek to infect me, but the older Mary, the Hebrew Grandmother of Mary is capable of an immaculate conception which I cannot permit you to fathom, Joan of Ark burns on Christ's cross, Celia, put that in your enactment if you can, show how God masturbated his own son Lee, no wonder He died for Him. I will not have you chasing after my virgin with a knife, Lee says tightly to Esther Goldstein, thats not your prerogative, its mine, solely; and if Im halfChrist then its questionable that I can take her virginity, I certainly cant half do it, can I? and theres no use in your screaming at me that you can jail me for corrupting a minor in retaliation to my threat that I will inform the Pennsylvania Society For Prevention of Cruelty To Children. Its the Goldstein Family that wants to take Rena's virginity, certainly not I. I will except Esther Goldstein, but she herself is culpable as well in her wish to preserve her daughter's virginity so that she herself can kill it by bringing down the telephone on her daughter's cunt:

IT WILL PHONE NOBODY MEIN KINT/

it will phone nobody, your hymen, your virginity, nobody will it phone because Lee as he sits on the toiletseat remains constipated,

so that virginity cannot be defecated;

481

because Carla Coffman is undergoing surgery, and the great friendship between the two of you is utterly betrayed as Dr Jaredleeclifford triumphantly discovers the congenital condition of an atavistic tooth growing steadily within Carla's brain so that it can gnaw on a picture of Red's purity within it, a picture presented as Red's hymen, Red's virginity expanding within Carla's brain, which is precisely what Carla desires, Red's virginity, that is, so that Carla can endure the sight of St Red himself, that big brawn of a girl offering her protectiveness to Carla, I will protect you, small and dark and delicate as you are, but the offering is unacceptable without Carla's certitude that Rena is keeping herself intact, keeping herself unattached to any male, restraining herself, Red restraining the juices of her own sex so that she will not then flaunt herself superiorly, acquisitively, before friend Carla, that Carla be not demeaned, be not made a laughingstock before the male, in her case her fiance Sonny Bond, for only then are her own headaches things bravely to be borne, and she can deceive herself as to their seriousness, dismiss them altogether, for they are throbbings only because they incorporate the intense loyalty of St Red Goldstein, a loyalty now seen exactly for what it is when Dr CliffordJaredLee opens it up and exposes it as a ruse for Rena, a convenience she utilizes to fool her mother when she permits a male, any male, to make abortive love to her, the ruse of being at Carla's, in Carla, so that the small, dark, delicate girls jawhinges fly open as the surgeon discloses Red's perfidy existing within Carla herself, and friendship an expanding Golem of a tooth, a fantasy artifact constructed by Rena to amplify in her friends brain and gnaw safely away at Rena's virginity within Carla, a disclosure with which the surgeon cannot cope, being quite beyond his powers, quite beyond Lee's knife, here in Carla his Red's virginity even as it grows being gnawed away, so that even as the great gargoyle flickerdog of him plunges in his firemanspole knife while he crouches behind himself in the Wildwood Wildcats' boardinghouse room on the Goldstein supper table and urges himself to persist, nevertheless, as the young girl singer is spuriously terrified beneath him, its too big she blabs, Im sorry I tantalize you in the alleyway, its only because my mother

482

and father dont like animals that I do this, Vince, and I know that a fourfooted beast such as you are Lee Harrison unlike a human can be restrained on a leash so that even if it is broken you will automatically halt at the end of its length, which is the length of your penis, watch out for gods sake, that chainpenis might snap in two and Id be utterly ridiculous walking out of here dangling a length of genitalchain from my crotch, besides which Im suffering from a severe concussion and you will derive no pleasure at all, being a dog and recognizing that your mistress to be enjoyed must be conscious, must, in fact, live, live, and here am I in the extremity of my passion already approaching death, so that you cannot possibly fornicate with me, but Lee forcing it nevertheless while his boy holds back, his boy masturbating as his man thrusts his prick into Rena, the ideal male fantasy even as the fantasy is rudely being dispelled by practically the whole team of the Wildwood Wildcats rushing up the Goldstein stairs, his brother Clancy Mann in the lead, furious and brandishing a breadknife and leaping on to the table yelling get off of her you prick, you blackeyed son of a blueeyed bastard, Levi Harrison, the Lithuanian Jew Nordic, Im not going to let you give me a lousy reputation simply because youre my younger brother, as my younger brother you have no rights with Rena St Red at all, get off of her, you want to kill her with your abnormally long dogprick, no, mein kint, there is nobody your hymen can possibly call, its burnt to a crisp and Carla Coffman is dead on the operating table and nobody can possibly handle it, why Charlotte Nathanson in her littlegirl's irony bets on it, knowing her cousin Lee prefers her and not you, not St Red at all, because it slips from Lee's fingers, the little white rubber hymen ball she throws from her own thighs on her Grandfather Nathansons Lansdale farm, throws high into the summerhot air, Lee backing away, running, running down the grass lawn in an effort to catch it, running down the mocha grass lawn of St Red in the snowy heat of his parents Roosevelt Boulevard Frankford Avenue bedroom combination diningroom, the fecal brown swirls on the Goldstein walls, the magenta and white stripes on the Emanuel walls, please catch my hymen Saint Nathanson groans, fizzing a thick white icecream soda in such enor-

483

mous quantity in her vulva that it overflows the black curls of
her mount, I told you Milkbottle H is toppling over Levi groans
from the bed beside them, yours is no method to revivify a dying
man, it is a method which cannot possibly work Norma insists to
Lee because it is basically unrelated to your father, you cannot
possibly justify the act of fucking Rena as a method of persuading
Levi to live, I told you Milkbottle H is overflowing, you can see
the fluid appearing at your first wife's door, prop her up for
christ's sake, dont bother with me, LIFT LIFT LIFT, if you can
raise her up high enough your father wont be drowned and you
wont accuse him of swimming in her flood, the only man alive
you can swim in her flood, but Lee, straining with all his might,
still cannot shit, hes got the dry toilet heaves, its possible he has
no shit within him at all, that hes pure, a virgin anus through
which no turd has ever been impelled and, as Rena's little white
Charlotte hymen plummets down from the blue ceiling he touches
it with the tips of his fingers far out on the heaving Rena-
sea, touches, catches, clutches, but it bounces off and away,
Renas cunt pouting at him childishly, it may be too hot for you
to handle as a child, she taunts him, but his belief in the efficacy
of orgasm as a method of bursting through and destroying the
hymen has not yet been dispelled, so that he lunges up again at
the girl, again and yet again, wishing that his father will die once
and for all, for death certainly as it has been versified countlessly
must take a woman's virginity, which would enable Lee to hold
death responsible for the hymenectomy, ruling out human beings
altogether, which must make his revenge upon Rena that much
simpler, he need not entangle himself with any human at all, but
Levi refuses as yet to die, he is quite adamant that he will not
expire in the act of the removal of a girl's virginity, a commedia
e finita even he will not bargain for to please his son. But birth is a
curious matter, and nobody knows this more yearningly than
Lee himself who, as he thrusts one leg over Rena's enamelled thigh,
finds that his other foot is caught in Rena's vaginadrain and that
the accumulated filth of his bathing in her, which he avoids up to
this point, is rapidly advancing upon him. If he will force his
foot out of her drain, on the other hand, he runs the risk of pull-

ing out her hymenstopper, and no evidence will be more clear
than that which is entered to show Lee, at the moment of his
birth, causing thereby the loss of Rena's virginity. Lee sweating,
then, on Rena's balustrade, a chorus of highschool dancergirls
chanting around the Goldstein midnight supper table the envoi
of Betty Emanuel's, that their plant hymens be watered by un-
matured champagne, Betty Emanuel herself leading the pack,
for nothing is in store for her life now but to lead highschool girls,
her own daughter married now and with two children, her son
himself married to a greatnosed thin skip of a girl named Norma,
the same name, oddly enough, of Lee's second wife, and her son
a partner now with Henry Feinstein and Gene Hertzog in the
Levi Coal Company as Betty becomes the chief buyer, a great fat
wax plant, in an upstate Pennsylvania dress shop, Lee considers
the possibility that the only way he might extricate himself from
his own birth, a possibility a magnificently radical notion never
before encountered in the history of humanity, will be by making
a certain declaration to Rena, a declaration she has been wanting
him to make for the whole afternoon evening of her adolescence,
the declaration, in short,

of love,

love, if you will, he rolls the idea around in his parched mouth :
love can be the preventative of birth.

Which is all very well. Indeed. But what will his mother say
to this idea?

What will Rachel Emanuel say to the idea of Lee declaring
his love for Rena to avoid through the avoidance of birth the
avoidance of the loss of Rena's virginity and thereby his responsibility for that loss?

The issue is inexorably clear : he must not hold himself culpable for the loss of the girl's virginity.

But, again, what will his mother say?

And, of equal importance, since Lee will be in love without
being born, what must be the consequences of his links to the
men, women and children of his world?

How do you plead, Russell of Zion inquires, a smile leaning
back softly from his lips—in love or no?

Eightyseven empty tables. Three hundred fortyeight empty chairs.

Gashwool, gakwhoosh the United Gas Improvement streetlamps flare up their yellow radiance under the leaping sorrel gargoyle dogs in St Red's eyes, the tantalizing being done to them by Lee Emanuel, the floppy wet moths of snowflakes sticking to the summerscreen of his eyes, the CAPITOL RECORDS building in Los Angeles, constructed in the form of a multistoried platter of discs, spinning in everincreasing velocity as the CONSTELLATION bearing Lee to his father's funeral circles the city in rising hoops how do you plead

in love or no/

THE FIFE OF THE DANCING ANT AXES OFF THE SURF

LETS CHANGE PARTNERS

SANTA LUCHEEYA

I HAVE TWO HUGE SUPPURATING BLACK AND RED BEDSORES FROM THIS FANCY FUCKING LEE BELLOWS AT RENA

IN LOVE OR NO

HOW DO YOU PLEAD

BORN OR NO

HOW DO YOU PLEAD

VIRGIN OR NO

THE FRANKENSTEIN MONSTERGOLEM MISTER MACLENNIHAN HIMSELF HIS PURPLE RED GREEN AMBER FACE CURLING OFF IN PATCHES my uncle you see Rena Volpe her milkfed walleye slowly dripping cream cancer of the skin my uncle dies of cancer of the skin caused by the Baltimore fire. But the susceptibility is present in the entire family. In the sexual fire my hymen itches. I have cancer of the hymen. My hymen peels itself off. So its all right for Lee to be born. Except that the sexual fire is caused by Lee. We find the accused in his original position Mister MacLennihan youve got to give me another chance to tie the knot in the string to secure the flat cardboard boxes you take the string of the penis around thumb and forefinger and give it two turns clockwise, loop it, then one turn counterclockwise, then two turns clockwise, loop twice and youve got the fallopian tubes perfectly tied in order to avoid conception and

486

thereby avoid birth Barry Handler the sonofabitch must hate me inordinately so much so that he patiently teaches me how to tie the MacLennihan knot so that I shant be born nor take therefore Rena's virginity, a masterstroke of Barry Handler's hate dont threaten us Lee Emanuel we dont have to listen to your threats about our daughters virginity, the threat in taking her virginity an act against the entire Goldstein family. No act at all. The girl wants to sing, shes got a voice, she enjoys it, I believe in her. A fuckin free ride is what you believe in Nate stammers. I warn her its her money well be living on, she doesnt want to discuss it, she insists on it being taken for granted, granted, grant the blue superjock Lee how the hell do I know you want to assail the blue-jock chastity belts of men I dont have to go to Dr Newman to have my virginity prepared to be taken. Understand that. But I dont understand, St Red, that you resent the ease with which you take my virginity, and that all men's vaginas must thereafter constitute a challenge, that you must alter the male genitals into the female. But it is an act, Lee, of causing Lee himself to be born through himself, the greatest boon woman can do for man. Except that what ensues is a gratitude in the man toward the woman, that Lee thank Rena for his birth, that he thank her for the motherhood of Lee, a violation of Rachel Emanuel herself, a violation, worse, of the condition of the past, extruding the past into the present, against which there is no more powerful taboo youd better reconsider Esther cries, youd better think twice three times about letting her support you not that it isnt right a mother should support you, true, but that the mother should be my daughter is something you should think about, you got a good head, Lee, you shouldnt use it between my daughters thighs suicide suicide suicide I cant breathe Rena swears its very hot I CANT BREATHE I WANT YOU TO STOP TALKING ABOUT ME BUT ITS FOR YOUR OWN GOOD MEIN KINT BUT MY HEAD IS SWELLING

SWELLING youre not taking my father Levi into account. I rather you wouldnt, its my

account, Rena mumbles.

Im talking to your family.

Dont talk to my family. My head is swelling.

Dont bring me into it, Carla rises from the bed.

If theres any money difficulty Lee assures them my father will be able to take care of

Well thats another story Solomon spreads his hands

Theres no need for him to bring in his father Rena squeezes the champagne glass, youre forcing him to bring in his father, youre permitting his father to be involved in the taking of my virginity and thats exactly what I want Lee to avoid;

if I can tie the knot, Lee thinks, the whole issue will be avoided Mister MacLennihan TEACH ME TO TIE THE KNOT BARRY; but you hate me; Im willing to use hate in order to avoid being born. you cant use hate

you cant use hate in the taking of my virginity.

There, you see, Im already attached to the taking of Rena's virginity by virtue of hate. But you hate the entire assemblage Hoppy Zitin points out triumphantly, which is precisely why you take the girl's virginity, you see kotex all around you. Your sister has got to clear up the entire matter, Lee pleads with Russell, youve got to rip the kotex from her thighs and let me fuck her. But thats impossible Russell sweetly objects, shell interpret that as a direct desire on my part, not on Lee's, so that I cannot admit that as evidence; besides, her husband, Roy Lindauer, will certainly remonstrate, with both of us, and I cannot incur the wrath of his realestate, the only real wealth in this world, it is fixed, permanent. Then you ask that my sperm gush out upon realestate and not within Rena at all, so that at last I must accuse the very existence of property as land as the taker of Rena's virginity, I cant tie the knot I cant

tie the knot youre

fired

f:

Wait a moment Silas interrupts. Youve got to think of the women preceding Rena as flatchested

SILENCE SILENCE SILENCE Mark Fahn demands

AS OPPOSED TO MY RHAPSODY RHAPSODY RHAPSODY Cornelius Nuri counterattacks ON MY FIONA MY RHAPSODY TO THE BABIES OF THIS WORLD

flatchested, too. Babies are, male and female. Women equal

babies, Silas eagerly continues. Their boxes are flatchested, isnt that so Mister MacLennihan? so that Lee should be able to make the knot and tie up all his preceding women and put aside their boxes so that he can in all conscience take Rena Goldstein, morally and legally cancer of the bone Timmy Lascar nudges Lee Rena's bones in the fucking are turning to mush/no no, turning into a labyrinth Jay Grays irritatedly objects/no no Myra Burroughs frowns Rena's bones in the fucking are turning blind I know I know when you go back and forth across the Levicontinent with your man looking for a job Rena's looking for a job singing, you see, back and forth Lee's father, shuttling back and forth, the blind girl in a hoop, Lee whirling the hoop about his hips/no no Minnie Doyle shakes her head Renas bones in the fucking are turning into a comic dance/no no Lloyd Engle and Noah Hudsen shrilly interpose her bones in the fucking are turning into mice and theyre running up Lee's thighs as we as mice want to run up his thighs/no no Levi objects Rena's bones in the fucking are turning into milk sveet sveet milk/no no Duke Montaigne avers Rena's bones in the fucking are turning into cats running after homosexual mice/no no Clement Lichtenstein thinly purses his kinks Rena's bones in the fucking are turning into dry hot sand so that shes going to be

SCULPTURED

YOU LIE LEE SCREAMS YOU LIE YOU LIE YOU LIE/no no Barry Handler insists Rena's bones are turning into leather cant you hear their smooth processed hides slide one upon the other/no no Lionel Shafkin remonstates her bones are turning dumb/no no a woman's bones in fucking Anne Kanovsky insists turn altogether into heart/no no Gail Greene a womans bones turn into coughing during intercourse/into little pomeranian scamperings Danny Naroyan testily says/into idiot rockingchairs Helen Nathanson says/into Joan of Arcs/into ballet postures suffering from ringworm/into high foreheads Rhona Lyrian says sadly/into plant leaves Betty Emanuel says/into leukemia Sue Emanuel opines

)sculpture);

no no Nina Tarassoff says, a woman's bones in fucking turn into monkeys)

nude poses Sy says on flat surfaces

SCULPTURE Lee screams, not nu
rena's bones in fucking turn into troika bells
into moving pictures Marcus Kronthal
dice/pass me the bones Lilly/into knives Harry Ring derides/
pass me the bones
/into squeezed blackheads Diane Valin
/rena's bones Terry Shannon says turn into freckles
HOOPS
HOOPS
HOOPS Norma whoops from the beach HOOPS pass me the
bones, Lilly, Walter says/into boxes of kotex Donna Zion sneers/
women's bones in fucking turn into sneering noses Nadine Gratz
says/
into teeth Dr Gratz says
into Lee, Rena says/into knives Jared says/into rhythm Silas
says/into suings against the male/into whiteness says Bella Zion/
into me Lee says/into fire Mrs Sherman says
MINUS THIRTEEN THOUSAND TWO HUNDRED AND EIGHT
ONE
RENAS BONES IN THE FUCKING TURN INTO MOTHS
but her limbs like great crutches are flung against me;
Then Rena's bones in the fucking, Terry Shannon Lyrian
hushes everyone, turn into the wounded gull. Yes, Nina Brody
agrees, perched atop my boyfinger, the bird with the black matted
hair of a monkey, one wing crumpled Lee tacking up the posters
on the Goldstein Emanuel windows MURRAYS ROACH DOOM
MURRAYS RAT DOOM MURRAYS FLY DOOM MURRAYS ANT DOOM
MURRAYS WORM DOOM;
its hopping away from us. What do you suppose is wrong with
it.
Hard to tell in this light amethyst mist there goes the sea in a
wounded cat the gull mightve been a little girl twirling a hoop
too many times around her. The fractured hoop of flight. The
broken arc hanging limply from the shoulder.
Lets go see.
Shes something like the winged victory, Terry, dont you think.

Well she has a head on her if we run then the gull frantically hops.

Doesnt it know were trying to help it.

Maybe its a virgin gull Donna.

Well mothers take care of virgins Alex.

Virgin mothers do, waiting in white on the boardwalk, like Bella Zion, white, edged in amethyst mist. Virginity is infectious, and is transmitted from the mother through her husband to the daughter.

No wonder Esther Goldstein is laughing, saying to each male in turn, Take me, take me, take

And that Im about to break the champagne glass orgasm in pure hysteria, knowing Im diseased with virginity through Solomon Goldstein and Sidney Zion, but that that disease never touches them, whereas the mother must die of it, all mothers, all daughters, all females; that theres no therapy for virginity at all; that each time a male tries to cure us, the virginity cowers, shrinks, backs away. Or, widens: so that the male goes right through it, never touching it and all I want to do is simply help the wounded gull.

Well will you put its virginity in a sling. Will you have virginity mend by a splint. I say that because at least I know virginity can be wounded in flight.

Im getting chilled.

But youre overwhelmed by the heat in Washington.

Well I dont want to go on the stand. Do you know its a revolving stand. That I play and sing as I slowly revolve, and that the walls of the club are panelled in elongated vanes of mirrors, and that colored lights play on them. What are you going to do.

Listen to the election returns.

But Im tired, I dont want to go on.

Shall I phone Clement.

Go on, phone. Are you satisfied we dont have to go back to Philadelphia.

Yes.

I had no rest all the way from Rochester.

491

Because we keep trying to catch that gull when it doesnt want to be helped.

Maybe because its shot down in Burma.

Do you try to help it because its shot down in Burma.

Yes.

Its suffering from amnesia because its shot down in Burma.

Yes.

It doesnt know what it is.

Thats true.

So that as the animal fucks you it has no idea of its identity.

Thats true.

And the amnesia of the poor fucking animal infects **Rena Emanuel.**

Yes.

So that she cant remember who she is.

Yes.

Out of pure sympathy you permit yourself to become infected with amnesia.

Yes.

And your brother Nate calls me a fool because I believe you, when I know very well that periodically you suffer from the loss of Rena Goldstein.

Yes.

And all that must occur in order for you to lose Rena is to be shot down.

Yes.

Which is precisely what Im doing to you now. Youre above me.

Yes.

And you want to be brought down.

Yes.

Because in the Rena Goldstein losing of herself is the engendering of a hatred at such a loss, a hatred toward the individual responsible for her selfloss, a hatred she otherwise would be unable to feel. You lose your knowledge of yourself for the prime purpose of being able to hate. You cannot hate out of the knowing of yourself. You can only hate out of the obliteration of your self.

It is not even important who the other individual may be—the one whom you hate. Once the hatred is released, the object towards which it is directed is immaterial. As a matter of fact, the less identity that object possesses, the more consummate your hate, and the greater your enjoyment of it. So that it just as well follows that you must seek to deprive the object of identity, that you must seek to have that very object experience an obliteration of self, the conclusion of which must be that the object hate you. And since neither can realize each other's identity, nor realize his or her own identity, there are great murders done in the dark, and no blood seen. There are vast butcheries accomplished in the dark, and no severances observed. It is by such a method that a self will pass a self, faceless and unutterably safe, and no harm done to the self at all because it has been lost. And, when the hatred has been totally discharged we regain our selves, remembering no hatred whatever; but, since hatred is coitus, we itch with the traces of ecstasy, which lick at us, so that we begin again to lose our selves. What more beautiful proof of the matter do we require when we see that the clear identities of children are the result of the ecstasy of the loss of self, and that thus through hatred we are reduplicated, but never again are we quite the same individuals. If we have no children, the consequence is that we are slowly maddened, for the butcheries in the dark have no chance to reconstitute, and hatred then is the most awful and stabbing of vanities, a narcissistic hatred that engenders monstrous children in ourselves, vistas of babbling foetuses, the awful born of the unborn, a league of ghastly infants who seek impossible shelters in us, racing from one organ to the next in us, searching for a locus in which to grow, but constantly being cast out and having once again to resume the babbling search, the monstrous children ever multiplying, slowly maddening us with their babble

Is that why you want no children, Lee

the milk from St Red's vagina threatening to engulf the assemblage, Jared advises that the only solution is to coalesce the dismembered Lee Emanuel, a denouement that will save everyone's life. But the fife of the dancing ant that axes off the surf will no

493

longer be operative, the various parts of Lee Emanuel object.

Nevertheless you will have to submit to the instruments, Jared replies. Surgery evolves away from dismemberment into amalgamation, very often, true, at the expense of the individual. But the drowning of the multitude in Rena's vaginal milkbottle h must be averted. We cannot permit the toppling over of a gigantic tudor cursive industrial symbol to a plane upon which it can be used between a womans thighs to snuff out the lives of all those humans to which you are related :

so that, the refusal of Lee Emanuel to be born, arousing the fury of everyone grouped about the tablebed, what after all is the extent of Lee's canniness as it strikes Lionel Shafkin, for suddenly Lee is overpowered at the impact his nonbirth must have on Shafkin in that each of the latter's cancerous cells is now attempting to crowd into a single corner of the man's body, in a very concentration of beginnings in the man's throat, and then back from the throat itself into the laziest of socialist ideations, retreating, even, from that point to lying abed and shrugging at the cabinetmaking craft that itself is slowly evanescing from the industrial scene, the whole making for an absolute repudiation in an absolute containment, just as Barry Handler, his lowleaning swart forehead smarting with pockmarks, his sealblack glistening hair disheveled over a cheekbone, unmercifully rasps at the brutal idealism of Lee, declaring that Lee would have Barry at Lee's nonbirth turn aside from joining the elder Handler at his leatherprocessing factory, I am not after all your choice, Barry rasps at Lee, none of us are. Youd have me declare against my father, Barry says, in my very pocket, and expose me in all my weaknesses of doing all that my father doesnt want me to do—simply for me to make a point of the independence and purity and miraculousness of my weaknesses, and lose myself even as Red Goldstein loses herself, be a Christian Amnesiac—in this sport you propagandize as the justifiable murder of fathers, not realizing that Oedipus kills himself in the killing of his father—he can go amnesia himself to Hell for all I care—he says he doesnt know who it is, that he knows not it is his father whom he murders. It is not every father who permits himself to be murdered without his son being murdered in retaliation. What is it, Lee? Is it that you believe you can escape your own murder after killing your father by yourself refusing to be born? That that, perhaps, is precisely what your father wants—that you not be born so that you wont suffer the inexorable and traditional consequence. Who, then, indeed will be the one to take Red's virginity? The answer is that nobody, then, can possibly take it, that then she must forever remain virgin which is perfectly sensible as far as I am concerned Silas Klein intervenes, because I should prefer to keep my picture of Rosa Caby as a woman untouched by a lad whose talent I considerably respect, I really dont know if I can continue to respect the lad if he lies down at Rosa's side, there is something of a cold naivete in the lad's action that does not quite belong with the ardent romanticism of Rosa, there is an insult involved which I should rather not entertain, so that as for me Lee need not be the one directly responsible for the loss of Rena's virginity, let him not be born at all as far as Im concerned, let there be no man born to assume relationship with Rosa, for such a relationship would assume that such a one take over the burden of that woman's suffering, which I absolutely forbid should happen to her, it would destroy her coarsely tragic air, already it is common knowledge that it is her farting that destroys her ballet career, which is something I can hardly bear as I trudge the streets back to my mother's house, the woman I adore prevented from her noblest consummations by her farting, information which it has been Rena Goldstein's amusement to report, amusement, mind you, the direct outcome of her amour with Lee, as if she herself cannot bear such an amour without pointing her sardonic fingernailbitten finger at a woman who preceded her with Lee, so that I entertain no particular compassion for Rena, let her bear her virginal weight all by herself, and let you, Barry, be a rebel, be antifather, be a suicide by killing your father, for there is nothing to be gained, as much as I support certain societal traditions, certain conservatisms, by your being a mime—oh, to be sure, a brilliant mime, a mime mocking your father even as you permit him to live, a cash in the bank mime, promoting, by the way, a typical sorcery in which the son permitting himself to be masticated by

495

his father little by little finds his, the son's, tensions being dispersed so that, even though his father may die, quite naturally, before him, the son—the son discovers that there has been no alteration at all, that the picture might as well frame no death of father occurring at all since the son has become the father to all intents and purposes, differing in no whit from his predecessor and remembering him not at all because there is no need to since he is the same himself, the mimicry demimed, so to speak, the very sardonicism the son used to assault and insult the father becoming a general sourness, a constancy of sneer of which the origin is no longer important, no longer, Barry, functional, so that if Lee, his organ now at its tumescent extreme, would have you crystallize your weaknesses, I am of no mind to oppose subscription to that. Except that, as St Red hurls it out, your support of Lee saves Rosa for your predisposition of her; but this means, you see, that Lee actually is doing the saving, and he lies beside her without lying beside her, because, actually, by his saving of her for you he must have to lie beside her in order to discover her for your discovering, for your very opposition to keep what you believe you must lose. And it is Rena who is managing to bring Silas and Rosa closer together, past the memory of the farts, Silas, because you must certainly realize that she would not be comporting herself as she does were it not for the farts, she would not be permitting your closeness if she were dancing and farting, Silas. This would be too much for you to bear. Rosa is fartless now. She does not dance. You would not have her at all, with her child, with her divorce from the commercial artist, were it not for her evolved fartlessness. Which should lead you to corroborate the evidence that Lee takes my virginity as my neck cords distend cant you hear everyone shouting hell kill her yet with his fancy fucking, bringing me down from above him to lie upon him, my hips alone upraised to receive him, the dog does it to me in my amnesia, the animal is taking me, taking Rena Goldstein on all fours as I lie unknown to myself on the cold flaming air, the dog is fucking me while my skull is cracked and my thighs are spurting such hugenessess of lubricating milk that it threatens to engulf the assemblage, but I swear to Im using Milkbottle H only

496

because Lee is in so many parts, his head is one place, his viscera is another, his lower limbs are thrashing about elsewhere in such disorganized abandon that Gladys Langdon Wallace Matthews, the hogsheadbodied wife of the Kensington Councilman, starts to rise from the tablebed in dismay, the whaleblubber of her bosoms heaving himalayilanly, her face dripping with magenta and white stripes, her watertank neck pulsing in hiccups of terror at the motions of Lee's legs and the abrupt explosion of shit from his anus in another corner of the room

LOVE

brown cockroaches of shit racing madly down the walls

she cant fuck you because your prick will one day fail to support her

Im going to fuck him anyway

mein kint mein kint think of what youre doing think FROM WHAT A GREAT HEIGHT A FEMALE MUST FALL IF A PRICK SUDDENLY CRUMPLES THAT IS TRULY THE CORRUPTION OF A MINOR LEE EMANUEL WELL HAVE YOU PUT IN JAIL FOR IMPOTENCE

AND ILL HAVE YOU PUT IN JAIL BY THE PENNSYLVANIA SOCIETY FOR PREVENTION OF CRUELTY TO CHILDREN BECAUSE YOU TRY TO FRIGHTEN RENA FROM BEING CORRUPTED BY IMPOTENCE BY PURSUING HER WITH A KNIFE I TELL YOU A FAILING PRICK IS NEVER A JUSTIFCATON FOR TERRORIZING A CHILD BY RUNNING AFTER HER WITH A KNIFE THE JUDGE WILL INFORM YOU THAT YOU SHOULDVE USED YOUR KNIFE ON THE ERECTIONLESS PRICK BECAUSE THAT IS WHAT YOU ARE AFTER IN THE FIRST PLACE ESTHER GOLDSTEIN TO CUT OFF MY BALLS AND SHOW THEM TO THE WORLD AND SCREAM TO THE WORLD

IT IS NOT ATLAS WHO HOLDS UP THE BALLS

BUT IT IS MRS ATLAS

The poor bastard is nuts, Herb Goldstein says, furtively. Furtively nuts, of course. Secret nuts. All lunacy hides. Even from itself. Doesnt know itself at all. Lunacy calls itself nuts, you see, and then says it isnt responsible for such an accusation. Excuses itself, then. Joins an open society, till the nuts hold up Mrs Atlas obviously the whole matter is a closed defiance of me, Terry Shannon avers, the ultimate consequence of my refusing to approve Rena, he now seeks to gain my approval by the withdrawal from the role of taking the girl's virginity, where the chips are down then I finally matter, or, should we say, where the prick is up he is faithful nonfaithful to me in his fashion, using a mere girl to prove it, to slap me in the face with it, slap me in the face, mind you, with Rena's hymen, as one would of old use a glove to make a challenge, that I will then duel in his mind, using, mind you, mind you, I adore that phrase mind you, it is so haughty of the mind to consider itself an admonitory finger—yes, in the duel, mind you, I will be using his penis to cross—what?—with Rena. Cross hymens? Hardly. I have none. I must use Lee's penis. And then? What does Rena use? His penis, too. We are both borrowing masculinity to fight over him—for what? So that he can withdraw in a fantastic retaliation as I tear aside Rena's mask—those are my legs, dammit, in a wild thrashing, the thrashing he borrows from me that I do in fantasy when he is seventeen, wild abandonment as I fling my lower limbs at him in an attempt to capture the youth, but even as I do so, my god, even so I must cause him the wildest damage which he must attempt to repair, to repudiate, because my maddened limbs at the height of my delirious ecstasy with Rena—how can I approve a woman who wants me—strike out chaotically and my ringwormed feet hit Gladys Matthews' skull and her hair—all her hair—flies off— because it is Gladys Matthews' wig Achille Volpe Matthews is revealed, the Roman senator with the completely bald dome whose milky eye is feeding Rena's thighs—

the wig settling on Rena's crotch just as Lee cracks her champagne glass hymen

the crystal hymen shattering in all directions pieces embedding in an eye here, in a navel there, on the wall there against the streaming brown cockroaches of shit from Lee's anus;

and the wig of Rena's virginity neatly transfixed on Lee's prick

GET OUT OF IT NOW YOU BASTARD IF YOU CAN THE ASSEMBLAGE ROARS.

BALD BALD BALD THE WHOLE OF RENA'S LOINS FRONT AND BACK

I LOVE YOU BALD BALD BALD

I TOLD YOU TO STOP TALKING ABOUT ME RENA SCREECHES AND
RUNS FROM THE ROOM OUT INTO THE BACKYARD FILLED WITH
TROPICAL SNOW LEE RACING AFTER HER AND SLAPPING HER FACE,
Carla Coffman staring after Rena incredulously, whispering but
shes bald, and this after she tells us, Rena does, on the moonlit
Rose Valley road, to redheaded Hedda Myers and myself, Rena
whispers, we virgins must be in league together as we crawl after
the hymen on the moonlight road, because we cant be friends if
were not virgins, we must stand together against those monster
dogs rearing at us because they easily go through specially constructed magicians hymens, but we really dont want to be friends
with such a girl who talks about virginity as if its a piece of magic
because after all shes wearing a wig all the time, there it is on
Lee's penis, shes been using us to keep her wig on straight, an act
of faithlessness in itself, so that Lee must stop himself from not
being notborn; he must be notborn to such a female; we hate her,
so that Lee is attempting to take her virginity out of her hate; and
there she is cracking her hymen all by herself, as if it is ten nervous knuckles. Her retention of our friendship is contingent on
Lee not taking her virginity, so that we must hate him if he super-
imposes his taking her virginity on top of her taking it herself;
and he, in the hating of us, destroys the friendship Carla and
Hedda have with Rena, the fact of the matter being that it is
actually Lee's desire to destroy all of Rena's friends so that there
can be no testimony as to her virginity or nonvirginity, no testimony as to her affability or sweetness or loveliness to other girls,
no testimony as to her connections with other females if he is
desirous of such connections with them himself, as, witness, Russell of Zion begins to swear, how Lee fucks the petite redhead
Hedda Myers once he is released of relationship to Rena, three
times in one night in the studio of Nina Tarassoff, the girl Hedda
but recently recovered from her one year incarceration at the Byberry nuthouse for dementia precox, she herself eluding her
lunatic husband Bernie Lefkowitz from whom shes separated,
Bernie wanting custody of the child, Lee fucking the girl once
Rena's closest friend in perfectly safe treachery, Nina becoming
intimate with Hedda after an introduction by Rena, I want you

499

to have Rena's virginity, Nina informs Lee, as a trophy, keep it as a trophy, think of it no more than as a trophy, it should be as an act of revenge that you should hold yourself responsible for the loss of Rena's virginity because Hedda finds Rena's virginity treacherous in that a whole friendship between Rena and Hedda is founded on their league against the prick, in Rena's spurious virginal front, in a magic she argues the female has against the male, that the male seeks to dispel that magic. But dispel it, then, Lee says, and in so doing cause the fracturing between Hedda and Rena, a fracturing that Rena actually desires once she does know a male sees her bald of virginity. Which is why Im so terribly sorry for you, Nina says, in that Im so indebted to you for separating Rena from Hedda, and yet must hate you because of the wound done to Hedda by Rena. But I cannot accept either your affection or your hate if it is founded on my effecting Rena's loss of virginity; and in my nonaccepting it must be assumed Rena's virginity can be said to have been taken by Nina herself, SANTA REDCHEEYA

SANTA REDCHEEYA

LETS CHANGE PARTNERS.

Just because my parents change partners, Lee, doesnt mean that you are equally able to do so.

SANTA LUCHEEYA.

Change pricks, you mean.

Yes.

DO YOU LOVE ME

Z

CHIRP CHIRP

DO YOU LOVE ME

PEARL HARBOR

BATTLE OF BRITAIN

NAZIS ADVANCE ACROSS THE UKRAINE

TWO TRILLION AND NINE

MINUS EIGHT HUNDRED AND THREE

Z

DO YOU LOVE ME DO YOU LOVE ME DO YOU LOVE ME

DONT ANSWER DONT ANSWER DONT

500

Saint Donna Zionstein. You dont care for cancer.

No, I dont. It gives me itchy skin, Aunt Bella.

You dont want to see me dying.

No, I dont.

Thats an error.

I know. My skin itches.

But not Renas.

No, not mine.

Alex Bradlows a very patriotic fellow during the war, mein kint. He flies for the United States of America and is shot down in Burma.

But Im married to Roy Emanuel.

Dont worry. Roy Emanuel obtains a divorce and marries Terry Shannon. Shes Irish, yet.

How can he marry a woman who has no head?

Because she poses for the American Victory, a symbol taken from the Victory of Samothrace, now an American missile. She poses in the nude.

I will win back Roy Emanuel. I will pose in the nude.

Without a head?

Oh no. I will put on a head.

But in the meantime you have license because Roy doesnt want to go to Philadelphia to witness my burial. Certainly you should retaliate against Roy through me. Because of Terry Shannon. You hate Roy.

Yes. Because I love Alex Lindauer. He owns realestate, he owns land. Sperm is spilt on land to insure fertility.

And Roy doesnt want to give you babies.

Because hes got a mean prick, Aunt Bella. Everything about him is mean. His bodys narrow.

A man should have wide hips and sloping shoulders and a high feminine voice, dont you agree?

Yes.

And Roy Emanuel is thus constructed, mein kint. Thats why hes so patriotic, and the United States of America wants soldiers who resemble women because the USA realizes how brave women are, much braver than men, but they cant put women into fighting uniforms, they cant send women to kill, so they find men who are the most closely patterned after women, and that is why the United States wins the war: because how can the men of the opposing nations fight women? Its not gallant, mein kint.

Brilliant strategy, mother: you manage to destroy Donna altogether by having her marry Roy Lindauer.

But I repent, Russell of Zion. Because in my dying I must be a man. You understand that, Saint Donna of Zionstein?

I remember nothing of your dying, Aunt Bella.

Thats good, then you will have no conscience about accompanying the ex-Burma flier, Alex Bradlow, to the Rochester hotel room. Its a good error you dont want to see me dying.

My skin itches.

But not Rena's.

No, not mine.

Go with Alex, then, forever. Let him fuck you, forever. Let him forever sleep in you after he fucks you. Because hes a woman, and its all right for a woman who has a prick to slumber within you forever and ever. It is a legend, and for legends we must forget who we are. In legends, mein kint, are the amnesiacs. I want my daughter a legend of forever being with Alex Bradlow, because Im dying. For only a legend can forgive me now. For only legends forgive the human beings. Walk with him forever by the rustgreen sea far from Atlantic City, down on the Margate beach, white as my flesh now, as the amented amerced amethyst mist comes in. Stop your giggling.

But the children are making such noise on the porch. Youre not going to die, mother.

Not for Donna, NO. NOT FOR DONNA, NO, NO. YOURE GIGGLING BECAUSE I HAVE NO HEAD. YOURE GIGGLING AT THE SIGHT OF THE AMERICAN MOTHER VICTORY

WILL LEE LOVE ME IF I HAVE NO HEAD

CUT OFF MY HEAD LEE

CUT OFF MY HEAD. OH, THANK YOU, THANK

IM SIMPLY SLAPPING YOUR FACE

IM SO COLD

IM SO COLD ITS BECAUSE IVE LOST MY HEAD

ONLY YOUR VIRGINITY

YOUVE CUT OFF MY VIRGINITY YOU MUST LOVE ME YOU MUST

L

YOUR VIRGINITY IS NOT YOUR HEAD

YOURE IN LOVE WITH AN OLDER WOMAN LEE THATS WHATS

THE TROUBLE YOURE

GIRLS ALWAYS THINK THE BOYS THEY LOVE ARE IN LOVE WITH

OLDER WOMEN BUT THE PERFECT I LOVE YOU ISSUES FROM THE

FOETUS

YOURE SLAPPING MY FOETUS. Somethings been born.

No. Its a dead foetus. Feel.

No.

Feel

Terry youre always against me.

Darling.

You dont want me for Lee.

Darling.

But I cant make love to you. You have no head.

Darling, my head is between my thighs.

Thats a legend.

Ah, then you forgive me. Levi, Terry Shannon is your sister, come to replace the Polack Christine Novak the mistress then who causes Levi to oppose the marriage of Lee to Rena by virtue of Levi desiring Rena, for Levi must hate his son because of Levi's alliance with Christine who as Terry Shannon of course desires Lee. Be my sister, Levi informs Rena, and we solve all difficulties, for certainly you cannot commit incest with Lee, and it is therefore a forgone conclusion that Lee must be repelled by Terry Shannon by virtue of her being the sister to Levi. Naturally, Terry is considerably older than Lee; and, while the prospect of going to bed with an older sister would answer Lee's deepest desires, he cannot do so because Terry is already his father's sister, a contretemps to be sure, which has no solution except for Lee to marry Rena who has been given advices by Terry that she, Rena, is not the girl for Lee, and Rena should certainly take Terry's advice because Terry is Lee's older sister whom after all Lee would prefer to marry. Rena, in an act of revenge against Terry, marries

Lee, which enrages Terry and causes her to become Levi's sister instead so that she can influence Levi to behave amatorily though without actual consummation toward Rena, in turn causing Lee to suspect that his father is Rena's brother, for what else would cause Levi to stop short of actually making love to Lee's wife? And, of course it becomes impossible for Lee to make love to Terry in that she is now his aunt—Aunt Terry Zion, no less, who is burning her freckles in her advanced age on the California beach, leaving her skin dead white :

nauseated to the point of amnesia, St Red fucks the exBurma flier in the Rochester hotel room. This is justifiable, because, as she puts it, I HAVE NO HEAD

But Levi, dying, draws all the young dancers around him, Levi realizing that the skimlipped Jay Grays, toying with Achille Volpe's milky eye and sticking pins in it so that it spurts St Red's vaginamilk at Lee, we must blind Lee, Jay spicules his vertexed chin, for having first encountered and executing Red without her priorly satisfying Jay's lechery, a cleanchinned and pointed lechery, a hairless vandyked lechery of bone, which would have suited her better in that I would not now have to forgive Lee by wanting to blind him, a blindness serving both my abomination of him and my compassion for him since he will not then see Red posed in the nude, my pointed chin going beautifully by congruency with the shape of her mons veneris, Jay then committing the ultimate corruption and treachery by having drawn for Lee and later having it elaborated by Rhona Lyrian the picture of Rena's genitals as a labyrinth, Lee himself the variant Minotaur within, if you will, a monstrous halfman, halfboy, which the archetype might well have been, Jay skimmingly grins, Barry Handler nodding his head with delighted dottedline rapidity— Levi coming to the realization out of the sensing that his own shrunken body is slipping into a labyrinthine rubber tube, one end of which is attached to his dripping penis, and the other to the pissbottle beneath his bed

YOU UNDERSTAND JAY GRAYS SHRUGS CAVALIERLY I LET ST RED GO TO LEE BECAUSE SOMEHOW I MUST FIND A WAY BY WHICH

504

TO EXERCIZE BOTH COMPASSION FOR AND ABOMINATION ON HIM
EVEN AS EVERYONE CONGREGATED HERE MUST DO

AYE

AYE

AYE a process by which Levi himself is serving his son Lee, so
that it is after all quite possible that Lee has taken unto himself
the very regret Levi himself had, the regret that is the desire of
Levi to arrogate unto himself the birth process, that it is a Levi
who gives birth to Lee, his son then looking upon his fathers
dying as the natural retaliation of life upon Levi's desire by way
of Levi's shrunken body patterning into the labyrinthal female
genitalia but inexorably having to make payment by losing itself
into the pissbottle—that variant Minotaur, Rhona Lyrian picks
up the thread, stationed within Rena's labyrinth to devour all the
sacrificial males brought to the girl;

draw round me, dancers, Levi enjoins the highschool boys and
girls, comprising all mincing Frankenstein Monsters in illfitting
tuxedos, Flikker the Golemdog in two pairs of canvas sneakers,
spasmodic Miss Sherman in her burnt pink evening gown, the
ironjowled Melinkoff pulling up in his fathers sled under
the iciclehung tropical moon, the sled drawn by eight little baby
boys here to seek out eight little marriageable girls EIGHT TIMES
YOU NEED RABBI SILVER YOU GOT NO GRATITUDE YOU SHOULD
WANT TO RETIRE HIM FROM CONGREGATION BRITH MIKVEH BE-
CAUSE EIGHT TIMES HES GOT TO GET RID OF A DYBBUK SON IN
YOU BECAUSE EACH TIME YOUR WIFE GIVES BIRTH YOU GOT TO
STUFF THE SON SHE GIVES BIRTH TO INTO YOURSELF OUT OF
JEALOUSLY I UNDERSTAND

I UNDERSTAND

Rachel Emanuel in a legomutton satin evening gown trilling
to each of her male suitors in turn I dont tell anybody any more
Im born in Odessa because Im an American girl after all I come
to America when Im very young Im only three years old when
Im crossing on the boat and I run all around the boat making
friends with the passengers just like my son Lee does with the
ladies waiting for the trolley on the corner of 7th and Berks

505

Streets and hes just a baby two years old at the most and he says I want to look in your pocketbook to each one I want to see whats inside

Solomon Goldstein swinging up on Esthers troika vowing hes already a responsible youngster she should marry him because look already I got one ulcer/Fiona promising Cornelius Nuri if hell live with her she promises to communicate with him only in babytalk/Rosa Caby whispering to Silas Klein you just put your magnum opus on rhythm right behind my buttocks AND YOULL BE ABLE TO SWAT THE

FLY FARTS

AS THEY COME OUT OF MY HAIRSCREEN DOOR/Mark Fahn placing his ear next to Hedda Myer's clitoris tied with a blue ribbon telling her confidentially Beethoven is a liar you see hes deaf he cant hear a thing thats why since Im absolutely honest Im composing in silences each black and white piano key is a clitoris I press down on and what results actually is a twisting and a squirming in my ear Hedda thats what I feel but I hear absolutely nothing I understand that since Ive got six sisters and no brothers I must have clitoral silence/I promise you Myra says to Mike Burroughs as they group around Levi I will go blind in one eye and I will go mad in the other SO THAT THE BLIND EYE, DARLING, DARLING

THE BLIND EYE WILL TAKE THE ELEVATOR THIRTEEN STOREYS UP IN THE APARTMENT HOUSE ONE SATURDAY MORNING AND IT WILL JUMP OFF THE LEDGE OF THE ROOF BECAUSE DOWN ON THE PAVEMENT WILL BE THE ONE MAD EYE TELLING THE BLIND EYE TO JUMP

JUMP

JUMP

SO THAT THE BLIND EYE WILL DIVE INTO THE MAD EYE ON THE PAVEMENT BECAUSE THE MAD EYE IS SHRIEKING JUMP JUMP SO THAT YOU CAN SEE THROUGH ME AGAIN AND

THE BLIND EYE JUMPS

JUMPS

AND, STRIKING THE PAVEMENT AFTER IT GOES STRAIGHT

506

THROUGH THE MAD EYE, SCREAMS TO THE MAD ONE YOURE A LIAR
A LIAR BECAUSE MADNESS IS
   BL/Im young,
   Myra says,
   so I
   can
   tell you
   all
this/Im dancing with a cleftpalate gull in my arms Alex hums
into Donna's ear/Im not so excited Bella says to Sidney Zion :
   because my soul is colorblind/
   Celia d'Arc admits her face comes from a farm; my face, pig-
like, signifies I must save all the pigmen of this world; Im tied
to a cruciform pigtrough, nobody wants to dance with me; thats
why, burnt, Im waiting for a phonecall from my agent, so I can
be an actress/youll have to excuse me Harry Ring I couldnt steal
a tuxedo because today my father died and I cant dance too well
owing to the fact that the knuckles of my right hand are bandaged
you better watch out how you die Levi Im warning you somebodys liable to finish it for you if you dont do it yourself Im only
seventeen and I take matters into my own hands, oh, literally, my
fathers dying a raging man once he is a big rager he is so enraged he can get he takes a oak chair apart piece by piece,
slowly, with his hands, right before me, I have to watch, as a
child I have to watch, so now he dies, the sonofabitch, too slow,
the whole family around him, waiting, waiting, Im warning you,
Levi, take heed, but its all right hes dying slowly, that much Ill
give him, but let him die Mark Fahn
   sure, youve got a point, Fahn
   in silence, but that he wont do all of a sudden, he starts to babble,
to chatter, nothing you can make sense of, yes, even that we could
forgive him if his babble makes sense, but it doesnt, its all crazy
mixedup syllables, without symbols, yet, because even that we
could forgive him if he speaks like highly symbolic poetry, or automatic writing, but no, not even that, its got to be absolutely meaningless, and were listening, the whole family, mama, my brothers,

507

my sister, me, listening, he should make at least one word of sense
and well forgive him, well let him die slow, sure, but for an hour,
two hours, three hours the man babbles laying there in bed and
I say to my older brothers you got to shut him up, youre the
oldest I tell Adam, do something, make him shut up, but Adam
cant, he turns aside, he shrugs, so I turn to the next oldest, Mendel, I tell him shut pop up, that babble, its an insult, its a shame
to him, he cant help it, so help him, do something for him, Im
warning you, Levi, watch out, but Mendel shakes his head, what
can he do as my father babbles and chatters and dribbles from
the mouth, so I tell the whole family none of you are going to do
anything, I, Harry, will do it, so they all shake their heads, they
all turn away from my father, they cant look, well I cant blame
them, because only the man who is going to do it is allowed to
look, after all, thats right, so I go up to my babbling father, my
chattering father, my meaningless father now, meaningless, you
understand, and I draw back my fist and I smash him on the
jaw and I break the jaw and he stops babbling he stops chattering he makes no sound now and all of a sudden hes got all the
meaning because hes

dead youll pardon me my bandaged knuckles I cant hold the
highschool girls too well around the waist/

wheres my wig

Lilly pass me the wig

wheres my wig Gladys whimpers in her jubilee jordan sixteen-
yearold shape at the graduating dance/I dont have a mother
Herb Goldstein confesses Frances Im the most fortunate of young
men

I LOVE YOU

Marcus Kronthal dances with the girl in the wheelchair whispering to her so that she blushes : I never fucked a girl in a wheelchair. Youre the boy Im looking for, she replies. I once saw a
movie in my fathers moviehouse and the hero was a man in a
wheelchair, yes it was a foreign film because this could only happen in a foreign land and the wheelchair hero wheels himself into
the girl's bedroom and do you know how he fucked her Marcus?
By quarterturns of the two wheels on his chair, back and forth,

back and forth, wasnt that heroism Marcus/I lost all the hair between my legs the future Mrs Ackman says

wheres my w

i could get a little piece of fur Mr Ackman says I could sew right on your dotted line/I stutter Nate Goldstein confides to Hannah because just before Im born the obstetrician says to my father sign here on the dotted line or I wont deliver, and I see that dotted line from the hole in my mother and I try to tell her MOM TELL POP NOT TO SIGN BECAUSE IM ALL RIGHT WHERE I AM TO HELL WITH THE OBSTETRICIAN BECAUSE IM ALL RIGHT TELL HIM NOT TO SIGN BUT

I CANT GET THE WORDS OUT BECAUSE IM SO EXCITED IM SO ANGRY and thats why Im still stuttering in a dotted line Jared/ the reason Rhona Lyrian says nobodys dancing with me is because of my philosophers head on my aphrodite body I try to synthesize Greek philosophy with Judaism and thats wrong to do when youre young: I should wait till philosophy and Judaism are both dead; then you can marry them/all the phallus wants to do is to take a drink of water from me Diane Valin says, flouncing up to Levi, and thats not so very much to ask of me, I feel/I want to be a fourletter man like my brother, Lee says/oh, Betty Emanuel says, all the mauve skinthin of her, thats easy, because LOVE is a plant/and idealist Barry Handler, member of the Young Communist League, goes from girl to girl on the dance floor searching for the one in whose fallopian tubes love can be tied/ Im already sentimental in my bones Timmy Lascar tells a girl, theyre going soft on me/ would a girl take care of my all pussycats Duke Montaigne inquires/not a boy will dance with me Clement Lichtenstein complains, theyre all so young/I need to be stuck by your chickenbreastedness Kanovsky declares to Anne/Im too tall for all the boys Gail Greene says softly; perhaps—perhaps if I could have only one leg cut off, I would be/i promise you if you marry me, Sy, Nina says fiercely, Ill paint a mustache on your mother/Ive got all the girls following me, Jay Grays boasts, because Im trailing a labyrinth on a leash/I never worry about farting when I do my comic dances, Minnie tells Charlie Doyle, because I paint each fart into a colored balloon, and as the gas

509

gently escapes I float delicately down to earth; I love you, Charlie says, because thats how people should come down to earth, by the emission of their own gasses/Lionel Shafkin jokes with Harriet, you know how people like to get out of their own skins, well, thats me all over, if you can manufacture enough cells in yourself, extra ones, you can multiply right out of yourself; sure, sure, its a form of megalomania, Harriet, but a Jewish boy has to expand out of his ghetto, and each man's body, after all, is like a ghetto—you got to live a whole life in your own body; so, if you can find a way to burst out of this, you/all love dances are war dances Sue warns Dave Emanuel/why Lilly, Walter says, why you know the more fat a man puts on himself the harder it is for a girl to get around him/why you know Donna, Roy Lindauer philosophizes as he leads her to Levi, the more land a man buys the more his girl wants to trample that land, and you wont have to worry about where youll find a spot to trample, Ive got it all for you/the trouble is, Terry Shannon admits, that since I cant dance to Wagner Ive got to sing him/Achille Volpe whispers to a girl his deepest secret Im weaned far too soon so that one eye, permitted to search for the lactation I miss, is constantly having milk squirted into it by all the angry nipples I mistake for my mother's; hence, my milky eye/we dont want to dance with the girls at all Noah Hudsen and Lloyd Engle chorus because whenever we do we feel the females are nothing more than mice running up our legs/I see absolutely nothing wrong, Danny Naroyan avers ferociously, in playing a Bach fugue for these adolescents because if you condition them to that why thats what theyll dance to/the point is Cliff Gratz holds up Nadine's nose for silence that Rena's virginity is analagous as we all know to the notorious doughnut hoop

THIRTEEN THOUSAND MINUS NINE HUNDRED AND NINETY SEVEN)

I CANT GROW UP WITHOUT A WIG)

WHAT WILL HIS MOTHER SAY)

/which constitutes a very considerable lesson in love. At the time of my being the proprietor of a doughnut factory in Florida. To think, Harry Ring interposes,

HAD I BEEN ABLE TO SECURE A SIMPLE DOUGHNUT BY WHICH I COULD HAVE MANACLED MY FATHER'S BABBLING CHIN. But, you see, it requires something as ludicruous as a doughnut. If I think of an iron ring, or adhesive tape, or any such, because theyre all too serious I cannot use them; but a doughnut, ah, the sheer comedy of it would have made me apply one instantly to my father's chin/

I use a simple barrel in which to cast rotten doughnuts. Each time I have a rotten doughnut and pass by the barrel I cast it in. One day I happen to look inside the barrel of rotten doughnuts and I am horrified to discover that maggots are crawling in and around and through and between the rotten doughnuts, and instantly I sell the doughnut factory instantly I sell all rotted hoops what you dont seem to understand is that Rena is lying at Norma Emanuel's absolutely motionless feethoop, and that the blind boy jumping up and down while holding on to his parents hands

COME CLOSER BOYS AND GIRLS DANCERS WHEEL ME AROUND THE DANCEFLOOR WHEEL ME TO RENA AND THEN, PLEASE, ONE QUARTER TURN OF THE WHEEL BACK, AND ONE QUARTER TURN OF THE WHEEL FRONT, I

WILL SPECIFY IN MY WILL

LEE

THAT YOU ARE TO INHERIT THE WHEELCHAIR FOR THE PURPOSE OF HAVING INTERCOURSE WITH RENA

;has at last wrenched himself out of their hands and is flying to Philadelphia in the Constellation to attend the seeingeye death of his father. Well, no

PLEASE GIVE ME BACK MY WIG

A MERE MATTER OF DAYS BEFORE ENGLAND WOULD CAPITULATE TO HITLER THE CHIEF OF THE R.A.F. ORDERS THE BOMBING OF BERLIN/THREE OR FOUR OR EIGHT PEOPLE ARE KILLED AND INSTANTLY GOERING CALLS OFF THE BOMBING OF STRATEGIC POINTS IN ENGLAND AND ORDERS INSTEAD THE RETALIATORY AND STUPID BOMBING OF LONDON WHICH PROVIDES THE R.A.F. WITH THE NECESSARY RESPITE TO REGROUP REHOOP/

Well, no/Cliff smiles. Actually, of course, Rena has been tossing her hymen for years into the hymen barrel. That is to say,

each night she discovers shes got a rotten hymen from her hymen
factory and she goes by the hymen barrel she tosses in the rotten
hymen and one night when stopping by Leechance to look into
chance/the fife of the dancing ant
/the rotten hymen barrel she finds the rotten hymens swarm-
ing with crawling knives in and around and through and between
and over and under the rotten hymens because, after all, she cannot omit coming to the conclusion that Solomon Goldstein, looking for a place to hide his nest of ulcers, has finally hit on his
daughter's rotten hymen barrel, so that, in agony, without realizing it, Rena suffers from an ulcerated hymen promoting spicules
of pain similar to that caused by knives, by Mrs Sherman's burnt
high heels clattering along the dance floor, by the twoyearold
WHAT WILL RACHEL EMANUEL SAY

;Lee on the corner of 7th and Berks being very cordial to the
ladies waiting for the trolleycar as he himself boards one at Frankford and Orthodox in synthetic anger because he realizes he must
carry Rena's knife for her to her parents because she can no longer play classical knives on the piano, only jazz knives, so that he
must cut her family to pieces with popular music, the hysterical
effect, finally, on Rena's virginity being that Mark Fahn plays the
piano keys as clitorises in silence as Lee rummages around in the
pocketbook hymen to look for flying ants, itching all over him Ive
got to get out of the bathtub now now Ive got what will his
mother say if hes dirty and what will she say if hes clean, so that
the whole problem of disabusing Rena of her virginity, the success or failure of it, is directly related to the reaction of his mother,
the obvious lesson to be drawn is that Rachel drives her son toward Rena to take or not to take her virginity so that she can
make as the chairlady her speech to the Brith Mikveh Sisterhood,
while Dr Jonah Silver, inadvertently lingering his finger a moment
too long
THE BOMBING OF LONDON IS FUTILE FUTILE ACCOMPLISHING
NO STRATEGIC PURPOSE IN MAKING ENGLANDS HOOP INOPERATIVE
AND HITLER JUMPS UP AND DOWN UP AND DOWN IN BLIND RAGE
AS HE HOLDS ON TO HIS PARENTS HANDS WHILE THE ENGLISH
GIRL COURTSEYING PERMITS HER HOOP TO SETTLE AT HER FEET/

512

at the paperwrapped champagne glass under Lees feet suffers concentratedly spiculed agony as Lee brings down his heel on Rena's virginity and simultaneously on Jonah Goldstein's finger

MY FINGER

MY FINGER SOLOMON HOWLS PART OF IT IS SLICED OFF BY LEE'S MEAT SLICER YOU GOT TO PUT HIM TOGETHER JARED. So, as we see, Rena's hymen clings as well to her father's sliced finger, its got blood on it from the swiss cheese of Rena's many times perforated virginity constantly being put into the Goldstein slicer from which Lee

z

z

z(hero

must, as hoop, lying at secondwife's feet, rescue it while Lloyd Engle and Noah Hudsen inform Lee that many men are scurrying away with Rena's cheese, compelling Lee to search pocketbook after woman's pocketbook in a supremely valiant twoyearold infant search to find a substitute hymen and replace it instanter, fucking her

firemanpoling it in

the Renadog rearing, jaws emitting multicolored balloonfarts, retaliating in revenge against the male infant, knocking him down on the GoldsteinEmanuel tablebed, the dancers urging her on

UNBORN

UNBORN

so that, the childgirl dead, her hoop broken into

ONE THOUSAND TRILLION AND THREE MINUS TEN BILLION AND NINETEEN FRAGMENTS;

GOLEMONSTERGARGOYLEDOG ST RED ON ALL FOUR PLUNGES DOWN ON HER TO RAPE HER;

it is, Cliff facetiously observes, the rape of the man, precisely what St Red has been desirous of all along, but only possible for her to do on all fours, as you will see the female of the species most capable let me say in passing, what with Hedda Myers on all fours on the Rose Valley road, certainly you dont imagine for a moment that Red is unbeholden to her conscience in having driven Hedda mad, and Carla mad, by her treachery, a treachery

513

to be purified, friendship at the very least to be resumed in her
mind though it may not tally with reality, by the rape of Lee, her
mind quite willing to bear that she does not match it with reality,
having quite gone beyond it by having

THE MIND ON ALL FOURS

while at the same time accomplishing the miraculous by having me, Clifford Gratz, drop his chin into Lee's, which verifies
her multiple rape by extension, including as well Sy Tarassoff
who wishes to pose her but which is prevented by Lee's hysteria,
now Ill show him hysteria, Lee has no concept of hysteria, really,
Ill really make him hysterical by being on all fours on top of
him, the disappearance of his ringworm by his becoming enamored of me to begin with initiating the whole process of the
loss of my virginity, effaced ringworm giving way to my woman-
hood, so that she is drawn out of her virginity by his very cleanliness to be superseded by reinfection of the ringworm, which is
nothing, Harry Ring, nothing, compared to the crab doughnuts
infesting your East Side toilet seat by which Rena is infected,
though I must say I must give myself some credit, Cliff paren-
thesizes, by having dumped the whole doughnut matter in Harry
Ring's toiletlap, thereby playing some indirect role in Red's infection, that very indirection, the indirection of all maggoty hoops
causing the loss of the girl's virginity, the hoops whirled round
too many times, so that Red sweats and plunges to drop her hymen to her feet, such a big horse of a girl Esther Goldstein chimes
in her own vector, that she should still be playing with her hoop,
and by so characterizing she brings down the metal phone on her
daughters classical clitoris, Esther saturated with the malevolence
of her own yawningly loose cunt and demanding that that
malevolence have some gratification in her daughter's depri-
vation by Lee while contesting it in all grinning conscience I
dont want you to marry her if you cant support her, implying
that its perfectly all right for Donna Goldstein to be fucked but
not certified, so do it secretly but not before all these adolescent
dancers crowding around Levi's wheelchair, Levi himself, Bella
accuses, having Christine Novak ponderously on his mind, compelling his son to advance on St Red who, herself grinning, is

perfectly aware of her fatherinlaw's stimulus, death, death, death driving toward causing the loss of her hymen, so that Gail Greene, even by the loss of her leg, is a caroming force against Lee which he must transfer to Rena, for a moment the girl, Rena, horror-stricken, thinking of her uncle jumping out the window because of the insane itching of his skin cancer, Rena wanting to jump a billion storeys out of her own skin, she demands, then, that Lee's penis be xrayed so that she can rest easy and not be terrified by the idea of cancer of the hymen, get it out, get it out she screams hysterically at Lee, and the very insistence by Lee that, whatever he has, is noninfectious, has her topple down on him GODDAMN YOU ILL DROWN YOU WITH MILKBOTTLE H UNLESS MY WIG MY WIG MY WIG ITLL GO FLOATING AWAY ON THE FLOOD

WHAT WILL RACHEL EMANUEL SAY

TO HELL WITH MY WIFE LET HER GO FUCK HERSELF LEVI EMANUEL ROARS FROM HIS WHEELCHAIR

ON THE PROMISSORY NOTE OF WALKING DOWN THE CORRIDOR ON THE SECOND STOREY OF THE EMANUEL HOUSEHOLD ON ROOSEVELT BOULEVARD THAT LEE WILL OVERHEAR THAT HE IS ESSENTIALLY THE GHOST AND NOTHING MORE THAN THE GHOST OF LEE THE FIRST THEN LEE THE SECOND KNOWS THAT, UNBORN, HE CAN LIFT HIS LAST LEG OUT OF THE RENATHIGH BATHTUB AND EMERGE PERFECTLY CLEAN, THE CLEANEST GHOST THIS SIDE OF PARADISE

and, therefore, as the dancers chant : UNBORN, UNBORN,

Rena and Lee, lying side by side on the flagstoned bedroom-livingroom patio of the GoldsteinEmanuel highschool dance, /because : only as a ghost can Lee fuck Rena and deprive her of her virginity without ascribing the instrumentation to himself/ sigh, one to the other :

I love you

UNBORN UNBORN the antiphonal flows from the dancers DONT FORGET THE FLOOD GLADYS MATTHEWS CALLS AND MY WIG THATLL FLOAT AWAY OH SAVE A YOUNG GIRL FROM THE SPEC-TACLE OF BALDNESS Jared, working against dottedline time,

515

swiftly coalesces Lee against the latter's thrashing savage protests in and around and through and over and under Rena

wheres he screwing me from now she asks

I got to know from what direction a man is screwing me you cant ask a girl to be screwed from all directions

the fuck you cant Lee says

the fuck you can Rena retorts because if youre doing it to me from all directions I cant then feel it from any direction

yes, thats his trouble Norma says

thrashing savage protests : if Im all in one piece, Jared, goddamn you, thats a distinct disadvantage in coping with living problems. Its much easier to defend oneself if one is separated into many pieces BESIDES WHAT WILL MOTHER SAY

Im plural

MY WIG

IF A MAN DOESNT FUCK A WOMAN BY BEING A SINGLE PIECE THEN THE WHOLE CONGREGATION OF MEN AND WOMEN WILL BE DROWNED A MULTITUDE OF HUMANITY MUST PERISH IF ANY MAN AMONGST IT IS SEPARATED INTO MANY SECTIONS

BUT IT WONT WORK I SWEAR TO YOU LEE BELLOWS AT HIS COUSIN

I cant take the advice of a man in sections Jared growls as he at last stitches all of Lee Emanuel's bloody parts into an absolute whole

I TOLD YOU YOU GODDAMN BASTARD SURGEON ONE MORE OF YOUR SYNTHESIZING ERRORS Lee curses as, plunging his whole self as the fucking apparatus into Rena's cunt inundated with the vast sea of Milkbottle H viscous milk so as to stopper up the tidal wave back into the woman, Lee collides with the unborn, the cleanest ghost this side of paradise emerging from Renas vulvatub, the whole of Lee living and the whole of Lee ghost in smashing collision in Rena's cunt, flesh and ghost and ghost and flesh in shattering orgasm

I GOT MY WIG BACK I GOT MY WIG BACK THE TENTON GLADYS MATTHEWS SPRAWLS HER ECSTATIC BULK OVER BOTH NAKED BODIES and laps up in gratitude whatever milkbottle h leaks have occurred from Rena's cunt flesh

and ghost and
flesh and
ghost in icy tropical mothwings hummingbirding through St Red's genitals so that she peers at Lee in the nakedest of obligations.

Youre naked, he says, rising on an elbow.

Yes.

Youre very beautiful, he says, in the nakedness.

Yes. Flesh and ghost, she says.

Im going to take a shower after this, he says inanely. I will never take a bath in a tub again. Because, even though Im clean, I itch all over. Showers, he nods at her.

All right, flesh and ghost, Jeanne d'Moth climbing cruciform trembles in her genitals—Rena leads vast hordes of men, vaguely, vaguely, from her vagina, indistinct mothshapes lightly beating against her crotch, slowly subsiding. Showers, darling. Ghost and flesh and ghost
and flesh, What will my mother say, Terry? Mrs Gladys L Wallace Matthews a hippohumpbacked cat, Councilman Matthews dazedly stroking her fur wig. Kitchens should be painted all in red, Frances Goldstein plumply avers, because thats where all the food is prepared.

Look what I married, husband Herb says, so I could be tied to a whore's apronstrings. The buzzer. Theres a customer, Solomon says, knocking on the plateglass window yet. In the dark, the customer shades his eyes, making his fingers like spyglasses. Binoculars, pop, Rena corrects. Its wartime, Solomon counters, so in this neighborhood, against Jews, the momseren use spyglasses. Nearly six million Jews have been exterminated, Norma Emanuel says; theres a hoop for you, Lee

MINUS SIX MILLION

she stands in the doorway of Lees room at 119 West 75th Street, her breasts heaps of pale blue and green flowers, her nipples buttoned all the way up her highnecked summerprint, the petticoats puffing out the hipskirt, bluegreengrayeyed, a touch of Levi's longshort stare in them, Norma the princess of the somnambulists, Lee thinks, who walk wobblethighed in their sexual

517

sleep, her irises plucks of pale gray, green and blue flowers of course I remember you he grimaces his shaving lathertorso toward her.

She shakes her head in a nipped modification of no. No you dont.

Of course I do. From Philadelphia.

She delicately kicks a smile behind her ear under crescents of blond canoecurls, tipping, a pair of blithe crimson cheekmuffs on either highbone, sometime scuffling for a blush against the fairflesh, her nose a touch of skipup over lucklips, luckalip princess with the chipapoint chin skipping pebbleflouncing over the gray-green blueing waters, the rose in the sunspray Norma, holding fast with nimble fingers to her heart its all Ive got, sir

one heart. Nay, then, hurt not my fingers well Lee after all the note I leave you says Philadel

But I do remem

You cant, not really. Its years

Please come in

Well. My girlfriend, Claudette, shes down on the street

I know I meet you in

Youre drunk, Lee. At a party. With Rena. I want to talk to you. But youre mean to me. You tell me to go away. Its a big party. The girl with the grandma face is there

Yes, the party a grimace of blood under his ear. True, I dont remember you

You say youre only interested in Rena. But she's telling everybody she

has a clogstocked medicine cabinet oil of cloves, belladonna, Rena doesnt need any medicines, only a diaphragm Lee searching for it frantically amongst the whitenesses of the shelves you see Rachel nods knowingly if she kept all her medicines like I do you wouldnt have any trouble in the first place Lee I dont know whats the matter with you sometime you act like you got no brains hes not too smart my Lee, sometimes, the brilliantly deep blue cup for washing the eyes, the dropper for the nasal spray gargle if your throat hurts its the best thing the doctor says I got a touch

of arthritis but I dont trust him your Doctor Newman he likes
to talk too much why dont you see him more often hes somebody
you can really converse with Lee he told me you should come in
any time of course Im proud my son out of five hundred patients
he picks Lee and doctors are always saying they got no time no
    a man who loves Tolstoi stuck away on Wyoming Avenue a
textile mill and cartracks Tolstoi in Feltonville well Dr Newman
says in Russia its not so different so instead of twostorey houses
and cartracks its Chekhov helping with the plague;
    here I got a black plague of twostorey houses. Black. Black car-
tracks, Lee, shining black cartracks, its a dread disease, believe
me, ask Nina
    he said I should ask you about your sinusitis and your sneezing
its a little better since he nearly kills me with those allergy tests
thats what I mean Lee he didnt notice what he was doing so he
had to make you sick yet but its your fault too why didnt you
tell him how you were feeling I dont know where my sons brains
are sometimes
    on Levis hornrimmed spectacles the Philadelphia streetlamps
gakwoosh gashwool. He depresses the brake in his Buick for a red
light. 2nd and Lehigh, freightyards, Pennsylvania, Reading, an
infinite series of hooknosed houses and the hornrimmed spectacles
rest on top of the five coal silos LEVI COAL COMPANY anthracite
dying out as a fuel Dr Silver uses gas, I use oil sulfa cant help
Christine Novak, amber Christine, yellow, green pneumonia the
traffic goes. But she tarries at the yellow, her flesh, no resistance
her skin so yellow I recognize you Levi greenly she smiles
yellowly :
    they havent killed this Polack yet, her teeth green trafficlights
    who wants to drive in such traffic Rachel irritatedly objects.
Besides, I got a touch of arthritis what do you expect I got such
pleasure from my life Victor its something I should be proud of
where he is I only hope you never hear those iron doors of a prison Lee better youre not born
    for Rena Goldstein
    but then I got to remember the first Lee he looks just like Levi.

A real question if the second Lee should be born so I should forget Levi, Rena laying beside the first Lee you make me remember Levi, I distrust you, Rena
naked. Sy Tarassoff. Na
BECAUSE THE GHOST OF THE FIRST LEE MAKES ME THINK OF THE GHOST OF LEVI. Rena frightens me, Rachel thinks. This is the payment I get, losing a tenyearold boy, a girl comes along and prefers the ghost of my tenyearold made into the living Lee, to remind me of the first Lee virgins should be excommunicated : theyre not really Jews. Underneath, Rena must be a Christian, because Jewish women, no matter what everybody says, by the very act of being born, arent virgins any more; in the womb theyre virgins. Its the mother who takes the daughters virginity, just by giving birth—because, whats a girl? Girls arent even supposed to be born; so they should have some kind of ridiculous virtue? So, Rena acts against her mother, through me, and accidentally grabs my first Lee whos coming home for lunch, I have a sandwich ready for the boy, hes such a blond, and if moths could be graygreen, those are his eyes, graygreen moths deepset,

but how would camphor feel in my womb? his hair parted in the center just like Levis

you love a little boy, him, the first Lee, its like youre shattered into a smoothness, and the shatter is smooth thats the love through my whole body that shatters a smoothness around the boy but all of a sudden not so smooth like Joshua Nathanson is phoning. Yes, a grandfather of a boy calls for his son, the second Lee knows this just like Im phoned about Joshua is very sick

a little boy leaping up in bed at 236 East Roosevelt Boulevard is a little boy leaping into the air in the park the second Lee tries to catch the white ball, Rena, hes trying to stop it from going in the direction of the boy hes named after because Joshua his grandfather is dead and he knows the white ball next is going toward, and after all hes got to stop it because theres a little boy coming out of you, Rena, you, too, you, and you grab his hand, you see, so I understand your feeling that the second Lee shouldnt be born, youre already protecting yourself against another birth, the birth

520

from the semen of the notborn in you THAT WILL RESULT IN THE NOTBORN OF THE NOTBORN

from the hospital, hes hit on the head by a baseball and Levi not once kills me with his fancy fucking hes never

fancy. Baseball, I say.

But thats Dave, Dave plays baseball, Lees not so interested but they tell me thats what the boy says his name is, and Lees smart, I can believe him, and I should come over and I call Levi and tell him and he says in his Lithuanian accent thick, thick Youre sure its Yes. Yes I say, a hospital should lie. And sure enough we can get Dave out of school, Daves in school sure enough Mrs Goldstein why dont you slam down the phone on my hand thats where it belongs I dont want to call anybody a phone isnt even invented because there isnt time for such an invention rushing to the hospital and sure enough theres my baby a

mother no matter how old her child is hes always the baby

the graygreen eyemoths and his hair parted in the middle, Levi.

A big bed for a baby.

Well, hes ten years old Mrs Emanuel.

Camphor. Pregnant women should use camphor, first. Because the world is winter clothes does it hurt I ask him Im worried because moths like the dark and thats the way they got the hospital room.

Just a little dizzy he says hes good with figures and his hands and in school and with Hebrew, he looks a little like Russell Zion but stronger, bigger why did you have to cross the park I scold him you know the kids play baseball Dave why didnt you tell him youre his big brother you got to warn a child

Mom how could

Im sorry mom, Lee says.

You got to watch out for the moths, they eat through everything, isnt that right, Gertrude.

Thats right Mrs Emanuel

And moths have eyes, graygreen all right its past, its forgotten, the main thing is you should get better thats right Levi says thick,

521

thick, his accent is worse than ever I thought it was improving but all of a sudden its like hes an immigrant right off the boat I run around myself making friends with everybody, the passengers Lee standing against the fence looking into ladies' pocketbooks hes not afraid of anything but the doctors are telling me I should be prepared for the worst what is the worst that can happen to a person is that her baby

ALL RIGHT

ALL RIGHT SO HE ISNT A BABY BUT THATS THE WAY A MOTHER THINKS

IM

NOT

A

SCULPTOR

IN

CAMPHOR/

Rena, is that her baby should die, you should know that, so maybe its right the second Lee shouldnt be born but how can you be sure yes in return for not being born he says I love you but dont you see he says I love you like its a thanks, and

what am I to do without him, there should be a baby a mother can scold, a boy with Levi graygreen eyes make all the holes you want in winter clothes the main thing you should get better. All right he says, but he says it like hes doing me a favor, like its a thanks.

A favor.

What can I do.

I sit.

Dave I tell he should go out, youll see Dave later.

Lee he says you get better Ill teach you how you should play ball and youll hit somebody else

Is that a way to talk I scold my firstborn. Wait in the Buick.

Every day he comes home for lunch Levi says you can hardly understand him the accent is so thick, as if its my fault he comes home for lunch he gets better food home I say, its healthier.

Healthier Levi says, healthier. His big muscles my husband's he dont hit anybody with them, its from his work, he can build, at the business.

522

How do you feel now I ask my tenyearold.

Still a little dizzy everything on him in the dark room is white like Bella Zion hes laying in Bella's whiteness Im frightened Rena Im my skin is so rosy Im a rosy afraid how can fear be so

rosy I dont like his Bella whiteness maybe if I could get him out of the bed and get some color in his cheeks a little Levi like I tell the physiotherapist when Levi is sick and dying it would do Lee good but no the doctors say. Call a specialist, but they did concussion, a fractured skull so if I get rose in his cheeks hell be afraid I dont even want to ask my baby if hes afraid god of my fathers please Im praying to you that much give him. That much. He shouldnt be afraid.

I cant even tell him Lee you shouldnt be afraid. He shouldnt even have an idea

god must be punishing me, Aaron Emanuel. Aaron has his ear to a cloud, and I have my ear to a moth.

God is in a moth.

God eats through everything, God eats

through :

all :

our :

winter :

clothes

MAKE MY WOMB INTO MOTHBALLS OH LORD GOD JEHOVAH OR ILL STUFF CAMPHOR INTO YOU OH LORD AND THROW YOU LIKE A WHITE MOTHBALL INTO THE HEAVENS TELL MY LITTLE SON ABOUT YOURSELF OH LORD INTRODUCE YOURSELF TELL MY SON ITS LEVI'S BROTHER AARON YOURE AFTER BECAUSE LISTENS TO THE GUNS GO BOOMBOOMBOOM AND A GOOD JEW SHOULDNT LISTEN TO GUNS INTRODUCE YOURSELF OH LORD TO MY LITTLE BABY

DONT BE SHY WITH THEM

PLEASE OH LORD I DIDNT HAVE TIME TO CAMPHOR MY LITTLE BABY IN MOTHBALLS and already hes got bandages around his head so tight I cant stick in the mothballs I want to see his hair

HIS HAIR HIS HAIR I GOT TO SEE HIS HAIR

Mrs Emanuel.

Rena, let him go, its no use, ghosts are no good, the second

523

Lee not born so I can see the first Lee again, how cruel and kind Rena is to me, a daughterinlaw I fill the whole medicine cabinet but there isnt any medicine for the first Lee how do you feel now but he dont answer hes unconscious the nurse says his nose has a thick accent its your nose Levi BLOW YOUR NOSE YOUR square-chinned Harry Ring says he cant do anything either because Lee isnt babbling Harry goes away I got to smash the chin of some-body whos spouting nonsense LEVI WHERE ARE YOU WHERE DID YOU GO I GOT TO SEE HIS BLOND HAIR GRAYGREEN MOTHEYES theyre

shut. Nurse. Hes unconsc

Where is unconscious, I ask her. What part of unconscious is he. What. Maybe hes with Dave waiting in the Buick Levi start the car already lets go home the second Lee must be home wait-ing, hungry, grungry, waiting, darkeyed what shall I do with the notborn? HOW DO YOU FEEL NOW, HES UNCONSCIOUS WHATS YOUR

NAME UNCONSCIOUS HOW DOES YOUR

UNCONSCIOUS FEEL ANSWER

ALREADY I GOT TO LOOK IN THE MIRROR RIGHT NOW HOLD THE MIRROR CLOSE TO ME ITS SO QUIET NOT A BREATH CAN YOU HEAR NOT A BREATH CAN YOU SEE

mom you cant see a breath you can only hear it the second Lee says

thanks for telling your mother so she wont sound foolish. I can see myself without a breath thats what mothers are for : seeing themselves breathless, its me whos holding my breath, not my little baby no no what should he be in suspense about/

excited about to hold his breath

after all wheres he going

whats he going to see

its me whos holding my first Lees breath IM HOLDING HIS LUNGS IM HOLDING HIS CHEST IN THE MIRROR THATS WHERE A WOMAN A MOTHER SHOULD ALWAYS LOOK FIRST

MY SON WHY ARENT YOU HOLDING THE MIRROR SO I CAN HOLD YOU?

Hes

Rena dont let him be notborn as much as I hate him that much you shouldnt love him TAKE BACK YOUR VAGINA ILL GIVE HIM A BATH it

hurts. too. much. to. have. him. back

Levi

Yes

Ask him

Who

Lee

What should I

How hes feeling

Hes uncon

No hes not. Ask

Rachel he cant

Ask him how

Its not time Lee isnt home yet hes not hungry

We got

Ask

Rachel for gods

Gods. In the synagogue. Ask the Golem to get the camphor

Rachel

The Dybbuk is mothballed for the summer. The Dybbuk wears winter clothes. Tell Dr Silver hes got to get the Golem to take off the clothes from the Dybbuk. Only a woman knows how powerless is a naked Dybbuk. A Dybbuks got to wear winter clothes, and all the Jews take him down to South Street to get him a new G.G.G. suit, we got such mercy on devils who possess us, we got to keep them warm, we cant let GOD EAT THROUGH THE DEVIL YOU GOT TO KNOW THAT LEVI YOU SEE THE DEVIL FLASHING FROM THE SPIRES OF THE CHURCH IN N'MUXT BECAUSE GOD KEEPS THE WHITE CAMPHOR SKY AROUND HIM AND YOURE AFRAID AND YOU PUT YOUR OWN SON ON THE HORSE TO RIDE BAREBACK AND HE DOESNT KNOW ANY BETTER SO HES RUSHING TOWARD THE DYBBUK ON THE CHURCHSPIRE YET YOU GOT TO COME TO AMERICA LEVI ITS THE ONLY WAY YOU CAN SAVE YOUR SON

. . . . yes . . . . save your little semens . . . . . yes . . . put

525

away one little semen a day .... yes .... a copper semen ....
in a little testicle bank .... yes .... the little semens will
grow .... yes .... assets :

> SIX MILLION SEMENS IN THE BANK
> liabilities :
> SIX MILLION SEMENS

... yes .... save ...
... save ... the little semens .....
.... yes ... i will thank you ....
.... yes ... i will take out a little son ....
.... yes ... and i will put him back ....
.... yes .... when youre bankrupt ....
.... yes ... dont you worry .... when youre short of cash ....
.... yes .... little lee .... wake him up ... you have money levi
.... wake him up .... we dont have to put the little semens
back ...
 Do we?
 Rachel.
 Wake him up.
 We cant.
 Yes. I will. Ill get him out of bed you prick, you sonofabitch
Levi, you nonfancy fucking bastard, wait and see, Ill get him out
of bed, just like you when YOURE DYING so if you dont want to get
out of bed yourself you goddamn well better get my little boy out
of
 Mrs Emanuel, you cant
 I can lift him. Im young, I dont need a penis to lift anybody,
whats a woman need with such a thing, I can lift my boy in my
arms
 Mrs
 Rachel
 He has passed away, Mrs Emanuel. Im sorry.
 He didnt answer me. Hes a good boy. A good boy answers his
mother. Lee
 He
 Lee my baby boy, you tell your mother how you feel, your own
mother, she has a right to know, dont you dare keep your mouth

shut, Im talking to you, a mother talks to her son he should answer, because all of a sudden you cant be a bad boy

Hes

A bad boy, such a bad boy, all of a sudden. What did I do to
deserve such a bad boy in a coffin yet. Thats what he gets for being
a bad boy who didnt answer his mother : so I got to give birth,
Rena, I pity you and your I love you because its a Leeghost the
first and how can a ghost get along in me all those years, what
kind of pleasure can a ghost have, yes? second Lee?

Im sorry for you, Rena, that a ghost should take responsibility
for the loss of your virginity. But, I guess thats the way young
girls the world over are :

87 empty tables, 348 empty chairs. Lesbian and fairy mannikins in the Chestnut Street clothing store windows.

Gakwoosh, gashwool. Ice, never.

Milkbottle, h.

Chirp, chirp. Morning.

A dying man's leaking pissbottle can throw SIX MILLION AND
ONE into Achille Volpe's milkeyed panic.

Chirp, chirp. Morning. And Terry Shannon, leaning against
the doorway, remarks to Lee, You see, your love, your Rena, your
Saint Red—shes taken me over completely, hasnt she? Posing in
the nude, Rena is Terry Shannon's American Winged Victory.
Shes put a head on my headless nakedness, hasnt she? Well, now,
do you think her immortality can be cured by your breaking off
her head?

Instead of answering after the fuck he has had with Rena, Lee
sneezes. Presumably, that is an evasion. Pressed, however, he replies that only ghosts sneeze.

Yeh Gertrude Forsten says Im tellinya Mrs Emanuel my husband suffers from hayfever somethin awful, rose fever I think
they call it around this time of year her narrow freckled brow a
series of skinny skeletons reclining in angularly contorted positions
waiting for black highheeled phonecalls, her orange hair in pin-
curls, orange tubercles being cultured in a cloudless blue medium
Lee remembers the bronzehaired deepbreasted girl of a few doors
away being drawn on a sled by a St Bernard along the snow-

527

tufted Roosevelt Boulevard strip separating the highways. Not Gertrude, and not in June

so hot for this time of year Rachel Emanuel complains, the querugirltone in the mockfrown, the cheek satinrouged, the flowered apron that sneaky Hertzogs got the Buick the next time Levi wakes believe me I wont wait a minute Im not afraid Ill tell him all about the Buick, all about

Mrs Emanuel Gertrude gently chides you shouldnt be out hangin wash

What? What? Rachel childshrills, snapping, one wrinkled nylon on a bonying leg, the other leg perfectly smooth by virtue of a rubber fleshcolored stocking the doctor says I should wear it for the arthritis you know I aint got such pleasure from my life its washday Gertrude. What day its washday, Gertrude Im getting so, her apologetic giggles, Im forgetting what day

But at least you could get the nurse. Shes a practical nurse aint she Mrs Emanuel?

Sure sure shes practical but shes a nigger and what can you expect you know she had the nerve, Rachels voice croaks down to a simulated whisper wavering, wash dishes she had the nerve to tell me thats the most shell do can you imagine Im tellin you Gertrude theyre all alike dont believe a word from them

Yeah thats right. Gee, yeh thats right Gertrude squeezefrowns her truncated gothicwindow forehead, her cormorantbeaked nose woodpeckering her upperlip, her orange freckles bleating against the flushed flesh, the scrawneck ditch tunnelling into the green apron snag cramped around the tall bonewillowed figure transelbowfixed on the ironblack fence, rustrazzed, scalloptopped, narrowshoulder hunched the metaltops even as Gertrudes and it is the evening and the morning of the sixth day, dim white vaporsigns of Constellation jets approaching Philadelphia oh them apples aint no good Lee Gertrude tells the boy, theyre always little green apples and sour but my husband he enjoys the shade dont he Mrs Emanuel

Im telling you you got a good man grampop Nathansons farm in Lansdale you can get sicklepears Mrs Forsten theyre little all right but theyre awful sweet

528

sveet

its a w, pop. Sweet.

Sveet.

Oh, pop

sv

he snores you know I never hear him not snoring when he
sleeps the boy says. Always, sleeping, he snores. Now, sleeping, not
a snore

zzzzzzzzzzzzzzzzz zzzzzzzzz zzzzzzzzzzzzzzzzzzzzzzzzzzzzzzzzzzzzzzzzzzzzzzzz
zzzzzzzzzzzzzzzzzzzzzzzzz(ero;

All his life, sleeping, he snores. Its enough to wake the dead
Betty Emanuel laughs;

now;

well, you know, Gertrude says, when the men are sick theyre
just like babies what about the cherry tree oh you mean the one
near the garage Gertrude stretches thinly on the pavement three
feet higher than the pavement in the Emanuel backyard honeysuckle, rose bramble and low blackgreen hedge his fingers, unable to make complete circles, are abandoned hoops Its a perfect
day aint it Mrs Emanuel; abruptly, screwing up her eyes oh I
didnt mean, well. I mean it could be more perfect couldnt it Mrs
Emanuel? Yeh, it even the cherries aint no good they aint got no
juice Lee. Gee, you could try them you wanna try them Ill get a
couple for ya but Im tellinya even my husband

if I had more strength I would clean the garage but I guess
Im just not up to it today its a beautiful day a little warm for
June maybe but its

Yeh, aint it?

The honeysuckles are nice aint they Gertrude. They smell so

sv

Yeh, they sure do.

You can hardly see the garage window now.

Yeh.

That damn Hertzog he took the Buick can you imagine such
gratitude my husband gave him everything in the business if it
wasnt for Levi he would be starving Rachel snaps, snivels, curses.

But you shouldnt be doin the wash.

529

It gives me something to do its even a lousy day Rachel curses if it would be more dry the sheets would dry in no time but there aint even a breeze.

Yeh its a shame a white sheet catercorners above the white-speckled hunchclumps of unmown grass, a gray retch of bare-assed earth here and there, a prayingmantis Rena her green cunt oozing white snot at a cautious gartersnake whose crimson red-dogpricktongue flicks, a boy scooping out semen from his nostrils and kneading it between his fingers, webbing it, then, to cast the gray rubbernet over girl and snake you cant even go out now in the yard because of the vermin Rachel complains, scolding the boy get back into the house I dont want you even watching such

Mom.

I said get back into

Yeh its the weather, Gertrude adenoids.

You got a cold, Gertrude?

Nah its my adenoids I got my tonsils out but never my adenoi

Lee got them both out the same time Dr Kitzmiller except he took out too much from the throat hes got a hole

Im tellinya Mrs Emanuel those doctors

You cant trust not one.

Yeh.

My eyes are watering again Rachel says. What did you say rose fever?

Yeh. Maybe you should see Dr Newman, hes the one you always

Well. Maybe soon as the mister, Rachel giggles, frowning, gets well I'll see Dr New

Gee, Mrs Emanuel, Im so sorry to hear about Mr Emanuel.

In some ways Hertzog is all right you cant deny, whats right is right, Levi has airconditioning on account of Hertzog got the unit.

Thats nice. In this weather thats a lot more comfortable.

Yeh, well, Harry Ring says, that hum from the airconditioner thats like my father its meaningless Levi watch out. Watch the Mediterranean is a long low blue swell between the Roosevelt Boulevard and Ruscomb Street one Jew unfolds his prayershawl, the tallis you shouldnt do that Rachel Emanuel Harry says, not wash a tallis and hang it out to dry and its not even a Monday morning it is the evening and the morning of the sixth day

The colored girl wont do it so I got to do it Rachel defends herself, its dirty from all these years hes going to use it this morning you think? Let it hang from the line

LET IT HANG HARRY RING LET IT

Sure, I understand, Gertrude says worriedly.

I cant understand Bella his own sister she dont even come over to see him, Rachel shakes her head at Gertrude. Theyre so close Levi and Bella more than the other sisters and brothers and yet she dont even that rose fever I better blow my nose already youll think Im crying Gertrude.

Oh no thats all right. I wont think that.

Im not crying.

I know, Mrs Emanuel.

Its the rose fever. The little bramble roses theyre so pretty aint they I should get a vase.

Yeh that would be nice.

The mister likes flowers. If I let him hed live in the country hes that crazy for fresh air and flowers.

Yeh that was my father all over. You couldnt get him out of the garden.

My fathers no different, Danny Naroyan sniffs. You cant get him out of the dirt.

Thats why he likes to drive in the country on Sundays, Rachel smiles. Smell, he says. Its a secret, Gertrude, but I say the same, smell, I say. Sure its all right for driving on Sunday, but who wants to live in the country, except the mister, he likes to.

My husband, too. Im sure sorry to hear

And do you know whos really the nurse, Gertrude? Its me, lowering her voice conspiratorially, snapping, wavercroaking, not that nigger, she curses, that lousy nigger she wont do nothing you cant get them to do nothing ooooh theyre so lousy she says without pausing for breath, rushing, girlquerulous, snagnagging, and what do you think Levi he dont agree? Of course he agrees, I want a nurse he says I got Rachel he says. Who makes him the

531

soup? I do, Rachels voice highs, laughing, astonishgratified ooh I cant even look at those airplanes up there Im telling you you couldnt get me in an airplane for a million dollars, not me, Im oldfashioned she giggles.

I feel the same way, Mrs Emanuel, Gertrude says very seriously, yeh.

But Im worried if I got rose fever maybe we cant drive in the country. What do you think, Gertrude?

Thats something to consider, Mrs Emanuel, all right.

And you know its a question can Levi drive with those bedsores, you should see them, Gertrude, he cant sleep right, with them. It gives him pain Lees coming home on furlough

STALINGRAD

Thats six million and one times shes whirled the hoop around her, Lee, Norma shakes her head incredulously. I cant bear watching any more.

Its sure good to know the wars over, Mrs Emanuel, Gertrude says carefully. Its been fourteen years

That long already, Rachel says incredulously. It just shows my mind aint what it

Well you got a lot on your mind, Mrs Emanuel.

Sure, Harbison's milk is all right, but we always used Supplee. Levi likes Supplee. He likes to drink from the bottle. I always tell him that aint right, you should take a glass. Sometimes, Gertrude, he takes a glass, he listens to me

You know how men

Men, men. Well, you got to overlook a lot. I scold him, though, if I see him drinking from the bottle

MILKBOTTLE H,

precarious;

Yeh well you got to tell them

Oh, I scold him

I cant bear watchi

six mill

I cant bear

Youd think hed know by now wouldnt you Gertrude.

Yeh well you know how men.

532

Theyre like children sometimes. You got to pick up after them oh. My eyes. She shakes her head. Age, she says, giggling.

Pennies.

Semens.

Do you think the prayershawl will dry in time, Gertrude?

LETS CHANGE PARTNERS BECAUSE ICE NEVER FAILS ON GUADALCANAL AND PEARL HARBOR AND MINDINAO

In time for what, Mrs Emanuel, Gertrude says, guardedly, her little orange hair nodules perking against the thin discharge of white semen against the cloudless blue sky as Mrs Sherman puts forth her hand to pick up the telephone my husbands calling but her charred penisfingers drop off one by one MILKING TIME MILKBOTTLE H MILKING TIME BUT I CANT MILK THE TELEPHONE WITH BLACK CHARRED FINGERS;

chirp,

chirp I better go in I hear him calling me in time for me to put it in the cedarchest let me tell you Gertrude that cedarchest in our bedroom certainly comes in handy for storing things of course its some job for me now to climb those steps,

Norma, billowing gently, her petticoats floating her up the stairs on 75th Street, pauses on the landingway. Lee Emanuel, she speaks quietly to the latherfaced figure in the doorway.

Yeh, I guess it is, Gertrude says.

Of course before Levi got sick we would sleep in the bed in the breakfast room so I wouldnt have to climb the stairs but now

Im sure sor

Its so hot in the shed Gertrude you cant imagine Im telling you dont ever buy a gas refrigerator.

Oh no, I wont.

Well I better get started, Gertrude. If I cant put away the prayershawl the least I can do is get the rest of the winter clothes in the cedarchest. Oh I hate to climb those stairs but what are you going to do.

Yeh.

Its getting dark already. The streetlights they ought to go on soon.

Yeh, thats right. My husband should be home soon.

My mister too,
gakwhoosh, gashwool/
Yeh they like a hot supper.
It gets so dark so early now.
Thats what happens when daylight saving time is over.
My goodness, I forgot to put the clock back. Im telling you my
mind isnt what it.
It happens to everybody, about the clocks.
I guess youre right, Gertrude. Hows your daughter.
Oh I didnt tellya. Theyre gonna make plastic fingers, two of
them, for her. Nobodyll know the difference.
I told you they wouldnt.
I was afraid maybe the kids.
Theyll make a joke even if they do. And kids get over it. Theyre
young. You know how it is.
I guess itll be all right.
Believe me. So I better get to the winter clothes and put them
away in the cedarchest. I hope I didnt forget to buy camphor-
balls.
If you forgot give me a call, I got some.
No, why should I borrow.
But I have plenty. Extra.
Well Ill pay you.
Oh please Mrs Emanuel. I wont take it.
I cant stand not paying. Even if its a few pennies.
Im tellinya I wont accept.
Its nothing. A few pennies.
Well Ill have to borrow from you, maybe something else,
another time, so thatll make it even.
All right, Gertrude, that way I can do it.
If I dont have mothballs, will the camphor flakes be all right?
Well, ordinarily, I use camphorballs.
The flakes do the same thing.
I guess flakes will be all right. Just so the moths wont get in
and eat the winter clothes. Those moths eat right through, and
then I got to sew up